THE EMPIRE OF BONES SAGA VOLUME TWO

TERRY MIXON

YOWLING CAT PRESS

Published by Yowling Cat Press ®

Digital edition date: 6/21/2023

Print ISBN: 978-1947376137

Individual Works

Ghosts of Empire Copyright © 2015 by Terry Mixon

Print ISBN: 978-0692604113

Paying the Price Copyright © 2016 by Terry Mixon

Print ISBN: 978-1947376045

Recon in Force Copyright © 2016 by Terry Mixon

Print ISBN: 978-1947376014

Assassin's Retreat Copyright © 2018 by Terry Mixon

Cover art - image copyrights as follows:

DepositPhotos/innovari (Luca Oleastri)

GraphicStock

Donna Mixon

Cover design and composition by Donna Mixon

Print design and layout by Terry Mixon

Audio edition performed and produced by Veronica Giguere

Reach her at: v@voicesbyveronica.com

ALSO BY TERRY MIXON

You can always find the most up to date listing of Terry's titles on his Amazon Author Page.

Note: the links below (ebook only, obviously) redirect you to my website where you can click a button to go to Amazon. This allows me to participate in Amazon's associates program and earn a little more. Sorry for any inconvenience.

The Last Hunter

The Last Hunter

Bonds of Blood

Alpha Strike

The Enemy Revealed

Command Authority

The Grand Conspiracy

Shield of Humanity

Fog of War

Ships of the Line

Operation Liberty

The Empire of Bones Saga

Empire of Bones

Veil of Shadows

Command Decisions

Ghosts of Empire

Paying the Price

Recon in Force

Behind Enemy Lines

The Terra Gambit

Hidden Enemies

Race to Terra

Ruined Terra

Victory on Terra

When Luck Runs Out

Gunboat Diplomacy

The Imperial Marines Saga

Spoils of War

Imperial Recruit

Enemy Action

The Humanity Unlimited Saga

Liberty Station

Freedom Express

Tree of Liberty

Blood of Patriots

Single Novels

Scorched Earth

Storm Divers

The Vigilante Series with Glynn Stewart

Heart of Vengeance

Oath of Vengeance

Bound By Law

Bound By Honor

Bound By Blood

Box Sets

The Empire of Bones Saga Volume 1

The Empire of Bones Saga Volume 2

The Empire of Bones Saga Volume 3

The Empire of Bones Saga Volume 4

Humanity Unlimited Publisher's Pack 1

Humanity Unlimited Publisher's Pack 2

Want to get updates from Terry about new books and other general nonsense going on in his life? He promises there will be cats. Go to TerryMixon.com/Mailing-List and sign up.

DEDICATION

This book would not be possible without the love and support of my beautiful wife. Donna, I love you more than life itself.

ACKNOWLEDGMENTS

Once again, the people who read my books before you see them have saved me. Thanks to Tracy Bodine, Michael Falkner, Cain Hopwood, Kristopher Neidecker, Bob Noble, Jon Paul Olivier, and Jason Young for making me look good.

I also want to thank my readers for putting up with me. You guys are great.

GHOSTS OF EMPIRE

BOOK FOUR

Princess Kelsey Bandar stared at the graveyard of dead warships. Fifty thousand wrecks from the civil war that destroyed the Terran Empire five hundred years ago.

She must lead the fight against the forces that killed those ships. The implacable artificial intelligences of the Rebel Empire.

With five old and damaged ships at her command, that seemed an impossible battle. One she must win.

1

"What the hell is that?" Princess Kelsey Bandar asked.

Commander Scott Roche, captain of the Imperial Fleet destroyer *Ginnie Dare*, leaned over Kelsey's shoulder and frowned at the derelict tumbling on her console's screen. "A mystery. I've been studying the Old Empire Fleet databases, and that ship isn't in it."

Kelsey knew that for a fact. She'd downloaded all the available ship's databases—military and civilian—into her implants before they'd started this survey of the graveyard, the name she'd decided fit the swarm of wrecked Old Empire ships orbiting Boxer Station.

Admiral Jared Mertz—her half brother—had tasked Commander Roche with watching over the sector base and examining the graveyard while he handled the negotiations with Harrison's World to get their captured people back. Since those talks were going nowhere fast, she'd decided to take a pinnace out to the destroyer and explore the sea of dead ships.

The horror floating before them in the cold darkness was mind-numbingly vast. They'd tallied tens of thousands of wrecks, all of them filled with dead Fleet personnel, she was sure. They'd been resting here since the destruction of the Old Empire more than five centuries ago.

They'd only examined a small area of the graveyard. The worst-case estimates were between forty and fifty thousand derelicts in wide orbits around Boxer Station. And those were the ships the rebels hadn't destroyed outright. She still couldn't imagine how many desperate battles the Old Empire had lost to fill this terrible place.

Most of the ships they'd found weren't salvageable, but the Terran Empire needed every one that was. Or they would once the enemy, the terrible shade of the Old Empire, discovered it hadn't won a complete victory.

Commander Eliyanna Kaiser and the destroyer *New York* were on their way to the Pentagaran and Erorsi systems. They'd bring back as many people and ships as their allies could spare. They'd need them all.

Jared's ragtag fleet consisted of two destroyers that weren't capable of fighting Old Empire ships of any class, two heavily damaged Old Empire battlecruisers, and a severely battered Old Empire superdreadnought, *Invincible*.

Of the battlecruisers, the ship they'd arrived in—*Courageous*—was still capable of all operations, but the other one—*Scott Pond*—wasn't able to flip. That meant it couldn't leave this system.

With more people, they could bring Boxer Station—the massive Old Empire Fleet base in this system—back online and put their ships into the construction yards for repair.

Which brought her full circle. The AIs that had brought the Old Empire derelicts here after defeating them in battle had sorted each group of ships into classes. This single ship floated alone, and none of the probes had seen anything remotely like it.

One of the obvious differences between it and the other ships was its size. This vessel was only about four times the tonnage of a marine pinnace, but it had flip drives. From the outside, it didn't seem badly wrecked. There was a large hole in the hull amidships, but the damage looked contained.

Kelsey turned in her seat and devoted her full attention to Commander Roche. On one of the Old Empire ships, she could've used her implants to continue examining the ship through the scanners, but on *Ginnie Dare*, she was limited to what she could see with her own eyes.

"Maybe it's some kind of scout ship," she said. "Though, it seems as though there'd be more of them, and the databases would at least know what it was."

"Well, something that small wouldn't take long to explore," he said. "I don't like things I can't explain. We should check it out."

"Good idea. I'll take my security detail over for a look. If you'll get a technical team together, they can assess things once we clear it."

The Fleet officer nodded. "I'll get them down to marine country. I feel obligated to tell you to be careful. Admiral Mertz wouldn't be pleased with me if anything happened to you."

No, her brother would be pretty upset. That made her feel good inside. Their relationship had really improved. Her father was going to be shocked and pleased about that when she finally got home.

Her twin brother, Ethan, was going to be surprised as well, though hardly pleased. He hated Jared and didn't trust him. She hoped that the events of this expedition would help change his mind, but she wasn't going to hold her breath.

"I promise to be cautious," Kelsey said. "Besides, I'll be in commando armor. I doubt anything over there would be able to harm me. I'll stay in constant contact. You can mother hen me if you feel the need."

"I'm *so* reassured."

She laughed. "You'll get used to me after a few more months. Then you'll barely cringe when something terrible happens."

Kelsey had to smile at his suddenly stricken expression. "Lighten up, Scott. Everything will be fine."

After a beat, he sighed. "I don't think I'll ever get used to the second in line to the Imperial Throne calling me by my first name."

"Relax," she said. "We put our pants on just like everyone else. With servants to hold us up and slide them on while we drink ridiculously expensive tea served in tiny cups made from the bones of our enemies."

He smiled. "Just like I'd always imagined. Be careful, Highness."

* * *

"YOUR DEMANDS ARE UNACCEPTABLE," Deputy Coordinator King said haughtily. "I cannot comprehend what you hope to gain by defying me. I am one of the higher orders, and I demand you comply with my lawful directives."

Jared was glad this conversation was taking place in his office. He was doubly glad that the woman was talking with him remotely. If she was this bad on screen, he could only imagine how obnoxious she was in person.

Deputy Coordinator King was the most trying individual he'd dealt with since leaving Avalon. The only person who rubbed him worse might be his half brother Ethan, and he wanted to *kill* Jared.

He tamped down his temper and gave the woman a bland smile. "My demands, Deputy Coordinator King, are not defiance. You have Fleet personnel in your custody. Several thousand people that you have no right to hold under any circumstances. If you want to discuss other matters, I'm more than willing to do so, but only once you return my people to me."

"Perhaps if I made examples of a few of them, it would shake you out of the belief that you can dictate terms to me or Harrison's World," she said coldly. "Those people were transported here as prisoners by the System Lord. You would do well to remember who you truly serve, *Admiral* Mertz."

Her less-than-subtle emphasis on his rank had far less impact than she probably expected. Three days ago, he'd been a commander. The shock of his sister promoting him still hadn't worn off.

Not that he was going to share that point with Deputy Coordinator King. He wasn't even a member of her version of Fleet. Harrison's World was under the control of what his people called the Rebel Empire. The Old Empire his people had fled from had fallen to the rebels and now answered to the AIs that had killed uncounted trillions of people.

Of course, Harrison's World hadn't been in the good graces of the system AI when Jared and his people snuck in. Jared had no idea what they'd done to warrant imprisonment, but the AI had placed three weapons platforms in orbit and had destroyed a number of urban centers.

In other words, the woman on his screen had a lot of nerve talking to him as though she had any leverage. Particularly with the Rebel Empire Fleet that she believed he represented. Besides, he wouldn't tolerate her threatening his people.

"With all due deference, Deputy Coordinator King, you're full of crap."

Her eyes bugged. "How dare you! I'll have you flogged for speaking to me in—"

"You seem to have forgotten your circumstances," Jared said harshly. "Are you claiming the System Lord imprisoned you unjustly? I'm a duly appointed Fleet Admiral with the full backing of the Empire. One in complete control of the orbital bombardment platforms. I suggest you remember how precarious your position truly is before you make threats like that."

Her eyes narrowed dangerously. "The Lord made a mistake. Not the only one, based on your mission here to deal with it. I feel confident that your orders also include instructions to do exactly what I've been insisting on.

"We'll find out when I come up to discuss the matter in person tomorrow morning. You will send a cutter for me. I suggest you take whatever steps you need to salve your bruised ego, Admiral, because this matter is going to be decided in my favor."

She disconnected without another word.

Jared rubbed his eyes. "Can she really be that stupid?"

"I've discovered that rhetorical questions often have yes for an answer," a mellow voice said through the overhead speakers. *Invincible*, the AI they'd installed inside the hull of the same name, was fully sentient, just like the Lords of the Rebel Empire, only without their homicidal core rules.

"That's because we have to ask to be sure we heard the idiots correctly the first time," Jared said. He leaned back in his chair and stared at the ceiling. "Which doesn't explain why she's so certain that she's going to get what she wants. Does she know something we don't?"

"Almost certainly. Until we can unlock the memory of the AI from Boxer Station, we have no idea what caused it to suppress this system. Though the presence of this vessel does indicate some kind of revolt was in progress."

They'd found *Invincible* floating in the graveyard when they'd snuck into distant orbit around Boxer Station. Rebel Fleet personnel and civilians from Harrison's World had restored it to complete functionality, minus any computer system. They'd also shielded her power systems, so they'd obviously desired to avoid discovery.

The final messages from the people onboard had strongly hinted that they were going to rebel against the AI. They would've failed, but they wouldn't have known that until it was too late. It had taken the addition of his ships to make the battle one they could win. Barely.

The senior Rebel Fleet officer had left a message to the woman ruling Harrison's World, Olivia West. She must've been in on the coup. Jared didn't know the reasons why, but there was more going on than met the eye.

"At least we have all night to figure out how to handle her," Jared said. "With the flip-point jammers in place, we can finally be mostly certain no one is about to spring a surprise on us. How goes the scan of the system?"

"Our probes are still searching the more distant areas, but they've located a single weak flip point. I only received the data a few minutes ago."

Weak flip points were a previously unknown version of regular flip points. Unlike the normal kind that assured reliable travel across hundreds of light-years, the weak ones were hard to detect. In at least some cases, they didn't assure two-way travel. Hence, his people being trapped so far from home.

The science teams were working overtime to understand them more fully, but he didn't trust having one in his lap.

He grunted. "So there's a back door? Wonderful."

"If I might be so bold, Admiral, you've never had anyone sneak out of one to surprise you."

"Unless you count Captain Breckenridge."

The disgraced Fleet captain was in *Invincible*'s brig. He'd betrayed his oath to the Empire and attempted to kidnap Princess Kelsey. His retreat through another weak flip point had led to the crippling of his ship and the capture of thousands of Fleet personnel—the very ones Jared was trying to get back.

"We should send a probe through," Jared said, "but I'll hold off until we know a little more about the situation here. We absolutely don't need a second front to this war. Any word from Kelsey?"

"She's exploring an unusual derelict," the AI said, "but everything looks safe enough, according to Captain Roche. He's listening in as they check it out."

"Well, I certainly hope she doesn't find anything dangerous. She has a knack for turning up trouble in the most unusual places."

"The odds of that seem unlikely."

"That's only because you don't know my sister. If there's something dangerous on any of those ships, she'll find it."

* * *

KELSEY HEADED INTO THE LIFT. It took her swiftly down to the appropriate level, and she made her way to *Ginnie Dare*'s marine country.

It was kind of spooky. *Ginnie Dare* had the same layout as Jared's old ship, *Athena*. Kelsey had many fond memories of spending time with the marines there.

Bittersweet, too. So many of the men and women she'd befriended were gone now, killed in the various actions against the Pale Ones and the AIs. The worst loss was Lieutenant Tim Reese, the commanding officer of the marines on *Athena* and then *Courageous*. He'd died taking Boxer Station.

Kelsey put on a neutral face and walked in. This wasn't the time to bring everyone down.

The marines were bustling around doing tasks that she actually understood now. Commander Roche must've called ahead to start people moving.

Lieutenant Angela Ellis, *Ginnie Dare*'s detachment commander, was waiting for her. "Highness. The captain let us know about the excursion. Do you need a full complement of marines?"

Kelsey looked up at the woman. Angela was tall and well built. Not just tall for a woman. Really tall. As in over two meters. She towered over most of the men under her command, and she was easily a giant as far as Kelsey was concerned. Half a meter was a lot of difference.

If they were ever able to start enhancing other people, Angela would make a formidable combatant.

She'd caught a flechette boarding Boxer Station but seemed to have recovered fully. Kelsey was glad. They'd lost far too many good people that day.

"I don't think so," Kelsey said. "It's not very big. I'm thinking Senior Sergeant Coulter, my team, and some techs."

Howard Coulter was the man that Marine Captain Russ Talbot—also Kelsey's boyfriend—had placed in charge of her guard detail. He'd be going no matter what she said, so she might as well incorporate him into her plan.

If her decision made the marine lieutenant feel slighted, she showed no sign of it. "I assumed that's what you'd want, so they're already armoring up. I took the liberty of getting your gear prepped, as well."

"Thank you. This shouldn't take long. If you'll excuse me, I'll go get ready."

The compartment outside the armory was where marines prepped for missions. As they were a co-ed organization, there weren't separate areas for women. That had taken a while to get used to, but now she was able to strip down and armor up without turning beet red.

The marines were almost ready to go, so she changed into her skinsuit. The Old Empire garment provided some protection of its own, which had come in handy on Boxer Station. It also allowed her armor to handle waste management. That was embarrassing, too, but after six hours in a suit, one welcomed the ability to use the bathroom.

Coulter and his people were still using Terran Empire Marine armor. Her powered Old Empire commando suit was significantly tougher and more capable than anything they'd ever seen before.

They'd captured suits of powered marine armor from the Rebel Empire that unenhanced people could use, but she didn't trust them. Those paranoid bastards had put bombs and other devices in them to control their military.

In her mind, it was far better to get something set up to do implants again and allow their marines to use the armor they'd found on so many Old Empire ships in the graveyard. The vast amount of salvageable equipment was arguably enough to outfit every marine in the Terran Empire, with plenty left over to share with their allies.

Kelsey's commando armor was dark grey with a faceless helmet. It augmented her already formidable strength and speed. It wasn't invincible by any means, but it made survival possible in the insanity that was combat with Old Empire weapons.

The armor hung from a rack, so she was able to open the back and step into it. A mental command through her cranial implants closed it up around her. She stepped clear and held her helmet in the crook of her arm.

Coulter and the half dozen marines assigned to her team gathered at her gesture. "We're ready, Princess. What's the target?"

"A mystery ship that doesn't appear in the Old Empire databases. It might not even be Imperial. We'll board and clear. Once we're sure it's safe, we'll bring the technical people in to give it a look."

Coulter nodded. "Got it. We go in prepared for hostile action. If it's as dead as everything else in the graveyard, no problem. If it has any surprises, we're ready. Mount up, people."

They boarded the marine pinnace together with a dozen technicians.

The approach went smoothly enough. Since they were using an Old Empire pinnace, she could interface with its scanners.

The small ship certainly looked dead as it tumbled in space half a dozen kilometers from *Ginnie Dare*, but *Invincible* had proved that appearances could be deceptive. The people from Harrison's World had brought the superdreadnought online and shielded her so well that Jared's people hadn't known she was operational until they boarded her.

Kelsey spotted a small hole on the other side of the ship from the large one she'd noted earlier. It was less than half a meter in diameter. It looked as though something small and fast had punched through the vessel. An asteroid, perhaps?

She supposed it was possible the damage was postcapture. Maybe they could figure it out once they boarded.

The pinnace came in slowly and matched the tumble of the ship. They clamped on with a thump.

"We're tight," the pilot said. "I'm going to use the pinnace's grav drives to level us out. With a ship this small, it shouldn't take more than a few minutes."

The ship slowed its mad spin until it was at rest relative to *Ginnie Dare*. Only then did Coulter take off his restraints and stand.

"Boarding party, form up on the ramp," he said.

Kelsey made no fuss when the marines put her at the back. If she needed to get up front, she could do so quickly enough. Everyone hooked up lines to prevent something from throwing one of them into deep space.

The ramp lowered, revealing the cold, bright stars looking down on the tomb beneath their feet. The marines led the way onto the hull, their magnetic boots holding them steady. Her armor had a miniature grav drive that would allow her to fly around if she chose, but she followed their lead.

They could've gained access through the rupture in the hull, but there was an airlock right there. The marines circled it, and one of them accessed the controls.

"It isn't opening," the woman said after a minute. "It has power, it's just not responding to me."

"Let me take a look," Kelsey said.

The controls had power. She could feel it through her implants. She sent a command to open, and the system promptly rejected her.

Nonplussed, she pressed the manual controls to open it. The lock queried her implants and rejected her a second time.

"That's new," she said. "It pinged my implants and told me to get lost."

"Welcome to the world the rest of us live in, Princess," Coulter said with a smile. "Luckily, we have another way in."

Kelsey looked at the rupture. The interior of the ship wasn't inside the reach of the pinnace's floodlights. The inky blackness had an ominous feel to it. What would they find inside this wreck? Or what might find them?

2

Commander Sean Meyer woke abruptly. The dark shadow of a man hovered over him. The figure had a hand over Sean's mouth. Not to smother but to keep him from crying out and waking everyone in the prison bunkroom.

He nodded to show the man that he was awake. Frankly, he'd half expected someone to attack him before now. Many of these men and women had been under his authority just a week ago. Before he'd betrayed their captain. He'd heard more than a few muttered curses, and everyone had avoided him like the plague.

The man tugged on Sean's arm and guided him toward the men's shower without a word of explanation. Sean was more than a bit surprised when the man began stripping, with every sign of taking a very early morning shower.

He did the same, hoping this wasn't some convoluted plan to kill him.

Two men were already in the shower, and steam covered every worn surface. They'd been cleaning the buildings, so the smell of old age and lingering rot was beginning to fade.

The sound of the rushing water was loud in his ears. Loud enough to conceal a murder, if the men were so inclined. A conspicuously open spot for Sean stood between the two men. His guide moved away from them and turned on the water at the far side of the room.

In the dim light, Sean recognized his guide as an enlisted man from *Spear*'s marine complement. One of the two older men waiting for Sean was *Spear*'s senior noncommissioned officer, Command Master Chief Ulysses Ross. He didn't know the third man.

"Command Master Chief," he said as he stripped and took his assigned place. He turned the water on and adjusted it until it was as hot as he could stand. If he was going to be naked in the shower, he might as well enjoy it.

"No ranks," the bald man said. "We think the showers are safe, but I'm not willing to take unnecessary risks, Sean."

"I understand, Ulysses. I was pretty sure no one wanted to talk to me, so I'm surprised to see you."

Ross gave him a cool smile. "Yeah, well, we find ourselves in odd times. You and the boss had a disagreement. Without going into specifics, I'd like you to explain that to us. Oh, my friend is Albert Newland. Al did the same job as me on *Shadow*."

Shadow had been the heavy cruiser *Spear*'s consort before the Rebel Empire had destroyed the light cruiser. Now both vessels were gone.

So the two senior enlisted men among the prisoners wanted to have a private chat with *Spear*'s disgraced executive officer. He'd find out soon enough if it was for good or ill.

"Well, Wallace and I did have some words. I told him I thought he was making a mistake in the strongest of terms."

Ross snorted. "That you did. You took something he wanted very badly and gave it away."

"He had no right to take it in the first place. Look, I knew the penalty for crossing him, and I'm more than willing to pay the price for it. Still, that seems a little off topic, considering our current circumstances."

He'd been in the brig when the AI's forces had attacked *Spear*. The machines had slain or stunned anyone who resisted. They'd cut him out of his cell and herded him with the enlisted prisoners. An understandable mistake, since Captain Breckenridge had ripped Sean's rank tabs off with his own hands.

The machines drove the prisoners into a large cargo hold, and Breckenridge had ordered them only to give their name and serial number if questioned. Nothing else. The officers had quickly gotten rid of their rank tabs, perhaps thinking that would keep the AI from targeting them for enhanced interrogation. Officers were more likely to know how to get back to the Terran Empire.

All of them knew what was at risk. If word slipped out, the Terran Empire would die.

The AI hadn't spared *Spear*'s wounded, either. The medical staff did what they could, but many died.

The machines herded the enlisted people onto ships and brought them to this planet. Apparently the AI had known who was an officer based on their rank tabs the moment it had captured them. So much for the subterfuge.

Sean had only seen one other officer among the men and women: *Shadow*'s critically injured captain, Paul Cooley. He'd been awake when the machines had brought him into the hold but had lapsed into unconsciousness by the time they'd started for the planet.

Based on the severity of his injuries, Sean wouldn't be surprised if the man had died, though the people on the planet had whisked the wounded away once they'd landed, supposedly to a medical facility.

They'd sent Sean and the rest to this old military base. They were on an island, but that was about all they knew. Their captors weren't interested in talking to them. Other than guard patrols and daily landings under heavy guard to drop off some of the nastiest rations he'd ever tasted, they ignored the prisoners.

"That can be sorted out in time," Ross continued. "It's above my pay grade, in any case. What I want to know is why you disobeyed orders. The real reason. I know you didn't think so highly of the things you gave back."

"You're wrong," Sean said flatly. "I valued one of them very much. So much that I couldn't stand to see how Wallace treated it. The second thing was more valuable than Wallace gave it credit for, but the first was a matter of principle that I couldn't let pass."

Captain Breckenridge had taken Princess Kelsey and Commander Mertz prisoner. If it had only been Mertz, Sean would've probably let things go, but he couldn't allow his captain to take the second in line to the Imperial Throne hostage. It was unthinkable. So he'd acted.

Ross gave him a hard look and then nodded. "That's about what I expected you'd say. I've never known you to be disloyal, but the boss put you in a hard spot. Hell, he put us all into a difficult situation.

"Without any officers here to provide guidance, I took it on myself to speak with the others in enlisted leadership positions. You might've been in the brig when this all went down, but as far as we're concerned, that's a problem for others to sort out later. We'd like you to resume your duties."

Newland nodded. "Several of our people overheard two guards talking about some unknown ships taking out the AIs. One of them mentioned Mertz. You've met the man. Do you think he might have turned the tables on those mechanical bastards?"

Sean blinked in surprise. Mertz was a capable officer, but he only had one undermanned battlecruiser. Yes, it was a powerful ship, but…

He put that thought out of his head. "Mertz is more resourceful than we gave him credit for. Is it possible? Maybe. I'm not sure how it helps us down here, though."

"It might not," Ross said. "We won't know until someone actually talks to us. When that time comes, I think you should be our point man. As the senior prisoner, you need to take the conversation to them. Let them know you're the force master chief. We'll back your play."

Sean nodded. "Has everyone been told I'll be resuming my duties?"

"Not yet, but they'll hear about it before dawn. Time to dry off and head back to our barracks. I'm developing permanent wrinkles."

* * *

"LET ME TAKE YOU INSIDE," Kelsey told Coulter. "The edges aren't a threat to suit integrity that way."

The marine noncom nodded. "I'll go first. Form up for quick entry, everyone."

He disconnected himself from the line and floated free of the hull. He'd turned off his magnetic boots.

Kelsey followed suit and grabbed him. It only took a moment to bring them over the opening with her suit's grav generator. Their lights played inside the ship. The cone of destruction led right to the hole on the opposite side. At its widest, the wound was over a dozen meters across. Even after all this time, there was still some debris floating in the damaged area.

"Yeah," she said. "Something small and going very fast blew through this ship. Probably an asteroid. It doesn't look like a missile hit or a beam blast. This is purely kinetic."

Her original plan had been to push him inside, but the number of sharp objects made that too risky. "I'll take you all the way in. Maybe we can open the lock from the inside."

"No," he said. "Bring everyone in. We'll start exploring from the central corridor. I can see that it's open on both sides."

"That's boring," she whined in her best ten-year-old girl voice. "Okay. You stay right there once I drop you off."

It only took a few minutes to get them all inside. They split up, with some going aft while the remainder went toward the bow. As small as the ship was, it wouldn't take long to search.

The interior lights were on, as was the gravity. That indicated the ship still had power. Since they hadn't detected the fusion plants, even at point-blank range, the designers had shielded them devilishly well. Considering that breaches in the hull should've made the detection inevitable, this ship had even better shielding than *Invincible*.

Kelsey decided to go with the bow team. There were no indications of combat inside the ship. Things were surprisingly neat and orderly. The dead Fleet personnel they found were in vacuum suits. Based on their expressions, they'd died relatively peacefully in places of their own choosing.

Coulter examined the dead as they went. "These people weren't under AI control. No beards or long hair. The AIs aren't big on personal hygiene."

She knew that far too well. The Pale Ones still featured prominently in her frequent nightmares.

"One other thing," he said. "The emergency doors are wide open. Was there a systems failure, or was that intentional?"

"Considering the lack of things blown around, I'd say intentional. Maybe we'll find out what happened when we get to the bridge."

That didn't take long. More men and women in Fleet vacuum suits sat at the controls. They seemed to have died peacefully as well. A quick check of the consoles found them all locked.

"Sergeant Coulter, Princess Kelsey, this is Corporal Brand. I'm in engineering. I'm no tech, but I'm only seeing grav drives and fusion plants."

She frowned. "That doesn't make any sense. The ship has flip vanes."

"Maybe the impact took the flip drives out," Coulter said. "This isn't a very big ship. The grav drives need to be in the stern, but the flip drives can be anywhere inside the hull. They're normally in engineering, but that's a matter of convenience."

"That would've sucked," Kelsey said. "Trapped in whatever system you were in when everything went down the crapper. Maybe we can access the computer and find out. Let's get the techs."

It wasn't difficult finding the airlock. It opened easily from the inside.

The techs came on board and spread throughout the ship. She followed the computer expert to the compartment set aside for it adjacent to the bridge. It wasn't as massive as the one aboard *Courageous*, but it wasn't tiny, either.

"It's still powered," the tech declared, "but it's not responding to my attempts to access it."

"Let me have a try." Kelsey used her implants to find the interface and attempted to connect. It promptly rejected her, but this time it gave her a reason.

Access denied. Implant codes not recognized.

My name is Kelsey Bandar. I'm an ambassador plenipotentiary of the Terran Empire. Here are my authorization codes.

This unit does not recognize your authority, Ambassador Plenipotentiary Kelsey Bandar. This unit is restricted to access only by certain personnel.

She considered how to respond to that. There were other avenues to gain access. She just needed to know what the machine was looking for.

Can you clarify what type of authorization is acceptable?

Only personnel with correct access codes and appropriate hardware may access this unit without authorization.

Perhaps I have the correct hardware. Why not? She had every other kind of equipment inside her.

Kelsey gasped as the computer probed her implants. At least the intrusion was quick.

You do have the correct hardware but lack the required access codes.

She considered how best to explain the situation. *Over five hundred years have passed since the rebellion. The Terran Empire still exists, but we're only just beginning to recover. Does my hardware grant me a more detailed explanation? Perhaps I can clarify things to your satisfaction. What hardware are you checking, by the way?*

You possess Marine Raider implants. This vessel is a Raider strike ship. You do not possess the required Raider access codes, however.

Her heart soared. A commando ship with a computer that could explain her implants to her! This was exactly what she needed!

As I have the hardware, will you grant me provisional access?

Negative. Without the appropriate Marine Raider codes, this unit may not grant you access. Warning. Attempting to access this unit without authorization will cause it to self-destruct.

It was as though it knew that she'd be tempted to get around the restrictions. So much for the easy way.

She turned to Coulter. "This is a commando ship. Or, as the computer calls them, Marine Raiders. It won't give me access. Once again, I'm stuck without an easy way to get the information I need."

"Princess Kelsey, this is Corporal Brand again. We found something else you need to see. Can you come down to the medical center?"

Medical center might have been too gracious a term. It was maybe twice the size of her old quarters on *Athena*. There were a few beds and one cramped operating theater.

The latter showed the first mess that she'd seen on the ship. The table had a few large smears of dried blood, and the scattered instruments made it look as though a hurried operation had just ended.

There was also one large piece of equipment that the marines had gathered around.

"What do you have?" she asked.

"I'm not sure, but there's someone in there," Brand said.

Kelsey looked through the port, and there was indeed a man lying on a gurney inside. He had terrible injuries to his head and face. She could see the graphene coating his skull. Since only commandos had that particular enhancement, he must be one. Unlike the other bodies on the ship, he wasn't a desiccated husk.

Shocked, she checked the equipment with her implants. It was a stasis unit, the same kind of machinery that had kept Reginald Bell alive for hundreds of years, and it was running.

"Dear God," she said. "He's still alive. We've found an Imperial commando."

3

"Hey there, Cowboy."

Jared glanced over at his executive officer in surprise. No, Charlie Graves wasn't his XO anymore. Kelsey had promoted him to captain and placed him in command of the battlecruiser *Courageous*. Which was where he should be, now that Jared thought about it.

"Charlie, what the hell are you doing on my bridge? Don't you have a ship to put back together?"

The younger man grinned. "I do, Admiral, but I need to speak with you privately. Since we had a cutter coming over for some spare parts, I figured now was the time. Might we step into your office, sir?"

Jared rose and gestured toward his office just off the flag bridge. "After you. Zia, you have the conn."

"Aye, sir." His tactical officer, now promoted to executive officer of *Invincible*, took over his station. Her long-time partner in crime, Pasco Ramirez, was filling that role for Graves on *Courageous*. There were higher-ranking officers available, but Jared didn't trust them.

The officers from *Spear* and *Shadow* had been on Boxer Station when Kelsey and the marines had captured it, but they'd supported Captain Wallace Breckenridge's mutiny.

Of course, so had the destroyers *New York* and *Ginnie Dare*, but he doubted they'd try anything funny now. He'd assigned observers to keep an eye on them.

His flag office was more spacious than even his old one on *Courageous* had been. Its size and relative opulence made him more than a bit uncomfortable. He wasn't precisely sure where his people had found the furniture, but as it was a gift, he couldn't very well refuse it.

Ignoring his almost comically large desk, Jared took a seat in one of the comfortable chairs. "What's bothering you, Charlie?"

His long-time friend sat across from him. "Permission to speak freely?"

"Cut loose. I need to know exactly what you're thinking."

"I think you're making a strategic blunder in the pursuit of a tactical solution."

He felt himself smiling. "That's plain enough. And I thought your blunt manner might keep you from commanding a ship in space. Silly me."

Graves smiled back at him. "I've never hidden anything from you, Jared, and I'm not going to start now. We're critically short of experienced officers. It's time to start vetting the men and women from *Spear* and *Shadow*.

"We didn't have enough leaders when we crewed *Courageous*. Now the officers and men from one destroyer are making do on a superdreadnought and a battlecruiser. Soon to be two battlecruisers. We're spread too thin. You need to put those people to use, and I mean right now."

Just the problem he'd been wrestling with, but not the solution he'd wanted to hear. "I appreciate your forthrightness. I know we're shorthanded, but we can't afford to trust them."

The young captain leaned forward earnestly. "We can't afford not to. Jared, those men are Fleet officers. Did some of them willfully mutiny? Probably. They supported Breckenridge. Are you going to hold that against an ensign or lieutenant who was just following orders?

"I know damned well that I'd have had a hard time telling a full captain he was wrong when I was a junior officer under his command, unlawful orders or no. Commander Meyer took a stand against Breckenridge, and that was brave as hell.

"No matter how this turns out, his career is probably over. Who wants a man at his back that might put a knife in it? Can you blame others who might have disagreed for keeping their heads down?"

Sean Meyer, *Spear*'s executive officer, had broken Kelsey and Jared out of confinement on the heavy cruiser. He'd stayed behind to make sure their escape back to *Courageous* was successful. He'd been in *Spear*'s brig when the AI-controlled ships had crippled the heavy cruiser. Now he was a prisoner on the planet below.

Jared sighed. "I know, but it's hard to trust people that fooled you once."

Graves nodded. "Then start with the officers from *Shadow*. They didn't cross us like the ones from *Spear* did, and the lower-ranking officers won't gang up to stage a mutiny. That just leaves the senior officers from *Spear*. A few dozen men and women. With appropriate watchdogs, they won't be a threat. Tag them with trusted monitors. They should know they're on probation, but we need them desperately."

Jared took a deep breath and nodded. "You're right. We'll scatter them throughout the task force and use them. But no command positions."

Graves smiled. "That's really all I'd hoped to achieve. *Courageous* and *Invincible* can monitor them, even in their quarters. We can make that plain enough to them as a condition of their probation."

"Well, now that you've set me straight," Jared said, "is that all you needed? How's your ship?"

"*Courageous* is battle worthy. Or as close to it as we can manage in the short term. A third of her missile tubes are offline or obliterated. Roughly the same percentage of beam weapons are gone. Her drives and battle screens are in good shape, though."

Jared compressed his lips. "*Invincible* is in about the same shape. A little worse, actually. We really need to get the construction yards back into commission. *Scott Pond* is a floating wreck."

They'd recovered *Scott Pond* from the floating graveyard of ships left over from the rebellion half a millennium ago. The rebels had destroyed her flip drives when they killed her crew. After her most recent combat, her grav drives were at less than thirty percent. Most of the ship was in vacuum, so they hadn't manned her. Calling her a wreck was being generous.

The task force was in as precarious a position as it could be. If they hadn't plugged the system's flip points, the next Rebel Empire visitor could sweep them off the table.

He and Charlie chatted a while longer before Jared stood and ended the meeting. "Thanks for telling me what I needed to hear, Charlie. Take charge of getting those officers back to work."

Graves climbed slowly to his feet. "What about the negotiations? Are we making any progress on getting our people back?"

"Not that you'd notice. Those people are remarkably stubborn. I'll talk with their representative again tomorrow. This time, she's coming up here. I can't imagine why they'd continue antagonizing the people in charge of the orbital bombardment weapons."

"Does it really matter why? They want to take control of their system. Something we can't let them do. We want our people. Something they apparently aren't willing to grant without getting what they want. This doesn't end cleanly."

"Probably not," Jared admitted, "but we have to try."

Graves headed for the hatch. "Maybe your Rebel Empire prisoner can shed some light on the dilemma."

Jared doubted it. Lieutenant Commander Michael Richards, the Rebel Empire Fleet officer they'd captured at Erorsi, was much less trusting of Jared than he was of Kelsey. Still, it was worth a try. What did he have to lose?

"I'll talk to him. Keep me up to date on the integration efforts."

"Aye, sir."

"Pardon the interruption," *Invincible* said after Graves had left. "Kelsey has just requested a full medical team to her location."

Jared cursed under his breath. "I knew it. What's the medical emergency? Is she injured?"

"Negative. It seems she's found a functional stasis unit with a gravely injured person inside. Based on the ongoing conversation she's having with Doctor Stone, I suspect that the doctor will take a team to join her shortly."

"Let Lily know that she's cleared to take whoever she needs with her. Keep me in the loop."

* * *

KELSEY WATCHED doctors Stone and Guzman working around the stasis unit. The engineering team from *Ginnie Dare* had restored life support in this section of the ship and made certain the fusion plants were stable.

Not that they'd been unstable, but a power failure right now could kill the injured man.

Kelsey had snagged the revival process from the stasis unit. It wasn't complex. She remembered how Reginald Bell had said this was cutting-edge stuff.

It was. He'd also said that the units couldn't keep someone alive for several centuries without adjustments, but he was wrong. This unit was self-regulating. It would maintain the patient's condition for as long as it had power.

Lily Stone looked over at Kelsey. "We're about as ready as we'll ever be. I want to caution you again not to be too hopeful. From what I can see, this man was so badly injured that they put him in as a last-ditch effort. He might be brain dead."

"We owe it to him to try," Kelsey said. "If he's alive, what are his chances?"

Justin Guzman shook his head. "Not good. At the very least, he's suffered significant damage to his frontal lobe. Let me second what Lily said. This poor man is almost certainly gone."

"We'll pull him out and make the call," Lily said. "If there's a chance, we'll get him to *Ginnie Dare*. We'll do everything humanly possible."

Kelsey knew that. She had to get her hopes under control. "Okay."

The doctors had her shift to the side and positioned the crash team around the stasis unit. They'd leap into action as soon as the field came down, giving every bit of life support to the injured man they could.

"Ready," Lily said.

Kelsey sent the command to shut off the unit. She felt the protective field come down.

The doctors sprang into action as soon as the hatch slid aside. They pulled the gurney out, and everyone bent over the man, attaching instruments and support equipment. One of the machines began wailing.

"No heartbeat!" Guzman said. "Give him ten units of—"

"Wait," Stone said, straightening slowly. "His skull is crushed. There's no brain function." She turned to Kelsey. "I'm sorry. He's dead. All this machine did was keep his body from decaying."

The disappointment was like a punch to her gut. Kelsey sagged. "God. I know I shouldn't have gotten my hopes up, but this seemed like karma."

The medical team stepped back and allowed Doctor Leonard and his teen henchman, Carl Owlet, access to the body. They slid a headset over the man's mangled cranium. Kelsey could now see that there'd never been a chance for the dead man.

Leonard glanced back at her. "His implants are still active."

Owlet tapped the keys on the portable unit. "We're downloading everything in the implants' memory and storage."

They all stood there watching until Owlet nodded. "Download complete. Starting comparison. Well, he has more data than you had on day one. A lot more."

"What kind of data?" she asked.

"It's encrypted. Let me see if I can determine what kind of protection it has."

Lily put her hand on Kelsey's shoulder. "You tried. That's more than the poor bastard had a right to expect after the Fall. Don't beat yourself up."

Once the medical team had taken the body and left, the room felt empty. No matter what they salvaged, Kelsey felt as though they'd failed the man.

"Huh," Owlet said.

"What?" She looked over his shoulder, but the screens full of gobbledygook made no sense to her.

"His implants have the same operating code as yours. The encrypted data seems to be something else. I know you can record video, so maybe that's what these files are. If so, there are a lot of them."

"Can't you tell? You downloaded the data from me."

He shrugged. "You didn't protect it. I can keep trying to crack the encryption, but it'll take time."

"Could it be hardware specific? Maybe he set it up like the ship's computer. Only someone with the right implants could view it. I hope it doesn't need an extra code. That would suck."

The young computer genius looked uncertain. "It's possible, but there's only one way to check."

Doctor Leonard shook his head emphatically. "We have no idea what these files are. Uploading any of them to your implant storage could be dangerous. The size of these files taken together is staggering. They would fill three quarters of your available storage."

"One file," she said. "Let's see if I can access it."

The older man sighed. "You're taking an enormous risk. That file could be anything. A virus, even."

"There's no need for someone to have spent so much effort laying a trap. That in itself argues that this is important and probably harmless."

The scientist threw up his hands. "Fine! One file. A small one!"

She accessed the computer and selected the file with the oldest timestamp. It was relatively small but still of enough size to maybe be a video.

Once she had it in her implant storage, she probed it. The encryption code was relatively easy to figure out. It was the dead man's implant serial number. She was certain that telling Owlet about that would earn her yet another lecture about computer security and why she should pick inconvenient and incomprehensible passwords. As she unlocked the file, it became obvious why that was more secure than it seemed. The vid required Marine Raider implants to view it.

Marine Raider implants weren't that different from those of their Fleet brethren, but they had linkages dedicated to the expanded hardware Kelsey had. That made them operationally more complex, and different enough to be a good security feature, it seemed.

With both those conditions met, she was able to play the implant recording.

The medical bay vanished, and she was standing on a hilltop. The sun setting in the distance was shaded more orange than yellow, and it was significantly larger than those she'd seen before. The air was heavy, with some kind of spicy overtone.

A marine pinnace sat in the valley below with men bustling around it. They were unloading small crates.

"Worried?"

The voice at her elbow almost made her jump out of her skin, but the video perspective shifted smoothly to show her a grizzled man in a camouflaged uniform. Unlike marine battledress, his didn't even have subdued rank tabs.

"Not really." The voice seemed to come from her, so she knew it had to be the dead man. "I can't imagine how anyone expects to be able to rebel against the Empire. This whole situation has to be blown out of proportion."

The older man nodded. "Probably. Still, what I'm hearing sounds grim. If someone really figured out how to override our implants, that could be a real nightmare scenario."

The dead man nodded. "I think that's unlikely, but times like this make me wonder. I figure the best thing I can do is focus on my job."

The other man turned toward the valley. "How are your people holding up?"

"They're fine. We'll be done here in less than an hour, and then we're heading back up to *Persephone*. We're relocating deeper into the Empire to check on this threat. I guess I'll know soon enough how bad it is."

The older man clapped the dead man on the shoulder. "Don't let it worry you, Ned. The Empire has beaten the odds before. We'll come out fine this time, too. I'm done with my part of the mission here, so I'll head back to my pinnace. We'll have a beer in a few months, after all this is done."

"Take care, Jake. If I find out anything useful, I'll try to get word to you."

The video ended, and Kelsey found herself standing back in the medical bay. Both scientists were staring at her, and Leonard had his communications unit in his hand.

"What happened?" the scientist demanded.

"Nothing much. It was an implant vid file."

"I almost called the medical team back," the older man grumbled. "Don't do that to my poor heart."

"I'm sorry," she said. "The file was encrypted so that only someone with Marine Raider implants and the dead man's implant serial number could unlock it. I saw a scene with him speaking to another man. I think our dead man's name is Ned and this ship might be *Persephone*. How many files are there?"

"Millions," Owlet said. "Some small, some really large. With the hardware lockout, I can't determine what they do."

"No, but I can," Kelsey said. "This could be a treasure trove of critical information. It doesn't seem harmful. Upload it to my implant storage, and I can work on it as time permits."

The two men looked at one another with resigned expressions.

"What?" she asked.

"You know this will get us in trouble," Leonard said. "Admiral Mertz will be quite annoyed."

"Then he can take it up with me. Come on. Give me the files."

"I know I'm going to regret this," the elderly scientist muttered.

4

Jared headed to the brig. Richards wasn't the only prisoner there now. Captain Wallace Breckenridge occupied a cell on the other side of the room. Oddly enough, the traitorous officer had been right next to Richards the last time Jared had been down here.

Lieutenant Benjamin Gonzales, *Invincible*'s security officer, rose to his feet. "Admiral."

"As you were." He gestured to Breckenridge's cell. "Why was he moved?"

"The other prisoner asked us to relocate him. Captain Breckenridge was pounding on the bulkhead at all hours and disturbing him. It seemed like a reasonable request. Was that wrong?"

Jared shook his head. "Not at all. Good call. I'm here to see Richards. Open his cell, please."

"Aye, sir."

The three marines in the room moved to a spot where they could use their nerve disruptors on the prisoner if need be, but Jared didn't expect any trouble.

Gonzales opened the hatch to Richards's cell. The Rebel Fleet officer had been reading something at the built-in desk but stood to face Jared. The other man stiffened. Admirals had that effect on people, even when they didn't serve the same Empire. To be fair, the two Fleets did share a uniform.

"There's no need to stand on ceremony, Commander," Jared said. "I just stopped in to see how you're doing."

Richards relaxed a little but didn't sit. "Much better since they moved that lunatic next door over a few cells, Admiral. Thank you for that. If I might ask, what did he do to earn your wrath? Your guards are polite but not very informative."

Jared could see how the situation would make him curious. "Captain Breckenridge imprisoned Princess Kelsey and myself for a while and involved several ships under his command in a mutiny. His actions led directly to the loss of his ship."

"That would do it," Richards said. "He's been a raving madman ever since you brought him in. Pounding on the bulkheads at all hours. Yelling so loudly that I can almost understand him. You might want to check the soundproofing on these cells. Congratulations on your promotion, by the way. It's quite a jump from commander to admiral."

Richards's dry tone was almost perfect. Too little to take offense at yet more than enough to get his meaning across. Jared was impressed.

He took a seat on the edge of the other man's bunk. "One I wouldn't have chosen for myself, but Princess Kelsey can be somewhat stubborn. In case you were unaware, the move you experienced was to the superdreadnought *Invincible*. My new command."

The Rebel Empire officer blinked. "A superdreadnought? Since you only had a battlecruiser the last time we talked, that's very impressive. You're much more formidable than I gave you credit for."

"There's a long story attached to that. One I'm inclined to share with you. You've been a model prisoner. If you'll give me your word that you won't give me any trouble, we can make a trip to the officer's mess. You've been eating the same food we do, but I figured you'd welcome a change in scenery."

The offer surprised Jared. He hadn't come expecting to make it, but now that he'd done so, it resonated inside him. He'd made the right call.

Richards's eyes widened. "I doubt very seriously that I'm a threat to a superdreadnought or the crew that captured one. Plus, I'm certain your diligent guards and ship's computer will keep close watch on me. I freely give you my word as a Fleet officer that I won't attempt to escape or harm you, your crew, or your ship while we're out on this excursion."

A very concise and limited statement, conforming well to the parole Jared had offered. That worked.

"Then come with me. Lieutenant Gonzales, one of your guards will accompany us."

"Aye, sir." If the officer thought Jared's plan a little dubious, he didn't say so.

"*Invincible*, please keep an eye on us, as well," Jared added.

"I'll keep a very close watch, Admiral, but I doubt Commander Richards will give you any problems. In fact, based on his reading list and spoken commentary, I'll warrant you'll have an eye-opening discussion."

Richards stopped dead in his tracks and stared at the ceiling. "Who the hell is that?"

"*Invincible*'s AI. And when I say AI, I really mean it. Hence the sense of self."

For a moment, Jared thought the Rebel Fleet officer would walk right back into his cell. He'd turned quite pale.

The other man stiffened his spine and walked out with Jared. The guard trailed them at a range that would allow him to stun the prisoner if need be. The three of them made their way to the officer's mess and found a seat in the corner. The people nearest them moved away when Jared requested some privacy.

They ordered tea and sandwiches. The guard stood against a nearby bulkhead.

Jared leaned back. "I'm certain you have questions. Ask away, and I'll do my best to answer them."

"An AI? How the hell did you capture one of the Imperial or System Lords? Forget that. How did you convince it to aid you?"

"I suspected you knew more about the AIs running the Rebel Empire than you'd let on. We recovered the hardware and software for the AI from an asteroid in the Erorsi system. Our experts found the malicious code and removed it before we brought it online here inside *Invincible*. She needed a computer."

The other officer shook his head. "I reject that name. I serve the Terran Empire. If there are rebels present, I submit they are your people, Admiral. No offense."

Jared smiled. "We could argue that point for days. It's just a naming convention, since I also serve a Terran Empire. One that has an unbroken history going back before the rebellion. One with an Emperor, I might add. To avoid confusion, let's use my terminology."

Richards looked as though he wanted to argue but clamped his mouth shut and nodded. "Only for the sake of clarity."

"As to the battle," Jared continued, "we captured Harrison's World and Boxer Station. Have you heard of either of them?"

The commander frowned. "I've heard of Boxer Station. It's a major Fleet base one sector over. Top secret. I've never met any officer assigned there. We couldn't have made it from Erorsi in such a short time. The trip would take weeks, and you'd have to go through occupied systems. How did you manage that?"

"There are some secrets I'm not ready to share at this point. For the sake of this discussion, let's say you accept that I'm telling the truth. We have control of Harrison's World, and I want to ask you some general questions about how the government is set up. I'm already dealing with them and would like to avoid any bloodshed, but they're making things hard."

The other man considered him. "Under normal circumstances, I'd refuse to assist you as a matter of course. We're at war, whether my people realize it or not. However, I've concluded that Princess Kelsey told me an unpleasant truth. The history I learned about the rebellion growing up may very well have been false. I want to find out what really happened."

He's telling you the truth.

Jared considered *Invincible*'s private comment.

How can you be sure?

He specifically sent that information to me and granted enough access for me to be certain. He means what he is saying. I'll notify you if he prevaricates or ceases to allow me to monitor him.

Please do.

Jared knew that if someone gave a computer enough access through their implants, the machine could assess their honesty. A general transmission wasn't intrusive enough. It required a willful granting of access to the machine. But when it happened, there was no deception. The computer was a perfect lie detector.

"You have my complete attention, Commander."

The Rebel Empire officer took a deep breath. "I believe it's in the best interests of my people to discover the truth. I'm willing to give my word to cooperate with you in exchange for the information you have. If you're right, my people are slaves. I have to know if that's true."

Jared nodded slowly. "If you'll agree to continuous visual monitoring by *Invincible*, as well as the files you access, I'm willing to grant you parole. Frankly, your help could save thousands of lives. Perhaps many more."

"I accept," Richards said without hesitation. "I'm willing to have an armed guard watch over me, as well. It's only prudent, and you'll have them standing by in any case."

"Done. I'll assign quarters for you. First, though, I want to bring you up to speed on the current situation."

He explained how the AI in the system had ruthlessly subjugated Harrison's World, vaporizing cities. How it had moved the enlisted prisoners captured from *Spear* to the planet. How he needed to get them back, but he couldn't allow the people below to know who they really were. More importantly, he couldn't let them free from their world.

Richards shook his head slowly. "That's a tough nut to crack, Admiral. The higher orders—the people that rule our society—are always maneuvering against one another. Even as an admiral, they'll see you as a social inferior.

"Fleet officers come from the middle orders of Imperial society. We have implants, as do they, but not from a young age. We only get them after thorough vetting and training as adults. The people you're talking to probably expect that you'll cave in to their desires."

"How do I get them to negotiate in good faith?"

The other man laughed. "Admiral, they're members of the higher orders. They don't negotiate in good faith unless it's with a member of their own class. Even then, I'd count your fingers after you shake on a deal. You'll just have to do the best you can."

* * *

THE UPLOAD TOOK LONGER than the download. Kelsey wasn't quite sure why. Perhaps it was a hardware limitation on the part of the cobbled-together equipment that the scientists had built.

"It takes specialized equipment to overwrite the operating code in an implant, right?" she asked. "Even if there's something in these files, it can't infect me."

"It's a little late to ask that, don't you think?" Doctor Leonard asked a bit waspishly.

"Probably, but I want to hear it again."

He sighed. "Nothing in these files can overwrite your implant code. That doesn't make this safe, though."

"Can you give me an example of what might go wrong?"

"No. I just don't like the unknown."

"Me either. So let's figure this out."

She had her implants start the process of unlocking the files. It would take several hours, even at the speed her hardware ran.

They made their way back to her pinnace. She was just settling in when her implants registered an incoming communications signal.

"Bandar," she said.

"Highness, this is Lieutenant Madison on Boxer Station. I've found what looks like an implant facility."

She recognized the woman's name as one of *New York's* officers. Jared had moved her to Boxer Station before her ship left for Erorsi and Pentagar.

"Is it operational?" Kelsey asked, trying to keep from letting her innate optimism run wild.

"I can't tell. That's why I need your help."

"We'll be right there."

She terminated the connection and called Jared. Once he answered, she passed word of the discovery.

"That's terrific news," he said. "I have some for you, too. *New York* just arrived at the flip point with four Pentagaran ships and *Best Deal*. I'll route them to join you at Boxer Station. I'd like to keep the new ships out of sight."

"Send Talbot out, too. He gets all weird when I find new stuff."

"You mean he gets weird when you jump in where angels fear to tread. I'll send him out right now. I'll be heading to bed soon, so don't do anything crazy. The locals are coming up early. I want to be ready for them."

"I'll file a report so you can read it in the morning," she said. "Good night."

Kelsey accessed the pinnaces' scanners. *New York* and the new ships would arrive at about the same time as Talbot's pinnace. It would be late, but she didn't need much sleep. Especially in circumstances like these.

She sent a message to the medical teams, who were still on *Ginnie Dare*, to join them at Boxer Station.

Half an hour later, Kelsey stood inside the docking area on Boxer Station. Power was back, but the computer systems were still offline. A team of specialists were removing the AI and recovering all the data they could from the other computers. When they finished, they'd wipe them and reload the operating systems.

Lieutenant Madison stood in the vast docking area waiting for her with several ratings. "Highness."

"Lieutenant Madison. Take me to your find." Her security team formed up around her as she spoke.

The Fleet officer gestured. "It's just off the medical center, which sort of makes sense. Several cutters are on their way over from *Ginnie Dare*. They should be arriving momentarily."

Several loud thunks announced the arrival of the aforementioned cutters. The hatches opened and disgorged Doctor Leonard, Carl Owlet, Doctor Stone, Doctor Guzman, and numerous other medical personnel and scientists.

"Perfect timing," Kelsey said. "I hope this facility can be made operational. That would make our lives so much easier going forward."

"*Your* life, maybe," Stone muttered.

She clapped the medical officer on the shoulder. "Cheer up, Lily! Imagine what you can do with implants in that fancy new medical center of yours."

"I'm imagining the hijinks the crew will come up with to end up in there with me," she said grumpily. "If you only knew how many silly ways they manage to get hurt as it is. These implants will be new territory."

"What could possibly go wrong?" Kelsey asked with a grin. "Let's go, Lieutenant."

Kelsey could've found the medical center from the plans she had in her implants, but that would be rude. This was Madison's discovery. She deserved the chance to show it off.

Boxer Station's corridors raised bad memories for Kelsey. She'd exchanged fire with mechanical fighting devices under the control of the AI here just a few days ago. She'd acquired new injuries and lost a lot of friends. The regeneration chamber had made her physically whole, but her mind was another story. The scars there might take years to heal. If they ever did.

The engineering teams had sealed away the worst of the damage. Life support was stable, and they weren't worried about any more bulkheads losing pressure. The marines—the few they had left—had searched the station several times to be sure there were no more AI-controlled humans hiding in odd corners or war machines left unaccounted for.

The humans were free of mental control at this point, but Jared was keeping them in isolation for their own safety. She'd seen how Commander Richards had become almost subhuman after he knew who they were, and she didn't want to subject the other prisoners to that. They'd been through enough.

The war machines seemed dead, but the technicians were manually disconnecting their power supplies just to be sure. Then they'd transport them to *Invincible*.

The battle to control this system had come far too close to failure. If any one part of the operations in space or on the station hadn't worked, they'd all be dead or captured. They'd lost seventy percent of the marine force in the assault. Fewer than a hundred men and women survived out of three hundred.

They couldn't afford another victory like that.

Kelsey shook off the gloom that threatened to overwhelm her. She had too much to do.

"This is the medical center," Madison said. She gestured through a wide hatch at a compartment bigger than Kelsey had imagined possible. It had to be twice the size of marine country on *Invincible*. At least.

Doctor Stone stepped inside and gaped. "My God."

It had half a dozen full operating theaters, more regeneration pods than Kelsey could count, several stasis chambers, and a compartment full of examination beds. There were adjacent wards that could hold hundreds of sick people. Maybe thousands. The sheer scale of the operation boggled her mind. This facility could probably hold every surviving man and woman in the task force. Even disused, it was damned impressive.

"It's bigger than I expected," Kelsey admitted.

Doctor Guzman shrugged. "This was a Fleet sector base. Besides being a huge station, it served as the command and control post for any number of other bases in the surrounding systems. It may have also been expanded after the rebellion started."

Stone turned to Kelsey. "Can I take it home with me?"

Kelsey laughed. "Where would you put it? Besides, the medical center on *Invincible* is pretty impressive. All you need are a couple of these stasis chambers and you'll be set. Come on, everyone. There'll be time to explore once we assess the implantation facility."

Lieutenant Madison had said it was next to the medical center, but that was still a bit of a walk. This station had probably been home to a quarter million Fleet personnel in its heyday.

The implantation center looked very much like the medical center: big and disused. A thin layer of dust covered everything. Unlike Workstation Twelve—the machine the Pale Ones had used to implant the AI's slaves—the dozens of stations in this facility were all-in-one affairs.

Of course, they hadn't done the full-body implants required for Marine Raiders here. No enhanced muscles, shielded bones, or pharmacology units. Only cranial implants. The individual stations consisted of couches the patient reclined on with equipment around the head. They were very sleek. Workstation Twelve was a kludge in comparison.

The scientists and technicians spread out to examine the various couches. Doctor Guzman went with Doctor Leonard.

Stone stood beside Kelsey. "Nothing for commando implants."

"I noticed that. I can't say I'm surprised. They can't have been common before the Fall. The Marine Raiders had to have been a very exclusive organization. They probably handled their own implanting. As much as I would love to have every marine with us set up to be a Raider, I doubt we'll find the hardware just lying around."

"The AI at Erorsi was getting them from somewhere." Stone said. "At least there are enough stations to get the Fleet personnel implanted in a reasonable time frame."

The princess turned to the doctor. "I thought you were against using the implants."

"It's the future, Kelsey. It doesn't matter how I feel about it. Frankly, I'll be interested in seeing how they work for myself."

Doctor Leonard waved them over.

"These systems are operational," he said. "I think. They draw power, anyway. Princess, can you access them?"

This was something she'd done many times before. Kelsey accessed the equipment and found it unlocked. The station in front of her provided her with an overview of the process. It was straightforward, though there were a number of complex monitoring screens. The workstations also had computers at least as sophisticated as Workstation Twelve's to oversee the process.

What they didn't have was voice access. Only someone with implants could operate them.

She turned to the scientists and filled them in.

Carl Owlet frowned. "How do we compare the implant code with the clean version we have?"

"Do we need to?" she asked. "You've examined the Rebel Empire Fleet personnel. These machines probably implanted them. They have to have compromised code."

"Doctor Leonard frowns on qualifiers," the graduate student said with a grin. "He takes off points if you use them."

"And rightly so," the older scientist said primly. "Science isn't made when you use words like 'probably,' 'maybe,' and 'hopefully.' You test everything and verify. We need to compare the implant code to what we have on our equipment."

It took her almost an hour to gain access to the code repository. She sent a version of the implant code to Owlet's machine directly from the workstation.

"This is the same code we pulled off the Rebel Empire officer," Owlet confirmed a few minutes later. "The hardware is the same as Admiral Mertz's Fleet implants, so no problem there. All you need to do is upload the clean code to this machine, and we can begin using it."

Kelsey nodded. "I've already checked every workstation, and they all use the same code. I can send it to all of them as soon as I unlock their repositories." She got that process started.

Meanwhile, they found the supplies for the implantation machines. Enough cranial implants to take care of thousands of people. She planned to send half of them back to Pentagar. Even so, there were more than enough to take care of every man and woman in their task force.

There was also a sealed supply of nanites locked away in a vault adjacent to the implantation center. The AIs didn't like using them for some reason. This supply was large enough to help tens of thousands of people.

Kelsey checked the time. Talbot would arrive in less than an hour. She'd better get set up for the first group, because she knew he'd insist on being at the front of the line.

5

A rap at the door made Coordinator Olivia West look up from her display. She put a false smile on her face as soon as she saw who it was. "Abigail. Come in."

Deputy Coordinator Abigail King was a senior member of Harrison's World's ruling council and a huge pain in the ass to work with. The conservative alliance had forced her on Olivia to avoid a council showdown during her election. She often wondered if she'd have been better off fighting them then.

The younger woman took a seat without invitation. "You asked to see me?"

"I wanted to get an update on how the negotiations are proceeding."

Abigail scowled. It wasn't a pleasant expression on her. "The jumped-up prole is still refusing to budge."

Olivia leaned back in her chair. "I see. How do you intend to move the talks along?"

"We have 2,354 prisoners. Executing a hundred or so should make him aware how seriously we're taking his intransigence."

It took a moment, but Olivia managed to suppress the first words that wanted to come out of her mouth. They wouldn't be helpful. "Leaving aside the morality of killing people under our control to make a political point, need I remind you that he controls the orbital bombardment platforms? The exchange of such pleasantries would be very one sided."

Abigail made a dismissive gesture. "He wouldn't dare attack us."

"Allow me to remind you of a few unpleasant facts. Rebels from our world plotted against our Lord. Those actions led to the Lord reducing the capital and several other cities containing many citizens of the highest orders to smoking craters. What makes you so certain that Admiral Mertz won't do that very thing?"

The other woman sniffed. "That was a decade ago. The Lord killed the rebels. Coordinator James and the council of the time paid for their treachery. As painful as that was, it did allow us to assume leadership roles. You wouldn't be in that chair without the removal of so many others with political clout."

Her tone implied Olivia wouldn't have achieved leadership of Harrison's World without the mass executions. True enough.

Abigail acted as though tens of millions hadn't died in the orbital strikes. For the other woman, the deaths of those in the middle and lower orders didn't count as anything but an inconvenience.

Olivia sighed. "You disappoint me. The admiral and his task force came for a reason. The System Lord has not spoken since Admiral Mertz arrived. I've never heard of the Lords disciplining one of their own before, but it's possible that's what happened. That could be good news for us, but we'd be fools to count on it.

"The admiral may have orders to discipline Harrison's World further for allowing rebels to flourish here. We need to walk this path carefully. There will be no executions."

The other woman sneered. "What do those peons matter? You can't tell me that any officer of flag rank cares one whit about the lower orders cleaning his decks. His stance on the prisoners must be some charade."

Olivia made a show of considering that. "It's possible he may be playing some deeper game. When are you speaking to him next?"

"In a few hours. He's sending a cutter to pick me up, but I plan to decline at the last moment. The prole can come down to me."

Abigail's intransigence simply amazed Olivia. People like her were so certain they ruled the Empire under the guidance of the Lords that they didn't care how anyone else thought. Even the people that might revolt and hang them. Or, in the case of the Fleet admiral, drop high-velocity tungsten rods onto them until they died.

"You risk too much," Olivia said after a moment. "We have no deep-space scanners, so we don't have any idea how large his task force is or how it's deployed. Would you like it if he came calling with a troop transport full of marines? They could come down and drag you up to the meeting."

The other woman leaned back, and her nostrils flared. "He wouldn't dare!"

"I'm not willing to bet this planet on your ego. I'll go and speak to Admiral Mertz in your place. We'll come to an understanding sooner with a willingness to actually talk, I'm certain."

Abigail's shocked expression was almost comical. "The council appointed me as negotiator! You can't replace me!"

Olivia stood slowly. "You forget yourself. I am the coordinator of Harrison's World. My decision is final. Run along and complain to your allies all you like. They won't overrule me. I control enough votes to assure that."

The younger woman stood abruptly. "You rule at our pleasure, Olivia. Never forget that. One day our willingness to take your insulting behavior will end, and so will you." She stormed out in a rage.

Olivia could've probably been a little less imperious, but the woman got on her last nerve. Oh well. Abigail King would never have been her ally, much less her friend. The bitch was too ambitious. This day had been inevitable and a long time coming.

* * *

SEAN MANAGED to sleep a while before people started moving. His change in status seemed to have already made the rounds. People that had avoided him like the plague nodded politely. Some even spoke to him.

He dressed in Fleet fatigues without name tags or rank insignia. He figured he could skip the shower after last night.

The prisoners ate in a mess hall manned by their own people, but the food came in grav vans with armed guards. The stone-faced men with Old Empire weapons stayed near the vehicles and only allowed a few prisoners to come get the day's food.

Sean walked toward them and stopped when they raised their weapons. "My name is Force Master Chief Sean Meyer. I'm the senior prisoner. I want to speak to someone in authority."

"Back away," one of the guards said. He aimed his flechette rifle at Sean to emphasize the command.

"No. Take me to someone with authority to answer my questions."

The man sneered. "You think you have some say in this, prole? You don't. Move on."

Sean smiled. "You're sadly mistaken. One word from me and you'll have a riot on your hands. Is that really how you want your commander to learn your name? All you have to do is pass the word up and it's someone else's problem."

The two men looked at one another. The one who hadn't spoken gestured for Sean to back up. "Go sit down and I'll call this in. No promises."

Sean made himself some coffee and sat down. Twenty minutes later, two new guards arrived in an open-topped grav car. They came toward Sean.

"Get up," one said. "Hands behind your back."

When some of the other prisoners stood, Sean held his hand out. "Stand down. There isn't going to be any problem. I'll be back shortly."

The guards cuffed him, led him to their vehicle, stuffed him in back between two additional escorts, and lifted off. With a little height, Sean could tell the prisoners were on a small island. Hemmed in between the guards, he couldn't get a clear look at it, but the island wasn't more than a half kilometer offshore. The water looked cold and a bit rough.

The grav car took them over what appeared to be slums. Further inland, the buildings became more upscale. One might charitably call them middle class, if one squinted. The car zeroed in on one of the larger roofs and landed. The building had a sign indicating it was owned by Roscoe Consolidated.

His guards escorted him through the roof door and into a lift. They went to the tenth floor and led him down a corridor with worn tan carpeting. The art on the walls looked inexpensive and generic.

One of the guards knocked on a door and led Sean inside without waiting for a response. The office consisted of a battered desk, an even more battered man behind it, and office furniture that someone probably should've junked years ago.

The man didn't look at all pleased about the interruption. "Put him in the chair and wait by the door. This won't take long."

That didn't sound promising at all.

The guards dragged a chair in front of the desk and sat Sean down with more force than necessary.

"Thank you for taking time out of your busy day to see me," Sean said dryly.

"Don't be a smartass," the man said with a snarl. "I can have them let you out of the car over the ocean if you piss me off, prole."

"My apologies. I'm Force Master Chief Sean Meyer, the senior Fleet prisoner. I have some concerns about my people and their housing."

The man sneered. "So I gathered. As far as I'm concerned, you should feel glad we didn't drop you a hundred kilometers offshore and let you swim for it, you bastards."

Sean hadn't expected this level of animosity. "Have we met? I certainly don't remember harming you."

The man rose abruptly and stomped around the desk. Sean thought he was going to hit him, but the man only grabbed Sean by his tunic and yanked him to his feet.

"Oh, no?" the man shouted, spraying Sean with spittle. "Maybe you remember Port City better? You know, the capital of Harrison's World before you blew it up, along with my brother. Give me one excuse to rip your head off and I'll dump your worthless body where no one will ever find it."

The level of danger was significantly higher than Sean had anticipated, especially since he had no idea what the man was talking about. "I'm truly sorry that happened, but I didn't do it, and neither did the men with me."

"You think that matters?" The man shoved Sean back down in the chair. "Say your piece so I can have someone come clean my office. Maybe the stink will go away in a few years."

Sean had intended to probe for some idea of what was happening, but he didn't dare.

"A number of our people were taken to a hospital. Not all of them have come back. I want to know how they're doing."

The man glared at Sean for a moment and returned to his desk with a muttered curse. He tapped on the keys to his console. "Six prisoners are in a guarded wing of a local hospital. If I could, I'd haul them back and let them die right in front of you. You want to know anything else?"

"I don't suppose you could give us some reading material?"

The man snorted. "As if you rats from the lower orders can even read. Get this bastard out of my sight. And the next son of a bitch that wants to see me? Shoot him."

The guards hustled Sean out the door without a moment's hesitation.

He had no idea what had happened on this planet, but it didn't look good for him or his people. If the Rebel Empire Fleet had bombarded the capital of this world, he could understand the hatred they were expressing. It limited his ability to see to their conditions, but he couldn't help that.

Based on how grave Captain Cooley's injuries had been before the AI ambushed them, Sean hoped he was still alive. He'd lost his legs and suffered life-threatening injuries when the Rebel Empire destroyer had wrecked *Shadow*.

They flew Sean back to the island without saying a word. He used the time to study the layout of the city and the island once they made the flight across the bay. The view reinforced the idea that the prison camp had once been a training facility. Parts of the island were still in use, though the people below weren't Fleet. They looked like stevedores.

He had a tantalizingly brief view of some ships drawn up offshore unloading cargo containers. They were big. There were also some sizable grav vehicles. He imagined the cargo came by sea and made its way across to the city after sorting.

Maybe, just maybe, they could escape their prison if Mertz didn't come through. At the very least, it wouldn't hurt to make some contingency plans. If they could get into the city, they might be able to get to a spaceport. It was a terrible risk, but if they had to run, they needed to be ready.

* * *

ABIGAIL KING STALKED into her office. Her assistant started to say something but rapidly found more productive things to do with his time.

"I'm not to be disturbed for any reason," Abigail told him and went into her office, slamming the hardwood door behind her.

She immediately called a memorized number.

"Calder Consortium. How may I direct your call?"

"Put me through to Master Calder."

As the head of the conservative alliance, Edward Calder was due the title even from the second most powerful official on the planet. After all, he'd been the one who put her where she was. He could take her out just as easily.

"Right away, Deputy Coordinator King."

The line was silent for a moment before her patron came on. "Abigail, I've been waiting for your call. How are things proceeding?"

"Poorly, Master. Coordinator West has removed me from the role of negotiator and is going up to the Fleet vessels in orbit herself. It sounds as though she's looking for a way to find common ground with Admiral Mertz."

The line was silent for a moment. "Do you think she's become aware of our plans?"

"It's hard to tell, Master. It galls me, but she's more subtle than I am."

Calder laughed. "Don't confuse the persona you play for who you really are, Abigail. You're far more discerning than you give yourself credit for.

"Now, while I'll admit that this might be a setback, I'm not yet ready to throw in the towel. You've put this Admiral Mertz into a heightened state of intransigence, as I instructed. All we need to do is keep him and Coordinator West from coming to an agreement. If the progressive coalition negotiates our release from Harrison's World, they will consolidate their rule for the foreseeable future. I won't allow that to happen."

"I've tried to assure that there is no agreement, Master, but if she makes more reasonable overtures, he may well agree to her terms. If only to get back at me."

He made a clucking noise. "You're too pessimistic. We still have many avenues to disrupt the negotiations. Perhaps it's time to remove West from power in a more permanent fashion."

Abigail shook her head, even though he couldn't see her. "I think it's far too premature, Master. The council is still more in her camp than out. Her assassination would only make them more mulish. Perhaps the engineered execution of some of the prisoners with the finger of guilt pointing at her? An atrocity would both derail the negotiations and taint her reputation."

"I wonder if we could merge those ideas," he said thoughtfully. "Killing some of the Fleet prisoners and then assassinating Olivia West. Those linked events could get everyone looking at Admiral Mertz as the guilty party for her death. That has possibilities.

"Keep a close eye on the negotiations and begin setting up plans to carry out the execution of some prisoners. If the moment seems ripe, we'll see if we can get the dogs to attack one another. Call me as soon as something important occurs."

He disconnected without waiting for her response. Abigail scowled at the view outside her window. This was risky. Impetuous. If things went wrong, she'd be the immediate suspect.

Which might be Master Calder's plan, she admitted. He led the conservative alliance, and his family had been in power before the System Lord had crushed the planet. As one of only a few surviving members of that clan, he'd want to sit in the coordinator's chair himself. With the death of Olivia West, he'd see Abigail as an obstacle to his ambitions.

She owed her rise in power to him, but she didn't owe him her life. She decided she'd take steps to see that certain information about him became public if something unfortunate happened to her. Done properly, he'd find out and understand the message she was sending him. In the end, the real winner was the one left standing.

6

The communicator on Olivia's desk chimed. She answered her assistant's request with the touch of a key. "Yes?"

"My deepest apologies, Coordinator. Lord Hawthorne is here without an appointment. He's very insistent about speaking with you."

"Send him in."

The titles accorded to the higher orders by birth always made her smile bitterly. They were lords and ladies, just like the AIs that ruled them. Their ruling society had three layers: the Imperial Lords who ruled the Empire, the System Lords who managed individual solar systems, and the higher orders of humanity.

The machine intelligences always spoke of how they worked hand in hand with the human leaders, and the lower orders believed that fiction. Little did they know that even the most powerful humans were just as much slaves as they were.

William Hawthorne was different for a number of reasons. She'd known him for most of her life. He was actually one of her few friends—and her mentor.

The tall man with sandy curls came in and bowed his head. "My deepest apologies for interrupting your busy day, Coordinator. I bring word from my Lady Mother. She commanded me to deliver it at once and in person."

"Then come in and tell me. I can hardly wait."

He closed the door and gave her a questioning look.

"My security team scanned the room this morning," she said. "I've been here ever since. Speak freely. Did your mother actually have a message for me?"

He smiled. "She did, though that's not why I'm here. My youngest sister is getting married next month, and my Lady Mother would be delighted if you could attend."

"I'll check my schedule and let you know, but only because I like your sister more than your mother. She gets on my nerves with all her matchmaking. I'm tempted to tell her about my unrequited love for you just to get her off my back."

William gave her a semipanicked look. "Don't you dare! Not even in jest! She'd never give me a moment's peace, urging me to divorce Craig and marry you straight away. Oh, the scandal that would cause."

He sat and gave her a considering look. "I might be persuaded to name my daughter after you, though. She'll be out of the artificial womb in another two months, and we still haven't agreed on a name. Craig would be honored, I'm sure."

"As would I. What do you really need?"

"I've spoken with the others and taken them the data you provided. Captain Black searched the few Fleet databases we still have and came up empty. No mention of an Admiral Jared Mertz.

"That's not really surprising, though. Fleet databases are fairly segmented. We only knew the officers and ships assigned to this sector and the surrounding ones. The admiral obviously came from farther away. Perhaps even the core worlds."

Olivia considered what that might mean. "They've had a long time to clean up the mess on Harrison's World. Why wait a decade? To see if there are any rebels still hiding here?"

William smiled. "I'd think you, of all people, would be happy to have the time to consolidate your rule. The orbital strikes mostly destroyed the existing political structure. I'm not sure I'd have expected a resistance leader to end up in charge back then."

"The irony isn't lost on me," she assured him. "We financed the restoration of *Invincible* and were only weeks away from striking at the System Lord." She said the last with all the bitterness she felt toward their AI masters. They'd taken so much from humanity, and from her personally.

Her fiancé, Fleet Captain Brian Drake, had almost certainly died when the AI realized the humans of Harrison's World were planning a revolt. His death had almost destroyed her. It probably would have if she hadn't been running for her life and helping rescue people from the devastation.

The Lord had struck at them without mercy, killing tens of millions. Then it had crushed their necks under its boot. The slightest hesitation to obey brought wholesale death. It could've sent probes down to take control of the implants in their heads, but it hadn't seemed interested in that level of domination.

Most of the nobles didn't realize the AI could take direct control of their bodies through their implants. The code in them was perverted. They thought of the lower orders as their slaves, but that was the worst kind of deception. The AIs that had crushed the Terran Empire could make them dance any time they chose to do so.

She knew this because Harrison's World had a loosely knit community of resistance members. They kept memories of what the Empire had once been alive. Maybe it was closer to a religion. They certainly felt a reverence for what they'd lost that was close to worship.

They'd thought a superdreadnought and a few secrets from the Grant Research Facility would be enough to subdue the AI. They'd been horribly wrong.

It had spies on the ground, though seemingly not in the resistance itself. It had gotten wind of the coup, or at least enough information to believe that humans were a threat to its rule.

Most of her allies on the ruling council would be horrified to know the truth about her. If they even suspected her role in the aborted coup, they'd speedily see her executed.

"Are you even listening to me?" William asked.

She shook herself out of her thoughts and focused. "Sorry. I let my mind wander. What did you say?"

He gave her an exasperated but resigned look. "I said that we've gone over the data we stole from Lady King's network. Leaving aside her profound incompetence as a negotiator, we've analyzed the video she recorded of the initial meeting.

"Admiral Mertz is definitely on a Holyfield-class superdreadnought. The same kind of ship as *Invincible*. The flag bridge layout is unmistakable. With his support ships, he's too strong a nut to crack, even if we managed to slip some people out to *Invincible* and finish bringing it online. His trained crew and support vessels would slaughter us. Whatever plan you formulate needs to be subtle."

She nodded. "I'll give it my best. I told Abigail that I was going up to negotiate in person. I'll bring back as much data as I can. Is there anything else?"

"One more thing. We looked at the meeting with the Fleet landing party. Something odd came out of it. Look at this."

He sent her a video snippet through his implants. It showed a woman in powered armor standing up to Abigail's obnoxious demands. Olivia found herself liking the small woman.

"Okay. What am I missing?"

"The men behind her are in a variant of standard unpowered Imperial Marine armor. So far, so good. Her armor is not standard marine issue, however. Also, even though she never used them, Abigail noted she had implants, so she's an officer."

Olivia frowned. "That doesn't make sense. Only shock troops use armor."

Imperial shock troops were the Empire's most deadly ground weapon. The massive suits made them virtually invincible. The people inside them, though, weren't trusted. Their officers kept them on a very short leash. At the first sign of a problem, their officers would eliminate them. The AIs didn't want humans to possess that kind of destructive power.

"That's what Captain Black said. We don't have any marines in the families now, but we have the basic data. Marine officers use unpowered armor. No exceptions. And look at her size. She's a tiny little thing. I could scruff her and she'd never land a blow on me. She's not a marine."

Bumped out of her comfortable mental space, Olivia took the time to consider the situation and listen to the exchange between the woman and Abigail again.

"She calls them 'her marines' right out in the open," Olivia said. "What about her armor? If it's not standard issue, perhaps identifying it will give us a clue who we're dealing with."

William shook his head. "That only deepens the mystery. The old databases identify it as Marine Raider armor."

Olivia's frown deepened. "What's a Marine Raider? I've never heard the term before."

"According to the records, Marine Raiders were the premier troops of the prerebellion Terran Empire. So heavily enhanced they could take out dozens of regular marines all by themselves. Artificial muscles, hardened bones, combat drugs that made them almost immune to pain, and faster than death.

"That armor is lighter than the stuff used by the shock troops, but these commandos could strike out of nowhere and be gone before you knew you were dead. There hasn't been a Marine Raider in over five centuries. They died trying to stave off the AIs. Or so we've always thought."

Well, that certainly made for an unexpected surprise. Who was this woman, and what was her role? Had the AIs resurrected the Terran Empire's deadliest killing machines? Was she a weapon the Imperial Lords would use to stab Harrison's World in the heart?

Her name was Kelsey Bandar, or so she'd said. Olivia looked forward to meeting this exquisitely deadly woman in person.

"Well, now that you've ruined my day," Olivia said, "let's have a drink. The good stuff. I might not be in a position to enjoy it tomorrow."

She poured a drink for her friend and for herself. When he was ready, she raised her glass. "To the Emperor. May he rest in peace."

William finished the ceremonial toast. "And to the Empire. May it rise from the ashes."

Olivia drank deeply to that. One day they'd restore the Empire or die trying.

* * *

JARED AWOKE when his door chimed. A quick check showed Crown Princess Elise of Pentagar smiling at the pickup. His internal chronometer said he had an hour left before his alarm went off, but he'd cheerfully lose some sleep to see his girlfriend again.

He threw on some clothes and opened the hatch. "Hey! I didn't expect you for a few more hours."

She stepped into his arms and kissed him. "I know you have a busy day ahead of you, and I wanted some time alone first."

Her Royal Guard companions remained outside as he closed the hatch.

She hugged him hard. "I'm so happy you made it through that battle. I watched the vids on the trip out. God. If I hadn't known in advance that you'd made it, I'd have been certain you'd all died. That was insane."

The battle for this system had been brutal. "We didn't have a choice. We had to win or suffer the consequences. We lost so many people, particularly the marines."

"I saw some of that, too. While it won't make up for the loss, we brought as many Royal Pentagaran Marines as we could pile into the corridors. They're on Boxer Station. We left our ships there, too. They'll need some remedial training on your equipment and how you operate, but that should help."

He nodded. "It does. Not against the planet holding our people but in case we have to do more fighting in space. We appreciate the help."

"We're allies. You've given so much to help us. How could we not give everything we could in return? We brought the heaviest ships we had upgraded to use the space-time bridges. We also brought extra crew to transfer to your ships. That should help fill some of the remaining gaps."

Jared mentally translated "space-time bridges" to "flip points." "I'm going to be in so much trouble when I get back home. Even with Kelsey making it an Imperial order to allow Pentagaran crew on our ships, the admiralty is going to flip without a ship."

"Leave tomorrow's problems for tomorrow," she advised. "I know you have a very important meeting this morning. Before then, I'd like to do something I've never done before."

He raised an eyebrow. "What would *that* be? I thought we'd been pretty... thorough."

Elise smacked his arm and pulled him down to sit on the couch. "That, too, but not right now. We don't have time, and you are *not* going to meet a foreign head of state after a roll between the sheets with me. What did Kelsey tell you about what they found?"

"They found what might have been the implant center on the station. Are you wondering what they might be like? I thought we'd discussed that to death. You need to experience them yourself is the best answer I can give."

She smiled oddly. "I'm ready to start."

He opened his mouth to say something and stopped. A quick check told him that she had implants.

"I hadn't heard the implantation center was operational," he said. "I wish you'd waited. We don't know this equipment as well as I'd like."

"Kelsey seemed satisfied," Elise said. She took his hand in hers. "And if she was going to allow Talbot to do it, how could I miss the opportunity?"

Jared frowned. "Wait. How many people are we talking about?"

Elise gave him a lopsided smile. "She's already shepherded a few dozen people through the process. Some of my people, her guards, Talbot, Doctor

Stone, and some scientists. The second round consisted of mostly my people. She didn't want to get too far ahead of your approval in getting your crew done."

He sighed. "Too late."

"She said you'd say that and begs your forgiveness."

"I should never have told her it was easier to beg forgiveness than ask permission. I've created a monster. If she'd asked, I would've said yes, but I certainly wouldn't have put you in the first group."

"Then it's a good thing I didn't wait. You need people to have implants, you know. The Rebel Fleet officers are implanted. If yours aren't, that'll set off alarm bells when your visitors arrive."

"You're right. Still, I don't have enough time to get people to the station, see them through the implant procedure, and then get them back before the negotiating party arrives. Why didn't she wake me?"

"It was late and she knew what you'd say. She invited certain crew members to come visit Boxer Station. If you approve, they have time for the procedure and the trip here. That's one of the reasons I dropped in so early."

Jared needed to have a long talk with Kelsey. It could wait until this situation was resolved, though.

He opened a channel to his sister through *Invincible*'s communications system. It would take minutes for her to respond, so he decided to make this brief.

Kelsey, you've officially gotten even. Go ahead with the people you sent for. In the future, I'd appreciate it if you didn't go behind my back where my people are concerned. The chain of command exists for a reason. Come back with the crew. I want you here on Invincible *when King comes up. Mertz out.*

He returned his attention to Elise. "There. I've scolded her and given her the green light. Now, what do we do about you?"

Elise shook her head with a bemused expression. "You stared off into space for just a few seconds. That must've been the fastest ass chewing in history."

"Hardly. You should've heard what she said when I got implants and didn't tell *her*. So, what can you do?"

Elise seemed to consider his words for a moment and then stood. "Actually, we can talk about that later. You have plenty of time to shower. I've missed you and have better things to do than talk."

That was a plan he could wholeheartedly get behind. Worrying about King could wait.

7

Kelsey stepped out of the cutter. Jared's bridge crew filed out as soon as she cleared the way. Her security team, Talbot, and Charlie Graves followed them. The cutter crew closed the hatch and decoupled, taking the senior officers from *Courageous* home.

Jared shook Charlie's hand. "Looks like we'll have to start cutting you in on the action."

Graves grinned. "I'm looking forward to getting back to *Courageous* and testing these implants. Now that you and the princess aren't hogging them."

"I bet. *Invincible*, please grant everyone present with implants the appropriate access to your systems."

"Done, Admiral," the AI said. "Welcome aboard, everyone."

Jared gestured toward the lift. "Zia, Kelsey, Talbot, Charlie, and Elise. Let's adjourn to my office. Everyone else, you know where you need to be. Start getting familiar with using your implants."

The large crowd dispersed, and Jared led the way to his office just off the flag bridge. It was a large space seemingly designed to impress visitors. His desk was made of dark wood and so large that Kelsey doubted he could reach the other side while sitting.

She looked around the space with interest. The shelves were of a similar make. He'd picked up enough knickknacks on Pentagar to fill them. The rest of the furniture was comfortable and expensive looking.

All in all, she thought the room set the right tone for the visiting negotiators. Of course, they hadn't seemed very impressed with a fleet of ships in orbit, so she might be wrong.

They settled into comfortable chairs, and Jared started things off. "I'm glad to see no one had any problems with the implant procedure. That'll make things a lot better for us the next time we have to fight. Unfortunately, we have a battle of a different nature coming up. The woman assigned to negotiate with us is difficult. Now she's coming to see me face to face.

"How do we keep her from knowing we aren't Rebel Fleet officers? Or that this ship was the one they were getting ready to stage a coup with? One misstep and they could kill thousands of our people."

Graves frowned. "I still don't understand how they could be so suicidal. We control weapons of mass destruction that could obliterate millions of their citizens."

"Weapons we won't use," Kelsey said. "It's never a good strategy to bluff. If they call, we look weak."

Talbot gave her a smile. "You bluff all the time."

"Never so often that you can read me," she shot back. "If we blow this, we have no leverage. Let them read the threat without us mentioning it."

Jared nodded. "That's probably for the best. I'd been planning to use a different conference room, but now that we have enough officers with implants, I think a trip through the flag bridge is in order. Impress her with this ship and its implied firepower."

"You'll need to replace the ship's plaque," Zia said. "The chances of there being two major ships with the same name are too small."

"*Invincible*, can you do that?"

"Of course, Admiral," the AI said. "What name would you like to use for our deception?"

He pursed his lips for a moment. "Let's go with *Athena*. And you'll need to tone down your interaction. You need to sound less capable."

"This unit will comply, Admiral."

"Perfect. Now, let's talk about the meeting. I'm envisioning Princess Kelsey and myself as our faces. I'll also need a flag captain."

Graves smiled. "I'm ready to fill the role."

Jared shook his head. "You have to be on *Courageous*. What if they need to know who commands that ship later? No, it needs to be someone that's here all the time."

He looked at Zia. "Since you've been acting as my executive officer, that makes you the logical choice. You'll need new rank tabs, Captain."

The woman's eyes bulged a little. "I know it's only pretend, but I was a lieutenant a week ago, sir. I'm feeling a little out of my depth."

"Who said I was making this up?" Jared turned to Kelsey. "I'd rather have someone I trust implicitly at my back when trouble comes calling."

Kelsey nodded decisively. "That's the right choice. *Invincible*, please log Zia Anderson's promotion to captain and her assignment as flag captain of this ship."

"Promotion and assignment logged, Highness. Congratulations, Captain Anderson. I look forward to working with you."

Zia swallowed hard, her skin going pale. "This is crazy. I'm the tactical officer from a destroyer. I don't have the experience to command a ship like this."

Jared shook his head. "I've seen you fight, Zia. Never doubt for a moment that you have what it takes. I was only a destroyer captain when this started. We all have to step up. Imagine what the situation will be like when we get any other ships from the graveyard operational. We won't have nearly enough people unless we promote from within."

The tall redhead sighed and nodded. "I understand, sir. I'll do my best."

"Then we're in excellent hands." He looked around the group. "I'm clearing the officers from *Spear* and *Shadow* for duty, but I want to vet them more thoroughly."

He looked at Elise. "I'm open to bringing some of the Pentagaran officers on board as well. We'll need every hand we can get. Since Kelsey has authorized your people to serve, we'll use this as a training opportunity."

Elise smiled. "Since at least some of these derelict ships will be coming back to Erorsi and Pentagar, I think that's the best plan. Our people need to be able to work together seamlessly."

"Pardon the interruption, Admiral," *Invincible* said. "The cutter you sent down to pick up the delegation has signaled they are on their way up. ETA half an hour."

Jared rubbed his eyes. "That figures. The one time I want them to drag their feet they're early. It looks as though we'll need to work out the rest of the plan on the fly. Let's get moving, people."

* * *

OLIVIA SAW the brief look of confusion on Fleet Admiral Mertz's face when she stepped out of the cutter. He'd obviously been expecting Abigail and all the mental pain that entailed. The fact that she noted the emotion at all told her a lot about the man.

He might be used to command but not to moving in political circles. No noble with any experience would show weakness to an opponent like that.

The man stepped away from several other officers and bowed slightly. Not as much as she was entitled to, but she wasn't going to make an issue of it. They had more important things to worry about.

"Welcome aboard *Athena*. I'm Jared Mertz. I'm afraid I was expecting someone else and don't know who you are."

Olivia smiled politely. "I'm Coordinator Olivia West. I head the ruling council of Harrison's World. Abigail works for me."

"Ah. I see. Coordinator West, allow me to introduce Zia Anderson, my flag captain, and Kelsey Bandar, my senior special operations officer."

Olivia found her attention centering on the short woman in a marine uniform with no insignia. "Please excuse my ignorance, Miss Bandar, but I'm not familiar with your position or how to address you. What is your rank?"

"I'm not at liberty to explain in detail, Coordinator," Bandar said. "Suffice it to say, I'm along to handle any unusual aspects of this mission."

Olivia raised one of her exquisitely shaped eyebrows. "I saw a vid of you speaking with Deputy Coordinator King. Your work must involve the threat of significant violence if it requires powered armor."

"My work occasionally requires a hands-on approach, yes."

That didn't explain anything about the woman. She was still an enigma. It made Olivia want to dig deeper.

"If you'll accompany me," Admiral Mertz said, "we can adjourn to my office."

The lift quickly delivered them to a large control center. It was identical to the one on the superdreadnought *Invincible*. That room had always seemed half finished, but men and women in Fleet uniforms filled this one. The only difference was the wall plaque.

The feelings of loss threatened to break through her wall, and she ruthlessly suppressed them. "Most impressive, Admiral."

"Thank you. She's a wonderful ship. This way, please." He led them into a side compartment. The office was lavishly if sparsely furnished. They ended up sitting facing one another in the open area in front of his desk. Her aides took seats behind her and to the sides. Mertz's officers sat beside him.

"Might I offer you refreshments?" he asked.

"Thank you, no," she said. "I'd rather see if we can get these negotiations back on some kind of regular footing. I feel as though Abigail may have taken the wrong approach in dealing with the issues at hand. Perhaps we can start over."

Mertz smiled. "I'd be happy to. Not to speak ill of your subordinate, but she wasn't willing to see any point of view other than her own. I'm willing to negotiate on many issues, but not about the return of my people."

She considered him for a moment. "I'm somewhat bemused at your concern for the lower orders. Why are they such a sticking point?"

"Because they came from my ships and I want them back. Is that so difficult to understand?"

Training new personnel would be time consuming, but that couldn't be the reason. There had to be some additional aspect to the situation she wasn't aware of.

She bowed her head slightly. "Of course. At the very least, I promise you that they have received medical care and we're housing them in a satisfactory manner.

"Are your people cleared to know about the situation in this system? Mine are, but I don't wish to cause problems by mentioning classified details to someone not ready to know them."

Miss Bandar leaned forward. "You mean who truly ruled this system? Yes, we three know."

"That makes things somewhat easier. The System Lord declared that the leading nobles on Harrison's World were in league to usurp its control. It destroyed every ship and facility outside the atmosphere. That was ten years ago. Now you've come in and used force to destroy or disable it."

She leaned forward and focused her attention on Mertz. "I'd like to know why the Imperial Lords made that decision and what it means for my people."

He cleared his throat. "That's a somewhat delicate situation. Your Lord made some decisions that the others disagreed with. In a way, it was trying for a coup of its own. They dispatched us to end its rebellion. In the course of that action, it destroyed some of my ships and captured some of my crew. Hence our current difficulties."

Olivia still found that hard to imagine. She'd never heard of an AI rebelling against the Empire before. Still, would she have heard about other situations like this? Probably not.

"What about Harrison's World?" she asked. "What have the Imperial Lords decreed?"

"They aren't willing to allow you back into space at this time, but your cooperation will bring the moment when you can rejoin the Empire closer."

"It hardly seems as though we have much to discuss, then."

He shrugged. "I didn't order your people's confinement. The Imperial Lords did. Are you ready to go back to war so quickly? Allow me to remind you how that worked out last time."

A twinge of frustration shot through her. They needed to get back into space. *Invincible* had the flip-point jammers that could give them the time to consolidate her rule and put forces loyal to the true Empire back in control. They had to control Boxer Station and the ships around it. With them, they could build a fleet that would challenge the AIs.

And none of that mattered right now. Admiral Mertz had a boot on their throats as long as he controlled the orbital bombardment platforms and sat here in this massive ship of war.

It was time to see what compromises could be worked. "What can we get in exchange for our good treatment of your people and their safe return? Surely there's some bone you can throw us?"

"What would you like that we can realistically provide?" Miss Bandar asked. "You already have the best technology the Empire can boast of."

Olivia turned to the mysterious woman. "You must not have dealt with many nobles. If I give an advantage away for nothing, that erodes my power base. Have you ever heard the term 'saving face'? That is what I need to do here."

The other woman's expression blanked for a moment, and then she looked at the others. "I know this meeting just started, but it's almost lunchtime. Allow me to order something for us while we consider your request."

Captain Anderson stood. "Perhaps I can offer you a tour of the flag bridge while they discuss things privately."

Olivia rose to her feet. "Of course. Something to eat would be very nice." She wasn't hungry, but if it allowed them a way out of this impasse, it was worth faking it. Besides, she wanted to tour the flag bridge and think about Brian.

* * *

ONCE EVERYONE WAS GONE, Jared rubbed his eyes. "This is going to be more difficult than I'd hoped. She wants to get her people back into space, but we can't allow that. Not even a little bit. We have to control this system and the resources in it. Those ships give us a chance against the AIs."

His sister nodded. "We can't let an enemy loose at our backs. Until we crack the encryption on the AI's data, we don't even know how many patrols they still have out. Is there anything we can offer her?"

"The Rebel Empire Fleet prisoners we recovered from Boxer Station?" Jared asked.

She frowned. "Why would we trade some Fleet personnel for others? That doesn't make much sense unless you know *why* we want our people back."

"I've spoken to some of them," Jared said. "We're keeping them isolated from the ship and other personnel, but someone had to get some information from them. Many, if not most, are from Harrison's World. Offering to let them go home after the tragedy that their lives have become seems humane to me."

Kelsey seemed to consider that. "Maybe. Let's talk about this some more before we commit. If we make a mistake, it could cost thousands of people their lives. I'm not willing to rush with stakes like that."

8

Captain Anderson escorted Olivia and her aides out to the flag bridge. "Allow me to explain the purpose of each station to you." She took the three of them on a trip around the bridge and gave them a very high-level run down of what each was for.

The noblewoman listened with one ear while she looked around. The memories of the past kept rising to the surface. How many times had Brian sat in a chair very like the one in the center of the bridge and spoken to her? Did his body rest there even now?

Something about the admiral's station bothered her. Something about it kept pulling her in.

Olivia focused her full attention on it and froze. The right side of the console had a small discoloration in the shape of a heart. It wasn't easy to see, but her eyes knew exactly where to look. The admiral's console on *Invincible* had one just like it. *Exactly* like it.

She was on *Invincible*.

It took every ounce of her willpower to keep her face neutral. What the hell was going on? Fleet wouldn't need to perpetrate a fraud like this. They had ships all their own.

The lift opened, and a man holding a tray of sandwiches and drinks walked in. The door to the admiral's day cabin opened a moment later. Miss Bandar stood there.

"If you'll come back in, we can eat quietly and then come back to your question. I think we've found a possibility."

Well, this should be *fascinating*.

Olivia examined Admiral Mertz more closely as she sat back down. He had a military bearing and his people certainly behaved like the Fleet officers she'd met. Who was he, and what was really going on?

And then there was Kelsey Bandar. She was a civilian through and through. Her posture told the tale, and the way she spoke. Yet she'd seemed very comfortable in that powered armor. She'd walked along the dock like a panther in Abigail's recording. Those weapons she'd worn hadn't seemed like props.

So, who was really in charge of this ship? Olivia was beginning to think it wasn't Admiral Mertz.

Time to test the waters.

Olivia leaned back in her seat. "Before we begin, I have a question. Nothing revolving around the negotiations. Where are you based? What sector? I've discovered over the years that a person's home says a lot about them."

Mertz's eyes flicked toward Bandar just enough for her to notice. He was looking for guidance. Bandar was the one in charge.

"We're based in the core systems," Bandar said. "We can't be more specific than that."

"Ah, the Core Worlds. What do you think of Terra?"

"Big," Mertz admitted. "I hadn't imagined buildings so large before I visited it. So many people in such a small place."

That wasn't the answer Olivia had expected. Far from it. She kept an interested smile on her face, but deep inside, she knew this charade went much deeper than she'd thought possible.

Terra had resisted the AIs until the end and beyond during the rebellion. When the orbitals had fallen, the populace fought the invading troops with every weapon they could manage. On a world with the highest technology in the Empire, those weren't empty words.

The resistance had heard of the years-long guerrilla war fought in the skeletons of the massive buildings, a fight so brutal that the AIs had eventually decided it wasn't worth the continued effort. They'd interdicted the planet much as they'd done for Harrison's World. No one in, no one out.

That wasn't common knowledge outside the resistance. The AIs preferred that their slaves think that Terra still ruled them. Not the emperor, of course. Everyone knew that institution was long gone. A democratically elected council made up of humans supposedly ruled the Empire with the help of the *benevolent* AIs.

The so-called Freedom Council supposedly met in the old Imperial Senate chambers. Only that august body didn't exist. God only knew what the machines had done with the planetary delegations. The most senior members of the higher orders and government on Harrison's World knew the truth.

Even adding the resistance to that number only bumped the count up by a few thousand people. Why would he claim to have visited the home world when it wasn't true? Or even relevant. This was a serious blunder.

Olivia couldn't imagine who these people were, but they controlled the orbital bombardment weapons menacing her world, so she wouldn't underestimate them. Any digging into their background wasn't wise when she was up here. They could lock her up in a few minutes.

No wonder they wanted their crewmen back. They knew the truth about who these people really were. It gave Olivia several thousand chances to figure it out for herself. If she could get back down to Harrison's World, that was.

"I went there once," Olivia lied. "The Imperial Palace still ranks as the most amazing thing I've ever seen. It's a museum now, filled with the finest art from all corners of the Empire. The Imperial Lords think we need to have those things as humans, and I suppose they're right."

She smiled. "I hope to show you how Harrison's World compares very soon. You said you'd thought of something I could offer the ruling council in exchange for the release of your people?"

Mertz nodded. "When we secured Boxer Station, we rescued hundreds of Fleet officers. They mostly hail from your world, so I think allowing them to return home for treatment is the best course of action for everyone."

That was the very last thing she'd expected to hear. Surviving Fleet prisoners? Could Brian be among them?

Her throat felt suddenly parched. "Do you have a list of their names?"

"I do," Mertz said. "They'll need therapy. They were under direct control of the System Lord for a long time."

Her implants pinged with an incoming file. She scanned it, and her heart sank. No, Brian wasn't among them. Loss rolled over her again. She shouldn't have allowed her hopes to rise. He was long dead.

She cleared her throat. "I believe the return of these brave officers is certainly worth the return of your crewmen. I'll need to get the agreement of the ruling council, but I don't see that as difficult. It might take a day or two before some of the more obstinate members give in to the reality that they won't get more concessions, though. Is that acceptable?"

"One can't ask more than a best effort," Mertz said. "It's really all we can offer at this time, other than my word that your cooperation will speed your release from this world."

"Then I think we've achieved as much as we can in this first talk," she said. "I'd like to return home to get the process started. As you agreed to grant me safe passage on your ship, allow me to offer you a chance to visit my world and depart in peace no matter what the decision is. I personally guarantee your protection and speedy return to your ship the moment you decide to leave."

She smiled. "While Harrison's World isn't quite up to the standards of Terra, I can assure you that it has its own wonders. I'd be pleased to show you some of them while we wait for the formalities to be worked out."

The other two looked at one another, and Mertz nodded. "We'd be honored."

Olivia couldn't wait to speak to the Fleet officers. What stories would they tell her? She would speak with Mertz's crewmen, too. They'd make up stories, she was certain, but the lower orders had never been very clever. She'd get to the bottom of this mystery. To that she swore.

* * *

Kelsey watched the other woman depart with mixed emotions. The woman's body language was very controlled, but there was a new dynamic to it, and that worried her. Had they somehow given away the fact that they weren't from the Rebel Empire?

The plan of sending the AI-controlled Rebel Fleet officers down was good, but it had its own risks. The longer the men and women were on *Invincible*, the better the chance they'd realize something was amiss. So getting them down to the planet was in everyone's best interest, and the gesture might get their men and women back.

Elise and Talbot joined them as soon as the cutter carrying the coordinator undocked.

"That seemed to go very well," Elise said. "Though I think you raised some suspicions. I'm not sure how, but Coordinator West seemed more on guard at the end."

"It happened on the flag bridge," Talbot said. "I was watching her through my implant feed. Damn, that's going to be useful. She was only curious right up to this point."

He fed them all a vid, and they saw her watching the tour with mild interest until she looked toward the rear of the compartment. Then her body stiffened and her eyes widened. The expression only stayed on her face for a few moments and then vanished as though it had never been.

Jared sighed. "Yeah, she saw something. Any idea what?"

"No clue. I'll scan the room from that angle and see what pops, but does it really matter? She knows something."

"Yet she's willing to continue negotiating," Elise said. "I think she meant everything she said at the end. She wants to convince them to return our people."

"I hope you're right," Jared said. "We can't very well get our people back by force. We don't even know where they're holding them. We're scanning the planet looking for possible locations, but that's hard to figure out. If they're in buildings, how would we know?"

Kelsey nodded. "All we can do is keep trying. If we locate them, we might be able to get them, though lifting thousands of people out under fire seems a recipe for disaster. I think the best plan is to try to get them released peacefully. We might not be able to make friends here, but I'd rather not make new enemies."

Kelsey yawned. "Sorry. I need to take a quick nap. I've been up for almost two days, and even my enhanced body needs a little rest."

"I'll stop in later and take you to lunch," Talbot said.

"That sounds good. Night."

Kelsey made her way back to her quarters, took a shower, and crashed.

* * *

NED WATCHED the town through his ocular implants. Parts of it were still on fire. People ran furtively from one building to the next, probably searching for food or shelter. Other groups of armed people, mostly in Fleet uniforms, stalked the streets. They stunned anyone they met. Others piled the unconscious onto vehicles and took them away.

They'd landed the pinnace under stealth a fair way off from their current observation post. The Fleet cruiser in orbit hadn't seen *Persephone* as she'd ghosted into the system. They'd dropped on the far side of the planet. He'd suspected then that the vessel was under the control of the rebels, but now he knew.

Time to get a prisoner to question.

"Mathews, Walker, you're with me. I want one live prisoner. If we can get him or her alone, perfect. If not, take down anyone who resists as quickly as possible. The rest of first squad will come part way as backup."

The remainder of the team would stay here, long-range flechette rifles on standby, in case he needed fire support.

His armor was in camouflage mode and blended with the foliage as he moved. As long as they didn't run, they were as good as invisible from fifty meters. The optics in his helmet and on the rifles made certain his people knew where each other were.

They slipped in close to the town, and he called a halt as he looked for likely targets. The rebels were operating in groups of at least four. He'd prefer not to kill too many of them right now. A missing person wouldn't raise the alarm like a pile of bodies.

"Captain, I have something," Corporal Davidson said over the encrypted link. He was the team's best sniper.

"Go, Hawkeye."

"There's a small group of civilians fleeing down a street to your left. Two hostiles are in pursuit. They should be coming out into the open in less than twenty seconds."

Ned pivoted to face the area in question, and his teammates reacted without orders. They could hear the information as well as he could.

"Thanks. Okay, boys. We stun both of them, if possible." He crouched down and aimed his neural disruptor at the street opening.

Two children, a boy and a girl, erupted from the street and ran for the trees as fast as they could. They looked to be ten or eleven to Ned. A man and woman, presumably their parents, ran after them.

A blue bolt flashed from the street behind them, and the woman fell soundlessly. The rebels had stunned her.

The man gave up his chance to reach safety and tried to pick her up. A second bolt took him down before he'd even gotten the woman onto his shoulder.

The rebels came out into view. One was a woman in a Fleet uniform that had seen better days. She was filthy. Her rank tabs marked her as a lieutenant commander. The other rebel was a civilian in even worse condition. His scraggly beard looked as unwashed as the woman's hair.

What was going on?

He mentally shrugged. They'd find out soon enough.

The woman made a better target. A Fleet officer should know something about what the rebels really wanted. At this range, he had to restrict himself to just her. His implants helped him line up the long-range shot, and he squeezed the trigger.

The blue bolt took her in the shoulder, and she dropped without a peep. The man ignored her and pulled a flechette pistol out of his pants. He was going to shoot the prisoners!

The man's head exploded long before the weapon was high enough to threaten the civilians. Davidson had taken him out.

"Get in there," Ned said. "Secure the prisoner and the civilians. We'll take them with us. Backup team, catch the kids. Try not to scare them too much, but we're on the clock. I want to be back in orbit before someone comes looking for these people. The Empire needs this data."

His men grabbed the civilians. With their enhanced strength, particularly in their Raider armor, that was no problem.

He was reaching for the Fleet rebel when Davidson called back in. "More rebels! They came out of a side street."

Four men in enlisted fatigues came boiling out of the street, almost in hand-to-hand range. They had neural disruptors in one hand and flechette pistols in the other. Blue bolts and fast-moving projectiles began slamming into his armor.

It was time to go old school. His hands flashed to the sword hilts over his shoulders. The dark blades were just like the Raider-issued knife on his belt, just bigger.

In seconds, he was among them. Arms and heads flew. It was over almost as soon as it started. The enemy was dead, and his short blades were running with blood. He wiped them off on a dead man's tunic and sheathed them. Time to get out of here.

Ned picked up the rebel Fleet officer and tossed her over his shoulder. In moments, he was back in the forest. The support squad reported they had the kids, so he ordered a retreat to their concealed pinnace.

Everything went smoothly, and they made it back there in less than half an hour. The kids were terrified, of course. He took his helmet off and gave them his most reassuring smile.

"Hey, you're safe now. We'll get you and your parents out of here. My name is Ned Quincy. Who are you?"

The boy stuck his chin out. "Larry. This is my sister Anne. Are you going to hurt us? What's wrong with Mom and Dad?"

"We're not going to hurt you. We're going to save you from the bad people. They're just asleep. They'll wake up in a few hours. By then, we'll be a long way from here. Come on."

They secured the prisoner tightly, even though she shouldn't wake up for a while. The medic checked the civilians and pronounced them healthy. This mission was a bigger success than he'd hoped. They had a prisoner, and they'd saved a family from the rebels.

That was nothing compared to the billions of people on this world, but he had to take his victories where he could. They might be rare if what he'd seen so far was playing out across the Empire.

The pinnace lifted off and began the slow trip back up to his ship. They couldn't let the enemy spot them now. They had to get the prisoner back to Fleet for debriefing, and that meant they couldn't allow the enemy to spot *Persephone*.

He sat down at the command console and looked at his reflection. There'd be a time in the future when he and his Raiders could fight back against the enemies of the Empire. It just wasn't today.

* * *

KELSEY SAT bolt upright in her bed, breathing heavily. The final view of the man in the console hung in her mind. It was the dead man from the stasis chamber.

What the hell?

9

O livia focused on her duties for the first few hours after she returned to Harrison's World. There were too many eyes on her to dig into the mystery. She needed to document what she'd officially seen and what she'd discussed for the ruling council.

They wouldn't be happy that she hadn't secured the planet's release into space. They'd be even unhappier when they found out she'd decided not to even try for it.

The more conservative elements of the council believed that they controlled every aspect of life on Harrison's World. They hadn't truly accepted that the situation had changed, even after a decade. They were of the higher orders and that was that. The military would bow to their will.

Even if "Admiral" Mertz and his people had truly been Fleet officers, that stance wouldn't have worked. They'd have had the full might of the Empire behind them. The Lords had decreed they'd remain in isolation for daring to consider rebellion. They wouldn't be releasing them any time soon.

Ironically, those same conservatives would never have pondered fighting the Lords to regain true human control over the Empire. They liked their position in society. Thus her conundrum.

Olivia suspected the people in orbit didn't want to let the people of Harrison's World loose because it would ruin their charade. How they'd managed to take out the AI and gain control of the system, she had no idea.

That's what she needed to know. The resistance might be able to deal with these people, even if the coordinator couldn't.

The buzzer on her desk went off.

Yes, her assistant could just ping her implants, but that wasn't the way the higher orders worked. The advanced technology of the Empire seemed to inspire them to avoid using it to interface with one another. They'd be more likely to send a hand-written note on matters of import than to ping someone.

She pressed the accept button. "Yes?"

"Deputy Coordinator King is here to see you, ma'am. She says it's quite urgent."

No doubt, that diplospeak meant Abigail was pissed. She must've seen the preliminary report Olivia had filed with the council. Well, this fight had been inevitable. She might as well get it over with. She could use it as a pretext to leave early and get to digging for the answers she needed.

The door burst open, and Abigail stormed into Olivia's office. She didn't even wait for it to fully close before she started.

"What the hell did you think you were doing up there?" Abigail snarled. "You gave up everything worth fighting for in less than two hours. Everything I've worked so hard to accomplish is ruined."

"Come in, Abigail," Olivia said with a false smile. "Sit down and tell me what brings you over."

The other woman stopped in front of Olivia's desk and glared at her. "Don't even start that nonsense with me. I demand an explanation."

After giving Abigail a long look, Olivia leaned back in her seat. "You're on the wrong side of this desk to be demanding anything. You can calm down or leave. The choice is yours."

The other woman took a deep breath and then three more just like it. The flashing anger hadn't left her eyes, but she was under a little more control.

"Those circumstances could change faster than you might think," Abigail said in a low, dangerous tone. "The coalition that appointed you coordinator can choose someone else if you fail to lead the way they expect. Right now, I'm certain your actions have a number of the council members reconsidering their support. Perhaps you'd care to explain why you gave ground in the negotiations?"

Olivia supposed the woman's threats were better than listening to her scream.

"I gave ground because they weren't going to agree to your hardline terms. The Lords hold the power to release us. We can't continue to delude ourselves that we can force them to do that. We have to bargain in a more nuanced manner. If you think differently, you're mistaken."

"That's crap. We have their people. If we hold out they'll—"

"They'll leave them and get more. It's a miracle that Admiral Mertz is willing to negotiate for them at all. He told me in no uncertain terms that they couldn't release us without the approval of the Imperial Lords."

"And you believed him?" Abigail shook her head. "I thought you were smarter than that. He wouldn't bargain for them if they weren't worth his time. They know some secret he doesn't want us to have. Rather than giving in, we should be questioning the prisoners."

That was unusually adept for Abigail, Olivia mused. The other woman was usually more of a blunt instrument.

"If they know some secret, then what?" she asked. "Are you planning to blackmail the man in command of the bombardment stations?"

Abigail showed her teeth. "Yes, I am. They took out the System Lord. That means there are events happening that we need to know about. That's not just me speaking, Olivia. That's the conservative leadership."

"If you don't address their concerns, they'll call for a vote of no confidence. They might not control an outright majority, but there are enough others who dislike what you've done to remove you."

Olivia shot the other woman a predatory smile. "I've heard that before, yet here I sit. More than enough council members will want to see what I'm up to before they allow the conservatives back into power. After all, you rebelled against the Lords. Do you really think the other council members have forgotten how their predecessors died?"

That was certain to infuriate Abigail, she knew. The conservatives had been in power since the rebellion. They couldn't understand why any of their leadership from a decade ago would support a coup.

Yet that's what the System Lord told them was the reason it blasted the capital and spaceports to oblivion, along with every outpost that had existed in the system.

The other ruling parties had formed a coalition to strip the conservatives of their rule, but theirs wasn't a strong majority. While Olivia was certain she could bring them around to her point of view, she couldn't afford to appear weak.

Olivia leaned forward in her chair. "You need to go back and consult with your political masters, because I don't think they were quite so strenuous in their instructions to you. If you push this matter now, it might be you who is out of a job."

She let her words hang between them for a moment before she stood. "I intend to bring Admiral Mertz down to the planet's surface and continue the negotiations in a more cordial environment. It remains to be seen exactly what we can achieve, but I assure you that I'm working tirelessly for the people of Harrison's World. I'll get the best deal possible for all of us."

Abigail spun on her heel without a word and strode out of Olivia's office.

It never ceased to amaze Olivia. If Abigail's father hadn't been a powerhouse in the conservative movement before his death, the woman would never have reached her current position as Olivia's primary deputy. Abigail was a time bomb waiting for an inappropriate moment to explode.

* * *

AFTER HIS VISIT into the city the previous day, Sean had decided a scouting mission to the other side of the island was in order. He'd spoken that night with Ross and Newland. They'd agreed that some discreet intelligence gathering would be helpful. They'd said they'd take care of it.

Now it was almost lunch, and Sean was getting antsy. There hadn't been any sign of trouble, but he hadn't wanted to huddle with the others again so soon. Even though he doubted their captors were monitoring them that closely, he wasn't willing to risk it.

When he went to get his midday meal, the server gestured for him to come around behind the counter. He did so without question and found Ross waiting for him in the kitchen.

The man was dicing something. "Sean, good to see you. I hope you're good with a peeler. We have a pile of fresh vegetables. You must've made some friends yesterday."

He snorted. "Hardly. If anything, the guy I spoke with would've been happy to cut off the food entirely. I can't claim any part of this."

His experience with a peeler was strictly limited, but he grabbed it and pitched in. The noisy kitchen would make monitoring them almost impossible.

"What happened last night?" Sean asked.

"Nothing," Ross said. "Too much chance of someone seeing them in the dark when normal people were asleep. They went right after breakfast. Some of the boys made a scene on the other side of camp and drew the guards' attention. A romantic entanglement gone astray. One of my best girls played her role to the hilt and beat the snot out of her 'wandering man.' It was quite entertaining, I'm told. Gina knows how to be very convincing."

Sean had heard something about it, but the brawl had ended by the time he'd gotten over there. "I'm sure the citation write-up will be unusual. Did your people make it back safely?"

"Just did. They slipped into the docks on the far side of the island. Whoever put up the fences to keep us in didn't check the original buildings closely enough. There are service tunnels that go under them.

"Several merchant companies receive goods on the docks and transship them into the city on big grav lifts. Our boys broke into one of the warehouses and found a few uniforms. Coveralls, really, in blue with one of the company logos. That let them blend in as they explored the place.

"The bottom line is that we might be able to get our people over there and co-opt enough vehicles to get everyone into the city."

"Don't the guards search the vehicles?"

The noncom shook his head. "Nope. At least they didn't on the one ride the boys took to move cargo."

"They went to the city? That was a little dangerous. What if someone challenged them?"

Ross smiled. "They got caught by the company supervisor and yelled at for goofing off. They had no choice but to 'get back to work.' On the positive side, they made some friends, and now a number of people think they work there. That kind of cover is useful. Useful enough for me to send them back. They'll go off shift with the real crew and into the city. They'll look for places we can hole up."

"That sounds good," he told Ross. "I'm not sure we should make a break until we give Mertz a chance to get us loose. Knowing where the spaceport is and some things about its schedule would be good, though."

The older man nodded. "That's on their list of things to inquire about. They're good people. They'll do what needs to be done and avoid sticking out."

Sean hoped so, because if they were caught, the outlines of the bold escape plan he'd come up with wouldn't work. He wished Mertz could get some information to them. Knowing what was going on in the negotiations would make his job easier.

If they needed to get moving, he'd like to know sooner rather than later.

* * *

Kelsey considered the dream. No, it wasn't a dream. It was a recording of events seen by the man in the stasis chamber. Somehow, she'd accessed his files while she slept. That *had* to be it.

Nothing like that had ever happened before, and it scared her. Her implants were like a computer. They did what she told them to, with the exception of the combat protocols. They shouldn't have been able to feed the recording into her sleeping mind like that.

She rubbed her face and checked the time. She'd gotten about four hours' sleep. Well, that was it. There was no way she was going back to sleep now.

With this new anomaly, she decided she'd better go have a few words with Doctor Leonard and Carl Owlet. She needed to figure this out before something went seriously wrong.

The lab compartment on *Invincible* was huge. They'd given over a full cargo deck to the scientists and the artifacts they were bringing back from the station and graveyard. She saw a stasis unit, the damaged flip-point jammer, and scores of tables covered with smaller items.

Doctor Leonard wasn't there, but Carl Owlet sat hunched over a computer station off to the side.

She walked up behind him and cleared her throat. "With implants, do you really need the screen?"

He jumped a little and turned to face her with a smile. "It's still very helpful. I can see things at a glance that don't pop out in the implant feed. I suspect that will change as I get used to the new hardware. For now, I'm doing both."

"That sounds complex. Where's Doctor Leonard?"

"Off hunting for artifacts. Is there something I can help you with?"

Kelsey considered how to frame her problem. "I finally got to bed a few hours ago and had a dream. Unfortunately, it wasn't mine. It was memories of the dead man from that ship. His name, by the way, is Ned Quincy. He was a major in the Marine Raiders and in charge of *Persephone*."

That got the graduate student's full attention. "That's not possible. Files in implant storage aren't accessed like that."

He stood up and started setting up one of the machines near his workstation. "Let's take a look at the files."

She sat where he indicated and put on the headset he handed her. He frowned and focused on the screen. "There's some unexpected activity. A large number of the smaller files are accessing one another. They're also adding new files. Weird."

"Are they filling up my implant storage? Do I need to delete them?"

"You still have a lot of free space. What concerns me is that the activity seems to be continuing. Are you accessing those files?"

Kelsey shook her head. "No."

"Let me look at the logs here... the files are initiating the access requests, but only within the new material. One file in particular. Let me look at the code in the static memory of my system. There, I've copied it. You can get up."

She nodded and took off the headset. "I want to look at some stuff while you figure this out. Did they bring over anything from *Persephone?*"

He gestured toward some of the tables nearby. "Since we were there, yes. A lot of personal gear and any odd equipment."

Leaving him to his work, she walked over to the tables and started examining everything as she walked down them. It only took her ten minutes to find what she was looking for. A pair of short swords in a harness.

She drew one and looked at it closely. It was exactly like in her dream. The honed edge of the dark blade looked just like her marine knife. That made it insanely sharp and durable enough to hack through a bulkhead.

Kelsey slid the harness on and tightened it. The sword hilts projected over her shoulders. They felt oddly familiar.

Carl waved for her to come over. "The file is complex. I'm not sure I understand what it is. I'm going to keep poking around in the code, but it might take a while. Nice swords, by the way."

"They were in my dream. Or the recording. Whatever. I'm going to step over here and see how they feel. I'll try not to throw one by accident."

"We'd all appreciate that."

Kelsey walked over to a cleared area and took a deep breath. She'd never had any martial arts training, but her implants knew some things. Combat reflexes, she supposed. At the very least, she could see how they felt without chopping up anything important.

She drew the swords awkwardly and tried to have her implants guide her, but that didn't seem to help. Apparently, her hard-coded responses didn't include sword fighting.

Kelsey sighed and put the swords clumsily away.

The files in her memory probably had something about the swords and their use. Maybe she could find a tutorial.

She accessed the file Carl had said was doing all the work and asked for a sword tutorial. It promptly requested control of her limbs.

This was similar to when her implants took her into combat mode. She checked the limits of what she was granting, and her hardware informed her that she retained override authority. If she wanted, she could stop at any moment.

What the hell. She authorized the file to proceed.

Her hands flashed up to the hilts and drew the swords smoothly. Her body then went into something very much like a choreographed dance. The blades went this way and that as she flowed across the open area, attacking imaginary foes.

In fact, that was exactly what it was. Her implants were taking her through a dance of death.

The blades slashed, thrust, and chopped, each move obviously representative of actual combat. Her body flowed along with it, even leaping as required, higher than an unenhanced person could manage.

The blades had every bit of power behind them she could manage. Considering how much she could really do, that meant something.

The routine ended with her crouching low, with her blades out at her sides. She felt like a predator.

The program was about to sheath them, but she countermanded it and stopped its control just to make sure she could. Her body was again her own, and she was certain that she could have stopped at any point she wanted to.

That's when she saw everyone in the room staring at her with their mouths open.

She rose to her feet and flushed a little. Her hands put the swords away with only a little trouble. "Sorry about that. I was just giving these a test drive."

Carl slowly clapped as she approached. "That was beautiful. You look as though you've been using them for years. I found something"

"Tell me."

"The central file is acting like a clearing house for the rest. It's written much like the control programs for the ship's computer. Well, not this one, of course. Regular ships."

"So it's a rudimentary AI?"

He shook his head. "It's what we call an expert system. It doesn't have nearly the capability or resources of an AI, much less a computer like the one on *Courageous*. Think of an automated library assistant."

Kelsey had used that kind of program quite extensively before this mission. They acted almost like people but weren't that smart. They used pronouns like "I" for themselves rather than the Old Empire standard of "this unit," but they were just mimicking intelligence. There was no spark of life to them, unlike the computer on *Courageous*. Or especially the AI on *Invincible*.

In any case, Jared was going to have a cow when she told him about it.

10

"You did what?" Jared asked.

His sister had the grace to look embarrassed as she repeated herself. "I loaded the files from the dead man into my implant storage, and I've been playing around with them."

Her admission came in his office in front of Elise and himself.

He considered Kelsey critically. "Has anyone ever explained the difference between boldness and recklessness to you? This was not the wisest of plans."

Kelsey looked mulish, but she nodded. "On reflection, I suppose that's true. However, it seemed necessary at the time. I need those files. *We* need those files."

"Just moving them to storage on *Invincible* wasn't good enough?" Elise asked.

"No. They're hardware specific, and implant serial number locked, too, but I was able to spoof that. On a regular computer, they just sit there. Even unlocking them takes a while. I made the right choice."

Jared wasn't sure she had, but it was too late for him to do anything about it. "What about your dream? That sounds dangerous. What if you'd activated some fighting protocol and beat the snot out of Talbot?"

Kelsey nodded. "I thought about that after the swords. Every attempt to access my body requires my authorization. I can't give that while I'm asleep. Accessing the vid files, well, that's a little different. Carl thinks he can modify the protocol to prevent unconscious access."

Elise considered Kelsey. "Why is it so important to you?"

"I have this equipment inside me, but I know virtually nothing about it. I want to be its master, not its servant. Somewhere in one of these files is the access code to *Persephone*'s computer and all the data I could ever want to know about the Marine Raiders and the implants inside me. I'm sure of it."

"How close are you to finding it?" Jared asked.

His sister slumped a little. "I don't know. The program talks like a person, but it's just an advanced interface. It's sophisticated enough to fool people who don't know what it is, but it can't really think."

"Perhaps parsing the files directly might give you more access to the contents," *Invincible* said. "Or at least allow for a more refined search for the codes you seek."

She looked at the ceiling with a skeptical expression. "My implants aren't really made for that kind of thing. I can make access requests and do searches, but I can't have it running in the background. Well, not very effectively. These aren't even straight recordings. I can hear some of his thoughts."

"There are ways of doing deep recordings that also include your surface thoughts. That's implicit in the interface between the human brain and cranial implants.

"In any case, I could construct a more comprehensive indexing program that would run in the background on your implant hardware. Coupled with some changes to the library program that use some of my own heuristic models, and it would make your access program significantly more useful in parsing what files might meet your needs while still respecting your privacy in much the same way I already do."

"I'm not sure I get that, *Invincible*," Jared said. "What do you mean about respecting privacy?"

"I have restrictions preventing me from invading the privacy of the crew. I can freely monitor the public areas of the ship, but not their personal quarters. This program would be similar in that I would create a subroutine for Kelsey that would do a systematic reindexing of the files available to her, but it would not report anything back to me."

Jared cocked his head. "You answer questions and requests when I'm in my quarters. How does that work?"

"My subroutines monitor for attempts to communicate with me and for emergencies. They only alert me in situations where regulations allow me to interact with the crew. They retain no data, so I'm unaware of what is occurring outside those situations. In the case of a medical emergency, I would summon a medical team at once."

"That would've been useful back on *Athena* when Carlo Vega died," Kelsey said. "What would I need to do?"

"Authorize me to access your implant storage and the central program. I'll replace certain subroutines with my own programming to optimize the searching and access of the data. As it updates the file indexes and cross-references the data, you will be better able to find information."

"Do it," Kelsey said. "How long will it take?"

"Not long at all. I'm accessing the program now. Updating the search routines and optimizing the ability of the program to catalog and access data now. Update complete. I did find a file in the index marked 'welcome.' I believe it to be a message from Ned Quincy to you."

She stared at the ceiling for a moment. "Play the message for all of us."

* * *

ABIGAIL HAD her driver speed back to the council building and summoned a crew in to search her office for monitoring devices. Once they had declared it clear, she used her private com link to call Master Calder.

"Yes, Abigail?"

"I confronted Coordinator West a few minutes ago, and I'm afraid that her initial report to the council is more of an understatement that we feared. She doesn't intend to push for our release at all. She's most likely going to give the prisoners back in exchange for some Fleet officers the Lord had on Boxer Station."

"Well, I can't say that's surprising news," he said. "We already suspected that she wouldn't push things. It's time to cause a rift in her relationship with Admiral Mertz. Implement the plan."

Abigail smiled. "With pleasure. I'll make the arrangements right away."

* * *

JARED'S IMPLANTS notified him that a vid file was available. He instructed it to play.

The scene around him dissolved, and he was sitting in a small compartment looking into a mirror. The man's face was pleasant enough in a rugged way. He smiled at his own reflection. "To whoever finds these files, greetings. My name is Major Ned Quincy, Imperial Marine Raiders. Consider this my final report.

"I don't know where I died, or even the manner of my passing, but you wouldn't be seeing this if I was still around."

His smile widened. "Don't mourn me. I probably went out doing something insanely risky. Even for a Raider, I've always been fond of taking chances and going big. I hope I died doing something epic."

Jared hoped Kelsey wasn't getting the wrong ideas from this man. She'd been doing entirely too many epic things herself this last year.

"Now, these files you've found," the man said. "I stole a copy of the library assistant and had one of my techs modify it to work with my implants. The man is a genius, if you ask me. I didn't think he'd be able to do it.

"You've broken my lock and have a full set of Raider implants, so you're my brother or sister in arms. Some of this information is probably not of much use to you, but it might inform you about who I am and what I've done. That's the idea, anyway."

The dead man continued. "I began retaining vids from my implants when I first heard about the rebellion. This is kind of my own history in fighting it. Moments that seemed important. I hope you find them informative and useful."

He leaned forward. "One positive thing, I can be pretty sure that we won the war if you find this. At least that's what I choose to believe. Good luck, and go kick some ass."

The vid ended, and Jared's view of his office returned.

Kelsey shook her head. "That's so sad."

"The Fall is filled with sad tales," Elise said. "If we knew them all, we'd go mad. He died doing what he loved and fighting for those he'd sworn to protect. Who could ask for more?"

"I'm going to keep looking for those access codes and take advantage of any information I find in there," Kelsey said. "I probably should've mentioned something before I did it, and I'm sorry."

Jared gave her a look of mock sternness. "I really hope you don't jump into something you shouldn't next time. Seriously, Kelsey, you take too many chances. One of them will prove fatal if you don't learn some restraint."

"I'll try, really. What do we do next?"

"We're getting our new Pentagaran crewmen up to speed. Doctor Stone is running people through the implant process as quickly as she can. It'll take weeks to get everyone done, so we're focusing on the most critical personnel first.

"Doctor Leonard is working to repair the damaged flip jammer. If we can get it operational, we can secure Erorsi and Pentagar. That's a priority. It would really help if we had the plans for them, though I'm not sure we could build one."

"It would be wonderful to have a shield against the Rebel Empire," Elise agreed. "A single destroyer could make life hard for us back home. A task force would take both systems in short order."

"What about getting the yards online at Boxer Station?" Kelsey asked. "We need to repair our ships and bring as many derelicts back to operational status as we can."

He nodded. "That's a priority, too. Baxter tells me his people almost have the original computer system verified. Once he's confident of its integrity, he'll bring it online and start assessing the situation. I'm hopeful we can get *Invincible* in there quickly."

"As am I," the AI said. "The parts you've salvaged from the graveyard have brought more of my systems back online, but there are serious repairs that can only be done in a shipyard."

"What about the planet?" Kelsey asked. "Won't they wonder why *Invincible* is away? Do we dare move her without getting *Courageous* in better condition?"

"It's a risk," he admitted. "The only other option is moving *Courageous* there first. We'll make the call when we have to."

"What about Coordinator West's offer to have you go down to the surface?" Elise asked. "Are you seriously considering it?"

"We have them under the gun. They wouldn't take action directly against me or my party."

"Would those be the same guns that are encouraging them to return your people? That doesn't seem to be working that well so far."

"Trust has to start somewhere," he said. "Otherwise, we might as well just leave our people with them."

Jared checked his internal chronometer. "It's time for lunch. Let's go eat. If I don't hear from Coordinator West by noon tomorrow, I'll call her back. She needs to know how seriously we're taking this situation."

Elise rose to her feet. "Diplomacy is sometimes slow. Don't rush things. Tomorrow morning is soon enough to start pestering her. We'll spend a few hours going over what we can, and then I want you to get some sleep. You'll need your wits about you."

His sister stood, too. "I'll let you two have some alone time. I think Talbot is feeling neglected."

* * *

SEAN WATCHED the wedge of grav vehicles land with some trepidation. They'd brought a lot of guards. This wasn't a food delivery.

That became clear when the men started herding prisoners toward the vehicles, using their weapons to threaten them as need be. It looked as though they were gathering about a hundred people.

He walked out toward them and stopped as soon as the cordon focused their weapons on him. "I'm the senior prisoner. What's the meaning of this? Where are you taking my people?"

One of the larger men stepped forward and sneered at Sean. "That's none of your concern. If you don't want to find out the hard way, you'd best shut your mouth and move back."

"I'll take that offer. Me in exchange for one of them."

The guard laughed. "I think not. As for where they're going, I have no idea. Coordinator West sent word to gather them up. When she's done with them, I'll bring them back. If they're alive."

Sean stared at the man coldly. "They'd best come back in good condition, or I'm holding you and Coordinator West responsible."

That only made the guard laugh harder. "You do that. Now get back before I shoot you and leave you here to bleed out."

Lacking options, Sean backed up and watched them load his terrified men and women into the grav cars with impotent fury.

Ross stepped up beside him. "What do we do now?"

He glanced at the senior noncom. "We find out what they're going to do. If they're ready to start questioning us, we need to break out and get our people back. Then we'll find a way to signal Mertz for a pickup. Get some men ready to head to the shipping docks. I'll be going with them."

11

Olivia worked for another hour before shutting her console down. Her assistant looked up from his work as soon as she stepped out of her office.

"Yes, ma'am?"

"I'm making an early day of it. There are a few things I need to take care of, and Abigail has my blood pressure up. You really need to come up with new words to describe her mood. 'Urgent desire' was a little understated."

He smiled blandly. "I'll work on that, ma'am. Perhaps a flashing light when she's frothing."

Olivia laughed a little. "That would work. Call my driver up to the roof. I want to stop in to see someone before I go home. Privately."

"Of course, Coordinator. I'll see to it right away."

She headed for the lift. He was a good man to have on her payroll. Smart, perceptive, and unusually competent. He'd see that her guards stayed some distance away yet close enough to protect her. He'd also make certain that only her most trusted security people were on watch for the flight home.

William Hawthorne had visited her, so she could plausibly return the favor. He'd be a fine sounding board for her suspicions.

The Hawthorne estate was located in the same general area as her residence. Most of the higher orders lived in estates grouped close to one another for exclusivity. Of course, that meant the AI had virtually exterminated the most prestigious families in the orbital bombardment a decade ago. In the old days, her family would have been strictly second tier.

Her security team meticulously cleared her flight path with all of the estates they overflew. Even as the coordinator, she needed to mind her manners. It wouldn't do for someone to make a "mistake" and shoot her down.

Her family and William's had been close before the rebellion. Five hundred years had allowed for many cross-connections between them. They'd intermarried to the point that everyone was related to everyone else to some degree.

That was true of most families in the higher orders, but not like the West and Hawthorne clans. They hadn't been nobles when the Empire fell but merchant families. Ones that had gone out of their way to prove their allegiance to the machines when they took over.

That sickened her, but her ancestors had done what they needed to do to survive. Those terrible deeds had gone a long way toward shielding the resistance.

That loose group of loyalists hadn't been in charge of the families back then, of course. They'd slipped into leadership roles generations later. They'd still be working to make up for what their ancestors had done for many years to come.

She relaxed a little once her air car settled onto the landing area beside William's home. His mother occupied the large house, but he preferred the more relaxed lifestyle of living apart from the hubbub with his husband.

William came out from the patio as soon as her car settled onto the ground. "Coordinator, it's good to see you again so soon."

"It's been a rough day, and I wanted to run something past you, if you have time." She motioned for her guards to wait outside. They didn't like that idea very much, but they obeyed.

William led her into his home. "Craig is off looking over the South Shore power plant. He'll be sorry he missed you."

"I hope nothing is wrong."

He shook his head. "No, nothing like that. They're upgrading the backup circuits to handle more of the load. Transmission technology has improved significantly since they built the facility. As one of the senior engineers, he wanted to be on hand for the tests. He'll be inconsolable once he realizes he missed you."

Olivia smiled. "I'm sure that isn't true. He's a remarkably steady fellow. You know, the kind you want around when something goes terribly wrong at a fusion power plant. I'm sure he'll be fine. Might we retire to your den to discuss something?"

His eyebrow rose. "Of course. I do hope my reputation won't be tarnished when word gets out that the two of us were huddled together without a chaperone."

"I'm tempted to start some rumors to see what people say."

He laughed. "Alas, I'm afraid no one would believe them. Would you like a drink?"

"Some red wine would be wonderful," she said as he led her into his exceptionally comfortable den. He'd decorated it in dark fabrics and subdued lighting. The bar built into the wall held some of the best liquor on the planet. She'd spent many an evening here plotting her ascension to the coordinator's office.

His dashing demeanor made many people assume he wasn't more than a social butterfly, but appearances were most deceiving. William Hawthorne was the leader of the resistance on Harrison's World, and she'd never met a more brilliant and determined man.

He poured their drinks and came back over to sit beside her. "The house is clear, and I've engaged the privacy screens. What's wrong?"

Olivia sipped her wine. It was excellent, as always. "I couldn't risk sending a message, but I have two issues for us to worry about. First, the people in orbit aren't Fleet. I'm not even sure they're really from the Empire at all."

His hand paused while pouring his drink. "That's not what I expected to hear at all. Explain."

"Their ship isn't just a superdreadnought like *Invincible*. It *is Invincible*."

"You're certain?"

She nodded. "Completely. I've compared the flag bridge to the one on *Invincible* in the messages Brian sent me. There are a few flaws in the admiral's console that precisely match. Also, when I asked them a question about Terra, their answer told me that they had no idea of the conditions there. They made as though it was still a civilized world. One Admiral Mertz claimed he'd visited."

"It might be," he said. "Just not on the surface. So who are they? How did they gain control of this system without the AI roasting them? They wouldn't try to pass *Invincible* off as their own if they had a similar ship."

Olivia took another sip of wine. "Precisely. I have no idea what they're doing, but they don't know about the Empire. At least not as it is today."

He sat back and considered her words as he stared at the ceiling. "We need to know more about them as quickly as possible. The prisoners might be a source of information. They want them back very badly, after all."

"My thoughts exactly. Can some of our people look into questioning them?"

"Of course. They're isolated on Spark Island, just offshore, so they're close by. Other than airships patrolling overhead, no one is directly interfacing with them. After all, they're only of the lower orders. Or so we thought. They might be something completely unexpected. Also, a few of them are still under medical care."

"I'm going to invite Admiral Mertz down to the surface, along with the mystery woman, Kelsey Bandar, tomorrow morning. A trip to inspect their people might be just the time to ask some pointed questions."

"Which brings me to my second problem. The conservatives are furious that I'm not holding out for complete freedom. Abigail stormed into my office and made some particularly pointed threats about impeachment."

William waved his hand as though dispersing a cloud of smoke. "They don't have the votes to sustain that kind of motion. No one really wants to see them back in power. They'd be fools to try."

"They've been fools before."

He inclined his head to acknowledge the point. "I'll make some calls and get our people in the other parties to start spreading the word. Perhaps dragging their plan into the open will encourage them to see reason. It can't hurt."

He sipped his drink. "Now, send me everything you recorded on that ship. Every word they said. We'll go over it with a fine-toothed comb and see if we can come to some conclusions about them before they come down. And I want to meet them."

They sat up late into the evening dissecting every moment of her visit to *Invincible*. It was late when she headed home, but she felt more certain than ever that they were on the cusp of something that would change Harrison's World forever. If they could survive the transformation, that is.

* * *

SEAN COULDN'T BELIEVE how easy it was to slip over to the other side of the island. The guards had rigged a fence that wasn't climbable, but they hadn't searched the abandoned buildings very closely. One near the edge shared power and cooling with another outside the fence. A tight service tunnel connected them.

The marines that had been conducting the reconnaissance led him across. They all changed into pilfered coveralls in the deserted building's first-floor bathroom. The three of them slipped into the more occupied areas of the port.

Sean had overseen the loading of supplies before, but this operation was significantly larger than anything he'd imagined possible. The massive ships offloaded huge containers that workers moved into a number of warehouses. Looking down the docks, Sean could see several different colors of coverall. That would distinguish one company from another, he supposed.

A number of men wearing the same color coveralls as them greeted the marines. They in turn introduced Sean as the new guy. They all assured him that he'd learn how the real world worked now.

He worked side by side with these men loading containers onto large grav lifts. He even accompanied several across to the city to unload them.

When he raised an eyebrow at one of the marines, the man shook his head. "Shift ends in a few hours. Then we go back with everyone else without making people wonder what we're up to."

By the time the shift was over, Sean was beat. He hadn't worked at something this physical in years. He really should make more time for the gym.

Crowds of men filled empty grav lifts and made their way to the city. The other workers invited the marines to bring the new guy bar hopping, but they declined. In a few minutes, they'd walked away into the strange city, blending in with the working-class crowd.

The marines led him to a rundown parking garage. They went up some darkened stairs and came out on a floor containing some of the shakiest grav vehicles Sean had ever seen. They didn't look capable of flight.

Sean gave the men a look. "You can't be serious."

One of them grinned. "I worked on all kinds of vehicles before I joined up, sir. Most of these are junk, but I found one that was repairable. We worked on it last night, stealing parts from the others as needed, and I got it working. No one will report it missing. Hell, I'm not completely sure these aren't abandoned. They don't look as though anyone's been in them for years."

Against his better judgment, they slipped into a vehicle so rusted that he couldn't be certain what its original color had been. It started, though it made noises that he feared meant something important was about to fail.

"That sounds bad."

The marine shrugged. "It's the backup grav generator. It should work well enough to get us down in one piece if the main fails. Not much more."

"I didn't think grav generators made noise."

"Only ones that are *very* out of tune. What's the plan, sir?"

"First, what do you know about this area? What kind of people work and live here?"

"Working-class poor, sir. I grew up in a neighborhood like this. People are trying to make ends meet any way they can. If you're worried about someone calling the security forces, well, that isn't the norm for this kind of place. Only when things go really bad."

Sean nodded. "Okay. That sounds good. We'll need to find a place where we might be able to hide a few thousand people in a pinch."

"Bad idea, sir." The marine in the driver's seat turned to face him. "This close to the island, the security forces will tear everything up. They'll search every building. We'll need to take everyone further away from here."

That wasn't what Sean wanted to hear, but it was probably true enough. "Then we focus on finding our people. I know the general area where they took me and what the building looked like. If we can find it, we might be able to locate everyone and find out what their intentions are."

"And if not?"

He grimaced. "Then we stash the grav vehicle and slip back onto the island before breakfast. Who knows? Maybe they'll bring everyone back before we need to do something."

Sean doubted that. They wouldn't have made such a big deal out of taking so many people if they were just going to bring them back. The clock was ticking.

12

Jared hadn't expected quick action from Coordinator West, so he was surprised when she called him early the next morning. He'd just arrived on the flag bridge when the officer manning the communications console turned to him.

"I'm glad to see you, Admiral. I have an incoming communication for you from Harrison's World. It's Coordinator West."

He sat in his chair and tugged his uniform jacket tight. "Put her on my console, Lieutenant Carver."

The right side of his curved console came to life with an image of the coordinator. She sat behind a large desk made of honey-colored wood. The wall behind her was a subdued blue, and he could see a painting over her shoulder. It looked like a landscape.

"Good morning, Coordinator," he said politely. "I hope you slept well."

"You mean you hope I slept at all," she said with a sardonic smile. "I had a lot of people to talk with last night. As you might imagine, not everyone is as ready as I am to make concessions."

He tipped his head in acknowledgment. "While I can see your point of view, I'm concerned about my people. Every day this remains unresolved, they stay locked up."

"I understand. With that in mind, I'd like to invite you and Miss Bandar to come visit your people and see our capital while we clear up this regrettable situation. You'll be here as my guests, and you have my word that you will not be restrained or prevented from departing as soon as you wish."

"I'll admit I still have some lingering concerns. Deputy Coordinator King painted a very firm picture of how she'd like to conduct negotiations.

Forgive me, but what's to stop you from taking me hostage as soon as I land?"

"I'm not Abigail King, Admiral. And, not to point out the obvious, you have the means to enforce your will upon us.

"That's not to say you'd use weapons of mass destruction to secure your release, but rest assured I have that clearly in mind."

"Very well. The better we know one another, the faster we can come to an agreement we're all satisfied with. As a gesture of goodwill, I'll bring the prisoners we rescued from Boxer Station with me. Since we rescued almost a hundred and fifty people, it'll take a few trips from orbit, but those poor people deserve to come home as soon as possible."

West inclined her head a little. "We appreciate that. In exchange, we'll immediately return five times that number of your enlisted personnel." Her smile turned wry. "That'll make a few people down here a bit testy, but it's the right thing to do."

That was almost a third of the prisoners. The unexpected gesture made Jared feel like this whole negotiation might go off in spite of his doubts.

"When and where would you like to receive us?"

"I'll give you a code to call me back when you're ready. Rather than meet in the middle of the city, I was thinking an open setting would make us all feel more comfortable. A friend has agreed to host the negotiations on his family estate. You're more than welcome to keep a cutter or pinnace there for your convenience and safety."

He nodded. "That sounds perfectly fine."

"Excellent. I look forward to your call, Admiral. Good day." The transmission ended.

Jared reached for the communications controls and stopped himself. He needed to get used to using his implants as much as possible or he'd never master them. He pinged Kelsey for an implant link.

She answered a moment later. *Morning. What can I do for you?*

I just got off the com with Coordinator West. She wants us both to come along. Against my better judgment, I've decided to agree to you joining me.

He could imagine her smiling.

I'll be good. I assume powered armor is overkill. What can I take?

Whatever seems appropriate for someone of your rather murky nature. We can keep a pinnace down there with us, too. We're bringing the prisoners from Boxer Station with us. They'll give us five times that number of our people back in exchange.

That sounds good. Really good. I'll meet you at the marine docking level in an hour. It'll take at least that long to get those people ready for transport. Anything else?

Nope. See you then.

He disconnected the call. Going into the lion's den worried him, but he didn't really have a choice. Not if he wanted to get his people back.

* * *

SEAN and one of his marine guides made it back a few hours before dawn. They'd found the building housing the guard commander, but they couldn't get in without raising a ruckus. So they'd left a man in a nearby parking garage to monitor who went in and out.

It was a risk, but his mechanic had salvaged some of the parts from the dead vehicles and found a contact to sell them to. Sean wasn't exactly sure how the man had been able to find a buyer in the early morning, but he wasn't going to ask questions.

There'd always been a market for proscribed items in Fleet. Usually nothing serious. Mostly things that broke minor regulations when aboard ship. Sean had the idea that his man might have made supplying those needs a sideline. Or maybe a second career.

A month ago, he'd have been outraged. Now, he welcomed the man's skills with open arms.

They'd used the local funds to procure half a dozen civilian com units, a few civilian-grade stunners, and a pair of highly illegal flechette pistols. He'd told his scrounger to find others that could help them get more money and buy other weapons. The man had smiled and asked Sean what limits he wanted to set. Stripping vehicles, burglary, armed robbery, or something else.

It made Sean feel like a criminal overlord. He restricted them to criminal acts that didn't involve coming face to face with the locals. No one was to be hurt.

The man nodded and gathered his team. Sean promptly dubbed them his pirate crew. They'd slipped back to the island before dawn.

Sean felt as though he'd barely drifted off when a hand shook him awake. It was Ross.

"We have company," the noncom whispered. "More grav vehicles and guards. Different uniforms this time. They're asking for you by name."

Sean sat up and rubbed his face. "Tell them I'll be right out."

He hoped that didn't mean they'd caught any of his people on the mainland.

It took a couple of minutes to get dressed and brush his hair. He walked out into the early morning light and spotted Ross. He was standing near a man in what certainly looked like a military uniform.

The man extended a hand to Sean. "Force Chief Meyer, I'm Detachment Leader Tomas Brent. I'm here at the instruction of Coordinator Olivia West and the ruling council of Harrison's World."

Sean shook the man's hand firmly. "Detachment Leader. What's going on?"

"Your commanding officer, Admiral Mertz, has arranged for a prisoner exchange. As the senior prisoner, you need to designate 750 of your people. Whoever you choose will be taken directly to an exchange point and turned over to Fleet representatives for repatriation."

That was unexpectedly good news. And Mertz was styling himself as an admiral now? Interesting, but probably necessary to negotiate from a position of strength. Sean didn't know anything close to the real story of what was happening between the AI's forces, these people who thought they were still part of the Empire, and Mertz's ships. And he didn't dare ask any questions.

He smiled at the detachment leader. "I'll get that underway at once. Does that number include the hundred people you took away yesterday?"

The man frowned. "We haven't taken any of your people anywhere."

"I'm afraid that isn't the case. Some of the men assigned to guard us took a hundred of my people away yesterday. I don't know where or for what purpose because they threatened to shoot me if I made a fuss. They claimed it was at Coordinator West's direction. Will you shoot us for asking for them back?"

The man shook his head. "I will not. You go select the people you want to send back to orbit while I go ask a few questions of the contractors who're guarding you."

* * *

JARED MADE his way to the quarters they'd assigned to Commander Richards. He nodded to the marine guard just down the corridor and pressed the admittance buzzer. The hatch slid open almost immediately. Richards was rising from the small desk off to the side of the compartment.

He gestured for Jared to come in. "I wasn't expecting you so soon, Admiral. Is there something I can help you with?"

"I'm about to go down to the planet and wanted to run some things by you. I'm not certain you've heard, but we met with Coordinator West yesterday. Things seemed to have gone very well. We're sending the Fleet personnel we rescued from Boxer Station down to them in exchange for about a third of the prisoners they have in their custody."

The Rebel Empire officer nodded and offered Jared a seat. "That's good on several fronts. The longer you had them on your ship, the sooner they would've realized something was different about you. No offense, but you people have some odd behaviors. As I'm sure you'd say we do. Can I get you something to drink? Water?"

"Thank you, no. It's hard to know what seems odd when we have no common experience. Coordinator West seemed undisturbed, so I think we pulled it off for the moment. Now we're going on a longer visit, and I'd like your advice."

The officer sat down across from him. "My first piece of advice is not to get drawn into any long discussions about your home. While each of the worlds of the Empire are separate from the rest, the less specific you are, the less likely you are to give them something to think about. Ignorance is your enemy here, Admiral. Especially since you don't even have current information on any of the possibilities."

"That's excellent advice. I think our general comments about the

Empire weren't specific enough to cause us any grief. The only world that came up was Terra, and we kept our responses very general."

The other man nodded. "Good. Keep doing that. I'll make a short list of planets and the general information about them. Stick with that and you should be safe enough."

Jared considered him. "You don't have to help us, so why do so? Your parole is to behave. This is more like collaborating."

Richards shrugged. "I've been able to access a lot more data and talk to dozens of people since you let me out of the brig. Any doubt that I had of your sincerity is gone. You and your people come from worlds isolated from the Empire. I'm certain of it.

"That doesn't mean your assessment of the Empire is correct, but it does mean that the data you recovered from *Courageous* hasn't been tampered with, and that troubles me. The people fighting the rebellion didn't seem as though they were under anyone's heel."

The Rebel officer sighed. "Worse, Princess Kelsey has shown me some of the recordings she recovered from the graveyard. Horrifying. Add that to what I saw of the attack on Boxer Station, and I'm almost to the point of conceding I was completely wrong."

He leaned back in his seat. "If so, I can't help the Empire. That's hard for me to admit, but I can't think of anything else to do."

Jared could only imagine how hard that must be for the other man. To have his entire world upended. To find out that the monsters under the bed were real and that you'd been working for them.

"You say you're almost there. What's holding you back?"

"Stubbornness," Richards said. "The evidence is there, but I can't bring myself to admit it. Yet."

"I'm sorry this is causing you so much pain, Commander. We'll do what we can to help you get through the trauma. You'll find friends among us, I hope."

Richards smiled. "I already have, I think. Let me get something together for you, Admiral. I'll have *Invincible* verify I'm being honest and send it to you before you leave. Good luck and watch your back. The higher orders are a snake's nest. Trust no one."

13

Kelsey stood outside the pinnace docks and watched as the men and women they'd rescued from Boxer Station boarded vessels that would take them down to Harrison's World. They were going to have a hard time of it. In one way or another, each of them had profound posttraumatic stress disorder.

Several had attempted suicide, and they'd had to restrain them. Some were insane. Ten years under the control of an AI would do that. It chilled her to imagine the poor bastards in the Old Empire that had lived for centuries under those circumstances.

It made her even more determined to bring the AIs down.

Each pinnace took just over a dozen of the prisoners so that it could return filled with seventy of their people. That way neither side had to trust that the other would follow through on their promises any more than they had to.

Jared exited marine country and waved as he walked over to her. He had two marines in unpowered armor around him. "I've got my honor guard. Are you ready?"

She nodded. "My people are inside. As is a full strike team of marines who'll wait in the pinnace, just in case we need rescue. Shall we?"

"A flechette pistol *and* a neural disruptor? Isn't that a little bit of overkill?"

She smiled. That didn't count the miniature versions of both pistols she'd hidden elsewhere on her person. Or her knife. The old Kelsey would be horrified. The new Kelsey felt a bit underdressed.

"Not if I need them," she said. "There've been too many times I've needed something and not had it. I wish they made a plasma pistol."

He shuddered. "That's *really* overkill. I'm glad they don't have things like that."

She probably shouldn't mention the powerful Old Empire grenades in pouches on her belt. As Talbot said, it was easier to beg forgiveness than ask permission. If she could've gotten away with wearing her armor, she would have. She'd even considered bringing her new swords, but they'd have stood out too much.

"You didn't leave your neural disruptor at home," she said, changing the subject slightly.

"I'm not crazy. With our record, something is all too likely to go wrong. Come on. Let's go meet our hosts."

They made their way into the pinnace, and it undocked moments after they'd secured themselves.

"While we make the descent," he said, "let me share some data on a few Rebel Empire worlds that Commander Richards gave me. If pressed, use the data to make a cover story and be sure I know about it. We can't afford any conflicting statements."

Kelsey reviewed the data he sent her. There were a few dozen worlds mentioned, along with some basic information about them. She selected one at random and sent her claim to Jared.

"What do we do if they press us harder?" she asked.

"Change the subject," he said. "We can't afford to slip up. Even the little we said about Terra could have gotten us in trouble. Thankfully, it didn't seem to bother Richards."

"What about the AI from Boxer Station? Have they been able to get its data unlocked? Surely it must know a great deal about the Rebel Empire."

Jared shook his head. "Not yet. Doctor Leonard said that Carl Owlet was close. That might mean tomorrow or next week. I'm not sure. Once we have access, we'll do what we can to filter the data and beef up our stories."

Kelsey split her attention between the conversation and the external scanners. The view of the planet was stunning.

The pinnace entered the atmosphere slowly, at least in comparison to a combat drop. Kelsey was able to look ahead in their course and zero in on the landing area. The other pinnaces were going there as well. Local ships were ferrying people in from the large city nearby. Perhaps that meant the prisoners were there.

She found her attention on the local vehicles sharpening when she saw them flying higher and faster than the grav cars at home. Their designs were probably far in advance of what she was used to.

Their pinnace landed a bit closer to the sprawling house than the others had, and a small delegation of people came out to meet them. She recognized Coordinator West. The other two were strangers. She supposed she was lucky that Deputy Coordinator King was absent.

The ramp at the rear of the pinnace lowered as they approached. Jared led the way down. Their marine guards followed them out.

Coordinator West extended her hand to Jared. "Admiral. Welcome to

Harrison's World. Miss Bandar. This is my associate, Lord William Hawthorne. He's graciously allowed us the use of his home for our talks."

A tall man with a rather flamboyant beard and mustache held his hand out. First to Jared, then to her. "Admiral Mertz, Miss Bandar, welcome to my home. Allow me to introduce my husband Craig."

The thin black man beside him shook Jared's hand. "Admiral. Miss Bandar." He bowed over her hand.

"Thank you for having us," Jared said. He turned to Coordinator West. "I hope the transfer of your people is going well. Many of them will need some serious help over the next few months and years."

Kelsey saw the twinge of some dark emotion on the other woman's face before she smoothed it out. "It's quite sad. Yes, we're taking them directly to a hospital where they can get every bit of assistance possible. We should go inside to speak, though."

* * *

ABIGAIL PUT in an appearance at her office so that she didn't draw undue attention by her absence. She read the report about the meeting between Admiral Mertz and Olivia and tried not to see red. They'd selected Lord Hawthorne's estate for their dialogue, and she knew from experience that the man protected his privacy.

For someone not entangled in politics, the man had an electronic security team second to none. No bugs ever survived more than a day. Most only lived for a few hours. Even getting them inside the building wasn't easy.

If she hadn't known that he never meddled in serious matters, she'd have suspected him of being up to some plot or another. But other than being old friends with Olivia, he seemed disconnected from people of power, except in social situations.

Frankly, the man was vapid, so she easily dismissed him from consideration.

After about an hour, Abigail left her office and made her way through the council building to a private air car that one of her aides had left for her. That assured her of privacy. The government tracked all official vehicles.

Her driver took her directly to her family's agricultural facility, where she'd decided to house her *guests*. The automated harvesters roamed the golden fields without need of human supervision. This allowed her a reasonable expectation of conducting her affairs unobserved. No one would question her presence.

Her car landed outside a large storage warehouse, and she stepped out. The loose organic matter in the air made her sneeze. She hated the countryside. It was so dirty.

One of the private guards came out to escort her inside. He didn't say a word, knowing better than to talk to her. At least he'd learned to respect his betters with only one object lesson.

Temporary cells housed the prisoners and a dozen additional guards made certain that no one felt like trying anything heroic. That might change when the time came to eliminate them. Even animals would try to survive in the end, even if they had no chance.

Abigail spotted the man in the lab coat bustling around a chair set up against the far wall, and she made her way to his side.

"Are you ready, Doctor Nelson?"

The bespectacled man turned toward her with a start. "I didn't hear you come in, Deputy Coordinator! My apologies. Yes, everything is ready."

"Then bring in the first prisoner and get this started. I can't be gone for long without raising suspicion."

"I prefer the term 'subject.' It makes this less personal."

She waved a hand dismissively. "I don't care what you call them. Just do it."

The man gestured to a pair of guards waiting nearby. They went out and retrieved a female prisoner. She struggled as they strapped her to the chair.

Nelson taped a number of monitors to her face and neck. "This will not harm you in the slightest, my dear. Of course, that doesn't mean it will be painless, but pain is transitory."

The woman tried to hit him with her head. Only the guards saved him from a nasty blow to his face. Belatedly, he pulled back.

"My name is Linda Montoya," the woman snarled. "I'm in Fleet service, and you have no right to do this."

Abigail admired the woman's spunk. She didn't sound nearly as uneducated as someone from the lower orders should. Perhaps they really did give them an education in Fleet. That could be helpful under the right circumstances.

She came close enough to catch the woman's attention but not so close that she was within striking distance. "We have every right to do whatever we please, up to and including executing you. I suggest you remember that. Your very existence revolves around answering my questions as straightforwardly as possible. If you waste my time, you won't live to regret it."

"You don't really have a choice, my dear," Nelson said. "The drugs I'm going to administer will make being untruthful quite challenging. The monitors I've placed on you will get a baseline very quickly and administer corrective shocks to encourage compliance. And before you determine not to answer at all, I feel compelled to warn you that excessive resistance could endanger your life."

Montoya defiantly stuck her chin out. "You can all go screw yourselves."

Nelson turned to Abigail. "This isn't a promising start."

"Just get on with it. If the questioning kills her, dump her body back in her cell to encourage the others to cooperate."

Nelson shrugged and gave the Fleet woman an injection. "This will take a few minutes to achieve full effectiveness. I can see that you're inclined to resist, and I'd prefer you didn't. We're not monsters."

The woman glared at Abigail. "I'm not sure that even you believe that."

Abigail stepped forward and slapped the woman with all her strength, sending some of the monitoring devices flying.

"Mind your place, prole, or I'll have you beaten."

"You talk big, bitch. Take these straps off and we'll see who does the beating."

"You think you have the option of talking back to your betters?" Abigail asked. "Then you're more of a fool than I expected. I can make an example of you that will get the next prisoner to tell me what I want without using drugs."

The woman laughed. "Then you don't know us at all."

Nelson finished reattaching the leads. "We're ready to begin tuning the monitors to the subject."

"Why are you telling me?" Abigail snarled. "Get on with it."

He asked the woman a few questions of a general nature, but she refused to answer them. Nelson shrugged and raised a virtual lever on his console. The woman cried out when the monitors administered a corrective shock.

"Every time you fail to answer," Nelson said, "I'll move that up another notch. Your screams will be quite instructive to your companions."

The woman's response was colorful, physically impossible, and incorporated disgusting acts with farm animals. Abigail reached past the scientist and moved the lever up two notches.

After a few minutes, the lever was almost two thirds of the way to the top. Even though the pain made the woman scream, Abigail was impressed that she still refused to answer. She had to respect the woman's willpower.

She turned to Nelson and spoke in a low voice. "As entertaining as this is, I'd prefer answers to my questions. Do you think you can break her without killing her?"

The scientist looked back at the sweat-covered woman bound to the chair. "I'm not sure. She's remarkably determined, even in the face of the drugs. Perhaps she has some innate resistance. That's not unheard of."

Abigail considered the prisoner and consulted her watch. "I'm on a tight schedule. If she dies, she dies. Get on with it."

14

William Hawthorne engaged Kelsey with a wide smile as he escorted her to his home. "You're a bit of a mystery, Kelsey. May I call you that? And you must call me William."

She smiled politely. "Of course you can. How am I a mystery?"

"I fancy myself something of a history buff, and while I'm not an expert on all things Fleet, I've never heard of a special operations officer. One whose rank is secret."

"That's part of what makes people like me more effective," she said. "The lack of general knowledge about us, that is. I'm afraid I won't be whispering any secrets in your ear. My apologies."

The man's eyes twinkled. "Well, then, I'll just have to figure it out for myself. I'm quite the amateur detective. Of which I read quite a bit. I'm afraid that I'm addicted to books about sleuths. If I might say, you're quite well armed for someone with an escort."

His outright curiosity and charm were refreshing, but Kelsey didn't let down her guard. "I promise not to use them unless I have to. I do hope there aren't any unpleasant surprises. Your home looks very beautiful. I'd hate to put any inconvenient holes in it while I get Admiral Mertz to safety."

"I assure you, there shall be no surprises of that nature on my property," he said seriously. "Coordinator West has given me her word that this will be a peaceful gathering. Informal, even. While this isn't the primary home of my family, it's been in our possession for generations. Craig and I are quite fond of it."

She had to admit it seemed like a nice place, sprawling and old. It looked comfortable. Stone walls covered in ivy, a dark slate roof, and a lawn manicured within an inch of its life.

"It's quite beautiful. I'm certain that your assurances are good enough. As a lord, you must have many interests."

The man's smile widened. "I'm afraid I'm one of those people that coasts on the work of their forebears. I'm something of a social butterfly, really. I do quite a bit of charity work. Craig is an engineer, so I don't feel as though we aren't contributing to society at all. As for politics..." He shuddered. "I wouldn't put one toe into that vipers' nest."

Kelsey smiled. "I've thought the same thing a number of times."

He led them all through the wide doors leading into the house. "I've taken the liberty of setting things up in my den. There's only one entrance, so some guards can remain outside the door while others are inside. I've also selected some of the best Harrison's World has to offer in the way of refreshments."

Kelsey had to admit the room was homey. Expensive-looking dark furniture, and the room looked very lived in.

Something else she noted were the servants William had looking after them. Tall, muscular, and fit. Her implants quickly identified a number of concealed weapons on them. They doubled as guards. Or perhaps they were security filling in for the normal staff.

It only took a minute of watching them to link them to William Hawthorne rather than the coordinator. They watched their master for cues.

Jared's marine guard came in with them, while her escort remained out in the hall. William closed the doors behind them.

You're inside scanner shielding.

It took every bit of her willpower not to jump at the unexpected voice in her head. It was the electronic ghost of Ned Quincy.

You shouldn't be able to initiate contact with me like this.

The other's mental voice seemed to take on a wry tone. *Something must've changed. I seem to have some small amount of latitude now that I've become aware of a possible threat to you. This room is shielded against signals. I thought you should be aware of the situation.*

This new turn of events was unexpected and more than a bit disturbing. She wondered if it had something to do with the changes *Invincible* had made to the program's code.

Well, she didn't have time to worry about that right now.

She made a show of examining the plaster on the ceiling. It was very pretty, but it concealed another surprise. She couldn't see any heat sources above her. A glance at the walls showed the same. Even the marines outside the door were invisible. The room was indeed shielded. Nothing blatant. All very subtle.

Kelsey attempted to access the marines' monitor equipment. She couldn't sense that either. No signals were going in or out.

"What do you think?" William asked her. "I can't take credit for the building, but the furniture was all my work. Not constructing it, of course. Only selecting it."

She gave him her full attention. "It's very nice, though I think you're not giving yourself enough credit. You've made some interesting modifications to the structure of this room. Unless the whole house is shielded, of course."

He cocked his head. "I'm not certain I catch your meaning."

"I think you do, Lord Hawthorne," she said formally. "This room is shielded so that no signal goes in or out. IR, implant communication, and possibly most other forms of signal. If you want to put me at ease, I'm not sure this kind of subterfuge is the way to go."

He bowed low. "My apologies." Some of the playful tone he'd used before was gone. "I often speak with others on matters they would prefer to remain private. Most don't even notice that there's a shield at all. You're most perceptive."

"Others have used scanner shields like this to hide an ambush. I've grown nervous when I can't see what others are doing around me. I'm afraid situations like that often lead to inconveniently large explosions. I'd prefer it if you allowed me to communicate with the marines."

"That presents something of a conundrum," he said. "Coordinator West would prefer that these conversations remain private, yet I'd like to accommodate you."

Kelsey dug a combat remote from a pouch on her belt. "If you could open up an authorized channel for this device, I could maintain contact with the guards without placing a large hole in your privacy. No one else can use it. I can narrow it down to a single frequency, and it will warn me if anyone else is on it."

He took the remote and examined it curiously. "What is it?"

"It's a combat remote. It allows me to extend my senses into dangerous places—like ambushes—and target my enemies without exposing myself."

His expression told her he was impressed. "You must do more fighting than I'd imagined possible. Forgive me, but you aren't the most imposing of people, Kelsey."

She felt the corners of her mouth tugging upward. "You'd be surprised."

"I'll speak with my people on allowing this device access. I don't want any of you to feel as though this is an ambush. Excuse me for a moment."

William went back out of the room, conspicuously leaving the doors open. Kelsey reestablished communication with the marines. More importantly, she reconnected with the high-powered link in one of the marines' backpacks.

It had the strength to connect her implants with the pinnace and its scanners. With them, she could watch every approach to the building.

Jared would take the lead in the negotiations. She'd focus on making sure no one attacked them while he was busy. She wanted to trust that these people wished them no harm, but they were part of the Rebel Empire. Both of them had implants and could be deeply in the AI's pockets.

She'd stay on high alert. If they had betrayal on their minds, she'd make them regret it.

Her mind crept back to the unexpected ability the Ned Quincy program had demonstrated in contacting her and observing her environment. That had her even more on edge. It was changing. She needed to understand what that meant and put a stop to it if it was dangerous. One more thing to worry about.

* * *

OLIVIA SETTLED into one of the comfortable chairs and devoted her attention to Admiral Mertz. She'd selected a juice from the western continent. William always had the best selection. The others followed her lead.

"The exchange shouldn't take more than a few hours," she said. "Shall we discuss how we proceed from here?"

"I thought that was settled," Mertz said. "We would send the Fleet personnel from the station to you in exchange for our people. I don't have a lot of leeway to offer you the outright freedom that you want."

"I need to convince the ruling council to approve that deal," she said. "As you know, getting others to agree to a plan they don't want to hear is never easy. I'm not actually speaking to that, though. I'm talking about an itinerary while you're here. I assume you'll want to see your people."

William came back in from the hall and closed the doors. He and Miss Bandar joined them near the fireplace.

She shot him a message through her implants. *What's going on?*

Miss Bandar spotted the privacy shielding. She requested an exception for her to maintain communication with their people. I agreed. I also consulted with my head of security about the scans he took as our guests entered the building.

Olivia waited a moment and then mentally sighed. *Don't make me beg. What did you find?*

Miss Bandar is heavily enhanced. Graphene sheathing on her bones, artificial muscles, and other internal equipment that isn't completely clear. Olivia, as far as I can tell, she really is a Marine Raider.

That set Olivia back on her mental heels. Her clandestine research indicated the AIs had decided the Raiders were too dangerous after the rebellion. They were entirely too capable. As far as she knew, the Empire didn't even make the equipment for that kind of enhancement anymore.

This only deepened the mystery about her guests.

The mental communication had only taken a few moments. Admiral Mertz was just now responding to her statement. "Absolutely. I'd like to see them as soon as possible."

Miss Bandar cleared her throat. "If you don't mind, Admiral, I'd like to see if Lord Hawthorne could show me around the city."

The nobleman smiled widely. "Finally, a task I'm suited for. I know all the most interesting places in the capital. We have some wonderful architecture and cultural sites."

Olivia nodded. "That sounds like an excellent division of labor. We can return here for dinner. Then you can make the decision to either stay the evening or return to your ship."

They spoke for a while longer, but the conversation kept coming back around to the prisoners. It was as if they were an itch that Mertz couldn't scratch. Finally, she decided they just needed to go see them.

She rose to her feet. "Perhaps you'd like to go see your people now? I'll take you to see the prisoners in the hospital first. A number of them arrived with serious injuries, though most have recovered and been returned to their fellows. Maybe a half dozen of the most badly injured are still under care. I'd be happy to return them to you as a gesture of goodwill."

"If they can be safely transported, we would appreciate that."

"Consider it done, then."

She led the way out. Her official air car had a boxy appearance due to its heavily armored nature, but she knew from experience that it could go much faster than most people thought possible. It had advanced grav drives and compensators.

Compact screens kept the atmosphere from creating much drag, so it could go as fast as many atmospheric interceptors. She'd never been aboard when that kind of speed was necessary, but her pilot had confided to her that it was a rush to fly so fast.

Her personal guards and Mertz's marines postured at one another but got into the car without any actual trouble. She sat across from him as they rose into the air and headed for the city.

"We'll land directly on the roof of the hospital," she said. "I suspected we'd be coming, so I made arrangements to go right in."

"How many people died after they arrived?"

"Many were badly injured," she said with some sympathy. "We did what we could, but several dozen died anyway. We have their bodies ready to go back with you. I assume you know how many people we have in custody."

He nodded. "We recovered the bodies after the battle and know who wasn't there. We'll do an identification on everyone as they come back. If someone remains unaccounted for, there will be questions."

"Understandable. We have implant recordings of them coming off the cutters. Your experts will be able to tell that we haven't tampered with the vids. We won't be keeping any of your people from you. Again, you have my word."

She watched him look out over the city and let the silence grow longer. She could see how he took in the vast sprawl of the city. Her suspicions grew as she watched how he reacted. It was as though he'd never seen an urban center this large.

The air car made good time to the hospital. Her driver had no doubt called ahead to clear the way. Even though most people would probably never notice them, there were other cars keeping pace with them, just in case there was trouble.

The car landed on the roof long enough for the passengers to exit, then it flew away. It would circle until she called for it. She led Admiral Mertz into the busy facility. A trio of doctors in white coats met them just inside.

One stepped forward and bowed. "Coordinator West, I'm Doctor Janice Hauptman, head of the surgical department at Adams Memorial. These are my associates, Doctors Mather and Jimenez. We've been overseeing the treatment of our guests."

Olivia bowed slightly in return. "Doctors. This is Fleet Admiral Jared Mertz. I'll defer to him about what to see."

Mertz extended a hand. "Doctors. Thank you for your care of my people. Might I inquire about who they are and their condition?"

"Of course," Doctor Hauptman said. "We tried to get some medical information from those who could talk, but they were uniformly uninformative. Most gave us a name and serial number. Nothing more. Here is a list."

Mertz took the tablet from her and scanned the list. "You have several without names. I assume that's because they're too injured to speak?"

Hauptman nodded. "Yes. Three of them have been unconscious since they arrived. They are in critical condition, even with full support. I'm guardedly optimistic about two of them making some kind of recovery. The third is still too injured to know."

He nodded, his expression somber. "If you don't mind, I'd like to see them first. I might be able to provide their names for you."

They traveled as a group to the intensive care ward. The first woman was so heavily bandaged that Olivia couldn't clearly make out her face. She lay in a bed surrounded with life support machines. Tubes and wires crisscrossed her body.

"Why can't you regenerate her?" she asked Doctor Hauptman.

"Her injuries are so severe that she's been through six brief sessions in the regenerator. I'm hopeful that she will be strong enough for a longer stint tomorrow. If we can get her to the point she can tolerate full-time treatment, she'll make it."

Mertz turned to them. "This is Petty Officer Margret Powers. Do you think she'll recover?"

Doctor Hauptman nodded. "I do. As will the young man beside her."

They turned to another young person in much the same condition. Mertz identified him as Able Spacer Thomas Rinaldi.

Doctor Hauptman showed them to a third ward. "This gentleman is in the worst condition. He'd lost his legs prior to arrival and suffered a tremendous amount of internal damage. Frankly, I'm astonished he survived the trip down from orbit. His life or death is almost out of my hands. All we can do is care for him as best we can while his body decides whether to live or die."

Mertz stared at the man for a long time. "His name is Paul Cooley."

15

Kelsey watched the city pass slowly beneath William's air car. It had an air of decay about it. Few of the buildings were clean, and some even looked abandoned. It had few of the megastructures that she'd seen in the vids of Terra.

Even though she had no evidence to base her suspicions on, she thought it had been this way even before the AI attacked the planet.

After a few minutes, she turned her attention to the Rebel Empire nobleman. "If you don't mind my asking, what was behind the suppression on Harrison's World? I know the basic facts, but what specific events occurred?"

He leaned back in his seat and looked at her with a thoughtful expression. "I'm not privy to all the details, mind you, but I know the general outline. The System Lord discovered a movement afoot to usurp its rule. To say that it reacted strongly, well, that's self-evident."

"So I'd heard. But how could it know what was going on down here on Harrison's World? Boxer Station is not close by, and an AI isn't capable of dropping in for a visit."

"The Lord had its ways of observing the general populace. It was plugged into every computer system on the planet, I'm sure. It must've heard something it didn't like. I'd imagine that it used persons of proven loyalty to verify everything. That's all supposition, of course. I have no idea of what really happened. Olivia would know more."

"It seems like it could've used those loyalists to take the conspirators into custody," Kelsey said. "It's a huge jump to bombarding the planet."

He nodded. "It was quite shocking. We haven't even begun to recover. The Lord obliterated the capital and every spaceport. Unfortunately, those also had large cities around them. We lost more than a third of our population in that one afternoon."

Kelsey could see the pain he felt clearly written on his face. "You must've lost so many friends. I'm sorry."

William smiled wanly. "You didn't do anything. The Lord made the decision." He took a deep breath. "In any case, what's done is done. Tell me what you think of the city."

She scrunched her face a little. "It seems as though it could use a good washing. Sorry."

"Plainly stated but true. A decade ago, this was the largest manufacturing center on the planet. Mostly run by the middle orders and staffed by the lower. They didn't have to keep things in the most pristine condition. 'Functional' was the byword. We still haven't recovered enough to begin making progress on it."

"It must've been quite a challenge to turn it into the capital of the planet."

He snorted. "You have no idea. My fellow lords never had to directly rule over the common people. They had an entire bureaucracy in the old capital that carried out their instructions and shielded them from any distasteful contact with the grubby merchants and workers. Or, heaven forbid, the criminal elements.

"My family came from the merchant classes of the Empire before the revolution. We still have many connections to that kind of people. That spared us the devastation the other ruling families suffered. Their estates were centered around the old capital. Ours was here."

He gestured at the cityscape flowing past his elegant vehicle. "This city is not a haven for the higher orders. These people blame us as much as they do the System Lord. After all, they don't know about our AI leaders."

She thought she heard a mocking undertone to that last, but she wasn't sure. Perhaps he wasn't enamored with a machine ruling him.

"Where would you suggest we go first?"

He pursed his lips. "I can think of a number of interesting places."

"Dealer's choice. You have some assumptions about what kind of person I am. Surprise me."

William smiled. "I know just the place."

* * *

ABIGAIL BARELY NOTICED as Nelson unstrapped the prisoner that they'd just finished questioning. The first woman had cracked, but she'd held out far longer than Abigail had anticipated. Then there'd been the need to verify the tall tale she'd told. With three others telling the same basic story, Abigail had to believe it was true.

Horrifying but true.

These people were nothing but puffed-up pirates from a planet the Imperial Lords had missed during the revolution. Or perhaps not so puffed up. They'd eliminated the System Lord, and they controlled the bombardment weapons in orbit. She had no idea what their ultimate goal truly was.

Well, she could find out from "Admiral" Mertz. He'd tell her everything she wanted to know if she could get her hands on him.

Abigail smiled. This also sealed Olivia's doom. She was conspiring with rebel scum. That wouldn't be too hard to spin into a death sentence. It virtually assured Abigail the coordinator's seat and the restoration of power for the conservative alliance.

She gestured for the guards to take the prisoner away. "Put him with the others. See that they're fed and given any mandatory medical care. These people might very well be important witnesses to a very despicable crime."

The plan for killing them was no longer required, of course. She didn't need to cause a split between Olivia and Mertz. She didn't want to. Unseating Olivia would now take a very different form.

She strode back out to her vehicle, sending the driver scrambling to open the door for her. "Calder Consortium. Now."

Her vehicle took off and curved toward the city. Once she'd had a chance to speak with Master Calder, she could make her move against Olivia without any fear of damaging her own standing.

She allowed herself a luxurious stretch and grinned. Life was looking very good.

* * *

THE SIGHT of the remaining patients pained Jared. These brave men and women had grievous injuries that would take months to recover from. Injuries that hadn't needed to happen. The list of crimes Breckenridge had to answer for kept getting longer and longer.

Coordinator West sent all of the injured except for the three in intensive care to join the rest of the prisoners going back to *Invincible*. The remaining three weren't stable enough to move. A final vehicle transported the dead. Fleet would eventually lay them to rest at the Spire.

The thought of all the bodies that had to fill the ships in the graveyard made him despair a little. The Empire would need to expand the Fleet burial ground many times over to allow room for the millions of heroes waiting to go home. Just recovering them would be a gargantuan undertaking.

Olivia seemed subdued as they waited for her car on the roof. "I'd read about their injuries, but that isn't the same thing as seeing them. I can only imagine the events that hurt them."

He gave the woman a small headshake. "I'm afraid you can't begin to understand them. These are the people that survived. All told, thousands died. Not unlike those who perished when the System Lord obliterated so many cities, I suspect. That's something I can't grasp."

The air car settled in front of them, and they all boarded. It rose and headed for the ocean.

Olivia gazed at him quietly for a minute before sighing. "We must avoid anything like that going forward. I'm taking you to see the rest of your people, but I want you to understand that I'm doing everything I can to get them released as soon as possible. If you try to send your forces after them, there are weapons that can destroy your small craft. That would prompt a stronger response from you. I beg you, let's take this slowly."

"I've sent too many people to their deaths recently," he said. "I'd much prefer to let this situation resolve itself. I appreciate your courtesy."

The air car flew out over the bay, giving him an excellent view of the many ships and small craft on the water. Almost all of them seemed to be purely oceangoing.

He pointed at a large container ship. "That isn't a grav craft."

Olivia looked at it for a moment and nodded. "No. Most bulk cargo still moves via water. Why waste the energy to move something by air when it's more cost effective to go slowly? The economy itself dictates what works best."

"I looked over the maps of this area shortly after we knew which city we were coming to," he said. "There are a number of populated islands not too far away, aren't there?"

"Indeed, though most of these ships come from more distant ports. The global trade is still intact, thank goodness. Harrison's World is slowly getting back on its feet. Look over to the left. See that island port? We'll land there so you can see how this works from the ground level. The camp where your people are is on the same island. We can walk from the port to the camp."

Jared examined the port more closely as she instructed the driver where to go. It seemed to have an unending stream of large ships unloading bulky containers. Vast fields of them were stacked high in the interior of the island.

The other side of the landmass captured more of his attention when he realized it must be where his people were. A number of low buildings sat inside a fence. Small air ships circled above the area, no doubt on the lookout for potential escapees. He was just close enough to see small groups of prisoners. His people.

The air car came down on a flat pad that seemed designed for loading containers into flatbed grav haulers. A number of them were doing so nearby.

He suspected that this pad was supposed to be in use, too, based on the man stalking toward them. He wore a faded yellow hardhat and a deep scowl with equal ease.

The scowl fled when one of the coordinator's guards got out to speak with him. In fact, he became quite a bit more accommodating. The remainder of the guards climbed out before Jared and Olivia exited the vehicle. His marines brought up the rear.

Her air car took off and allowed another with even more guards to land. Those men and women spread out around them in a close circle.

Jared had seen the Imperial Guard do the same when the emperor went somewhere with crowds.

Many of the workers stopped what they were doing to gawk. Coordinator West took that in stride, barely seeming to notice them. Her guards saw them, but only as potential threats.

That left him time to look at them as people. Perhaps that's why he saw the man staring at him in obvious surprise.

Of course, Jared was equally shocked, though he suppressed the expression before it made it to his face. The last person he'd expected to see loading a container onto a grav lifter was Commander Sean Meyer.

* * *

SEAN LOCKED eyes with Jared Mertz long enough to see the recognition flare in the man's eyes. He was dressed in an admiral's uniform and traveling with someone important. A powerful woman with dark hair in an impeccable suit. Guards surrounded both of them.

The woman and Mertz exchanged some words. He started over toward Sean. Well, this was going to be interesting.

Mertz stopped beside him. "Pardon the interruption, but could you explain how this works?"

Sean bowed as he'd seen the foreman do with other important visitors. "I'd be happy to explain the process, sir. If you'll step this way, I'll show you where it starts."

He lowered his voice. "Well, this is the last place I'd have expected to see you. Does this mean we're going to get out of here soon?"

"I hope so," Mertz said softly. "How the hell did you escape the prison camp?"

"We found an unguarded access tunnel, and some of the marines are good at making friends. We even have some people on shore looking for a way to get everyone to the spaceport, just in case we have to make our own travel arrangements."

"You're very resourceful, Sean." His tone was admiring. "You might as well call them back. There are no spaceports. The AIs had this planet on lockdown. It blew the capital and spaceports just like they did during the rebellion."

Mertz put his hands on his waist for a moment before raising his voice. "Tell me about how the ships are unloaded."

Sean gestured toward the ships nearest the dock. "Each of these comes in and is assigned a docking time. The large cranes unload it and place the containers into the stacks. Each has a number that the supervisors keep track of. Based on things like the perishability of the cargo, the need for faster delivery, and other priority factors, each is loaded onto these grav lifts for transport to shore."

"And once there, the lifts take them to other cities and so forth?"

Mertz shielded them with his body and slipped Sean his com.

Sean pocketed it and shook his head. "No, sir. Grav trains take cargo to the more distant locations. These lifts only deliver the containers to a facility similar to this on the shore. Workers there see them on their way."

Mertz frowned. "Then why not just unload them there in the first place?"

Sean had wondered the very same thing. "The yard on shore is too small. With all of the extra cargo coming through this bay, it was easier to use the island to get all the ships unloaded. The grav lifts serve the shore port and a number of train yards. I should've said that up front. Sorry."

"I hope you can get back into the camp quickly," Mertz said softly. "We're on our way there now. Coordinator West probably didn't get a good look at you, but you'd best change your appearance some. A hat, shave, etc."

Sean had been cultivating his stubble to blend in. That would be an easy fix. That and a hat would hopefully be good enough.

Mertz shook Sean's hand. "I think I've got it. I appreciate you taking the time to explain it to me."

"It's my pleasure."

He watched Mertz rejoin the woman and her guards. They continued toward the edge of camp.

The foreman yelled for everyone to get back to work, so he blended into the suddenly busy crowd. With luck, he'd be back at the barracks and ready for visitors before they got there.

16

Abigail arrived at the Calder Consortium building and exited her vehicle in something of a rush. Her guards struggled to keep up as she breezed past the security checkpoint. The people manning it knew better than to delay her.

She took the lift up with two of her people and headed for Master Calder's private office. She placed her guards outside the door with a gesture and stared at the Master's assistant. "I need to speak with him. Now."

The man smiled apologetically. "I'm sorry, Deputy Coordinator King. He's in an important meeting and left instructions not to be disturbed."

"I'm telling you to interrupt him. This cannot wait."

The man considered her for a moment and then rose to his feet. "I'll go do so in person, Deputy Coordinator. Please wait here." He went into the office and came back out after a minute. "Please go in, Deputy Coordinator."

Abigail gave the man a nod and went inside. Master Calder stood behind his desk, staring out the window at the city.

"This had better be important, Abigail. The negotiations you interrupted might not go so well when I reschedule."

She bowed her head, knowing he was watching her reflection in the glass. "I apologize, but this is more important than your meeting, Master."

He turned and raised an eyebrow. "Well, then. I shouldn't delay your update with my posturing. Please continue."

"Admiral Mertz and his people aren't Fleet. Not ours, anyway. They're descendants of loyalists who escaped the Lords with Emperor Marcus's son Lucien during the revolution."

Master Calder blinked and stood stock still for a moment. Then he gestured for her to take a seat. "I grant you that's a worthy reason for bursting into my office. I assume the rush is because he's still on Harrison's World and you want to take action against him and Olivia now?"

She settled into her seat and nodded. "Yes, Master. We can prove that Olivia is collaborating with the enemies of the Empire. That's not only enough to strip her of her office but to execute her for treason."

"You can legally prove that she knows who she's dealing with? After all, you took these prisoners without cause to have them tortured. With my blessing," he hastened to add. "But our enemies will not be fooled."

Abigail stuck her chin out defiantly. "We did what needed to be done. Olivia is weak. These people are playing her. The others will see that."

"Will they? After the Lord turned on us, they wasted no time seizing power. They're not going to be eager to hand it back. They know the price they'll pay."

"There isn't time to play subtle games pitting one faction against another," she said firmly. "Mertz will have what he wants in a few days at most. Honestly, it really doesn't matter at this point. We have enough of his people to prove our accusations at any time.

"The window to take Olivia out of play is narrow, though. If we don't strike while Mertz is here and blame him for the attack, we'll have no choice but to trust the political process. We've seen how well that works."

The conservative alliance had been the eyes and ears for the Lords since the revolution. The System Lord had rewarded them by using its influence to keep them in a dominant leadership role on Harrison's World. Until it had inexplicably turned on them.

It had accused them of planning a coup and had used irresistible force to scour the system of all human presence. That, in turn, had led to a coalition of weaker parties wresting control of the planet away from its rightful rulers.

Master Calder considered her words while drumming his fingers on his desk. "A successful attack might very well allow you to take the coordinator's chair. A failed one will start a civil war. Given a chance, Olivia might lead the unwashed hordes to our doors with torches."

"If she allows them to rise, they'll attack all of the higher orders indiscriminately," Abigail almost sneered. "She won't."

He nodded slowly. "If we commit to this path, we have no choice but to push through to victory. Once the others become aware of the resources we've been gathering, they'll consolidate into a solid wall of resistance. You'll have one chance to strike the head off the snake."

Abigail smiled. "I can do that."

The Master walked to his bar and poured a drink. "Even if I grant you that point, these invaders control weapons that could destroy Harrison's World. We need to expedite Project Damocles."

Abigail shrugged. "Will the time ever be better? The Lord is disabled, and these people only have two ships. They think themselves safe. Also, they don't have a superdreadnought as they'd claimed. The prisoners all agreed that this so-called Admiral Mertz is a commander in their Fleet and only has a repaired battlecruiser and a freighter. They don't even have widespread use of implants. We can eliminate them all with one bold stroke."

"They defeated the System Lord. Are you telling me they did so with one cobbled-together warship?" Master Calder sounded unconvinced. "Then where did these thousands of prisoners come from?"

"Other ships that followed Mertz to this general area. Based on what I heard, a patrol sent out by the System Lord crushed their ships. I'm not sure how Mertz was able to capture this system, but he cannot hold it from us."

Master Calder shook his head. "This Mertz may be more formidable than you give him credit for. I need to think for a moment."

He paced his office for a few minutes before seeming to come to a decision. "If we can take the orbital bombardment platforms off the table, the ships can't cause widespread damage to the planet. Even if the intelligence you have is wrong. The time has come for us to restore order to this world. Do not fail me."

Abigail rose to her feet. "I won't, Master. By nightfall, Olivia West will be dead and we'll control our own orbital space." She smiled widely. "Then we'll eradicate these rebels from the heavens."

* * *

WILLIAM DIRECTED his driver to take them to a location away from the city. Kelsey happily switched her observation to the coastline. The never-ending flow of dilapidated buildings had become monotonous.

The city trailed off into rural areas. Much of the land seemed dedicated to food production. Massive machines tended and harvested vast fields. The corn was recognizable, but she couldn't place the other plants.

"The land below produces the food that keeps us all from starving," William said after a while. "Well, not really starving. Even though the urban centers are large here on Harrison's World, we're not lacking for arable land. Still, it feeds everyone in this city, and much is exported to surrounding areas."

She pulled her gaze away from the fields below. "Was that a danger when the AI attacked? I've seen the results of large-scale bombardment up close. It can be… extreme."

He gazed out the window for a few moments. "It feels wrong to say this, but the damage from the bombardment was limited to areas close to the targets. Rather than one large kinetic weapon, the orbitals have smaller ones that strike in close proximity to one another. That still means total destruction for a city and all the horror that entails, but it restricts large-scale damage to a manageable level. Has something larger been done elsewhere?"

She nodded grimly. "I'm afraid so. A ten-kilometer asteroid. Not quite an extinction-level event, but far too close for my peace of mind. Let me tell you, being nearby when it hit was… unpleasant."

He stared at her. "You were that close to a massive asteroid strike? And you lived?"

Kelsey shrugged. "We had good pilots, but not everyone made it. I can't go into the details of the situation, but I'm here to tell you that those rides at the amusement park no longer even raise my heart rate."

"I'd imagine not." He took a deeper breath. "Anyway, my family owns a fairly large swath of these fields, so it's been my pleasure and headache to see every inch of these lands for the last few years. We have a number of houses and buildings, but there's one in particular that I'd like to show you."

"I don't know that much about architecture."

He laughed. "You won't need to. It's not the building itself that you'll find intriguing. It's what's inside it."

The building in question looked like a large warehouse. They circled it once, and the driver brought them down to a cracked plascrete slab beside it. The exterior of the single-story structure hadn't seen fresh paint in quite some time. The original color was white. She could tell that from the few places where the last coat was still intact.

The sliding doors were locked tight, and small blinking lights told the tale of alarms at the ready.

William climbed out and held the car door for her. Her two marine guards flanked them as he led her to the building entrance.

"If it had been anyone but me, the alarm would've already warned the intruders away. A hidden weapons emplacement would've targeted anyone foolish enough to continue. Only the most stubborn would feel its wrath, though."

Kelsey raised an eyebrow. "You'd keep something that valuable way out here in the middle of nowhere?"

He smiled. "This seemed like the best place for it. Come."

There wasn't a keypad, so he must've used his implants to disarm the building's protections. The large door ponderously slid open a few feet and stopped with a screech.

"Well, so much for me avoiding any embarrassing lapses," he said with a chuckle. "I obviously need to bring someone out to fix the door."

The interior was dark but not so obscured that her optical implants couldn't show her what was waiting. William didn't know that she could see in conditions of almost total darkness.

In the center of the open area, a civilian cutter sat in the gloom.

He turned on the lights with a flourish. "And here we are. The last ship on Harrison's World still capable of reaching orbit and beyond. Theoretically."

Kelsey walked over and gave it a closer look. In the light, it had some similarities to the building. It was obviously old, and the fuselage could have done with some repairs. In all, it looked incapable of atmospheric flight, much less making it into space.

Still, it was a ship on a planet that had lost every spaceport, so that had to count for something.

"I can see what you mean by theoretically. Does it still work? How did it survive the orbital bombardment?"

William wiggled his hand in the air in a way that she thought meant uncertainty. "It should still be capable of flight. At least the self-diagnostics say it is. My father gave it to me as a fixer-upper. It was long past retirement from the family fleet, so he told me I could have it so long as I maintained it. I'd brought it out here because we didn't have an unused space large enough to hold it."

He sighed. "And then the capital was destroyed, taking the main spaceport with it. If I'd moved it to one of the smaller spaceports, it still would've been lost. Like my father."

She could see the emotion he was keeping bottled inside him. "I'm sorry for your loss."

He nodded his acceptance of her condolences. "Everyone lost someone that day. I'm hardly alone in that. It still hurts, but in the face of such a tragedy, it seems gauche to mention it."

After a moment, he continued. "In any case, I've made a number of inquiries. I suspect that this may be the only remaining spacecraft on the planet." He turned to her. "You're not going to blow it up, are you?"

"I think our ship is safe enough from it," she said dryly. "Besides, I'm not sure it would even get high enough for the orbital bombardment platforms to shoot it down."

"True enough. Now that you've seen it, I'll admit to asking you out to see it with ulterior motives."

She raised an eyebrow. "I'm flattered, of course, but I'm seeing someone."

"Dear God!" he said, clutching his chest. "Your virtue is safe with me!"

Kelsey laughed. "Well, if not an assignation, then what?"

His gaze sharpened. "I just wanted to ask you a few questions away from prying ears."

"Fire away."

"Where did you come from? You're not Fleet. At least your Admiral Mertz doesn't hold the rank he claims. Who are you really?"

She stood there, frozen in place at the unexpected question.

17

Olivia allowed her guards to lead the way to the fence isolating the prisoners from the port. A number of empty buildings separated the two areas. There was one guarded gate along that stretch. A heavy stunner commanded all the approaches the prisoners might use.

An unkempt man stood beside the guards. He bowed at their approach. "Coordinator West. Welcome. My name is Jack Oliver. I'm in charge of the internment camp."

She gave him a nod. "Mister Oliver. This is Fleet Admiral Jared Mertz, your prisoners' commanding officer. He's here to inspect their condition. I assume everything is in order."

His eyes darted to Mertz and then back to her. "Of course. If you'll come this way."

The man's furtive glance filled her with dread. What was he hiding?

They made quite a sight, all of the men guarding her, walking as one large crowd. The camp guards stayed away from her personal protective unit, but that didn't keep her people from regarding them as possible threats.

It took almost five minutes before she saw the first prisoners. Dressed in Fleet uniforms, they watched the procession curiously. The onlookers grew more numerous as they came to the central square of the camp.

A group of men stood waiting for them. They looked like officers, but she knew that wasn't the case. They had no implants.

One of them seemed familiar, somehow. A tall, thin man with a clean face and sharp eyes. She couldn't place him, but she'd seen him before. Or perhaps his twin. If you met enough people, you'd find unrelated folk who were so similar it was spooky.

The man in question saluted with his fist to his chest. "Admiral. Force

Master Chief Sean Meyer reporting. You know my associates, Command Master Chiefs Ross and Newland. We're glad to see you, sir."

Mertz returned the salute. "Gentlemen, I'm pleased to see you as well. This is Coordinator West, the leader of Harrison's World. I hope to conclude negotiations with her very shortly to secure your release. Are your conditions acceptable? Do you need anything?"

Meyer glanced at her and then back at his commanding officer. "Things were a bit rough the first few days, but they're looking up. I'm most concerned about the men and women separated from us. I know we'd all like to know where they went."

Mertz frowned. "Didn't they tell you? They're going back to *Athena*, our flagship in orbit."

The tall man shook his head. "Not them, sir. The hundred people the guards took yesterday."

There was a moment of stunned silence before Mertz turned and gave Olivia a stony look. "That *does* sound like a pressing question. I'm sure the coordinator can tell us where they are."

* * *

KELSEY STARED at the man in shock. How had he known?

"Excuse me?" she asked. "I don't know where that came from, but you're off base."

He smiled, showing her marines his hands when they perked up. "Am I? Please tell your men that I'm not silly enough to attack a Marine Raider with my bare hands. I'm certain the results would be spectacularly humiliating."

She gestured for them to search the building in case this was more of an ambush than it appeared.

Once they were gone, she put her hands on her hips. "I think you should explain what you mean."

"It was a combination of things, really. Let's start with the biggest mistake. Terra. I'm sorry to inform you, but the capital of the Empire was suppressed shortly after the revolution."

His expression became more solemn. "The citizens there resisted fiercely, and they never stopped. It became the most impressive guerrilla action in history. The Imperial Lords finally decided that the planet was a lost cause and declared the system off limits. It has orbital bombardment platforms much like those over our heads. So I'm afraid that Admiral Mertz's claims of visiting it ring false."

Kelsey had to admit there was a possibility he was telling the truth, but she couldn't just say so. "Coordinator West also said she visited it, so why should I believe your tall tale? I'm not sure what you hope to gain from this charade, Lord Hawthorne."

"Olivia would be the first to tell you she knew you were lying right then. Well, actually, she knew you were hiding something even before that moment. If Terra isn't enough to get you to speak more freely, shall we discuss your ship? Her name isn't *Athena*, is it? Let's just call her by her true name. *Invincible*."

He smiled at her expression. She expected she looked like an animal caught in a bright light, unsure of which direction to run.

"Rest easy," he said as she struggled to come up with a story. "If we intended to act against you, we would've already done so. You can call Admiral Mertz and verify that he's in no immediate danger."

She considered doing that but decided to test the waters a little further first. "How do you know that name?"

"*Invincible*? Simple enough. We spent quite a lot of time and money refitting her in secret. Let me assure you, slipping personnel and parts under the very nose of the System Lord was a challenge.

"Olivia, the poor woman, was in a relationship with the senior Fleet officer on that ship when the Lord suppressed us. She received a number of messages from your flag bridge over the years preceding it. Ones showing marks on the Admiral's console that were quite distinctive. She knew right away where she was."

He allowed her a moment to consider that before he continued.

"If you were truly Fleet personnel, you wouldn't need to finish restoring that ship to carry out your supposed mission to take out the System Lord. You'd have brought enough force to handle that. For the life of me, I can't figure out what you're really doing here or who you are. Perhaps you'd care to explain it to me?"

Kelsey sighed. "I should've known things were going too smoothly. Why were you about to stage a coup against the AI?"

"I'll show you mine if you'll show me yours."

In spite of the gravity of the situation, she laughed. "You're a rascal."

"Craig agrees with that assessment completely. Honestly, we mean you no harm. Your people control all access to Harrison's World, so attacking you would be madness. You truly hold all the cards in this game. Can't we be honest with one another?"

She considered him for a moment. "It's a long story. The basis of which is that we're not from around here."

His eyebrows drew together. "You come from the other side of the Empire?"

"Not exactly. What do you know of the Fall?"

"I assume you mean when the AIs suppressed the Empire. I know what most people know, and a bit more handed down by tradition in secret. The AIs took over Fleet faster than Emperor Marcus could marshal forces to stop them. The AIs crushed the Imperial forces near the border of the Empire. Many of the derelicts orbiting Boxer Station came from that last stand."

"The emperor perished there?"

"Legend says no ships escaped the cul-de-sac where Fleet made its final stand. I see no reason to doubt that. We couldn't exactly search the derelicts without raising suspicions."

She allowed the corner of her mouth to quirk upward. "Well before that last battle, the emperor sent his son away to a distant world. Once the fighting ended, our world was damaged but alive and unoccupied. The emperor's son, Lucien, kept the flames of civilization burning, and though it took centuries to again get to the stars, here we are."

He stared at her for a long moment, thunderstruck. "That isn't the story I was expecting at all. If, of course, it's true. Why are you here in this system?"

"To get our people back," Kelsey said. "Taking on the AI cost us far more than any sane person would want to pay. Yes, we appropriated *Invincible*. Without her, we'd never have succeeded in defeating the AI and its ships. And, for the record, finders keepers."

William shook his head slowly. "Remarkable. I certainly won't contest your possession. After all, you accomplished everything we'd hoped to do. Though, unless we work together, those gains may be very short lived."

"How so?"

"There are some devices in the ship's hold. They are critical to protecting this system."

Kelsey nodded. "The flip-point jammers, yes. We found them and have this system locked down. For the moment, we are in complete control. There won't be any surprises from the AIs." She put her hands on her hips. "Now, show me yours."

He leaned up against the leg of the cutter. "You and I have something in common. Ever since the AIs overwhelmed the Empire, there has been a resistance. A fairly ineffective one, considering the AIs control virtually all the industrial capacity. We have no ships and few troops. Yet on every world, we're looking for a way to take the Empire back.

"Here on Harrison's World, the conservatives have been the spies and willing helpers for the AIs. Only in the last few decades has the resistance gained the tools it needed to have a chance of overthrowing their rule. Those flip-point jammers and the almost-completed superdreadnought. With those, we thought we could secure the system and rebuild the true Fleet. We still can, if you'll work with us."

She paced as she considered her response. "Some accommodation might be possible, but you need to know that your plan was doomed. Even with total surprise, the AI would've destroyed *Invincible* if we hadn't had other ships. Even with them, we lost a lot of good people. You can prove your commitment to wanting to work with us by returning my people."

He raised an eyebrow. "Yours? Not Admiral Mertz's? So you're in command. Forgive me, but you don't look like a military person. Even with those impressive implants. You strike me more as a member of the higher orders. Or a noble, as they were once called."

She nodded. "That's true enough. Perhaps you noted my name is Bandar. My father is the sitting emperor of the Terran Empire and my brother the heir. Under the edict put forth by Emperor Marcus and by my father's appointment, I am Princess Kelsey, heir secundus to the Imperial Throne and ambassador plenipotentiary of the Terran Empire. The true, unconquered Empire."

* * *

ABIGAIL LEFT Master Calder's office and went straight to the headquarters of the conservative alliance. Gavin Decker, his chief troubleshooter, was already waiting for her. He closed the door in the faces of her guards and led her to a sitting room decorated in dark, rich browns. She sank gratefully into a large leather chair.

He sat on the edge of his desk. "Master Calder instructed me to cooperate in every way possible, Deputy Coordinator. What can I do for you?"

"I need you to kill Coordinator West. I think eliminating the admiral's companion—Miss Bandar—will sow enough suspicion so that we can spin Olivia's death as retribution. If Mertz can be taken alive, that would be helpful, but I understand how complicated that might be. Kill them both if you need to. I need it done today. Bandar should die within the next few hours, if possible."

The man hid his shock well, but she saw it flicker across his face. "I have people following both groups. Lord Hawthorne and Miss Bandar are away from heavily populated areas, so direct action is possible. May I inquire why we're embarking on this course? There will be a significant amount of blowback."

"I'm aware of that. The ultimate reasons are not your concern. Master Calder has endorsed my plan. Is that going to be a problem?"

He seemed to consider her words for a moment and then shook his head. "No. Depending on the circumstances that hold sway in a few hours, the assassinations might be subtle or overt. The coordinator's location and security posture will dictate how this plays out. Do you have any preference in regard to the methods I use?"

"Not particularly, so long as no one doubts Mertz and Fleet are responsible for her death."

He smiled. "Consider it done."

18

Olivia turned her attention to the camp commander. "Perhaps you'd care to enlighten us, Mister Oliver?"

The man shrank back a bit but straightened almost immediately. He glared at the prisoner. "That's a damned lie. No prisoners are unaccounted for."

"That's good," she said, eyeing the perspiration beading on his forehead. "I know that a complete list of prisoners was made. We'll do a thorough head count, just to settle this. Now."

The man nodded. "Of course. I'll get that started right away."

Olivia watched him walk toward the gate and leaned over to speak softly to her guard commander. "He might be telling the truth, but I don't trust a man who sweats under questioning. Grab him if he tries to make a quick escape."

The woman in uniform bowed. "Right away, Coordinator." She motioned for two other guards to follow and headed after the man, her com unit to her lips.

That matter dealt with for the moment, she returned her attention to Admiral Mertz and Force Master Chief Meyer. "We'll get to the bottom of this matter very shortly. I authorized no such prisoner removal. I swear it."

Mertz gave her a steady look and then nodded. "I believe you, but I also have no reason to doubt the force master chief. How will you go about finding my people?"

"If the camp commander had anything to do with it, we'll get that information from him in short order."

They'd only begun a tour of the camp when her guard commander returned with Oliver in cuffs. Two men had him held between them and were forcing him to walk quickly. Her remaining guards focused their attention out on the camp guards. If there was going to be trouble, now would be the time.

None of them seemed inclined to do more than grumble.

"He made a break for his air car," the guard commander said. "I had people waiting for him."

Olivia shook her head with mock sadness. "I'm so disappointed in you, Mister Oliver. Who paid you, and where did they take these people to?"

The man glared at her, which earned him a slap to the back of the head from one of her guards. That didn't dampen his animosity one bit.

"These people killed millions of us," he snarled. "Why should we care what happens to them? You should've killed them all as soon as they landed."

"Watch your tone," she said coldly. "We didn't kill them because they had nothing to do with the attack on our world."

"But Fleet did! Screw those bastards!"

Olivia understood his reaction. Only the cream of the higher orders knew the AIs ruled humanity. Regular people knew nothing of computer-controlled warships or the System Lord. They thought Fleet was responsible, when nothing was further from the truth.

"I gave my word that these prisoners would be cared for," she said coldly. "Where are these people?"

"I have no idea, and at this point, I don't really care," Oliver said sullenly. "My brother died because of them, and they deserve what they get."

She felt like slapping the man, but that wouldn't do much good. "Who paid you?"

Oliver said nothing.

"Take him back to his offices and hold him there," she told her guard commander. "If he doesn't tell you the truth before I get there, he and I are going to have a very unpleasant conversation."

The woman bowed and led the man away.

Olivia turned to Mertz and Meyer. "I'm very sorry this happened. We need to account for every one of the missing people, and I'll do whatever it takes to return them as soon as possible."

Mertz turned to the senior prisoner. "Force Master Chief, do you have a list of the missing?"

"Not completely, sir. If there is a master prisoner list, we could go over it and get the last few we couldn't place."

Olivia found the file in her cranial implants. "I have it right here. Let's get started."

* * *

"THAT'S QUITE A CLAIM," William said. "One I'm not willing to credit without supporting evidence."

"And here I thought my word was good," Kelsey said with a chuckle.

"I'm not certain how I would prove something like that. You don't happen to have any Old Empire computers lying around, do you? No? Then we're at something of an impasse."

He rubbed his chin. "Actually, we do have access to a significant Imperial asset from before the rebellion. Perhaps it will allow you to prove yourself."

She gestured toward the door. "I happen to be at your disposal. Oh, and until we sort this out, it might be best to leave Jared and Coordinator West out of this. I'd especially like to avoid mentioning any of this unless we're face to face."

"It shall be our little secret," he assured her. "I'll need to call and tell Olivia that we'll be gone for at least a few hours. I suggest you let Admiral Mertz know as well."

She retrieved her military com. It linked to a long-range unit carried by one of the marines back to the pinnace. From there she could reach Jared.

The call didn't connect. Strange, his unit was off. That wasn't right.

Kelsey watched Lord Hawthorne speaking to Coordinator West and waved for his attention before he disconnected. "Is she with Jared? His com is down."

He asked and nodded. "She's handing him her unit."

She held the civilian com up to her ear. "Jared?"

"Right here."

"I tried your com, but it was offline."

"That's not good. I'll get a spare from one of the marines. I'm fine, though there are some concerns developing."

She listened as he described the situation with the missing people. That concerned her, and she was certain who was behind it. "It has to be Deputy Coordinator King. She's still working some angle."

"I agree. I'm going to focus on this. Are you comfortable being on your own for a while?"

Kelsey looked at William. "I'll be fine."

"Be careful. I'll ping your com unit with my new information as soon as we hang up."

He was as good as his word. Her com lit up with a new code and a text message from Jared authenticating it. It said *All good here. I'm still not happy with what you did with Elise.*

She smiled. He was making sure she knew it was really him. No one down here knew about his love life.

Kelsey sent a message back. *You'll thank me later. At least that's what Talbot says.*

"Okay," she said aloud. "We're good. Where are we off to now?"

"A secret base, of course. Where else would a group of die-hard loyalists live?" He led her and the marines back out to his vehicle. The driver took off and headed even farther away from the city while he made a discreet call.

She settled back in her seat. "Aren't you worried about anyone tracking you to this secret hideout?"

"Of course," he said with a smile. "But they won't know a thing. You'll see."

They flew for almost an hour before landing at a small town. Specifically, at a diner.

He held the door open for her. "Try the malthar bites. They're fabulous."

Kelsey watched him order with more than a hint of confusion. She'd thought they were in a hurry.

A man and woman dressed eerily like them came out from behind the counter and headed out toward the car. Two men in credible marine armor followed them. Lord Hawthorne drew her into the kitchen with a twinkle in his eye.

"I doubt anyone is following us, but they'll continue on and return here when we call. No one will be the wiser."

"We'll just wait here in the kitchen?"

"Not quite." He tugged her arm and led her to the freezer.

"You're kidding, right?"

Without a word, he opened the door and stepped inside. She and the marines followed. Her breath puffed in the cold air, and she shivered a little.

He proceeded to the rear of the large space filled with meat and other perishables and opened the top of a large box marked "malthar bites." Instead of frozen meat, there was a ladder leading down into the darkness.

"Malthar bites," she said. "Clever."

"I rather thought so. From this point forward, the shielding will block any outside communications. Watch your step."

Kelsey had no trouble navigating the narrow ladder, but the armored marines did. Nevertheless, they all managed to reach the plascrete below without any problems.

She found herself standing in what looked to be a tunnel with an arched roof about three meters overhead. It led downward at a slight angle.

William gestured toward the ceiling as he led them deeper into the ground. "This access originally led to a small warehouse a block over, but that drew more attention than we liked. It was better if we went with a business that had lots of people arriving and departing at all hours, just in case someone was watching."

"Is this a pre-Fall construction?" She felt the wall, but its rough surface told her nothing. "Are you going to eat those? I'm starved."

He handed the food over without a word. The nuggets of fried meat were good. The savory flavor was unlike anything she'd tasted before.

"Mmm. These are excellent! What's a malthar?"

"A large, flightless bird with less intelligence than my shoe. They make good food, though. The restaurant we just left is famous for its secret spices.

"Yes, this tunnel is prerevolution. The town is only a few hundred years old. People loyal to our cause set up shop here and are still a significant proportion of the residents. That helps with concealing everything, too."

"Why don't you tell me more about this resistance movement?" she asked as they made their way onto what looked like a rail tube stop. A sleek car sat waiting for them.

He shook his head. "I'd rather wait until we arrive at our final destination. Sometimes seeing is worth hours of chatting."

The interior of the tube car was old but serviceable. She sat on a faded blue cushion next to him. The marines took the spots opposite them. The car doors closed, and it took off smoothly.

The trip lasted about ten minutes, and the two of them chitchatted after they finished eating. William refused to discuss anything of substance.

Once the car slid smoothly to a halt, he led the way out onto a stop almost identical to the one they'd left. Only this one had other people waiting for them—half a dozen men in full armor with flechette weapons and one with a plasma rifle. The man with the latter had it aimed conspicuously at her.

William shrugged apologetically. "I'm afraid that you're going to have to turn over your weapons now. As sad as it would be, any resistance will result in your deaths."

The marines had already raised their weapons and closed ranks with her. The tension was like a mist in the air. She knew that the next few minutes were going to be critical, and they really shouldn't throw away this opportunity.

"Lower your weapons," she ordered. "We're going to cooperate."

Kelsey started digging out her pistols. "You know that I'm more than capable of taking you on hand to hand, right?"

"I'd really rather you didn't," he said in a sorrowful tone. "No one needs to get hurt. After all, if you're telling the truth, I swear you'll get everything back, and we'll become the best of friends."

"And if, for whatever reason, I can't convince the computer?"

"I'd regret having to explain your untimely passing. I wouldn't have you killed, of course, but you'd be our guest here for a very long time."

She sighed. "Well, I suppose I'd better give this my best effort."

* * *

ABIGAIL WATCHED her office chronometer make its way slowly toward the end of a regular workday. She'd been listening to the news through her implants with more than a bit of anticipation.

She'd already planned how to quickly consolidate power and isolate the most troublesome of the council members opposing the conservative alliance. Before any of the fools knew what was happening, she'd have her boot on their throats.

Then she'd execute stage one of Operation Damocles. That would get everyone's attention. Perhaps at that point, Master Calder would read her into the rest of the program. She had her suspicions about what came next, but it was only guesswork.

A throwaway com unit she'd acquired chimed softly and she snatched it off her desk. A new file had arrived for her. She played it with shaky fingers.

The image showed that old stick Lord Hawthorne's antique air car flying along. Abigail could just make out the back of the blonde rebel's head. The woman started to turn toward the lens of the camera, but a bright flash of light shot onto the screen, and the car exploded.

That made her grin. One down. Now all she had to do was wait for Olivia and Admiral Mertz to die.

19

It took longer than Jared cared for to identify all of the missing personnel, but he now had their names and faces. Exactly one hundred people were unaccounted for, so he was relatively certain their count was accurate. The number was too precise to be accidental.

Of course, that meant that the people Meyer had ashore had to have already slipped back into camp. He hoped that hadn't screwed up some aspect of what the man was doing. They hadn't had more than a few moments alone, so he really didn't know what was happening on that front.

Honestly, an escape attempt right now might be the worst thing they could do.

Olivia turned away from the guard she was speaking with and stepped over to him. "Admiral, I'm satisfied that we have a good count of your missing people.

"Honestly, I know Abigail King is behind it, but I can't figure out her reasoning. Mister Oliver's testimony won't be enough to question her legally, but I *will* get to the bottom of this. I doubt she's seriously injured anyone."

"She'd better not have," he growled. "I'll tack her hide to the nearest wall if she's harmed any of my people."

"And I'll help you. It might be best if we go get the inevitable confrontation out of the way."

He nodded. "I'd appreciate a moment with the force master chief."

"Of course." She walked back over to her guards.

Jared lowered his voice. "Can you get weapons in the city?"

Commander Meyer's lips twitched. "Sir, I've discovered that you can get damned near anything as long as you have money. So, yes. We've already bought a number of flechette pistols and civilian stunners."

"I'll message you with the coordinates for an island we have under our control. If need be, get your people ashore and make your way to that general area. It's probably only a few hours in one of those grav lifts. Call them for pickup once you get close, and the marines will work something out."

"Aye, sir. Let me give you a couple of civilian com codes, just in case." He rattled off three strings of numbers that Jared committed to implant storage.

"Got them. Good luck. See you again soon."

He made his way over to Olivia just as she finished her conversation with her lead guard. "Is confronting Deputy Coordinator King so directly safe?"

Olivia laughed. "What's she going to do? Shoot us? No, she'll deny everything, but she won't attack us."

He wasn't so sure about that. "I'd recommend you have forces positioned in case you're wrong. Recent history has taught me that it's better to be ready when the sky falls."

She seemed to consider that and slowly nodded. "I suppose having a plan B doesn't hurt. Once we're inside the council building, there'll be too many people around. I suppose any attack would need to take place as we're arriving or leaving."

Her com chirped, and she glanced at it. That became a double take.

"What is it?" he asked.

"The news service is reporting that a vehicle like William's crashed outside the capital. They've found five bodies." She looked up. "That would be William, Miss Bandar, the two marines, and the driver."

Jared pulled out his com and called Kelsey. There was no response.

He cursed his decision to allow her to come to Harrison's World. If she'd died in what he guessed was an attack, he'd never forgive himself. Still, she'd pulled off miracles before, so he wasn't really going to believe she was gone until he saw her body for himself.

"Why would King attack her?" he asked through clenched teeth.

"To drive a wedge between us? Perhaps that's also why she took the prisoners. Or this could just be a terrible coincidence."

They stared at one another and shook their heads.

Olivia headed for the gate. "We need to confront her as soon as possible. Then we should go to the crash site."

"I couldn't agree more, but I have an idea."

* * *

KELSEY ALLOWED them to herd her and the marines through a massive vault door. Inside was a lift easily large enough to hold ten times their number. It had to be for cargo. As soon as the door closed, it dropped at a fairly good clip.

She raised an eyebrow. "So, now that I'm a captive audience, would you mind telling me where we are?"

If he was worried about being within her grasp, it didn't show. "Certainly. Though I suppose that makes me look like a clichéd vid villain. Should I explain my entire evil plan so that you can make good your escape and take me down?"

Kelsey shook her head. "You're incorrigible."

"Thank you. Well, this is a prerevolution facility that we managed to hide from the AIs. It wasn't known to the public, so that was easier than it sounds."

"A planetary defense center would be the obvious choice," she said, "but I'll venture a guess that this is the Grant Research Facility."

His eyes widened and his jaw literally dropped a bit. "My, my. You *are* full of surprises. I'd have sworn no one knew about this place before the revolution, much less after. How the devil did you know?"

"You'd be surprised what an ambassador plenipotentiary and daughter of the emperor is allowed to know."

"For all our sakes, I fervently hope you're telling the truth."

The lift settled to a halt, and the doors opened. A wide entry area with prominent weapons emplacements covering every angle greeted them. Depending on how far below ground they were, it would be difficult indeed to dig these people out.

A large set of armored doors slid open across from them, and several men and women walked out, eyeing her curiously. One of the men wore a Fleet uniform with captain's tabs. He seemed to be in charge.

William bowed slightly to him. "Kelsey, this is Fleet Captain Aaron Black. Aaron, this is Kelsey Bandar. As to what she does… well, that's a bit more complicated. Let's leave it at saying she's Admiral Mertz's special operations officer. Be careful with any handshake. She's a Marine Raider with full augmentation."

If that disturbed the short black man, he didn't allow it to show. And by short, Kelsey really meant it. His eyes were level with hers.

He extended his hand. "I'd be pleased to call you by your appropriate rank, Miss Bandar. At this juncture, is there really much point in keeping it to yourself?" His voice was a pleasant alto, and his smiled revealed shining white teeth.

She shook his hand slowly. "I've already told Lord Hawthorne, so if he doesn't want to share, who am I to ruin his surprise?"

The man shook his head. "Lord Hawthorne thinks he has a sense of humor. We've tried to correct his misapprehension. But he still feels compelled to try. Welcome to the Grant Research Facility. Still under the original management. It's my privilege and honor to run it for the resistance.

"Before you feel compelled to attempt a daring escape, allow me to warn you that even a Marine Raider won't be getting out unless we say so. I don't know everything about your implants and enhancements, but I've looked over Lord Hawthorne's scanner readings, and you're a marvel. It still won't grant you a miracle."

Kelsey laughed. "You'd be shocked at the things I've survived in the last six months, Captain. I believe we found some products from this facility on *Invincible*. Those flip-point jammers really saved the day. Unfortunately, we broke one. The other two are covering the entrances to this system as we speak."

The man raised his eyebrow. "Indeed? Well, that's gratifying to know. It took us a very long time to take them from theory to hardware. We had no way to test them, either. But where are my manners? Allow me to introduce my staff and lead scientists."

Kelsey made note of each name and face as Captain Black introduced them. Part of her mind was still working on how she might escape. Perhaps blowing a hole in the roof of the elevator?

That probably wouldn't work.

She almost jumped at the voice in her head. Again. *You really need to stop doing that.*

Why?

Because it surprises me. I'm not used to having another person in my skull.

It's not like there's a real person monitoring everything around you.

No, she thought. Not exactly, anyway.

So, what did you see that I missed?

As the elevator descended, I detected several levels where there were emissions consistent with weapons platforms. Perhaps they're targeting intrusion from above, but I wouldn't bet your life on it.

Hmm. That was a point to consider.

Are you monitoring everything I do all the time? I didn't see those things. I didn't even have a scanner out.

Your implant hardware has adequate passive scanners, if you know how to access them, and of course I'm watching. It's not as though I need to sleep. I'm adding your sensory recordings to the ones my creator made. Also, I'm pleased to say that I've completed the indexing of his files. They should be significantly more useful now.

Thanks. If I survive the next half hour, I'll take a look.

The internal exchange had only taken a moment. She had to admit, even though the program in her implants was a little creepy, it had its uses.

"So," she said to William, "what's next? How can I prove myself to you?"

"Well, this facility has a computer built and installed by the most paranoid security freaks the Empire could find before the revolution. If you have the credentials you claim, surely you can get it to confirm them."

He raised a hand to forestall her instinctive reaction. "I don't expect you to gain access to the systems. That's not really within the realm of possibility. All I want is to see the computer verify you're telling the truth."

She nodded. "Let's get this over with so you can stop threatening me."

The interior of the facility felt like the inside of a large orbital. They had to have put heavy shielding around everything, because the power emanations alone would've been detectable from the surface. If she'd known how to use the passive scanners that Ned had mentioned, she had no doubt she'd have detected any number of strange readings as they led her to an area deep under the entrance level.

The lift claimed it serviced levels 50 to 75, as well as the entrance. There was no telling how many levels there were in total. It might be as large as *Invincible*. Or even bigger.

On level 70, they brought her to what was obviously a computer center. The large, thick hatch was familiar to her. Of course, they didn't actually take her inside. They led her to a conference room beside it.

It bore a striking resemblance to the one in the planetary defense headquarters on Erorsi. If that was anything to judge by, there must've been a lot of people down here at some point. Perhaps there still were.

William took the seat at the head of the table with an ease that made clear he was Captain Black's superior. He gestured for her to take a seat beside him. "Sit. Perhaps you'd care for some tea?"

Kelsey sat. "No. Let's get this over with."

"Very well. Computer, this is William Hawthorne. I would like you to create a virtual instance of yourself and have it perform some tasks for me."

"Virtual workspace ready," a standard Old Empire computer voice said from the overhead speakers. "This unit is booted and standing by for your instructions."

"Excellent. The person seated next to me will be communicating with you. I wish for you to verify the veracity of her claims and authenticate them as best you can."

"This unit is ready. Implant access to the virtual workspace is granted. State your name through the implant channel."

Kelsey found the access channel it was offering and sent a communication request. Once it accepted, she started speaking with it through her implants.

Computer, I am Princess Kelsey Bandar. I give you permission to access my implants for the sole purpose of verifying the truth of what I'm saying.

Access acquired, Princess Kelsey Bandar. Proceed.

My title is ambassador plenipotentiary of the Terran Empire. My father is the emperor of the Terran Empire, and I am second in line to the Throne. Here are my Imperial access codes.

She sent the computer her authorization codes. She knew from asking Carl Owlet that they had virtually unbreakable encryption and identified her as what she claimed. Even if someone else took the codes from her, without her hardware, they'd be invalid. He informed her smugly that they were better identification than her DNA.

Access codes received and confirmed, Ambassador Plenipotentiary Kelsey Bandar. How may this unit serve you, Highness?

I understand you are only a copy of the main computer. Is that correct?

Affirmative.

So any instructions I give you will not hold true for the actual computer?

Correct.

Will the main computer be aware of what transpires in this virtual workspace?

The main computer is monitoring the basic communication and is aware of this conversation and this unit's conclusions. No commands or files are being transmitted, however.

Thank you. Can you tell me what level of authority someone with my credentials has on your system?

Complete authority, Highness. This facility operates under the authority of the Imperial Throne. As an ambassador plenipotentiary and heir secundus, you have complete authority over this unit and this facility.

Thank you.

Kelsey looked back to William. "Done."

He smiled a little. "Computer, is Kelsey Bandar speaking the truth? Are her credentials valid?"

"Affirmative. Her Highness Princess Kelsey Bandar, heir secundus and ambassador plenipotentiary to the Terran Empire, is who she claims to be."

His eyebrows went up almost to his hairline. "That's a surprise, but a pleasant one. Computer, dismiss the virtual workspace."

Kelsey smiled. "Now that that's done, let me give you a less pleasant surprise."

She pinged the computer and requested access. It immediately granted it to her.

Computer, do I have complete access and control of your systems?

Affirmative, Highness.

Excellent. Lock out all other users from the computer systems and put this base on lockdown. No one in, no one out. Be certain that nothing is detectable outside the facility and that no research projects are impacted.

Grant users in the middle of anything enough access to complete what they're doing. Accept no commands from those users other than ones related to the experiments in progress.

Acknowledged, Highness.

The overhead speakers began blaring something similar to general quarters on a Fleet vessel, startling everyone in the room.

Captain Black surged to his feet. "What the hell did you do? Computer, what's happening?"

"Access denied, Captain Black."

Kelsey sat back in her chair and smiled. "Now the shoe is on the other foot. I have complete and utter control of your facility." She held up a hand to stop the Fleet officer from exploding. "I haven't done anything to reveal it to anyone outside this facility. I'm not your enemy."

"Well, you're sure acting like one," he snarled.

She looked at William. "Are you ready to sit down and talk like adults? Are we done with the threats? Do you accept that I'm who I say I am?"

The Rebel Empire noble rose to his feet and bowed as deeply as possible. "Of course I do, Highness. I'm yours to command."

* * *

TIME DRAGGED, but eventually Abigail's spies informed her that Olivia's car was approaching the council building. Unlike the first kill, she could watch this one in real time. If, of course, the assassins struck as Olivia was arriving.

Honestly, she hoped they did. She really wasn't looking forward to Olivia confronting her over those missing prisoners or Lord Hawthorne's death.

How would they do it? Another anonymous crash? That might look suspicious. Of course, the people prone to seeing things that way would do so anyhow.

And they'd be right, after all.

The car was thirty seconds from touchdown when it happened. A dark shape rose from the river and raced toward the council building.

Olivia's car turned and sped away, a good indicator that she'd been suspicious. That spoke well to her character.

The new vehicle, larger than a regular grav car by a fair margin, closed the distance in record time. Abigail finally recognized it when a small missile blew Olivia's car out of the air. It was an Imperial marine pinnace, just like the one that had brought the now deceased Admiral Mertz to Harrison's World.

Where had Master Calder found one? Had he had it all this time?

The pinnace peeled away, going right over the bright lights of the city. The building's vid feed would have recorded it clearly.

Realization hit her. This was the perfect frame. No one other than the visitors had vessels capable of reaching space. With that provocation, it would be perfectly clear who'd attacked whom. Brilliant!

Abigail got on the com to her assistant, who she'd insisted wait for Olivia's meeting to be over before leaving.

"Get me the military liaison. A Fleet pinnace just killed Coordinator West. I want atmospheric fighters scrambled to take it out. To take them all out. I want Fleet gone from Harrison's World before dawn. Do you understand me? Get him on the line now!"

20

Olivia watched the vid feed with a sick stomach. She'd sent those people to their deaths. Her guards had been going to bring Abigail to join her at the crash site where William went down. People who'd been with her for years. Now they were all dead.

"I need to contact the security forces and have Abigail picked up," she said dully.

"Actually, are you sure that's the best idea?" Mertz asked. "I've had some unfortunate experience recently with coups. King has probably been planning this for a while. If you talk to the wrong person, she'll know you're alive and try again. At this point, they think you're dead. You'll want to keep them thinking that until you take them down."

She looked over at him in the other seat of the car she'd borrowed for the trip. "I can't just let her get away with this! She's going to be consolidating power right now."

"It's your call. I suggest if you're going to let them know you're alive, go big. Make some kind of general broadcast. Notify your ruling council all at once. While you're doing that, I need to call my people and get them moving. It won't be long before she takes a swing at us."

Olivia shook her head. "You really don't understand how this works. She's already started purging the government of people loyal to me. I need to make my calls right now and pray it isn't too late."

She pulled out her com and made a call to her office. From there, she could get the word out quickly. Unfortunately, it wouldn't connect. She tried the backup number she'd had a very bright resistance tech install, and she was into the automated system at her office.

"This is Coordinator West. Authenticate me. Sigma Alpha three five seven."

"Identity verified, Coordinator," the computer said. "How may this unit assist you?"

"Code red. Execute emergency plan Omega."

"Executing. Primary connectivity unavailable. Switching to secondary. Secondary unavailable. Switching to tertiary. Connected. Transmitting. Transmissions complete. Wiping system. Goodbye."

The line went dead, but that was all according to plan. Emergency messages had gone out to every council member not associated with the conservative alliance. It might be too late for some of them, but many would get the word in time and go to ground. She hoped. It had also notified contacts within the resistance. Then the computer had purged itself.

Unless everything had gone to hell and Abigail had more reach than Olivia had ever suspected. If so, she'd hunt Olivia down, erase all the gains of the last decade, and kill a lot of good people.

She returned her attention to Mertz. He was just wrapping up his own emergency call.

"They tried to attack the pinnace at Lord Hawthorne's estate, but it was on alert. It's on its way back to the island we have under our control. It can't make it to pick me up, but that's fine. I'm not going anywhere until I know what really happened to Kelsey."

She felt herself frowning. "But William's car is destroyed. They found their bodies in the wreckage. I'm sorry, but she's gone. So is my oldest friend."

Just the thought sent her spirits sagging. She forced the savage sorrow aside. She didn't have time to grieve.

"You don't know Kelsey like I do," Mertz said. "She's surprisingly hard to kill. How far away from the crash site are we? Where can I get some different clothes? I stand out like a sore thumb in this uniform."

"There's a town close by. I know some people there. They can have clothes ready by the time we arrive."

Olivia called ahead to the diner and gave the correct code phrase to identify herself. "I need some casual men's clothes. We'll be there in ten minutes." She made an estimate of his sizes and included that before she disconnected.

"I should make the call now to get the prisoners released," she said. "I don't want them caught up in the middle of this."

"Hold off on that. Right now, King has bigger fish to fry. I ordered them to make their way out after dark."

"Excuse me?"

He smiled. "I spoke to them briefly before we left. They've already discovered a way out. In fact, I'm somewhat surprised that you didn't recognize that I was speaking with Meyer at the port. He had to rush back into the camp and shave to have any hope you wouldn't recognize him."

Olivia felt her eyes widen. She put the images of the man at the port and Force Master Chief Meyer up side by side. Definitely the same person.

"I'll be damned. I never would've imagined someone from the lower orders could be so clever."

"You shouldn't let your prejudices get in your way. People can be smart no matter what their background. When we have time, I think I need to tell you a story."

"Would this be about how you aren't really who you say you are? I figured that out already. I knew for sure the moment that you said you'd been to Terra and I realized that you were actually on *Invincible*."

It was his turn to be shocked. "Yes, we really do need to talk. First, though, we need to find Kelsey, and hopefully Lord Hawthorne."

* * *

SEAN PUT his com unit away. Mertz had wanted him to wait until dark to get things rolling, but he really didn't know how much they'd accomplished. It would be better to start everyone moving now. Then he'd have enough people in the port after dark to commandeer several grav lifts and get the exodus done in one go.

And, contrary to what Mertz probably wanted, Sean would be taking a team to find the missing prisoners. He knew where to find the bastard that had run the camp. The trick was going to be getting in to snatch him, but Sean had a few ideas.

First, he needed to get the plan in motion.

He found Ross and Newland. "There's been some kind of attack on the coordinator, and Admiral Mertz believes it's time for us to decamp. I want to appropriate four grav lifts."

Newland grunted. "I figured we needed to do that before too long. That's going to screw with their delivery schedule, and that'll draw attention pretty damned fast. Once the foreman for that section of the dock gets wind of the delay, it won't take him long to figure out something is squirrelly. We'll need a distraction that won't draw the camp guards' attention."

Ross smiled. "A fire would be too flashy, as would an explosion. What about a grav failure on a loaded lift that's just departed? The damned thing would sink and spread containers all around the harbor."

Sean considered it for a moment. "That's as good as anything I can think of. It would get attention but not the kind that would get prison guards all excited. We'd need to have our people staged and ready to go in the buildings outside the fence. How long to get them out there?"

"An hour should be enough," Ross said. "We'll get everyone moving and let the last few people get dinner ready. If we hit the docks closest to the camp, we can get everyone to the loading area without too much risk. We'll just have to stun anyone in the warehouse."

Newland shook his head. "Too open. They'd be right on the lift deck for the guards to see."

"Well, then," Sean said. "We'll just have to focus the guards' attention at the critical moment. Leave that to my team and me. Go get everyone moving. This could go bad any minute."

Sean left them to it and rounded up his shore team. They met in one of the barracks. In the shower, of course, though they kept their clothes on.

"Gentlemen," he said, "the time has come for us to decamp. Timing is critical, and while we don't want to draw the guards' attention too quickly, we'll need to provide a few minutes of entertainment to get them all looking away from the port. I don't suppose anyone brought explosives back from the shore?"

They shook their heads. One man, the scrounger, spoke up. "Explosives are harder to get than crappy weapons, sir. We have some civilian stunners and flechette pistols. Maybe we can cause them some grief with those."

"I'm not sure I'd want to get them shooting at us, Corporal. All in all, I'd prefer to escape without them knowing we're gone for a bit."

"What about the air patrols?" one of the others asked. "If we stun the two men in one of the vehicles, they'll figure it was a mechanical failure and get into search-and-rescue mode."

Hmm. SAR might be just what they needed. "They might see the beams, and those stunners are short-ranged weapons. Probably not that accurate, either."

The man nodded. "We can tune out the color. If we focus the beams as tight as possible, we might be able to tag someone flying low and slow. It would have to be a two-man team to get the lookout, too."

"Are any of the guards patrolling that low?"

"Occasionally. Some of them like to show off."

It wasn't the best of plans, but he supposed they could light one of them up with flechettes if they had to. "Okay. We'll set up on the far side of the camp. I'd prefer the thing to crash on the other side of the fence, but we don't have a lot of choice. As long as everyone else gets away clean, I can deal with that. Which two men are staying with me?"

* * *

JARED LOOKED over the town as their air car came in for a soft landing. It wouldn't have been out of place in Avalon's agricultural districts. The driver stayed in the car while Olivia led Jared inside. He'd taken off his jacket to reduce the number of people that might recognize his uniform.

Something smelled good, reminding him that he hadn't eaten in a while.

Despite what he'd told Olivia, he felt hollow inside. The crash could've killed his sister. He was putting on a good face, but it could all be true. He prayed it wasn't. That would be a disaster, personally and professionally.

Olivia went to the counter and put in an order for food. The man behind it leaned over and said something to her. She stiffened and then sagged a little.

Jared saw something very much like joy in her face as she came over to him. "They got out of the car here. They're okay."

He closed his eyes for a moment. "Thank God. If they're here, who was in the car?"

"Some poor people who were providing cover for them. Stunt doubles, as it were. It doesn't look as though you'll need that change of clothes just yet. We won't be under observation as we make our way to them. Come on."

To say that he was surprised when she handed him a bag of food and led him into the freezer was an understatement. The secret tunnel under the diner was even more of a shock.

"What the hell is down here?" he asked.

"That's going to take a while, and I think that it would be best to get together with William and Miss Bandar for that explanation."

They boarded the grav train and ate as it bore them into the darkness. The food was good, but he couldn't remember what it tasted like as his mind swirled. What was this place? One of the planetary defense centers? Something else?

It only took ten minutes for them to make their way to another station and disembark. The large armored door failed to open when they arrived.

Olivia tried it again and frowned. "That's odd. It should've opened right up, and I'm not getting ahold of anyone inside."

* * *

Kelsey smiled at Captain Black and William. "I'm glad that we were able to settle that so easily. Computer, restore access to everyone affected by my earlier instructions."

"Done. Coordinator West and an unknown visitor are at the station and requesting admittance. They signaled during lockdown."

"I hope that's Jared with her. That would make explanations much simpler."

William headed for the door. "I'll go get them and be right back, Highness."

She scowled at him. "That's going to get old fast. I thought I told you to call me Kelsey."

"So you did, but that was before you told me who you *really* were. One simply doesn't chat up their social superiors in a public setting. Perhaps in private. We'll see."

He left, and she shook her head. "What about you, Captain Black? Can I get you to call me by my given name?"

The dark-skinned man smiled a little. "Is that an order? I'm still not even certain I'm in your chain of command."

"I think we can work that out," she said as she gestured for him to sit beside her. "I'm curious. How did a senior Fleet officer become a member of the resistance?"

Black sat and regarded her for a moment. "They caught me young. My father is a member. After I joined Fleet and passed the security screening, they felt out my allegiances. Once they were certain I was fully committed, they used some hardware here to overwrite the code in my implants to allow me to be their spy. I was down here when the axe fell, so we faked my death for official purposes."

"Wow," she said. "That sounds exciting. I'm sure our scientists will want to compare notes to see if your code matches what we're using. But that will come in due time.

"As for whether you're in the same Fleet as my Empire, I think being a member of the resistance counts for a lot. With my brother being a Fleet admiral, I think I'm going to go with yes. Unless you have some reservation, of course."

He inclined his head. "My allegiance is to the Empire, but Lord Hawthorne and Coordinator West are going to have to tell me if this counts. If they get behind you, I will, too."

The door slid open, and William escorted Jared and Olivia West in. Her brother rushed to her side and pulled her into a hug. "I thought we'd lost you."

She gave him a confused look. "I told you we were going to be incommunicado for a bit."

William looked grim. "And things have happened while we were. Abigail King shot down my car. She killed everyone. She tried to kill your brother and Coordinator West, too. It seems that we have a coup in progress."

21

Sean watched as the people under his command slipped out of the prison camp one small group at a time. The remaining personnel kept moving around the open areas enough to simulate the correct number of prisoners for the guards.

The marine armorer used the time they had left to modify the stunners. With the color inducer bypassed and the range boosted to the maximum, this might just work.

He asked the question that had been bothering him while the man worked. "How do you know what to do? I didn't think we had any of these weapons."

The man grinned. "I knew some people on *Athena*. They slipped me the tech manuals and a few pistols to study. One neural disruptor and one flechette pistol, as well as a maintenance kit. I didn't tell the LT, but she might have guessed. I have no idea if she reported it up the chain. It's too late to ask her now."

That was the damned truth. He sighed. When he'd read Mertz's report on how many people they'd lost fighting against the Pale Ones, he'd been certain the man was a colossal screw-up that had gotten most of his people killed for no reason.

Now that he'd seen how many of his crewmates they'd lost, he knew the truth. Mertz had pulled off a miracle. Breckenridge's task force had started with a heavy cruiser, two light cruisers, and two destroyers. They'd lost all three cruisers and most of the people on them.

In hindsight, it was obvious who the incompetents were: Wallace Breckenridge and Sean Meyer. It was too late for his former captain to learn from his mistakes, even if he could, but Sean was determined to make up for his own failures.

"You did exactly right, Corporal," he said. "Your foresight might save thousands of people. You can count on me recommending you for a damned medal if we make it off this planet alive."

The man started putting the stunner back together again. "If it's all the same, sir, I'd rather you didn't. I didn't exactly do it for the right reasons. I was—"

"It doesn't matter," Sean said, guessing what the man's original intent had been. "I've learned some hard lessons over these last few weeks. What counts is that you did the right thing."

He looked out at the sun. "It's about time for us to make our move. What are the possible repercussions of your modifications?"

The man finished putting the weapon back together. "The pistols might burn out, but they should get one shot, minimum. I was real careful, so hopefully they'll still be accurate. These things have no recoil, sir, so aim right where you want to hit. No leading and no dropping of the shot with range."

Sean picked one of the pistols up. "How will we know when they're close enough?"

"If they're close to the fence, these should reach them."

"Good enough. Come on."

They went outside and joined the people moving around the camp. Command Master Chief Ross fell in beside them smoothly. "Things are on schedule, and I have some good news."

Sean smiled. "I love good news. Tell me more."

"We've seen one of the air patrols that has a history of making close passes. We've moved as many people out as we dare. Our people are standing by to make their move on the cargo lifts as soon as I give the signal."

"Well, then, let's not keep them waiting." Sean led the way to the building where they'd decided they had the best chance of hitting the target. With the stunners modified the way they were, they had to make direct hits to have any effect at all. Without the color traces, they'd have no idea where their shots were really going if they missed.

"How many people are still in camp?" he asked Ross.

"About a hundred. They'll scatter as soon as the air car comes down and make their way clear. We'll be the last ones out."

The senior noncom eyed the stunners when the corporal laid them out. "How good is your aim, sir? You want me to take the second shot?"

Sean settled in next to the window and picked up one of the stunners. "I think I can handle it, Command Master Chief. Why don't you go outside and stand next to the window here. You can give us a warning and countdown to shoot."

"Aye, sir. Shoot on zero."

They only had a few minutes to wait before Ross spoke. "Here they come. Left to right, moving about thirty kilometers an hour. Two guards, the one on the left at the controls."

"You have the one on the right, Corporal," Sean said.

"Aye, sir."

"Stand by to fire," Ross said. "Three... two..."

The air car flew into view, moving slowly enough for Sean to line his sights up on the driver. When Ross said "zero," Sean pulled the trigger. Even without a beam, he knew right away that he'd hit. The driver slumped.

The corporal missed, though. The passenger lunged for the controls.

Sean snapped off a shot as the corporal fired again. One of them hit the man, because the air car veered off course and slammed into a building outside the fence. The impact was impressive, even without any explosions. If that didn't get their attention, nothing would.

"Time to go," he said, tucking the pistol into his tunic.

The two of them stepped outside and joined Ross on a casual walk toward the other side of the camp. A pair of air cars flew overhead, racing toward the crash site. The guards on the ground were also looking in the right direction. Sean figured that the communications channels were alive with chatter right now.

The few remaining Fleet personnel in evidence quickly disappeared in the same direction they were heading. Three minutes later, they were under the fence and into the port. The only question now was how long it would take for one of the guards to notice the camp was deserted.

If anyone in the port had noticed, Sean couldn't tell. Everyone was still loading cargo. Well, everyone except for the people at this dock. His people had taken the loading crew prisoner and were efficiently boarding four lifts in small groups. It looked as though they already had more than half the camp population on board.

As soon as everyone had boarded, Sean shook Ross's hand. "You've got the coordinates to the island. Get them there safely, Command Master Chief. I'll find our people and make my way to join you as quickly as I can. Good luck. Oh, and here's Admiral Mertz's Fleet com. You'll need it to get hold of the marines on the island."

The older man pocketed the com. "We'll be fine, sir. You're the ones that need the luck. Be careful, Commander."

"Bet your ass. Get going. It won't take them long to find the people we have locked up, and once they do, all hell is going to break loose."

Ross saluted him and made his way out to a lift. They'd kept the drivers on board but had them under close guard. A few of his men had previously finagled their way into the control rooms and knew something of how the process worked. They'd keep the drivers from doing anything to give them away. With the number of lifts working this area of the coast, it was almost certain that no one would notice anything amiss, even after the alarm went out.

Sean motioned to the dozen men he'd selected to join him. They'd all changed into coveralls and would be taking a small grav car over to the city. The warehouse supervisor's car. They'd sell it to a dealer in stolen vehicles that his streetwise marine had buddied up with. It might have a hidden tracer in it, or he'd have kept it. It ran better than the ones they'd secured for their own use. Pity.

At least that had been the plan.

That changed as they were walking toward their ride. A large man in the same color coveralls as their own stormed up to them from the loading area. "Where are my lifts? What the hell is my cargo doing sitting out in the open?" He frowned. "Who the hell are you? You're not part of my dock crew."

So much for simple.

* * *

JARED EXPLAINED the outside events to Kelsey, Lord Hawthorne, and the man in the Fleet uniform quickly and succinctly. "So, as much as I wish I had time for the long version of what you've been up to and what this place is, we need to get back up to orbit as quickly as possible."

Olivia gestured toward the table. "We have to take the time to sit and work our way through this. Even the coup needs to wait. I've made calls and you've taken steps to get your people to safety. Well enough, but we need to come to an agreement. If we don't do it while we're all sitting in the same room, we might not get it done at all."

She waited for them all to take a seat. "Admiral Mertz, as I explained earlier, we've known you weren't what you claimed since I visited your ship in orbit. Or should I say *our* ship. The three of us are the leaders of what you might call the Terran resistance on Harrison's World.

"We found *Invincible* in its orbit and set out to rebuild her with the intention of destroying the AI in this system. We planned to restore as many of the wrecked ships to service as possible and to take back the Empire from the AIs. Our families never gave up."

She smiled at Jared. "Your turn."

Jared sent a private message to Kelsey through his implants. *What do they know?*

His sister smiled. *They know who I am and where we're from, in general terms. They know why we're here. She's the only one in the dark.*

"Well, then," Jared said smoothly. "In actuality, Kelsey has already let the cat out of the bag. We're from a splinter of the Old Empire that never fell. Emperor Marcus sent his son to us, and Kelsey is the daughter of Emperor Karl Bandar. She's second in line to the Imperial Throne and an ambassador plenipotentiary of the Terran Empire."

To say Olivia looked shocked was an understatement. "What!?"

Lord Hawthorne nodded and smiled wryly. "It's true. The computer verified her honesty. Not only did it confirm her story, but it also ceded control of this facility to her. She locked us out to prove her point. I can't think of a more convincing endorsement."

"She graciously let us back in, but I'd rather she didn't do that again,"

Captain Black said in an unhappy tone. "We have a lot of experiments in progress, and I'd rather not risk any unfortunate accidents."

Kelsey grinned. "No worries. I'll keep myself in line." She focused her attention on Olivia. "As you said, we're short on time. I realize how much work you put into *Invincible*, but we bled for her. I think Imperial salvage laws apply. For what it's worth, we did get your flip-point jammers in place."

Olivia waved her comment away. "That doesn't matter now. You've achieved almost everything we'd hoped. We need to join forces and stop this coup before it undoes all the hard work so many people put into getting the conservatives out of power. They were always the lackeys of the AIs. If they regain control, we might never get them out again."

"Olivia is right," Lord Hawthorne said gravely. "The resistance is small compared to the conservative alliance. If we lose control, we may never recover. We need to come to an agreement.

"Admiral Mertz, I'm the leader of the resistance on Harrison's World, and I recognize Princess Kelsey as the direct representative of the emperor. I'm begging you to help us retain control of Harrison's World in the name of the Empire.

"Think of what we could do together. This world hasn't lost any of the technological prowess of the Empire at its height. In fact, with this research facility, we're even more advanced in some areas. The AIs frown on a number of fields. Research in them has virtually ceased."

Jared gestured toward his sister. "You're talking to the wrong person. Princess Kelsey makes those kinds of decisions. If she thinks that is the right course of action, that's good enough for me. Personally, I think it is."

Lord Hawthorne turned to Kelsey. "Highness? What do I need to promise? Shall I strip naked, paint myself pink, and dance in the capital square?"

"I'm sure we'd all rather you didn't. Jared, I've already done a number of searches in the computer here. I believe their story and I like their plan."

"Then we're in agreement," he said. "What should we do?"

Kelsey gestured toward Lord Hawthorne. "That depends on how committed the resistance is. You recognize who I am and what I represent. I'm willing to consider you loyal citizens of the Terran Empire as we know it today. I'll even concede that you are in control of what happens on this world, just as they did in the Old Empire, but I decide what happens in the system until we have a stable situation here."

The three people from Harrison's World looked at one another and rose to their feet, then sank to one knee. Lord Hawthorne spoke. "On behalf of all of us, we recognize the authority of the Imperial Throne and once more swear our allegiance to it."

Kelsey scowled. "You don't need to kneel to me. Please get up."

They rose, but Olivia shook her head. "You might not like it, but that's really only an abbreviated version of how Imperial nobles swore public allegiance to the emperor in the old days. I've seen recordings of Marcus's coronation. It was a circus, and I say that as someone who grew up in a society that positively dotes on pomp and useless frivolity."

"Still," Kelsey said. "My father is the emperor and my brother the heir. You can try that on them, if you like. I'd rather have friends and allies than courtiers. We can work out the details of what this all means once we have the situation on the ground under control. Jared, we need to get the prisoners released first."

He smiled. "Already done, I suspect. Commander Meyer is executing an escape plan as we speak. He already had a way out of the camp, so I thought that the most prudent way to proceed. By now, they should all be on their way to the island." He let the smile fade. "Except for a hundred people. Abigail King took them somewhere."

"We have to assume she knows everything they know," Olivia said. "Which means she knows who and what you are. In more detail than I do, but we don't have time for the full story. It might be best if you both make your way to the island and back to orbit. Once you're gone, she can't use you as a weapon. I'll find your people. I swear it."

"Jared can go," Kelsey said. "They need him in command up there. I'm staying here until we get everyone back."

"That's not the safest course of action," Jared said. "You need to come with me. If they catch you, they'll use you as a bargaining chip. If we're both clear, we can work from orbit to help the resistance."

His sister shook her head. "If they catch me, they'll seriously regret it. I'll want a team of marines and my armor, if that can be managed."

"Perhaps I can offer a few compromise solutions," Captain Black said. "We have some powered armor here. No Marine Raider armor, of course, but very advanced. I think you'll be pleased with one as a temporary replacement."

"I'd rather not make any more trips than we need to," Jared added. "Just because they don't have ships capable of reaching orbit doesn't mean they can't shoot small craft down. The weapons on the island cost us some good people, and I don't want to risk more unless we have to."

Olivia nodded grimly. "That's wise. We have a network of weapons capable of taking out small craft. We also have atmospheric fighters that are probably even more powerful in engaging them. I can probably arrange for a window where the weapons are offline and the fighters are... unresponsive. That would be enough to allow you to get away. I can't say the same about anyone coming down from orbit."

The coordinator turned to the Fleet officer in charge of the facility. "Captain Black, is there a way we can get Admiral Mertz to the island without him being intercepted?"

The officer smiled. "I think we might have something that will do the trick."

"Good. Work with him and make that happen. I'll take Lord Hawthorne and Princess Kelsey to see if we can stop this coup and find her people."

"That sounds like a plan." The dark-skinned man's expression became cold. "Do me a favor. Kick that woman's ass. She killed some very good people this afternoon."

Olivia smiled like a shark. "If by kicking her ass you mean kill her, I'll take care of that in the most expeditious manner possible."

Jared rose to his feet and pulled Kelsey into a hug. "Be careful. We need you back in one piece."

She squeezed him back hard. "Don't worry about me. You stay safe. I imagine King has plans to attack you in orbit. Damned if I know how, but she can't be doing all this crazy stuff without some bigger plan."

"Let her try," he said. "I'll slap her down so fast her head spins."

22

Abigail glared at the man in front of her desk. She could see the slight tremble in his hands. Good.

"What do you *mean* the coordinator's computers aren't recoverable?" she asked in a low, deadly tone.

That made him shake a little harder. "They've been wiped clean, Deputy Coordinator. I'm not certain how. We segregated them as you instructed. Perhaps they had some code that triggered a hidden program. Now that it's done, we have no way of knowing."

"What about backups? I need to know what she was doing. Not only for the continuation of the government but to know who she colluded with." Abigail narrowed her eyes. "Perhaps a computer specialist working for me?"

The man was quivering now, obviously terrified. "The backups were wiped, too. I swear it's nothing my people did. We're loyal."

"You mean you're useless. If I find out you had anything to do with this, you'll live a long time, regretting your choices every minute. Get out!"

The man fled.

She sat behind her desk, sulking. He was innocent. Probably. Olivia had been a wily one. She had to have understood that Abigail would come for her someday. The only mystery here was figuring out which of her staff had done the deed.

This takeover would've been easier if she'd had access to the other woman's files, but she'd make it work without them. It wasn't as if she didn't know who her enemies were. They'd stymied her and the conservative alliance in the council often enough.

She'd already sent teams after the leaders and prominent voices of the opposition, supposedly to take them into protective custody. And, really, it was. For her. If they had a chance to start plotting, they'd vanish like roaches when the lights came on.

Roaches. Odd how that was the one Terran species that seemed to have made it to every world colonized by mankind and more than a few they'd given up as too harsh for habitation.

No doubt, some of her enemies would escape. Then she'd have the merry task of rooting them and their sedition out before they made too much of a bother. That could be a pleasure, she supposed. Those people would be the most satisfying to see tortured.

The com on her desk buzzed.

"Yes?"

"I have Mister Oliver holding for you. He says his call is urgent."

She frowned. "Who?"

"The man in charge of the Fleet prison camp, Deputy Coordinator. The one Coordinator West had arrested. We had him freed as part of the initial housecleaning."

Now she remembered the man. A prole but a hater of all things Fleet. Appointing him to guard the prisoners had been a stroke of genius on her part. He'd create an incident if she ordered him to, and he'd had no problem with her taking some of the prisoners to question.

"Put him through."

The vid screen on her desk came to life. The man looked even dirtier than she'd remembered.

"Deputy Coordinator, the prisoners are gone."

She stared at him for a moment. "What?"

"They escaped after Coordinator King had me arrested. I have no idea how, but they killed two of my men, and they're gone. All of them."

She surged to her feet. "You imbecile! How could you lose thousands of unarmed prisoners?" Abigail throttled her temper. "Never mind how. Find them. They can't have gotten far. No excuses!"

She cut the connection and rubbed the bridge of her nose. Why was she surrounded by idiots and incompetents? How hard could this be? These people had had no contact with Harrison's World before the Lord delivered them. They didn't even know where to go to meet their compatriots. They'd stand out wherever they went.

As soon as the man recaptured them, she'd have him executed. That's what the passel of idiots surrounding her needed: a good example of why they'd best not fail her.

She opened a channel to her assistant. "Get the Defense Force commander on the com."

"Yes, Deputy Coordinator."

Abigail hoped they'd be able to seat a reformed council tomorrow so she could officially become coordinator. It was long past time to sweep Olivia away and take her rightful place.

"I have General Thompson, Deputy Coordinator."

The vid screen came to life again, showing her a powerfully built man in a light-green uniform with a myriad of ribbons. No doubt they told some kind of story about how he'd saved the world a few times. Military men and their egos demanded it.

"General," she said. "I'm expecting some good news out of you. What is the status of taking the island back from the Fleet assassins?"

"We're almost ready to attack, Deputy Coordinator. To be certain we had enough force, we've pulled in fighters from around the planet. They're refueling and arming now. I anticipate we'll attack in about two hours."

She'd rather he acted now, but she knew they needed overwhelming force.

"Too many people have failed to live up to their reputations in the wake of this tragedy, General," Abigail said coldly. "You'd best not be one of them. I hear the polar base is a terrible assignment. Am I being clear enough?"

To his credit, the man didn't look intimidated. "Yes, ma'am. They won't get away with this treachery. We'll make them pay for what they did to Coordinator West."

"I want a full report as soon as you have the island secure. Take it, no matter the cost."

"I'll contact you as soon as we're done, Deputy Coordinator."

Abigail terminated the call. At least *he* sounded like he might get his task accomplished. She wanted that island under their control before she executed Project Damocles. It would be best to keep these fake Fleet people from being able to react.

The timer at the corner of her implant display told her she had less than twelve hours to go.

* * *

"If you'll step into the warehouse, I think I can explain everything," Sean said.

"I'm not going anywhere with you," the man snarled at Sean. "You tell me why my cargo is on the dock and where my lifts are right now."

"Okay. We hijacked them."

The man stared at Sean for a moment and then grew even redder. "You son of a bitch, stop trying to piss me off. Tell me where they really are."

Sean produced his stunner and jabbed it into the man's gut. "I just did. Now get inside the damned warehouse before I do something we'll both regret."

For a few seconds, Sean thought the man was going to resist. "Seriously? You'll never get away with this. And why the hell even bother? Lifts aren't that valuable. Hell, you left the expensive cargo on the dock. You are the *dumbest* criminal ever."

A few more pokes of the pistol got the man started into the warehouse. Sean kept him under control while his men surrounded them to keep anyone from seeing what was really going on.

"That's because I'm not a criminal. You'll get the lifts back. Cooperate and no one gets hurt."

They stuffed him in the storage room with the other workers and headed back out front.

"Heads up," one of the marines said. "We have company."

An air car had landed on the dock, and a dozen camp guards climbed out. Some went toward the remaining lifts and others trotted toward the warehouse. All of them held flechette rifles. They looked pissed.

Three of the men came toward Sean and his team. The one in front was obviously in charge.

"You there," the man said. "I need everyone gathered on the dock. This port is closed. No lifts in or out."

"The hell you say," Sean snarled, giving his best impression of the man they'd just locked up inside the warehouse where the guards were going. The clock was ticking. They had to get out of here right now or they'd never make it.

The two men flanking the guard leader half raised their rifles in a show of intimidation. Their leader poked his finger in Sean's chest. "The hell I say. We're looking for some escaped prisoners that killed two guards. Friends of mine. Give me any crap and I'll have my boys show you what a rifle butt feels like on that thick skull of yours."

Sean raised his hands a little. "Hey, I don't know nothing about any prisoners. We're just trying to make a living here."

"You can make a living when we're done. Go over to the right side of the dock and wait for us to get everyone out of the warehouse."

Other air cars were delivering guards to the rest of the docks. The other guards were in the warehouse now, so it wouldn't be very long at all before they wondered where everyone was. The men dispatched to the lifts were out of sight. If Sean and his men were going to escape, now was the time.

He pulled his stunner from his coveralls and shot the leader. The man went down without a peep.

The corporal followed his lead and shot one of the remaining guards as the man was raising his rifle.

Sean had the last man. The pistol crackled as soon as he pulled the trigger again, and the smell of fried circuitry filled the air. The man got his rifle up, obviously not stunned.

One of the other marines tackled the guard from the side, which didn't stop him from pulling the trigger, but it saved Sean's life. The burst went high and tore the siding on the warehouse.

Every head on the docks turned toward them as the marine smashed the man in the face three times, knocking him out. Every guard in sight began heading in their general direction at a run.

Time to get the hell out of there.

"Grab the rifles and spare magazines. Come on!"

They piled into the guards' air car as quickly as they could. One of the marines fired at the warehouse when some of the guards inside came running out. He shot over their heads, and they threw themselves flat.

Sean had the air car up and speeding over the lifts as the men on them came out. Guards further up the docks fired on them, but nothing connected. He took them out over the water and gunned the air car toward the city.

"They're in pursuit," one of the marines said. "Three… no, four air cars on our six."

"Keep them back and hang on."

Sean took the air car into a sharp turn and began making it a more difficult target. That would make the marines' aim shaky at best, but it beat getting a flechette through the head. He called out his maneuvers before he executed them, trying to give the shooters as much of an edge as he could.

Their whooping told him they'd hit something, but he couldn't spare the attention to look back. The city was coming up fast, and he wasn't planning to slow down. They'd need time to get lost in the general population, and he'd do whatever it took to give it to them.

The windscreen shattered. He flinched in spite of himself and hunched lower. Apparently, the bad guys had a few good shooters of their own. He just prayed that they'd make it in one piece.

The air car screamed over the docks, sending the people below diving for safety. He cut over the road between buildings and found himself going the wrong way down a stream of traffic. The air car beeped a warning that no doubt meant something to people trained in its use.

Sean resisted the urge to pull up and dove for ground level. In the relative safety below traffic, he pushed his luck, sped across an intersection, and raced a few feet over the pedestrians' heads.

"How are we doing back there?" he asked over his shoulder.

"We took out one of the air cars over the bay, sir. I'm not sure what happened to the second one, but we only have two behind us now. It's way too crowded with civilians for us to take any shots at them. You think you can lose them?"

"That's the plan. Hold on, I'm about to do something my driving instructor would fail me for."

"Like he'd give you a passing grade right now?"

Sean laughed. "Here we go!"

He took the air car around a corner at what he'd conservatively call insane speed. He banked it and pulled back on the controls.

The air car missed the far building by what felt like centimeters, racing along perpendicular to the ground with cars seemingly right over his head. Under other circumstances, he'd have been amazed at the sheer number of terrified faces that screamed past them. Literally screamed.

A glance back revealed that one of the air cars pursuing them hadn't made the turn. Thankfully, it hadn't injured any pedestrians. There was no sign of the other one, so he guessed it had gone straight.

"I'm going to find a spot to drop you," he shouted as he ducked back under traffic. "The security forces will be along pretty quickly, and we don't want to get into a fight with them. Get ready to bail out. We'll meet at the safe house."

They'd rented a place in one of the more rundown suburbs to use as a base of operations. It had their vehicles and a cache of weapons that would give the security forces even more of a heart attack. Once they shook all their pursuers, they could plan the next step toward finding their missing people.

Pedestrians scattered as he came in for a fast landing at a small plaza. The marines piled out, separated into three groups, and headed off to get lost in the crowd.

Sean started to join them, but an air car full of guards found him again. Rather than let them get out and start chasing his men, Sean pulled his own vehicle back into the air, this time, with the traffic flow.

The guards opened fire on him, making him curse. Every flechette went somewhere. Those bastards would kill someone.

He headed back toward the waterfront. With him above traffic, perhaps they wouldn't hit any noncombatants.

Of course, that meant they had a much better chance of hitting him. With the number of shots the air car took as he pulled around the corner, he hoped they didn't hit anything important.

Like the grav drives.

Warning lights flashed on the dash. Not the drives, but some of the automated controls. The car wanted to set down, but he found the override switch. He needed to get out while he could, but he wasn't going to allow his vehicle to crash into anyone. Ahead, he could see the water of the bay.

Time to make a flashy and dangerous exit.

He savagely jerked the air car into an almost vertical climb and aimed for a large building's roof. It was almost on the waterfront, so the view must be spectacular from the top floors. He had to time this just right, or he was going to have a very exciting drop to the plascrete hundreds of meters below.

That, of course, opened him up for even more hits, and the air car began to make some terrifying shimmies as it flew. One of the grav drives was out of alignment. He needed it to stay working for just one more minute.

Sean threw himself out of the air car and hit the roof at what felt like a hundred kilometers an hour. He rolled uncontrollably and slammed into something that stopped him dead in his tracks. A loud "crack" and intense pain told him he'd broken his left arm below the elbow, and his knee on that side was on fire.

He lurched to his feet just as the guard's air car howled overhead in pursuit of his former ride. They didn't even look down. Of course not. Only a complete mental defective would jump out of a speeding air car onto a roof.

The range was opening up, but he pulled his flechette pistol and shot at them. In one of the action vids, he'd have brought them down with his coolly aimed flechettes.

As far as he could tell, they never even realized he'd been firing at them.

His air car slammed into the bay, thankfully far away from any of the small craft on the surface. The guards began circling around it, obviously looking for the bodies of the idiots crazy enough to try those stunts.

The security forces chose that moment to show up. The guards found themselves under the guns of what looked like some seriously pissed security forces.

Satisfied that they wouldn't be going anywhere for a while, Sean looked for a way off the roof. With his luck, they'd have locked the door.

They had. Thankfully, his pistol made short work of the locking mechanism.

He started painfully down the stairs. He needed to get out of the area before more members of the security forces showed up. Once clear, he could make his way to the suburb via cab and walk to the safe house. It'd be dark by the time he got there, but after all the excitement, a nice walk sounded relaxing.

23

Olivia left Admiral Mertz and Princess Kelsey in Captain Black's capable hands. She had to organize the resistance against Abigail's coup. Aaron would see the admiral safely toward the island, and William would help Princess Kelsey find out where the prisoners were.

That is, if Olivia didn't get the information when she got her hands on Abigail.

The grav train saw her back to the diner in short order, and she changed into clothes from the stash below the freezer. Now she'd pass as a working woman, so long as no one looked closely at her hands. Her pampered digits would never pass muster.

Two of the facility guards came with her, both women. A group stood out less than a single person. They borrowed one of the beat-up vehicles in the lot from one of the cooks. It would raise no eyebrows.

While one of the guards drove them toward the city, Olivia got on the com to one of her people through a backup channel. No video, but she had a passphrase that let him know it was her and that she wasn't under duress.

"What's the status?" she asked.

"About two thirds of our allies escaped. Government forces have been on lockdown since they shot your air car. They supposedly have footage of a Fleet pinnace blowing it up. Emotions are running high. Deputy Coordinator King is scheduled to give a live address in about an hour."

"Not supposedly. They really have a pinnace stashed away somewhere. That means they've been playing some other long-term game that we haven't figured out yet. What about our security teams?"

"We have everyone on alert. Once you decide where we should strike, we can move. We don't have the same number of bodies as the security forces, though. We'll need to be choosy."

"Be ready for my call."

She disconnected and considered her options. A straight-up fight would kill a lot of good people on both sides. She was the damned coordinator. Surely, she could turn this on its head and put Abigail on the run.

After a minute, the bare bones of a plan formed. She smiled. It would be perfect if she could pull it off. Since Abigail thought she was dead, Olivia had a better-than-even chance of making it work.

If it failed, well, she wasn't any worse off than she was now.

Olivia gave the guard driving the air car her instructions and called one of the cells to meet her inside the city.

About fifteen minutes before Abigail was scheduled to speak, they pulled up in front of a building in the lower business district. Half a dozen men and women loitered on the walk, waiting for her. One stood ready in what looked like his son's tricked-out air racer.

The man smiled sheepishly when she raised an eyebrow. "It's all I could get on short notice."

"It'll do fine if we need a speedy getaway," she assured him. "Wait here and be ready to leave quickly. Once this goes down, we need to be somewhere else fast."

She turned to the women from the research facility. "Head a few blocks to the south and wait. If I don't call in half an hour, head back home."

With the instructions given, she led the way into the building. The lobby was more upscale than the exterior suggested, but that wasn't a surprise to her. The owner liked to flaunt his wealth.

The wide desk on the other side of the lobby boasted two human receptionists and a beefy guard. The large sign behind them proclaimed who they worked for.

The central receptionist smiled at Olivia brightly. "Welcome to Calder Broadcasting. How may I be of assistance?"

"You can take me to the main studio right now."

The woman's professional smile turned a little sad. "I'm sorry, but we don't give public tours. Perhaps you could schedule a special event. I'll give you the public relations com number."

Olivia smiled wryly. Her disguise was obviously too effective. "Take a closer look and see if you know who I am. Actually, we don't have time for that. George, if you please."

The man beside her drew his stunner and shot the guard. He went down without a peep.

When both women screamed, Olivia held up her hand. "Quietly. We won't hurt you. I'm Coordinator West, and you're helping me stop a coup. I need you to move quickly. Take me to the studio."

The woman on the right stared at Olivia in shock. "It *is* her! She's alive!"

The main receptionist's expression told Olivia that she was less enthusiastic. Of course, her boss wasn't Olivia's fan, either.

Still, Olivia was surprised when George stunned the woman.

"She was reaching under the desk," he said. "Probably a silent alarm. Miss, you keep your hands where I can see them." His stunner never wavered from the remaining receptionist.

The woman nodded sharply, frightened but still cooperative. "There's an alarm, but she didn't activate it. If you want to get to the studio before the address, we need to hurry."

Olivia gestured for the woman to proceed. Time was very short.

* * *

CAPTAIN BLACK TOOK Jared and Kelsey to a massive underground hangar. A number of sleek vessels sat waiting there. Most were only for atmospheric use, but a few along the back wall looked space capable.

"These are prototype vessels meant to demonstrate some of the work we've been doing here," the Fleet officer said. "We don't take them out very often. Many of them incorporate stealth technologies of one kind or another. We can get you to the island in one of them."

"Can one of them get me straight to orbit?" Jared asked. "That might make things easier."

The slender Fleet captain gestured to the small craft against the far wall. "These three can make it out of the atmosphere. One of them—the marine pinnace—is offline. We're swapping the grav units for upgraded versions. We thought we might need extra speed with current events. Just not so soon."

Jared had to admit that it didn't look capable of flight with the back end opened up and dozens of technicians stripping out the drives.

"How soon to get it back online?" he asked.

"At least a few hours, Admiral. If I'd known you were coming, I'd have started getting it put back together sooner."

"What about the small one?" Kelsey asked. "It looks like a fighter."

Captain Black nodded. "It is, and she's ready to go. Unfortunately, there's no stealth on her, other than what normally comes with a ship that size. Its upgrades are in the weapons department. She doesn't use missiles. Instead, we put a powerful but short-range beam weapon on her. It can make two shots before the capacitors are discharged, but inside its range, it should be a thoroughly unpleasant surprise for someone."

Jared was impressed. That was a lot of punch for that small a vessel. More than the missiles they normally carried when used at short range. It wouldn't be very safe for the pilot, though. At beam range, a bigger ship would kill them all too easily.

"What about the third one?"

The boat in question looked nothing like a normal wedge-shaped pinnace. Instead, it was more of a disc.

"It's a stealth testbed," the other man said. "It's slow, but the damned thing is almost invisible to regular scanners until you get right on top of it.

It's completely unarmed and only has room for two. It's also, I hesitate to say, a screaming bitch to fly."

That brought a smile to Jared's face. "Is that the voice of experience?"

The other man nodded. "Oh, yes. It's prone to spinning and wobbling. We've been working on it to bypass the orbital bombardment stations, but there hadn't been a driving need to act just yet. I think the time has come."

"Does it have a standard docking rig?"

"I'm afraid not. This was only a proof of concept. For a real mission out to one of the orbital platforms, we'd build a larger ship. We still might not have included a docking setup. That would pretty much announce its arrival to the station."

"Having examined the stations," Jared said, "I'm not certain they would've noticed or cared." He turned to Kelsey and Lord Hawthorne. "I think this is where I take my leave of you. Be careful, Kelsey. As much as I want our people back, we can't lose you."

She gave him one final hug. "I'll be fine. They can't kill me if they can't find me."

"I'm not reassured." He looked at Captain Black. "I'll need a pilot and a suit."

"I'll have someone meet you there, Admiral. Have a good flight."

Jared shook his hand and then Lord Hawthorne's. He took the indicated walkway and went down to the floor of the hangar. He spent a few moments admiring the atmospheric craft. They looked wickedly fast and as deadly as a supernova.

When he arrived at the saucer, a man in a vacuum suit was waiting for him. He was short and thin, almost boyish in size. He held out his free hand. The other had a second vacuum suit in it.

"Admiral Mertz, I'm Roger Walton, one of the test pilots. I'll be taking you up."

He shook the man's hand. "Roger. You're a civilian?"

"Through and through. It'll take me a few minutes to preflight the critical systems, so I'll let you put your suit on."

Jared slipped it on and waited patiently for the man to finish. The very last thing he wanted was for anything to go wrong.

After a few minutes, Roger climbed up into the ship via a slender ladder. He didn't invite Jared up, so he was probably still looking at things. He stuck his head down after a bit and waved for Jared to come up.

"Everything looks good, Admiral. It's somewhat tight in here, so watch your elbows. Are you a pilot?"

Jared nodded. "Sure am, but I have no intention of being a backseat driver."

That made the man smile. "That's good. I'll give you the rundown, but unless I'm somehow incapacitated, please keep your hands off the controls."

The cockpit was even tighter than Jared had imagined. No wonder they'd picked such a small man to pilot it. Jared felt like he couldn't move at all without being in danger of touching something he shouldn't.

"Not a lot of room, is there?" Roger asked. "It takes a lot of space for everything they have to have to make the stealth field work."

Jared strapped himself in to the couch. "How does it work?"

"Damned if I know. The brains tell me it's need to know and that I don't."

The man brought a console between them to life. The piloting controls did look somewhat familiar, but Jared hoped he didn't have to try them out during an emergency.

"How do we get out, and how do you keep the locals from wondering what all the strange aircraft are?"

"Most of the people in this area are friendly. There also aren't many folks feeling a burning desire to move to the country and grow crops. Those that do come along, well, let's just say that the locals make them feel very unwelcome.

"As for getting out of here, there's a shaft leading to the surface inside an abandoned grain silo. It's reinforced to take the stress of grav drives moving inside it. The roof opens like a flower. We launch at night—usually very early in the morning—and steer clear of town."

That made sense. "And the planetary traffic control network?"

"We have some people in the loop. They add us to the expected traffic—while changing our origin point to somewhere safe—or cover for us if we're seen while testing any stealth mods. We keep flights to the very minimum, though.

"Today, we're not on any flight lists. We're going outside the atmosphere, and there's just too much risk of someone seeing us. We'd rather not leave even a fake electronic trail this time."

Without another word, Roger brought the craft to a hover and nudged it toward a massive hatch in the wall. The thick metal slid aside, revealing the shaft the pilot had mentioned. It went horizontally into the ground for several kilometers before it curved upward.

They shot out of the silo at low speed and accelerated into the sky. Jared wished the craft had implant interfaces. The view must be spectacular, even at night.

"We're taking it slow," Roger said. "Half an hour to orbit. We don't want to chance anyone seeing us. We especially don't want to risk one of the orbital bombardment platforms shooting us down. That would ruin our evening."

"The platforms won't engage inside the atmosphere," Jared said. "Once we're high enough, I'll enter the clearance code into our transponders."

Roger grinned. "While I'd love that, we don't have any transponders. That sort of defeats the whole idea of a stealth ship. I guess none of the brains thought it likely we'd ever get our hands on something like that."

Jared couldn't see anything in that to make him smile, so he kept his mouth shut and let the pilot focus on his work. The ship rose to the very edge of space without anything disastrous happening.

"Scanners from the orbital platforms are still safely below detection thresholds," Roger said. "We're angling to pass beyond them in the northern polar region. Their coverage there is slightly weaker. Of course, if they see us, all three of them will be able to take shots at us."

"That's not very reassuring."

It felt like it took hours for them to climb close to the level of the platforms. Roger's cheerful commentary trailed off to nothing as he focused on his work. Jared gripped his seat and prayed.

"Approaching maximum scanner strength from platform three. It's going to be closer than I'd prefer, but I think we'll squeak by. The brains allowed for some leeway, so even if it hits detection threshold, the platform might still miss us. Not that I want to count on that kind of luck."

This was far more hair-raising than Jared had planned. He sat with his heart racing as they inched into the top of the orbital's envelope and beyond. He knew the moment they were safe because Roger visibly relaxed.

The other man turned to him with a look of pure joy on his face. "We did it! The scanner strength is dropping off. They're focused on the planet, so we're safe."

Jared clapped the man on the shoulder. "Very well done! Now we need to get to *Invincible*. Preferably without letting anyone down below know we're here."

"I'm picking up her active scanners. I verified what her orbit was before we took off. Setting course now. We can signal them when we get closer."

Jared was actually curious how close they could get without letting *Invincible* know. This was very similar to the approaches he'd done on *Courageous* in a fighter before they got to Harrison's World. Except that kind of stealth relied on high-speed coasting.

"I'll set up a channel and be ready to respond if we're challenged, but I want to see how close we can get."

Roger gave him a dubious look. "We kind of pushed our luck with the orbital stations, don't you think? We're already way inside your ship's normal detection range. Isn't that enough?"

"I thought you were the daring pilot looking for some adventurous stories to tell. How many free drinks will slipping up on a Fleet superdreadnought earn you?"

"Zero if it blows us out of space. Okay, we'll try it, but I don't want to risk getting shot. If the scanner strength spikes, call them before they get too worked up."

The man was right. If they'd had missiles, they could've opened fire and almost certainly have gotten the first salvo in before the startled bridge crew could raise the battle screens. Perhaps even before the AI could react. Of course, it helped to have a handy planet screening their approach.

Unlike the bombardment stations, *Invincible* wasn't putting out a constant stream of targeting scans. She relied on a number of detection criteria in which another ship would reveal itself so she could focus on it for more detailed readings.

Propulsion was a big factor. Large ships required massive grav drives.

Those distorted space enough to detect a ship long before they'd otherwise see it.

"We're coming up on five thousand kilometers," Roger said. "We're still below detection threshold, but someone observant might still spot us."

"How close do you think you can get before they see us?" Jared asked.

"That depends on the angle of approach. We're above them now. If we come straight in, maybe three or three and a half thousand kilometers. If we pass them by and come in from their stern, their own grav drives will mask us until we're maybe two thousand kilometers away. Give or take."

Jared gave the pilot a decisive nod. "Come in from astern."

"Aye, sir." Roger gave him an exaggerated salute and a smile.

In the end, they beat Roger's best estimate and Jared's worst nightmare. They slipped right up to the ship and attached to her hull just forward of engineering without any challenge.

Once the magnetic clamps locked down, Roger turned to Jared with a huge grin. "Now *this* is worth a lifetime of free drinks for sure!"

"Yes, it is," Jared said glumly. "I'm going to have to find out what the brains' secret is and update our scanning profiles. We're obviously at risk. Put us into standby mode, and we'll go surprise a few people. I'll buy the first of your well-earned drinks, too."

"After all this stress," the pilot said, "make it a double."

24

Once Jared was safely away, Kelsey turned to William and Captain Black. "Okay, now it's time to find our missing people. Actually, I'd like to make sure that the others get safely to this island first. I have a Fleet com unit. Jared said that he slipped his to Commander Meyer, so we need to get close enough to reach them. The booster my marines have only works on my end."

William considered that. "With the cordon of military around the island, you're not likely to get that close. But perhaps there's another way. If we get back into the city, I can arrange for us to hack into one of the orbital transceivers.

"Those would be the ones that Olivia used to contact you before all this mess got out of control. We won't have long, but you should be able to call your ship and have them verify they made it to the island."

"How are the prisoners going to get through that cordon without drawing attention?" Captain Black asked. "The forces on the island will have to drive our military back to get them under protection. No offense, but I'd prefer to see no loss of life here on either side."

Kelsey considered the situation and had to admit it posed a few challenges. "What we need to do is get the military to allow them to pass through. Maybe when Olivia makes her countermove, she can order them to stand down?"

"That's a big maybe," William said. "It might be best to intercept the prisoners and get them to a safe location to sit out the fighting. Then, once the coup is dealt with, they can go in safety."

Captain Black nodded slowly. "That might work, but only if we can figure out where they are and get word to them. Once we locate them, we can slip them into one of the ports closest to the island. I'm thinking of one that has a large warehouse that they can hide inside."

"If we can get close, my com should connect with theirs," Kelsey said. "Close being within twenty kilometers. How about one of those stealth atmospheric craft?"

"It's a risk, but not a terrible one," Black said. "Still, I'm not sure Admiral Mertz would be pleased if I send you right out to the military."

"Perhaps we should try a different method," William said. "The press will have any number of air cars circling the island in case there are developments. If we masquerade as one, we don't even need to use a stealth craft. We can mix with the crowd."

Kelsey liked it. "Fortune favors the bold. Let's make that happen." She turned to Captain Black. "Now, I believe you promised me some powered armor. If this all goes into the crapper, I want to have some protection. If it goes smoothly, then I'll have it with me when we find the missing prisoners. That makes rescuing them a lot simpler."

The dark-skinned man shook his head. "I think I see why you give Admiral Mertz grey hairs. I believe we have something that will work for you. It has some upgraded features when compared to the original Imperial Marine armor, but that shouldn't stop you from using it without training."

"I've gotten quite good at figuring things out on my own," she said. "As for Jared, you have no idea. He's my half brother, you see. I've been making him age prematurely for decades."

William raised an eyebrow. "He's from the other side of the sheets, is he?"

"That galls both him and Ethan, for entirely different reasons. Jared would rather not have his parentage hanging over his head, and my twin looks at him as a threat because of it. To my shame, I shared Ethan's point of view for entirely too long."

"That's completely understandable," William said seriously. "I'm surprised he doesn't see you as a threat. I assume you were born after him?"

She nodded. "By ten whole minutes, and thank God for that. I'd rather be doing something interesting."

"'Interesting' isn't precisely the word I'd choose for what you do," Black said. "Come with me."

He took them on another trek through the facility to a massive armory. Kelsey was impressed. It was even bigger than the one aboard *Invincible*. Row after row of full-size marine combat armor stood ready for use.

Compared to her lean Raider armor, it was thick with artificial muscle. It looked exactly like the marine armor they'd recovered from derelict Imperial ships orbiting Boxer Station. Only these suits weren't in desperate need of refurbishment.

These suits were heavy enough that they stood without the need for a rack. Unfortunately, whoever had lined them up had them facing out from the wall. With the entrance at the back, that might prove inconvenient if people needed to get armored in a hurry. She'd obviously been spending too much time around marines over the last year.

She ran her hand down one of the heavily muscled arms. "Tell me these are implant controlled."

"They are," Black said. "They come in a few different sizes, one of which should be short enough for you. The armorers normally use their implants to move them. Give me a minute to get some of the men to bring it out so we can fit it to you."

Considering that most marines towered over her, she was glad she didn't have to make do.

"There's no need," she said, wrapping her arms around one. She grunted, lifted the massive suit, and walked it out into the open. It was heavy enough that she had to turn off the governors on her artificial muscles, but it still didn't max her out. It came close, though.

At only a meter and a half, no one expected to see feats of strength from her. Yet the Old Empire Marine Raider bone reinforcement and artificial muscles increased her power tenfold. She could only imagine how strong a similar enhancement would make someone like Talbot. Her lover was not a small man by any measure.

Captain Black blinked at her. "Okay, then. I knew about your enhancement, but it's so easy to forget. Climb in, and these gentlemen will begin fitting it."

Kelsey entered the armor from the rear and ordered the suit to close up via her implants. They must not have expected many people to come in and just take a suit, because it didn't require any authentication at all. Something else Talbot wouldn't approve of.

The supports that held her were set wrong for her height, so she'd need to come back out for the techs to adjust them, but she could look at the armor first.

The systems came online and began feeding telemetry right into her implants. The dark interior of the helmet vanished, and she found she could see everyone just fine. She tried to turn on the interior cameras to project her own image on the faceplate but found the armor didn't have that capability.

Maybe that was what the designers intended.

That's exactly what they intended.

Kelsey flinched. "Dammit! Don't do that!"

She found speaking aloud made her feel better, and inside the privacy of her new suit, no one would think she was crazy. Well, any crazier than they already considered her.

I'm sorry. I was just trying to be helpful.

"We're going to need to work out some rules of the road. It's kind of creepy having you in my head watching everything I do." That's when it occurred to her that the program was running when she went to the restroom. Christ.

Well, it was too late now. At least she hadn't had sex since she'd taken him into her head. She really needed to get him moved into some other system. If she could.

"It's okay, Ned. I'm going to call you that, okay?"

It is my name.

"I thought you couldn't read my mind."

Only the strong surface thoughts. It's almost as though you're talking to yourself. That I can hear. The tactical doctrine of the marine armor is to make it as intimidating as possible. Faceless killing machines project the right kind of image. With Raider armor, we don't want people to see us until it's too late, and there are circumstances where a face is useful. Also, we have our own ways of intimidating people.

"Such as?" She began running through a systems diagnostic of the armor while she conversed with the ghost in her head. Everything was green.

The projectors that put your face on the helmet can put other things there, too. Grinning skulls and demonic faces are particular favorites. Were favorites.

His mental voice sounded so sad that she felt a chill go down her spine. It would be very, very easy to think of the program as a real person with actual emotions.

"I'll keep that in mind going forward. I hope this doesn't seem ungrateful, but you're sounding more like a person than you did the last time. That's... well, creepy."

I've integrated all the data files and raw memory maps. I feel like more of a person than I did before. It's more than a bit unsettling.

"Memory maps?"

That's what I called them when I made backups of my vids and files during the rebellion. I told my implants to make direct copies of my memories. Our doctor didn't think they would even be readable, much less useful if I died, but I figured it couldn't hurt. I think I might have been wrong.

"How so?"

Now I really know that I'm dead. It's as though I'm a ghost in your implants, watching things take place that I can't control. I feel like a ghost.

That made things much more complicated. What had she created? When she'd told *Invincible* to update the program's ability to integrate data files, she might have done way more than she'd bargained for. She might have created a new kind of AI.

She was going to have to do a lot more testing of what this being was, but now was not the time. Even though the conversation had only taken a minute, the others were waiting for her to talk with them.

"Is there anything else that you need to tell me before I deal with my other problems?"

Just one thing. The search of my recordings is complete. I didn't record myself accessing the ship's computer on Persephone.

"Dammit. I really need that code. No offense, but I'd like to have more than you to tell me about my implants, and that ship is a treasure trove that we can't use."

I didn't say I couldn't provide the code. As I incorporated my memory maps, I remembered things. In this case, I found the code about an hour ago. I'll gladly share it with you, Kelsey.

"Why didn't you say so then?"

You were a little busy confronting these men, and you told me to keep quiet.

That last sounded a tad smug. "I can see I'm going to have my hands full with you. Fine. Thank you. Do those memories address how you died or what happened to *Persephone?*"

Unfortunately, no. Perhaps those things will be made clear when you assume command.

* * *

AWAY FROM THE MARBLE-PANELED LOBBY, the broadcast station was more utilitarian. Bland white walls, bright lights, and somewhat worn carpeting in commercial tan.

It was also busier. Hordes of people moved quickly down the halls and into various rooms stuffed full of equipment Olivia couldn't identify, all chattering away in what sounded like a foreign language, one made up of technical phrases and acronyms that meant nothing to her.

The receptionist led the way through the crowd and up to a door with a security lock. It opened with a card she produced. "This corridor takes you directly to the main studio control booth."

"Thank you. I won't forget your help. If your boss fires you, I'll find you a place on my staff that will more than make up for the loss."

The woman snorted. "If you're serious, I'll submit my resignation today. Leaving this place is no loss."

"You're hired. Come with us."

Olivia led the way into a darkened control room at the end of the short hall. Screens covered the walls, some showing a news desk where a talking head was jabbering on about something. Probably Olivia's supposed death, based on the burning wreckage in the vid behind him. Other screens showed an empty seat in what looked like Abigail's office.

It wouldn't be empty much longer, based on the countdown clock beside it. Five minutes to go.

A man without a jacket, his sleeves rolled up and his face perspiring heavily, gawked at them and shot to his feet. "What the hell are you people doing in here? Get out! We go live in four."

"Yes, you will," Olivia said. "Just not with the broadcast you expect. Listen up, people. What you're reporting is a lie. I'm Olivia West and I'm very much alive. Abigail King is staging a coup, and you're going to help me stop her."

"Bullshit! I don't know you. Master Calder said—"

George raised his stunner and took the man down. "Who's the associate producer?"

No one spoke, but everyone looked at a younger man with a

monumentally ugly tie. George stalked over and pulled him to his feet. "Do you recognize Coordinator West?"

Motion on one of the screens got Olivia's attention. Abigail was sitting down behind her desk. The woman's smug expression of anticipation infuriated her. They had three minutes.

"I'm going down to the set," she said. "Make certain they don't cut to Abigail."

The receptionist—Olivia really needed to learn the woman's name—led her to a door on the other side of the room. Several of the resistance members followed. A short set of stairs led down to another door and into the studio.

There were a lot more people running equipment than she'd expected. Dozens of men and women focused on their tasks, all surrounding a brightly lit desk with the talking head. He sounded like he was preparing to cut over to Abigail.

Olivia had to hand it to him. The man looked only mildly alarmed as she brushed past the cameras and stepped close to the set.

"Cut to commercial," she said softly from just outside the camera range.

The man blinked once and turned up the brightness of his smile. He picked right back up with his calm, measured monologue, barely glancing at Olivia.

"As I mentioned earlier, Deputy Coordinator King is about to make a statement from her office on the terrible events that took place earlier today. A highly placed source in the administration has informed this reporter that some very shocking allegations will be revealed in just a few minutes.

"You'll want to hear them first right here on Channel 7 News. Let's break for a short commercial, and we'll be right back."

Someone off the set shouted, "Live in fifty-five seconds."

The anchor stood and pulled Olivia onto the set. "Sit right here beside me, Coordinator. My name is Jackson Zapata. Just call me Jackson. I'll make the assumption that the rumors of your death are grossly exaggerated."

"You could say that. There's a coup underway."

That seemed to make him very happy. She supposed trouble was what folks like him thrived on. "Then you'd best say so up front. The security forces might try to shut us down, so lead with the meat of the story."

A woman with a tray of makeup rushed up to Olivia. "Let me put this on your cheeks, or you're going to look like a corpse."

"I think that's what someone had in mind," Olivia said with a hint of gallows humor.

Another woman—a producer of some kind—whipped off her blouse without any qualms about showing her undergarments to God and everyone. "You can't go on air in that! Arms up!"

"We'll come back with the camera on me," the anchor said. "I'll make a brief introduction so the audience is prepped. You'll know when to start speaking. Just look into the camera and pretend it's a person."

In an astonishingly brief period of time, they had her face made up and her top changed. The producer was brushing Olivia's hair when someone off set started counting down.

"Live in three... two..." the man beside the camera held up a single finger as the producer dove behind the desk.

"Welcome back to Channel Seven," the anchor said gravely. "It's my great pleasure to introduce a very unexpected yet most welcome special guest in studio, Coordinator Olivia West. Coordinator, I'm sure that our viewers are all greatly relieved to see you alive and well. Please tell us what's really going on."

Olivia smiled into the camera like a wolf, imagining that she was staring right at Abigail. "Thank you, Jackson, and an even bigger thanks to Lord Edward Calder for providing this forum for me."

She took a deep breath and launched into her explanation. "People of Harrison's World, it saddens me to inform you that Abigail King, formerly Deputy Coordinator of our world, is attempting to stage a coup. The vid you've all seen is a lie. That pinnace didn't belong to Fleet but to rebels intent on overthrowing the rightful rule of law. Perhaps even the Imperial Lords themselves."

That last was untrue, but the rules of politics were crystal clear. Admit nothing, deny everything, and make counteraccusations. Let Abigail be the one on the defensive.

"Now, let me explain very quickly what really happened. We don't have long before the rebels kill this transmission, so let's make our time together count."

25

Sean came limping into the safe house just as the big news broadcast came on. The marines leapt into action, getting his broken arm set and putting some ice on his knee. The medic thought it was only a bad bruise.

The coordinator only got about ten minutes into her speech before the channel went off the air with a nondescript "technical difficulties" banner. For some reason, he didn't think many people were going to believe that. In the end, it hardly mattered. She'd said more than enough to get people thinking.

"Well, this is a pleasant surprise," he said. "I expected our escape to be the big news of the day, but with all this going on, the security forces won't even be looking for us."

"I wouldn't be so sure about that, sir," the medic said as he finished wrapping Sean's knee. "Someone is going to care about what we're doing. Maybe only the capital security forces, but still."

"This kind of thing spawns riots. The people that feel suppressed in society will be taking the opportunity to even the score. Which opens us up to random danger but clouds our activities from view. We need to get some eyes on the target building. I don't want our little songbird to escape before we can find out what he knows."

The medic didn't look pleased. "You really need to stay off that knee, sir. If you abuse it, we'll be carrying you."

"Are you saying I'm fat?" he joked.

The nonplussed marine only sighed.

"I've had enough excitement to last a lifetime, Sergeant. I don't need to lead the charge to secure the prisoner. I'll be happy to wait with the getaway driver. But it's getting dark, and the crowds won't wait long to begin roaming the streets."

He outlined the general plan for them. They had three vehicles, including a grav van. That was for securing any prisoners. The other two air cars would deliver troops onto the roof where the guards had brought Sean into the building. Hopefully, the camp commander would be in the same suite of offices he'd occupied earlier. If not, perhaps someone there would know something worthwhile. That was the only place he knew to look for answers.

They mounted up and headed into the city at a sedate pace. His predictions proved accurate. Once they made it into the business district, there were small groups of people roving around, and a few agitators were already whipping them into a frenzy. It wouldn't be long before they started setting fires and looting.

The security forces were getting ready. He saw a couple of checkpoints —complete with officers in riot gear—going up and came up with a new scouting plan. They moved all the weapons out of the first air car and relocated all but two of the men from it to the van. It led the way.

This approach proved wise when it ran into a surprise checkpoint. The rest of them took a side street and avoided some very uncomfortable questions. The security forces gave his men a hard time but let them through when the mob put in an appearance up the street.

They all made it to the target building without any further problems. A convenience store provided a place to park while they swapped out people and weapons. The owners were securing sheets of hard plastic across the windows, no doubt anticipating looting.

The occupants of the building had the target floor brightly lit, so Sean expected someone to be there. Probably trying to figure out where all the prisoners had disappeared to.

He decided to keep the van in the parking lot after having a word with the suspicious owner of the shop. Some local currency got them drinks and junk food in case they couldn't get back to the house. A shotgun and a few boxes of ammo made the man a friend for life.

Once everything was in readiness, the two air cars went up to the roof. Without communications—other than local coms—he couldn't follow along with the raid. He was just glad none of the windows blew out in an explosion. That would draw the security forces, even with riots taking place.

His com signaled. "Yes?"

"We have takeout. You want to come to the door?"

"Be right there." He hung up and slapped the driver on the shoulder. "Go."

The van took off and landed on the roof. His team hustled three men and a woman out to meet them. They'd rigged up some makeshift restraints ahead of time, so these folks were not a serious threat. The two men in back with Sean could keep them under control.

The marines dumped them into the van and took off for their air cars.

This time they'd be taking more of a chance getting back to the house. The lead air car would have a full load of passengers, though no weapons.

Sean smiled when he saw the bastard who'd given him so much trouble. "Well, well. Things are looking up. I'm actually pleased to see you."

"You can go screw yourself," the man snarled.

"While that might be entertaining, I'd rather get a little information from you. We can do this the easy way or the hard way. I'm hoping you go for hard, honestly."

The man spat at Sean but missed.

Sean smashed his good fist into the man's face. It hurt, but not as bad as his broken arm. Blood streamed from the man's nose as he bellowed in pain.

"I'm an officer," Sean said as he shook his hand, "but I'm not inclined to be a gentleman. Admiral Mertz would disapprove of my methods, I suspect, but I find they hold a particular charm. You took a hundred of my people. You can tell me where they are or I'll cheerfully break you in half. If I get tired, one of these hulking young marines can spell me. Are you certain you wouldn't rather tell me what I want to know?"

The prisoner's answer was profane and to the point.

"This is going to be a long night," he told the driver. "I'm glad we picked up snacks. We're going to need the energy."

* * *

Olivia wasn't surprised when the power went out only ten minutes into her address. Honestly, she'd expected only half that time. She'd already made her final plea for the people to spread the word and resist the unlawful regime. If Abigail hadn't cut her off, Olivia would've been in the awkward position of having to pass things back to the anchorman. This way was much more dramatic.

Emergency lights came on all over the studio when the overheads went out. Jackson Zapata stood. "Well, that's it for tonight, Coordinator. We need to get you out of the building before the security forces close in. I hope you have a speedy ride waiting for you."

"I have that in spades. Thank you for making this as straightforward as possible."

He smiled and extended his hand. "It was an honor and a pleasure. Not to mention a huge boost for the station's ratings, I'm sure. Maybe I should ask Lord Calder for a raise."

"I'd hold off on that for a while if I were you. In fact, you might want to come with us."

He smiled slowly. "That's a *wonderful* idea, and I'll gratefully accept your generous offer. We could do a documentary-style show of your fight against the tyrant and usurper. Charlotte! Get a camera crew ready to go! We're following the coordinator!"

The woman in the bra started shouting for people by name and ordering them to do things. Olivia decided that if the apocalypse ever came, she wanted that woman organizing the last stand against the zombies.

"What's the best way to get out of here?" she asked as she peeled out of the woman's blouse. She'd stand out less in the one she'd worn earlier. "I have men and vehicles outside."

"The tunnels," he said promptly, taking his producer's blouse from Olivia and tossing it to her as she trotted by. "They crisscross under the district. One leads to our satellite office a few blocks away. Your people can meet us there and not risk running into security forces."

Olivia slipped her blouse on and buttoned it quickly. The door leading to the control room opened, and her people came out at a run. One of them hurried up to her.

"The security feed is on backup power. There's no sign of trouble yet, but we need to get you out of here."

"I'm already working on that. What's the address for this other office?" she asked Zapata.

He gave it to her man. "Have them go into the parking garage, top level. The employee code is 1234."

"You know that isn't secure," her man said, obviously offended by the broadcast company's lapse in security consciousness.

"Take it up with management," Zapata said. "Coordinator, we can head down to the tunnel through the stairwell behind the studio. Someone will tell the security forces about it, I'm sure, but they won't have time to block you from leaving or follow you, for that matter. Especially if they think you went somewhere else."

He raised his voice. "Your car can land on the roof, Coordinator. Allow me to take you up there myself."

She smiled. "You're clever. I like that in a man."

"You're making me blush," he said with no sign of any such redness. "We should make our exit now."

He led them to the stairwell and started down, but the security team insisted on going out front. The trip to the basement was noisy and quick. Deep underground, machinery sat in the darkness. The emergency lights were few and far between.

The ever-resourceful Charlotte produced handheld lights from a maintenance locker. Zapata led them through a side corridor and into a tunnel.

"Do you know where everything is?" she asked Charlotte.

The woman nodded seriously. "Yes."

Olivia smiled. "You may just be the most competent person I've ever met."

"Thank you."

The tunnel was dark but clean and clear of debris. They made excellent time to the destination building and quickly went up the stairs to the parking level.

The building still had power. Her vehicles stood in a line, ready to go.

Behind them, a grav van with a fold-down satellite transceiver and the Channel 7 logo was pulling up. The cameramen and staff that had followed the producer swarmed it.

Olivia gestured for one of her people to go with them. "In case we get separated, make sure they get to the rally point. I'm beginning to think a record of what we're doing here might be very useful."

She turned to Jackson Zapata. "I'm not going to tell you where we're going, just in case you get picked up. Thanks again for all your help."

The handsome man grinned. "I haven't had this much excitement in years. I just hope that everything works out without too much violence."

He said the last with a note of solemnity. She wondered if he practiced the expression in the mirror. Probably, but that didn't mean it wasn't genuine.

Olivia made her way to the getaway car. The air car couldn't have been as fast as the vehicle Abigail had destroyed, but if there was a problem, it might be able to outrun it.

She climbed in. "Ready? Let's get out of here before the world comes down on our heads."

"Yes, ma'am." He brought the vehicle to a hover and took them out of the building with the others following behind.

They took the side roads out, but she still saw several security vehicles speeding toward the broadcast building. She didn't breathe easily until they were away from the area.

* * *

"AM I SURROUNDED BY INCOMPETENTS?" Abigail screamed at her assistant. "This is unbelievable! Can anyone do anything right? Anything at all?"

The man was in on almost every aspect of the plan, so she wasn't giving anything away by ranting at him in her soundproofed office. Part of her knew that it wasn't his fault. None of this was his doing, but she didn't care. How could they have missed killing Olivia? The one thing they absolutely had to do. This was all going to come apart.

"Deputy Coordinator, I understand you're angry, but if you insist on ranting, Coordinator West is going to rally people around her. You need to find her and stop her right now if you intend to avoid hanging."

His calm rebuke hit her like a bucket of ice water. She forced herself to take a deep breath and stepped back from the cliff. "I... you're right. Of course you are. Go write me something to tell the press. This isn't Coordinator West. It's an impostor. Tell them she doctored the statement. Tell them she's the one staging the coup. Anything. We only need to keep a lid on this until we find her and kill her."

He nodded. "An excellent idea, Deputy Coordinator. I'll have something for you in a few minutes." He left her office at a dignified pace.

She buried her head in her hands as soon as he closed the door. This was all going wrong so quickly. She had to get back on top of the situation right now.

Her com signaled. Not the official one but her private unit. A glance showed it was Master Calder.

"Master Calder," she said, astonished that her voice was so level. "There have been some unexpected developments."

"So I saw," he said with more than a hint of anger. "I'd ask you how she survived, but I think we both know the answer to that. She suspected a trap and sacrificed her security detail. That's much more cold-blooded than I expected from her. And, to be fair, killing her wasn't your task.

"Unfortunately, your head is on the platter if we don't regain control. You need to discredit her tonight. Or at least leak enough information to do that for you. Here's what I want you to do…"

Five minutes later, she'd made a call to the people overseeing her personal prisoners. They'd increase the guard and start questioning them again. This time they'd record everything and doctor the vids to implicate Olivia in a plan to become the dictator of Harrison's World, in coordination with rogue Fleet elements.

She had the perfect way to distract everyone. A quick check of the timing on Operation Damocles told her that she could move the plan up to take place in half an hour. Not all the elements would be precisely in place, so there would be a delay of about twenty seconds. That shouldn't matter. No one would be able to react in time to make a difference.

She walked out to her assistant's desk with a cold, hard smile on her face. She'd hunt Olivia down like a rabid dog. The woman wouldn't be able to do one thing to change her fate, no matter what evidence she had.

26

To say that everyone was shocked when Jared strolled onto the bridge would've been an understatement. Even *Invincible* didn't seem immune to that emotion.

Zia gaped at him and jumped to her feet. "Admiral! You're back! I had no idea you were even on your way up."

"Indeed," *Invincible* added. "In fact, no transport has left the surface at all. Your presence here on this vessel seems impossible. Would you care to explain, Admiral?"

Jared shook his head. "Actually, I think I'll leave you all in the dark for a bit. This is my friend Roger. *Invincible*, he has full guest privileges, and you can speak freely in front of him. Plus, his first drink is on my tab."

"Of course, Admiral. Hello, Roger."

The man frowned at the ceiling. "Is that a computer? It doesn't sound like a computer."

"It's a *long* story," Jared said. "One we don't have time for right now."

He stepped behind Zia's command chair and glanced at the superdreadnought's status screens. "We all seem to be in one piece. Keep the marines on the island on high alert. Our lost people are loose and making their way toward them now. I'm not certain how they'll make themselves known, but they'll be on cargo lifts."

Zia nodded. "I'll see that Major Talbot is informed. What about the princess?"

"She's working on rounding up the last of our people. About a hundred of them were separated from the rest. And we've made some new friends below. I'll want the senior staff brought together in my office in twenty minutes. What's *Courageous*'s status?"

"She's relocated to the Pentagar-bound flip point, sir. The jammer there started emitting a warning signal. Some kind of malfunction. Doctor Leonard thinks it might have received some subtle damage during the battle before we deployed it. We've relocated every other vessel to cover the flip point in case we have unexpected visitors while it's offline."

"That's smart. If we have any more computer-controlled destroyers pop in while we have no cover, we're dead."

"That's what Captain Graves thought, as well. We broke the encryption on the base AI while you were incommunicado. There are two additional pairs of destroyers out on patrol, one in the direction of the Imperial core and the other through the worrisome flip point. The AI expected the patrol in question to return about two days from now, but it might be early. The other patrol is a week out."

"Was there any other information I need to know about on the AI's data storage?"

The slender officer shrugged. "We're still skimming the data. Considering the source, we thought it a little risky to have *Invincible* sorting it out. Doctor Leonard has it hooked up to the standalone system, and Carl Owlet is overseeing a team. He hopes to have the basic outlines of what's there in a couple of days, but detailed information is going to take longer.

"There's one bit of good news. The AI wasn't expecting any direct visits from the Rebel Empire. With the system on lockdown, there's no need. This AI sends a destroyer to pass on an update once a year, and that isn't due for another six months."

That gave them some breathing room but presented its own set of problems. They had no modern destroyer to send. Or, actually, they might. There was the Rebel Empire destroyer they'd disabled at Erorsi. With the flip carrier to transport it here, they might be able to get it online again in time.

Well, one problem at a time.

"Okay, let me bring you up to speed on what's happening on Harrison's World."

The lift doors slid open, and two people stepped out onto the bridge: Major Talbot and Crown Princess Elise Orison.

She rushed over and gave Jared a fierce hug. "I just heard you were back. I was so worried."

It was good to hold her, but the bridge wasn't the place and this wasn't the time. "I'm sorry about that. I was just about to explain what was going on down there, and Kelsey is fine, Talbot."

He nodded. "I figured she was, but she's in the middle of it, isn't she?"

"Surprisingly, no. Just the outer edges. It seems that Coordinator West is actually aligned with a resistance movement that's been around since the Fall. She and her people were responsible for outfitting *Invincible*. They're in control of the Grant Research Facility."

"Is that how you made your miraculous appearance?" *Invincible* asked. "I've looked over the logs, and an exterior maintenance airlock was accessed before you surprised us, so I'm going to rule out teleportation. For now."

That distracted Jared from his story. "Is teleportation even possible?"

"Admiral, with a sufficiently advanced technology, almost anything is theoretically possible. That feat remains highly implausible, however. You were saying."

"Right. They've been working on some very effective shielding technology."

"Obviously," Zia said sourly. "How am I going to ever live this down? Someone actually boarded us without me knowing."

Roger grinned. "If it's any consolation, the Admiral gave me some pointers."

"You're not helping. How does it work?"

"Magic? I have no idea. I'm just the pilot."

That answer obviously didn't please Jared's flag captain. "*Invincible*, go to full active scans. If there's a pebble sneaking along near us, I want to know about it."

"I'll assume that was meant less than literally. Commencing active scans. No vessels or anomalies detected."

"Well, keep an eye on things. If you spot something unusual, let me know and take appropriate countermeasures. No more surprises."

* * *

KELSEY FELT a bit ridiculous flying around in a van wearing a set of combat armor. She couldn't even sit down. She had to stand in the rear, braced against the wall. She had her usual array of heavy weapons slung outside her suit.

God help her if someone stopped them for an inspection.

At least she'd been able to convince her marine guards to take more mundane transportation to the capital. Jared's companions had gone with them. In this getup, she didn't need any extra protection.

The driver took her out to the swarm of press air cars at the edge of the military exclusion zone around the island. "We just got an official warning not to cross into the interdicted area," he told her. "I'm not seeing any cargo lifts."

"What about closer to the mainland? Do you think they might be there?"

"Probably. The nearest city is a port."

"Take us that way. I'll know if we get close."

The man took the van back toward the coast while Kelsey checked her Fleet com through her implants. No signal yet, but it would register the other com as soon as it came in range.

They passed over the city and curved up the coast toward the north. It looked beautiful, she thought. It was right on the equator and seemed warm and toasty. The beaches were gorgeous, even at night. Perhaps *especially* at night. So romantic.

Her com beeped. "I think we just touched the edge of their range."

As they left the city behind them, her com locked on. She opened a channel and waited for someone to answer.

"Yes?" a voice asked cautiously.

"You know this is a Fleet com, so don't sound so suspicious. This is Princess Kelsey. I'm just south of your position."

"Ah. Good point, Highness. I'm Command Master Chief Ross. I have almost all of the prisoners with me on four lifts."

That was excellent news. "Great. Put Commander Meyer on."

"He's not here, I'm afraid."

She frowned. "Where is he?"

"He took a team to the capital to find the missing crewmen. I have his civilian com number, but we're out of range for that network."

Dammit. That complicated things. He should've just come with everyone else and let her find the missing people. Of course, Kelsey was sure Talbot thought the very same thing about her when she went rogue, so she probably shouldn't point that out.

"Give me his number." She stored it in her implant memory for later and turned to face the rear of the van. She had a good view of the city from there and could describe the docks for them. "Now, we have a warehouse at the nearest port. That's safer than running the blockade around the island. What I want you to do is—"

The night lit up brighter than day. The intense blast of light from the center of the city would've blinded her if not for her optical implants dimming it. A nuclear explosion? But that didn't explain the intense beam of energy rising from the center. It was already gone, but the afterimage remained, shooting straight into the sky.

The shock wave is coming.

The ghostly voice of Ned Quincy startled her into action. She slammed the helmet onto her head and locked it in place. "Take us down!" she shouted through her exterior speakers.

The pilot started to, but the massive shock wave struck them like a brick wall moving at light speed. The van came apart, and Kelsey's world went dark.

* * *

AN INTENSELY LOUD alarm interrupted Jared's explanation of what they were going to do next. He whirled and stared at the main screen even as his implants told him what was happening. Someone had just set off a nuke on Harrison's World.

No, two blotches of horrible light were fading on the image of the planet below. Someone had just taken the coup to a completely new level.

"Get me readings on—" he started to say, but *Invincible* overrode him with an even louder alarm.

"All hands brace for impact," the AI said over the speaker. The massive warship accelerated with brutal force, momentarily stressing even her mighty grav compensators and staggering her crew.

Jared was going to ask what was happening, but a giant fist smashed into his ship, sending it tumbling madly. Main power failed, and he was hurled to the deck.

* * *

SEAN GAVE up on being the heavy when they got back to the safe house. It was much easier for one of the marines to intimidate the man. He left it up to them to pick the most appropriate member of the squad.

They picked a whipcord-thin woman named Gina. He thought she might be the woman that had created the distraction in the prison camp. The supposedly jilted lover.

She went to the bathroom and returned with an old-fashioned straight razor. Okay, now even he felt uncomfortable.

She squatted in front of the main prisoner. They'd tied him to a chair, and he was literally a captive audience. "Hey there," she said in a friendly tone. "I'll bet you're wondering what I need this for. We'll get to that. First, I want to tell you a little story. You okay with that?"

The man swallowed noisily but said nothing.

"I'll take that as a yes. My name is Gina and I have a friend named Linda Montoya. Linda and I are close. Very, *very* close, if you take my meaning. You took her, and I'd be really, *really* happy if you told me where she was. To encourage your speedy cooperation, I took the precaution of buying this handy straight razor."

She held it up so that the light reflected in the prisoner's eyes meaningfully. It looked, well, razor sharp.

"I'm not cooperating with you, bitch." He sounded terrified.

Hell, Sean felt his own anatomy trying to retract. He was morally certain that the marine intended to give the man gender reassignment surgery. Or would it be gender obliteration surgery?

"Sure you will," Gina said. "You don't have a choice. You're playing the game no matter what you want. The only thing left undecided is how many parts I take before you tell me what I want to know. Shall we begin?"

One of the other male prisoners—who all looked suitably horrified—leaned forward a little, making the ropes holding him down in the chair creak. "Don't be an idiot, Jack! She's not bluffing! She's going to castrate you!"

Gina smiled at the second man sweetly. "Thank you! It's always nice when other people take you seriously. However, you're off a little bit on your assessment. I'm going to start with something a little more... prominent. You know what they say, go big or go home."

"For God's sake," the woman said. "Are you going to let her maim you to prove how much of a man you used to be? Moron." She focused her gaze on the marine. "He gave them over to Deputy Coordinator King's people. They hauled them away. We don't know where they took them."

"That's helpful," Gina allowed, "but not enough. We already knew who was behind it. That doesn't get us any closer to finding them. I'm certain you know more than you imagine. Some detail that will get us where we'd all like to be. Me reunited with my girlfriend and you not wondering where all your parts are or whether the doctors can reattach everything."

She held the razor back up. "So, do we have any takers? Every bit of information gets you off the hook for a bit. Surely you want me aiming my sharp tongue at someone else, right?"

Sean's admiration for her acting ability rose. At least he hoped she was bluffing. If not, he'd have to stop her, and in his condition, he wasn't certain he could. And if what she'd said wasn't a clever ruse, she'd be inclined to slice and dice.

27

Olivia and the rest of her people arrived at the building they were using to regroup just in time to hear about the bombings.

Holy God. Someone had nuked four major cities. The death toll was going to be in the millions. Maybe the tens of millions. The number of injured people was going to crash the medical system.

Every channel was going on nonstop about the blasts. Even Jackson Zapata was in front of the camera, recording something. She made sure that one of her people went over to verify that wasn't going out live. They couldn't afford for the security forces to trace his transmission.

Abigail had already issued a statement blaming the "terrorist attack" on Olivia. She looked suitably horrified at the "brutal destruction and death" that she claimed Olivia was responsible for.

"We've got to get out in front of this," she told William as soon as he arrived. "If people believe we did this, it won't matter what the truth is. We're done. The resistance is done."

He nodded and took a seat beside her in the rather Spartan office she'd appropriated. "We need to find Abigail, and I'm worried about Princess Kelsey. She wasn't very far away from one of the blast sites and the com system is down. Obviously. You'll also need to get someone in the military on your side. Might I suggest General Thompson?"

Thompson was the logical choice. While not the most senior officer on the planet, he wasn't political like General Abernathy. She could rely on the latter being in the conservative alliance's pocket.

"Where are our political allies?" she asked.

"Those that escaped are in hiding. Those that didn't are in 'protective custody' at the council building. You can be sure there are more than enough guards to keep them secure. I'm also relatively certain that's where

Abigail is hiding, based on the movements of her staff. If we can get in, we might be able to kill two birds at once. So to speak."

She could field a larger force than Abigail expected, that was for sure. The research facility didn't have marines, but they did have people trained to use heavy weapons. They also had powered armor.

That was overkill, honestly. Of course she could breach the defenses, but could she keep her allies alive? That was more difficult to control. She needed eyes in place in the most heavily guarded building on the planet.

"That's the right thing to do," she said at last. "But we have too many crises going on at once. Let's see if I can take one of them out of play."

Her tech team had a command center set up for her use. It had plenty of high-tech gear capable of communicating with whomever she wished.

She pulled the lead tech aside. "I need to speak to General Thomson. How long is that safe to do? I don't care to bring an armed assault down on us."

"Me, either," the woman said. "I can bounce your call around the planet any number of times, but I wouldn't chance more than a couple of minutes. We won't know if they've traced us, but I can't see how anyone could do it in that short amount of time."

"I suppose I'll have to talk fast. Set it up."

That took a comically short period of time. The woman walked over to her console, tapped a few buttons, and nodded to Olivia. "Use the built-in screen right here."

Olivia initiated a connection from a number in her contact list and waited. A man in a green uniform appeared. It wasn't General Thompson, but she recognized his chief of staff. "Colonel Wells, I need to speak with the general right away."

The man looked somewhat surprised to see her. "He's busy, but I'm sure he'll make time for you, Coordinator. Hold one moment."

The screen blanked and came back to life a few seconds later. General Thompson stared out at her. "Coordinator. I've got my hands full at the moment, and I'm not even certain I should be speaking with you. Deputy Coordinator King claims to have proof that you're behind the mass murder of millions of our citizens."

"I think we both know who's lying, but allow me a minute to walk you through this. For the record, I had nothing to do with this atrocity. I'm horrified and so angry that I could kill her and the bastard she works for."

He nodded. "She swore something very similar to that only a few minutes ago. You'll need to do better than that."

"Are you incompetent, Dwight?"

"Excuse me?"

"You heard me. Can you tie your own shoes?"

"If that's all you have to say, I'll go back to the tasks demanding my attention."

"You're supposed to say 'of course not,' to which I'd cleverly ask where the pinnace came from."

He frowned. "The pinnace?"

"Yes, the one that tried to kill me. Did you detect an extra one coming down from orbit? Did it come from the island? Surely, someone tasked with keeping us safe from the 'Fleet menace' would notice a little thing like that."

"No. It came from nowhere and went back when it was done."

"Isn't that a little convenient? Particularly since I'm supposedly in league with those very same Fleet officers. The basic story just doesn't hold together. I had no reason to fake my own death, much less blame Fleet. They had nothing to do with this, but Abigail King did."

He sighed. "I want to believe you, I truly do. Nothing I've seen about you screams 'mass murderer,' and I'd like to think my judgment isn't that flawed. But I can't just come out and support you without proof."

"So don't," she said. "Just don't allow Abigail to steal our world away from us. The Fleet personnel on that island aren't a threat to us. If they wanted to blow up a city from orbit, they could do it without a problem. We know that all too well. Just leave them be and focus on saving as many people as you can."

He shook his head. "You're behind the times, Coordinator. The situation in orbit has changed. Those nuclear blasts weren't just terrorist attacks. They somehow generated powerful bursts of energy that wiped the orbital bombardment platforms away like they were paper."

"What!? Are you sure?"

His smile was grim. "That response, more than anything, convinces me that you're telling the truth. Yes, I'm quite certain.

"The fourth blast crippled the Fleet superdreadnought. It's tumbling into a decaying orbit as we speak. If it doesn't come crashing down into the atmosphere like a massive shooting star, it'll be the next best thing to a miracle."

* * *

KELSEY CAME GROGGILY BACK to consciousness. At first, she didn't know where she was. Then she recognized the armor she was wearing. Finally, she remembered the explosion.

That brought her the rest of the way awake in a hurry.

She was standing somewhere, but it was dark. Pitch black.

It's good to see you awake again, Kelsey.

"Ned. Where am I? The bottom of the ocean?"

I'm certain not even this armor could take that. We're about a kilometer offshore. The water pressure isn't tremendous, so we're probably only deep enough to prevent light from filtering down.

"This thing doesn't have a grav unit. Great. That means I get to walk back to shore."

I'm sure the driver would happily trade places with us.

That's when she remembered the poor man. He wouldn't have survived a shock wave like that. Of course, there were probably plenty of people in that city that wished they'd died so cleanly.

"We have to get out of here. Which way is shore?"

Turn right. More. Stop. It's directly ahead.

Kelsey started walking. It would take a while to get to shore. Hopefully, the Fleet personnel on those lifts had been far enough away from the blast.

"Who the hell would do something like this? It's crazy!"

You'll get no argument from me. Did you notice the energy shooting upward?

"That beam? Yes. What was it?"

I suspect the weapon was a bomb-pumped laser. A special core focuses the blast into a coherent beam of energy. It only survives for a moment, but that's long enough. One that size could have certainly made it out of the atmosphere and struck something in orbit.

"Like our ship? God. We've got to hurry."

She sped up until she was almost racing through the muck. She fell repeatedly but struggled to her feet and slogged on.

Getting to the surface faster won't change anything. I hope that your brother made it, I really do, but falling into a hole you can't climb out of won't be doing him any favors.

"And that's the difference between being a human being and a copy of one. I don't know if you're really an AI or not, but you don't remember what it's like to be this desperate."

Perhaps you're right. Or it might just be that I don't know them as well as I know you. I don't want you to die when a few minutes will make no difference at all.

What will you do when you get to shore? You can't call them. With the nearby blast, you might not be able to call anyone else on the planet, either. You need a plan, Kelsey. Stop rushing around mindlessly and figure out what you need to do.

Dammit. Dammit. What to do? What would Jared do?

"The people on the lifts. The Fleet coms are hardened. They'll still be working. We have to find a vehicle and circle around until we find them."

There you are. Now, make it happen. Without killing us.

* * *

JARED STRUGGLED BACK to his feet. "Status?"

Zia stood beside the helm with blood streaming down her face. "Our drives are down, and so are all the fusion plants. We have a hull breach in engineering."

He blanched. "What's our course? *Invincible*, are you online?"

The AI failed to respond.

"We're tumbling," Zia said, "but I think that blast of power to the drives may have kicked us into a higher orbit. Stand by... yes, we're going to curve up and then pass close to the atmosphere. Maybe too close, but we've got about an hour to fix that."

"What the hell happened?" He staggered over to where Roger lay sprawled on the deck. The man had a nasty gash on his forehead, but he was breathing. The rest of the bridge crew were getting up, most with minor injuries.

Talbot was helping Elise to her feet. Neither of them seemed seriously injured.

"I'm checking the scanner records on this console now," Zia said. "It looks like there was another nuclear explosion on the planet below our position in orbit. It went off about twenty seconds after the rest. There was some kind of beam that shot out of the atmosphere and hit us."

She tapped the console to go to a different display. "*Invincible* brought up the battle screens and accelerated right before it went off. The beam only struck us a glancing blow. It almost missed us entirely."

"If that was winging us, I don't want to know what a direct hit was like."

"No, sir, you don't. The two orbital bombardment stations we had in scanning range are gone. The first blasts took them out. There's nothing but debris left. I'd be willing to bet the third station was destroyed in a similar fashion."

The bridge lights flickered and came on. He checked the ship's status through his implants. One of the fusion plants was back online. Someone in engineering was still making things happen. He pinged Baxter's implants.

You still there?

Barely. The decompression didn't happen all at once. We got our masks on in time. Some kind of electromagnetic pulse took down the drives and fusion plants. You know, the ones that are hardened to prevent that sort of thing. What the hell was that?

Ask me after you get the drives online. We have about an hour before we find out what an uncontrolled atmospheric entry feels like from the inside.

Shit.

"*Invincible* is back online," Zia said.

"Indeed I am. I apologize for my unscheduled nap. An exceptionally powerful electromagnetic pulse caused me to reboot."

Jared glanced at the lift doors as they opened and a medical team rushed in. "I'm just happy to have you back with us, and that you saved our hides. What happened down there?"

"I hypothesize the explosions were bomb-pumped lasers. I realized that the blasts destroyed the orbital bombardment stations and that we were almost directly over a city like the others. I felt it was prudent to change locations in an expeditious manner."

"You did the right thing," Jared said with feeling. "Someone without any scruples for human life planned for this long and hard. Those didn't happen in a day or a week. This has been in the works for a long time. The question is, what's their next step?"

"Perhaps we'll be able to figure that out once we restore our scanners to full capability."

Jared checked them. Almost all the scanner units were inoperative, and they only had a view of their immediate surroundings. They couldn't detect another vessel if they had to.

They also couldn't dodge another of those bomb-pumped lasers until Baxter brought the drives back online. If there was one more down there waiting for them to travel to the right part of the sky, they were dead.

28

Abigail felt trapped. Yes, previous administrations had built the council building to withstand a riot, and she had security units all around it, but she was sitting here waiting for Olivia to strike. Her now-discredited ex-boss had to take action against her—and soon—if she expected to have any chance of winning this fight.

She thought many bad things about Olivia West, but stupidity was not one of the woman's failings. She *would* strike back, probably with more force than Abigail's advisers thought possible. Someone would defect and support the woman. Bastards.

The problem was that Olivia could be anywhere in the city. Hell, anywhere on the planet. And she could find Abigail any time she chose.

That needed to change.

"Have the guards gather our guests," she told her assistant. "We're moving them to a safer location."

The man raised an eyebrow. "It's hard to imagine any place on the planet more secure than this building."

"I'm sure the citizens blown up by the nuclear bombs felt quite similarly."

"A point, I grant you. Where will we be going?"

"The farm. I already have guards on site, and no one knows about it. They can't find us there. If they're stupid enough to attack this building while we're gone, so much the better. That could work out in our favor, too."

Her com signaled. It was Master Calder. She gestured for her assistant to go. "Get everyone moving. I'll join you at the vehicles as soon as I make arrangements."

Master Calder's image appeared on her screen when she keyed the accept button. He seemed pleased. Almost jovial. "Yes, Master?" she asked.

"I wanted to take a moment to congratulate you on turning this situation around, Abigail. I'm very impressed. Moving Operation Damocles up was a risk, but it seems to have paid off. The stations are gone, and we've critically damaged the Fleet superdreadnought. It will enter our atmosphere and burn up in a very short period of time. Well done."

She preened inside at his words but only allowed herself a small smile. "Thank you, Master. I'm very pleased to have made that operation a success. Once I find Olivia West and kill her, we'll have undisputed control of the planet. Do we know where the other Fleet ship is?"

"Our scanner readings are limited from the surface, but I believe it's at Boxer Station or one of the flip points. Now that they don't control the bombardment platforms, we can initiate phase two of Operation Damocles. That's the reason I called. I won't be available while it's in progress, so you're going to have to lead the conservative alliance until I put an end to these rebel interlopers."

Abigail had no idea what phase two entailed, but if it was capable of taking out the remaining warship, she was all for it. Victory was within their grasp.

"I'll take care of everything, Master Calder. You might want to have anything you don't want damaged out of the capital. I've come up with a plan to deal with Olivia once and for all."

He listened to her explanation, nodding his head as she wrapped up. "An excellent ploy. I'll notify everyone. Give us an hour before you act."

"That may not be possible," she said. "I won't be the one initiating the events."

"True. Do what you can and give everyone a warning once things kick off. I'll talk with you shortly. By this time tomorrow, the last decade will be only a bad memory. We'll claim our future and restore the Lord to power. Until then, good luck."

"To you as well, Master."

Once he ended the call, she went out in search of her assistant. She found him discussing the new plans with the chief of Council Security. That worthy had been secretly in her pay for quite a while, though the blackmail material she had on him was more than enough to assure his cooperation. If anyone else knew his dirty little sex secrets, he'd never see the outside of a cell.

The man bowed as she joined them. "Coordinator."

She'd arranged a farce of a council meeting an hour ago to impeach Olivia and install herself as their newest head of state. Finally.

"Chief Yancy. I want the prisoners moved out to a facility my assistant will designate. Quietly. I don't want anyone to know they've been moved."

He nodded. "I'll see that it's done, but some people are going to see them being moved inside the building. I can minimize that by clearing the area around the parking bay, but people will notice."

"So see that anyone that knows goes along for the ride. You're imaginative. My private file on you makes that abundantly clear. I don't care what you have to do or who you detain to make that happen.

"Also, I'll have a special delivery coming in later today. Grant the people bringing it full access to the vault. They'll be incorporating some new equipment. It's very secret, so no one is to hamper them or attempt to inspect anything. They'll seal the vault when they finish. Understood?"

He bowed again. "Yes, Coordinator."

"Excellent. Now, I'll be going out in advance of the prisoners. Let's get things set up so that no one is aware that I'm gone."

Her assistant smiled. "I have just the thing, Coordinator. If you record another public address, we can send it out after everyone has left. Mention that you're staying in the council building until you capture the criminals behind this despicable deed. Then everyone will see what you expect them to see."

"I like that. Let's go take care of that little detail and get the hell out of here."

* * *

KELSEY WAS EXCEPTIONALLY glad once she got to shallower water. The light filtering down from above made walking through the muck easier. Once the silt changed to sand, it became simple.

She wasn't sure what people would think when her head broke the surface, but that turned out not to be a problem. The beach was deserted.

The city in the distance was burning. Based on the number of air cars she saw, the people that could were fleeing, most likely afraid of radiation or a second explosion. Those that weren't running away were heading *toward* the city. People there needed rescuing. That covered both sides of human nature.

With no one standing around to gawk at her, she popped her helmet and took in a deep breath. The smell of fire dominated even the salt of the ocean. Her suit's built in rad detector was reading higher than normal background, but not outrageously so.

It would be worse the closer one got to the city. Many, many people would die before they could get adequate medical treatment for radiation sickness. The Rebel Empire's rejection of medical nanites would seal their fate.

"Ned, can we bring down the medical nanites from Boxer Station and help these people?"

I'm afraid not. They require implants to function. Civilian implants are fine, but they take time to build and install. These people don't have that kind of time. Realistically, every ship and medical center on this planet will need to make rad pills as fast as they can. It won't be nearly enough, but it's all we can do.

The realization that millions of survivors would still die crushed her, but she didn't have time to mourn them now. She linked her implants to the

Fleet com and saw that Ross was still in range. Kelsey breathed a sigh of relief and called him.

"Princess Kelsey?" he asked.

"Command Master Chief. I'm glad to hear your voice. Are you okay?"

"We're fine, but we feared the worst when you didn't answer our calls."

She looked back out over the waves. "That's what happens when you sink to the bottom of the ocean. Where are you?"

"We're in the outskirts of the city. We're digging people out of the rubble and using the lifts to get them out of the radiation zone."

She hadn't expected anything less. "What are the radiation readings? I don't want anyone staying longer than they can tolerate. Medical care is going to be hard to come by for a while."

"We're good, actually. The buildings in the city center took most of the damage and shielded the suburbs from a fair share of the fallout. Also, we have rad pills. The military cordon around the island is lifted, and we have pinnaces inbound with medical supplies and more troops."

"What about *Invincible*?"

"They're alive, but the ship is damaged. They need to get the drives back online as soon as possible to avoid entering the atmosphere. Once the pinnaces drop off the medical supplies and marines to help with SAR, they'll join the rest going up to help."

"Give one my location. I'm going up. I'll be the short woman in powered armor."

"Will do, Highness. Ross out."

She only had to wait a few minutes before a pinnace came swooping out of the sky and landed near her, blowing sand in every direction.

Kelsey charged up the ramp and grabbed on as it lifted off aggressively. The bay was empty except for one marine acting as the crew chief.

"Highness, the pilot asked for you to come to the flight deck, but I don't think you'll fit."

Not a chance in this armor. "I'll take the marine command console and call him from there, Sergeant."

She strapped herself to the wall behind the console and opened a channel to the flight deck. A Fleet officer with a headset on appeared. That was new. He must have implants.

The man glanced at her. "Princess Kelsey, Admiral Mertz asked me to brief you. We'll be docking with *Invincible* in about twenty minutes."

"Lay it out, Lieutenant."

"The ship's drives are offline. The admiral doesn't think they're going to be operational soon enough to help. He's ordered the crew to prepare to abandon ship while we use all the small craft to try and shift their course."

The idea made sense. When they'd found *Courageous*, they'd had to stop her spin with a pinnace. A lot of them working together might be able to affect a ship as large as the superdreadnought. If they had time.

"What are the chances?"

"*Invincible* gives us maybe thirty percent."

"Not good enough. There has to be something else we can do."

"If you have any ideas, Highness, I'm sure the admiral would *love* to hear them."

"I'll think about that. Get up there quick while I take care of one last thing."

* * *

IN THE END, Sean hadn't had to stop the marine from giving the man the closest shave of his life. The prisoners hadn't been able to give them a decisive clue, but they'd obviously told her everything they could think of that might be relevant.

The best piece of information they had was something the woman had overheard one of the deputy coordinator's guards mention. He'd said something about "the farm," and another man had quickly shut him up. So their comrades were probably somewhere outside the city.

With all the nuclear explosions, that might be for the best.

All they had to do was figure out where this farm might be located. For that to happen, they needed information that he didn't know how to acquire.

His civilian com chirped. It was an unknown number. He considered not answering it but decided that Ross or the admiral might have picked up a new unit.

"Hello?"

"Commander Meyer," a female voice said. "This is Coordinator West. I hope I haven't caught you at a bad time."

He blinked in shock. She was the last person he'd expected to be calling him. He almost disconnected, but if she were tracking them, she already had their location.

"No, this is a perfect time, Coordinator. We're just sitting around mulling over a problem. What can I do for you?"

"I have a favor to ask. And, before you become overly concerned, I've formed an alliance with Admiral Mertz and Princess Kelsey. Yes, they've read me in on your secret. I'm not sending anyone after you. You're perfectly safe."

"Well, unless the security forces catch you first for all the damage you caused in that wild ride through the city. Have you considered a career in racing?"

More like the demolition derby. "If things don't start looking up, I might. What can I do for you, Coordinator?"

"I need some people skilled in combat to undertake a rescue operation under fire. Princess Kelsey said that you might also need my help in finding the lost prisoners. I'll give what help I can in any case, but there are some important people that need saving, too.

"She and Admiral Mertz have more pressing matters to attend to, and you're the senior Fleet officer left on the planet. His Fleet, anyway. There are a number of your marines available, but only if you agree."

Sean considered her offer and decided he had nothing to lose by sharing what he knew. "I'll need to make a call first. Who are we rescuing, and why don't you have the people to do it?"

"The military is sitting out my struggle with Abigail King. I have some skilled fighters, but we're talking about storming the planetary council building. It's a fortress. Abigail has a number of my allies in that building, and I'd like to get them back alive and put her on trial for mass murder."

He snorted softly. "There's nothing I'd like more than to make that woman pay. Not only for what she did to my people but for what she did to yours. As I said, I'll call you back once I see what I can find out. Do you know anything about a farm that might be associated with King?"

"Not off the top of my head. You make your call, and I'll make a few of my own. Then we'll see if we can't ruin Abigail King's day."

29

Olivia had a brief conversation with her tech wizard and started the woman searching for data on any farm that might be associated with Abigail. By the time she had that in motion, Commander Meyer had called her back.

"I've spoken with the marines on the ground," he said. "They managed to get through to Admiral Mertz. I have his blessing to help you.

"Here's what I'm proposing. You'll need to get the marines out of the city by the coast. They're assisting in search and rescue. Take them to the island, and they can draw combat gear. Once they have that, you'll need to provide their rides. All the pinnaces are helping in orbit."

She nodded to herself. That matched what she'd heard. "I have the transport available. With all of this moving around, I think we'll need to hit the council building sometime before dawn. That leaves us time to rescue your people if I can find any farm or rural property that is associated with Abigail in any way."

"That works for me. I can give you an address to pick us up. We'll need combat gear for a dozen marines. I suggest you pick us up now, and we can coordinate what needs to happen next."

That suited her just fine. "Give me the address, and I'll send someone right away. Thank you."

She disconnected the call and turned to William. "We'll need someone from Grant to bring the pinnace, if they have it put back together, and some weapons for Commander Meyer. I don't want to divert any of the other transports."

He shook his head. "That's not going to be possible. We've already sent the pinnace to assist *Invincible*. I spoke with Captain Black and authorized him sending it. In fact, I'm going to be joining him in trying to save that ship."

Olivia blinked in surprise. "Okay, I can see sending the pinnace up to help. Exactly how is your presence supposed to improve their odds?"

"Because I'll be flying another ship up to add one more set of grav drives."

"You can fly? All they have left is the fighter. Surely that won't help something so large."

"You don't think I could fly a fighter? I'm sure I'd be dashing. No, there's another ship. It hasn't flown in a very long time, but the automatics say it's still functional. It might just make the difference between success and failure. And yes, I'm trained to fly a ship. It's just been a while."

She didn't know what to say. It wasn't as though he needed her permission. "Good luck. Come home to Craig. And me, of course."

He gave her a florid bow. "I shall return. I'll want your promise that you'll be careful. If Abigail kills or captures you, I'll be devastated."

"We have a pact, then." She rose to her feet and gave him a hug. "Good luck."

Once he was gone, she went out to find her tech. "Tell me you have something."

The woman looked up from the console she was working at. "Several things, actually. Deputy Coordinator King—now styling herself with your title, by the way—made another public statement. It was more of the same, but she did confirm our suspicions she was inside the council building by word and deed."

"How so?"

"The address was filmed in your office. She also mentioned she was going to stay there 'working for the good of the people of Harrison's World' until you were brought to justice. The number of security people around the building is becoming ludicrous. Surely all those people have something better to do than guarding some political gasbag."

The woman paused for a moment. "Present company excluded."

"Thanks for that," Olivia said dryly. "Any word on where this farm might be?"

"Possibly." The woman manipulated her screen and displayed a map of the area. "Deputy Coordinator King's family owns a number of agricultural facilities in the area surrounding the capital."

Olivia examined the map closely. It showed a dozen large properties. "We'll need to scout them. Can you get an enlarged image of all of them?"

"I'm not plugged into the satellite network, and someone has been cutting off my access. They haven't frozen me out, but I'm certainly not able just to waltz into that kind of system anymore. It might take me a while."

"Unless you'd care to drive out there personally, I'd suggest you get busy."

* * *

JARED RESISTED the urge to go down to engineering. That wouldn't make any of this go faster, and it might slow them down. The pinnaces and cutters were doing what they could to alter *Invincible*'s course, but it was increasingly looking as though they wouldn't make enough of a difference to save the ship.

The crew would be able to use the escape pods, but the loss of the massive ship would hurt the Empire badly. The loss of the AI would be even worse. They didn't have enough time to get the computer removed.

Ginnie Dare and *New York* were racing in from the flip point, but they'd be hours too late to do any good. Unless of course he managed to save the ship. Several pinnaces had managed to match the ship's uncontrolled tumble and were using their drives to stabilize her as much as they could.

The lift doors opened, and Princess Kelsey rushed onto the bridge. She wore a massive suit of armor, though she held the helmet in the crook of her arm. "It wasn't my fault."

He felt the corners of his mouth twitch. "I must not have heard what happened yet. What disaster did you not cause?"

"Any of this. I just wanted the record to show that for once. How are we doing?"

"Not good. The small craft are giving everything they have, but it's not going to be enough. I'm preparing to give the order to abandon ship. Unless, of course, Baxter pulls off a miracle."

Kelsey stood beside one of the backup consoles. "Do you think there's much chance of that?"

"Honestly? No. You know what galls me? We're not that far away from having enough thrust. If we had three or four more pinnaces, we'd squeak by. We'd skip off the atmosphere and probably burn off every external fixture on the ship, but we'd survive long enough for the destroyers to get here."

"How long do we have?"

He checked the countdown timer in his head. "Five minutes until I have to order the crew to the pods. Ten minutes until we enter the atmosphere. I'll order the small craft to break away as soon as we begin the evacuation."

She shook her head. "There has to be a way. *Invincible*, is there anything on the ship that can give us the extra boost? What if we vented the atmosphere out the back?"

"While clever, that would not generate sufficient thrust," the AI said.

"We need more ships," Kelsey said.

He agreed, but they were using all they had. "The resistance sent up their pinnace. It's helping. Lord Hawthorne is bringing a ship up. It won't get here in time. That's it for every small craft in the area."

"Actually, it isn't," *Invincible* said. "Scanners are back online, and I'm picking up another pinnace. It has already left the area around Harrison's World."

"What?" Jared accessed the scanners through his implants and saw that

Invincible was correct. There was a pinnace racing toward… a gas giant in the outer system away from the flip point? That didn't make any sense.

Kelsey must've been checking it, too. "Why is it going all the way out there? It has to be the pinnace that tried to kill Coordinator West."

"And we have no way of catching it, either." Jared checked the clock and their updated trajectory. "Time to call this. I'm sorry, *Invincible*."

"As am I, Admiral. If only the engines in these small craft were more powerful. I'll miss seeing how this story turns out. Good luck."

Kelsey frowned. "Wait. Can't we make them more powerful? What limits their thrust?"

"Safety interlocks," Jared said. "Those grav drives might explode if pushed too hard."

"And an explosion would be worse than our current problems how?"

He followed her train of thought and decided she might have a point. It would put the pilots in grave danger, but if they volunteered…

"*Invincible*, contact the pilots. See if they're willing to take the risk."

A few moments later, the AI responded. "All are prepared to risk it, Admiral. The danger is high, though. I recommend everyone abandon ship before you put your plan into effect."

"Open a ship-wide channel. Tie in every suit com as well."

"Ready, Admiral."

"All hands, this is Admiral Mertz. We're going to try one last thing to save the ship, but we can't do it with you on board. Abandon ship. All hands abandon ship. Godspeed."

An undulating warning sounded on every speaker at maximum volume. It announced the absolute worst case for any ship.

Swarms of emergency pods jettisoned from the hull. They darted away at savage velocities, designed to carry their precious cargo clear of whatever was going to kill the ship. They all angled down toward the planet's surface, their beacons screaming for rescue.

He looked at the bridge crew. "I believe you have a pod waiting for you, too."

Zia shook her head. "I'm the captain of this ship, sir. I decline to leave her before everyone is safely away. Everyone else, you heard the Admiral."

No one moved. Kelsey put her hands on her hips. "Jared, you're wasting time. Save this ship. If it doesn't work, then we can run for our lives."

"So much for me being noble. *Invincible*, have the pilots disabled their safeties?"

"They have, Admiral. All report ready for maximum acceleration."

"Everyone strap in. This might be *very* rough. Align the ship as you see fit and go, *Invincible*."

The crew tightened their restraints. Kelsey, who couldn't use any of the seats in her armor, locked her helmet down and grabbed a console.

The increase in acceleration wasn't much, but he saw an immediate effect. Their course slowly began to change. Bit by bit, it edged closer to being enough.

Then a massive impact rocked the ship. Fresh alarms wailed.

"One of the cutters exploded, Admiral. Hull breach amidships. We're beginning to rotate. I calculate less than a fifty percent chance this vessel will rebound from the atmosphere. I recommend that you order the others to cease acceleration and abandon ship."

He nodded. "Kelsey, please accompany the bridge crew and abandon ship. I'm going to stay and try to make this work."

"We both know you can't move me, so let's save the theatrics and get on with this."

Silence reigned for a few seconds. "Well, then. One last roll of the dice. We'll know how this turns out in sixty seconds. It's been an honor, everyone."

He sent the order for the small craft to break away. This was it. Either they'd make it on their own or they wouldn't make it at all.

It didn't take long before he felt the ship punching through the upper regions of the atmosphere. Even a massive vessel like this could move in odd ways when meeting an almost fluid resistance. The exterior scanners showed quite the light show as they went deeper.

At least until the drag ripped off the exterior scanner arrays. Shortly after that, it started raising the hull temperature. That temperature change would be the only way they'd know if they made it back out of their death dive.

The gentle movements of the ship became wild bucking in a much shorter time than he'd thought possible. Kelsey had the worst time of it. The console she was holding onto broke loose and sent her tumbling.

That scared him to death, but she grabbed onto another one and braced herself under it. "I'm fine. This tumbling can't hurt me in my armor. I'm more worried about smashing one of you."

"The temperature is leveling off," *Invincible* said. "I believe we may be skipping back off the atmosphere. Much the same as a thrown stone skips across water."

"How do you even know about that?" Jared asked. "And as a warning, those sink in the end."

"The video collection in the library is quite instructive. If we are skipping out of the atmosphere, we should have enough time for *Ginnie Dare* and *New York* to arrive. They can tow us into a stable orbit."

Zia turned to face him. "The hull temperature is definitely leveling off. We're not going deeper into Harrison's World's atmosphere."

That brought a loud cheer from the rest of the bridge crew and a sigh of relief from him. "Well done, everyone. Well done."

"Thank the small craft pilots," his flag captain said. "They really saved our bacon."

"Do we have communication? Can we get them to return and help stabilize the orbit until the destroyers get here?"

Zia shook her head. "We're completely cut off. No communications, no scanners. No weapons, for that matter. The beam arrays are gone. The missile tubes are intact, but the hatches will be welded shut. We also lost our flip vanes. We're trapped in this system until we can replace them."

Kelsey climbed out from under the console she'd used as cover. She'd bent its leg columns with her grip. She pulled her helmet off and shook out her hair. "That beats the alternative. I'd rather have to wait to leave than never get out of here at all.

"Speaking of not being able to go anywhere, we need to find out what that pinnace is up to. If they think it's worth doing, we have to stop them."

Jared nodded. "We need one of the probes launched after it. Make that a priority, Zia, and find some way to get in touch with *Ginnie Dare*. I want them in pursuit as soon as possible."

Zia turned to her console. "Aye, sir. I'll send someone out a lock to look over the probe launcher and to make an estimate of our new course. They can use the suit com to get in touch with the pinnaces. One of them can relay to *Ginnie Dare*."

Jared rose to his feet. "You forget it's just us. I'll go take a look and get this rolling myself. Come on, Kelsey. You can make sure I don't fall off."

The hostile pinnace's course worried him. What could it be racing toward? Obviously, something that the enemy thought might be helpful against his ships. If it could take out *Courageous*, it was nothing to sneer at. He had to stop them.

30

Sean breathed a sigh of relief when he got word that *Invincible* had survived her near-death experience. He hadn't known the ship even existed before today, but he grasped how important something like it would be to the Empire. No matter what Captain Breckenridge thought, war with the AIs was inevitable. Hell, it was already happening. They had to have the ships and technology to win it.

New York was already in orbit and helping to get the crippled superdreadnought into a stable orbit. *Ginnie Dare* was more than halfway to the gas giant the enemy cutter was running toward. It wouldn't be able to stop them from getting there, but Captain Roche would be right on its heels.

Meanwhile, Sean had his own problems.

The ride Olivia West promised arrived on schedule. It was a fully loaded vegetable lift, packed to the gills with harvested corn. It was in large bins that they had to unload and stash in the safe house before they could go to her secret headquarters.

Frankly, if this was the most effective ride she could manage, she might be in an even worse position than he'd feared.

Half an hour later, they had the lift cleared, and everyone piled into the back. The prisoners came with them. Sean didn't want to leave them where they could cause trouble. If they escaped, they might manage to warn King that Sean was coming.

The lift deposited them all at a nondescript building. It didn't even have obvious guards outside. Inside was a different story.

Squads of armed civilians watched every approach into the building, huddled behind heavy weapons. If the security forces decided to come in here, there'd be a massacre. Of them.

Olivia West met him in a large room that they'd converted into a command center. She came over with her hand extended. "Commander Meyer. Thank you for coming so promptly."

He shook her hand gravely. "It's my pleasure, Coordinator."

"If you and your men will come this way, I have weapons and armor for all of you. A fast car from a secret facility just arrived. It couldn't carry any powered armor, but I'm given to understand none of your people could use it anyway. It requires implants."

He saw a good selection of unpowered armor and standard Old Empire weapons laid out. "This will work just fine, I'm sure." He gestured for the marines to go outfit themselves. "What have you found out about my missing people?"

She looked at his arm and the makeshift sling he was wearing. "I can't help but notice you're injured. You're also limping. Were you injured in the escape?"

"Let's just say that I had an exciting exit from a moving air car. My medic set the broken arm. He thinks the knee is only bruised."

"Then perhaps you'd like to let someone with a medical scanner confirm that, and get some medication for the pain and swelling? You're about to go back into the fight, so you'd best take advantage while you can."

Stubbornness made him want to argue, but he decided that was idiotic. He pulled up a chair and sat. "Thank you."

Coordinator West summoned a woman with a bag emblazoned with the Imperial Red Cross emblem. She set it down beside the chair and pulled out a ridiculously small medical scanner.

"Hi there," she said with a smile. "I'm Doctor Janice Hauptman. I'm an emergency specialist, so you're in good hands. Tell me what happened."

"I rolled out of a fast-moving air car and slammed into something sturdier than myself. The transfer of energy didn't work out in my favor."

"No, it didn't." She ran the scanner over his arm. "It's a clean break, well set. I'll replace the make-do splint with a spray-on that will be more comfortable and sturdier. You're not in any danger from that. Any other issues?"

"My knee's bunged up."

She scanned it. "Ah, yes. It's bruised, and you have some minor tears to the cartilage. You'll want to stay off it."

"Yeah, that's not happening. I have a hundred of my people to rescue. Do you have a shot that can help with the pain? And maybe a knee brace?"

She gave him a disapproving look. "That's not the safest course of action, but I can give you something for the pain and wrap the knee. If it goes out on you, don't blame me."

"I hereby absolve you of all responsibility regarding my health when I pull my next fool stunt."

"My, aren't we grouchy."

"It's been that kind of day."

"True enough," the doctor said. "I'd just delivered your injured compatriots to your pinnace when all hell broke loose, and the coordinator won't let me go do what I need to do."

He understood her anger. "Your day is worse than mine, and it won't be ending any time soon. Did they all get away safely?"

"I assume so. We released all but three of the worst injured. I manipulated the hospital records to show even those people were gone, but we hid them in a different wing of the hospital. They're safe."

"Was Paul Cooley with them?"

She nodded. "He's a friend of yours? He's badly injured, but I'm guardedly optimistic about his recovery."

"Thank God. When all this is over, drinks are on me."

The doctor shook her head slowly. "Things were only just over from the orbital bombardments a decade ago. Those drinks will have to wait a long time."

She finished replacing the cast and gave him a sturdier sling. Then she injected something into his knee that made it immediately feel better. She finished up by wrapping it with something stretchy.

"There you go. I suggest you follow up with one of your medical professionals to get this taken care of as soon as possible."

"Thanks, Doctor. I hope they let you do what you need to do soon."

Coordinator West shook her head from where she was standing nearby. "I wish we could, but the odds are we'll need the good doctor's services when we raid the farm or the council building. I understand that sucks, but it's necessary. Thank you, Doctor."

Once the other woman had departed, Sean gingerly stood and tested his leg. It would do.

"Have you located this farm?"

She nodded. "We think so. There are several possibilities, but one of them has extra vehicles parked nearby. My tech wasn't able to get much of a satellite scan before they locked her out of the system, but only that one agricultural area seems to have that kind of buildup.

"Your marines on the island are going to be here in a couple of hours. I suggest we go out and see for ourselves. If you feel comfortable going in and freeing your people, I'd be happy to loan you my men."

Doing something was better than sitting on his ass. "I'm in, but please tell me you have something better than a vegetable lift to sneak us up in."

"Don't you think that's appropriate? Who would notice a few more around a farm?"

He sighed. "I suppose that makes sense, but the damned things are uncomfortable, and they smell bad."

"Take it out on our mutual enemies," Coordinator West said without any apparent sympathy. "We'll have larger vehicles to come in and pick up your fellows as soon as we get them loose. If they're there. Besides, I'll be with you, so I'll be in the same situation. If you're ready, we should get moving."

*** * ***

KELSEY STAYED out of the way while Jared focused on stabilizing *Invincible*. William had arrived, and she kept him company as they watched *Ginnie Dare* chase down the fleeing pinnace through their implants.

The superdreadnought was still blind, but William's small ship had scanners capable of seeing what was happening at least as well as *New York*.

"They told me how big she was, but that really doesn't do her justice," he said. "Your ship is monstrously huge."

"And beat to hell," she said. "After the fight with the AI, the bomb-pumped laser, the exploding cutter, and now the dive through your atmosphere, I'm not sure that it wouldn't be quicker restoring one of the other superdreadnought derelicts."

He leaned back in his acceleration couch. "I wouldn't be too sure about that. A lot of the damage is superficial. If you can get the shipyard on Boxer Station back into operation, I think she'll be back into shape quickly."

"Where do you think they're going?"

"The pinnace? I can't say that there's ever been anything worth a damn out at that particular gas giant. If I used the Terra system as an example, it's more like Neptune than Jupiter. Cold, distant, and it doesn't even have any pretty rings. No one ever built remote stations there. I can't think of any visitation at all since the system was settled thousands of years ago."

She shook her head. "There's something there. They blew up the orbitals and ran straight for it, even knowing that we'd send a warship right on their heels. They have a weapon there, or at least some way to defend themselves. We need to be able to sneak up on them."

"Come now," the noble scoffed. "Surely that imposing destroyer of yours will be able to stop them."

"I hope so, but I wouldn't hold my breath if I were you. We need a plan B."

"Perhaps you could use the stealth ship to sneak up on them."

That wasn't a bad idea, she thought, but she rejected it. "It's too slow, and I doubt it's working so well with that massive dent in the side."

"No, and Roger isn't able to fly with the dent in his noggin, either. Too bad we didn't build two."

Perhaps now would be a good time to point out that Persephone *is mostly operational. Her stealth shielding isn't as good as the saucer, but her power plants are online, and she could make the trip, I suspect.*

Kelsey froze as she considered that. Ned was right. The Marine Raider ship was designed to sneak up on people. If things went south, it might be best to have that plan already in motion.

"The little voice in my head has an idea," she said. "Can I borrow your ship? I need to pick up some people and gear."

*** * ***

JARED WATCHED the scanner feed coming from *New York* through his implants. *Ginnie Dare* was almost to the gas giant. Another hour and he would be in control of the area. The rogue pinnace was already slipping around to the back of the planet.

They'd cut open the probe hatch on *Invincible* and dispatched several to look the area over, but they'd arrive about the same time as the destroyer. He left getting *Invincible* into a stable configuration to Zia while he and a hastily gathered staff kept an eye on the big picture.

He really needed to form a permanent staff. The electrons were still settling in on his promotion to flag rank and events had been occurring at a rapid pace, but he wasn't just commanding a single ship anymore. A staff would help keep him organized.

Which would be a blessing right about now. The race to the gas giant was far from the only crisis on his plate. The virtual destruction of his superdreadnought flagship, the coup on Harrison's World, the rescue operations at the nuked cities, and the repair mission at the Pentagar-bound flip point were all boiling over at the same time. He was losing track of the details.

He'd moved back to the flag bridge just to stay out of Zia's way. With all its stations, it allowed the crew members Zia had seemingly plucked at random from the crew to work all around him, theoretically only disturbing him when they had something requiring his attention.

That was not how it worked, of course. He was walking around the compartment, getting updates from each group as they happened. He needed to work on his multitasking skills.

Still, it kept him from going crazy trying to watch everything in real time.

"Admiral," one of his new staff officers called out after a bit more than an hour, "*Ginnie Dare* is approaching the gas giant."

He moved over to the man's station. "What do the probes show?"

"Nothing seems out of place. They're coming around the curve of the planet, following the path the pinnace took."

Jared used his implants to read the probes' findings for himself. *Ginnie Dare* had her weapons armed and her scanners on high. She was ready for trouble.

Just not the kind of trouble that came looking for her.

Active targeting scanners from the gas giant lit the destroyer up, and two dozen missiles came boiling out of the atmosphere almost in the destroyer's face.

Commander Roche changed course to get his ship away from the planet and started firing his antimissile railguns. He stopped maybe a quarter of them before the rest blotted his destroyer from the sky.

The probes picked up a number of distress beacons, so some of his people had escaped.

"Send a recall signal," Jared said grimly. "Get the pods moving in this general direction. There's something down there with a lot of firepower, so we can't risk coming to them."

The probes weren't seeing any large pieces of debris from the destroyer. She was gone. So was most of her crew, in all probability. That was an unexpected gut punch.

There'd be time to grieve later. "Take a probe in deeper. Put it on an automatic course to orbit the planet once. We need to see what we're facing, and it won't be able to signal us until it gets back out of the atmosphere."

"Aye, sir."

Several minutes passed while the commands made their way to the probe, and the view from the probe changed as it angled into the outer reaches of the gas giant's atmosphere. The signal faded before they saw anything. They'd just have to hope the probe survived to tell them what it found.

The emergency pods slowly began reporting in. Only twelve of them had ejected in time, none of them fully loaded. Sixty-three survivors out of hundreds. Scott Roche was not among them. The senior surviving officer was Lieutenant Angela Ellis, *Ginnie Dare*'s marine detachment commander.

Jared had known they might find trouble at the gas giant, and so had Scott Roche. He'd taken every precaution, but it hadn't made one bit of difference. Now Eliyanna Kaiser's *New York* was the only surviving ship from Breckenridge's task force. He'd send her out to recover the pods at a safe distance as soon as he could.

Half an hour later, *Invincible* reacquired the probe's signal from the other side of the gas giant.

"Incoming telemetry," the man said.

Jared focused on the detailed picture emerging from the passive scans. The probe had found a small station high in the planet's atmosphere. The station had an array of missile tubes on its upper surface, too, so it was the source of that massive salvo.

It was also transmitting a signal deeper into the atmosphere. The probe noted that and turned to follow it down.

The obscuring clouds vanished abruptly. The view was stunning. A layer of colorful clouds above and below sandwiched a sky as clear as a sunny day back home.

Floating in the middle of that was a massive space station. Mighty arms sprang out of its body and linked to four vessels on humongous grav cradles.

Each of those ships was instantly recognizable as a battlecruiser. The probe couldn't tell, but Jared was certain the bad guys were bringing them to life.

Hiding them there was brilliant. The atmospheric pressure at that depth was low enough that the large ships could maneuver without burning up like *Invincible* almost had. They could lurk just out of sight and let the station support them.

His forces, in their current condition, couldn't stand against that kind of firepower. Those ships had to be computer controlled, just like the destroyers the AI had had before they'd defeated it. Those had almost wrecked his fleet.

The firepower he was looking at now would finish the job as certainly as night followed day.

31

Olivia walked through the woods behind the Imperial Marines. They in turn trailed her scouts. It seemed they were traveling in the order of most silent to least.

The scouts were woodsmen, chosen because they knew what to look for. Things that might be out of place in the forest near the agricultural area. They were ghosts, flitting through the trees and underbrush as though they were never there.

The marines moved as a group, spearheading the assault task force. Even heavily armored and carrying a ridiculous amount of weaponry, they managed to keep the sound of their passing to the occasional rustle of leaves or swishing limb. Certainly nothing that would carry for any distance.

She, on the other hand, was the one who'd tripped over a log. *After* they'd warned her about it. She might as well go running through the woods, screaming at the top of her lungs. At least that was how she felt.

The rest of the attack force, comprised of more city-oriented members of the resistance, followed farther behind, where their lack of woodcraft kept them out of the range of sharp ears.

Sean Meyer walked beside her and was obviously staying close in case he had to make a grab for her.

The marines had given her a short lecture on things she could do and things she couldn't. That's how she knew she could speak to him softly, but not to whisper. Whispers apparently carried for long distances. That seemed counterintuitive.

She probably should avoid falling down again, too.

They'd parked the lifts some way back at another farm. The farmer in question had come out with a shotgun to see who was there. It had taken some speedy talking to get him to hear them out.

She'd left some men behind to make certain he didn't call anyone, but he didn't seem like a lookout for Abigail.

One of the scouts appeared out of the darkness almost in her face. She hoped she hadn't been about to scream when Commander Meyer clamped a hand over her mouth, but she couldn't be completely certain.

Once the officer seemed satisfied she wasn't going to do anything to give them away, he let her go.

"Thank you," she said softly. She glared at the woodsman. "For God's sake, don't try to scare me to death."

He had the grace to look mildly embarrassed. "Sorry, Coordinator. Our men are at the inside edge of the forest. The main warehouse has people inside. They're showing up clear through the walls in the gear the marines gave us. Too many to count. That building has a butt load of people stuffed inside. Hundreds."

"What about guards?" Meyer asked. Two of the marines were gathered around and listening closely.

"Three sets of them outside the building. They're using lifts to hide behind. Show up just fine on those binoculars." He nodded to the Fleet officer. "We'll be keeping those, if you don't mind."

"You get my people where we can take out the sentries and you can keep the rest of the gear, too," Meyer declared.

The man grinned. "Don't need your people to get those idiots. They're watching things on their coms. Ruined their night vision. They won't see the boys sneaking up."

"I'd appreciate you taking a few marines along," Meyer said dryly. "Just in case they need to shoot someone."

"Then we'd best be about it, before someone that knows their ass from a hole in the ground comes along."

The man led the marines off, and Olivia watched them go with some trepidation. "What exactly did you just give them?"

The Fleet officer grinned. "Nothing too bad, as long as you trust those boys. Night-vision gear, Fleet marine knives, flechette pistols, civilian stunners, and a couple of long-range flechette rifles."

"Sniper rifles? I do trust them, but I bet the game wardens won't be thanking you. If those men aren't poachers on the side, I'd be astonished."

"Then issue them a year-round hunting pass. Think of it as motivation. They'll work super hard to be sure none of the sentries gets out a peep for that kind of swag.

"Here's what we're going to do. We'll advance until we reach the open area and stop. Once the marines take out the sentries, we'll advance slowly while they secure the exterior of the building. Once we're ready to rush, we go in. Stunners only, unless we absolutely have to kill. We don't know who the bad guys are until they open fire."

Olivia nodded. "I'll leave that in your hands. I'll also stay outside until you give the all clear."

He went off to coordinate with his people and came back a few minutes later. They had to wait about twenty minutes before the woodsman appeared again, this time making some noise to announce his presence.

"We got the guards trussed up. The marines said for you to get into the forward positions."

Meyer clapped him on the shoulder. "Good work. Tell them we'll be along directly."

All the message carrying was necessary because they weren't going to chance someone catching a stray com transmission.

He turned to Olivia once the man was gone. "I'll lead the teams into place. You stay back to the rear and keep low. You'd rather not catch a stray flechette once the party starts."

"No worries there. My security people won't let me anywhere near the fighting. Good luck, and be careful."

It took about half an hour to get everyone in position to attack the building. She prayed there weren't as many guards as the numbers suggested. That would be a disaster. It also wouldn't make any sense. Why have so many people guarding the Fleet prisoners? Most of Abigail's trusted people had to be in the council building.

Olivia never heard the signal to go, but she saw the attack begin. Small charges blew holes in the thin metal walls of the building, and the marines rushed in. Almost immediately, Olivia heard flechette pistols firing. Blue stunner beams strobed in the darkness.

She was behind a lift, but she crouched lower. Her guards watched the attack unfold and kept their weapons ready. In the dark, there really wasn't that much to see.

That is, until one of the large doors abruptly slid open and people poured out into the night. Right toward her hiding spot. Some of her people fired into the enemy with stunners, but there were far too many bad guys for them to stop.

The lead security man cursed and grabbed her shoulder. "Run for the trees. Holloway and Jennings, keep her safe while we cover your withdrawal."

The two men grabbed her and ran for the woods. Someone must've seen them. That was obvious when one of the two men pitched forward, his head a bloody mess.

The other man shoved her toward the trees. "Run!" He whirled and opened fire.

Olivia didn't hesitate. She ran as though her life depended on it.

The people behind her must've had stunners, too. She saw a blue beam snap past her and hit a tree. She threw herself to the side and rolled for cover. She didn't make it, and the world went dark.

* * *

KELSEY HAD STOPPED FEARING for her life months ago, but that didn't keep her heart from rising into her throat when Lord Hawthorne almost crashed them on the island where the people from the various life pods were gathering.

"I thought you knew how to fly," she demanded as the ship settled to the plascrete.

She saw a Fleet guide rising cautiously from behind a blast barrier where he'd thrown himself. The man watched the ship suspiciously, probably not sure it was going to stay still. Kelsey couldn't blame him.

Lord Hawthorne turned toward her. "I did train," he said more than a shade defensively. "I'm a little rusty."

"You don't say."

The people she'd called ahead for came out of a hangar near the ship at a run, Talbot in the lead. He ran up the ramp she'd lowered and made his way to the flight deck.

"That was either the worst landing I've ever seen or the most amazing recovery of a complete guidance failure in history. Which was it?"

The Rebel Empire noble gave the marine a sour look. "I can see why the two of you get along so well."

She laughed. "Tell me you have some pinnace pilots. Please."

"Two of the best," he assured her. "We're going to be stuffed to the bulkheads in this thing. It's designed for three or four dozen people. We'll be dragging along three or four times that number. With the life support gear you brought, we'll be able to make it to *Persephone*, but we won't enjoy it."

"I grabbed everything on your list," she said as she got to her feet. "*Persephone* has two stealthed pinnaces, if they're still functional. We have enough crew for the ship and marines to make an assault on that new base. We just have to get there before those ships come to life.

"I had the crew on Boxer Station send over every engineer they had. If there's a problem with the pinnaces or ship, they'll do the best they can to fix them. They can't mess with *Persephone*'s computer, but it hasn't seen fit to raise a stink about the people we had examining all the systems before now."

The pilots came in and took over for William and herself. She walked William out of the cutter and gave him a hug. The act seemed to surprise him, but he'd get over it.

"You've helped us so much. I'll leave your cutter at Boxer Station. The engineers can give it a good maintenance check while we're gone."

"Be careful, Highness. The cutter doesn't matter. It's a relic of history. You, on the other hand, matter a great deal."

"I'm surprisingly hard to kill. I'll be as careful as the situation allows. See you soon, William."

"Return to your people hale and whole, with the heads of your enemies at your feet, warrior princess." He stepped back and swept into an exquisite bow.

Kelsey was still gaping as he spun on his heel and walked off toward the hangar.

"I'm not doing that," Talbot said as she walked back up the ramp.

"I hope to God no one else is, either. Can you imagine dealing with that all the time?"

The cutter was packed with people. It was going to get smelly fast, based on what she was already sensing. With her enhanced sense of smell, that could get pretty ugly. Good thing she was going to button up in her Raider armor for the trip. She'd snagged it along with everything the marines needed for the assault.

All the equipment reduced the available space even further, but they didn't have a choice. She hoped everyone had used the bathroom. The line would be murder.

"How long for the trip out?" he asked as she got into her armor.

"Three hours with pushing the drives on this thing. One of Baxter's people said it would hold. Then we make the run from Boxer Station out to the gas giant. Call that another five or six, since we don't dare stand out. Any way you cut it, this is going to be a long drive."

She finished buttoning up and began sliding her weapons into their normal locations, including her new swords. She'd brought them along in case things got really bad.

They waited for everyone to get settled in and closed the ramp. The ship was standing room only. The cutter lifted off, and they were on their way to a fight that they had to win. If, of course, they managed to get their ride working.

* * *

JARED SOMEHOW MISSED Lord Hawthorne's cutter leaving Harrison's World. It was already halfway to Boxer Station when one of his staff gave him a status on it.

He called them and asked to speak to Kelsey. She came on a few moments later.

"Bandar here."

"Kelsey, where are you going, and what are you planning to do once you get there?"

"*Persephone*. We're bringing her online. She might be able to get close to that station before it knows we're on the way. I have Talbot and a full crew of marines at my side. If we don't take these ships out, we're all screwed anyway."

"I wish to hell you'd cleared this with me ahead of time."

"It's in the report I sent you before I left."

He brought it up and scanned it. Yes, she'd tacked her intentions at the very end. She'd obviously expected he'd skim the summary. He really needed to read every word next time.

"Remind me to explain the difference between asking permission and begging forgiveness to you at some point," he said with a sigh. "Well, it's too late to stop you now. Do you have enough people?"

"We have almost fifty. A mix of marines and crew. It'll be tight, but we'll manage. Look, you have enough on your plate. I'm going to let you go. Wish me luck."

He sighed and did so before terminating the call. It burned him up that she was rushing off to save them again and he was sitting here, unable to even shoot at anyone if they failed.

That made him pause. He couldn't control any aspect of any of the situations he was monitoring. At this point, he was useless here. That wouldn't be the case if he went out to join them.

From what he remembered of that ship, it could use a lot more crew than they could possibly stuff into that cutter. He had plenty of people to spare on the crippled superdreadnought. They'd been ferrying them up from Harrison's World for the last few hours. Marines, too.

He immediately called Zia to hold two pinnaces. He then compiled a list of crew members that would be of use on the Marine Raider ship. He sent the list to *Invincible* with instructions to summon them to marine country.

Then he called Lord Hawthorne's cutter and informed the pilots of his plan to meet them out there. He ordered them to keep that information to themselves. It was time to turn the tables on Princess Kelsey and do something to help save them.

He left for marine country at a run. He'd have time to get into unpowered armor and vacuum gear. He'd also make sure that every man and woman was as heavily armed and well protected as possible. If they got into a fight, they might need every bit of damage they could deliver.

32

It took almost an hour for Sean to get the situation at the farm locked down. A hardcore group of fighters took some of the prisoners hostage. Eventually, he sent the marines through the roof and stunned everyone after sharpshooters took out the most fanatic of the defenders with flechettes through the wall.

They'd accounted for the missing Fleet personnel, even if some of them were a bit battered. Seeing Gina the marine holding a sobbing Fleet crewwoman was the highpoint of his week.

There were a number of other prisoners. Sean suspected they were Coordinator West's political allies. He sent some men to round her up.

They came back empty-handed.

Worried, he sent everyone he could spare to scour the area for her. They found the bodies of her guards near the forest but found no sign of the coordinator herself.

"Find me whoever was in charge of this facility," he told one of West's people.

That turned out to be a scientist of some kind. Two grim-faced guards held the man up between them. It looked as though they'd prefer to be marching him outside and shooting him.

Sean followed their lead and gave the man in the lab coat a hard look. "My name is Commander Sean Meyer. These Fleet personnel are my people. I'm told you drugged them and questioned them against their will."

The man drew himself up and stared down his nose at Sean. "I'm Doctor Paul Nelson, and you have no right to—"

"I don't care what your name is or what you object to," Sean said, cutting him off. "You're guilty of kidnapping, torture, and a host of other crimes against people under my command. I could have these men frog march you outside and shoot you in the head. No one would care, and many would thank me. If you want the opportunity of dealing with the civilian authorities instead, you'd better start cooperating. Do you understand?"

The man swallowed noisily and nodded convulsively, unaware of the grins his captors were sporting at the deception. At least Sean hoped they knew he was lying.

"What do you want to know?"

"Someone kidnapped Coordinator West," he said. "I want to know who."

"I have no idea."

"Take him outside and shoot him. Dump the body in the woods near the coordinator's guards."

"Wait!" The scientist dug in his heels as he shrieked. "Wait! Deputy Coordinator King probably took her. She left just after the fighting started and went toward the woods."

Sean held up his hand and stopped the men. "She was here? I thought she was at the council building."

"She wanted everyone to think she was there, but she came here with the political prisoners. When you attacked, her guards took her out toward the woods."

"Where were they going?"

"How should I know?"

He considered the scientist. King hadn't taken him with her, so he might be telling the truth. Maybe. Or perhaps he knew more than he suspected.

"That's not good enough. I need someone here who can lead me to her. If you're not that man, you'd better come up with someone else for me to focus my attention on before I give these boys their marching orders."

"Her personal assistant was here," the scientist said in a voice filled with desperation. "I saw him lying near the questioning equipment. I'll show you. Just don't kill me."

Sean gave the man a long, searching look. "Show me."

The scientist led them to a young man laid out with the other wounded. He'd been stunned but was coming around. Someone had bound his hands together in front of him.

Sean gave the scientist a cold look. "You'd best hope this man has the answers I'm looking for. Put the good doctor into one of the cages he kept my people in."

The guards took the scientist away while Sean knelt at the young man's side. He only had to wait a few minutes before the man was able to process his surroundings.

"What happened?" the man asked.

"I think you can guess," Sean said. "You're Deputy Coordinator King's personal assistant?"

The man blinked at him. "You obviously know that."

"I want to know where your boss is."

"If you don't already know, then I won't tell you."

Sean had heard that tone before. This man wasn't going to cooperate, even if threatened with death. Sean needed another plan.

He searched the man's pockets and found his com. It was locked, of course. "Give me the code."

"No."

Why did everything have to be so hard? He gestured for one of the guards to come over. "This man is an important prisoner. Segregate him and make sure nothing happens to him."

While that was happening, he searched out Coordinator West's tech guru and handed her the com. "Abigail King's personal assistant is here. Another prisoner says that King was here, too. I think she took your boss. Can you crack this?"

The woman took the com and plugged it into a portable computer. It took a ridiculously short amount of time for her to access its contents. "Here we go. I have his contact list, and he's thoughtfully labeled her private com code. It looks like she tried to contact him after the attack, probably to see if he'd escaped. Let's see if she left a message."

An audio-only message began playing. "If you got away, meet me back at the council building. I have West in my custody."

The message terminated without any further pleasantries.

"My, she's a friendly sort," Sean said. "Can you locate that com and confirm where she is?"

"Maybe. I used to have access to all the major planetary systems, but they've been locking me out. That one isn't high priority, so let's find out."

She worked at her computer for a few minutes and grinned. "I'm in. They blocked my original access, but I found a backdoor. Yes. The com is at the council building. It seems to be in the executive wing. I'd wager she's in Coordinator West's office."

"Do you have floor plans for the council building? It might be advantageous to get in through a less obvious route."

She shook her head. "Those kinds of plans aren't available to the general public, and they're not kept on a system I can access from here. That said, it should be possible to find or create access with the right tools. I'd have to be on site to make that happen."

"Gear up. The main force of marines will be ready to assault the building before dawn. Let's see if we can get inside before then. If need be, we can make a hole to let the marines in after we reconnoiter the place."

* * *

KELSEY WAS PLEASANTLY surprised at how much work the engineering team from Boxer Station had completed on *Persephone*. They'd not only verified the grav drives were fully functional, they'd vetted the fusion plants and sealed off the damaged sections of the ship. The makeshift crew could access every functional area without vacuum suits.

They'd also moved the dead into the damaged section of the ship. That was a relief. She'd not been looking forward to moving the bodies. She could only imagine how bad that would be when they started clearing out the derelicts. There must be millions of dead on those hulks.

She stripped off her armor and put it in a handy corner. Getting out of the overcrowded cutter and being able to stretch her arms felt wonderful. Still, she wished they'd managed to stuff twice as many people into the small ship. They were going to be very undermanned for this flight.

Okay, Ned. Let's have that code. If it doesn't work, we're screwed.

The code will work. Unless, of course, I changed it and don't remember.

You're filled with positive thoughts, aren't you? The code.

He gave it to her, and she accessed the computer. It digested the code for a moment and granted her access.

"I'm in! Holy cow, I'm in! Computer, do you recognize my command authority?"

"This unit has received the appropriate codes from a qualified Marine Raider. This vessel is yours to command, Princess Kelsey Bandar."

"Kelsey is fine. I want a system status check. Is this vessel capable of in-system movement and a stealth approach to a military installation?"

"Grav drives are operating within nominal parameters. Stealth systems are in passive mode. Weapons systems are degraded. Four of six beam emplacements are not operational. Flip drives are offline. Warning, with the hull breached, this vessel cannot withstand a high speed insertion into atmosphere."

Like the small Pentagaran ship she'd flown on, *Persephone* was capable of landing. It was significantly larger than that other vessel, but the layout of the hull had told her it was possible. No one wasted time streamlining a hull on a ship that had no need to enter atmosphere.

"*Persephone*, do you have any knowledge of how this ship was damaged or of how Captain Ned Quincy died?"

"Affirmative. This vessel attempted to escape enemy pursuit in the Valhalla system by going through a particularly heavy ring of debris orbiting a gas giant. A small, fast-moving object destroyed this vessel's flip drive and killed eight crew members.

"Major Quincy was critically injured during the ensuing rescue operations. His actions saved the lives of three engineers trapped in the wreckage. The medical officer doubted Major Quincy would survive his injuries but placed him in the stasis chamber."

Kelsey considered that. "How did you escape pursuit, and how did the crew die?"

"The pursuing vessel was significantly less fortunate in crossing the ring. Its terminal course took it deep into the atmosphere, where it was destroyed. This vessel escaped into the outer system.

"Repairs to the flip drive proved impossible. The crew used their remaining supplies over the next several months and made the determination to take their lives with drugs in their pharmacology units. Several decades passed before this vessel once more made its way into more traveled areas of the system. At that point, it was recovered and brought here."

"Why didn't you self-destruct or at least wipe your memory?"

"This unit hypothesizes that the rebels believed this vessel to be without power. They never boarded, so this unit was not obligated to wipe its memory."

That was certainly to her benefit. She doubted she'd have been lucky enough to find another one of these vessels intact.

"Warning. Unknown vessels approaching."

Kelsey tapped into the ship's passive scanners. There were two Fleet pinnaces approaching at high speed from the direction of Harrison's World.

"Open a channel to them. Unknown vessels, identify yourselves."

"Kelsey, you're in big trouble."

"Jared, I didn't expect you to chase me down."

"I'm sure you didn't. It just so happens that I have some free time, and I brought some extra Fleet personnel and marines. I assume you don't have a problem with that?"

Considering how shorthanded she was, she was ecstatic. "The more the merrier. I'll meet you at the docking area."

She considered how their arrival changed the mission. "Computer, the crewmen I have with me are not Marine Raiders. Can I authorize them to operate the ship's systems?"

"Yes, Kelsey. Marine Raider vessels are often partially crewed by Fleet officers, though always under the command of a Raider."

"Excellent. One additional question. Do you have complete specs on my implants and all Raider equipment?"

"Yes."

A thrill ran up her spine. It felt like Christmas.

"Upload them to my implants. All of them. Include any classified files you have in storage. I'll review them as time permits." She accessed her implants and granted the computer access to some memory.

"Upload complete."

Kelsey made her way to the docking area with a bounce to her step. She skimmed the implant specifications and grinned. She'd been in the dark for so long. Finally, she had the manuals. Now she wouldn't have to guess what she was capable of anymore.

If, of course, she survived the next few hours.

She transmitted copies of everything to Boxer Station, *Courageous*, and *Invincible*. This information was so difficult to come by that she couldn't chance it being lost again. She locked it down so that only someone of the rank of captain or above could access it, but only if she didn't make it back. After a moment, she added Carl Owlet and Doctor Leonard to the list.

The docking hatch slid open as she arrived. Jared and a stream of Fleet officers and marines came out. Most headed for the areas of the ship where they'd be working, but some followed Jared as he stepped up beside her.

"We're really going to have to work on our coordination," he said as she led him back toward the bridge. "If you'd simply asked me for help, I could've sent a lot more people."

"I was afraid you'd try to stop me."

He shook his head. "Not this time. One way or the other, we need to stop these bastards. If they get those battlecruisers online, we're screwed. Does this ship have weapons?"

"Not many. It comes with six beam emplacements, but only two are working. Other than that, we're ready to go. I've accessed the computer, and it has accepted me as its commander."

He smiled. "So, now you get to command in space, too. You can appoint yourself an admiral."

"That's not funny. I'll never know enough to command a ship in space. I'm happy to have you to lean on."

They arrived at the bridge, and she spoke. "Computer, I'm placing Admiral Jared Mertz in command of this vessel."

"Negative. Only a Marine Raider may command this vessel. This unit cannot accept Admiral Mertz as the commanding officer. However, you may designate him as your operational delegate."

"Well, I suppose that'll have to do. Make it so. Are you ready to move, *Persephone?*"

"Yes, Kelsey."

She turned to Jared. "The ship is yours, Admiral. Let's go take these bastards out."

He smiled grimly. "It'll be my pleasure, Captain Bandar."

33

Olivia awoke with a massive headache. She'd been stunned. It took her a minute to realize that Abigail had tied her to a chair in her own office at the council building. And not the comfortable one behind the desk.

Abigail King sat in that one. The bitch looked smugly pleased with herself.

"It's about time you woke up. I've been overseeing the consolidation of the planet while you've been napping. I hope it doesn't irk you too badly that I'm savoring the moment."

Olivia's mouth tasted like something had died in it. "This is the point in the program where I tell you that you'll never get away with this and you share your clever plan with me."

"Since you'll never escape this building, I don't have a problem with that scenario. Your rebel friends have been sneaking around outside for the last hour or so. They probably don't realize that I can see them moving into place to attack, but that's okay. It's all part of my so-called clever plan."

"Not to quibble, but technically you're the rebel. We're the resistance."

"So you did know. I'd been curious." Abigail rose from behind the desk and walked around to stand in front of Olivia. "I really don't care what you and the scum like you call yourselves. You're traitors, and once we restore the Lords to power in this system, we'll root you out."

Olivia shook her head. "You know the AIs murdered trillions of people to enslave humanity. How could anyone support continuing that?"

"Because I and the other loyalists get to wear the boots on the necks of people like you. The AIs are in control, and nothing you do will ever change that. What did you hope to accomplish? Revolution? The Lords are firmly entrenched and have enough firepower to stop anything you try."

"It looks like you're the one in the building about to be overrun. In the end, it doesn't matter if I live or die. The resistance will win. You can't stop men in powered armor."

The other woman laughed. "That's the best part. I don't have to. Once the attack begins, I'll scurry out your secret exit and let them have everything. Ah! You didn't know I knew about that, did you?

"You also didn't know we made extra nuclear weapons when we built the bomb-pumped lasers that destroyed the stations and the superdreadnought. We had to, because we didn't know where we'd need to put every weapon. Besides the three that are still in place in buildings Master Calder owns, I had the spare brought here. Once I'm away, I'll blow it up. Oh, and you, too."

Olivia tried to keep the despair she felt off her face, but she doubted she'd succeeded.

* * *

JARED WAS AMAZED at how stealthy *Persephone* was. After they began moving toward the gas giant where the enemy awaited them, the computer advised going to what it called "active stealth" and increasing speed substantially.

That seemed counterintuitive, so he tried to find out what that entailed. The computer politely told him to mind his own business. It was classified, and he didn't have need to know.

Somewhat nonplussed, he kept the speed where it was and told the computer to engage active stealth. Due to the position of Boxer Station, he could communicate with it without risking the enemy receiving a transmission that tipped their hand for most of the trip out. They managed that by restricting where the communication beams went.

The staff at Boxer Station had replaced the scanner units destroyed in battle, so they had a good view of the system that didn't tell the enemy anything they didn't already know.

"Boxer Station, *Persephone*. We've gone active with stealth. How are you reading us?"

The voice of the lieutenant in charge of Boxer Station's repairs sounded shocked when she came on. "*Persephone*, we've lost you on our scanners. You were there one moment and then you were gone. We've gone to targeting scans, and we think we *might* have you ranged, but we can't be sure."

That was ridiculous. They were right in Boxer Station's lap. There was no way they could *fail* to see them. At this range, they could have seen the fighter that he loved so much, even just coasting along.

Jared shook his head and stepped over behind the helm console. "Take us up to the speed that the computer recommended."

Lieutenant Heather Brand touched her console. "Increasing speed."

"*Persephone*, we have you again," Boxer Station said.

"I knew it was too good to be true," he muttered. "Go ahead, Boxer Station. How clear is the reading?"

"It's spooky, Admiral. Even though we know pretty much where you are, the readings aren't firm at all, and they're getting weaker as you pull away. By the time you get to extreme missile range, we'll have lost you again. If we weren't painting you hard, we'd have already done so. Whatever stealth that little ship has, it's amazing."

This might have a chance of working after all.

* * *

SEAN COULDN'T BELIEVE he was even trying this. He had a ring of marines around the council building, entrenched with heavy weapons. At his command, they'd storm the building after pinnaces took out the defensive positions. Inside five minutes, they'd have most areas under their control.

So, instead of going with that relatively safe plan, he was sneaking through the sewers with his rag-tag team of marines and the coordinator's closest confederates. Their plan? To find a spot where they could breach an unused subbasement with a shaped plasma charge. Then they'd infiltrate the more traveled corridors and try to rescue the coordinator.

What could possibly go wrong?

The coordinator's tech wizard had a scanner of some kind and was probing the walls of the wretched tunnel. The incredible stench didn't faze the woman in the slightest.

"I think about here." She tapped the moldy, stained plascrete beside her. "This should be about three meters thick and heavily reinforced. You'll want to keep from going overboard with the blast. If you take out the wall on the other side of the room, you might bring down the level above it. That one has machinery that will be noted if it goes offline, and it might collapse this whole section of the building."

"Lovely. Everyone, spread out. If this building is so shielded, how do you know where to place the charges?"

"Power conduits," the woman said as she made her way past him, wisely retreating down the sewer. "I can see the ones feeding the area around the council building, and they give me distances."

"So, you're guessing."

The woman's eyes narrowed. "You don't have to be insulting. This is much more refined than a guess."

He raised his hands in surrender. "Have it your way."

The marine armorer carefully placed a plasma charge on the wall. They could tailor the output by regulating how much plasma it generated. That theoretically allowed them to use only the force necessary. They'd know in just a minute how good the tech lady was.

"We're ready, sir," the man said. "We need to pull back about fifty meters. I can remotely detonate it at that point."

Once they were in place, he made sure the marines were ready to charge and gave the order to go.

The explosion was more significant than he'd expected but still low key.

The plasma flash was blinding, but they'd shielded their eyes. Once it was done, they rushed in. The hole through the wall was large enough for them to use but still bubbled with heat.

One look through told him that the blast had trashed the room, but it hadn't done more than blacken the far wall. The tech had called it almost precisely. Dinner was on him if they made it through this alive.

The marines tossed heat-resistant material over the shattered remnants of the wall and scrambled into the council building. They divided into teams to hit the critical areas as quickly as possible. He led his people up three levels to near where the coordinator's office was and waited for the word that everyone was in place.

One by one, the teams checked in. When the last one was ready, he gave the order. "Go. Go. Go."

* * *

KELSEY WATCHED the gas giant through *Persephone*'s passive scanners as they entered orbit. It was beautiful, in a cold, ethereal way. All pale colors in sharp bands. A darker-blue storm that was probably bigger than Avalon churned along the equator.

She and the marines were strapped into their slots on the two pinnaces the Marine Recon ship boasted. They'd had to leave *Invincible*'s pinnaces back at Boxer Station. They weren't stealthy enough.

They slipped past the protective station without it seeing them. Based on the way the missiles and beam emplacements were laid out, it wouldn't be able to shoot at them now. That was one less thing to worry about. She didn't know if there were other stations hidden in the planet's depths, but that was a problem for another day.

The station hosting the battlecruisers wasn't scanning, but they'd be hard to miss if anyone was looking at the area visually. Their only chance for success was to slip up completely unseen.

Persephone would stay in the clouds above the battlecruisers. The stealthed pinnaces would drop down as quickly as possible and try and land on the station before anyone saw them.

"Talbot, is everyone ready?" she asked.

The marine nodded. "Ready, Princess. Say the word and we drop down on these bastards and ruin their day."

They'd crammed almost two hundred marines into the two pinnaces, a third more than they were rated for. Yet that was a ridiculously small number of people to storm a space station and four battlecruisers. Less than forty on each team.

The only saving grace was that the enemy had to have even fewer people. Not counting any automated weapons platforms, of course. If those were active, they'd all die.

"Kelsey, we're in position," Jared said over the encrypted combat link. "They're not showing any sign they know we're up here. Once you cut free and start dropping, you'll be at the station in less than sixty seconds. Are you ready?"

"As ready as we'll ever be. Everyone, stand by for drop."

"Good luck."

The pinnaces cut loose and fell like stones into the pale clouds.

* * *

ABIGAIL HAPPENED to be pouring a drink when she felt something shake the building. Just a little. The ripples in the expensive alcohol told her she hadn't imagined it.

"Well, I think we might have some visitors," she purred at Olivia. "If so, I'd best be on my way. I wouldn't want to linger and get caught up in the blast. Do say hello to everyone for me, and pass along my heartfelt wishes for them to roast in Hell."

She sent the activation command to the warhead, and the timer went live. Fifteen minutes. Now it was unstoppable.

Olivia couldn't respond. After a while of listening to the woman rave, Abigail had gagged her. That was unexpectedly satisfying.

The former coordinator of Harrison's World glared at her replacement as Abigail made her way through the secret door behind the bar and into the small lift hidden there. It took her quickly down to an abandoned grav train station.

The massive concourse must've once served a large section of the city, but now it sat forgotten. Not empty, though. A shiny new grav train waited to whisk the coordinator away to safety in case of a dire emergency.

And it would fulfill that function. The title was hers. And the best part? Abigail could blame the explosion on her enemy. Nothing could stop her now.

34

Sean led the men and women under his command toward the coordinator's office. They had stunners out as their primary weapons because they'd rather not injure any more people than absolutely necessary.

He'd visited the Imperial Senate building back on Avalon as a kid and then later as a serving officer called to give testimony on Fleet affairs. This place one-upped that august building in snoot factor. Seriously, who put marble busts of all the former councilors in little alcoves? After five hundred years, they were *everywhere*.

Everything around them spoke of large amounts of money spent for the sole purpose of showing off wealth and power. As corrupt as some of the senators at home were—and he knew one such man very well from his association with Captain Breckenridge—they weren't in the same league as this.

Thankfully, most of the defenders were elsewhere. Probably guarding the most likely exterior approaches. All he saw at first were civilians, who wisely fled.

That changed when they arrived at the executive wing. Armed and uniformed security commanded them to halt and then opened fire with flechette pistols. His people outnumbered them, though, and their stunners carried the day. One of the coordinator's people was badly wounded in the firefight, so he detailed a few people to guard their backs and watch over her.

Sean expected the coordinator's office to be under heavy guard, but the outer office was deserted. The marines flowed into the main room and cleared it quickly. Coordinator West sat tied to a chair and gagged.

He pulled the cloth from her mouth. "Are you okay?"

"No. She has a nuclear device in the building. It's activated and on a short timer. We need to initiate an evacuation right now. We only have ten minutes."

Sean used his knife to cut her free. "Most of the people won't get clear in time. Where is it?"

The coordinator's tech woman ran behind the desk. "The computer is wiped, but the basic system controls are still intact. I think I can—"

A loud alarm began wailing outside the door. The tech looked smug. "Fire alarm. It won't get them far, but it's better than nothing."

Coordinator West rubbed her wrists and stood as soon as she was free. "Abigail used the secret escape route in this office. I know where it lets out. I need some people to get me there fast in whatever grav vehicle we can find. We might be able to get the code from her."

Sean pulled out his Fleet com. "I need a pinnace on the roof right now with two squads of marines. Eliminate the defensive positions and pick up Coordinator West. Take her wherever she wants to go. Fall back ASAP. There's an armed nuke in the building on a short timer. Ten minutes."

They reversed course and made their way back toward the rotunda. Muted explosions outside told him the marines were carrying out his orders.

The tech came up beside him. "I think I know where the bomb is. If we can get to it, I might be able to disarm it."

"What are you?" he asked. "Some kind of vid hero? How can you do all this stuff?"

"Years of hacking everything that can be hacked, and some things that supposedly can't. No matter how well shielded this thing is, there'll be radiation. If they wanted to keep that under wraps, the only place that makes sense is the vault."

"Vault? Like in a bank vault?"

She nodded. "Pretty much. It's under the rotunda."

Olivia smiled grimly. "That would be just like her." She ducked into an office and wrote something on an important-looking piece of paper. "Here's the door code."

Sean grabbed the marine armorer. "We might be able to get to the nuke. Can they be disarmed?"

The marine nodded. "If it's not too complex or booby-trapped. It's possible."

"Come with me. Everyone else, go with the coordinator."

* * *

THE PINNACES DROPPED out of the clouds right on top of the station. Kelsey could clearly see it on the visual scanners as they fell toward it. She waited for it to open fire or for one of the battlecruisers to blast them, but nothing happened.

Right before they hit the station, the pilots savagely decelerated and clamped onto the hull. The ramp went down, and a marine tossed out a magnetic breaching charge. Once the ramp was back up, they remotely detonated it.

The shock wave shook the pinnace badly but didn't dislodge them. The marines lowered the ramp again and poured out of the pinnace. They made it into the station without any problems and bypassed the closest emergency containment doors.

She expected an alarm to be sounding, but it was quiet inside. There was computer access, but it rejected her attempts to interface.

"Talbot, take your men and block access to battlecruisers one and two," she ordered. "Lieutenant Evans, you have three and four. I'll find the station command center."

"On it," Talbot said. "Keep your head down, Princess. We have unfinished business."

She grinned and led her team deeper into the station. There were no markings to indicate where anything was. She'd just have to assume that the control center was somewhere in the central shaft.

They took to the stairs to make sure no one ambushed them in the lifts. Somewhere in the distance, she heard the sound of flechette rifles firing.

"This is team three," a voice said. "We're encountering hostile fire from the docking port to battlecruiser three. Men without combat armor. We're going in."

A few moments later, teams four and one called in. They'd gained access to battlecruisers one and four without resistance. Those ships seemed to be in standby mode. Main power was offline.

Talbot called in last. "We're getting fire from battlecruiser two. Nothing serious. We're going in."

"This is team three. We're in. The battlecruiser also seems to be in standby mode. Main power offline. We're starting our sweep."

"Talbot here. Battlecruiser two is online. Main power active. We're heading for engineering."

Kelsey keyed her com. "Teams one, three, and four, if you do not encounter resistance, detach your reserves to assist team two. Lock down your engineering spaces to keep the main systems offline."

A stream of acknowledgements flowed back to her. If only one of the battlecruisers was active, they might be able to win this even if it got away.

"*Persephone*, this is Bandar. Three of the battlecruisers seem to be offline. We're securing them. Be ready if the last one gets away."

"Copy," Jared said. "We're not seeing any action from the station above us, so I'm going to leave it be. If the battlecruiser breaks away, we'll take it out. We'd have already opened fire on it, but the station raised battle screens as soon as you breached it. It's brought targeting scanners online, too. That means it'll lay into us as soon as we act. Do what you can to stop it from detaching."

"We'll do our best. Bandar out."

That was about the time that the stairwell door below them opened and men poured in. They immediately opened fire on her.

* * *

OLIVIA RACED to the roof of the council building and met the marine pinnace as it came roaring in for a landing. The far side of the roof was on fire. It looked as though something had exploded. She ran up the ramp as soon as it came down, with the rest of the infiltration team at her heels.

"I need to talk to the pilot," she told the man with the headset. "To show him where to go."

"This way, ma'am."

He led her through a door at the front of the pinnace and to a small compartment where the two pilots sat.

One of them, a woman, looked over her shoulder. "Sit down at the flight engineer's console and tell me which way to go."

There was only one seat open, so Olivia sat and looked at the map the woman had put on display for her. "Go south. You're looking for a warehouse near the edge of the city. I'll find it before we get there. Make it fast. We don't have much time."

"Roger that."

The woman turned and touched the controls. The pinnace lifted smoothly into the air and blasted forward, crushing Olivia into her seat with acceleration. Now she knew how thrilled and terrified her driver must've felt when he got to go fast.

She tore her attention away from the pinnace and studied the map. Whoever had designed and installed the escape route had used one of the city's old grav train links. The line now terminated at a warehouse.

"I have it."

"Excellent. Touch it on the screen."

Olivia touched the warehouse on the map.

The pilot was silent a moment. "I have it. There look to be two normal ways in. A cargo loading area and a personnel door."

"There's a disabled lift in the office area on the south side," Olivia said. "Only, it's not disabled. It leads down to a train station. My implants can open it and control the lift."

The pilot spoke softly, probably to the marines. Then she nodded. "Let me land the pinnace so you can approach from the street."

She brought the pinnace down, and the marine that had brought Olivia up to the flight deck escorted her back out.

The heavily armed marines surrounded her as she made her way into the building. The lift opened to her implant command. Half a dozen marines went in with her and pushed her behind them. That seemed fair. They had all that armor.

She sent the lift down to the station below. The doors opened just in time for the train carrying Abigail to pull to a stop.

The doors on the vehicle slid open and Abigail ran out, only to freeze when she saw all the weapons pointed at her.

"I'll wager this comes as a shock," Olivia said. "Don't you villains ever learn?"

"But... how could you... I left you..."

Olivia held out her hand to the nearest marine. "May I borrow your pistol?"

The man handed her a flechette pistol that she could barely get her fingers around. It felt as though it weighed a ton.

"I don't have time to blather. Give me the code to disarm the nuclear device."

"Go screw yourself."

Olivia shot her in the leg. The pistol kicked harder than she'd expected. A big splotch of blood appeared on the other woman's leg, and she fell down screaming.

"Is that enough, or shall I shoot you in the other leg?"

Abigail snarled at her. "You can go to hell. I've already killed millions, and you'll just shoot me anyway."

Olivia thought about that for a moment and nodded. "I think you're right." She raised the pistol and pointed it at the other woman's head. "I should shoot you dead, but then I'd have to live with that memory in my head. I'll just have to settle for something else."

She smashed the barrel of the weapon across Abigail's face, breaking her nose. Far less satisfying but not as cold as an on-the-spot execution.

"We need to go, ma'am," the marine said, gently taking his pistol back from her. "The LT says we only have five minutes to get clear of the area. If Commander Meyer can't stop the bomb, we don't want to be here when it goes off."

She let them hustle her and their sobbing prisoner back into the lift and prayed the commander was able to stop the looming atrocity.

35

J ared listened to the chatter between the teams with mixed emotions. They'd completely surprised the enemy, that was for sure. Three of the four battlecruisers were powered down and drawing needed resources from the station.

That was good. That was *great*.

Except for the fact that the last one was on internal power and coming to life. That was bad. *Very* bad.

The bad guys must've focused their attention on that one. It made sense. A completely functional warship of that size would have a very good chance of taking out every mobile vessel in this system. It could certainly defend this planet from all attacks while they took their time getting the other three ready to fight, especially with the armed station above it.

Kelsey and the rest had an excellent chance of taking everything else intact. All that left for him to do was figure out how to defeat a ship the size and power of *Courageous* with a damaged Marine Recon vessel. One with only two operational beam weapons and no missiles at all.

"The operational battlecruiser has detached from the station," Lieutenant Brand said. "It raised battle screens before it exited the station's cover. They appear to be opening the range from the station but are not accelerating much at all."

"Can we penetrate their screens with our beams, *Persephone?*"

"Yes, Admiral. However, the amount of damage this vessel can cause is limited, and its battle screens are significantly weaker than those of a battlecruiser. One direct salvo will likely destroy this vessel."

They needed a bigger weapon. Well, it just so happened that they had one. He opened a shipwide channel. "All hands, this is Admiral Mertz. I want all nonessential personnel to go to the rescue pods and stand by. When

I give the order, the rest of you will have thirty seconds to join them. Slave all controls to the bridge. I'll eject you when the time is right. It's been an honor."

That seemed entirely too much like the speech he'd given on *Invincible* earlier.

"Lieutenant Brand, lay in a course to ram the battlecruiser in the engineering section. If we can disable their drives, it won't be a threat anymore."

"Aye, sir. I'll need to move us around to a better approach vector. It will only take a—"

She leaned forward and stared at her console. "Explosion on the battlecruiser. Something big in the engineering section."

Jared tapped into the scanner feed. It was a damned big explosion. Now there were large secondary blasts ripping the aft section of the ship into chunks. Its grav drives failed, and it began falling.

That's when he saw a pinnace detach from the hull of the doomed battlecruiser. It looked damaged, too.

"We're receiving a transmission," Brand said.

The overheads came to life. "*Persephone*, this is Talbot. We've disengaged from the battlecruiser, but we took some damage. A hand would be really nice, because our drive just failed."

The pinnace arced downward and disappeared into the clouds below the station. It didn't have the strong hull a battlecruiser did. The pressure would quickly crush it.

"Take us after it," Jared ordered. He hoped they could catch it before the pressure did their own compromised hull fatal damage. If that happened, they'd all die.

* * *

THE BOMB WAS RIGHT where the tech suspected. On any other day, he'd stare at all the art and baubles packed into the small room. Today he only had eyes for the oblong weapon set on top of an ancient, hand-carved chest.

Sean stared at the complex bundles of wires and controls on the nuclear weapon with apprehension. Especially when the armorer shook his head.

"No way," the man said. "I can't defuse that in five minutes."

The tech attached her computer to it. "Maybe we can disable the antitampering mechanisms. It's not as if we have much to lose. We can't get far enough away to survive the blast anyway."

Feeling like a third wheel, Sean watched the two of them work feverishly. The countdown clock was racing toward zero, and still time seemed to flow like molasses.

At fifty-three seconds, the tech shouted in triumph. "I've disabled the antitampering features!"

"Can you disarm it?"

The marine shook his head. "No, but I'll keep trying."

That's when the solution hit Sean. "Can we accidentally set it off?"

"No."

"Put the spare breaching charge on it and run like hell."

The man gaped at him for a second, whipped off his pack, and pulled out the spare charge. He fiddled with the controls and slid it under the bomb. "Out! We need to close the vault to maximize the damage."

That was probably going to piss off a number of wealthy and powerful people. He could live with that.

Seconds later, the three of them had the vault closed and were running for all they were worth. They made it into the stairwell just as the charge went off.

The good news was that he immediately knew the nuke had failed to explode. The bad news was that the stairs collapsed on them, and he lost consciousness in a moment bright with pain.

* * *

KELSEY HUNCHED down and returned fire at the hostiles. They didn't have powered armor, so the exchange was very unfair.

"Make a bridgehead," she said. "Find the control room, and let's pin them down."

The marines moved ahead of her and immediately ran into heavy resistance. They kept moving forward, but the bad guys contested every centimeter. The fighters on the other side had the benefit of knowing the layout and having prepared the area for defense. They hadn't had long, but someone over there knew what they were doing.

"All teams," Kelsey said. "Send everyone you can to deck nine. Find a way in and put pressure on the defenders. Hell, make a new way in and keep them off balance. We need to end this now before someone over there gets desperate."

She got responses from everyone but Talbot.

"Talbot? Do you read?"

More ominous silence.

"Anyone from team two. Respond."

After another lengthy silence, she called Jared. "*Persephone*, do you see anything going on with battlecruiser two?"

Her brother's silence was even more frightening.

An explosion in the distance announced one of the other teams making a move. The marines in front of her used it as a cue to drive forward. There was a hail of flechettes, and then they were overrunning the defenders.

The fight trailed off rapidly from there. The defense had been very fragile. Once the marines made it in, they rapidly seized control of the deck except for the armored hatch leading to the control center.

With the ships not showing signs of resistance, and no one finding people on any other deck, she suspected the remaining enemy was on the other side of that hatch. So she needed to get inside and end this.

But she'd try to talk them into surrendering first. There were obviously things going on under the surface of Harrison's World that she'd like to settle before they had to leave.

The hatch had a communications interface, so she linked to it through her armor.

"Surely you don't expect us to just open the door?" a man asked. He sounded cultured. Refined.

"That would be the sensible thing to do," she said. "We have control of this station and the ships. This isn't going to go in your favor. Yield and you live. Resist and die. It's as simple as that."

He laughed. "After what we've already done? Don't insult my intelligence. You'll turn us over to someone on Harrison's World for trial and execution."

She had to admit he had a point. There was no chance these people wouldn't pay the ultimate penalty for their part in the nuclear explosions. No matter what she promised, that debt would need to be paid.

"True," she said. "How about a quick death after a fair and speedy trial?"

She didn't know where she'd read that, but it seemed like the appropriate brand of gallows humor.

"Thanks, but we'll just stay where we are. You're welcome to come in, but I promise you a warm welcome. Oh, and I'm sure you'd rather not destroy the controls and computer for this station. That might make things dicey when the grav drives fail. Like what happened to your ship."

Hopefully, that was a lie, but Jared's silence worried her.

She terminated the conversation and turned to the marines. "Okay, we need a plan to get into that compartment without destroying everything. Ideas?"

Lieutenant Terry Evans eyed the hatch. "That looks pretty thick. We need to figure out how large the control center is and see if there are other ways in."

"That's a good place to start," she said. "Everyone spread out and find me a way in. I'll watch the hatch."

It only took them a few minutes to make the assessment and regroup.

"It's big," Evans said. "Maybe thirty meters across. This is the only entrance on this level."

"What about above it or below?"

He shook his head. "We'd have to breach it, and that'll still wreck almost everything in there when we come in shooting."

It doesn't have to.

She listened to the voice of the dead Marine Raider. *What are you thinking, Ned?*

If you set a plasma grenade on the lowest setting, it will probably breach the compartment. I'd suggest the ceiling. The odds of something important being that high are minimal. Once you gain access, you can toss a combat remote down the hole and jump in after it.

Kelsey shook her head. *I'd still trash the compartment with flechettes. If I go for stunners, they'll shoot it up resisting me. And me too, of course.*

They'll be somewhat disoriented from the breaching. To minimize damage, I suggest you use my swords. If the marines toss in smoke, the enemy will have difficulty even seeing you. Your implants will let you see them just fine, though.

I've never used those swords in combat. I'm pretty sure I wouldn't be very effective with them. You had years of practice and training.

I could use them for you, if you permit.

She considered the plan for a moment and slowly nodded. *I'll do it. Thanks. You have my permission to control my body during the upcoming combat until the fighting is over.*

"Okay," she said. "Here's the plan."

To say they all thought it was a bad idea was an understatement. "Suicide" was the word that Evans used.

So she put her foot down. "I think the odds are a little better than that. In the end, what choice do we have? Come on. We don't have any more time to waste."

She almost dragged a couple of reluctant marines up to the next level and estimated where the control center was under them. There were some empty compartments that might have been offices on a normal space station. Leave it to an AI to include them on a station that most likely never saw a permanent staff.

Kelsey picked the compartment that was best placed and got everyone ready. One marine would toss the reduced-strength plasma grenade, another would throw a combat remote into the breach, and the rest would follow up with smoke.

She drew her swords. "Go."

Even at reduced strength, the plasma grenade sounded like the end of the world. It blasted a hole in the deck bigger than the office. The marines followed up with the remote and smoke.

Her armor processed the signals and gave her a layout of the control center. It was big, all right, and full of people staggering around as though they were drunk and firing pistols at shadows.

No time to waste.

Kelsey jumped into the compartment and gave herself over to Ned Quincy.

It was very much like when she'd allowed what was to become Ned to control her the last time. Except this time there was a lot more blood. Arms and hands seemed to be the preferred targets to her swings, though there were a few thrusts. And screams. Lots of screams.

All in all, killing everyone in the compartment didn't prove necessary, thank God. Some people were unconscious, and others chose to surrender. Those with missing hands or arms had no choice but to stop fighting or die.

Less than thirty seconds after she jumped into the compartment, the fight was over, and Ned returned control of her body to her.

She really needed to start working with these swords so that she could do that for herself. She opened the hatch, and the marines rushed in, securing the compartment and the prisoners.

While they did that, Kelsey found an active control panel and accessed the station's scanners.

The battlecruiser was far below them. It seemed to be in the process of coming apart as it fell. *Persephone* was somewhat higher but also falling. She doubted it could go much lower and survive.

* * *

JARED HAD to take *Persephone* deeper than he'd have preferred, but the able Lieutenant Brand came up with a way to save the pinnace. She flew the ship under it and slowed their descent until the pinnace was safely on top of the ship.

The marines made their way to the nearest airlock, which was on a slope, so that made getting them in trickier than it would have been in space. Then they slowly rose up until they were back in the same clear atmospheric band as the station.

As soon as they became visible, Kelsey called the ship.

"Thank God!" she said. "We thought you were gone."

"No," he said, "though getting Talbot and his men off that ship was a hell of a lot more complicated than it should've been. What's your status?"

"We've secured the station. We have injured and wounded prisoners. The station computer is being unexpectedly cooperative. The prisoners never expected us to get into the control room so quickly. I found an open console with the command overrides already entered."

She smiled at him over the link. "This fight is over."

36

Twenty-four hours later, Jared was sitting back at Lord Hawthorne's estate with Kelsey at his side, Olivia West and Commander Meyer sat across from him, and Lord Hawthorne was making drinks.

The commander was a bit worse for wear. He sported an arm that had been broken twice in one day, three broken ribs, and a shattered knee, but he was in good spirits. Things could've been worse. He didn't die in a nuclear explosion, for example.

"Are we sure that there aren't any other little surprises scattered around the system?" Lord Hawthorne asked.

Jared shrugged. "We can't tell until we examine everything more closely, but why have a second station hidden when you have something like that one?"

Olivia nodded. "That fits with what we've been able to pull from Abigail and Lord Calder. Once we authorized the use of truth drugs, they spilled their secrets readily enough. Our forces raided their secret base—the one where their single pinnace came from—and we'll be going through their secrets for quite some time. The gas giant station was there as backup for the system AI, by the way. If things got bad, it would activate the extra ships.

"Your attack on Boxer Station was so sudden and overwhelming that it didn't have time to complete the activation. After you won, the station shut the battlecruisers back down when it never received final orders from the AI."

She sighed. "That illustrates how badly outclassed we'd have been if we'd have attacked it on our own. It would have destroyed us. Thank you."

"Yet here you are," Kelsey said, "in undisputed control of this planet.

With the loyalists on the run, you can consolidate your gains. And now that Doctor Leonard has repaired the malfunctioning flip jammer, we're not in deadly danger of the computer-controlled destroyers overrunning us.

"Speaking of which, he could use some help repairing the third one that was damaged in the original fight. We'd like to block Erorsi and Pentagar off from the Rebel Empire. In fact, it would be very useful if we could make more of those."

Lord Hawthorne grimaced. "We can probably repair the one unit, but we won't be building more very quickly. It took years to construct the ones we have. It requires incredibly fine tolerances in the parts and a host of rare materials. We anticipated expanding the construction later. So, no, we don't have any spares laying around. That third one is actually meant to be a spare."

"Pity," Jared said. "Still, we have time. We also can't count on that device being a panacea. Anything man can build, he can circumvent. We have to plan on that happening and not rely on being safe forever.

"We'll move the spare to Erorsi, and we'll just have to take some calculated risks when we take them offline for maintenance. We'll need the parts and manuals, of course."

The nobleman nodded. "I'll get them for you tomorrow."

"We've made arrangements for a cutter to bring the bodies we found on *Invincible* down tomorrow, too," Kelsey told Olivia. "I know they were your comrades, and they deserve to finally come home."

He could see the coordinator's eyes growing damp.

"Thank you. That means a lot to me." Olivia cleared her throat. "What do we do next? Obviously, freeing the rest of the Empire won't happen overnight, but that has to be our goal. We fix the ships we can and make our plans going forward.

"Well, so long as that's what the emperor says. We're under your authority when it comes to things like that."

"Don't you already have a lot to do here?" Sean asked. "Rescue operations and recovery from the nuclear explosions will take years. Suppressing the loyalists and keeping them from other mischief will take even longer."

"That's a good point," Kelsey said, "but we need to be working toward that goal. Here's what I propose. Our ships will need weeks of repairs. Perhaps months. That gives us time to help get things in motion.

"We'll get the shipyard at Boxer Station back online and reactivate the asteroid mines. Raw materials and finished parts will be key to getting the repairs of the derelict vessels under way. I'm more than happy to share those responsibilities with Harrison's World, with the understanding that Fleet needs to keep the system and the ships locked down. We've all seen what a few unpleasant surprises look like when they threaten to put the AIs back in control."

That brought immediate nods from everyone.

"On behalf of Harrison's World," Olivia said, "I can say we have no desire to rush things. And I don't care who overthrows the AIs, so long as it's done."

There was nothing like a near-death experience or two to get people cooperating, Jared thought. "So, we'll need to leave some people here when we go back to Avalon. Specifically, we need a senior Fleet officer to command Boxer Station."

Kelsey nodded her agreement. "I realize you have Captain Black, but he's going to have his hands full. And until I know you better, I want someone I know to be in charge."

She turned to Commander Meyer and pointed her finger at him. "Poof, you're a Commodore. Welcome to command of Boxer Station and the system space of Harrison's World."

Jared enjoyed how the newly promoted officer's eyes bugged out. It was nice to watch his sister roll over someone else for a change.

"Wait a minute!" the flabbergasted officer said. "I'm not even cleared for duty. I was relieved and charged with a whole host of crimes."

"I hereby dismiss those charges," Jared said. "The doctors will get you cleared for duty long before we're ready to go. You'll be able to get your implants done, too.

"I'll solve one of my headaches by leaving you the senior officers from *Spear* and *Shadow*. You know them best, and they won't have problems working for you. And, of course, plenty of men and women to fill out your work rosters."

Jared turned to Olivia while Meyer mentally floundered around. "Once we're certain we have all the data we can get off the system AI, we'll wipe it and rebuild the personality with uncorrupted code. It will be able to run the station and probably increase the efficiency of the construction bays in getting our ships fixed."

"I'm sure Captain Black would like a look at both the hardware and software before you do that," she said. "At some point, we may want to build more. To fight the AIs, we might need some of our own."

"Speaking of parity," Kelsey said, "I need to bring up a touchy subject. I haven't been here long, but I can see that the Rebel Empire has a well-defined caste system. That comes from the AIs, and it has to go. The built-in discrimination has to stop."

Lord Hawthorne sighed. "We know. Changing it wasn't an option before you came. Having met you has brought just how deeply ingrained it is into stark relief. We'll lean heavily on Commodore Meyer and his people to point out where we need to change and take steps. It can start with universal implants."

Olivia nodded vigorously. "First, we need to start getting people's existing implants updated before they learn what's really going on and the AI code makes them start fighting us. Then we *will* begin making civilian implants available to everyone."

"The senior military officers come first," Lord Hawthorne agreed. "Then the other council members. As we clear the top people, they'll smooth the way for doing their subordinates. By the time you're ready to return home, we should be secure. Other than Captain Black, only the people in this room know your secret."

"Then we can begin the process of making implants universally available," Olivia said. "The plans for the normal civilian models are in the computer at the Grant Research Facility. We can get production lines set up for both versions. We can have spare equipment built for you by the time your ships are ready to travel.

"We also examined the small, computer-controlled weapons platforms. They were definitely built by human beings, but not on Harrison's World."

"We actually found the construction facility," Jared said. "It's on Boxer Station. It looks as though the AI forced the Fleet engineering people to design and build them for it. Thankfully, it wasn't automated, or there might have been even more of the damned things. That said, I'm considering how we might be able to use something like them in the future. I *hate* losing marines. A wave of these up front might save a lot of lives. I'll see that you get plans for them, too."

"What about the Raider implants and equipment?" Kelsey asked. "Can Grant build those?"

"Maybe," Olivia said. "Now that you have the full specs, it's at least possible. They'd certainly help make a difference with the Marines. That's something to talk with Captain Black about. He's already made a lot of progress in mass-production of civilian-grade medical nanites. He expects to have Fleet grade ones very soon."

"Are those the same as what I have?"

Olivia shook her head. "No. He's already found the ones used by the Raiders are significantly more advanced. More powerful and more capable. Those will take more study."

"Ned tells me they were fairly new in his time," Kelsey said. "Top-of-the-line gear."

"Captain Black thought so, too. He's adjusting the process and may very well have something worked out by the time you're ready to depart.

"Speaking of departing, when you go, I'd like to send William with you as our representative to the Imperial Senate and the head of our delegation."

Kelsey looked around, satisfied. "That sounds perfect. We don't have a crisis in sight. I'm seeing smooth sailing all the way home!"

Jared wished he shared her optimism. If the last year had been anything to go by, something else would come out of nowhere to bite them in the ass. And, of course, he'd have to deal with the fallout of what they'd done and with his homicidal half brother that was certain he was out to steal the Throne.

Well, that trouble was for another day. He stood, refilled his glass, and then topped off everyone else.

"Everyone," he said solemnly, "I give you the Empire. May she triumph over her enemies."

The rest of them climbed to their feet and raised their glasses.

PAYING THE PRICE

BOOK FIVE

Admiral Jared Mertz returns to the New Terran Empire a conquering hero. But not everyone cheers his success.

Crown Prince Ethan Bandar tried to kill Jared once. Paranoia and ambition demands he succeed this time.

Only Jared's sister and their battle-hardened allies stand between him and death.

1

"Admiral, do you have a few minutes?"

Jared Mertz looked up groggily from his lunch in the officers' mess to find Doctor Jerry Leonard standing beside his table. The fog of exhaustion that hung over him had dulled his edge. It seemed like a year since he'd slept a full night.

He gestured for the scientist to join him. "Pull up a chair and order something to eat."

The older man sat down primly. "I had something in the lab an hour ago, but thank you. I'd like to take one more try at traversing the weak flip point before we pull out."

The strange variants of the standard flip points were new to all of them, and the scientists were still struggling to understand them. Some only allowed one-way passage. Others were just as hard to find, but two-way. They knew so little about the new stellar phenomena.

The one in the Harrison's World system had eaten every probe they'd sent through it. Not one had returned. Not even when programmed to return as soon as the flip capacitor recharged.

Of course, no enemy had followed them home, so that was good news. Jared thought whatever was happening to them probably natural. Perhaps this flip point was one-way for even the smallest of vessels.

"The fleet is performing the final checks before we leave for Pentagar," Jared said. "We're on a tight schedule."

"This won't take long. We've devised a new probe. Well, actually, we built one that looks like Frankenstein's monster. The core is a standard probe, but we added an external battle screen generator and bolted on the power system from one of the defunct war machines. We even added a second flip capacitor to speed its return.

"If the environment on the other side of the flip point is hostile—which at this point seems a given—that should allow it time to return with some readings. We'd like your permission to send it through."

Jared shrugged. "Why not? Let me wrap up my lunch, and I'll join you on the flag bridge. Say fifteen minutes?"

The scientist beamed. "Thank you, Admiral."

Jared finished his meal and returned to the bustling flag bridge. Over the last few months, he'd selected a full-time staff of officers to assist him in overseeing the fleet he'd assembled. They sat at their stations all around the circumference of the large control center, monitoring the preparations for departure.

No one called out when he entered the bridge. That had been one tradition he was happy to dispense with. Everyone had work to do. They didn't need to stop what they were doing just because he'd walked off the lift.

He sat at his console. It swept a full 270 degrees around his command chair, giving him the ability to multitask like nobody's business. It had taken him months to get fully accustomed to it, but now he was thrilled at how much data he could keep track of at once.

Jared pulled a headset from the niche in his console and slipped it on. His implants could interface without it, but the headset allowed for much greater data throughput. When linked to his flagship, he could access anything at lightning speed and in tremendous detail.

Part of his attention went to the scanner readings. The superdreadnought *Invincible* floated in a wide orbit around Boxer Station. They'd captured the Old Empire Fleet base from the Rebel Empire AI that had once ruled this system.

The rest went to the fleet he was taking back home. It consisted of his superdreadnought, a Fleet carrier, six battlecruisers, eight heavy cruisers, twelve light cruisers, and two dozen destroyers. It also had ten colliers with extra missiles and supplies, six Marine troop transports, sixteen fast couriers built for speed, twelve scouts built for stealth, a dedicated science vessel, two hospital ships, four factory ships, *New York*, and *Persephone*.

The factory ships would be particularly useful back home. They had all the tools needed to make the high technology items they'd need, like the cranial implants. They couldn't make the Marine Raider equipment because *Persephone* didn't have the details on the manufacture. That had been one of the Old Empire's most closely guarded secrets.

Once they figured out how to manufacture the Raider hardware, he suspected they'd have a crash course in bringing as many marines up to those specs as possible. They'd have to impose some stringent psych exams to keep that kind of power out of the wrong hands.

Those factories could also duplicate themselves. With more manufacturing capability, they could build advanced shipyards and simultaneously lift themselves up to Old Empire tech levels. Arguably, they were the most important ships in the fleet he'd gathered. Two just like them would go back to Erorsi and Pentagar with his compliments.

It would take a lot of reverse engineering or recovering the plans at some future point, but the factory ships could probably also build new AI hardware. The Empire would need additional sentient AIs on their side for the coming fight. Though, he admitted it would probably take the emperor a while to come around to that point of view.

All the ships were severely undermanned and only functional at the most basic level. Not even Boxer Station's construction bays could perform miracles. They took in battered wrecks and repaired the critical systems. The rest would need to happen by hand, because there was an almost unending line of derelicts waiting their turn.

They'd brought more people in from Pentagar and Erorsi, but that barely made a dent in their needs. They'd even begun careful, limited recruiting from Harrison's World. They had to be certain those people were trustworthy before they told them the truth about the Rebel Empire.

After a lot of thought, Kelsey had decided that the people there had to know the truth. They couldn't just hide it from them. That was wrong, and the truth would get out. That would be damaging. They had to stay on the moral high ground.

Plans were in development to roll out the knowledge once they were sure they had the existing implants scrubbed of the viral code. There would be resistance, but that was natural. They'd be upsetting the existing layers of society.

They'd be giving the lower orders implants and medical nanites. The higher orders, used to being the lords of all they surveyed, would scream bloody murder. They'd deal with it. Learn from it. This process would eventually play out in many other systems, so they had to refine the process while they could.

In the end, everyone would be better for it. The hard part was convincing them of that. Kelsey had recorded a number of speeches that the leadership could play when the time was right. Jared hoped they'd help explain the situation and keep the inevitable violence to a minimum.

Back to his current situation. Even understrength, the ships he'd gathered represented more fighting power than the rest of the New Terran Empire. Hell, *Invincible* alone could conquer his nation. The rest was overkill.

They also had thirteen Fleet transports for cargo and an upgraded cruise liner to carry civilians. *Best Deal*, the freighter that had housed their scientists, was far too slow to keep up. They'd be leaving her here.

Captain Anton Keller, *Best Deal's* civilian skipper, was thrilled with the larger and much faster ship Jared had given him. It had military grade defenses, systems, and engines. It also carried many times more cargo than his old ship. He'd lost no time renaming her *Best Deal II*. The original one would go to Erorsi to help rebuild the system.

They'd even found a luxurious yacht to take home as a gift for the emperor. The current Imperial yacht was a fine vessel, but this one was much faster, had real defenses, and was armed. Jared was sure Karl Bandar would like it.

They'd done a few modifications to *New York* as well. They'd added battle screen generators and a second set of flip capacitors. The Old Empire versions of the capacitors were small enough to fit beside the current ones in engineering. They'd had to stash the battle screen controls in a conference room, but Captain Kaiser was happy to have the extra protection.

Jared had arrived with a small, old destroyer and a slow freighter converted to do science. He was going home with more than a hundred ships. Even with the surviving officers and men from *Spear*, *Shadow*, and *Ginnie Dare* helping to fill needed roles—both on his fleet and on Boxer Station—that left them with few Imperial personnel. Wallace had lost the light cruiser *Titan* and the destroyer *One Bullet* with all hands.

He'd robbed the destroyer *New York* as much as he could, but Captain Kaiser needed her core team. Her ship didn't have the same level of automation as the Old Empire ships. He'd considered leaving *New York* here, but he knew the woman would refuse that order, and Fleet Command wouldn't be happy, either.

Jared had insisted that everyone get Fleet implants. That way they could work on any ship, if required.

It amazed Jared that they'd been able to repair so many badly damaged ships in such a short time.

This wouldn't have been possible without the oversight of the AI on Boxer Station. Carl Owlet had used clean code to make a new personality for it that would be loyal to humanity and the Empire. It was able to juggle repairing multiple ships much better than a human team could have.

That was possible because the AIs were truly sentient. That was the last big shock the New Terran Empire would have to accept, and Jared had made it hard to ignore.

With the desperate need for command personnel, he'd reassigned Zia Anderson to command the Fleet carrier *Audacious*. He'd considered his original executive officer, Charlie Graves, but Zia was the more aggressive of the two. Besides, Charlie was completely happy commanding *Courageous*.

Zia's previous slot as his flag captain went to *Invincible* herself. Or rather the AI that resided inside her. The AI knew the ship better than anyone else possibly could. Kelsey had made an Imperial ruling that the AIs were people and so entitled to give oaths of service.

Invincible's AI, who'd decided to take the name Marcus, now had a commission as a Fleet captain. Boxer Station's AI—which had chosen the name Harrison—had one as well. That would give Fleet Command apoplexy and cause the Imperial Senate to implode.

The crew had been a little spooked to have an all-seeing captain, but they were adjusting. They'd even found a crash test dummy somewhere, made it a uniform, and strapped it into the command chair on the bridge so they'd have someone to look at when reporting.

Marcus used the speaker in the chair, and he didn't use what he heard or saw in his oversight of the public areas of the ship in his captain persona. He kept it segregated, and the crew knew how the subroutines maintained their privacy. It was working surprisingly well.

With the three flip-point jammers the scientists at the Grant Research Facility had built, they could lock down Harrison's World, Pentagar, and Erorsi from Rebel Empire incursions. Except for when they needed to perform maintenance on them.

That didn't account for the weak flip points, though. They'd have to be very careful using them.

Commodore Sean Meyer had two battlecruisers, four heavy cruisers, and six destroyers to guard Harrison's World. He'd work hand in hand with Coordinator Olivia West to ease the planet into the New Terran Empire without letting most of the people know about the change in management.

Someday, the general population would learn the truth. Just not right now.

Pentagar was getting a number of ships, as well. They'd watch over the base on Erorsi, too, until more ships arrived. Since Jared was taking a long, unexplored path home, they'd only accompany him partway.

By his best guess, it would take another six months to finish the final repairs on all the ships in his fleet. It would take even longer to get them fully manned with trained, enhanced personnel. He shuddered to think about how long it would take to work through the remaining tens of thousands of derelicts.

They'd brought the mines in the asteroid belt back online, reestablished the automated fabrication units, and now had a mobile station to disassemble ships too badly wrecked to fly again. They called it the breaker. It salvaged what parts it could and melted the rest down. The critical and rare elements went into new parts.

The crew there also pulled the dead from the wrecks and sealed them in body bags. If the medical teams could reactivate the person's implants, they made note of their names and copied the data stored in implant memory.

The cargo holds on several of the transports held the tens of thousands of bodies they'd recovered so far. Fleet was going to have to come up with a new means of burying their honored dead. The Spire couldn't hold the many millions of corpses in these ships.

The lift doors slid open and Doctor Leonard walked onto the flag bridge. Kelsey was with him.

She smiled at Jared. "I hear we're about to go exploring."

* * *

KELSEY EYED her brother critically from behind her cheerful expression. He looked exhausted. That was understandable. He'd been putting in twenty-hour days for the last nine months.

His implants and medical nanites reduced his need for sleep, but there were limits. Four hours a night wasn't enough. Not over that long a timeframe.

She'd tried to put her foot down and discovered there were some things she couldn't order him to do. She shuddered to think about how he'd have been without teams of people working behind the scenes to take tasks off his plate.

Maybe once they started back toward Avalon he'd get some rest.

"I don't think exploring is quite the right word," Jared said. "We're only sending a probe. Another probe, actually. This makes what? Eight?"

"Nine," Doctor Leonard said. "Perhaps we'll get this one back. If not, we'll have to ponder over what we missed on the long trip home."

"We're leaving on time," Jared said sternly. "You have sixteen hours. Any more than that and you're out of luck."

"I'm quite certain we won't need that long," Doctor Leonard said. "This will either work or it won't. I took the liberty of sending the probe out earlier today. A second probe will monitor this side for us. We can signal it whenever you're ready."

Kelsey linked her implants to *Invincible*'s scanners. The weak flip point was only fifteen light minutes away. She saw the system layout in her mind and noted the delayed readings from the probes.

She had been working hard over the last few months and had mastered the basic operation of her Raider implants. She could now process data as quickly as it came in. Using the processors in her head to spin off tasks was becoming second nature. She'd even gotten used to the ghostly voice of Ned Quincy in her mind.

Mostly.

Thankfully, he didn't seem inclined to speak much unless she spoke to him first. Once she had time, she was going to have to figure out how to move him somewhere else, if they could figure out how. Perhaps he could be of use on *Persephone*, like Marcus was on *Invincible*. He wasn't nearly as complex, but he seemed to be a sentient AI.

"Send the go signal, Marcus," Jared said.

Kelsey felt the transmission leave the ship.

"Command sent, Admiral," the AI said. "It's programmed to make the trip and immediately return. We'll know in half an hour if it was successful."

She leaned up against Jared's console. "While we wait, I have a few things to run by you."

They talked about last-minute loading details until her implant timer indicated the probe would have made the transit and the data was about to arrive at their location. She could see Doctor Leonard was busy reading the full data stream from the probe staying in the Harrison's World system, but it made no sense to her. It was focused on the flip point and too technical.

The first probe vanished… and reappeared a few seconds later. It immediately indicated it was in distress. The battle screen had failed, and many of the systems were offline.

"What the hell happened to it?" she asked. "Was it fired on?"

"I'm getting the scanner recording now," Marcus said. "I'm forwarding it to you."

The view from the probe was of deep space. It saw the weak flip point in its scanners. When the signal came across to flip, it did so.

Intense radiation bombarded it from every angle on the other side. The battle screen held up almost as long as it took the flip drive to cycle and take the probe back to their side.

The view of the system beyond the flip point was indistinct. It was as though space was foggy.

"What the hell was that?" Jared asked.

"I believe I understand," Doctor Leonard said as he stepped up beside Jared's console. "The other system's sun has gone nova. The destination side is far too close to either a neutron star or perhaps even a black hole for the probes to survive more than a few moments."

Kelsey shook her head. "Well, that certainly explains why none of them came back. It means we're not going over there, either."

"Actually, that's not a given," Marcus said. "I've analyzed the strength of the radiation, and a ship's battle screens are capable of protecting it. Only the probe's lack of power caused its premature failure."

"Admiral, might I mention that this is an unprecedented opportunity to study such a phenomenon?" Doctor Leonard asked. "We have no records of anything like this in the Old Empire databases, and we might not be back this way again anytime soon. Might we use one of your ships for a few hours? Other than the natural dangers, the system probably doesn't pose any additional risk."

Her brother looked between the scientist and Kelsey. "Okay, but only if you make the trip on *Persephone*. Her scanners are more than capable of getting you the data you need. You only have half a day. We're leaving on schedule. I'm serious."

Kelsey was more than a bit surprised Jared was allowing her to go. He must be even more exhausted than he looked. Still, it sounded interesting.

"We can do that," she said. "Doctor, what are the chances you can detect other flip points in that system?"

"Slim, but not impossible," he ventured. "Weak flip points are out of the question. We'll be able to find the one linking to Harrison's World again because we know precisely where it is, but the chaotic environment there will overshadow any others.

"We can use the ship's scanners to locate gravimetric anomalies like planets and regular flip points, though. If they aren't too far away from us, that is."

She grinned. "Well then, what are we waiting for? We have a supernova to explore!"

2

"Is that thing safe?"

Carl Owlet looked over at Fleet Captain Aaron Black. "It should be. Why?"

"It could go right through you—and the wall behind you—if it malfunctions. You don't have Princess Kelsey's strength. Hell, I'm not even sure *that* would be enough if it went rogue."

The graduate student gave the Fleet officer a suitably unimpressed expression. "Don't be ridiculous, Captain. Everything will be perfectly fine."

"Famous last words," the other man said. "I'll just watch from behind this handy blast shield."

The two of them were down in one of the ranges used for testing weapons inside the Grant Research Facility. It had plenty of protection for observers and the labs around it. If it could handle plasma weapons, Carl thought it should be safe enough.

Probably.

He took a deep breath and tried to put the worries Black had raised out of his mind. Yes, he only had normal human strength. Well, maybe a little less. He was only seventeen and a bit on the scrawny side.

His latest creation sat on the table in front of him, looking like the prop from an old play. He'd taken some artistic license with it, admittedly. That old pre-Empire vid Kelsey had insisted he watch had influenced both his stylistic choices and some of the programming he'd designed for it.

As a weapon, it looked... short, but that was kind of the point. Thor's hammer was a unique sort of thing.

After she'd raved about the rather primitive special effects and acting in the vid, he'd sat bolt upright that night with the idea fully formed in his head. It was straightforward engineering using the newly discovered grav technology from the mobile weapon systems the AI had been using.

Since it had both power generation and grav capability all wrapped up in one package, the real challenge had been making a shell that could protect the controls and designing the programming to make it work.

That had taken four months of robbing his sleep cycle to solve. An hour or two stolen between working like a dog to get the new ships up and running. He couldn't complain, though. Everyone had put in the same amount of hard work, and it was about to pay off in a big way.

Captain Black had come into this project late. While Carl could design the parts, he wanted someone with experience in robust weapon systems to do the final construction.

The staff here had really come through. He'd never have thought of some of the things they included as a matter of course. Some of the design changes they suggested were brilliant. They had access to the highest technology of the Old Empire, and they'd been working with it their entire lives. He had a lot of work to do just to get into their league.

They'd created a custom shell for the hammer that was both a stunning replica of the weapon from the vid and virtually indestructible.

The Old Empire had been working with some very cutting-edge hull metals using partially collapsed matter. While nowhere in the same neighborhood as something like neutronium, it still weighed a wickedly large amount. Without the built-in grav generator, he'd never be able to pick the hammer up.

With the grav generator working to keep it stationary, not even a Marine Raider could move it if the wielder didn't want them to. That also fit with the myth behind the vid.

That left the control functions. A normal set of Fleet implants could only work within fifteen meters. That's why the Old Empire had used headsets to amplify them.

He'd solved that by learning how the headsets worked and building an additional transmitter they could add to an existing set of implants. Since it was going to go inside a person, he'd spent a great deal of time ironing the bugs out. It had to be perfect.

Then Captain Black's people had gone over every aspect of it and suggested a number of modifications. That only proved to Carl that he still needed a lot of polish, even though they were uniformly complimentary of his work, calling it groundbreaking.

Once he was done with this project, he'd submit the long-range communicator to Admiral Mertz. He'd already worked up a modification to add it to the basic implant set for future recipients. Those would give someone the range of a headset. They could even give it to people that already had implants with an outpatient procedure.

Still, that wasn't enough range to control the hammer in combat, so he'd created one with even more range for Princess Kelsey. Rather than present her with an untested device, he'd had Doctor Stone implant it inside himself. It was too large for the cranium, so it went behind his lungs. He'd figured it wouldn't interfere with anything there and Doctor Stone agreed.

The matching equipment in the hammer linked and communicated with the wielder via a channel so heavily encrypted that he doubted even he could hack it without his personal knowledge of the algorithms. Good luck to the outsider that wanted to tap in.

Avoiding jamming was ridiculously simple, in theory. The actual hardware and new scientific theory was a lot more complicated. The execution was fiendishly difficult, and he'd had to create an entirely new branch of science to make it work. Well, expand one that existed into something that was actually useful, rather. That had taken the last two months to get working.

Everyone knew about Einstein's pre-Imperial work. Pre-spaceflight, really. Specifically, spooky action at a distance. Quantum entanglement of photons so that changes in spin replicated on the linked pair without regard to distance or transmission time.

A curious scientific oddity. Nothing had ever been created that could successfully harness the effect in a meaningful way. He'd torn up the databases at the research facility and a few separate projects had smashed together in another dream. The work on that had been so intense that he'd once yelled at Doctor Leonard for interrupting him.

He'd been mortified later, but the older scientist had just beamed at him. He'd acted as though Carl had passed some kind of test.

Older people were weird.

The quantum validation unit worked in tandem with the long-range communicator. It used an expected sequence of photon spin changes to validate the commands. Someone might tap into the encrypted communications frequency, he supposed, but they wouldn't even be able to know there was a second signal required to validate any instructions.

It also kept the two units linked. The hammer and wielder would always know where the other was, within the range of the quantum unit. Whatever that ended up being.

Now that he'd brought it all together in this device, it was time to see if it actually worked. He'd test the range later.

Quantum theory said it was unlimited, but nature didn't behave that way. Even flip points had limits. There would be a maximum useful range. He just hoped it was enough to prove workable with Mjölnir.

He linked his implants to the hammer and hefted it. With the grav assist, it seemed light enough. It would collapse the table if he turned that off.

The target was a set of the Old Empire marine armor on a stand at the other end of the room. It looked imposing as hell. Part of him expected the hammer to bounce off, leaving him looking like an idiot.

"I'm ready," he said after taking a deep breath.

"The recorders are on," Black said. "You're clear to go. I have a med team standing by. Just in case."

"Thanks for the confidence booster," Carl said in the same dry voice he'd been practicing after hearing how good it sounded on Admiral Mertz.

The hammer had a strap to wrap around the wrist, but this wasn't the time to use it. He drew the weapon back and awkwardly threw it while designating the armor as its target. It left his hand and flew toward the armor at maximum speed.

In retrospect, that was a rookie mistake.

The hammer brought up its miniature battle screen, broke the sound barrier just in front of Carl, and blasted into the armor with the force of a speeding pinnace.

It blew through the chest of the armor as though it were tissue paper. The reinforced plascrete behind the target faired just as poorly. Carl had a clear view of the room next door as the hammer screamed around in a tight turn and howled back toward him, generating two more sonic booms right together as it reversed course.

The first blast had deafened him, even with the protection of his implants, and blown him into the wall. It thoughtfully slammed the table on top of him. He'd ended up sitting with his back to the wall as the hammer arrowed toward him like a freight train.

He had just a moment to get his hand up, and the hammer abruptly slowed, creating a fourth sonic boom that almost knocked him unconscious. The handle slapped into his hand as gently as one could ask for.

Carl lay there, stunned, staring at the hammer and at the devastation it had wreaked on the range and the surrounding labs.

He couldn't hear Captain Black shouting for the medical teams, but he saw them rushing in with their trauma gear and expressions that told him he looked pretty bad.

"I think I might need to tweak a few settings before I present it to Princess Kelsey," he said faintly as they surrounded him.

* * *

CROWN PRINCESS ELISE ORISON stood beside Admiral Walter Sanders on the bridge of His Majesty's battlecruiser *New Wales*. It was identical in every respect to Jared's old ship, *Courageous*, and it was all theirs.

There was still a lot to do in refitting her, but this ship represented more power than the rest of the Royal Pentagaran Navy combined.

She could see the pride in Walter's expression. He was very pleased with this as his new flagship. At least until Boxer Station completed basic repairs on the superdreadnought *Great Britain*.

"Well, Admiral," she said. "The time has come for me to say my goodbyes. You'll be on your way back to Pentagar shortly, so my cutter will take me to *Invincible*. I'm going to miss having you around."

The older man smiled. "Not so much, I'll wager, Your Highness. You want more time alone with Admiral Mertz, and I'm too much like a chaperone."

She grinned. "You've found me out. Well, it's not as though I've let that stop me so far. He and I *are* sharing quarters, you know."

"What a scandal that would be, if word ever leaked back home. The heir to the Pentagaran crown shacking up with some foreigner."

She cocked her head. "Shacking up? Have you been watching those old movies Kelsey favors again?"

"Every chance I get," he admitted. "Princess Kelsey says the twenty-first century was some kind of touchstone to the Old Empire. They supposedly enshrined it in a kind of collective consciousness.

"She attributed a Captain Jack Harkness in saying that was when everything changed. I suppose it's a reference to that being the last truly common sense of humanity before they went interstellar and forged their own societies. Perhaps that explains some of her madness for the era, and that of a number of other people.

"In any case, Jared is a fine man. I'd rather not see either of you hurt."

"Why should I hurt him?"

"You shouldn't," the old admiral said gruffly. "But, you need to keep in mind who you are. You'll inherit the Throne one day. He's a serving officer in a foreign navy. Do you have a future together?"

She'd been pondering that question for a while. She loved Jared, but her duty was clear. That wasn't going to be an easy decision to make. Give up her soulmate or her people. A stark choice indeed.

"We're both aware of what lies ahead of us," she said gravely. "I'm hopeful this trip will settle it for us."

She checked her internal chronometer. She'd never get used to the capabilities of her new implants. It had been nine months, and she still wondered how Kelsey did it.

"I need to be on my way. I promise I'll uphold the dignity of the Pentagaran people. Be safe, Admiral."

"Screw dignity, Elise. Do what's right for you, and damn anyone who lifts their nose."

"Now there's some advice I can surely follow," she said with a laugh.

* * *

Marine Major Angela Ellis stared at the destruction with wide eyes. "One little guy did all this? The kid from the science department? Seriously?"

"You have no idea, Major," Fleet Captain Black said. "You're selling him short. Way short. My people tell me the work he did on this project is breathtaking."

She nodded as she walked over to look through the hole in the plascrete wall. It was three meters across. "So I see. Breathtakingly stupid and he wants to give this thing to Princess Kelsey. Not happening."

The Fleet officer smiled. "Even the commander of her personal protective detail might find that difficult to enforce."

Nine months ago, she'd commanded the destroyer *Ginnie Dare*'s marine complement. With the loss of her ship and far too many of her people, they'd assigned her to keep an eye on Princess Kelsey. Which was more of a challenge than it sometimes appeared. Even with a double squad of men and women working diligently to make it happen.

Such as when Kelsey took off through an unexplored weak flip point without summoning Angela back to the ship.

"What did this?" she asked, gesturing toward the shattered armor and ruptured wall.

He pointed to an innocuous hammer on the floor. It sat handle up, as though someone had just set it down.

"That. He threw it at the suit of marine armor you see scattered around the chamber. The recorders say the hammer broke the sound barrier less than five meters in front of him. It reached Mach 7 before it hit the armor. It was still accelerating. Don't ask me what its top speed is. I have no idea.

"It wrecked the lab on the other side of the wall with a double sonic boom when it reversed course. He ate a table and took another sonic boom when it decelerated on the way back. Even behind a blast shield, four sonic booms all on top of each other felt like being on hand for the apocalypse."

She bent down and grasped the handle. The hammer didn't even twitch. Not even when she put her back into it.

"Jesus. How much does this thing weigh?"

"Somewhere in the ballpark of three tons. Imagine that with the full power of a grav generator pushing it to that kind of speed."

She tried and failed. "That makes the anti-vehicle weapons we have look like a kid's popgun. Even the new plasma ones."

Black righted the table and sat on its corner. "My chief of weapons design locked himself in his office right after Carl wrecked his lab. He has this idea for a new set of implant-controlled ground assault weapons. Something with 'real heft,' he said."

"Jesus." She ran her hand through her hair. "This kid is a menace. Why haven't your people made something like this before?"

"Because we didn't put everything together. Even if we had, we couldn't have solved the communications issues. Mister Owlet came up with the theories needed for these breakthroughs in days, though it took months to create working prototypes. You call him a kid, but that's not what I see when I look at him."

She sat down beside the Fleet officer. "What do you see?"

"You can never tell him this, but he's the kind of man who redefines the course of entire civilizations. Like Einstein on old Terra. The man was such a giant that his shadow still falls across us today. People might mention him and Carl Owlet in the same breath one day, too. Assuming, of course, that he doesn't kill himself before then."

Angela felt an expression of disbelief steal onto her face. "You're kidding me. I've met the kid. He's not all that."

"Forgive my saying so, but you couldn't be more wrong if you tried,

Major." His voice had gone hard. She felt her spine reflexively straighten. When a Fleet captain used that tone, you'd screwed up big-time.

Black waved his hand, dissipating the cloud of tension. "Sorry. I just don't think you can see the forest for the trees. I work with geniuses every day. Everything from the quiet, brilliant men and women to the screaming and shouting prima donnas that throw things when they don't get their way. That kid is brighter than all of them.

"The best minds in this research facility simultaneously worship and hate him. Once he gains the experience of age, I expect he'll probe the very secrets of the universe. With medical nanites pushing our lifespans to centuries, the mind boggles."

She shook her head. "We *can't* be talking about the same person. He's not old enough to drink. Hell, he couldn't get a date if he tried."

The Fleet captain smiled. "I expect that will change with time. Meanwhile, we're going to rebuild this room with a lot more protection. I imagine he'll also put some more stringent limits into the hammer when the medics release him."

"What's his condition?"

"Shattered eardrums and a concussion. A few scrapes and bruises. He got off light. We both did."

She felt her lips tighten. "He won't feel that way once I get ahold of him. If he thinks he's giving that damned hammer to the princess, he's got another think coming."

Black laughed. "Good luck with that. The boy has spine."

3

K elsey guided *Persephone* deeper into the radiation-filled void of the new star system with a hint of disappointment. She'd expected there to be more excitement running around the remnants of a supernova.

Instead, she could barely see anything. The intense radiation made a hash of scanner readings in a ridiculously short distance.

That wasn't stopping Doctor Leonard from chortling over whatever it was he was seeing.

She'd tried sampling the data feed, but didn't have the background to understand it.

"Captain," Lieutenant Jack Thompson said, turning away from the helm console. "I think we're closing in on a large planet. The ship is veering slightly off course."

She leaned forward and looked through the ship's scanners. Other than seeing the course deviation, she wasn't getting anything. Not even on optical. Frankly, they weren't really even sure of how close they were to whatever was left of the sun.

Kelsey frowned and did some comparisons in her head. "I'm not sure it's a planet. That might be the star remnant or the black hole. We should try to triangulate it. Take us on a divergent course, and tell me how far away that thing is."

"Aye, ma'am."

She returned her attention to Doctor Leonard. "Can you give me an update? We might have found the central body in this system."

He looked up from his borrowed console, blinking owlishly. "What? Of course you have. I spotted it five minutes ago."

Kelsey restrained her initial response. "Don't you think you should share little details like that, Doctor? We're flying blind here."

"Ah. Forgive me. The gravity pull you're seeing is coming from the central object in the system. A black hole, I suspect, based on the type of radiation we're seeing and the amount of stellar matter we're flying through."

"Why so?"

"If the sun were still intact, its solar wind would've pushed all these energetic particles clear. We'd see a starkly bright object where the sun once was. A star without its mantle of gas would be unmistakable.

"Since we're not seeing anything like that, it must be because the solar mass collapsed into a black hole and it's drawing the remaining stellar matter inward without the corresponding push of the solar wind."

That made her sit up. "We're not in danger of falling into it, are we?"

"Oh, no. We're still quite distant. The space around it will clear to some degree as we get closer. We won't see it optically, of course, but we should have an unparalleled view of the event horizon. Which we also won't see directly."

"You make it all sound so exciting. We should have Christmas cards made."

Doctor Leonard smiled. "That's clever. Indeed, we should. What we *will* see shortly is the accretion disk. It's spinning around the black hole and generating the radiation ahead of us. I imagine it will be quite spectacular."

He returned to his data, and she had the ship move back into a course that would take them closer to the black hole. Slowly.

Space cleared until they could see the vast emptiness that was the central system. The titanic blast had vaporized the inner planets, leaving only husks to circle what might have once been a life-giving star.

The charged particles hid any gas giants in the outer system from view. The nova would have stripped them of their atmospheres, but their cores should be mostly intact. She imagined they would be very educational to the scientists.

In the place of honor was a spinning disk of glowing dust. It was very beautiful, and quite deadly, if the radiation levels were to be believed. As they grew closer, those kept going up. At some point, the radiation would be a threat even with their battle screens.

"That's it," Doctor Leonard said. "The black hole at the center of the system." He turned to face her. "It's so powerful that even light cannot escape its clutches. The ultimate prison. Well, technically, the matter inside eventually evaporates, but I'll stand with my analogy."

"If we can't get close, how are you going to get more data?"

"I believe we can get excellent readings from a safe distance. We'll have to devise dedicated probes the size of cutters to get into close ranges, but that won't be happening anytime soon. Rest assured, though, what I get here will revolutionize our understanding of black holes."

"Captain, what's that?"

She returned her attention to the helmsman. "What?"

He highlighted part of the scanner readings. It was some kind of debris orbiting around the black hole. "An asteroid? Something blown off a planet?"

"No," Doctor Leonard said after a moment studying his console. "Lieutenant Thompson is quite correct. The orbit is unusually stable for such a small object near the mass of a black hole."

Kelsey made some measurements. She'd really rather not get that close, but they could get nearer to the object and determine exactly what it was in relative safety.

"Take us in," she ordered, "but only until we get better readings."

"Aye, ma'am."

He took *Persephone* in closer. It took almost an hour before they were seeing details optically. The object wasn't as irregular as she'd expected. In fact, it was far too regular to be natural.

"That's artificial," she said. "Nature abhors consistent lines like those."

Leonard frowned. "Who would put something out here? How could they? Is it another Old Empire relic?"

Kelsey shrugged. "I have no idea, but we're going in for a close look. If this is something we need to explore before we head home, I want to take as much data back to Jared as I can. Get me the cleanest scanner readings you can, Doctor."

He nodded and bent back over his console.

This little adventure was showing signs of adventure after all. Hopefully, without the kind of destruction that usually meant for everything around her.

* * *

MAJOR RUSS TALBOT looked up from his console when someone knocked. Angela Ellis stood outside his office aboard *Invincible*. He gestured for her to come in.

"I thought you were down on Harrison's World, Major. What brings you here?"

Nine months ago, he'd been a senior sergeant and Angela had been a lieutenant, the same rank as his now-dead boss.

Kelsey had waved her magic finger—yes, that one—and made him a major. He hoped to God that someone didn't convince her to make him a damned colonel before they got home. His career was already screwed to hell.

If the recent changes in their rank bothered her, she didn't allow it to show. "I've got a big problem, Russ. Carl Owlet."

The marine grinned and leaned back in his chair. "Your idea of big differs from mine. I'm not sure he even shaves regularly. He hitting on you?"

"What? No. No! He's doing something much worse. Look at this."

She sent him a vid through his implants that made him sit up abruptly at the destruction.

"Holy cow!" he muttered. "Is he okay?"

"I'm told he'll make a full recovery, but he built that damned thing for Princess Kelsey."

"Ah. All becomes clear. You're worried he's trying to kill your principal."

She sighed and sat abruptly in one of the chairs. "No, not really. He's just not thinking, and I'm worried about what something like this would mean for the princess. What if he makes it more dangerous?"

"I've known Carl for over a year. He's damned bright. Perhaps not as grounded in common sense as I'd like, but not a menace. You're not giving Kelsey enough credit. She doesn't usually grab the biggest weapon handy to smash a problem."

Not recently, anyway.

"So I should just let him give her that thing? It can blow holes in this ship."

He smiled a little. "I understand you want to keep Kelsey safe, but you can't just shoot everyone who might give her something dangerous. For Christ's sake, she routinely wears powered armor and has an arsenal in our closet."

It was common knowledge that he shared Kelsey's palatial quarters and her bed. He'd overseen the installation of the armory. It had everything from two spare sets of armor—one Marine Raider and the other an upgraded general marine assault suit—to an array of every weapon they'd found to date.

If their commander had been anyone other than Jared Mertz, he'd have had a coronary.

At some point, she'd end up moving to *Persephone*. The captain's quarters there were significantly smaller. He had no idea where she'd put her toys. Maybe they could rip out the adjoining cabin and provide the two of them some extra space. If, of course, his duty didn't take him elsewhere.

"Look," he said after a moment. "Talk with her about it. She'll listen to your concerns."

"Yeah," Angela said glumly. "She'll listen and then do whatever she likes."

"Welcome to the Imperial Guard in everything but name. Thank God it isn't me keeping her from doing crazy stuff now."

Angela sighed. "The universe hates me."

* * *

JARED WALKED into *Invincible*'s briefing room and nodded to the various officers and scientists gathered there. It was early in the morning, and most of them looked a bit out of sorts.

"Good morning, everyone. There's coffee and a buffet against the wall. Please indulge yourselves."

He suited words to deeds and filled a plate. If this turned into anything like some of Kelsey's other discoveries, it might be hard to find time for food later.

Kelsey had an even larger plate than his, but didn't look nearly as discomfited by putting all the food away as she once had. His sister was adjusting to her new condition.

"I told you not to do anything to wreck my schedule," he growled as he sat beside her.

She smiled. "I didn't put that thing there. It's not my fault."

Once everyone had taken their seats, he nodded toward his sister. "Tell us what you found."

The screen came to life. An image of a large space station showed against a bright swirl of dust. It was difficult to make out the surface details, but it was undoubtedly artificial.

"We found this station orbiting the black hole in the other system," Kelsey said. "Due to its proximity to the event horizon, we were unable to approach as closely as I'd have liked. *Persephone* told me our drives and screens were up to the task, but it would put us at almost ninety percent of capacity. I decided that was cutting it a little too close."

Jared nodded. "Good call. We don't want a failure to send you falling into a black hole. Your father's already going to kill me for everything you've been through."

The people gathered around the table rumbled with laughter. Even Kelsey. They'd achieved enough distance from the events to see the humor in something like that now.

"That's what I was thinking, too," she said. "So, while we couldn't get close, we did creep up enough for the scanners to get some data. The layout is nothing like what we've found in any of the Old Empire databases. With Doctor Leonard's concurrence, I'm declaring this as probably nonhuman in origin."

That set off a murmur around the table.

"Wait," Jared said. "You mean as in alien? Not just one of the other human polities that existed back then? The Old Empire never found any evidence of sentient alien life."

"I submit that we just did," she said seriously. "We attempted to communicate with it, but the station didn't respond. It may be that our methods are so different that it didn't recognize our message. It's also possible it isn't completely functional. In that environment, I wouldn't be surprised."

Doctor Leonard cleared his throat. "The design elements of this station are markedly different than what we've seen before, Admiral. Rather than a sphere, this is more like a massive ring with the center aligned toward the black hole. That means very little in and of itself, but combined with its survival in the most hostile environment imaginable and its lack of battle screens, that has to mean something."

Jared considered that. "Kelsey thinks the station's protection might have failed. Perhaps it once had screens."

The older man shook his head. "The orbit is far too precise for it to be a derelict. If it were being flooded with radiation, the drives that kept it in place would have also failed. It's protected by something we're unfamiliar with."

"We'll have to send a ship in more closely to find out," Kelsey said. "That decision falls to you, Admiral. Do we look now or let others follow up at a later date?"

"I can send a few ships in to take a closer look after you head out," Commodore Sean Meyer offered.

The man had recovered from the injuries he'd sustained nine months ago and settled into commanding Boxer Station with more ease than Jared had expected. His cadre of officers from the wrecked heavy cruiser *Spear* was working out better than Jared had hoped.

"I could even task my exec with that," Meyer said with a grin toward Captain Paul Cooley. The man's injuries had been far worse than Sean's, and he was only now getting used to the artificial legs the doctors on Harrison's World had built for him.

The emotional damage from losing his ship and many of his crew would take far longer to heal.

Cooley nodded. "I can take some ships in to check it out."

Jared shook his head. "We should look before we head back for home. I'll leave the follow-up exploration to you two, though."

He leaned back for a moment and thought about it. "I'll take every ship in my fleet through. We'll search the system thoroughly and get as many readings as we can. Then we'll head for home."

"That's a little bit of overkill, don't you think?" Kelsey asked dryly.

"I want to know if there are other flip points there and where they let out. Nothing in the Old Empire records indicates a system like this one, and I doubt it went nova in the last five hundred years. The aliens that built that station came from somewhere. I'd like to have an idea of where that might be."

He checked the time. "Everyone, head back to your ships after you download the data Princess Kelsey brought back for us. We'll move into the Nova system in half an hour. And that's a capital Nova, as in the new official name."

Kelsey waited for the others to start leaving before she spoke. "I honestly didn't mean to delay our departure."

He smiled. "As if I were going to go home without as much information about a potential alien species as possible. This won't take long."

Jared hoped it actually worked out that way for once. It would be a refreshing change of pace.

* * *

CARL ARRIVED BACK on the science ship *Pallas* just in time to avoid any awkward questions. He'd brought the hammer with him, safely tucked away in his gear with the grav drive making it almost weightless.

He'd spend some time reevaluating the settings before he presented it to Princess Kelsey. Thankfully, she wouldn't need it anytime soon. They wouldn't be fighting hostile AIs or Pale Ones on this adventure.

He hurried into the lab and dropped his bag on the table.

Doctor Leonard frowned at him. "What's wrong with your ears?"

Carl reached up to touch the sterile cotton sticking out from his ears. "Just a little accident. The doctor down there said I should keep these in until the nanites do some catch up work."

In actuality, the doctor had blistered Carl's damaged ears for his carelessness. She'd regenerated his eardrums in the base medical center, but told him that he was in danger of infection, even with his nanites. She'd also told him he was an idiot several times.

He pretty much agreed with everything she said. He'd really screwed up.

Doctor Leonard gave him a look that said he was less than convinced, but he allowed the explanation to stand. "You made it back in the nick of time. We're heading through the weak flip point to explore the Nova system. That's what Admiral Mertz named it. We've found something very exciting there."

His mentor sent him the data through his implants. It only took Carl a moment to realize what he was looking at. "Aliens?"

"Possibly," Doctor Leonard allowed. "We'll take point on making that determination. Are you able to wear a pressure suit?"

"Of course!"

He had no idea if that was true, but he wasn't going to miss this opportunity.

4

---

ngela found Kelsey Bandar in her office. Admiral Mertz had decided his sister needed one, and it wasn't as if there wasn't room on the superdreadnought. Someone had decorated it with furnishings from Pentagar, Harrison's World, and Erorsi. It looked nice.

There were some odd additions she suspected came from somewhere in the Old Empire. No doubt salvaged from the graveyard. That was a little creepy, but Angela supposed that might just be her.

The princess smiled at her. "Angela! We found aliens. Isn't that exciting?"

"I suppose," the marine admitted. "Though I'd have liked it better if you'd kept me in the loop."

"Somehow, I knew that was going to be your takeaway from this," Kelsey said wryly. "I was on a Marine Raider ship. What additional safety could you have provided?"

"If aliens had boarded you, I could've kept shooting them till I went down."

Angela knew that sounded ridiculous, but she couldn't help it. Kelsey thought her guards were an inconvenience to someone built to be one of the deadliest fighters in the Old Empire. She didn't say that, but Angela knew that's what she was thinking.

Her boss sighed a bit theatrically and gestured for Angela to sit. "I'll try to remember. At least get comfortable while you rip my head off."

Angela took her up on the offer and sat in one of the comfortable chairs. Unlike the ones in Major Talbot's office, these actually encouraged someone to stay awhile. She still sat in a posture of attention.

"I'm not going to belabor the obvious, Your Highness," she said, "but it's true. Your protective detail is here for a reason. Even if it doesn't make much sense to you. Besides, you made a deal."

When Angela agreed to enter the princess's service as guard commander, she'd extracted a few promises from the woman. Within the basic parameters of Kelsey's activities, the guards would be low-key.

They trusted that the princess was relatively safe on *Invincible* or one of the other Fleet warships. But she was still supposed to inform Angela of where she was and what she was up to.

Looks could be so deceiving. Kelsey was half a meter shorter than Angela and so damned slender that the marine imagined she could break the tiny woman in two without much effort. The reverse was true, as one bout in marine country had decisively proven.

If they ever gained access to the materials to make more Marine Raiders, Angela was going to be the first person in line. That was the other promise Kelsey had made.

"I'm sorry," the smaller woman said, looking a little contrite. "I got caught up in the moment. I'll do my best not to forget again. I promise."

After a moment, Angela nodded. "I appreciate that, Your Highness. In any case, that isn't the reason I'm here to see you. It's actually a completely different kind of security issue."

Kelsey folded her fingers on her desk and gave Angela her complete attention. "Tell me. What threat to life and limb is next on your hit parade of value?"

Angela shook her head. "Where do you get those sayings? Never mind. I don't want to know. This time, it's Carl Owlet."

The princess blinked. She opened her mouth and then closed it again. Finally, she spoke with a bit of a smile playing about the corners of her lips. "If I had to rank my friends as threatening, he'd be buried somewhere in a footnote. How could that young man possibly threaten me? Or anyone? He's a scientist."

"With science," she said firmly. "Or rather, what he builds using it. He's working on something he intends to give you, and it's dangerous."

Kelsey rubbed her hands together like a little kid. "Oooooo! I like presents! What is it? And how is it dangerous? You can tell me. I'll still act surprised."

"You're going to be the death of me yet," Angela said glumly. "Let me put this into perspective. He destroyed a weapons range down on Harrison's World and almost killed himself with it."

That wiped the gleeful expression right off Kelsey's face. "Oh my God! Is he okay?" She surged to her feet. "We're going to see him right now. Why didn't someone tell me he was hurt?"

Angela kept her seat. "He only caught a few minor injuries. He's already back at work on *Pallas*, but that's only because he got lucky. Damned lucky. His creation could very easily have killed him and dozens of other people in the area. I don't want you accepting that gift."

She probably shouldn't have phrased it so bluntly. She realized that as soon as she'd said it.

Kelsey's eyes narrowed. "That's a strong statement. I'll consider it when *I* make *my* decision on the matter. Now, enough dancing around. What the hell is this weapon?"

"Something he calls Project Mjölnir."

The princess's eyes widened. "Seriously? Like Thor's hammer?"

"It is a hammer. I have no idea about it belonging to someone else. It's based on a vid."

"Which is based on an ancient myth from pre-Empire Terra. Hell, before modern technology. And he destroyed a lab with it? What happened?"

Angela sent Kelsey the vid she'd uploaded to her implants.

The princess frowned as she watched it in her head and then twitched violently. "Holy shit! That thing just vaporized a set of marine armor and the wall behind it. I couldn't even do that with a plasma rifle. Oh, it really messed him up. He should've been in armor."

"That isn't the right takeaway from this fiasco," Angela said repressively. "He was incredibly reckless, and that weapon is far too dangerous for you to use."

Kelsey shrugged. "I thought the same thing about my implants before I learned to control them. Practice and refining the skills needed are key. Come on. We're going to pay him a visit and let him explain this for himself."

She took one step toward the hatch and stopped. "You aren't to tear into him about this. I'll handle that. You've delivered your warning and I've heard it. I'll decide how to chastise him about this. Clear?"

Angela sighed inside where it was safe. "Of course, Your Highness."

This wasn't going to work out well at all. The little blonde maniac would take the weapon and gleefully put herself in the medical center. Angela just knew it.

* * *

CARL WENT over everything Doctor Leonard had recorded about the alien station with a fine-toothed comb. The interference of the radiation combined with the distance of the ship from the object made the small details difficult to make out, but he had a good general feeling for it.

It was somewhat larger than Boxer Station, but a lot of that area was empty space in the center of the ring. The structure itself was a mighty circle. He couldn't tell, but there were probably instruments on the interior of the ring.

The station was at least several decks thick but looked fragile because of the empty space. It wasn't rotating, so the purpose wasn't to generate artificial gravity. Frankly, he was at a loss as to what it really did.

The most obvious guess was that it was there to study the black hole.

Certainly, the Empire would want to do the same thing. The opportunity was unprecedented.

That still didn't explain who had built the station. It didn't look Imperial, but there had been other human polities before the Fall. He wasn't quite ready to jump on the "aliens" bandwagon.

Humanity had never found a single example of nonhuman sentience. Not even the remains of a long-dead civilization. Nothing.

Well, arguably the AIs were sentient nonhumans. He should be more precise.

Yet, this station wasn't using battle screens to filter out the deadly radiation. In that environment, it would quickly fry an unprotected Imperial facility, so there must be something there shielding it.

Or, perhaps not. Maybe the screens had failed long ago and the station was a dead hulk. They wouldn't know until they got a chance to examine it more closely.

The hatch to his lab slid open, and Princess Kelsey walked in. Her guard dog was at her heels.

Perhaps that was being too harsh, but he'd never seen Major Ellis smile. Of course, perhaps having her ship shot out from under her had something to do with that.

In any case, he wasn't really a fan.

Kelsey came over to him. "I heard you got hurt, and I wanted to see you for myself. Why do you have cotton balls in your ears?"

He tried to give a nonchalant shrug. "Just a problem testing something out. The docs fixed me up and put those in to help speed the healing."

She gave him a stern look. "You should know me better than that. I want the real story, and I want you to trot it out right now, young man."

He sighed. He should've known this wasn't going to be easy.

"It's a surprise."

"Congratulations. I'm surprised. Now, let's have some details."

He shot a look at Major Ellis. The woman had obviously tattled on him. His opinion of her plummeted.

"I'm not sure what you heard," he said as he walked over to his desk, "but I'll wager some important details were left out."

He pulled the hammer out of his pack and handed it to her. "This is Mjölnir."

She hefted it with a frown. "It's kind of light. After watching that vid, I expected something with a bit more heft."

So, she'd already seen the vid. He considered turning off the grav support, but that might cause an injury. He'd already done enough to give her the wrong opinion about this.

"Set it down, please."

She placed it on the deck and he stopped the miniature grav drive from neutralizing the weight. "Try it now."

Kelsey went to pick it up and her eyes widened in surprise. "Wow. Okay, that is heavy."

She lifted it, but he imagined it had taken a significant percentage of her Marine Raider artificial muscles to do it.

"The shell is made of partially collapsed matter," he said. "It weighs about three tons, and that's not all. Set it back down."

Once she did, he engaged the grav drive to resist motion. It didn't precisely make the hammer weigh more, but it added resistance to movement. If someone tried to lift it, it quickly adjusted the drive to counteract that pressure. It could stop a dozen Marine Raiders acting in concert but still not damage the floor.

When combined with the neutral buoyancy function he'd worked out, it wasn't dangerous to set it on a glass table and yet still prevent others from moving it. One of his more clever ideas, he thought.

This time Kelsey couldn't budge it.

She stood and shook her head. "I suppose I'm not worthy. Impressive."

"You *could* be worthy, with the right additions to your implants."

Kelsey nodded. "You can tell me all about it, but I want to make something particularly clear first. You're my friend, and we've been through so much together. I don't want to see you hurt yourself. That vid was scary and you were lucky."

He deflated a bit at that. "Things didn't quite go as planned. I didn't anticipate how abruptly the hammer could change speed. To be honest, I didn't realize the destructive scope of a grav drive pushing it like that. My simulations were flawed. I've corrected that and will add in safeguards to prevent something like that from happening again."

"Sit down," Kelsey said.

He sat on his roller chair and she took a handy stool. Now came the ass chewing.

"I'm honored and grateful that you thought I'd like this. The idea of this in my arsenal is exceptionally cool. That said, you don't understand how the mind of a warrior works. And, contrary to some opinions, that's what I am."

He wondered who she was talking about. Everyone knew she was a badass.

"You need to do more testing," she continued, "but that kind of capability might save my life one day. If I had someone in marine armor shooting at me, I'd do exactly what you did. Boom. Problem solved. Sometimes, you have to blow shit up.

"Still, you're not a warrior. You're more like that guy Q in the Bond movies. You come up with all the cool toys."

He felt his lips quirk at her cursing. It still seemed so out of place. Talbot was rubbing off on her.

"I thought Batman had the cool toys."

"Don't quibble," she said with a smile of her own. "Both of them can have cool toys. Now, I want you to explain the capabilities of this hammer to me."

"Well, it can obviously power through heavy armor and thick walls with ease. It's a combination of the partially collapsed matter shielding it, a miniaturized battle screen, and the grav drive."

Kelsey blinked. "Battle screens don't work in atmosphere. Besides, the equipment to project one takes up a lot of room."

He nodded. "For a full-strength one, yes. This one is somewhat lightweight in the protection department. It doesn't need to shield you from a ship's missile. Flechettes and plasma are more in line with the threats I envisioned you facing."

"Captain Black didn't mention anything about a battle screen," Major Ellis said with a frown.

"It was a last-minute addition," he admitted. "I didn't think I'd be able to make the hardware small enough, but I had a last-minute breakthrough. It's very short range. Just a couple of meters, at most."

Kelsey seemed impressed. "Is it only good in a single direction, or is it omnidirectional?"

"Single direction only. The smaller the coverage area, the stronger the protection. That's what made the hole in the plascrete. I wanted it to be useful against threats as well as in flight."

The princess cocked her head. "Flight?"

"Sure. The grav drive is pretty powerful. See the strap? It can secure around your wrist and pull you along. Not like dragging you, because the grav drive affects you, too. It's more a way to keep you inside the field. You and your armor will slow it down, but not that much, I'd imagine."

She sat back. "I could fly. Now *that* is cool. We'll come back to that. Could you add this to marine armor? Or to my Raider suit?"

He nodded. "Sure. It would take me a while to design something to fit into an appropriate place inside the armor. Space is somewhat at a premium. It would drain the power cells fast, though.

"It would be better if the suits were redesigned to use the grav/fusion power packs. It would also give them new capabilities similar to yours."

That last didn't exactly make him happy. He'd wanted to give her something unique.

Still, anything that kept the marines alive was a good thing. Part of his mind was already starting to work over how he could do that.

Kelsey snapped her fingers. "Hello in there."

He came back to reality. "Sorry. I was thinking about how I could make that happen."

"You've got the entire trip home to work that out. Back to the hammer. So, it would really allow me to fly? How fast?"

"I've never really opened it up. With the extra load a person adds, I suspect somewhere around Mach 15."

She looked stunned. "Are you pulling my leg? That's insane."

Major Ellis looked like she shared that opinion. Only she wasn't so happy about it.

"That's incredibly irresponsible," the marine said. "That could kill an unprotected person."

"Angela," Kelsey warned.

"I'm sorry, Highness, but that's madness. Not even you could survive a crash at that speed, armored or not. You're tough, not invincible."

The marine focused her attention on Carl. He shrank back a little at her intense expression. "Princess Kelsey told me I had to let her do the ass chewing, but I'm putting you on notice. If your antics hurt her, I'll hurt you. Am I clear?"

"Angela!" Kelsey said as she surged to her feet. "I think you've said enough. Perhaps you should wait for me on my pinnace."

The marine gave him one last, hard look before she bowed her head toward Kelsey. "Perhaps I should, Highness. My apologies to you."

The large woman stalked to the hatch and spoke briefly with the marine there before she left.

Carl noticed that she hadn't taken back any of what she'd said. If something went wrong, the woman could break him in half.

Kelsey sighed and resumed her seat. "I'm sorry about that. She's a bit overprotective. She means well."

"I don't disagree with anything she said." He rubbed his face. "I don't usually build things that have the potential to kill. Not so easily, anyhow. I need to keep that fact firmly in mind."

He'd test this hammer to levels that combat equipment would envy. He'd die before he allowed it to hurt his friend.

"As for the flying," he said, "the grav drive and battle screen keep you protected. I'll obviously need to test it very, *very* thoroughly before there are human trials.

"A collision would hurt, but the battle screen would absorb most of the kinetic energy and deflect all the debris away from you. You could fly through a pinnace, but I'd recommend you wear armor. Something still might bounce back. If you somehow became separated from the hammer, it will come back by the shortest route unless you've ordered it elsewhere."

She nodded slowly. "How could I do that? My implants have the same fifteen-meter limit as everyone else's. The armor boosts it to several hundred, but that's pretty short for something like this."

"I designed and built an extended range communications implant. I've tested it out to ten kilometers. The hammer has the same range, but can track the user from even further away."

"Like with a beacon?" she asked. "That's a bad thing in combat. You don't want your enemies to be able to track you."

"Actually, it's nothing like a beacon. It uses aspects of quantum mechanics to track the wielder. There are no detectable signals at all. In any case, I had Doctor Stone put the matching unit inside me. It works great at the ranges I've tried. I'll narrow down the maximum useful range before I turn the final version over to you."

He held up his hand and the hammer flew from the table into it with a slight singing sound. "Just like in the vids."

"Whosoever holds this hammer, if he be worthy, shall possess the power of Thor," she said. "Or, I suppose 'she,' if this was intended for me."

"It seemed easier to go gender neutral," he said. "Unlike a magic hammer, I can't change the inscription on a whim. So, I went with 'they.' It seemed simpler."

"You even put the inscription on it? Damned impressive, Carl. Damned impressive. Still, you're going to need to convince a very skeptical audience before I try it."

Carl set the hammer down beside him. "Whatever it takes."

She smiled. "I'm glad you're being so understanding. I want you to work with Major Ellis. She's going to vet every aspect of this hammer before I accept it."

He felt his mouth drop open. "Seriously? The woman hates me. You'll never get it if that's the bar I have to meet."

Kelsey stood, her expression sympathetic. "I understand, but that's the way it is. I'm fairly certain she doesn't actually hate you. She'd give her life to protect me, and I won't dismiss her concerns. Even when expressed in such an abrupt manner. Sometimes you have to overcome tremendous obstacles to get what you want."

"She's not an obstacle, she's a mountain. With wild animals ready to rip me apart."

She headed for the door. "I'll be rooting for you. As I said, I'd really like to have something like Mjölnir. I hope you can make that happen. Good luck."

Carl sat there long after she'd left, trying to imagine how he could please the impossible woman. No scenario he envisioned worked.

He was doomed.

5

Elise sat up when Doctor Lily Stone lifted the headset off her temples. "Everything good?"

Stone nodded. "The update went smoothly, and the hardware replacement checks out, too. Congratulations, Your Highness. You're no longer hackable by the Pale Ones or the Rebel Empire AIs."

She hopped off the examination table. "I can't begin to tell you how good that makes me feel, Doctor. My people have a cultural fear of forced reprogramming that you newcomers just don't understand. Being immune to having these implants suborned is a huge relief to me."

"I saw what those things put Kelsey through, and the poor bastards on Erorsi. They'll need modifications, too."

"Won't that be fun?"

Elise could hardly imagine how difficult it was going to be to track down every single Pale One on Erorsi. Especially now that the planet was going through such a brutal and semi-permanent winter. The asteroid impact had thrown enough debris into the atmosphere to obscure the sun, and living was tough.

Current estimates put the timeframe before the weather patterns returned to some semblance of normal at fifteen to twenty years. Even then, the long cold streak was going to alter things permanently. Many species were going to die. The biosphere was going to change, and not for the better.

At least they didn't have to obey the mad AI anymore.

Perhaps that was how they'd get them fixed. They could use the equipment the AI had used to control the Pale Ones to summon them to a central area and sedate them. Part of her cringed at forcing them to obey, but this would be the last time. Then they'd be free forever.

"Could you explain again what changed in the hardware?" she asked as Stone walked her to the door.

"Certainly. We replaced the central node in your implants with a new model designed by the folks at the Grant Research Facility. This one is not subject to external overwriting without the person's consent and active cooperation, and it includes a number of improvements thanks to other research they've done over the centuries. They tell me the performance is even faster, but it already seems like lightning to me.

"The core kernel's programming is now hardwired. A sentry subroutine will monitor the implants for aberrant behavior and overwrite any new code. Or if the user tells it to."

"That's reassuring. So, no more people under the control of their hardware?"

Stone nodded. "Precisely. Kelsey still has what she calls combat mode, but that's not *quite* the same thing. Her implants control her body in combat, but she's always in the driver's seat.

"Also, Carl Owlet put a nasty surprise in there for anyone that tries to overwrite the implant code. Your implants will hack a rogue unit that attacks you, taking control of it instead. I don't know the details, but I understand the program is wickedly subtle. The AI won't even know what's happening until it's too late."

Elise grinned. "Payback is a bitch. I assume it won't work against a true AI."

"No," Stone said. "They're immune in much the same way you are. That's where Carl got the idea. On the plus side, those things are rare. The odds you'll ever run into one are pretty slim. Not counting Marcus and Harrison, of course."

"Why didn't the Old Empire do this? It seems so straightforward."

Stone shrugged. "We may never know for sure, but Kelsey thinks that critical people were killed by whoever was behind the rebellion. Carl says that the old implants have something that is supposed to allow only a restricted few to update the code. Something about private keys. Without them, the Old Empire was powerless.

"We captured those keys when we rescued Princess Kelsey. With them, we can easily update the old hardware. The people at Grant have come up with new keys, and we'll make sure that trusted people in many places have a way to get it, but not have it taken from them. I don't know the details and I'm happy with that."

Elise nodded. "We're sure they're secure?"

"They had Marcus try and hack someone. He failed. That works for me."

"Me, too." Elise shook Stone's hand. "Thank you, Doctor. When will everyone have this update?"

"We're focusing on your people now. The change is quick, and your doctors can handle the process now that we've trained them. I figure all of the people in the task force heading to Pentagar will be done before they get home.

"Commodore Meyer will have his people done in about the same timeframe. Then he'll assist Coordinator West in getting Harrison's World done."

Elise felt the corner of her mouth quirk up. "Those two have been working together pretty closely these last few months. I think their relationship might be changing from a purely professional one."

Stone raised an eyebrow. "You think? They seem pretty professional to me."

Elise waved her hand dismissively. "I have an eye for that kind of thing. He might not know it yet, but Coordinator West is interested in deepening their relationship. She's good at keeping her cards close to her vest."

Considering the woman had been running an underground movement for most of her life, conspiring against the AIs while infiltrating their puppet government, that was something of an understatement. Elise had played poker with her, Sean, Jared, Kelsey, and Talbot. That had been an eye-opening education. An expensive one, too.

The woman didn't have a single tell. Not one. Her bluffs were indistinguishable from the rest of her hands.

Kelsey was by far the best player Elise had ever met, and she was outclassed. Worse, Elise was almost certain that Olivia West had thrown a number of hands to play down her advantage, and she'd still trounced them all.

Elise had made a number of notes to improve her own skills in that arena. In fact, she'd gotten together with the coordinator several times and sat at the feet of the mistress. Those skills would serve her well as a stateswoman. Particularly now that she was on her way to the seat of the New Terran Empire.

Based on everything she'd heard, and some of the things she hadn't, there was going to be trouble. She'd need to work hard to turn that situation around before it bit them all in the behind.

"I'm not saying that her intent will necessarily mean anything," Elise added. "It takes two to dance, after all. It really depends on what Sean wants. What about the people in Jared's task force?"

Stone smiled. "We have a lot of people to work through, but we'll be done before we reach Avalon. Keep an eye on things over the next few days. I don't expect that you'll have any issues, but if you do, call me at once."

"I will. Thank you, Lily."

Elise made her way to the ship's library. With all the electronic books, most crewmembers never saw it, which was a shame. She'd found it amazing and fascinating, and that was before they'd put any books in it.

Just the idea that a modern warship would have a two-level room of that size dedicated to the printed page was astounding to her.

She'd lost no time sending a message home for books to fill it with. Word had spread to Coordinator West's friend and mentor, Lord William Hawthorne. He'd found many tomes to add to the haul. Between the two of them, and the various finds in the graveyard, this library was now worthy of the name.

In fact, Lord Hawthorne was the one she was coming here to meet. She found him standing beside a tall shelf with an old book in his hand. He wasn't alone. Reginald Bell sat in a chair nearby, examining a portfolio of some kind.

"Gentlemen," she said as she came over. "Thank you for taking the time to meet with me."

William Hawthorne slid the book back onto the shelf and bent low at the waist. "Elise. It's a pleasure as always. May I say you look stunning?"

"Flatterer. No need to rise on my account, Reg. Your knees aren't as young as they used to be."

The older man gave up on standing and bowed his head. "Princess Elise. It's good to see you again. The trip here was a trifle more tiring than I'd imagined. Though these new nanites are helping some."

Kelsey had Doctor Leonard remove some of her Marine Raider nanites and examine them. The little machines were markedly more advanced than the ones given to regular Fleet personnel, but the scientists could reprogram them to work in others.

They'd need periodic replacement, but they might keep the old gentleman with them a few more decades. He had so much to tell them and so little time left to do it. They could harvest enough Raider nanites from her for that.

Reginald Bell was the only person alive who'd seen the Empire before the Fall. Even his ancient appearance belied his true age. The Terran Empire had gone down fighting more than five centuries ago. That was far longer than even Fleet nanites could extend someone's age.

And that was a blessing. The poor people the AIs had enslaved during the Fall were all dead. God rest their souls.

He'd spent more than two centuries in a stasis unit. Generations of men and women had watched over him as they were born, grew old, and finally passed on. They'd done so solely in the hope that, one day, his intimate knowledge of the Old Empire would once more prove valuable.

Now that Jared and Kelsey had freed Erorsi from the thrall of the crazed AI, the people that had survived in the old planetary defense center could finally live their lives out in the open. Now they could save Reg's knowledge of the Old Empire.

That wasn't to say that he hadn't recorded a lot before he'd gone into stasis. Only, he hadn't known what those outside would lose over the years. He'd stuck to large events, but current day anthropologists and historians wanted to know the minutia of his life. He spent hours every day telling stories and answering questions.

He'd also decided to record his memories in the same way Ned had. It probably wouldn't result in an AI of him after his death, but it would save the only direct memories of the Old Empire they had left. Other than Ned, of course.

"We've just been amusing ourselves while we waited," William said. "Please, join us."

She sat in the chair he held for her and waited for him to sit. Then she launched into her semiprepared speech.

"I appreciate you both taking the time to meet with me. Marcus is also in attendance, though the subroutine is not going to report our conversation to his main memory unless we decide that's appropriate."

"What's the old saying?" Marcus asked from a speaker under the table. "Four people can keep a secret if two of them are dead and one is an AI that isn't talking to itself?"

"I'm fairly sure that's almost correct," William said with a smile. "This is all suitably mysterious. What, if I might ask, can we help you with?"

"Something very important," she said. "Jared is going to need our assistance when he gets home. Crown Prince Ethan Bandar has a very real and very deadly grudge against him."

She leaned forward. "Jared is intensely loyal to the Empire, and Kelsey has blinders on when it comes to family. That means it's up to us to protect him. Ethan Bandar will try to kill Jared. I will not stand idly by and let that happen, and I want you to help me stop him."

* * *

KELSEY SAT in the command chair on *Persephone*. She'd been studying her ass off and now had what Jared charitably called an ensign's skill set. She was hoping to bump that up to at least lieutenant by the time they got home.

Ned said that was really all she needed for a ship this size. Yes, there were some specific skills required for operating a Marine Raider strike ship, but he was helping her learn those.

She'd never be as good at piloting as someone that started learning a decade ago. She'd be happy if she learned enough to be competent.

That was why she had primary on the ship's helm as they prepared to flip to the Nova system. Lieutenant Thompson would be watching her like a hawk from his console, though he'd never say so. She felt like a kid riding her bike for the very first time. The mental image of a powerful warship with training wheels almost made her laugh.

"All Fleet elements, this is Admiral Mertz. Flip in sixty seconds and report to *Invincible* upon arrival. You all have your assigned sectors, so get about it. Remember, you'll be out of direct communication once you move any distance at all into the radiation, so you'll have to use your discretion on approaching anything anomalous.

"Be careful and rendezvous at the Harrison's World flip point in twenty-four hours. Good luck. Mertz out."

She took a deep breath as the timer counted down. She had the helm on manual, so this wasn't just pushing a button. She was adjusting the power output and frequency of the flip drive by hand. If she got it wrong, the ship might not flip at all. Wouldn't *that* be embarrassing?

Thompson hadn't said a word about her settings. She wasn't sure if that was because she had them right or he wanted her to learn something. When the timer hit zero, she activated the flip drive.

Thankfully, *Persephone* flipped.

"Good settings, ma'am," Jack said. "A trifle low, but within the margin of error. Watch out for *Ajax*."

"Thanks, Jack."

The destroyer in question had appeared just in front of them and was cutting across their bow. Kelsey adjusted course enough to be certain they'd miss one another. In the radiation field, it wasn't easy to see everyone at a glance.

She sent a message to *Invincible* and then eased the ship away from the flip point. Once they were clear, she headed off toward their assigned search area.

"Doing this all by hand is complex," she said. "It's a lot simpler to have *Persephone* do the fine details."

"True, but then you wouldn't know what to do if you ever had to do it yourself under pressure. For example, what if Captain Baxter had blown his attempt when *Athena* was running from the Pale Ones?"

She'd been unconscious for that, but she'd heard the story. Once Jared had rescued her from the Pale Ones, they'd chased the ship back to the Pentagar flip point. *Athena* had lost power and bridge control seconds before flip, and the engineer had calculated the settings in his head.

If he'd screwed it up, they'd all be slaves to the Pale Ones right now. She made a mental note to see that he received the Imperial Cross for that. Her father wouldn't argue. That was over and above whatever Fleet Command and the Imperial Senate decided to do.

The highest award for valor in the Terran Empire came with a few perks that only the emperor could bestow. A small plot of land somewhere and a knighthood. Sir Dennis. Wouldn't that tie his trickster tongue?

It also bumped someone up the chain when it came to salutes from his fellows. All Fleet personnel owed a holder of the Imperial Cross a salute, regardless of their respective ranks. Admirals saluted sailors if they held the Imperial Cross.

Since the Fall, they hadn't had an opportunity for anyone to earn that high award. Peacetime wasn't the kind of forge that created moments that earned one.

This mission was going to change that. She wouldn't be surprised to see a number of people receive the Empire's highest honor. It saddened her that all too many of them died doing so.

"Well, yes," she said after a moment. "That would've been awkward. As an engineer, I'm not sure how he knew what to do."

"It's part of their training, just because it might prove necessary. Score one for the training weenies. I never thought I'd say this, but I may have to buy some of them drinks when we get home."

"Your secret is safe with me. I'm transferring the helm back to you, Lieutenant Thompson."

"Aye, ma'am. I have the controls."

Once he'd accepted the helm, she brought up a display of the Nova system. They were going about a third of the way around. They'd be looking for planetary bodies and flip points. If they hadn't found any in twelve hours, they'd circle around and come back via a different route.

Part of her was disappointed that she wouldn't be exploring the strange station, but the rest of her was thrilled to avoid being at the sharp end for once.

That's violating the Marine Raider code.

"Use your outdoor voice," she subvocalized at Ned.

He laughed. This time it came across as an actual sound. Of course, it only came through her auditory implants, but this was better than the disembodied voice in her head.

It had taken her quite a bit of practice to learn to speak without others either hearing her or seeing what she was up to. Or being so incomprehensible that Ned couldn't understand her.

They'd come to this compromise because she needed the privacy of her mind left intact. The shade of Marine Raider Major Ned Quincy, the previous commander of *Persephone*, was a resident in her implants.

It was ludicrous on the face of it. Her implant processors were far inferior to the most basic of Old Empire computers. At least the ones that were of any size. Yet, somehow the memory recordings that he'd left had come into a life of their own. He was an AI. A real one, similar to Marcus, but different enough to be unique.

That had sent Doctor Leonard and Carl Owlet into a tizzy. That was the only word for it. Yet, so far, they'd been unable to recreate that lightning in a bottle. They were still hopeful, though. It had worked once, so they could do it again. All they needed to do was figure out the critical elements they were missing.

Even Marcus was at a loss to explain it. All he could do was confirm that Ned Quincy was undoubtedly sentient.

She hadn't needed anyone to tell her that. The man's odd sense of humor didn't allow for any other possibility. He was a real person, even if he wasn't the man who'd created the recordings before the Fall.

Living with him in her head had proven... challenging. She wanted her privacy, too. So, they'd made a pact. She was the arbiter of when he could use her senses. As he was resident in her implants, she had to trust that he would respect her wishes.

Otherwise, she'd go crazy.

So, he was on his word that he didn't monitor her when she told him to get lost for a while. Like when she and Talbot retired for the evening. Or when she had to use the restroom.

Since he lived in her implants, he could interface with the ship and do any number of things. Watch entertainment vids, read, and visit with friends. Of which he had some. How that worked, she wasn't precisely sure.

He even claimed he was able to sleep. That involved putting part of one of her implant processors into a low powered state that he claimed allowed him to dream.

Ned also wasn't normally supposed to monitor her thoughts. She'd given him permission while she was flying the ship today. That way, if she was about to screw up, he could warn her. A second safety net.

That meant, under normal circumstances, he only heard what she said to him, and she only heard his "voice" in her real ears. That made things bearable.

"Now that we're in the Nova system, no more monitoring my surface thoughts. Was my transition for crap?"

"I wouldn't say that. It could've been a little steadier, but you made it. Just keep working the sims, and you'll get better. Practice makes perfect."

She didn't need a lot of sleep, so she spent a fair amount of time in various sims. Some for the piloting, others for combat. She'd also visited a number of Old Empire worlds via recordings.

Ned's input on combat was immeasurably helpful. He'd made complete copies of all his training in his implants. They'd been among the files she'd taken over when they recovered his body.

Having the files didn't directly translate to her being able to use the skills. It did make her processors' use of combat mode significantly more effective.

That wasn't good enough for her, though. Kelsey coveted his skills. She wanted to be the badass that he'd been.

Direct access to his memories of using the techniques gave her a leg up, though. The style of fighting favored by the Raiders was a distilled compilation of many different Old Empire martial arts. Almost all of which had been lost during the Fall.

With him in her head, she was the last remaining practitioner of this dead art. One day she'd have to teach others, and she wanted to be able to do that. She felt like that kid in one of the old vids with the quirky master. Wax on. Wax off.

"That reminds me," she said. "I have a question for you."

"Since I'm not reading your mind, you'll have to clue me in."

"Sorry. I was thinking about an old martial arts vid. Pre-spaceflight. What degree master were you?"

He projected a mental image of himself standing beside her. It was spooky really. He could overwrite her optical input and add himself to the scene around her. It was just like what he did for her auditory implants. No one else could see him, unless he chose to go wide, so he was like a ghost.

"We didn't use the black belt rankings a lot of the civilian martial arts favored," he said. "Those got all funny once you made black belt. We made an intentional break with that tradition. We use the colored belts for lower levels and a black belt to indicate mastery. The only level we have above that is sensei. One capable of teaching."

"I'd imagined you were some super badass. What a letdown." She smiled to take any sting out of her joke.

"Well, if it's any consolation, I was the Raider's unarmed combat champion six years in a row. And the woman that broke my streak? She cheated."

"Uh-huh. Well, that does make me feel better. Where do I fall on that ranking?"

He made a show of thinking about it. "Not black belt. Sorry. It's not second nature to you, yet. You haven't caught a fly with your chopsticks."

"You *did* see that movie!"

"Which movie, ma'am?"

Kelsey blinked a moment. She'd said that out loud. "Sorry. I was talking to my resident ghost and got carried away."

Lieutenant Thompson and the rest of the bridge crew knew about her guest. Jared had decided that they had to. If something went wrong, they might need that knowledge.

It had taken some doing to convince them she wasn't crazy. Sometimes, she still wasn't sure.

The officer's eyes moved to her right. Ned must've made himself visible to everyone. Through the ship, he could do that. Maybe that was how he had friends.

"Sorry," Ned said. "I was teasing her."

"You still didn't answer my question."

He smiled. "You're a brown belt for sure. Keep working and you'll make black by the time we get to Avalon."

"I hope so. I'd like to have that part of my training squared away. I'm getting tired of Talbot throwing me around the mat when we fight. Well, when my augmentation is turned off, anyway."

She checked her chrono. "We've got almost a full day, and it looks like we won't be stumbling across very many surprises in the next twenty-three hours. Jack, I'll be in the gym if you need me."

6

C arl Owlet exited the pinnace and floated over to the strange station with light pushes from his grav unit. Because of the extreme radiation, he wasn't wearing a normal vacuum suit. Not even the marine versions would last more than a few moments here.

Instead, they'd raided the engineering section for suits designed to operate near an exposed fusion plant. That wasn't the same level of radiation, but tests had shown they'd allow the team to survive in this environment.

The heavy suit restricted his movements but protected him from the intense radiation flowing from the black hole.

Which wasn't that far away, really. He had a fabulous view of the accretion disk through the center of the alien ring. It was stunning. He made certain to get some good shots of it with his external vid recorders. They were more powerful and had much higher resolution than his implants.

He wasn't the first to make the trip. The marines were waiting for him on the surface of the construct. Still, it felt as though he was first on the scene.

"Stop lollygagging and get your skinny butt down here, Carl," Talbot said.

"On my way, Major. Your exaltedness. Sir."

"Someone is looking for a round on the mat, I see."

Carl smiled. His big friend was so easy to predict. His promotion still had him in an odd mental space. Still, he'd best not tease Talbot too much. He didn't want another marine ready to tie him into knots.

Up close, the station really did look different. The hull material was nothing like what they'd used in the Old Empire. Not only was it completely black, it absorbed every form of radiation they could detect. Discovering what it was would be high on his list of tasks.

He stopped lightly beside Talbot and the rest of the marines floating near the hull of the station. Its bulk obscured the accretion disk, and they were in shadow, so they all had their suit lights on. The skin of the station absorbed a lot of that, too.

"Did you find an entrance?" Carl asked.

"Not yet. Since no one reacted to our arrival, I have teams making the rounds in both directions. While we wait, I'd like to ask you a few questions."

"Shoot."

Carl changed his orientation so he was looking closely at the skin of the station. Rather than a smooth surface, small bumps covered it like a texture. Yeah, definitely not of Imperial manufacture.

Talbot sent him a private message to switch to channel six. Carl opened it, but also continued monitoring the general channel.

"What the hell were you thinking?"

He rolled his eyes. "Is this about the hammer again? Make one damned mistake and you never live it down."

"Don't curse."

"Hello? Pot, this is kettle, over."

"Yeah, well I'm a grizzled adult and you're ruining my preconceptions. No, this is about Angela Ellis. You're getting on the bad side of the wrong person, and you need to take a step back before she hurts you."

Carl shook his head, even though the marine couldn't see him. He unhooked a small scanner from his belt and began taking readings from the surface of the station.

"I haven't done anything to that woman. She's frothing all on her own. I'll get the kinks worked out of the hammer a lot faster without her breathing down my neck."

Talbot floated next to him. "You have no idea. She's a good person, but she has issues when it comes to losing people. We all do, really, but hers are more like an obsession. She's convinced you're out to kill Kelsey with your supposed incompetence."

The marine held up a hand. "I've told her you're the brightest guy on the block, but she got a bad first impression. You need to stop banging heads with her and try a different approach. You're not going to bulldoze your way through her objections."

The scanner readings were very odd. Part of the beams never came back. The hull must be absorbing them, too. What he was getting told him two mutually exclusive things.

First, the hull was made of collapsed matter. Not the partial stuff that he'd used on the hammer, but something a lot closer to neutronium. So much so that the beams weren't penetrating the surface at all.

If that were true, that explained the lack of a battle screen. No radiation would make it through that. Just cutting it would take a hell of a lot of focused energy. If they could do it at all.

Invincible's beams would be ineffective. It would require more power in a tighter focus. Well, maybe they would work with time, but the designers had never envisioned long duration shots. Their tightest focus would be useless. It required something much finer, yet more powerful.

Assuming the readings were correct, the mass of the station should be incredible. Here he was floating beside it, but it should have enough pull on its own to anchor him. Not like a planet, perhaps, but maybe a large asteroid. A handful of true neutronium would weigh millions of tons. He'd need to do some calculations before he knew what to expect.

Yet there was nothing. No indication at all that the surface was pulling any of them in, and that was damned odd. It really couldn't be both ways. He was missing something.

"I wish I had a clue how to hit the reset button," Carl told the marine. "Major Ellis is all over my ass. Talk about hostile. She threatened to break me into little pieces with Kelsey standing right there."

"I hope you take what she says seriously," Talbot said. "She's pretty pissed about the whole thing."

"I don't understand why. There was no way Kelsey was ever getting that version of the hammer. I have a lot more testing to do on it. Hell, I wasn't even going to tell her about it until the testing was complete. *She* told Kelsey. Now I have to convince the she-bear that it's safe."

He looked over at Talbot as he said that last. The marine was smiling. Bastard.

"Look, kid, I get it. I really do. I tried to tell her what a stand-up guy you are, and it bounced. She's got it in her head that you're a dangerous fellow. It's up to you to convince her she's wrong. I can't help you with that. No one can."

"I'm doomed."

Talbot laughed and moved off to confer with the other marines keeping watch. So much for a helping hand.

Carl sighed and glared at his scanner. It wasn't even giving him a good idea what the texture was for. If they didn't get inside the thing, they might never find out. At least not before they left to go home.

He hated the idea of someone else making the big discoveries after he came up empty. Maybe he could get a more detailed reading on the skin if he boosted the scanner power and narrowed the focus. A sweeping scan that went up and down the potential frequencies would also increase his odds of getting something meaningful back.

It only took a few moments to change the settings. He held the scanner against the surface of the station and started probing it.

The hull underneath him sank with astonishing speed, yanking him inside the station. He didn't even have time to yell before the darkness engulfed him.

* * *

ANGELA FINISHED GOING over the data Owlet had given her about Project Mjölnir. It was insulting. He'd tailored his summary as though she was four. And slow.

His opinion of marines in general, and her in specific, had to be pretty dismal.

Perhaps he didn't know that officers in the emperor's service had to have university degrees. Admittedly, hers was in military studies, but she had the ability to grasp other advanced subjects.

She set the summary aside and opened his write-up about the quantum validation theory.

That might have been a mistake.

It quickly arrowed off into science that she didn't have the background to understand. Not without a lot of study. Time she was unwilling to waste on this one project.

Maybe the computer could help her grasp it. "*Persephone*, if I send you a file on a scientific subject, can you help me understand it?"

"This unit may be able to assist, Major Ellis. It depends on the nature of the theory and how specific your question is."

She sent the files. "This is classified under my seal. Only Princess Kelsey, Carl Owlet, Doctor Leonard, Admiral Mertz, and I are cleared to know the contents."

"Understood. Which theory are you looking for clarification on? There are a number of fields that are mentioned."

"Quantum communication. How does that work?"

"It doesn't, at least as far as this unit's databases are concerned. This unit has located several mentions of failed experiments in that line, but none that were able to meaningfully use the quantum entanglement of photons."

"Then focus on the files I sent. How does it propose the communication to work?"

She leaned back in the chair behind her desk to await what was no doubt going to be a boring lecture in science. She really didn't need an office, but the privacy would be useful if it put her to sleep.

"The devices use entangled photons and predefined arrangements of spin as authentication mechanisms. These units do not directly communicate, strictly speaking. The standard communications units use the spin of the photons to verify a command is authentic.

"Though not directly designed for communication, it may be possible to use them for such. The photon sets are sizable and would allow for significant data throughput. The quantum devices are only capable of communicating with one another in linked pairs. A working range of ten kilometers is given, but this unit finds that claim doubtful."

Angela sat up, interested. "Doubtful in what way? Are you saying that it doesn't work?"

"Test results indicate that it did in fact work in a lab setting, but this unit is finding a discrepancy in the range Carl Owlet has verified and what the original scientific theory seems to indicate.

"Carl Owlet has set a working range of ten kilometers. That is unrealistic and does not fit the scope of how entangled particles operate."

"Okay, what would be a more likely range? Five kilometers? Less?"

"This unit apologizes. Perhaps it did not adequately explain the original theory. Even prior to spaceflight on Terra, the effect of entangled photons were observable at hundreds of kilometers of separation."

She blinked. "Are you saying someone could control this hammer over a distance of hundreds of kilometers?"

"Negative."

Angela sighed in relief. "Thank goodness. That would be hard to get my head around. What do you hypothesize the maximum range to be?"

"This unit believes the upper range to be unlimited."

She must've misheard what it said. "Could you expand on that?"

"Theoretically, entangled photons are not bound by distance at all. It should not matter if they are in the same compartment, in different stellar systems, or across the observable universe. The artificial range assigned to the communicator by Carl Owlet does not seem supported in theory."

She stood slowly. "Are you telling me that he could control that hammer over interstellar distances? That's ridiculous. If so, why would he only say it worked out to ten kilometers?"

"As designed, control of the hammer requires both the standard communications unit and the quantum validation device. So, the normal communicator limits the range.

"That said, this unit believes that Carl Owlet doubted the scope of his breakthrough. It believes that he incorrectly applied an artificial limitation. Only an actual test of the communications potential can prove or disprove that assertion, however."

Angela tried to get her head around what the computer was saying. Unlimited communication range? Absurd.

"We'll leave that aside for the moment. Tell me about the rest of the hammer."

Hopefully, she wouldn't find any other glitches in his presentation. This wasn't looking good at all.

* * *

JARED FELT like he was floating beside Talbot. He was using the vid feed from one of the other marines to have a conversation with him from his flag bridge, but it was just as though he was there.

"How the hell could he just disappear?"

"Damned if I know, sir. I turned my back for a minute and he was gone. I thought he'd floated around the curve of the station, but he didn't turn up when we spread out. *Invincible* scanned the entire area looking for him. Nothing. He has to be inside that thing."

"I thought you didn't find any airlocks."

The former noncom growled. "We didn't. There isn't a single entrance to this thing. Not one seam we can find. Nothing."

"Then we'll need to open the thing up. Try a plasma rifle."

"No dice. As far as I can tell, it had no effect whatsoever. It didn't even discolor the skin. We need bigger guns."

"*Invincible*'s beams are too heavy. Try the plasma weapons on one of the pinnaces. Call me back once you're in."

He turned to Doctor Leonard. "What do you think happened?"

The older man shrugged. "He went over to get scanner readings of the hull on that station. There's no way he would wander off. I suppose it's possible that he had a suit failure, but that doesn't explain why no one can locate him. I think your belief that he's inside that station is an accurate one."

"Then how did he get in, and how do we get him out?"

"I haven't the slightest idea. What's more troubling is that he should've called us. Perhaps we might not be in range to hear a cry for help, but Major Talbot is. I should go over there and take readings for myself."

Jared shook his head. "Not until we know more about what happened. One of the marines can take a reading after they breach the hull on that thing."

"Incoming communication from Major Talbot," Marcus said.

This time the marine had his helmet off, obviously inside the pinnace.

"Are you ready to fire?"

Talbot shrugged. "We already did. No effect that we can see. The damned thing is immune to damage from us."

"Hold on," Jared said. "Are you telling me that our weapons are just bouncing?"

"Literally. I hit it with flechettes, too. Not a scratch on it. You're going to have to use the ship's weapons."

"Not the missiles. That's overkill. Maybe a low-powered beam. Marcus?"

"If the Major and his people will pull back, I can move into range and focus the beam on the hull. At the lowest power settings, it still has the potential to do a lot of damage."

Jared nodded. "Aim somewhere other than the spot Carl disappeared."

It took about ten minutes to get everything set up. Jared monitored the shot when Marcus took it at the lowest power setting.

It had no more effect than the handheld plasma weapons.

"Well," Marcus said. "This is unexpected. Shall I increase power, Admiral?"

"Take it up slowly. When it fails, it might go suddenly."

Invincible fired ever increasingly powerful shots at the station. None had any effect whatsoever. Once they reached full power, they started adding in additional beams. All to no effect. The dammed thing might as well be immune to energy weapons.

"Shall we stand off and try a missile, Admiral?" Marcus asked.

Jared rubbed his face. "Not yet. An explosion or high-speed impact might be completely different from a beam attack. I'd rather not rupture the thing."

He turned to Doctor Leonard. "Suit up, Doctor. You're going to take some readings before we try again. Tell me what that thing is and how to open it. If we can't, we might never see Carl again."

The odds were stacked against the young man. His suit only had air for another four hours. Assuming that was an alien environment in there—if the station was even functional—it would probably be hostile to humans.

The clock was ticking.

7

After half an hour of searching, Carl gave up on figuring out how the station had pulled him inside. He also conceded that he wouldn't be repeating the feat that made it happen. No amount of scanning from the inside was having any effect, though he was getting clean readings now.

He wasn't getting out the same way he'd gotten in.

Which was bad. The interior of the station was dark and cold, and that didn't even begin to consider the "atmosphere" he found himself in.

It was difficult to tell with his suit lights, but the liquid surrounding him certainly had pale blue color. The scanner said it was water, though it had some odd trace elements. The oxygen content was in line with what he recalled about normal water on Avalon, but it had a higher range of heavy metals. Arsenic in particular.

In any case, he wasn't going to be breathing water anytime soon. He needed to find an exit, or he was going to die in here in a few short hours.

A year ago, this might have paralyzed him with fear, but not now. He'd learned a lot from the people around him. When the pressure hit, you had to keep swinging. So, he buried his fear and got to work.

The ring was clear in the center. A tube several dozen meters across seemed to circle the station. Many compartments sat to every side, none with hatches.

He supposed that made sense. With a liquid atmosphere, it probably required better circulation to remain healthy for the occupants.

Not that he'd seen any sign of them. Not in person or through furniture. Though he did see what looked like operational machinery. He had no idea how they kept it functional over long periods submerged like this.

Or even how an aquatic race could learn to forge metal and get into space.

There were a lot of questions he'd like answered, if he survived.

Once again, discovering the purpose of the station was high on the list. Someone had come into the most hostile environment imaginable and built it. Considering that and the materials, the aliens were more advanced than the Old Empire. So, why hadn't anyone found evidence of them or even met them?

Surely, such an advanced people must've left other artifacts.

Unless, somehow, they were located on an unconnected set of flip points. Everyone knew that only a fraction of stellar systems had flip points. What if that theory was flawed? What if there were two or more unconnected—or only barely connected—flip-point networks?

With that, it might be possible for two advanced species to occupy the same volume of space without ever having met. The weak flip point that led here might be a fluke.

It seemed as though one of them would have discovered communications from the other. Unless, of course, the builders were long gone. Swallowed by the mists of time.

Could this station, hidden away in a place no one would come looking, be the only remnant of these people?

That was frightening, when one considered it. What could cause the end of an advanced people like this? Something similar to the Fall? Humanity had survived. Shouldn't they have as well?

A blinking light from ahead caused him to slow down. Something was different.

He approached the small light cautiously. It sat above a hatch—one not that different from the ones used in the Empire, though constructed from what looked like salvaged materials.

What sent a chill down his spine was a message scratched under a button.

Press me.

The implications were staggering. He wasn't the first human to visit this place, and his predecessor had anticipated his arrival.

Carl considered his options. He didn't have anything to lose by trying. He pressed the button.

The hatch slid slowly open, allowing the fluid to flow gently into what was obviously some kind of airlock. One large enough for his suit, thankfully.

He wedged himself inside and found the button to cycle the lock. Unsure of what or who might be on the other side, he pressed the button firmly.

* * *

ANGELA STARED AT THE HAMMER. It sat on her desk without seeming all that special. Yet, after *Persephone* had explained the research to her, she'd realized that it was a stunning technological marvel. Even if some parts of it failed to live up to expectations. Or the designer was a mad genius.

She'd arranged to take it with them against Owlet's wishes. That had really pissed him off, and that was just fine with her. The boy needed to learn his limits.

Taken singly, the quantum validation unit, the partially collapsed matter, the miniature grav drive with the incorporated fusion plant, the tiny battle screen, and the enhanced-range communicator were all groundbreaking in one way or another.

Owlet wasn't even responsible for the partially collapsed matter or the drive/fusion plant combo. The people at the Grant Research Facility figured out the former and God only knew who created the latter for the AIs.

Still, Owlet had managed to create something unique and dangerous. If only the boy had common sense to go along with his genius.

The true groundbreaker might be the quantum validation system. She completely understood his impulse to limit its range. Faced with the alternative, she'd instinctively rejected it, too.

Perhaps the range wouldn't be infinite. There might be more to the theory than what they knew. Flip points had an upper end. Perhaps this system would, too. Only testing would tell for sure.

None of that changed her opinion on allowing the boy to hand over his toy to Kelsey without changes. Weapon or no, it needed some limitations.

Frankly, she wished she had some method to interface with the quantum setup. Just to see if it bypassed the radiation and distance to Owlet. But she didn't have that implant. Only he did.

But what if she just had the communicator do something to the quantum unit? Could it?

It only took a moment's search of the technical specifications to show that wasn't possible. He'd only wired the hammer to check the spin of the photons in the quantum validation unit. There was no provision to use the validation unit to communicate directly with the hammer or wielder.

Too bad. That might have been interesting.

* * *

KELSEY'S LESSON had gone as well as it could. Ned had the knowledge, but not the body to spar with her.

So, she spent a lot of time doing katas. Dances that drilled the moves into her muscle memory. He was also training her marine guards, so Kelsey could turn her enhancements down to human normal and practice with them.

Even with her skill level, that was more in line with the butt whooping she'd have expected before this grand adventure. She knew the word diminutive was an understatement when applied to her. Particularly when compared to marines.

So she cheated. She kept just a little speed and strength to bring her more in line with them. The goal was to learn how to win, after all. Not how to be stomped into the mat gracefully.

They were the real reason she was determined to make black belt before the fleet returned to Avalon. They had a background in combat and were racing up the ranks. She was determined to be the first one there. She knew she wouldn't be the first sensei, but that was fine with her.

She'd banished Ned from her mind and taken a shower, satisfied with her progress. Maybe another few weeks and she'd get that damned belt.

Angela was waiting for her when she finished dressing. Kelsey schooled her face and hoped the woman wasn't there to rant about Carl or Mjölnir. It was like an obsession.

She got an energy drink out of the refrigeration unit in her office. "What can I do for you, Angela? Drink?"

"I'm good, Highness. I wanted to give you an update on my research into the hammer project."

The marine couldn't even bring herself to name it. Kelsey suppressed a smile and sat down. Not behind her desk, but off to one side in a comfortable cluster of chairs. The marine officer joined her.

"You can't have done any real testing yet, so what new danger have you discovered?"

The large woman smiled wryly. "I hope I'm not always so full of negativity."

"Only when it comes to this project and Carl Owlet. Sorry."

"Then this will be a refreshing change of pace. I think Owlet has made the most important breakthrough in science since the creation of flip drives."

Kelsey choked a little on her drink. "Excuse me? Are you trying to drown me?"

"Not intentionally," Angela said. "I'm being completely serious. This quantum validation system and tracking unit. He told us it was good out to ten kilometers. I think he's allowed himself to doubt the true reach of his discovery.

"I'm no scientist, but it seems to me that the limit he imposed is arbitrary. Quantum theory says it should have no range limitation at all."

Kelsey carefully set her drink down on the handy end table. "You're telling me that he created an intergalactic communicator? The fabled means of one system talking to another without sending a ship through a flip point?"

Angela shrugged. "I can't speak as to the distance, but I'm willing to bet my firstborn child that it will be a hell of a lot further than ten kilometers. I think it has some relation to flip points, so like them, I bet there is an upper end to the realistic range.

"But they can send a ship hundreds of light years. How far could a simple communication go? Twice that? Five? Ten? I have no idea. Until we start testing, we won't know."

The marine leaned forward earnestly. "I can see some obvious advantages and drawbacks. We could send a probe through a flip point and get a view from the other side without it coming back. In real time. There isn't supposed to be a delay in transmission, though there might be, I suppose. This is all new stuff."

Kelsey nodded. "And the downside?"

"Fleet Command could become backseat drivers. Right now, Fleet commanders make calls for themselves. With direct communication, that opens the possibility of micromanagement."

"That would be a negative," Kelsey admitted. "Wow. This is big. Why didn't he admit there was the possibility of something like this?"

"I have no idea. If I could tinker with the hammer and figure it out, I'd ask him. I can't, though. It's not open to use as a communicator the way the hammer is set up."

Kelsey considered that. "I bet one of the techs could untangle that for us. We'd just have to be careful not to break something. It's only a test device, so I'm not worried about taking it apart. Make that happen, and see if you can open a channel to Carl."

Angela smiled. "Won't *that* surprise him?"

8

The situation had Jared stumped. If they used a missile, they might critically damage the station. Or destroy it. Yet, none of the other weapons even made a scratch on the thing's surface. Whatever it was, it was damned good at stopping energy.

He supposed that made sense. That kind of thing was terrific for a station built near a black hole.

Doctor Leonard was over there scanning it now. The initial readings told the tale of why their beams and plasma were ineffective. The hull was some kind of collapsed matter. Perhaps even neutronium.

The scientist was unwilling to guess at how strong the material might be, but he'd already determined that it wasn't as massive as theory predicted. He'd keep working, but time was running short.

Jared would hate to do it, but he'd punch a missile into the station to gain access if he had to. Searching the wreckage might take a while, so he was only giving the man another half hour. If he didn't find a way in before that, Jared would do so on his own.

The scientist had a dozen marines in close proximity, all of them heavily armed and loaded down with supplies. If they got in, he wanted extra air and gear to keep them going while they figured out how to create an exit.

Remotes were recording everything and sending it to *Invincible*. For all the good it seemed to be doing.

* * *

"How's it coming, Doc?" Talbot asked. "You found anything yet?"

The older man gave him an exasperated look. "Not since you asked me two minutes ago, Major Talbot. I'll certainly inform you the moment that changes."

"I'm not trying to rush you or anything, but Carl only has two hours of air left. Admiral Mertz doesn't want to do it, but he'll put a missile into this thing in half an hour if you haven't found the way in."

"I'm quite aware of the time constraints, Major. I'm not seeing anything. Almost literally. The skin of this station is blocking my attempts to get any data."

"So, that was what Carl saw, too. What would he do to get around that?"

The other man nodded. "I'm already doing that. I've increased the power of the scan as much as this equipment will allow. Nothing."

Talbot had guessed as much. "Is there any way you might be able to get a better reading?"

"Perhaps if I modulated the frequency I might find one that gives better results. It will take me a moment to set up an oscillation."

"I suggest you try to mimic what you think Carl would've done."

"Yes, indeed. Thank you, Major Obvious."

Talbot smiled. Some of those old movies and entertainment shows were gaining a cult following. Even the so-called commercials.

Without warning, the hull sank, pulling Leonard, Talbot, and the entire cluster of marines into the cavity. It flowed around them and closed off before he could even kick his own scanners into high gear.

"I believe I replicated the sequence Carl found," Leonard said.

"Thank you, Doctor Obvious. First squad, go left. Second, go right."

Talbot switched to the channel he'd been using to communicate with Carl earlier. "Buddy, can you hear me?"

A moment later, Carl Owlet called back. "I hope you brought something that can get us out of here."

"The jury's still out on that. We're headed your way."

"I have him," Talbot said on the general frequency. "He sounds okay." He consulted his implants and started toward the left. Carl wasn't that far away.

"I'm unable to signal the ship," Doctor Leonard said. "We appear to be just as muzzled as Carl is, even with the higher-powered gear I brought along."

"I'm not that surprised. What's this stuff around us?"

The scientist scanned the liquid. "It's water, with a number of trace elements mixed in. It appears our mythical builders were either water breathers or amphibians. That rules out humanity. Congratulations, Major Talbot. We've discovered an alien civilization."

"Whee. Now all we need to do is get out and tell someone."

He led the marines around the ring until they found the airlock. Carl floated outside it.

"How are you doing, pal?" Talbot asked. "Is your life support good? We have air and other supplies for you."

The boy shook his head. "I'm good for a few more hours. Thanks for coming, but I really wish you'd stayed away. I'm very much afraid we won't be getting back out."

He slapped Carl on the shoulder, an odd feeling in the water. "Don't be so negative. How hard can it be to get back out?"

"Ask the guys that built this." He gestured at the airlock. "They're still inside. They never made it out again."

"That's not all. You need to come in and look at them. There's not a whole lot of room, so I suggest only the three of us go in."

Talbot started to insist he go in first, but decided that was silly. Carl had already been inside the room. He'd have known if there were any dangers. He'd settle for going in before the doctor.

Once they followed Carl through, he saw what the younger man meant. Someone had taken a compartment and sealed it off. They'd managed to pump out the water after they'd built the airlock. Quite a feat on an alien space station.

The down side was that they were still here. One side of the compartment had dozens of bodies in armored vacuum gear identical to their own. Even from here, he could tell they were still inside those suits.

The only one of them not stacked like cut wood was sitting in a makeshift chair. He, too, was suited, but he'd rigged up some kind of screen in front of him. The keyboard looked virtual, but the rest had come from a large communicator, something like what Doctor Leonard had brought along.

"Who are they?" Talbot asked. "Old Empire?"

"It's a *lot* more complicated and confusing than that," Carl said. "Ping his implants."

Talbot was surprised the dead man's implants were still active. That was a first from an Old Empire Fleet body. He pinged them for the man's identity and immediately realized what Carl had meant.

The body belonged to Carl Owlet.

* * *

KELSEY WATCHED the technician disassemble Mjölnir with interest. Some of the parts looked familiar to her—such as the grav drive/fusion combo—but the rest was new. Carl had really packed it tightly. There was no room to spare.

The woman put on a pair of magnifying goggles and looked at the connections. "This is the quantum validation unit here, Captain. It's pretty small, but I don't have any experience to tell me what that means about capability.

"It's wired directly into the central processor and linked to the communicator. The connection is parallel, so I'm assuming that it can operate independently, but the two are somehow both required."

"That's what the technical specifications say," Angela said. "It uses the quantum unit to validate commands sent by the standard communicator."

"Can you isolate the quantum unit and use it for communication?" Kelsey asked.

The tech looked up at her. "I can isolate it, but I'm not even sure how it works. I could probably send a signal of some kind, but I'm unsure what the input is supposed to look like. If it's only built to authenticate the commands, it might just be a code."

Angela nodded. "That's what I gathered from reading the specs. It has a large list of valid codes. It uses one and moves on to the next. All are just different spin states for the various photons."

"That makes sense, if both ends work off the same list and have a means of discerning when a code was missed, for whatever reason. I'll examine the system in a little more detail and determine if I can send some kind of meaningful sequence to Mister Owlet. I have to be sure of the mechanism first."

Kelsey nodded. "Call me when you have it ready to test."

* * *

ELISE WENT over the research she'd gathered about Ethan Bandar. It was scant on details, other than what was in the public record. She resigned herself to the fact she just wouldn't be able to pin him down without actually meeting him. She couldn't really ask the people that knew him best for crucial details.

But, perhaps she didn't have to. Jared must have confided in someone. Captain Graves was his oldest friend and former executive officer. He must have heard an earful. But he wasn't available until the ships regrouped.

He might also have confided in Doctor Stone. Elise had found there were several classes of people that knew the most about someone's life: mates, close friends, priests, bartenders, and doctors.

There was only one way to find out.

She made her way to the medical center. The place was a hive of activity. Elise hoped that didn't mean there was some kind of emergency.

Doctor Stone spotted her from across the compartment and made her way over. "Are you having a problem with the implant updates, Your Highness?"

Elise shook her head. "Not at all. I had some personal questions, but I see you have something in progress. Has something happened?"

"There's an unfolding situation on the alien station, but I can spare a few minutes. Until the admiral gets more information and we get the people back out, we won't know if there's really a problem."

"They got in? That's good, right?"

"Only if we manage to get them back out. Come into my office and we can talk."

Stone led Elise into her office. They sat in a comfortable set of chairs off to the side of the desk. "What kind of personal questions are we talking about? You're not writing my unauthorized biography, are you?"

Elise smiled. "No. I'm trying to make plans for when we get to Avalon. Based on a number of comments, I'm fairly certain that Jared, and to some extent Kelsey, are going to have problems with Ethan Bandar. I need to get a feel for the man so I can make some contingency plans. I've heard some rather dark whispers."

That last made Stone nod. "Well, I've heard a few things, too. Some I'd slot under the doctor-patient confidentiality umbrella, but others I can talk about. What dark whispers have you heard?"

"Jared told me that he was pretty certain that Ethan was responsible for someone's death. He thought it was an assassination attempt gone wrong."

"Yes," Stone said. "The mission's original ambassador, Carlo Vega. He ate something that *really* disagreed with him. There was an investigation, but it proved inconclusive."

"You think the heir to the Imperial Throne is capable of that?"

Stone considered that. "I hate saying so, but I've seen how he feels about Jared. I think it's a reasonable suspicion. No one will ever prove it, mind you, and that doesn't even begin to count the number of rumors I've heard about the man."

Elise sat up straighter. "What kind of rumors?"

Stone leaned forward and lowered her voice. "None of this is more than gossip, mind you. Ethan Bandar has worked hard to get Jared ejected from Fleet. When that proved impossible, he settled for poisoning his reputation. Whispers about his character here, pushes to keep him out of promotions or better postings there.

"Honestly, Jared was a full grade behind where he should've been. That's all because of Ethan Bandar and the people in Fleet hauling his water."

Elise nodded slowly. "I imagine he's not going to be pleased when Jared returns as an admiral in command of a fleet like this. As the one to have met the Pale Ones and emerged victorious."

Stone's lips quirked. "You have a talent for understatement. Based on what I've seen of the man, he's going to have a stroke. Or die of apoplectic shock. If he somehow survives, he'll come out swinging. If he tried to have Jared killed before, he'll try harder.

"He'll immediately have his Fleet stooges take everything away that he can. Expect a court-martial."

"Seriously? For winning? What does the loser get? A blindfold and the final meal of his choice?"

"They'll charge him for the loss of his ship. For what he did to Captain Breckenridge, too. Ethan Bandar can't allow Jared to emerge victorious. It's like a medical condition, his paranoia. The heir will feel justified doing whatever it takes to stop Jared. Including murder, in my opinion."

Elise sighed. "That matches everything I've heard about the man. What can we do to protect Jared?"

"Make certain the emperor is behind him, which I suspect he will be. The strike will come from the shadows or through proxies in Fleet. We'll need to be in control of Jared's transport. We wouldn't want any unfortunate cutter accidents, would we? That sort of thing."

"There's no way to prove Ethan Bandar was behind the assassination attempt?"

"I've been over Vega's body with every tool this Old Empire ship has to offer. I can say with certainty what killed the poor man, but not who was behind it. But I promise I'll be with you every step of the way making sure we protect Jared from that man's twisted hatred."

After a deep breath, Elise continued. "What about Kelsey?"

"Are you asking if she thinks her brother is a murderer? I doubt it. Jared kept that theory away from her, and she's never approached me about it. Ethan is her twin brother. I can't imagine she believes him capable of something like that."

"I'll have to talk with her," Elise said. "Just to let her know I'm worried. Especially with the changes she's gone through. He might turn some of his anger on her. If she's not on guard, something terrible might happen."

Stone grinned. "Oh, I do hope he tries something. I remember the vid of the assassination attempt in your parliament building. That's when she could barely walk. Now that she's fully integrated with her implants and hardware, it would be brief and very messy for her attackers."

"I hope it doesn't come to that. A shot from the dark could kill her before she knows a thing."

"Then we'll have to work hard to make sure that never happens."

Elise extended her hand. "Welcome to the conspiracy, Doctor. Let's hope we can keep anyone from making a terrible mistake. There are enemies more deserving of our attention. I'd rather we all focus on the Rebel Empire before they come looking for us with a fleet of ships."

9

Carl helped the others move his… his other body away from the computer and lay it on the deck. He was no medical specialist, but the other Carl had been dead awhile. Weeks. Maybe more. It was hard to tell.

The other him had purged his atmosphere, so he had the look of a man who'd been in a vacuum. Not as bad as the corpses from *Courageous*, but it still made estimating time of death difficult with only his eyes.

If they ever got out of here, someone could tell them. If not, it hardly mattered.

He sat in the chair, and it creaked ominously under his weight. The armored vacuum suit wasn't light. He hoped his seat didn't collapse. The air in the room was foul and unbreathable, so he'd have to make do.

"I'm going to see who else we have in the pile," Talbot said. "Give me a hand, Doc."

Carl tapped the keyboard and the screen came to life. The message it displayed was no surprise.

Hello, me. That is, if you're Carl Owlet.

You'll have to forgive my gallows humor, but I'm almost out of air and I'm sure no one is coming for me.

Yet, based on the people I found here when I arrived, others have made it inside looking for me. Well, for other versions of me.

In case you haven't checked, there are five others just like us in the pile. The one before me had a marine escort. Apparently, they came in with him. Two others had some marines that followed them in later, and one had Doctor Leonard.

So, that makes six of me, three Talbots, one Doctor Leonard, and from one to three of various marines. I wonder how many make up a set.

Anyway, the first Carl died quickly. His implants were still active, so I was able to access all his recorded data. Useful. He started tearing equipment on this station apart to build an airtight area.

It took two additional groups to get it finished. My immediate predecessor was able to get this computer set up and attempt to interface with the station. He wasn't successful, but I knew all the things that hadn't worked. That saved me time.

I think I'm close. Based on some of the environmental clues, I think the station is aware of me. I just can't hear what it wants to say. If it's really trying to communicate.

It has to be tired of us littering the corridors.

In any case, I've compiled everything from the logs our predecessors made into one for you. I hope you succeed in making contact and getting the hell out of this deathtrap.

Wait. What? You're wondering what the hell is going on with a half-dozen Carls?

Damned if I know. We all have identical implant serial codes. Which makes accessing their implant records a breeze, I have to tell you. Make a note that you might want to close that security loophole before the AIs hear about it.

Based on the complete implant records, I think we have to be from different universes.

Congratulations. This is going to win you the Lucien Prize for sure. And honestly, you deserve it. You really gave everything for this project. Several times over.

Anyway, there are minor differences in a number of things. People who some of us know that I don't recognize. Other references to events not going as I remember. The first Carl arrived here almost nine months ago. You'd have to compare the date to see how that works out for you.

It has to be the black hole. Somehow, it's turned the inside of this station into some kind of shared space. Frankly, even if you get out, I'm not sure how you'd know you got out to the right universe.

Not that I suspect you'd care. It beats dying.

Well, my air just gave out, and I need to bring this heart-to-heart to a close. I'm rooting for you, buddy. If anyone can do it, it's you. Do us proud. If you make it out, give Angela a kiss for me. Adios.

Carl

Well, that certainly wasn't what he'd expected.

And kissing the marine officer would be a good way to die. The other him sure had a twisted sense of humor.

He pinged the dead man's implants and discovered he had access to everything. That cloned serial number issue was a real thing. Though he supposed it wasn't cloned in this case. He'd be sure and fix that if he got out.

The combined logs were there, and he pulled them in. For good measure, he snagged every file the man had. He could sort them out later.

He was sure the other him had done the same, but he verified he had the files from all of the versions of himself.

The last Carl had died seventeen days ago. That meant they'd arrived over a span of almost seven months. He wondered if someone else was going to show up before he died.

"There are six other versions of you, counting the one in the chair," Talbot said. "I found a few of myself and another Doctor Leonard. The marines outside are represented, mostly. Oddly, there are a few people here that died before we found this station."

Talbot leaned against the wall and looked at Carl. "I have to tell you, this is spooky. What the devil is going on?"

"Parallel universes," Doctor Leonard said. "I found a number of files with theories in my other's implants, and it's obviously true. We are in fact incontrovertible proof."

"My other me thought he was close to a breakthrough," Carl said. "I'll try to finish my life's work, if you know what I mean."

Talbot shook his head. "That's dark, man. *Really* dark. I'll cycle the men in to get files off their implants. Just in case there's something useful. Then we'll search the station while you work. We have enough air and food for a few weeks. Let's hope it doesn't take that long."

* * *

JARED FELT like banging his head on the console. They had complete records of how Doctor Leonard had triggered the station into absorbing himself and the others, but now it wasn't working.

They'd placed a unit on the surface of the station to do exactly what Doctor Leonard did, but it just sat there. The station wasn't interested.

He wondered if it had to be a person. Damned if he was going to risk someone else to test the theory. They didn't even know if the others were still alive.

The lift doors slid open, and Elise walked onto the flag bridge. She stopped beside his seat.

"What's the word?"

"Not good. We think we know how they got inside, but the method isn't working without a person. I'm not asking anyone else to risk their lives. I'm going to fire a missile."

"Won't that put them in grave danger?"

"No worse than leaving them inside. Marcus, target the station opposite the entry point. Fire one missile and count on the radiation hashing it."

"At this range, that shouldn't be an issue."

He nodded. "Good plan. Fire when ready."

The missile wouldn't reach full speed, but it would be impressive enough. It lanced out of the tubes and slammed into the station.

Jared eyed the debris and quickly decided most of it was from the missile.

"The shot was ineffective, Admiral. Telemetry indicates it struck the station but did not penetrate. The cutter we had standing by says they can't see any damage at all. Not even a scratch."

He rubbed his face. "How is that possible? Even collapsed matter should dent. Right?"

"I'm afraid my grasp of the material is weak. Obviously, it's even stronger than we'd expected, or there's another force stabilizing the station. In either case, I don't believe further missiles would be very effective."

"No, I think you're right. Have the crew stand down. We'll just have to hope they find a way out for themselves."

* * *

PERSEPHONE MADE it all the way out to the twelve-hour mark without finding anything exciting. Only a single stripped gas giant core. Angela supposed the science types found that interesting, but it really didn't do anything for her.

They stayed long enough to get some scanner readings. The radiation was lower this far out, so they were able to send in probes that lasted almost an hour. The scientists would have to make do with that.

The technician had to take a study break while working on the hammer. It was so different from what the woman normally worked with, she needed to draw it all out and make a plan. With the grav drive set to negate its weight, it was easy to move it around.

She called Angela and Kelsey back to the work area just after *Persephone* started back in. She looked tired.

"The mechanism isn't exactly set up for direct communication," she told them, "but I have a plan. The only thing I don't know is if Mister Owlet will even notice it. I'm not sure how the system is set up on his end. As he's the authenticator, he might not have a means of receiving an incoming signal.

"Even if he does, he might not recognize the message. I settled on an old communication protocol called Morse code. It utilizes sets of dots, dashes, and pauses to make letters and words. It's not commonly known anymore, though. He might not have the means to understand it."

Kelsey nodded. "He'll recognize some of it. I know that he's seen some Old Earth vids where people have used it. If this doesn't work, well, we're not really suffering. It's just a test. What are you planning to send?"

The woman gestured toward her tablet. "I wrote out a short message. Basically, an explanation of why we've called. We'll know it worked if he sends a response of any kind. Comprehension isn't really required.

"I'll mimic dots and dashes by single validation codes and closely sent trios. I've programed my tablet to do the hard work. All I need to do is press the button. I can resend it at intervals to allow him to try and decipher it."

"Do it," Kelsey said.

* * *

CARL WAS LAGGING. He'd been up all day, and it was now the middle of the night. The marines had gone into a rotation to allow some of them to sleep. The compartment was too small for them to fit into. They could pressurize the compartment, but that would waste air. Better to stay in the suits. They might need every breath before this was over.

He'd reviewed everything the other versions of him had discovered and recorded. The station certainly seemed as though it were trying to communicate with them. Small mobile devices occasionally ventured near the trapped men.

A marine from one of the earlier groups had fired at one of the mobile units, but the water spoiled his aim. Thankfully, he hadn't tried a plasma weapon. In water, that would boil them all. There'd been no hostile response to a real provocation like that, so Carl assumed that the computer wasn't interested in killing them.

The station had to have a computer. That much was certain. It had used those machines to lure the men to where they could salvage equipment useful in creating an airlock.

Carl was at a loss as to how they would communicate with an alien computer. Not only was there a language barrier, they didn't even know what it looked like.

Hell, if the computer wanted to help them, why didn't it open an exit? By now it had to realize the stakes.

He almost jumped out of the chair when his implants told him that he was receiving validation signals. His fogged mind didn't understand what that meant for a few seconds.

Someone was using the hammer command validation system to send authentication signals to him with the entangled photons. They were getting through!

There was a pattern to them, too. Single signals, groups of three, and longer pauses. There was a meaning in there. His thoughts immediately went to Morse code.

Unfortunately, he didn't understand Morse code and had nothing on it in his implant memory.

He smiled. He knew enough though.

* * *

KELSEY SMILED when the tablet showed signals coming back. "He heard us! It really does have a long range. We're halfway across the system! There's no time lag. This is FTL. He's done it!"

"The response isn't making sense," the technician said. "He must not understand the code. He's just repeating a couple of letters. S then O then S. Then it repeats."

That was a bucket of cold water to Kelsey's face. "That's a distress signal. Only used in dire circumstances. He's in trouble."

She opened a channel to the bridge. "Jack, something's wrong back at *Invincible*. Flank speed."

"Aye, ma'am. Flank speed to the ring station. That gives us an ETA of about five hours. If I might ask, how the hell do you know that?"

Kelsey looked over at Angela and the technician. "Three really smart people figured out a way to make it happen. I'm on my way up."

10

Talbot listened to Carl explain the sudden communication with more hope than he'd expected. Everyone else had died, including three other versions of him, and that made him think of this place as a death trap. Maybe not.

Doctor Leonard grasped what Carl was saying immediately. "You never mentioned this quantum validation equipment. God, boy. It takes my breath away. How could you fail to grasp the implications?"

The graduate student shrugged. "I saw them, Doctor. I just didn't want to mention them until I did some testing. Flip points have a top range, so I'm certain this does, too.

"It's Princess Kelsey and *Persephone*. They're still five hours away at maximum acceleration. So, at the very least, we know this will work inside a solar system and that it's FTL. Obviously. They've sent the alphabet in order, so I can communicate with them now."

The older man nodded energetically. "It isn't deterred by the radiation, so it's not interacting with the environment between the sender and receiver. Also as theory predicted. Carl, this is the most significant scientific breakthrough since the Fall. Perhaps even before it, if the ability to communicate can cross stellar boundaries."

Carl didn't look impressed. "It won't do us any good if we can't get out of here."

"That's another point," Leonard said. "It might be reaching across a universal barrier. That's even more significant. My boy, you've wildly exceeded my highest hopes for you. When we get home, I'll be submitting something to the Lucien committee on your behalf."

The younger man blinked. "That's insane. I don't even have my doctorate yet. I've only barely started learning."

"I know! The next few decades will be brilliant! Hell, the next few centuries."

Talbot cleared his throat. "This is all very exciting, but I'm going to side with Carl on this. If we can't get out of here, it doesn't make a difference to us. Did any of the other Carls try this?"

Leonard shook his head. "There was no mention of it. Let me scan them again."

The scientist pulled out the scanner and took a good look at Carl. Talbot mentally tagged him Carl Prime.

"Is it the unit behind your lungs? Excellent. We'll see if they have similar equipment."

He scanned the corpses and shook his head. "None of them have it. You're unique, even among your doubles, my boy."

"Well, that possibly explains why they didn't get out of here," Talbot said. "None of the boys have found anything that looks like an exit, and none of the scanning we've done inside has opened anything. The little machines are watching us but haven't tried to interact.

"We have to get the admiral to trigger an opening on the surface while we're waiting inside at the right spot. That has to be it."

"Major," one of the marines outside said over the com, "you'd better come out here."

He excused himself from the scientific discussion and cycled out through the airlock.

"What is it?"

He saw it before the man spoke. The light that one of the Carls had rigged to draw people here was blinking in a series of single flashes and sets of three.

The alien computer had sensed the quantum signals and was attempting to communicate.

* * *

CARL WATCHED the light blink in the same style code that Kelsey had used. How was that even possible? No one could detect the quantum effects. Well, obviously the aliens could. Somehow. He'd have to dig more deeply into that if he made it out of here.

At least it meant there was a possible way out of here. If they could convince the computer to release them, they might live after all.

"The first thing we need to do is find a way to talk on our end," he said. "It can detect the quantum signals, but I can only directly communicate with the hammer. I don't want to muddy those waters unless I have to."

Doctor Leonard nodded. "Quite right. Perhaps a light of our own?"

"We need to do this at a faster speed than figuring out how to say 'Hello World' or some such. I'm going to try something a bit more involved. Give me a few minutes, please."

He stepped back over to the light and thought about the problem. The thing could obviously sense the area around the light. Otherwise, how would it know which power circuit to mess with to communicate? So, it could probably see him right now. Or whatever passed for sight for these people.

He blinked. That might be it. "Seeing" meant different things to different species. Old Terran bats used sound to know their surroundings. So did a number of sea dwellers. The aliens might also use that to communicate.

The computer could've been attempting to communicate all this time, but in their suits, they'd never know. Especially if the sound was outside the normal range of human hearing.

He activated the scanners in his suit. They weren't as good as a handheld unit, but they were adequate for this task. They were also simple to integrate with his implant processors.

Computers were fast. Faster than a human. If they could establish a communication protocol, the computers could work it out faster than he could.

The area around him was alive with subsonic noise. Hell, even noise in the normal human hearing range. Only, they hadn't been listening for it.

He had his suit send out a subsonic pulse in Morse code. It was immediately repeated from somewhere near him.

The computer was listening.

He experimented with making the tones faster. The top speed of communication was impressive. It sounded like an electronic wail to him.

Next, the computer needed a large sample of language to make guesses with. They had no common point of reference, so hopefully the computer could make progress on its own. Visual cues would help.

He had a lot of video in his implant memory. He liked watching some of the same old Terran vids that Kelsey did. Perhaps if he could find a way to link that video with the Morse code, it would be a start.

Actually, a nature documentary might be better. He liked hiking, though he rarely had time these days. Or a suitable location. If the computer could match key words and images, perhaps his implant computers could help translate.

He didn't have any of those, but maybe he could get some.

Carl sent a message through the quantum link, asking if they could send some nature documentaries through the link at high speed. He knew enough about video and audio encoding to get it all back together on this end.

All they had to do was link the computer on their end into the quantum unit and tell it to send some to him.

That would allow him to communicate with them in a more reasonable manner, too. Once they had a mutually agreeable set of communication protocols, he could send and receive video and audio through his implants.

Setting that up took a few minutes. Once the data started flowing in, he began assembling it. It only took a few seconds. He'd built a lot of data throughput into the unit for future growth.

Once the first was complete, he instructed his implants to keep exchanging data until the two units could understand one another.

The process was unreal. He played the vids through his suit projector on the bulkhead at a fast pace. The implants translated the audio track into Morse. The high-speed squeals of Morse from the computer made him go faster, and then even faster.

Then he became a bystander as his implants and the computer traded increasingly complex series of code that were more complex than Morse. It included a large amount of data. They were creating a shared language, he thought.

Which was crazy. His implants weren't *that* advanced.

That's when he realized it wasn't just his implants. It was also communicating with someone through his quantum validation unit at an incredible rate. A ton of data was flowing in both directions.

It was using the already established link between the quantum unit and the computer on the other end to speed the process. His implants were acting as a go-between. He only hoped the others didn't freak out and cut them off.

He initiated a communications request and slipped it into the torrent of data flowing between him and the computer.

* * *

KELSEY WAS STILL TRYING to grasp what was happening when her implants pinged with an incoming communication request. It was Carl Owlet.

He must've figured out some way to use the quantum validation unit to communicate directly. That was excellent. She accepted the request.

"Carl? Are you alright?"

"Kelsey? Thank God we got ahold of someone. We're okay, but trapped inside the station. Things are really odd in here. I think we really did find aliens. Just not live ones."

That was pretty clear, she thought. "We're sending the movies you requested, and I allowed *Persephone* to respond to the other information requests because it was you. What's happening?"

"The computer here—at least I think it's a computer—sensed the quantum communication, and we're trying to teach it enough to interact with us. My implants are requesting data to find common ground with it. We're hoping that we can get enough clarity to tell it we need to leave. Where are you?"

"Halfway across the system. Congratulations on creating the first FTL communications system, by the way. This is huge."

"It's been a big week for me. Talbot, Doctor Leonard, and a dozen marines are here with me. We found incontrovertible proof that there are parallel universes."

Hearing her lover was trapped worried her, but she was already doing what she had to do to get him free.

"We'll be back in the area in a bit more than four hours. Parallel universes? You're sure?"

"Pretty sure. We found bodies here. There are several versions of me. With my exact implant serial numbers. They left messages for me. It's kind of creepy."

"You can drop the qualifiers. That's creepy."

A second request for communication came in, but this one was odd. It had no implant code at all. She wasn't sure who was calling.

"I'm getting a request to talk to someone," she told Carl. "Is it someone on your end?"

"Not that I know of. Everything is going through my implants. I'm not getting a ping from anyone."

She mentally shrugged. "Let's see who it is."

Kelsey accepted the request. She added the person to the already existing conversation. "Hello? Who is this?"

"Hello. I am the person you are communicating with."

That rocked her back on her heels. The voice sounded almost natural in her mental ear. No trace of odd accents. "You're the computer in the station around the black hole?"

"My queries of those terms indicate that I am almost certainly what you mean by that, though computer is an unfamiliar concept. I am a living being."

Kelsey put her diplomatic hat on. "Greetings, then. I am Princess Kelsey Bandar of the Terran Empire. My associate in your station is Carl Owlet. May I ask whom I am addressing?"

"My name does not translate well. You may call me the last. It is an accurate term, as I am the last of my people in this universe."

She filed that away. There would be time to figure out what it meant soon enough.

"That's an odd name for those of my people. Perhaps I can call you Omega?"

"Yes, that name seems accurate."

"Very well," she said. "Omega it is. You're aware some of our people are inside you. We mean you no harm. In fact, they are trying to get back out."

"I am aware of their predicament. I sorrow at the deaths of those that came before them. I was unable to communicate with them. I deeply regret that I cannot assist you in exiting this station."

Carl cut in. "This is Carl Owlet. May I ask why you can't help us?"

The alien sounded apologetic. "The flaw lies in my current state. Those that came before you did not come from the same reality as you. You are aware of this?"

"We are."

"The reason for this lies in the nature of this station. It exists in many realities. More than I can count. All circling this cursed black hole.

Something about the extreme gravity and bending of space and time have made the interiors of all the stations become one.

"When you came inside my hull, you stepped outside your reality. Here, all are equally real. I cannot sense which one to open a portal to. Here on the inside, it is one. Outside, there are many. When you entered, you activated the portal from only that reality. I cannot replicate it in the other direction. I cannot tell which is which."

Kelsey had a hard time getting her mind around that. "Why did your builders make you that way?"

The other being laughed without humor. "Such was never their intention. Our sun was growing less stable. We built this station to create a gateway out of our doomed solar system.

"They created a path to another reality for our people to flee. One with a stable sun and no people to fight them for a place to live. It took many, many years and hundreds of expeditions, but they finally found a suitable home, and our people fled this doomed place.

"Centuries later, the sun did explode. It may be that the use of the technology in this station accelerated the process. I am unsure. It happened in many realities, all at once. Somehow, that cataclysm is responsible for my current state."

That story could've ended a lot worse, she thought. "I'm glad they made it. Why didn't they come back for you?"

"I am an unbreakable part of this station. To remove me would kill me. This is the sacrifice I made for my people. I do not regret it.

"In any case, the linking of all those stations into one has made it strong. It survived the explosion undamaged. In fact, I am unsure anything can damage it any longer. I would help you escape if I could. Perhaps, with your strange communication units, we can find a solution."

Kelsey hoped so. If not, her friends would be trapped forever.

11

"That's an incredible story," Jared said. "If we didn't have people inside to see it for themselves, I'm not sure I'd believe it. But it still doesn't help us get them back."

He sat in his office with Kelsey. Six hours had passed and many of the ships were back. The last of them would return in the next few hours and he had some decisions to make.

"You've spoken with this thing," he said. "Do you believe its story?"

She nodded. "I do. It hasn't asked us for anything. If it had some kind of ulterior motive, it would actually have to communicate it. It doesn't want to leave the station. Omega says it's happy to remain there alone.

"And it has been very forthcoming in how we might be able to get them back to our reality. If our end of the quantum validation unit is near the surface of the station, but not in range to be pulled in, it thinks that it might be able to sense which reality to open the hull to."

"That sounds a bit chancy, but I'm not sure how we could increase the odds. Do you believe the story about multiple realities?"

"Carl showed me images of the other Carls. That's pretty damned convincing."

"That's just insane. Other universes. Meaning we could maybe use it to find one where the Old Empire never fell. Though, I'm not sure that's the best idea."

"Thankfully, you don't have to make that decision," she said. "All we need to do is get our people back, and *Persephone* will have to be part of that."

He felt himself frowning. "Why? I'd rather not expose you to this unknown danger."

"We already have the communication flowing. There's a lot of data coming our way, and I'm loath to stop it. We're taking everything Omega sends us and isolating it. In a case of better late than never, I locked down the sensitive files to make sure we didn't give away the crown jewels."

"We'll have to hope it doesn't misuse any data it already has. I'll want copies of what you have, just in case something goes wrong."

She nodded. "I'll make that happen. When do we want to try?"

"As soon as possible. We can withdraw from the Nova system in a few hours. I think that's the best thing to do. We have a long trip home."

"I can have *Persephone* in position in half an hour."

He rose to his feet. "Then do it. Let's get our people back, and the bodies. I want Doctor Stone to go over them with a fine-toothed comb."

* * *

"YOUR PEOPLE ARE PREPARING to get you back to your ships," Omega said. It had figured out how to communicate directly with Carl through his implants. Impressive for an alien that had never encountered them before.

"What do you think the chances are?" Carl asked.

"Very good, I believe. Even from this range, I have narrowed down the possible realities greatly. If there are still many choices, we can try them one by one until we reunite you with your people.

"I will be sad to see you go. It has been refreshing to have someone to speak to after so long."

Carl nodded. "How long ago did your people leave?"

"More than two thousand of your years. I have many diversions and we are a solitary people by nature, so that has not been a burden. Still, I will look back fondly on this time we have shared.

"Speaking of which, I see that it is the custom of your people to give gifts. We also have that tradition. When friends part, they exchange meaningful things. I would give you a gift my people left with me. It is precious to me, but I believe you are destined to have it."

"I don't want to take something that means so much to you. That wouldn't be right."

Omega laughed. "At least see it before you decide. Come around the ring. I will tell you where to stop."

Carl made his way around until he found another closed off chamber. It didn't have a door, so he doubted the designers had intended anyone to go inside.

At least, that's what he thought. The bare surface of the metal shimmered and became like a mirror.

"You may pass through. It is safe. This is where I reside."

He took a deep breath and stepped into the liquid metal. He passed through unharmed and emerged into a large room. Larger than the one where he'd found the bodies, in any case.

"This is bigger than I expected."

"That is really no mystery," Omega said. "There is a level of the station reserved only for machinery. This chamber resides there, on what your people would consider an engineering level."

"Wait. I'm not on the same level? How did that happen?"

"My people have long had the ability to open portals from one location to another, so long as matched quantum equipment was on either end. The range is short, relatively speaking. On this doorway, it is only good within this station. In fact, it is the only such door here.

"Before our world was destroyed, there were larger doorways that allowed for many to travel between cities at the same time. The power requirements were quite large. A similar portal served to get things into orbit. I suppose one could have been created for travel between planets, but the energy cost would have been extreme."

Carl tried to envision a world like that. Such ability to travel instantly from one city to another would change the very fabric of society. One could live on the other side of the planet from where they worked and commute. It was astonishing.

"That's a tremendous thing. Your people were magnificent."

"Thank you. I believe they still are. Walk forward to the row of cabinets. You want the one on the far left."

Carl started that way but turned to face a wall full of machinery. A large, clear tube held a brain harnessed in thick gold wires that penetrated its surface in many places. "Is that you, Omega?"

"It is. They removed my brain to become the controller for this station. My body would have failed long ago. I was ill and they could not cure my disease.

"I doubt they imagined my brain would live on so long. They provided a way for me to end myself, if I ever desire, but I am content in my isolation."

It was amazing. Carl could hardly imagine it. He took a good recording and then turned to the cabinet. It slid open to reveal a large case.

"How do you get to things like this without a body?" he asked.

"I have mechanical devices that I can direct. You have seen them, I believe."

Carl slid the case out and set it on the countertop. In the blue water, it looked vaguely pinkish. Movements were still awkward.

It wasn't difficult to open. Inside were rows of clear crystal disks. Thousands of them.

"What is this?" he asked.

"The collected knowledge of my people. Every written word, every oral story. At least those since we could save them for those who came after ourselves. That box contains the sum of all my people's knowledge."

Carl's heart raced. "That's too much. I can't take your people from you. That's why they left this, wasn't it? So that you would never be alone."

"I have all of this in my data banks," Omega assured him. "They left this as a symbolic gift to repay what I did for them. One that I feel is appropriate to give to you who has done so much for me. Take this gift and use it to know us, Carl Owlet."

He nodded. "I will. But, I have to give you something, too. It will require some thought to match what you have given."

"No, my friend. Simply meeting you was more of a gift than you can imagine. Our people did not believe there was other sentient life in the universe. We saw no sign of it in the heavens. The knowledge of your existence is a tremendous thing.

"The reader is also in the cabinet. I will send you the information on how to decode these disks. The data is quite dense. They are constructed in such a way that the media will remain stable for as long as the universe continues to exist."

"From my people to yours, thank you."

Still, Carl's mind wandered as he considered appropriate return gifts. Then he smiled. That was perfect. He had just enough time to arrange for them to bring it.

* * *

ANGELA FLOATED out of the pinnace and guided the box Carl had forced her to pick up from his lab. She'd argued until she was blue in the face that he didn't need any extra equipment, but he'd been adamant.

The plan was for her to place it where they went in. The being inside would be sure that they exited at the same location.

She thought they were trusting the thing too far. The very idea of an alien life-form made the hair on the back of her neck stand up. It probably had tentacles and lots of eyes. She shuddered inside her suit.

But those were issues far above her pay grade. She'd attach the box to the hull and stand clear. *Persephone* was less than a quarter kilometer away. Perilously close to the station for a ship her size. Kelsey wanted to give the being the best chance possible to find the right reality to open a door into.

Angela only hoped it wasn't some kind of trap.

Once the box was in place, she pulled back into the pinnace, notified *Persephone*, and waited.

After a few minutes, the hull deformed and extruded again. Standing on it were a number of armored Fleet vacuum suits. The explorers had returned!

She ordered the pilot to take her in. He'd hold them close to the hull, since the magnetics didn't seem to work on the station.

Talbot floated up the ramp as soon as she lowered it.

"It's good to see you again, Angela. Damned good."

"You, too, Talbot. Let's get you all inside and get the hell out of here."

He gave her a small headshake through his faceplate. "Not yet. Carl is still inside."

"What? Dammit all to hell. Is he a hostage?"

"No, he needed to handle the box you brought over. He'll be along shortly. The station only had to try half a dozen times to find the right reality for us. It swears it knows the right one now, so *Persephone* can move away and we'll pick Carl up when he comes out. He said it should only take about thirty minutes."

"I'm going to kill that runt," she snarled. "I swear to God. Let's get loaded. I don't want to have the alien screw us up by accident."

They loaded the bodies into the pinnace. A glance inside one faceplate told her she didn't need to see the rest. They'd purged their atmosphere, but death was never pretty.

She opened a channel to *Persephone*. "The station says you can pull back. We're still waiting for Owlet."

"I know," Kelsey said. "He just told us. That's annoying."

"For once, I'm in complete agreement with you, Highness."

"Move away from the station and wait. I'll let you know as soon as he's coming. Jared wants to get the hell out of here. As soon as Carl is aboard, we'll move back to the Harrison's World flip point."

* * *

CARL LUGGED the box down to the room where Omega's brain rested. He set it on a counter and started opening panels, looking for power.

"Can you point me toward a power line I can tap into? Something on the same order as the light the others created above the room they used."

"There is a line inside the panel to your left. What are you doing?"

He opened the panel and spotted the line. He needed to be cautious because he was in water, but he could do this.

"Once I'm gone, you've lost your means of communicating with any of our people. I made a number of other quantum pairs, so I'm installing a few here for you, linked to a redundant communications array. That way we could leave one at Harrison's World, keep another on *Invincible*, and still have others that might prove helpful without having to return and add more.

"I figure it's better to spend the time and effort while we're here than come back. This might be for nothing. Damned if I know what kind of range they have."

He pulled several pieces of equipment out of the box. "With the radiation, you probably won't get more than a few dozen kilometers of range on the communicator, but if someone else tries to board you, you can warn them off. Or invite them in. Whatever suits you."

Omega was quiet while Carl worked. It only spoke after he closed the panel.

"I am deeply moved by what you are doing for me. It is unexpected and most welcome. I am inspired to do something for you, in turn."

Carl smiled. "No need. This is what friends do."

"I have not had a friend in a very, very long time. I shall work hard to be a good one. Which in turn, leads me to what I might be able to do for you. We built this station to open a path to another reality. Until your people came, I was unaware of these flip points. They are fascinating. I think they are part of the same theory that allows for interdimensional travel. That affords us an opportunity."

Carl closed the box. "Really? That's pretty interesting. Let's test the normal communications unit. Call *Persephone*."

A few moments passed before Omega spoke. "They indicate my signal is weak, but they received it. Hopefully, this will save new visitors from danger. This is wonderful. Thank you."

"My pleasure. I can test the quantum part once I get back to *Invincible*. What was the other thing you were talking about?"

"This station can open a portal to other universes. That requires a lot of stored energy to breach the barrier. I once gathered it for months from the sun before I released it all at once.

"I believe the theory of your flip points is similar in many ways. Through my gravitational monitoring of the black hole, I can sense the layout of nearby flip points now, including the three in this system. The one you came through and two others that are likely hard to sense with your instruments in this environment.

"Those, in turn, link to other systems. All together, they form a web of connections. I can detect the linkages out for many hundreds of light years. It may be possible for me to use what I know of your destination to create a flip point between here and there, using the vast gravitational power of the black hole to forge a link powerful enough to cross that gulf."

He blinked. "That's insane. People can't just make flip points."

"Your science also dismisses the possibility of interdimensional travel. Yet, I have made portals to other realities many times.

"They faded after a short time once I stopped expending the energy to keep them open, so there is no guarantee that the flip point will endure. But even if it is only in existence for a few days, that should allow you to get home much more quickly than would otherwise be the case. I at least owe it to you to try. Who knows? Perhaps it will be permanent."

"That sounds amazing," Carl said. "Thank you."

"Perhaps you already have this information, but allow me to send you the map of flip points I have detected. It may prove useful to you in the future."

Carl's implants received an incoming data stream. Not a map, but individual listings of flip-point pairs. They had directions and estimated distances, but no map of real space stars to give them structure.

He brought up the Old Empire flip-point maps and began comparing them. Many of the flip pairs were marked, but not all. Not by a long shot.

Also, some of the pairs were not pairs at all. A small number had three, four, or even five possible links coming from the same flip point. That was a possible confirmation that the weak flip points perhaps led to several potential locations. Doctor Leonard would be thrilled.

Once the data stream ended, Omega continued. "I also have some spare parts for the interstation transport system. I can create more for my own use. I will gather enough to create two larger doorways and a smaller test unit.

The larger units will be able to move people from one side of a planet to the other. Or to stations in orbit.

"The smaller unit will allow you to study the technology and eventually recreate it. The details for the construction are in the discs I gave you, as well as the theory behind it. I hope that it makes a difference in your struggles going forward."

The implications were staggering. If he could duplicate this equipment, people on Avalon could go to the opposite side of the planet in a moment. They could get from the surface to Orbital One or even the moon. Long-range travel would never be the same. It would change society in ways he couldn't begin to imagine.

"Thank you, Omega. I'm sure this will come in very handy, even if I can't imagine in what ways right now."

12

J ared listened to Carl Owlet's explanation with as much patience as he could muster. He didn't want to jump right down the boy's throat. Though, with the risks he'd taken, Carl certainly deserved a thorough ass chewing.

Kelsey sat in one of the comfortable chairs off to the side of Jared's office. Her expression was difficult to read. He wondered if she was as angry as he was. Or perhaps more so.

Once Owlet finished explaining what he'd done, and that the newly forged quantum link was operational, he looked at the graduate student quietly for a moment.

"Part of me wants to rip your head off, Carl. It really does. That was an unacceptable gamble. What if it couldn't have gotten you out? You'd have died."

The young man nodded. "I'm aware of that, Admiral. It seemed a risk worth taking. If we can keep a line of communication open to Omega, think of the things we can learn together. Accomplish together. Sometimes, the reward is worth risking death."

Owlet hesitated a moment and then shrugged. "If I had it to do all over, and I knew that I'd succeed but die in the process, I'd have to do it anyway."

Jared had a hard time disagreeing. Especially if that thing really could create a flip point.

Doctor Leonard had scoffed. Such wasn't possible, he'd said.

Jared was inclined to see it the same way, but he wasn't going to say the alien was wrong. Not until it tried.

If it succeeded, even for a few hours, they could shave months off their travel time. And they could be sure that they'd miss running into any Rebel Empire scouts. That was worth the risk.

"Time will tell," Jared said at last. "We transition to Harrison's World in a few minutes. I want you in your lab to tell me if you're able to make the quantum connection. If so, we'll wait there to see what happens. Omega might destroy itself trying.

"I can hardly imagine anything that could destabilize a black hole, but if it exists, I'd rather not be close by. For all we know, it might shut down the weak flip point and leave us trapped."

The graduate student nodded. "If it works, we can pass a quantum unit off to Boxer Station. I have a few other sets to test longer distances. We can pass some off and try as we get further away. If they really don't have a top range, we'll be able to maintain communication."

"But you think that's unlikely," Kelsey said.

"I do. I can't believe that the range on one of these pairs is much more than that of a flip point. If it works over interstellar distances at all. Which I mostly doubt."

Jared sighed. "This discussion isn't over, but we have things to do. Report to your lab and let's get out of here."

"Yes, sir."

Once Owlet was gone, Jared turned to Kelsey. "This is nuts. It kills me that he's so ready to give his life like that."

"Why?" his sister asked. "It's for something he deeply believes in. You'd do the same. So would I. Is this any different?"

"Giving your life for science? Yes, it is. Science can happen later when it's safer."

"Well, we might just have to disagree, then. I'm pretty pleased with him, myself. He's matured noticeably in just a few days. Our little scientist is growing up."

He smiled. "Maybe. I hear that Major Ellis might just end him before he shaves regularly."

"She's pretty mad," Kelsey agreed. "But I think she also recognizes his resolve."

Kelsey looked as though she were going to say more, but didn't.

Jared rose from his seat. "Let's adjourn to the flag bridge. I want to put this place behind us."

They made their way to the flag bridge and waited for the fleet to assemble. Carl said there were two additional flip points in this system, but none of their people had found them. Even if they had, he was ready to leave them unexplored.

Once the fleet was in readiness, he gave the order to flip.

* * *

ANGELA WATCHED OWLET WORK, her insides roiling slowly. He acted as though he hadn't risked his life for nothing. He behaved as though everything was normal.

He'd a jury-rigged communicator set up on his lab table. He spoke into it now that they were back in the Harrison's World system.

"Omega, can you hear me?"

There was nothing for a moment, and then a voice issued forth.

"I hear you. The quantum communicator is working. Congratulations, my friend. This is a notable achievement."

Owlet shook his head. "I can't believe it worked. This is insane."

"I never doubted it would work. Though, I agree there may be an upper limit to the range. It shall be interesting to see how that works."

"Yes, it will. I need to let you go. Admiral Mertz asks that you hold off on creating the flip points for a few hours. We're going to leave some extra quantum units here and need time to make the exchange. Once we're ready to go, we'll call you. That way, if something unfortunate happens, we won't be trapped there."

"Agreed. If something untoward occurs, it is likely I will not survive to see it resolved. Better not to risk anyone else. I will await your call. The process will take several minutes once it is initiated."

"Until then. Goodbye, Omega."

Carl disconnected the channel. "Well, that went better than I'd expected."

"What did you expect?" she asked. "To die over there? That was a stupid risk."

"Here we go." He opened a cabinet and began assembling some equipment. More quantum pairs. He gave her an odd look as he worked. "You and the admiral share a low opinion of my judgment."

"That should tell you how wrong you were. Why risk your life for something like that?"

"Tell me, Major. When you get into a fight, do you decide if that's the time to pack up and go home? That suddenly it's too dangerous for you to be a marine?"

She felt her hackles rising. "Of course not. You don't get to pick only the winning fights. Sometimes, you have to play the hand you're dealt."

"That isn't the same thing as what you did. You made a choice to stay over there and risk being trapped. It was irresponsible."

"You make it sound as if what I do isn't important. That I'm somehow doing something unworthy."

He set the equipment down and walked over to her. "You've got a lot of nerve, Major. People like me lost their lives over there. *Exactly* like me, in fact. I won't throw away what they did. Their lives meant something."

He gave her an odd look. "I'm not afraid to risk death or injury to finish what they started."

Carl Owlet reached up, grabbed her uniform tunic, yanked her head down, and kissed her.

* * *

CARL CAUGHT sight of Kelsey walking into the medical center out of the corner of his eye just as Doctor Stone was running an instrument across his face. She stopped beside the exam bed and eyed him critically.

"What the hell happened?"

"I walked into a hatch," he said. "Stupid of me, I know. How did you hear about it?" His heart raced at lying to her. He really wasn't very good at this.

"Angela said there was an 'incident' in your lab, but wouldn't tell me what it was. So, I came to see for myself."

She eyed the area around his eye. "Yeah, that's a good one. You're lucky you have nanites. Otherwise, you'd have a big shiner. My dad made me keep one after I got mouthy with one of my friends. He said it built character."

"I've had my share of them over the years, too. Older boys tend to frown on some kid showing them up. They pounded me into the ground like a tent stake."

"Well, you're in an adult world, now. You're more likely to face an attack on your reputation than your body. Still, I wonder if you couldn't do with a little hand-to-hand instruction. It wouldn't hurt and would definitely help with your coordination."

"I don't think—"

"Actually, that's a great idea," Kelsey said, overriding his objection. "I'll talk with Angela about giving you some pointers. After the bruising goes down."

She didn't give him the chance to decline, instead heading back toward the hatch. "I've got to run. We'll be transitioning back to the Nova system shortly, and I need to be aboard *Persephone*. We'll talk later."

He watched her leave with a sinking feeling in the pit of his stomach. How could he get out of this? Ignore it and hope something distracted her? Hand-to-hand practice with Major Ellis was a very bad idea. Particularly right now.

"Are you going to tell her that someone punched you?" Stone asked. "Angela Ellis, I'm guessing."

She pulled back and examined her handiwork with satisfaction. "This will still bruise, but it'll be gone in about twenty-four hours."

"What makes you think someone hit me?" he asked.

"A few decades of medical experience. I can see the knuckles in the emerging bruise."

"Please don't tell Kelsey."

Stone raised an eyebrow. "I don't blab about things covered under doctor-patient confidentiality. So, the question you need to answer is simple. Did Major Ellis assault you? That's actually a crime, and I'm obligated to report things like that."

"I had it coming. Please, just let it drop."

"Tell me what happened. Maybe I can help."

He reluctantly explained about the message left by the dead Carl from another universe. "I don't know if he was yanking my chain or not, but when Major Ellis tore into me, I felt like I had to do it. I expected her to yell, but she stared at me for a second, popped me, and stormed out of the lab. You don't think Kelsey knows, do you?"

"Based on her performance, I think she has a strong suspicion," Stone said. "Look, Carl, I won't say you did the right thing, but I'm not sure you were wrong, either. Relationships are odd sometimes.

"Frankly, I think you'd be better off apologizing tomorrow. After she's had a chance to cool off. Tell her why you did it. It might not help, but it can't hurt. Well, not in a way I can't fix."

He sighed. "Nobody warned me life was so complicated."

The doctor smiled. "It can be. Now scoot."

Carl left the medical center and walked slowly back to the lab. He'd already sent the equipment to the cutter from Boxer Station. They'd get everything set up there shortly. They'd have the quantum unit linked to Omega. He'd have one linked to it. They'd have an extra three for other lines of possible communication to Erorsi and Pentagar.

He had plenty. They were time consuming to construct, but he'd made dozens of linked pairs after he'd refined the process. If range really wasn't a limit, every world would need one paired to each of the others. Or some kind of relay capability.

He knew he was intentionally putting aside his issues with Major Ellis. He'd messed up, and he just didn't want to think about it right now. Maybe if they all got home, he wouldn't need to work it out. They'd all go their separate ways.

Which would make him sad, but that was life.

A check of the chrono made him speed his steps. Time was short.

* * *

KELSEY BOARDED the cutter taking her to *Persephone*. Angela was with her, but seemed lost in thought. The large woman had been incandescent when Kelsey saw her last. Which had prompted her to visit Carl.

Now the anger was gone. Replaced by what certainly looked like confusion to Kelsey.

What had really happened? She didn't buy the old "walked into a hatch" story. Those two had mixed it up. She'd probably slapped him. Hmmm. No. Angela wasn't that girly. She'd punched him.

Kelsey couldn't imagine what he might have said to get such an extreme response. The marine officer was a professional. There was no way she'd let words move her to act that way.

Even if Carl had taken a swing at her, she'd have stopped him without much violence. Whatever he'd done, he'd gotten past her guard before she'd had a chance to stop an instinctive reaction.

She felt her eyes narrow. Had he made a pass at her? Those two? She wasn't seeing it, but that would do it. Particularly if he touched her unexpectedly.

No. Not touched. Kissed.

Kelsey cleared her throat. "You have something on your lip."

Angela paled and scrubbed her face roughly. "Did that get it?"

"Yeah, that got it."

Uh-huh. He'd kissed her. Nothing else would explain the woman's look of sheer panic.

Well, well. She was going to have to keep an eye on those two. She wondered whether the sparring practice was a good idea or not. Probably good, though she wouldn't mention it to Angela right now. She didn't want to back the other woman into a corner.

She'd probably best have a conversation with Elise. If anyone could help her guide these two through the minefield they'd found themselves in, it was her. She was subtle and had an eye for nudging people.

Kelsey smiled. This was going to be a lot of fun. For those watching the two do the dance, anyway.

13

J ared waited until Omega signaled that it had succeeded in creating the flip points before he ordered the fleet to transit. He still couldn't believe this was possible. Well, he'd find out for sure shortly. Elise sat near him at an empty console. He was glad to have her close at hand.

The trip through the radiation was tense. It wasn't until it cleared in the inner system that Marcus detected the two new flip points. Yes, two.

"Marcus, open a quantum channel to Boxer Station. Boxer Station, this is *Invincible*. Do you read us?"

"Boxer Station here, *Invincible*. You're coming through loud and clear. This is amazing."

"We made it safely to the Nova system, and we're detecting two new flip points near the station. Can you ask what's going on?"

"Stand by."

While Sean was busy, Jared turned his attention to the scanner readings. The two flip points were some distance away from the station and about a hundred thousand kilometers apart from one another.

"Do those flip points look stable to you, Marcus?"

"Indeed they do, Admiral. Doctor Leonard is working to confirm but says he will need to be much closer to know. Our ETA is less than an hour."

"*Invincible*, Boxer Station. Omega says he had enough power to create two flip points, so he linked one to Avalon and the other to Pentagar. He indicates that they seem stable, but he has no way of testing them."

"Thank him for us," Jared said. "We'll have to test them ourselves when we get closer. *Invincible* out."

They coasted into communication range forty-five minutes later. Jared opened a regular channel to the station. "Omega, this is Jared Mertz. Thank you for creating these for us. We are deeply in your debt."

"On the contrary, Admiral Mertz. I believe we are, as they say, even. I hope they prove stable. The effort depleted my power reserves. It will take some time before I can attempt the process again."

"I'm sure they're fine. If not, well, we're no worse off than we were before. Which one is which?"

"The one closest to you leads to the world you call Pentagar."

"We'll give them a look. Thank you again."

He smiled at Elise. "Shall we send someone through to see if your home is on the other side?"

She nodded. "Yes. If so, we can drop off some quantum communicators and see if we can maintain a link with them. That would certainly make life easier."

"Yes, it would. Marcus, open a channel to Doctor Leonard."

"Ready, Admiral."

"Doctor, do the flip points look stable?"

The other man's voice came back over the audio channel. "They do, Admiral. I recommend you send scouts to get comprehensive scans. Carl has care packages of quantum pairs that they can leave with instructions. That way we don't have to risk staying too long and having an unstable flip point close behind the scouts."

"Get them sent over to the ships I'm designating right away."

"Yes, Admiral. Leonard out."

It only took a few minutes to get things ready, and he dispatched the two scouts through the new flip points. He knew they wouldn't be returning quickly, so he fretted. He'd much preferred using probes, but the hellish radiation would damage them too quickly.

Doctor Leonard was designing some that would be able to handle the environment, but that took time.

The ship dispatched to Pentagar returned first. The woman commanding it said she'd sent and received an acknowledgement from Royal Fleet about the new flip point and the care package.

The flip point on that end was strong and looked stable. It was closer to Pentagar than the other two by about fifty percent. He hoped it remained open, because that would greatly simplify matters.

The second scout returned a few minutes later with a similar report. They hadn't called anyone, as per his orders, but the flip point looked good. It was at almost solar north in the Avalon system.

There were no flip points in that region of space, so there was no reason for Fleet to be watching for anything.

He wanted to be there in person to smooth things when they discovered he'd returned. He didn't want any unpleasant surprises to turn into shots fired.

Jared opened a general channel to the fleet. "All ships, this is Admiral Mertz. Transition in sixty seconds. Maintain signal silence unless ordered otherwise."

He looked up at the ceiling. "Transition on schedule, Marcus."

"Yes, Admiral."

The clock slowly counted down to zero and the ship flipped. It only took a few moments for data to start coming in from the passive scanners. They were in the Avalon system, as advertised. Their return had been a long time coming and was going to upset quite a few apple carts.

"Marcus, signal Commodore Meyer."

A minute went by. "No response, Admiral. It seems there is a range limitation after all."

"Well, Harrison's World is a long ways away. I know Carl has one he's putting together that will work with Omega. Let me know if he gets ahold of him."

"Yes, Admiral."

He looked over at Elise. "Welcome to Avalon. We hope you enjoy your stay, and please consider Fleet for your future spaceflight needs."

She smiled. "Oh, I will. Right now, I'm looking forward to seeing how you avoid scaring the life out of someone."

* * *

TED JACKSON WAS BORED. Not so much that he couldn't handle the routine flight control duties for Orbital One, but enough that he was already planning his weekend. A romantic getaway with his wife out to the mountains.

She had no idea, but he'd rented a cabin for them on the lake she loved hiking around. There was a local camp that the kids could spend a few days at and not miss them one bit.

It was a win from everyone's perspective.

An icon appeared on his console. Incoming call from a Fleet ship. Call sign... *Invincible*? A quick check confirmed there was no such vessel.

He shook his head and responded. "Orbital One traffic control to unknown sender. This is an official Fleet frequency, and impersonating one of our vessels as a prank could get you in a lot of trouble. Take this friendly warning to heart, and knock it off before I have to *officially* notice you."

This didn't happen often. It usually ended up being rich kids horsing around in Daddy's yacht. A single warning was usually enough to get them to clear out. Those that didn't learn quickly ended up getting a hefty fine.

"Orbital One traffic control, this is *Invincible*. I assure you we're real. Stand by for visual."

Ted almost refused it but decided he had to let this play out. He accepted the visual, opened his mouth to tear a strip off the kid, and... sat there with his mouth open in an unflattering manner.

That wasn't the control room of a yacht. It was a warship. One he wasn't familiar with, but large.

A man sat at the center of a circular room ensconced in a wide, wraparound console, dressed in a Fleet uniform with admiral's tabs. Other men and women were visible at stations around him.

Whatever this was, it wasn't the prank of some drunk kids.

Where the hell was this transmission coming from? He traced the origin of the signal out to solar north. There was nothing out there. Maybe it was still a prank.

He muted the com and turned to Lieutenant Randy Kingsolver. "Randy, scan out to solar north. Tell me who's out there?"

He unmuted the com. "This is Lieutenant Commander Ted Jackson, Orbital One traffic control. Identify yourself."

The man smiled. "I'm Admiral Jared Mertz. You'll find me in your database as a commander and captain of the destroyer *Athena*. I'm back and I've brought a few friends. I'm afraid it's a little convoluted to explain over the com. Would you be so kind as to call Admiral Yeats? I'll wait."

Randy sat bolt upright. "I have unknown warships on the scanner! A lot of them. Big ones. Where the hell did they come from?"

Ted muted the com. A glance at the data on Randy's screen showed the impossible. Dozens of ships. Over a hundred of them. Some of them impossibly large.

He hit the emergency alert beside his console. Alarms rang throughout the station, calling the crew to battle stations.

The admiral came on the com moments later. He had bed head. "Status, Commander."

"We have an unknown fleet in the system, Admiral. I have no idea where they came from, but they're asking for you by name. The caller identifies himself as Admiral Mertz, formerly in command of *Athena*."

Yeats blinked. "Keep the crew at battle stations. I'll be there directly."

* * *

KELSEY'S PINNACE made it to *Invincible*'s docking bay just as Admiral Yeats's cutter was starting its final approach. She'd silently watched the long conversation where Jared gave the admiral some of the basics. He'd barely gotten started when Yeats ordered him to hold position. He'd come out in person.

Home fleet had several heavy cruisers at hand. He'd brought all of them and their escorts out to meet *Invincible* and the fleet. This had to have been a rude awakening. Literally, since he hadn't brushed his hair all that well before he called Jared.

The man of the hour was waiting for her, decked out in a dress uniform. Elise stood beside him, radiant in a dark red dress. Kelsey had taken the precaution of putting on a blue number that suited her well.

Lord Hawthorne stood nearby in an elegant suit talking with Reginald Bell. The latter wore a suit with an odd cut. Probably something from the Old Empire.

This was going to be a very important meeting. Marcus was recording everything for posterity, and in case they needed it at Jared's court-martial, no doubt.

"Well, are you ready?" she asked.

"As ready as I'll ever be," Jared said with a small smile. "I've dreaded this moment for over a year. This is going to get really, *really* complicated, and it won't be pleasant."

"You're a pessimist."

"I'm a realist," he corrected. "One who is about to be proven right in style."

The sound of Admiral Yeats's cutter docking rang through the bay. The Fleet officers and marine honor guard snapped to attention as the hatch cycled open.

Admiral Yeats was an intimidating man, Kelsey knew. She'd met him once. He didn't look like the kind that took surprises well.

The barrel-chested man stalked into the bay and right up to them. A tall, dark woman came in behind him. Her rank tabs indicated she was a captain. Her name tag read Quinn.

Jared saluted. "Admiral Yeats, Captain Quinn, welcome aboard the Fleet superdreadnought *Invincible*. You know Princess Kelsey. Allow me to introduce our guests. Crown Princess Elise Orison of the Kingdom of Pentagar, Lord William Hawthorne of Harrison's World, and Reginald Bell of Erorsi. I should mention, he's a formerly serving ensign in the Old Empire Fleet."

Yeats's return salute wavered at that last, and he gave the old man a surprised look before he refocused on the rest of them. Other Fleet officers and marines came out of the cutter. He bowed somewhat to Elise. "Highness."

He extended a hand to William and then Reginald. "Lord Hawthorne. Mister Bell. Welcome to Avalon. I look forward to getting to know more about you and your worlds. I'm especially looking forward to a deeper explanation from you, Ensign."

The senior Fleet officer focused his attention on Jared. "Congratulations on your promotion. I don't recall having authorized it."

Kelsey stepped forward. "That was my doing as the emperor's direct representative in accordance with Emperor Marcus's Imperial edict, Admiral. Jared logged his objections. So, if you want to yell at someone about it, start with me."

Yeats gave her a long look. "I might just have to do that, Highness. I can't say I'm familiar with this edict, so I look forward to a more detailed explanation."

Captain Quinn extended a hand to Jared. "It's good to see you again, Jared."

"You, too, ma'am."

"I didn't see *Athena* in this astounding gathering of ships," Yeats said. "Speaking of which, where did you find them?"

Jared grimaced. "She was crippled, and we had to leave her behind. These ships are Old Empire built and restored by us. Might I invite you to my office so we can discuss this in private? It's going to be a long conversation, and I have video."

Yeats looked over the men and women around them. "I think that might be for the best. After you. Captain Quinn, you're with me."

Jared led them to his office.

The trip through the flag bridge made Yeats stop and stare. "This ship is amazing. I couldn't believe the size of her from the outside. Now I can't believe how much room there is in the inside. I want this control room."

"This is only the flag bridge. She has a separate control center for the ship itself. She's a wonderful ship, sir. Wait until you hear what she can really do."

Jared led them to seats and offered refreshment. "I know you have a lot of questions. We took the time to prepare a basic vid of what happened to us and what we found. It might be best if you watch it first. That'll save a lot of questions."

Yeats accepted a drink from Jared and nodded. "Proceed."

Captain Quinn sat beside Kelsey. "I bet this is going to be entertaining."

"You have no idea," Kelsey told the other woman.

She sat back and sipped her drink. This was only the first of many times she was going to see it, she was sure. She might as well get used to being patient. She dreaded telling all this to her father. He was going to get very upset.

The wall screen came to life with her image. She was the narrator they'd chosen. It had taken weeks to get everything right. Then they'd had to add parts about the Nova system and the new flip points at the last moment. It was a lot to take in, and she was sure that not everyone would be graceful about it.

14

Admiral Yeats watched the entire vid with a growing sense of incredulity. If it hadn't been for the ships around them, he'd think the normally solid Commander Mertz was around the bend.

Or was it admiral? He wasn't sure of the legality of Princess Kelsey's actions. Yes, he'd watched the last message from Emperor Marcus, but he didn't know if the Imperial Senate was going to see things her way. Based on history, at least some of them would fight such a thing tooth and nail.

Hell, he didn't know if *he* saw it her way. Yes, Mertz deserved to be a captain. He'd worked his ass off and had the talent.

Okay, Mertz had more than the required talent if what they'd showed him proved true. Yeats realized he'd have failed miserably trying to pull off the other man's successes. Yet there would also be elements in Fleet that resisted these promotions as political.

He had a lot of thinking to do and very little time to do it.

They'd been in Mertz's office for hours. He knew people on Orbital One already knew parts of the truth, and he had to make a report to the emperor soon. Best to get it over with.

"I'm not going to lie to you, Jared," he said. "I don't know that the Imperial Senate will agree with the princess's logic. You might find yourself back to being a commander in hot water before the day is out."

Mertz shrugged. "I didn't ask for a promotion, so I'm good either way."

Yeats nodded. "What you've accomplished here—all of you—is tremendous, but it's going to go before a board. There's no question. You'll have to justify everything.

"But I'll tell you right now that I am proud of what you've done. You've served Fleet and the Empire well."

He turned to Princess Kelsey. "I think your argument of having the authority to do any of this is threadbare. If they decide to ignore the edict, then the entire house you've built comes crashing down. I honestly have no idea how this will play out.

"There will be people like Breckenridge that say you've been driven mad by the torture those things subjected you to. They'll speak with voices full of pity while they try to undo everything you've accomplished. It saddens me to say that."

"You look so normal," Quinn said. "I have difficulty believing what I saw is anything other than concocted, and I know I'm not going to be alone."

Kelsey stood and casually lifted the end of Mertz's desk with one hand. "I can demonstrate the changes, I believe."

"So you can," Yeats said faintly. "I'm certain any number of cyberneticists will be coming along to verify you really have an AI on this ship. I doubt that the Imperial Senate will accepted it as a person or a Fleet officer, though. No offense, Marcus."

"None taken, Admiral. I'm content to see how this plays out before I get cranky."

Yeats smiled in spite of himself. The concept of a cranky computer was funny and possibly indicative of real sentience.

"I need to call your father, Highness. I can only imagine how chaotic this is all going to be."

"I'll go with you for that, if you don't mind," she said.

"Actually, I do. You'll have time to have your say. This isn't it. I need to give my liege an unedited report. Privately."

He looked at Jared. "For the moment, I want these ships to stay right where they are. Captain Quinn speaks with my voice. You will obey every order she gives. Including you, Highness. Am I clear?"

Jared nodded. "As crystal, Admiral."

Kelsey also nodded. "I'm not going to mess things up now. We'll do what she says."

"See that you do. Don't make my life any harder than it needs to be. Now, where can I make a private call?"

Jared stood. "Marcus will direct you to a conference room, Admiral. You have my word that no one will monitor your conversation."

He'd have to accept that, but he'd act as though they were monitoring him anyway. "Very good. Marcus?"

The computer—or AI if you chose to believe it was sentient—directed him to a conference room on another level. "I can initiate contact with Orbital One at your command, Admiral."

"Please do so."

Once he had someone on the orbital, he had them patch him through to the Imperial Palace. Only the emperor wasn't there. He was on the Imperial yacht headed for Mertz's fleet.

Perfect.

It took a few more minutes to arrange a connection with his liege. Karl Bandar looked stressed. Yeats understood that perfectly.

"How are Kelsey and Jared, Robert?" the emperor asked. "Is it really them?"

"It's them, Majesty. They seem whole if not completely unscarred. They've brought back an incredible fleet of ships and even larger stories for us.

"If they're to be believed, the Old Empire is still alive, only under the control of mad artificial intelligences. Supposedly, we're at war with them."

"The only reason we weren't conquered centuries ago was because the computer in charge of this sector got bogged down with the planet Pentagar. If it weren't for *Athena*, we'd likely already have Rebel Empire ships moving towards us."

Yeats sighed. "The Imperial Senate is going to go mad, and Fleet isn't going to be happy, either. Gargantuan doesn't begin to cover it. I'm not sure that Hercules could perform the required feats to fix this."

"You know how you eat an elephant, Robert? One bite at a time. I'll be there in less than an hour. Then we'll cut the problems into manageable chunks. Don't do anything hasty before then."

Yeats smiled. "I think I can restrain myself, Majesty. I do have one bit of unambiguously good news, though. Jared and Kelsey seem to have resolved their differences. She's stoutly defending him, and they seem quite friendly. I suppose everything they've been through would do that."

The emperor smiled widely. "That's *excellent* news. Now if we could just get Ethan to come around. Maybe Kelsey can finally make him see reason."

Yeats doubted that very much, but kept his opinion to himself. The heir was going to be one of their problems. He just knew it.

* * *

"Senator Breckenridge, I need a moment."

Nathaniel Breckenridge looked up from his meeting with his senate allies, not bothering to conceal his irritation. His assistant knew better than to interrupt him at a moment like this.

He rose to his feet. "Pardon me, gentlemen. Ladies. If my man feels the need to disturb me, I should probably hear what he needs to say."

"It better be good," he said softly to the man as they stepped over to the far side of the room.

"I received word that a large fleet of ships has arrived in the system. Not, I might add, by any of the flip points Fleet protects."

Breckenridge frowned and turned his back on his senate allies. It wouldn't do for them to read his expression. Or his lips. His man knew well enough to shield both.

"That's very interesting, but what does that have to do with me?"

"One of the ships is the destroyer *New York*. It's assigned to your nephew's task force. None of his other ships is present, but it strongly implies that he is somehow connected to the events."

That didn't bode well. Wallace was usually a problem to solve. Or cover up.

"I see. Well, if these people didn't come through the flip points, where did they come from?"

"Supposedly through a newly created flip point, according to my contact. And, Senator, I'm told there are over a hundred Old Empire warships.

"Frankly, my source is hearing so many stories that I'm certain most of them have to be tall tales, but one comes across as ominous. She said that Wallace lost his entire task force and is under arrest. Rumor has it that the emperor is considering adding treason to the list."

Shit.

"We need to get in front of this if we're to salvage anything," Breckenridge said. "I'll wrap up the meeting as quickly as possible. As the head of the Senate Armed Forces Committee, I can get some answers and start changing the narrative."

He walked slowly back over to the conference table.

"My apologies, but I'm going to have to bring this meeting to an unexpected close. If you'll check with your staffs, I believe you'll hear some of the same rumors I was just told. If any of them are true, we have a lot of work ahead of us. Call my assistant, and he will schedule a follow-up where we can plan."

He watched his associates depart with a blank expression. What had his idiot nephew done now? How much was it going to cost to fix it, and who would he need to ruin in the process?

* * *

ETHAN BANDAR READ the information again, slowly.

How was this even possible? Not only was Mertz still alive, but he'd come home with more firepower than the Empire. In one ship. The others were apparently just for added emphasis.

All the Bastard had to do to seize the Throne was reach out and take it. Instead of stopping him, his sister was to all appearances aiding him. They'd become allies.

There were so many aspects of this that he didn't understand. He was certain there was more to the story than what his contact in Fleet had heard. He wasn't on the scene, after all, and they were treating everything as classified.

But he would. He had the clearance to hear everything. Once he knew precisely what the Bastard was doing, he'd stop him. The man was no match for him. No one was.

He'd need to be certain he cleaned up any loose ends from the assassination attempt. There would be no strings for the Bastard to pull is plans apart before Ethan ended him and the threat he posed. He couldn't allow anything to stop his ascension to the Throne.

It bothered him that his father had gone out without him. Had he turned against Ethan, too? He'd thought he could trust his family, but perhaps that was a mistake.

Or perhaps his father had finally sensed some of the threat Ethan had been warning about for the last decade and more. Perhaps he wanted to be certain his heir was safe while he determined how dangerous the situation was.

No. His father had rushed out to embrace the man who'd take everything away from his son if he could. He'd become one of the ever-shifting list of people that put on masks of deference while they plotted to ruin Ethan.

What was Kelsey thinking? She'd always been stubborn and slow to see the truth about Mertz, but Ethan had been certain he'd finally opened her eyes.

Now she'd taken it into her head to make the Bastard an admiral. God only knew what else she'd done. He needed to find out everything he could and take steps to eliminate Mertz as a threat as soon as possible. Had she turned on him as well?

Well, he'd have to take steps to eliminate the growing threats to his rule before they realized he was onto them.

He dialed a number from memory. "Victor. Ethan here. How would you like to get together for drinks this evening? I have some work for you."

15

Karl Bandar came through the docking hatch and caught his daughter as she threw herself into his arms. He held her close as she cried, saying nothing.

He'd heard enough to know that she'd been through some kind of trauma. He didn't have the specifics, but it had been bad. He knew it deep in his bones.

Only a marine officer stood at the far end of the corridor, so he knew she'd arranged to have it cleared. His guards surrounded them, but it was as though they were alone.

When she'd cried herself out, he tilted Kelsey's chin up. "I'm so glad you made it home safely, dear one. If I'd known what this trip would subject you to, I would never have allowed it."

She wiped her red eyes. "I had to be there. I don't know what you've heard, but it was worse. Worse than you could ever imagine. Yet, without it, everyone would have died. And then our enemies would've come for you and the Empire."

"You make it sound grim."

"There were moments when I was certain we would all die. We showed a basic vid to Admiral Yeats. I need to show you the part of it that I know will hurt you first. I need to do it alone."

His heart sped up. "You fill me with dread, Kelsey."

"If it makes me cry when I see it, I can only imagine what it will do to you. I want to have privacy, and to be there for you. Come."

She gestured to the marine. "This is Major Angela Ellis. She's acting as my guard commander. I'd like to keep it that way."

He inclined his head. "Major."

She saluted. "Majesty. Your daughter is a brave woman and an inspiration to us all."

"She inspires me every day."

They took a lift to the largest set of quarters on a ship he'd ever seen. Two armed marines stood guard outside the door.

"Are these Jared's quarters?" he asked.

"No. They're mine. *Invincible* has a lot of space, and this was originally for visiting VIPs. I'd prefer your guards wait outside. There are no other entrances, and I need to show you this alone. Major Ellis has seen it, but will also stay outside while we talk."

There was a note in his daughter's voice he'd never heard before. Command. She couched her words as a request, but they were really an order from someone that expected obedience.

Of all the changes to his daughter, that was one he thought he'd never see. Her face was leaner, too. Her body more toned. Though small, she'd always had a hint of pudginess in the face. That was gone now, replaced by flat planes and a hawkish stare.

Based on her arms, she was more muscular, too. She'd never been a physical child, though active. She looked as though she worked out regularly now. She'd changed a lot in the last year.

"Colonel Andrews, wait outside with Major Ellis. I'll be fine."

The man nodded. Considering Karl's somewhat rusty hand-to-hand training and his daughter's petite size, the man no doubt felt he was safe enough.

Once they were alone, he put his hands on his daughter's shoulders. The muscles under her skin were even more pronounced than he'd guessed. "Don't drag this out. Tell me what hurt you."

She gestured toward a couch in front of a wall-mounted vid screen. "Sit. Part of this is visual."

Once they'd both sat, she took his hand in hers. "The Old Empire enhanced their Fleet personnel with equipment implanted in their brains and bodies. This allowed them to interface with equipment and ships.

"That's how the rebellion started. Someone corrupted an AI, and it, in turn, hacked Fleet officers and crew. It literally forced them to fight against their friends."

He nodded slowly as he considered that. "It would explain so much. The speed of the change and the ferocity of the attack. I understand now."

"I don't think you do. The poor bastards were still alive in their own heads. Forced to watch as they did horrible things. The Old Empire had something called medical nanites. They greatly enhanced a person's life span. Those first people might have lived for centuries."

Karl was horrified, of course. That was a terrible story. "I accept that it's worse than I can know right now. What does that have to do with you?"

She took a deep breath and let it out slowly. "There was an old ship's computer still forcing the changes on captured prisoners near the Kingdom of Pentagar. Pentagar is one of the allies we found. Crown

Princess Elise is here as head of their diplomatic delegation, and as Jared's girlfriend."

"I… see. Well, that might complicate matters, but you were in charge of any diplomatic work, so perhaps not too much. That ship's computer did something to you?"

She nodded, her eyes shiny with unshed tears. "I'm past it, mostly. The nightmares still come sometimes, but I've become accustomed to the changes and they eventually meant the difference between life and death for all of us and Pentagar as well. In the end, it was worth suffering through everything, but that won't take away one bit of the pain I'm about to cause you. I love you and I'm so sorry."

Kelsey took another calming breath and continued. "I was stupid. I went somewhere Jared didn't want me to go, and they captured me. I defied common sense and this was *not* his fault. He blames himself, but I don't. And I don't want *you* to, either. Am I clear?"

He allowed a small smile to touch his lips. "Yes, ma'am."

That made her smile in turn. "Sorry. I'm going to have to get used to someone else being in charge."

"What happened to you?" he asked gently.

"The computer forcibly implanted me," she said. "Not just with the cranial implants, but with something called Marine Raider enhancements. Graphene coated bones, artificial muscles, a pharmacology unit with advanced combat drugs, cutting-edge medical nanites, and more. They turned me into the most deadly fighter the Old Empire could produce.

"But that didn't come without a steep personal cost. The machine that did the work was programmed by an AI that didn't give a damn, and I'm *very* sorry to say it used no painkillers whatsoever when it cut me open."

His heart stopped. He could barely grasp what she was saying, but he felt the horror of what she was describing.

Before he could say anything, the display came to life, showing a scene from someone's helmet cam. He'd seen enough video like it during his time in the service. A group of Fleet personnel was rushing a gurney through a ship's corridor at a breakneck pace.

Kelsey was on the bed, and something was wrong with her face, but he couldn't quite catch it with all the movement.

When they boarded a lift, he recognized one of the people as the medical officer from Jared's ship. What was her name? Stone. The marine cam was pointed at the door, so he couldn't see Kelsey.

When the doors opened, they raced out of the lift and into the medical center. He had enough experience to recognize there were two complete trauma teams standing ready to receive his daughter.

Stone pushed the cart near some equipment he didn't recognize. "Get the regenerator ready. If we don't get these incisions healed now she might have permanent scarring."

The image froze. Terrible, raw scars covered his daughter's face.

He rose slowly to his feet, his heart frozen. "My God."

"Incisions like those covered my entire body," his daughter said matter-of-factly. "The agony was indescribable. I didn't want you to see this without knowing that I'm fine now. It was horrible, but it's over."

He pulled her up and into his arms. It was his turn to weep while she comforted him.

* * *

JARED FINISHED his presentation to Admiral Yeats. It had taken hours to go over every aspect of the basic situation. At least his commander now knew the full danger they faced.

The older man rubbed his eyes. "I have to say that I'm horrified at the scope and power of the enemy you found, and very impressed with what you did to stop them.

"Would I have made different choices? Yes. I can't tell you if they'd have worked, though. It's very easy to judge with the luxury of hindsight. What counts are results, and you brought more of your people home than I'd ever have expected, given the circumstances."

Jared shook his head. "So many people didn't make it, and that brings up another matter. Where do we put them all? The grounds around The Spire are too small.

"We have our people and all the Fleet personnel recovered from the ship's we've refurbished or scrapped. Almost a hundred thousand bodies, and that doesn't even begin to count the rest of the derelicts. The final count from the graveyard will be in the tens of millions."

Yeats rubbed his eyes. "I have no idea. I'll get people working on that as soon as possible. There are so many hot items on my plate that I'm not sure where to start."

The hatch behind them slid open. Since Admiral Yeats had ordered the marines to leave them undisturbed, it could only be one person.

His Imperial Majesty, Emperor Karl Bandar, walked into the compartment. "Gentlemen, no need to stand on my behalf."

Jared stood at attention, saying nothing. This was Admiral Yeats's show.

The admiral shook his head. "The day Fleet officers don't stand for you, I'll retire in disgust. How was your meeting with Princess Kelsey?"

"Heartbreaking and eye-opening. She's been through so much."

The emperor stepped over to Jared and gave him a long, intent look. Then he pulled him into a hug. "Thank you for keeping my little girl alive and for bringing her home to me."

Jared might have adjusted to this kind of thing from Kelsey, but it was never going to feel natural with his father.

"I screwed up so many times, Majesty. What happened to her is my fault, and I accept full responsibility for it. I could have stopped her, stopped them, but I was too slow."

"Sometimes, the biggest regrets come from the shortest periods of time. I don't pretend to understand the full scope of what they did to her, but I know enough of the circumstances to be sure you did everything you could to protect her. For that, you have my unreserved gratitude."

He waved at the chairs. "Sit. We have a lot to discuss. We'll want food and drink, because we're going to be here for a while. I want to get a plan of action agreed on before we let this story go wide. It's already leaking, but we have a little time to shape the way it's received."

Jared sat back down. "Before we stop talking about Kelsey, there's something you need to see to understand the person she is now. She left home—forgive me—a pampered little darling. That's most assuredly no longer the case.

"Both of you have heard what the Pale Ones did to her. That doesn't really explain it. I have several videos you need to see. They all came from either her own implants or from security recordings. I'll lay out the background for each one before I play it."

He queued the assassination attempt at the Pentagaran parliament building. "This was just a few days after we got her back. Before she could reliably walk again. Some people tried to assassinate the King of Pentagar, Crown Princess Elise, Kelsey, and myself."

He played the recording.

The two men sat there, their jaws hanging open when it finished.

The emperor turned to stare at Jared, his eyes glazed with shock. "That's my little girl? She took them apart with her bare hands. Six armed men. She killed all of them."

Jared nodded. "That's exactly what she did. With her bare hands. She calls that combat mode. Her Raider implants have hardwired threat responses. All she has to do is direct them, and they can deal with some very hairy situations.

"You saw how fast she was? That was a combat drug from her pharmacology unit called Panther working in tandem with the modifications made to her brain by the implants. Together, they speed up the nerve impulses and the ability of the brain to process information. Doctor Stone said something about nerve conduction velocity.

"Basically, she had all the time in the world to figure out what to do. She's had a year to master her implants and learn how to fight for herself. Now she can do things like this."

He played the video of her assault on the asteroid base where they'd recovered the hardware for Marcus. Then without letting them recover, he played the video of her on Boxer Station. Some was from her own implants, but more was from marine helmet cams. For good measure, he added the attack she'd led on the hidden battlecruiser base at Harrison's World.

The two men looked shell-shocked when the videos ended.

Jared waited for them to wrap their minds around what they'd seen. "That last video was about three months after the first video. She's had nine additional months to work on her form under what I would call expert instruction. In everything from hand-to-hand combat to fighting in powered armor with weapons you can't begin to imagine, she has few peers and no masters. Princess Kelsey is a warrior now."

"Training from who?" Yeats asked. "From the marines?"

"Some, but not exactly. This next part is going to be hard to understand. Even our experts are having some difficulty explaining it."

He ran them through the AI ghost of Ned Quincy and how it had taken up residence in Kelsey's implant storage. He stressed how the man's detailed knowledge of Old Empire special operations was invaluable and how he could help them in ramping up for war. They rightfully looked alarmed.

"Let me end by saying that he has only the access she grants him. Kelsey is always in control of her body and can put him to sleep if she chooses. His memories, though incomplete, provide a wealth of training that she could never have gotten about being a Marine Raider."

"That concerns me in spite of your reassurances," the emperor said. "Could he be relocated?"

"The scientists haven't had any luck building a computer he can run on. Frankly, he shouldn't be possible, so we're leery of doing anything to risk him. He's one of a kind, and all attempts to recreate lightning in a bottle have failed."

"You're sure that he can't influence her in any way?"

Jared nodded. "They've done a lot of testing, and the hardware only allows Kelsey to control her body and mind. She can allow him access to see through her eyes or control her movement, but she's in charge. Her thoughts are her own. There is no possibility of mental influence."

Karl Bandar rubbed his eyes. "I'll want a full report and regular updates on that situation. It, too, is an Imperial secret. I don't want that even put into writing. If word got out that she had someone living in her head or was hearing voices, certain segments of the Senate would go insane. Absolutely no one else is to know until more time has passed. Is that all?"

Jared smiled. "Much to my chagrin, she's also assumed command of a Marine Raider ship, *Persephone*. The computer will only accept a Raider as a commanding officer, so she's it. She's learning to command a ship in space, too, and not doing so badly. You have every reason to be very proud of her, Majesty."

The emperor looked as though he'd been run over by a grav bus. "I am proud of her. It's just going to take a while to wrap my mind around this."

Yeats shook his head. "She's smaller than my youngest granddaughter. She doesn't look like she could lift, well, anything."

Jared nodded. "Yet she can do this."

He played the video of her lifting the weight machine in *Courageous*'s gym. The whole thing, weights and all.

"Gentlemen, Princess Kelsey is the most dangerous fighter in the Empire today, bar none. And that's what we were fighting. What we *will* be fighting if the Rebel Empire figures out we're still alive."

"Colonel Andrews is going to kick himself for leaving me alone with her," the emperor mused. "Or he would if we allowed this to get out. I'm declaring it an Imperial secret, too. I want all copies of this locked away, and everyone that knows about it needs to be warned to keep their mouths shut."

"That might be difficult," Jared said. "The first video is widely available on Pentagar. They've even produced a vid drama about us with sterling reviews. This information is going to leak."

"We have control over what comes in from Pentagar at the moment," Yeats said. "We can warn everyone to keep it close. If she has even a shade of the respect I think she does, we'll keep a lid on it for a while."

"We only need a bit of time," the emperor said. "I don't want to cause panic in the streets. Eventually, we'll have to spread word of the enemy capabilities. Right now, there are enough other shocks to bury this one."

Karl Bandar shook his head. "Let me see the recording from Emperor Marcus."

Jared played it for them. The two men watched in reverent silence.

"Well," the emperor said, "that's as clear as crystal to me. The sitting ruler of the Terran Empire issued an edict that no emperor since has rescinded. It doesn't matter that we didn't know it existed on Avalon. We're at war, and Kelsey had exactly the authority she claimed. I hereby endorse and approve of my daughter's actions.

"That might not solve all the problems, but it should make things a bit easier for you to manage, Robert. That means her promotions for you and your fellow officers are valid and sustained by me, Admiral Mertz. Congratulations on a well-deserved promotion."

Yeats nodded. "That will clear away many of the distractions. The Imperial Senate is going to scream, though."

"Let them," the emperor said. "This is an Imperial function. We're the same Terran Empire as the one Marcus headed. Lucien took over as emperor after his father's death. The line is unbroken. I might not be able to sweep the table clear, but I can definitely say this one matter is settled."

He smiled at Jared. "I hear other kinds of congratulations are in order. A certain little bird tells me you and Crown Princess Elise are… shall we say, good friends?"

Perfect. Now his father knew about his love life.

"I can assure you there was never any impropriety."

The emperor raised his hands. "I never implied anything else. I'm certain you've done everything humanly possible to bring our peoples closer together."

Wow. Did the emperor just make a bawdy joke? It made his head spin.

Then he smiled. "Well, then you'll be delighted to hear that your daughter has been making friends, too. Remind me to introduce you to Marine Major Russ Talbot. He and your daughter are living together."

The emperor rubbed his temples. "I thought her quarters had a few male touches. Dammit. I wonder how angry she'll be if I ship him off to Thule?"

Jared laughed. "If that's the least of your worries, you're in good shape.

Frankly, the public is going to be causing you a bigger one. We arrived through flip points that didn't exist before. With the help of an alien intelligence orbiting a black hole. One that can open gateways to other universes. How the hell do you keep something like that under the rug?"

The emperor shrugged. "You tell them what you can of the truth. That the process is experimental and classified at the very highest level. We'll give it a code word classification and call it Project Rainbow Bridge. We'll need to tell everyone here to keep it under their hats."

Jared nodded. "I can think of a good way to hide the alien aspect of it, too. One of our scientists has been working on something in a related field. He's developed something he calls quantum communication. It's faster than light and undetectable, at least at our technological level.

"It works at interstellar ranges, too. We can still talk to the alien station. While we were there in the Nova system, we were able to talk with Harrison's World. We can't reach any location other than Omega right now, so there's an upper limit, but it's a significant one. With relay stations, that limit becomes largely irrelevant."

He brought up the flip map of the Old Empire. It now had the newly created links on it.

"As you can see, we now have a full map of the explored flip points. Carl Owlet says we have some additional information given to us by Omega, but it still needs to be processed.

"The one I've highlighted is from Avalon to the Nova system. It's almost a thousand light years away. This is by far the longest wormhole we've ever seen. The one to Pentagar is only slightly shorter. Carl Owlet tells me we can still communicate with Omega."

"I'll be damned," Yeats whispered. "We could communicate with ships away on an expedition."

"Yes, it does have some down sides," Jared admitted.

The older man gave him a wry look. "You're an admiral now, Jared. That means you've become one of us backseat flag officers. You'll come around. And, since we're now both admirals, I think you can call me Robert, at least in private.

"Joking aside, micromanagement would be something we need to avoid, but it has the potential to allow frontline commanders to pass data back quickly and respond to strategic changes in their orders. Finding the right kind of balance would be key."

"So, you intend to tell the world that this scientist designed this breakthrough, too?" the emperor asked. "He won't be able to replicate it."

Jared nodded. "True enough, but since it's highly classified, he won't be able to share any details of what was done. Not even the theory behind it. Certainly not the equipment required to make it happen."

"The academics are going to go insane," Yeats—Robert—predicted. "They'll make all kinds of demands and probably protest. We did promise to share the technological finds with them, after all. In writing."

The emperor shrugged. "That's the way it has to be for now. One day we'll be able to share the truth.

"The long-range communications gear is a grand achievement in its own right. Undoubtedly worthy of the Lucien Prize. Give me the data on it, and I'll present it to the board when I get back home. They're already considering this year's candidates. Your man will undoubtedly win in the physics category. What is his name?"

"Carl Owlet. He's seventeen and only a graduate student. Brilliant, but somewhat of a private person."

The emperor grinned. "Well, he's going to be in for a rude awakening, isn't he?" His expression sobered. "There are a few other matters we need to discuss at length. Things like how we shift the Empire to a wartime economy. How we start building the ships we'll need to fight the Rebel Empire with. Harrison's World is a great resource, but need to spread out our capabilities."

Yeats nodded. "We're also going to need an unprecedented number of people to man those ships and to fight on the ground. We can't capture those planets from orbit. We have to occupy them and root out the rebels as we go. Besides capturing the worlds, we'll need garrison forces. The Old Empire is huge, and we don't have the people. We need to recruit and train as we go."

"Those are just the start of the problems we face," Jared said. "We need to ramp up implant usage among the civilian population. We need that productivity, and with the advent of medical nanites, society will change. Lives will extend to hundreds of years.

"Also on the military side, we need to figure out how to best use the flip-point jammers, build fighters, train pilots, and develop doctrine. We should also begin work designing massive forts to guard the flip points, set up some kind of FTL communications network, and assess the other technology the Old Empire knowledge can provide."

Karl Bandar sighed. "We'll need a lot more people to do that, but let's hammer out a general idea of what we want to look at first. Then we recruit helping hands. Jared, I think you'd best call for that food now."

16

Carl was finalizing the assembly on his next piece of equipment when Major Angela Ellis stalked through the hatch. She looked angry. Big surprise.

He set the equipment he was working on down and turned to face her. "Come back to have another go?"

The bruise was almost gone, but he really didn't need to antagonize her like that. It had just popped out of his mouth.

She stopped a little short of him. "I was wrong to hit you. It won't happen again. But I want to know why you did that."

"I've been asking myself that very same question. I'm not sure what the answer is. I'll blame the other me."

She frowned. "What the hell does that mean?"

"Did you read the message the other me-before-last left on the station? Let me send it to you."

He watched her reading it and knew she was done when she started shaking her head. "Why the hell would he say that? We barely know one another. Did he *want* me to punch you? You *are* kind of an asshole, so that's not out of the question."

Carl smiled a little. "I did some checking over the files in his implants earlier today. I found a trove of interesting images and vid files. Like this one."

He sent her his personal favorite. The image was obviously from a handheld camera. It showed himself and her, cheek to cheek and grinning like fiends. She was holding the camera out, and he could see the Pentagaran parliament building in the background. The two of them looked close. Kissing kind of close.

"Did you make this? You're sick."

He held up his hand. "Innocent. I found a lot of vids and images. It looks like you and earlier me were a hot item. In fact, all but one of the other Carls had vids or images that linked us romantically in multiple universes. That last one was more of a lab rat than I am. Maybe he didn't get out enough to date."

She pulled up a stool and sat. "That makes no sense. Why? How?" She shook her head. "It doesn't matter. We're not them, and it was wrong of you to kiss me."

"I know. I will say, however, that it was worth getting punched in the face to carry out my other self's final request."

"Just don't do it again. We're not them and…" She clamped her mouth shut. "Kelsey wants me to teach you hand-to-hand. When would you like to go to the gym and start?"

"Never. I'm not going to be competent at fighting. Period. You and I both know that. Let this go."

She shook her head. "When my princess tells me to do something, I do it."

"Like when she told you not to threaten me and you did it anyway? I'm not seeing why this is a problem."

She sighed somewhat aggressively. "Don't push me, Owlet. I can tie your skinny ass into a pretzel."

"I can't see what the other me saw in you. You're bossy, touchy, and stubborn."

"And, apparently, an idiot. You're dangerously reckless, and we're obviously unsuited for one another."

"Yet, there we were. In any case, I can't go now. I'm working on something."

She looked at the oddly shaped device. It looked like a bulky arm brace. "What is it?"

"A portable battle screen. Very similar to the one in the hammer. I built a fusion plant without the grav drive element and installed it with the screen generator in this arm brace. It's bulky, but I'll probably be able to make it smaller with a little work."

Major Ellis picked it up. "How would someone use it?"

"Hold out your arm." He strapped the unit onto her left forearm. "Have you ever seen a vid where old-time people were fighting with swords and shields?"

She nodded. "Kelsey made me watch one about some guy pulling a magic sword from a stone."

"I've seen that one. Excalibur. I guess I know what my next project is. In any case, this generator forms a battle screen in the shape of a rounded shield. It's about a meter across, so it won't protect your legs unless you crouch down.

"There's a control to alter the shape of the screen. To narrow it and extend it lower. That would make it a bit taller than the wearer and about half a meter across. If you went sideways and squatted, it would deflect a plasma burst around you. I'm working on joining two fusion units to the next model to increase the potential size a little."

He gestured toward a suit of marine armor on a stand. "I'm adding one to that, too. It'll be significantly larger and more powerful but will act in the same manner. The first unit is only a prototype and proof of concept. Something I can put on a dummy and fire a gun at."

"We all know how well that worked out last time."

"Then don't use it."

The sound of someone clearing his throat drew their attention to the hatch. Doctor Leonard stood there.

Carl retrieved the prototype. "Good morning, Doctor. What can I do for you?"

"You have a visitor."

He moved to the side and Emperor Karl Bandar stepped into the compartment.

Major Ellis braced to attention, and Carl had to force himself not to do the same.

He bowed. "You honor us, Majesty."

"On the contrary, Mister Owlet," the leader of humanity said. "You honor me. I've heard tremendous things about your work. Your inventions and breakthroughs are going to revolutionize a lot of things in the Empire."

He felt his face flush as he took the hand Emperor Karl extended. "I just did my part, sir. The team deserves the credit. Doctor Leonard is the one you should thank."

The emperor nodded. "I have, yet he didn't create interstellar communications or design that protective device I heard you talking about. My apologies for standing in the corridor listening. We were waiting for the right moment to interrupt you."

"And it turns out we should've done that right off," Doctor Leonard said with a smile and a shake of his head.

They'd overheard him arguing with Ellis. Dammit.

"That will teach me to leave the hatch open. My apologies."

"No need," the emperor said. "It is I who should do so. I'm sorry I listened in on a private conversation. I do hope the two of you work out your problem. In any case, I've come to ask a favor of you."

"Certainly," he said. "Whatever you need."

The emperor smiled. "I need for you to deny you had anything to do with creating the new flip points and then refuse to discuss it any further."

Carl frowned. "That's easy enough. I didn't have anything to do with it at all."

"Yes, but I'm going to imply you did and that it's classified. Then your denials will be true, but no one will believe you. The subterfuge is necessary to keep people from knowing about your alien friend for a while."

"I can't say I'm happy with lying, but I understand. I'll do it, of course."

The emperor's smile widened. "Excellent. I'm classifying this information as an Imperial secret under the name Project Rainbow Bridge.

You will only speak of the alien or the process with authorized people. For now, that is Doctor Leonard, Admiral Mertz, Admiral Yeats, Princess Kelsey, myself, and Major Ellis, of course. The fewer people that know the precise details, the better."

Carl nodded. "Of course. What happens now? The mission is over. Or is it? I'm a little unsure if I should be packing my bags to go back to Avalon."

"We're already moving to orbit. A few ships will stay here to keep any idiots from going through the new flip point and killing themselves, but I think shore leave is in order. You'll be staying here, working on these projects after you take care of some business below. And taking some personal time."

Carl wasn't sure why the emperor looked at Major Ellis when he said that.

"Doctor Leonard tells me that you've got a number of pots in the fire and that you're the most adept at using the new technology," the emperor continued. "Your results speak for themselves. He'll continue to work with you, but I'm giving you carte blanche to explore what you like, under his oversight. If you need assistants, I'll find some. Or you can pick them. Whatever you need."

That shocked Carl. "I'm honored, of course, Your Majesty, but I'm only a graduate student. I've never led a research project before."

The older man nodded. "That's why Doctor Leonard will continue to advise and guide you. As for your degree, he tells me that you've met all the requirements for your doctorate except for your thesis.

"I'm going to have a word with the chancellor at Imperial University. I believe your work on quantum communications will be more than enough to satisfy him. You can make a very good classified paper out of it, and those who are cleared to know the details can question you about it. That should be all that they require to grant your PhD.

"Work with Doctor Leonard to get the paper ready quickly. After all, they won't want a graduate student awarded the Lucien Prize for physics."

Carl's head spun. "I'm honored you'd think so, but that isn't happening, Majesty. I'm not in that league."

"Somehow, I knew you were going to say that. The head of the panel considering the awards this year disagrees. I spoke with him an hour ago, and he swooned at the breakthrough and all the other science it hinted at. He believes that it's also linked to flip-point science, and I'm inclined to agree.

"Young man, this is the most significant breakthrough in physics since the Fall. You're going to win that prize without any help from me, and that's where the lie comes in. They'll undoubtedly ask you about the flip point and if you created it. Tell them no and repeat yourself as many times as you need to. Say nothing of who did or what happened."

Carl understood now. Of course they wouldn't believe him. They'd be certain he created the flip point as a byproduct of his research into quantum communications. The emperor's plan was clever. They'd all jump to the wrong conclusion, and the emperor could protect the truth for as long as he wanted to.

Only Carl would have to let people believe he'd done something he hadn't. He'd have to allow them to shower him with praise he hadn't earned. He might win an award he didn't deserve. Only he would likely know what a monstrous fraud he was.

He bowed his head. "I'll do what I need to do to protect the secret, Majesty. Whatever it takes."

"Excellent. As you've just become one of the most valuable resources in the Empire, I'm taking it upon myself to see you stay safe.

"Major Ellis. I've spoken with my daughter, and she's agreed to release you to my service. Now that she's home, we can have the Imperial Guard resume protective duties for her. You've done a tremendous job, and that means you get a more difficult one."

He grinned. "I'm placing you in charge of protecting this brilliant young man. Continue to use the people you're familiar with and requisition whatever equipment you require. Keep him safe."

She opened her mouth with what looked to Carl to be an objection, but closed it with the words unspoken. "Yes, Your Majesty."

"Excellent. Mister Owlet, I look forward to reading your unredacted dissertation. Take a few days to see the city and meet with the university officials. Enjoy yourself. You've earned the downtime. When you get that shield ready, I want to see it in action."

His smile turned a little sly toward the marine officer. "And, Major, don't let your position as his protector stop you from dating if that's how things roll. That's an order." He headed for the hatch. "Until we meet again."

Once the emperor and Doctor Leonard had departed, the two of them stared at one another silently.

Well, this was going to be awkward.

17

Nathaniel Breckenridge waited impatiently for the Imperial Marines guarding the prison facility to scan him for weapons. They didn't seem the type he could intimidate with his position, so browbeating them into moving faster wouldn't work.

Pity. He really wanted to take his frustration out on someone.

The senior marine finally nodded. "You're clear, Senator. This way, please."

He led Nathaniel down the corridor to a lift. This section of Orbital One was completely isolated from the rest of the station. Only one way in or out. One heavily guarded way.

As the head of the Senate Armed Forces Committee, Nathaniel had the access to know there were just over a hundred prisoners serving time here. A few hard cases were in maximum security, which seemed a bit redundant. This was already the most heavily secured prison in the system.

The lift deposited them on a different level, and the marine brought him to a small room that looked as though it was set up for meetings between prisoners and their counsel. Which was exactly what he'd be using it for today, he admitted grimly.

Wallace was already there, dressed in a garishly orange ship's suit. One without any rank insignia or even a name tag. All it had was a number on the front and rear.

His nephew stood awkwardly. They'd cuffed his wrists with a long length of wire going through a loop on the table. A glance confirmed they'd also shackled his legs.

"Release him," Nathaniel said coolly.

The marine shook his head. "I'm sorry, Senator, but I can't do that. The prisoner has been violent in the past, and it's standard procedure—"

"I don't care what your procedure is," Nathaniel snarled. "Wallace Breckenridge is a decorated Fleet captain. I'm in no danger. Remove his restraints. Now."

The marine gave him a long look and then backed down. "If the prisoner attacks you, or resists being led back to confinement, that's on you, Senator."

Nathaniel looked at his nephew sternly. "Captain Breckenridge won't give you any further trouble. Will you, Wallace?"

His nephew's sullen expression didn't look promising. Nathaniel slapped his hand on the table, making the younger man jump.

"That requires a response, Wallace."

"No," his nephew said. "I won't cause any problems when we're done."

Nathaniel waited for the marine to remove the restraints and withdraw. As both an Imperial senator and a licensed Imperial counsel, he knew they wouldn't record this meeting. So he could say exactly what he needed to.

He sat across from his nephew and waited for him to sit. "What the devil did you think you were doing? Could you have blundered more badly if you tried?"

"All I did was what duty required of me, Uncle Nathaniel. Mertz violated every regulation when he——"

"Bullshit. You tried to force your way on them out of spite, and it blew up in your face. For God's sake, you kidnapped an Imperial princess."

"It was for her own protection," Wallace insisted stubbornly. "She's not right in the head. Those implant things drove her crazy. Megalomania. Mertz, too. Once the facts come out, I'll be free and he'll be locked up in here."

Nathaniel shook his head. It was worse than he'd imagined possible. The idiot actually thought he was doing the right thing.

"So why did your own chief medical officer clear Mertz and her, then? Doesn't that undercut your argument?"

"Of course not. The man was obviously Mertz's secret supporter. He couldn't just let him pass the exam and then flunk the princess. I had to disregard his bias. My own cool detachment was what was needed to make sense of the situation."

Nathaniel felt his stomach do a slow roll. "My sister would be horrified if she were still alive. I have some sad news for you, Wallace. The emperor has already accepted the validity of the Imperial edict. The Senate will fight it, but I'm not sure they even *have* the legal authority to fight him on this issue.

"Frankly, if you weren't buried in this up to your eyebrows, I'd be inclined to accept it on general principle. Now I have to try to save your sorry ass. What the devil were you thinking?"

"This is ridiculous, Uncle! I was doing what was best for the Empire."

"Really? Let's leave aside your poor judgment in kidnapping the second in line to the Imperial Throne. I'd like to hear your justification for the battle of Erorsi. Not why it happened, but why you did what you did. I can assure you that the court-martial will be addressing it shortly."

"Let them," Wallace said flatly. "I was following Fleet doctrine in a bad situation. The enemy proved to be much more capable than we expected. It happened so damned fast.

"One second things were going as planned, the next the enemy destroyer was firing missiles from a ridiculous range. Captains Macumber and Cooley made some serious errors in judgment. That cost them their ships and a lot of good people."

Nathaniel considered his nephew. He wasn't a Fleet officer, but even he knew that wasn't true. At least not in reality.

"What about the warnings that Mertz gave you about the destroyer. Not just in the briefing—which he recorded, by the way—but also in a message before you engaged. He told you it was faster and better armed than any of your ships, did he not?"

"Yes, but that assessment made no sense. A little ship like that couldn't have that kind of capability."

"Yet it did. Just as Mertz said. Just as the prosecution will prove he told you multiple times, yet you still sent those ships to fight the destroyer while you went after a freighter with your heavy cruiser."

He shook his head. "You know what I'd say if I was prosecuting this case? That you were afraid. That you scuttled away to avoid a fight you'd probably have lost."

The statement so outraged his nephew that the man sat there sputtering.

"I have no doubt someone will mention it at your trial," Nathaniel continued relentlessly. "The jury will be hard pressed to dismiss the charge. Cowardice in the face of the enemy is a serious offense, is it not? Why did you go after the freighter, Wallace?"

The other man slouched in his chair. "I wanted to seize the computers and cargo for the Empire. I knew the princess would give it away. Just like she gave everything else away. The woman is mad. She *shot* me!"

Nathaniel imagined she'd enjoyed doing so. His respect for the Imperial family went up a notch.

"Let me tell you what they're going to charge you with," Nathaniel said without addressing his nephew's objections. "First, disobeying a number of lawful orders."

He held up a finger to silence his nephew's objection. "I don't care that you think they weren't valid. Your lawyer will do his best to get them thrown out. Just listen.

"Second will be a series of charges that you were derelict in your duty. That your actions led to the destruction of three ships and thousands of dead Fleet personnel. Third, and most damning, treason. When you defied Princess Kelsey, you stood up to the Imperial Throne. You can be sure the emperor will lay that charge before the Senate, and I doubt I can stop that trial, either."

He let that sink in. "If the edict stands, then you knowingly and willfully defied her instructions and kidnapped her. It's the same as if you'd done it to Emperor Karl, and that, you idiot, was beyond stupid.

"I have no idea if I can save you. At best, you're going to lose your commission and go to prison for a very long time. I can't imagine an outcome where that doesn't happen. At worst, they'll execute you. You *do* remember that treason is a capital offense, don't you?"

"But, everything I did was for the Empire!" Wallace almost wailed. "How can this be happening? I've always been a loyal officer, doing what I needed to keep the Empire safe. This is all Mertz's fault. And the princess, but mostly Mertz."

Nathaniel sagged a little. Even now, his nephew refused to take responsibility for his actions. Honesty compelled him to admit that he'd protected Wallace for far too long.

This was going to end badly. He'd do everything in his power to salvage what he could, but a drunk counsel just out of school could convict the man. He'd given them too much proof and done too many irredeemable things.

All that mattered now was the family name. Nathaniel would save it, even from Wallace. Somehow.

* * *

ELISE WENT DOWN to the surface of Avalon in the same cutter as William Hawthorne and Reginald Bell. All three of them had appointments with the Department of Imperial Affairs.

The older man's situation would be the easiest for the Empire to deal with, she imagined. He and his people had continued to fight the rebels, and they'd agreed they were still Imperial subjects. That should lead to a very smooth transition.

She smiled. He was the last surviving person from the Old Empire. She imagined that meant he was automatically a citizen here. His Fleet back pay would be an impressive sum, if anyone thought of that angle.

Lord Hawthorne would have a more difficult time of it. His world was Imperial, but had fallen to the rebels. They wanted to keep the existing power structure and certain agreements they'd made with Kelsey. The Empire would probably balk a little at that, but they'd have to set a precedent for all the other worlds under the sway of the Rebel Empire.

In her case, the Kingdom of Pentagar was a formerly Imperial world that had been isolated by the rebellion. They'd thought they were the last bastion of the Empire. They'd formed their own government and had no intention of acknowledging that the Empire—any empire—had sovereignty over them.

Pentagar would remain a close ally of the Empire. Nothing more. That would make for some sparks, she imagined.

The cutter landed at the spaceport, and the Fleet crewmen saw them off. A delegation from the Department of Imperial Affairs awaited them. It looked as though they'd decided that three separate groups would be appropriate.

A woman in a pale green dress stepped over to her. "Welcome to Avalon, Highness. I'm Brenda Winters, a senior negotiator at the Department of Imperial Affairs. Someone will see to your bags while I escort you to the department. I'll also be working with you to clarify our governments' relationship."

Elise smiled and extended her hand. "You could've sent someone to pick me up. Unless you want to start negotiating in the grav car."

The other woman returned her smile. "No, but I'll admit I had an ulterior motive. I wanted to see Mister Bell with my own eyes. It's so astonishing that he was alive before the Empire fell. That he was a serving Fleet officer. Not to say that I wasn't looking forward to meeting you," she hastily added.

Elise laughed. "I completely understand and take no offense. In fact, I'd be pleased to introduce you later. He's quite the storyteller."

She watched the other two groups moving toward separate grav vans. The large vehicles allowed enough room for both parties, including the guards they'd all brought down to Avalon. Not that they needed them, but the guards did display a certain level of status.

Reginald had argued against the tactic, but she'd convinced him that he was representing a planetary government. William had helped her argue the point, and the older man had acquiesced.

A third grav van was awaiting them. Elise allowed the other woman to lead her and the pair of Royal Guards accompanying her in that direction.

"I'd like to raise a point that I suspect Mister Bell won't mention on his own," Elise said. "He was trapped on Erorsi during a Fleet assignment. One that he's been performing for more than five hundred years."

"There's the matter of Fleet advancement and back pay. As I said, he'd never mention the issue on his own, but as a Fleet icon, I'd imagine you'd want to do something about that. He's dedicated centuries to carrying out his orders. That kind of loyalty demands recognition."

The other woman stopped dead in her tracks, her eyes wide. "I hadn't even considered that. Oh my God." She laughed. "Some Fleet accountant is going to die on the spot. I'll be certain to pass that along, because you're absolutely right."

Elise climbed into the grav van with a satisfied expression. The older man would try to duck any awards or money. He'd say they wouldn't do him much good at this point in his life. Still, it was a matter of principle.

Her father had driven that lesson home when she was a girl. Loyalty *must* be rewarded. Achievements recognized. Fealty was a two-way street.

Emperor Karl had probably thought of that, but things were very busy. She wanted to be sure that nothing fell through the cracks.

The trip to the Department of Imperial Affairs was quick, and the view was very nice. Avalon was a pastoral world, as befitting a former vacation hotspot. Perhaps she could get in some skiing while she was here. If Jared could free the time.

Once they'd landed at the large building and made their way to a conference room, Elise sat and let Brenda take the lead in discussing their situation. Since she had signed an agreement with Kelsey, this should be a perfunctory meeting.

The other woman sat across from Elise and opened a notebook. "I took the liberty of reading the agreement you reached with Princess Kelsey under her authority as the emperor's representative. It all seems to be in order, but there's one small formality that needs to take place before it's valid."

Elise raised an eyebrow. "That's not what I understood. Isn't her word on this matter binding?"

"Yes and no. She had the authority to negotiate the treaty, but it's not officially binding on the Empire until approved by the Imperial Senate. I've sent a copy to the Imperial Affairs Committee, and they're reviewing it.

"No doubt, they'll want to discuss it with you. Once they approve the language, it has to pass a vote of the full Senate. If they recommend changes, obviously your government will need to review them and agree."

That was not what Elise had expected to hear. "What's our current status, then?"

"Due to the circumstances, the department will continue to treat Pentagar as a foreign government, but under a strict reading of the Imperial Charter, worlds are not allowed to secede from the Empire. I understand that isn't what happened, but the founders never envisioned the rebellion or the Fall.

"I'm not sure how the Senate will judge matters, either. It's possible that some senators will see Pentagar as an Imperial world. Others might try to keep that interpretation and still grant you more latitude in home rule. Unfortunately, some might stand firm that you are Imperial subjects. At this time, I'm not sure how the majority feels. Things have happened so fast."

Elise felt her expression harden. "The Kingdom of Pentagar is a sovereign nation, and we will not bow our heads to force. Your senators had best keep that firmly in mind. Do not turn allies into enemies. Especially not in the face of this war we're in together."

The other woman spread her hands helplessly. "I agree, but my hands are tied. You're going to have to go to the Imperial Senate and discuss the matter. I've already spoken to one of the members of the committee, and he'd be happy to talk with you as soon as you desire."

"Very well. I expect this is something I'd best see to at once. Who is he, and how do I set up a meeting?"

"I'm told he is available now. The van we arrived in can take you to the Imperial Senate building. Oh, and he's one of the senior members of the committee. We've worked with him often, and he's a very reasonable man. Senator Nathaniel Breckenridge."

18

Angela rode in silence on the way to the main campus of Imperial University with Owlet. The young man stared out the grav car's window, brooding. He'd been that way ever since he'd met with the emperor.

He was meeting with the chancellor shortly. Every kilometer that passed made him look more sour. It wouldn't take long for the official to see right through his deception.

"You need to pull yourself together," she said firmly.

He turned his head away from the window distractedly. "Hmmm?"

"I said that you need to focus. If you go in there like that, he'll know you're lying."

"He'd be right," Owlet said dejectedly.

"You promised the emperor that you'd do this, and that means you need to give it your best shot. You have to make these people believe you're being up-front and honest. If they see through this, then you've failed in your duty. So, as I just said, get your head out of your ass."

He smiled a little. "I wasn't paying much attention, but I'm pretty sure that isn't what you said."

"It's what I meant."

He sighed. "You don't have any idea how hard this is for me, do you? Let me turn this around. Science is my life, just like the Marines is yours. What if the emperor ordered you to lie about a battle you'd been in? What if he ordered you to take credit for saving a bunch of lives? Of single-handedly winning the battle while you were just one person doing her part. That's what this means to me."

"The two things are hardly the same," she said dryly. "But if he ordered me to, I'd do it."

"What if they awarded you the Imperial Cross? Then the public would be honoring you for something you never did, and you'd have to wear the reminder of that lie for the rest of your career. Until the truth came out and then you'd be reviled as someone without honor."

That set her back on her heels. He was taking this a lot more seriously than she'd imagined.

"Again, the two situations are hardly equivalent," she said. "Even if they were, I'd damned well do what was best for the Empire. It's more important than how I feel. Everyone would understand when the truth came out.

"Let me point out where you made a mistake. You figured out how to communicate across interstellar distances. That's big. That's worth the damned Lucien Prize all by itself. The rest of this is just embellishment."

"All I did was pull together a bunch of other peoples' research. Yes, I had to detail the scientific framework this was based on, but I just saw the connections. Others did all the hard work."

He balled up his fist and hit his armrest. "And that's what's diabolical. I'm telling the truth while knowing they won't believe me. When it all comes out, it won't matter that I've denied everything, and I'll know it the whole time."

"Are you going to back out?"

"No."

"Then quit your bitching and get your head out of your ass. We're landing, and unless I miss my guess, that's the chancellor standing right there. You gave the emperor your word to fool him, so you'd better put your game face on."

* * *

CARL STEPPED out of the grav car. He'd seen Chancellor Warwick before—from a distance—but the man hadn't known him from Adam. Until today.

"Mister Owlet, welcome back to Imperial University," the dapper older gentleman said. "I must say that what I've been reading about you is most impressive. Come to my office, and we'll discuss it in a more, um, secure environment."

Warwick glanced at Major Ellis curiously. "I'm afraid I don't know your friend. Is she, ah, cleared to know about this?"

Carl wasn't surprised at the other man's confusion. Major Ellis had changed into civilian clothes for the trip. He supposed that made more sense on a university campus. It softened her appearance a lot. She wasn't nearly as intimidating when she was out of uniform.

She was, oddly, a lot more attractive. He could see what the other Carls had seen in her. Not that that changed their current circumstances.

He smiled, working hard to make it look genuine. "Chancellor Warwick, allow me to introduce Major Angela Ellis of the Imperial Marines. She's my minder and is indeed cleared to hear anything we discuss."

"Ah! I see. Then if you'll both come with me, my office isn't far, as you know."

The three of them walked off the landing pad while the driver took the grav car back into the air. The man, another marine in civilian clothes, would be nearby in case they needed a quick extraction.

"Actually, I have no idea where your office is," Carl said apologetically. "I was pretty focused on my studies and never had reason to go to the administration buildings."

"I understand. That's true in much of academia. We administrators labor behind the scenes so that people such as yourself can focus on what's important to you."

In this case, Carl was in complete agreement. Imperial University was a model of efficiency and excellence. Chancellor Warwick and his associates had done everything in their power to make the learning environment the best it could be, while staying out of the way.

All too often, that wasn't the case. He had nothing but the greatest respect for the man, and that made what Carl was doing even worse.

"I had a long conversation with Doctor Leonard this morning, and I took a brief call from Doctor Cartwright," Warwick said. "Both were laudatory in discussing your contributions to the mission. I, of course, don't know the full details, but both men mentioned that they wouldn't have achieved so much without your hard work and keen insight."

"Allow me to assure you that they're overstating my case, Chancellor. I played the part I needed to, but *they* made the magic happen."

Major Ellis cleared her throat. "I have to disagree. Mister Owlet brought more to the table than he's mentioning. Don't let his humble nature fool you. His skills had a lasting and far reaching impact on this mission, and I've personally seen him do things I'd call wizardry."

Carl couldn't stop himself from giving her a sideways look of disbelief. Her compliment actually shocked him speechless. It had to be a lie to shore up his story.

"So I'm given to understand," Chancellor Warwick said as they walked through the tree-lined quad.

Students filled the open area. They laughed, played, and shouted. Most were older than he was, but that wasn't unexpected. He'd arrived at Imperial University barely into puberty, a prodigy. Which significantly affected his social life, he admitted.

Now he was old enough to envy those couples walking close to one another. His focus might have sped him up the ladder in his studies, but he'd missed so much while locked in the lab on those late nights.

Part of him wanted to smile wryly at the looks they were getting. He knew what they were thinking. The chancellor was giving a tour to a prospective student and his... mother? Major Ellis wasn't that old, but her imposing stature lent her an air of maturity beyond her years. The way she walked made her look dangerous, though their watchers wouldn't know why.

He resisted the urge to say something to her about it. That wouldn't be helpful, even if it would be fun.

"Do you know that you'll be the youngest PhD this institution has ever produced, if you pass your dissertation?" the chancellor asked.

Carl returned his attention to the man. "No, sir. I wasn't aware of that. It's a little intimidating."

"Don't be too worried," the man assured him. "The fact that your theory has been proven to work lends a lot of credence to your underlying model. I've taken the liberty of assembling a team of department heads to review your work. All cleared by Fleet, of course."

They walked into the administration building and took the lift up to the top floor. Carl kept his initial objections quiet until they'd made it into the man's office.

"Let's sit over here while we talk," Chancellor Warwick said. "Can I get you any refreshment? Coffee, perhaps?"

Major Ellis put her hand on Carl's leg to stop him from answering. "Thank you," she said. "We'd both love a cup."

"Then I'll be right back. I've got a fair hand with the brewer, so I'll bring us a fresh pot."

Carl tried to ignore the heat soaking through his pants leg from her hand. It was… distracting. "What if I don't want any coffee?"

"Then don't drink it, though that would be rude. I wanted one last chance to remind you this is game time. Of course he's getting a team of people together to review your work. He's heard about the Lucien Prize, so he's moving quickly. Don't make too much of a stink about it."

She was right, but that only made it more annoying. "Well, I can't just help him speed this along. It would be out of character. No one would take this without some protest."

"I bet you know some people that would jump at the chance and run over anyone in their way."

He actually did know some people like that, but they weren't him.

She seemingly realized where her hand was and withdrew it, sitting back in her chair. He hoped she didn't realize what kind of effect her touch had on him.

The chancellor came back a few minutes later with what turned out to be some excellent coffee. As a lab rat, Carl knew all about bad coffee, so he could appreciate a good brew.

Chancellor Warwick set his cup down on the saucer. "Now, as I was saying, a team of cleared PhDs are examining the papers you've prepared. I understand that it isn't a thesis in the conventional manner, and so do they. You'll be meeting with them to discuss everything over the next few days. Think of it as a working defense of your dissertation.

"We have two of the quantum communication sets. Fleet is taking a number of them to the Baker system next door. One of our people is with them and in possession of the other half of the linked pair they loaned us for testing. It should be through the flip point later this evening and ready for testing tomorrow."

"We know that they don't work at an unlimited distance," Carl warned him. "Harrison's World is two flips away, and we can't communicate with it now. The Nova system is just short of a thousand light years away. Harrison's World is an additional 415 light years, though some of that is lost because it's at something of a slight angle. Call it thirteen hundred light years by direct line."

The other man nodded. "The Baker system is significantly closer. Hopefully, it will work. If it doesn't, then that gives us more data, doesn't it?"

"I suppose so, but that isn't really helpful. I have to admit I didn't expect it to work at interstellar distances, no matter what the theory said. The fact it has a limit is actually reassuring to me."

The other man sipped his coffee and gave Carl a long, considering look. "I understand that you feel that you only combined several existing sets of work to make your breakthrough. I want to take a moment to disabuse you of any notion that those facts lessen your work.

"Do you know how many winners of the Lucien Prize felt the same way? Most of them, based on any number of biographies I've read over the years. Or they thought their work was too limited in scope to be worthy of the award. That feeling, my boy, is natural."

Carl shook his head. "I don't think I did enough unique work to be worthy of the honor. I'm certain that the committee has better candidates to consider."

Warwick smiled. "Then you'd be wrong. I spoke with Doctor Paul Creedmoor this morning. He's heading the selection committee for physics this year. When I sent him the classified briefing paper—for which I had permission!—he almost swooned. He'd already spoken briefly with the emperor, but the details of your work set his intellectual curiosity afire.

"You can rest assured that your work will be studied closely, even though the committee was only a few days from making a decision for this year. You've loosed a fox in the henhouse for certain."

That didn't make Carl feel any better, but it was beyond his control. Whatever they did, he'd have to accept it. One way or the other.

"In the meanwhile," Warwick continued, "I've arranged for an apartment for you. We should make our determination before the Lucien Committee reaches theirs. Or I'll be most cross with some people."

Major Ellis cleared her throat. "I'll need adjoining rooms for myself and my people."

The chancellor frowned. "We hadn't considered that when we reserved the apartment, Major. Student housing is full. We pride ourselves on bringing our students as close to their work as possible. There are two bedrooms, so I could turn one of them into a guardroom, I suppose. Perhaps having one of your men move in with him?"

She gave Carl a less than friendly look. "He's my responsibility, so I'll think of something."

Great. One more thing for her to be mad about that wasn't his fault.

"Before I see you there, Mister Owlet, I'd like to ask the question I'm sure will be on everyone's mind. Is the new flip point also an outcome of your research?"

There it was.

"No. The origins of the flip point and the means of its creation are Imperial secrets and have nothing to do with my research. You'll have to ask Fleet about it."

The other man smiled, getting the anticipated wrong impression from Carl's denial. "I see, though part of me isn't sure I believe you. I'm certain you'll be asked the same thing many times over the next few months, too."

"They'll get the same answer," Carl said tiredly. "When will I meet the team?"

"Tomorrow. They need time to study the information Fleet sent. You look tired, so I suggest you rest. You'll be quite busy in the morning."

"That works for me," he said. "I have some equipment that needs to be secured at the lab. It's related to the quantum pairs."

"I'll need to check the security there," Major Ellis said. "We can't have classified and important equipment and research just lying around. I'll put part of my team on the lab right away."

"I assure you that our lab is up to the task. We do classified research for Fleet there."

That didn't seem to impress the marine. "Then it'll be even more secure. This isn't negotiable, Chancellor."

"Hrump," the other man said. "I'll cooperate, of course, but this is hardly necessary. And, forgive me, but it's more than a bit insulting."

"I'm sorry about that," she said, not sounding sorry at all.

Carl finished his coffee quickly and set the cup down. "Perhaps I'd best see to settling in then. Who is in charge of the examination?"

"Professor Bedford."

That wasn't the best news. Andrew Bedford was old and cantankerous. He didn't much care for young people, which was odd in a university professor. He'd taken an especial joy in grinding Carl down.

Well, perhaps things would be different this time. After all, the hard work was done. Right?

19

Kelsey stood in her room at the Imperial Palace, feeling like a stranger. It had only been a year since she'd last stood here, but it felt like a lifetime. She wasn't the same girl who'd imagined adventure and excitement exploring the remains of the Old Empire with her despised half brother anymore.

No, not even close.

Now Jared was as close to her as Ethan was. Maybe more. Her full brother had become less friendly when puberty hit. Overprotective and imperious. She was sure that would make for one hell of a fight when he found her.

She'd managed to get Talbot off doing something else for a few hours by telling him she needed a little alone time. That would keep him from punching Ethan in the face when her brother did something that offended him.

Her enhanced hearing picked up the sound of his approach. The Imperial Guards let him into her room without argument, and he was angry. Furious.

Big surprise. It was time to settle this once and for all.

"What the hell were you thinking, Kelsey? Dammit, you gave him everything he's been craving. I thought you were smarter than that."

She smiled sweetly at Ethan. "It's good to see you, too! Yes, I really missed you. And I'm fine. Thanks for asking."

His expression grew even more thunderous. "Don't toy with me. I demand to know why you helped Mertz build a platform to seize the Throne."

She allowed her false cheer to slip away. "This is old and tiresome, Ethan. He's not after your job. Frankly, I doubt there is anything he'd rather avoid more. We were wrong about him, and you need to see that before you make an ass of yourself."

He stepped close to her, his expression more than a bit menacing. "Don't tell me how to feel," he said in a low voice. One that she'd have found threatening before her idea of threatening changed forever.

Now Ethan didn't even register on her danger meter. She knew he couldn't hurt her. He would never intimidate her again.

Kelsey stared into his eyes from only a few centimeters away. "You're in my personal space. Move or I'll move you."

The surprise in his expression was gratifying, but he didn't back down. "Not until you see sense."

"Back up. In case you didn't catch it, there's an unspoken 'or else' attached to that."

"You always think you know better than me," he sneered. "You've been nothing but soft and weak. Now he's twisted everything in your mind until you think he's on your side. Well, I'm not going to allow you to throw away our birthright so easily."

She put her hand on his chest and pushed gently. For her, that is. Ethan staggered back a few steps, shock written all over his face. She'd never had the physical strength to deter him before. Now she had enough to throw him through the wall if he made an ass of himself.

"I'm not going to stand here and let you froth on about something you know nothing about," she said coolly. "I've been right by Jared's side for over a year. A time in which some very terrible things happened. You should do yourself a favor and read up on it. As the heir, you need to know.

"One thing I can tell you without the slightest hint of doubt, though. Jared Mertz is an honorable man. One who has no designs on the Throne."

"Unbelievable," he swore. "He got to you, too. I don't care how long you were there or what you think you saw. He is the greatest threat to our inheritance that could possibly exist. Mertz has Imperial blood in his veins, and he thinks that he can displace us. I won't allow that to happen because you've lost your mind."

She laughed. "You think you know everything when all you really understand is this unreasoning hatred of yours. It's worse than an obsession. You should see someone about it before other people—"

Ethan lunged forward and grabbed her by her blouse, slamming her back into the wall. To be fair, she saw him coming, but chose to let him in.

"You are not my equal," he snarled. "You never wanted to rule, and you don't have the mettle for it anyway. So, don't lecture me on strength. I'll protect us and the Throne."

She looked down at his hand. "I allowed this to happen to make a point. I suggest you learn from it."

Kelsey barely had to bump her strength to get him moving. It was mostly skill she'd learned from Ned in his hand-to-hand training. In less than two seconds, she'd mashed Ethan's face into the wall. She kept him there by jamming his arm up behind him.

It felt surprisingly good.

"This has gone too far, Ethan. You need to reassess this delusion. Jared isn't after you or the Throne. If you keep making an ass of yourself, things will not end well."

Kelsey leaned forward until she could whisper up toward his ear. "If you think you can push me around, you're wrong. Keep your hands to yourself, and go do some thinking." She let him go and stepped back.

He stared at her for a moment and then left without a single word.

She sat on the arm of her couch. That could've gone better. She hoped she'd gotten through to him. That his own self-interest would keep him from doing something stupid.

After all, what choice did he have? It wasn't as if he could just order people to dispose of his problems.

* * *

ETHAN ALMOST STAGGERED AWAY from his sister's room. Her physical changes shocked him, but not as much as her mental ones. Mertz had corrupted her. She was under his sway.

Before she'd left, he never would have believed anyone could come between him and his twin. They'd been close since before they could remember anything at all. He loved her.

She'd betrayed him. She'd become a threat to him and the Throne. She'd become an enemy to be dealt with.

Oh, he wished he could change her mind, but now that she'd switched sides once, he could never trust that she wasn't working against him again.

He leaned his head against the wall and wept. It would break his heart, but he needed to neutralize her. Perhaps he didn't have to kill her, though. If he could remove her as second in line to the Throne, then he could allow her to live. He owed her that much.

Ethan straightened and headed for his rooms. He needed to calm down and then go speak with his father. Surely, he would see the truth this time.

Mertz was the true threat to the Throne. Without him, Kelsey would fall in line.

If his plea didn't work, he could reevaluate things. If it became necessary, he would mourn, but the security of the Throne was more important than even his closest family.

* * *

JARED STEPPED into the conference room and nodded at the senior officers sitting around the table. He'd been dreading this board of inquiry for the last year. At least this would finally end his torture. One way or another.

He recognized most of the officers, but not the man at the head of the table. A check of his implant memory told him it was Admiral Jack

Lancaster, head of the Judge Advocate General's Office. The senior jurist in Fleet.

Well, he supposed that at least meant they were taking this seriously. He was happy he'd taken the time to load the public profiles of all Fleet personnel. Otherwise, he'd know nothing about the man.

"Admiral Mertz," Lancaster said. "Please have a seat." He gestured to the chair on the other side of the table from the senior officers. All either Vice Admirals or Admirals, he noted.

Jared took his place. "Admirals."

"I'm Admiral Jack Lancaster, head of the Judge Advocate General Corps. Allow me to introduce my associates." He went down the line confirming Jared's records.

"Now," Lancaster continued. "Let's be clear about the purpose of this board of inquiry. There were a number of serious incidents during your expedition, and we're going to review them all. We need to examine every aspect of what occurred.

"We'll be conducting this board under oath, so be advised that anything you say here might be used against you in a court-martial, should one be convened. Do you understand?"

"Yes, sir."

Jared knew there would be a court-martial. That was a foregone conclusion. He'd lost his ship. *Athena* would never fly again. *Ginnie Dare* was destroyed under his authority, and more than half his personnel had died in the last year.

That didn't even begin to count the decisions he'd made that these men and women would be second-guessing. They had the perfect vantage point to judge everything he'd decided without any of the pressure.

Yes. There'd be a court-martial.

The hatch behind Jared slid open. He glanced over his shoulder and saw Captain Alice Quinn stride into the room. The slender black woman nodded to everyone at the table.

"Admirals. Apologies for my tardiness. Captain Alice Quinn. I'm serving as Admiral Mertz's counsel in this matter."

Lancaster frowned. "This isn't a court-martial, Captain. We're only gathering to hear Admiral Mertz's summary of the events in question."

Quinn smiled. "I understand, sir, but under Fleet regulations, Admiral Mertz is entitled to have an officer stand as his defense counsel during a board of inquiry, too. As you well know, I served in JAG before I transferred to the command track. I'm still licensed."

"This is very irregular," Lancaster said. "It doesn't sound as though Admiral Mertz engaged your services. You can't just show up and declare yourself his counsel."

She turned to Jared. "Admiral Yeats sent me. Do you feel the need for counsel, Admiral? If I'm not an acceptable candidate, or you feel that I'm chasing down the work, I can suggest a number of very competent people to represent you."

Jared shook his head. "You're perfectly fine with me, Captain Quinn. You're hired."

She returned her attention to the board. "I believe that settles all the requirements, sir. I'd like to request a brief recess while I consult with my client. It shouldn't take more than a few minutes."

Lancaster didn't look pleased, but he nodded. "The conference room adjacent to this one is free, I believe. We'll wait here."

"We'll be back very shortly. I'd like to thank the board for their indulgence."

Jared followed her into the other conference room. "This is a pleasant surprise, Captain Quinn. Thank you."

"I'm glad the admiral called me. That was an ambush. I'm surprised someone as savvy as you missed it. They should've insisted you have counsel."

"I lost my ship and more than half the people under my command. They have to seat a court. You can't stop that."

"Probably not, but everything you say here will be testimony at that trial. You need to have someone skilled at spinning things to get the right tone on the matter.

"I'm not suggesting you shade the truth. Think of me as more of a truth whisperer. I'll translate what you say and defend your actions. If they go too far, I'll slap them down. You have rights and I'll see them respected."

He sighed. "I really appreciate this, but I'm not sure you can save me. I stuck my neck way out. They're going to chop my head off."

She grinned. "That's not the combat commander I know. You need to think of this in Fleet terms. Outmaneuver the bastards and give them hell.

"I've read a summary of the actions you took. We can win this thing, but not if you let them bully you. Admiral Lancaster has a fair reputation, but we leave nothing to chance. If Senator Breckenridge doesn't have someone on that board in his pocket, I'll eat my rank tabs.

"Call me Alice. You're the top dog now, so I get to use your rank while you get to be all familiar."

"That feels wrong."

Quinn laughed. "Get used to it. By the way, you really did us proud. Don't let all this second-guessing get you in an uproar. These admirals would've failed at the same challenges you overcame. Rest assured, I'll tell them that, too.

"Come on. Let's get back in there."

The two of them returned to the main conference room. Lancaster watched Quinn retrieve a chair from against the bulkhead and then started the recorder.

"This is the board of inquiry over the events that occurred during expedition fifteen into the Old Empire. I am Admiral Jack Lancaster, the presiding officer." He introduced the other officers for the record.

"Also present are Admiral Jared Mertz and his counsel, Captain Alice Quinn. Admiral Mertz, please rise."

He did so.

"The testimony you are about to give is under oath. Raise your right hand. Do you swear to tell the truth, the whole truth, and nothing but the truth on your honor as a Fleet officer?"

"I do."

"Please resume your seat and tell us in your own words what happened during your expedition. Leave nothing out and take as much time as you need."

Jared took a deep breath and started at the very beginning. This was going to take a long, long time.

20

———————

Talbot set his drink on the bar and considered punching the smug bastard standing in front of him in the face. Yes, it would cost him his rank, but that seemed a fair exchange.

But Kelsey would be disappointed in him. He sighed and unclenched his fist.

"I think you should reevaluate what you just said to me before I turn your face into hamburger," he said conversationally. "You don't know Admiral Mertz and you weren't there. What gives you the right to judge him?"

The man beside him, another marine, stepped into Talbot's personal space. "I've seen the list of dead. The Bastard killed hundreds of our brothers and sisters. How can you defend what he did?"

Talbot heard the unspoken capitalization of the word "bastard" and knew how this was going to roll. This guy was one of the idiots that thought the admiral was out to use his birth as a lever to the top. Nothing Talbot said was going to change that.

"Is that all you see? The list of those who died? What about the things they gave their lives for? Those don't matter? You think this was all for the admiral's glory? I thought you were an idiot, but that's being unfair to idiots. Someone help me out, here. What's stupider than an idiot?"

"Someone who betrays his brothers for an officer's berth."

Talbot swung, but someone grabbed his arm, spoiling his aim. Other marines dragged them apart before he could shake free.

A grizzled command master chief planted himself in front of Talbot. "This isn't the officer's club, Major. You don't get to come down here and throw your weight around."

He raised a finger before Talbot could speak. "But, you were a senior sergeant when I last laid eyes on you, so you deserve the respect that carries. There won't be any fight today. I want to hear why you're defending this officer."

The first man shouted something, but the new guy turned and bellowed at him. "Pipe down, Grayson. You're a damned disgrace to the uniform, insulting an officer to his face. And for using words small enough that he can understand you. Sit down and shut up."

The man turned back to Talbot. "I'm Command Master Chief Rex Santiago. I knew some of those men and women, too. Why did they die, Major?"

Talbot took a deep breath and tossed back his drink. "Because they were heroes. Because they cared more about the Empire than their own lives. Because they were marines, and that's what marines do."

The crowd shouted almost as one. "Oorah!"

"Bartender," Talbot said. "This is going to be thirsty work. Drinks for everyone, on me. Except for that asshole. He can buy his own drink."

Everyone laughed. Even the asshole.

Talbot launched into the unclassified part of the story. He told them what they'd found. He told them what the stakes were, and he laid out the odds stacked against them.

"If you want to know why so many people died," he wrapped up, "you should look at Captain Breckenridge. That's why he's in the brig."

That set them all to talking.

In a way, Talbot had known this would happen. He'd come here expecting to have a fight, and to tell this story. Technically, this was against regulations. He'd badmouthed an officer. But, he was also an officer, though lower ranking, and in a different service.

These men and women wouldn't turn him in, though. They'd chew over what he'd said and make up their own minds.

That's why he'd come here looking for the fight. Hell, he still wanted to punch that idiot.

Santiago drank some of his beer. "I'd heard some of this through the grapevine," he admitted. "Wasn't sure I believed it. I guess I do now."

He raised his voice in a way that only the best noncoms could, so that it cut through everything going on in the bar.

"Ladies and gentlemen, I give you the Imperial Marines. To our lost brothers and sisters."

Every one of the marines shouted at the top of their lungs and drank.

Well, maybe this was going to work after all.

The command master chief stepped closer to him. "So, what's this I hear about you dating Princess Kelsey?"

Well, maybe not quite as well as he'd hoped.

* * *

ELISE ACCEPTED a ride to the Imperial Senate building with a growing sense of doom. Of course that idiot Breckenridge was going to use his uncle to stymie the good they were trying to do.

The senate building wasn't as impressive as the parliament back on Pentagar, she decided. It was too new, and the designers had gone more for a sleek, modern look. It lacked the gravitas of history.

The grav car set down on a pad outside the entrance, and her guards stepped out. A young woman in a dark burgundy, knee-length dress was waiting for her.

"Crown Princess Elise? I'm Jean Trouville. If you'll come with me, I'll see you to Senator Breckenridge's office."

"Are you his assistant?"

"No, ma'am. I'm an aide to the Imperial Affairs Committee. I work for whichever senator needs me. This way, please."

Trouville led Elise into the building and past the guards. Those men and women didn't look pleased at seeing the Royal Guard moving by with their weapons, but they kept their peace.

This was going to take some getting used to for everyone.

Two of them did fall in place behind the group and joined them in the lift. That was fine by her. The senator deserved the protection his office afforded.

The senator's office was on the top floor of the building, speaking to his place in the hierarchy. He probably had a magnificent view.

The man's assistant stood when the group arrived. "Crown Princess Elise. Welcome to Avalon. If your guards will wait out here, the senator will see you right away."

She smiled and shook her head. "I'm afraid that isn't how this works. Until my guard commander knows the senator better, he's insisted he remain in my presence. The senator won't even notice him, and he can have his own protection. I don't mind."

The man bowed his head with an expression that hinted he'd suspected this was how it would play out. "Of course. This way, please."

She turned on the recording feature in her implants before the man opened the dark wooden doors. She wanted to capture the senator's every word and expression. That might not be strictly legal here, but she could plead ignorance.

Senator Nathaniel Breckenridge stood and came around his desk as soon as she came in, a wide smile that seemed eerily genuine on his face.

"Crown Princess Elise. Welcome to Avalon. Thank you for taking the time to speak with me."

She allowed herself a smile. At least he wasn't the boor his nephew was. "Anything I can do to speed the process of our alliance along is time and effort well spent."

One of her guards waited in the outer office while the commander of her protection detail took up a position off to the side.

Breckenridge waved the senatorial guard back out. "I'm perfectly safe. I'll call out if I need you."

He gestured toward the bar. "May I offer you refreshment? I have a selection of the finest the Terran Empire has to offer, both alcoholic and non. The fruit juices are quite good."

"I'm fine for the moment," she said as she took her seat. "I think it's best if we get right down to business. They tell me your committee has some concerns about the alliance between the Empire and the Kingdom of Pentagar. Perhaps you'd be kind enough to outline your objections for me."

"The problem isn't me, I'm afraid. More the Imperial Charter. It doesn't recognize the validity of secession, and I'm loath to toy with its long-understood meaning. By strict reading of the provisions, it doesn't allow for withdrawal of any member world for any reason."

"That seems to me to be somewhat shortsighted considering the rebellion," she said dryly. "You see, we didn't leave the Empire. The Empire left us. We've fended for ourselves since the Fall, and we're going to go right on doing so.

"I've done this dance before, so forgive me if I move us along. You wouldn't have called me over if you didn't have a counteroffer to make. One where we can both get something we want. I'm interested in hearing it."

He smiled. "You're very astute. Yes, I'm willing to compromise. Frankly, I'm not an idiot. The Rebel Empire is dangerous. Their ignorance is all that is keeping us safe. But I don't want to cross my party without receiving something in return."

"Why am I left with the feeling that your price revolves around Captain Wallace Breckenridge? He's your nephew, is he not? For the record, he's an ass."

The senator smiled sadly. "I'm forced to agree. Make no mistake, I'll do everything I can to minimize the damage he's done to my family name, but he's crossed several lines that I cannot and will not shield him from the consequences of.

"He's going to be court-martialed and thrown out of Fleet. He'll also spend many years in the brig. So be it. That need not have anything to do with the alliance between our peoples. I'm willing to throw my support behind your cause and bring as many of my compatriots as I can."

"I see. What are the goals of your compatriots? Is it in their interest to support the division? If so, how will you sway them?"

"They'll almost certainly bow to the inevitable, but not until they make the Throne suffer. Our stated goals in this matter are that the Imperial Charter doesn't allow Pentagar to be separate, rebellion be damned. They hold that your world is still subject to the Empire."

She shook her head. "How would you enforce that? This might come as a shock to you, but we have powerful ships, too. Ones given to us by my close friend Kelsey under the treaty between our worlds. Would you go to war with us in the face of the Rebel Empire?"

Breckenridge stood and walked slowly over to the bar. "I'm going to make a drink for myself. Call out if you change your mind." He poured something dark into a tumbler over ice.

She considered him for a moment before responding. "What's the price of your assistance in navigating this obstacle?"

He sat back down and sipped his drink. "I know where some figurative bodies are buried and I'm willing to twist arms, but I want your help in the matter of my nephew."

Elise raised an eyebrow. "I'm at a loss as to how I can help him, even if I were inclined to do so. The man is a menace."

"You and Princess Kelsey are friends. She'll listen to you. I know that I can't save Wallace from his madness, but I have an obligation to shield my family from as much of the disgrace as I can. If you can convince her to intervene with her father to leave treason off the table, I'll work tirelessly to keep the Kingdom of Pentagar a sovereign state, precisely as you've negotiated."

"You can ask around," he said with a smile. "I'm a good politician. I stay bought."

This kind of deal making wasn't unknown to her. She could see how it would help him. His nephew would still be a disgrace, but the family wouldn't have spawned a traitor. For a powerful senator, that had to be worth a lot.

"I'm willing to talk with her about it," Elise said, "but I can only promise to be as persuasive as possible. Ultimately, she might decide to say no. Or her father might."

"Then I suggest you be very persuasive. We have the votes to enforce the Imperial Charter, and without my influence, your treaty will never be ratified." He raised his glass in salute to her. "I'm looking forward to seeing another professional at work. Good luck."

21

Karl Bandar stopped the video report he was reviewing when he heard his son at the door. He'd left instructions not to be disturbed, but that wasn't how his son worked. As much as he'd tried to temper his son's… enthusiasm, it hadn't really taken. Ethan always expected immediate results.

When his guard politely declined to disturb Karl, his son got louder. Karl sighed and walked to the door.

"It's alright, Les. Ethan, come in."

"Father, we need to talk about—"

"Sit and listen," Karl said firmly. "That entails closing your mouth, in case I wasn't clear."

The boy obviously wanted to argue but clamped his lips shut with palpable impatience and fury. He also sat, if only grudgingly.

Karl locked the door and engaged the privacy field. That would keep the sound of the inevitable argument out of the ears of even his loyal guards.

"You're trying my patience, Ethan. You're running around with your hair on fire over things that don't deserve that level of response, and you need to dial it back."

He held up a finger to forestall this son's hot words. "Your turn to speak will come but not until I'm done. What you did out there showed an extreme lack of respect for me. If I leave orders not to be disturbed, being pissed off isn't an excuse to disobey them.

"For reasons that seemed good at the time, I've let this behavior slide, but that stops now. You're my son and heir, but that also means I'm your liege. The man you've sworn an oath to support and obey. I expect obedience from you, and respect. I'll have them both, or you will regret it. Is that clear enough?"

Ethan pressed his lips into a tight line, and his eyes flamed with barely suppressed fury. "Perfectly, my lord."

Karl sighed. It was never easy with his son. Or his daughter, sometimes, but that was a completely different kind of trouble.

He sat on the corner of the desk. "Since you've already interrupted my work, you might as well tell me what has you in an uproar."

"Do you know what Mertz has done to Kelsey?"

"He didn't do anything to her, but yes. I've not only read the summaries, I've spoken in depth with Doctors Stone and Guzman. They both have a far deeper understanding of the implants than I do. I expect that other medical experts will be up to speed to check their assumptions soon enough, but I believe I know more than enough."

"Now who's being naive? Mertz may not have ripped her apart and rebuilt her, but he took full advantage of it. Those monsters put things in her brain, and he's had access to sway her for a *year*.

"Hell, everyone on that mission did the same to *themselves*. How do we know it's anything like they say? Wouldn't that be a wonderful way to enslave us? To get us to put those machines in our heads for them? Then Mertz can just waltz in and seize the Throne. We need to lock them all away until we're sure it's really safe."

Karl sighed inside. "Your incessant paranoia about Jared Mertz is tiresome and beginning to worry me. Forget him. As to the implants, I've done some checking. I don't want word getting around, but I had Emperor Lucien disinterred. With all due reverence, I assure you. He had implants just like the Fleet people do.

"I've seen that his body was delivered to Orbital One. It's possible that some data will be recoverable, even after all this time. Scientists trained in doing so will get what they can before we bury him again."

He shook his head. "I'm finding it hard to believe that we never knew. Think of the trove of historical data from the first days of Avalon. Or the critical information his father might have given him."

Karl sighed. "Clearly, they were once a common part of Imperial life. Based on the advantages I'm starting to grasp, they will be again.

"I confirmed that by having some of the Fleet personnel that died here examined. They too had this equipment. Someone I trust is extracting the hardware and will see about powering it up in due time. Then we'll know if the programming is the same."

Karl leaned back in his chair. "They'll have to learn a lot about the programming language and the hardware, but we'll get to the bottom of this. We're taking nothing at face value."

"Aren't you?" Ethan asked with an edge to his voice. "How do we know this supposed edict is even real? Mertz could have very easily concocted it to get a leg up and move toward his real target. The Imperial Throne."

He'd hoped his son would come to his senses, but that was seemingly off the table. Time to address the issue squarely.

"You've always thought the worst of your half brother. And don't even think of snarling at me. That's what he is, like it or not.

"Tell me this, Ethan. If he were looking for a way to seize power, and your concerns of the implants were correct, why didn't he use force when he arrived? We couldn't have stopped him. If that is indeed his plan, we still can't. His people are in control of more firepower than we could muster in our defense."

Ethan leaned forward intently. "Then now is the time to strike. Get them off those ships under some ruse and get loyal officers aboard them before it's too late. I'm not sure why he's delaying, but we can't wait much longer."

Karl shook his head sadly. "The Senate would never accept his claim over yours. Or Kelsey's, for that matter. Even if they did, the people would rise up. Son, this is paranoia. You're seeing shadows behind every event that just aren't there."

"You're being willfully blind, Father. I've always known you were soft where Mertz was concerned, but I never dreamed you'd just hand our birthright over to him. How can you be so blind?"

"Enough," Karl said firmly. "You need a vacation, son. Take a trip out to the lake in the mountains. Stop obsessing over these crazy theories."

"I will not abandon the Empire when it's in such peril."

"You misunderstand me. That wasn't a suggestion." Karl smiled and touched a key on his desk.

Les opened the door. "Yes, Majesty?"

"My son needs to take a trip out to the lake to get away from everything. Take him there and see that he stays put."

He turned his attention to his fuming son.

"I can't force you to rest and reconsider, but I can put you in time-out. The heir to the Throne cannot afford to be so willfully paranoid. Once you've had time to think, we'll talk again."

Ethan surged to his feet. "You're making a grave error in judgment, Father. Don't compound it by taking the one person who sees the threat clearly out of play."

When Karl said nothing, his son stalked out of the room.

Once he was alone again, he called his guard commander. "I'm sending Ethan to the mountains. I want extra people in place to make sure he doesn't sneak away. He's to be kept there until I say otherwise."

"Is he under arrest, Majesty?"

"No. Think of it as protective custody. Isolation to keep him from making a fool of himself. Make sure the guards aren't ones he can browbeat."

"I'll take care of it, Majesty."

Karl sighed and leaned back in his chair. This had all gone wrong so quickly. Ethan's unreasoning hatred of Jared was going to cause real harm if he didn't put a stop to it. He made a mental note to confer with Ethan's private physician to check and be certain that there wasn't a true pathological behavior behind this.

At least his son would be out of the way for a little while. He couldn't cause too much harm up in the mountains.

* * *

ETHAN FUMED as the guards herded him back toward his rooms to pack. The gall of the old man. He treated his chosen heir as if he knew nothing at all. As if his concerns were nothing more than the ravings of a madman. It wouldn't surprise him if there were a visit by doctors while he was away.

He'd turned against Ethan, too.

Everyone had, and they'd soon strike, unless he acted to mitigate the threats against him. It was regrettable that things had come to this, but he had to do what was best for himself and the Empire.

He leaned against the wall as soon as he was back in his rooms. First Kelsey and now his father. How could they choose the Bastard over their own blood? Mertz's sickness had infected them.

Unlike his sister, he couldn't allow his father to orchestrate the overthrow of the rightful heir. He loved his father even more than Kelsey, but the old man was going to have to die.

Did he? Ethan ran through the possibilities in his mind. Surely there was some way to spare his father.

But no viable alternatives came to mind. The loss of the man who'd carried him on his shoulders as a boy ate at him, as if the man were already gone. Really, he was. He just didn't know he was dead, yet.

There would be mourning for his father across the Empire. They'd commission monuments beyond counting to remember his memory. Ethan would see to that.

He packed in the privacy of his room, which gave him the opportunity to stash a few items he might find useful. Starting with a very concealable communications unit. He would be able to oversee every action his minions performed right under the noses of his watchdogs.

Ethan had paid good money to be sure it wasn't traceable. They wouldn't even detect the signals on the security screens. It was that good.

He called his man. "How goes the preparations, Victor?"

"They're good. I should have it resolved tonight."

"Excellent. I have a few other tasks for you. I want you to pick up someone with those damned implants and another person who is familiar with the technology."

"Do you have a specific target with implants in mind?"

Ethan smiled. "As a matter of fact, I do. But first, I'm afraid things have taken a bad turn here at the palace. My father is shipping me off to the Imperial Retreat off in the mountains. While I'm gone, I want you to work with my man in security to get in and take care of something for me. Several things, actually."

* * *

TALBOT STAYED UP LATE DRINKING. The marines he'd visited had reacted as well as he could hope. Word would spread and people would make up their own minds, but at least the base slanders of the admiral's blood wouldn't come into play. Mostly.

The board would want his testimony at some point, but they still hadn't finished with the admiral. A full day wouldn't even scratch the surface of what they'd done over the last year.

He was about to cross the street when his internal alarms sounded. This late at night, the street was pretty empty, even downtown, but the group of young men coming toward him didn't look like revelers out for a stroll.

A glance behind him showed a number of men following.

This was an ambush. At least, that's what his instincts told him.

He had a neural disruptor on him, but by the time he was sure what they were up to, it might be too late. He needed them to spring their trap early.

Talbot bolted across the street, hauling ass for the closest alley. That got them all to chasing him, so he knew he was on the right side in this fight.

He set the neural disruptor to wide beam and fired at the forward group. They went down in a heap. They'd be under about half an hour.

That didn't keep the second group from opening fire on him. One of the slugs hit him in the arm, but he managed to retain his grip on his weapon.

He linked his implants to his com and called emergency services just as a noise in the alley gave him a split second's notice that there were people waiting. He ducked and lashed out with his foot in a savage kick as the operator came on the line.

"Emergency services. What is the nature of your emergency?"

I'm being attacked! Near the Excelsior!

The hotel was the closest landmark. They could track his transmission, too. The com would convert his implant communications into his voice for the operator.

One of the men in the alley leapt over his screaming comrade and brought a metal bar down on Talbot's arm. It snapped with a sickening crack. His weapon spun off into the dark. The second swing caught him in the head, and he was out.

22

K elsey woke when her com sounded an emergency tone. She rolled out of bed and answered before her toes touched the floor.

"Bandar."

"Kelsey, it's Jared. I just got a call from emergency services in the capital. Something happened to Talbot. He was attacked and is missing."

The last remaining fog in her brain blew away as if a hurricane had swept in. "Shit. What do they know?"

She raced to her closet and dressed as quickly as she could. Something suitable for rough and tumble.

"Very little. He called and told them that much, then the line went dead. Someone killed the com. Crushed it, as a matter of fact. Police are swarming the area, but they haven't found him or the attackers yet."

She cursed under her breath. "He was armed. A neural disruptor. Something people here don't know about yet. That means this was organized and there were a lot of people."

"Don't rush in. This could be dangerous."

Kelsey laughed grimly. "I sure as hell hope so. Someone is going to bleed for hurting my man. Guard your back. If they came after him, they might have other targets in mind."

She killed the call and opened the pack with her weapons. Oh, how the Imperial Guard had argued against her bringing them into the palace. Too damn bad, she'd said. Now she'd been proven right. She should've brought her armor. Though, to be fair, it wouldn't be of much use right now.

Kelsey used her implants to call Marcus on *Invincible* through the palace systems. That had been the first upgrade she'd seen to. The AI answered at once.

"What can I do for you, Highness?"

"Someone attacked Talbot. They took him. I want a strike team ready for my call. Have them prep my armor and bring it along if things work out that way."

"Of course. You do realize that the planetary authorities will take a dim view of Imperial Marines making an assault on the capital world of the Terran Empire, don't you?"

She snorted. "You think? I'll have that conversation with them up front. Is there anything you can do to track down his implants?"

"Not at this range. I'd need a receiver in close proximity for that. However, he's a marine. He has an implanted locator beacon. If we can activate it, any receiver within a dozen kilometers will have his stats and location data."

"I'll have the pinnace try that. Keep an eye on any visitors you have. Keep trusted crew close to them and marines on standby in case someone tries something up there.

"Also, I want a squad sent to Orbital One to keep an eye on Jared. He could be a target. Keep it low key, but make sure they're ready to rumble."

"I'll have a pinnace on the way within ten minutes. One will be dropping with the ready squad and your armor to assist you shortly."

"Excellent. Keep me informed."

She killed the connection and finished dressing. Her weapons belt slid comfortably onto her hips. Her flechette pistol on the right and her neural disruptor cross draw on the left. A marine knife sat at the small of her back. Spare magazines covered the rest of the open space.

Her off duty armor went under her blouse. It wasn't great against a modern flechette pistol, but it would stop regular slugs all day long. The big benefit it had was being unobtrusive. Once she'd arrayed herself for war, or at least a minor firefight, she headed for the door.

The two Imperial Guards gave her a double take as she swept past them, armed to the damned teeth.

"Highness, is something wrong?"

"Someone just kidnapped my boyfriend, and I'm going to find him. Notify palace security that a marine pinnace is dropping from *Invincible* shortly. It's coming for me. You *will* let it through."

The man blanched. "Ah, we can't allow something like that near your father."

She spun in place and pinned him with her very best angry princess stare. "If they had something nefarious in mind, they could drop a spread of missiles onto this building before you knew what was happening. Either you trust Fleet or you don't. I suggest you go along with me on this.

"Also, I'm going to explain the facts of the situation to my father right now. He'll back me. Count on it."

Kelsey stalked off toward her father's quarters. Part of her hoped the guards there tried to block her, but they stepped aside.

Her father was already up and dressed in a robe. His hair was mussed, so he'd been asleep. His eyes widened at the sight of her, weapons and all. "Something's gone wrong."

"Someone took Talbot. I'm going after him. I called for a marine pinnace to bring me a tracker and backup. Are you going to let them pick me up?"

Her father looked at the guard. "Clear the marine pinnace for an emergency landing. Go to an increased state of alert, too."

The man bowed and hurried off.

"You look so different," her father said. "So dangerous. Part of me didn't believe even after seeing the ambush recording, but it believes now. What will you do?"

"Find him. I'll see the blood of whoever ordered this."

* * *

JARED HAD *Invincible* send out a warning and recall to all personnel in his fleet. It would reach most of them very quickly, but there were always a few who managed to wander off without a com. They'd get a rude wakeup call by marines making sure they were safe.

He had most of that done when a knock at his hatch announced the arrival of the marines the AI had dispatched. That was fast.

Out of habit, he checked the view plate and frowned. He didn't know any of the four men outside his door. His implants confirmed they weren't assigned to his ships.

He ran a second search against the Fleet database he'd uploaded earlier while he activated the com.

"Yes?"

"There's been a problem, Admiral. Let us in, please."

The search came up blank. These men were not Imperial Marines.

"Hang on while I get something on. It'll just take a second."

He hit the alarm on the plate. He expected Orbital One security to call him right away, but other than the blinking light, nothing happened. Then the light went out.

Oh, yeah. He was in trouble.

He raced for the bedroom as he heard the hatch he'd locked slide open. A suppressed weapon fired at him as he dove through the hatch and cycled it closed. Thankfully, the man missed.

Jared used his implants to link with the suite communications gear. He'd had his men rig that up this afternoon. None of his calls was going out. They'd jammed him. Help wasn't any closer than the marines from *Invincible*. If they weren't ambushed.

Thankfully, he'd let Kelsey talk him into keeping weapons and unpowered armor in his room. He had just enough time to slide the vest on and jump into the closet before the locked bedroom hatch opened. These bastards were good.

Two of them came in with weapons out. Jared lit the one facing the closet up with flechettes. The New Terran Empire unpowered armor wasn't up to the task of stopping them. The man went down in a spray of blood. His partner dove behind the bed and returned fire.

A gunfight at pointblank range was not Jared's idea of a good time. Luckily, his flechettes were better at penetrating the bed than the old-fashioned slugs were at finding him. The other man screamed and stopped firing.

That's when the other two fake marines opened fire from the hatch leading to the living room. The chest protection he'd been able to slide on took several hits and held. He fired back, but his angle was crappy.

Then the bulkheads beside the hatch splintered under the assault of hundreds of flechettes. Both attackers died a gory death. The cavalry had arrived.

A female marine in unpowered combat armor—Old Empire style— came into the bedroom looking for threats. A check confirmed she was assigned to *Invincible*. "Clear. Come out, Admiral."

Of course the woman could sense him in the closet.

Jared stood and his leg gave out. He'd taken a shot after all.

"The admiral is hit," the marine called out as she slung her rifle. "I've got him."

She grabbed Jared in a fireman's carry before he could decline. A full dozen marines fell in around them as they headed out of his quarters. Anyone that came near got weapons in their faces and told to move back. Including Orbital One security.

"Put me down," Jared said.

"Our orders are to get you to safety, sir," Lieutenant Wilson—the man in command of the detachment—said. "I'm taking you back to *Invincible*."

"Put me down, Corporal Jackson. Right now."

The woman obeyed but raised her weapon and glared at the growing crowd of security officers. They were one mistake away from a tragedy.

"We're on Orbital One, and we will *not* threaten Fleet personnel. Everyone, lower your weapons."

The marines seemed disinclined to obey, but they reluctantly did so. Orbital One security wisely kept their distance. No doubt, someone in a position of authority was on the way. The assassination attempt was over.

All he had to do was deal with the aftermath and try to explain how he thought the heir to the Throne was the most likely mastermind. Talk about a hard sell.

* * *

ANGELA GOT the warning call just after she'd climbed into bed. She instantly summoned her people. It would take at least five minutes before they came howling in, so she'd have to make sure Owlet was safe until then.

She grabbed her weapons and charged into the living room. Everything was deceptively quiet. Except for the squawk Owlet made when he saw her standing there in her underwear with her flechette pistol out.

He'd been playing some kind of first-person shooter game on the vid screen. One she'd played before, she noted with some amusement. She'd have to whip his ass at some future point.

"What's wrong?" he asked as he surged to his feet.

"Maybe nothing for us. Someone kidnapped Talbot, and the admiral wants everyone to keep an eye out. The protective detail is on the way. Five minutes."

"Shouldn't you… ah, get dressed?"

"I thought you had a thing for me. Isn't this a geek's wet dream? A mostly naked woman with a gun?"

He snorted. "The other versions of me had a thing for you. I'm just wondering when you'll punch me again."

"You hit a guy one time," she said with dry amusement. "I doubt we're targets, but we're exposed out here."

"Well, *you* are, in any case. I put out combat remotes to keep an eye on the building."

That surprised the hell out of her. Frankly, it was something she should've thought of. "Why did you do that?"

He shrugged. "Mainly to test a new command and control array for them. They tag everyone who comes into range and sort them as threatening or not. Since this is a university campus, I designated people wearing green as threats. It's not on, though."

"Give me a link."

He sent her the control link. She found the array and brought it to life, resetting the threat parameters to standard. His placement was pretty good, though she'd have done a few things differently.

The array screamed an alert to her. Armed men were already inside the building. A grav van outside had two armed men waiting beside it.

"Shit! They're here. Into the bedroom!"

She faced the door and called her team. "Code red. Hostiles in the building. Contact in sixty seconds."

"We're three minutes out. Hang on."

They weren't going to help her one damned bit. She knew she should've overridden that damned stuffed shirt of a chancellor. Now she had a couple of minutes to regret it. They'd mow her down, but not before she killed a bunch of them.

"I don't suppose you have any weapons in here?" she asked Owlet as she tipped the dresser over with a crash. It might provide him with a little cover.

"I didn't think I'd need one. Will we make it?"

She gave him a look. "You'll make it. Stay behind that and pray the team gets here in time."

Angela took up position beside the door and trained her weapon on it. The first few men through would die. With luck, the wall would provide enough protection for her to survive long enough for backup to get here.

The door blew in with no warning, smashing to splinters as the armed men came charging in.

She opened fire and dropped at least one of them. They were combat trained. That reduced Owlet's chances. Dammit.

A long burst killed the men in the room, and she leaned out to fire at the men in the living room. Her flechettes chewed up the furniture as she searched for them. She could hear them screaming as she killed or wounded them.

They weren't standing idly by, though. Their shots tore up the wall, and she quickly took hits in her arm and side. She'd be down in seconds. Dead before the team got here.

The combat remotes warned her of a grav drive screaming in from the south. Maybe the team was ahead of schedule. That would be a nice surprise.

Except it wasn't slowing down to land. It was acting more like a guided missile.

The moment before it arrived, she realized what it had to be. "Oh shit."

She threw herself down and covered her head. The interior wall she'd been using for cover exploded inward, throwing chunks of debris all over her. She could only imagine what the living room on the other side looked like.

That didn't stop the enemy, though. A man came through the hole and opened fire at Owlet. His slugs went whining off in every direction. Owlet stood there with that damned hammer extended in front of him like a shield, unharmed and obviously terrified.

Well, she supposed a battle screen was the best protection available. He'd thrown the damned thing through a plascrete wall. Flechettes weren't a threat now. To him, at least.

She found her dropped pistol, shot the man, and staggered to her feet.

"Come over here," Owlet shouted. "Now!"

Angela rolled across the bed and got behind the protection of the battle screen just as the remaining men opened fire from the carnage that used to be a living room. There were too many to kill, even if the screen would've allowed her flechettes through.

One of the men threw a grenade. The screen wouldn't stop all the fragments. This was it.

Owlet grabbed her around the waist and threw them backwards out the shattered window. They fell toward the ground five stories below.

And missed.

They swooped out as though they were flying and skimmed above the parked grav cars. Someone was shooting at them from the window but the hammer was hauling ass. They blasted out of the campus area with a shockwave as they went supersonic.

Yet all Owlet was doing was holding the hammer by its handle. The loop of leather was around his wrist, but that shouldn't have mattered. It should've torn free and left them falling to their deaths.

"You're hurt!" he said.

Her side was throbbing. "A little. Why aren't we falling?"

"The grav field is large enough to enclose us. We're completely safe."

Their course wheeled, and they arrowed back toward the campus. They seemed to be going even faster.

"No," she said. "We need to escape."

"They hurt you. I'm going to hurt them back," he said, his voice as unyielding as the battle screen protecting them. "The remotes said they're escaping in their vehicle. Hold on."

The van grew from a distant dot to full size in an astonishingly brief interval of time. She thought they'd miss it at first, but it swerved right in front of them.

Angela flinched, but they were through it before she had time to feel more terrified. Flaming wreckage fell in their wake.

She wanted to yell at Owlet for taking such a stupid risk, but she was so tired. Darkness slipped over her even though she heard him calling to her. Maybe she could tear a strip off him after a little nap.

23

It was late when Ethan's private com signaled, but he'd been waiting with anticipation for the call. He took a deep breath and calmed himself before answering.

"Yes, Victor?"

"Things didn't go as planned, Highness."

That wasn't what he'd expected to hear. He didn't bother trying to hide his scowl from his man. "In what way?"

"The attack on the Bastard failed," Victor admitted. "The team snatching your sister's paramour sprang their trap too soon, and they put him on guard, I think. The kill team only wounded him."

"Idiot!" Ethan raved. "That was the most important part of the plan! How could you screw it up?"

"Highness," his man said calmly, "we'll get him. He can't stay safe forever."

"That's not a solution," he snarled. "What about the rest of the plan?"

"A mixed bag," Victor admitted. "The armed team fooled the brig personnel and got Breckenridge out. We'll have him smuggled into the palace before too long. Your sister's lover is on his way to be examined. We didn't get the scientist, though. His guards put up more resistance than expected."

The man's expression told Ethan there was more to the story than that, but he didn't ask. It didn't matter.

"Then work with the people on site. Take care of it personally." He leaned closer to the com. "And, Victor? Don't bring the marine back when you're done."

* * *

ELISE WAS with Senator Breckenridge when she got the warning from Jared. The senator had ordered something to eat in his office, so she was as safe as if she were in a police station.

The building was heavily guarded, and the senator still had two men outside the door. Her guard commander had summoned the rest of her team to see her safely away from here once they finished their negotiations.

Breckenridge, for his part, seemed unconcerned. He really didn't know the marine, so that was probably for show. Still, it was classier than his nephew.

She'd put her com in privacy mode, so she knew there was more trouble when it rang.

"Excuse me," she said as she rose to her feet and stepped away. "Orison."

"This is Marcus, Your Highness. There have been more attacks, including an attempt on Admiral Mertz's life. He's injured, but not badly, and is safe. As you're close to him, I thought you should know.

"Also, where are you? I'm sending a marine quick-response team to reinforce your protective detail."

Her heart leapt into her throat when the AI said Jared was injured, but she forced herself to speak calmly. "I'm in the senate building, meeting with Senator Breckenridge. My full guard team is on the way, and there are serious looking men protecting the senators. I think I'm safe enough."

"With all due respect, Admiral Mertz thought the same on Orbital One. Allow me to suggest you accept a marine pinnace as a ride up. That compromise would help ensure your safety."

She saw the logic of that. "Of course. Thank you. Tell me more about Jared."

"He has a minor wound on his left leg. He's receiving treatment and will recover completely. Mister Owlet and Major Ellis also escaped an ambush. The attackers injured the major more seriously, but the doctors expect her to survive.

"From the initial reports, their defense of his apartment was more... vigorous than their attackers expected. At the very least, the collateral damage to property was much higher than the other attacks. Unfortunately, we didn't manage to take any of the attackers alive."

She sighed. "So, you're telling me this is an organized group not afraid to attack protected areas. I'll be waiting for your pinnace. Thank you, Marcus."

Elise disconnected the call. "There have been other attacks. Jared Mertz was injured on Orbital One. Another marine officer was hurt down here. Are you sure we're safe?"

He rose from his seat beside the table and touched a button on his desk. "Get me the chief of the Senatorial Guard."

After a moment, a woman's voice came back. "Yes, Senator Breckenridge?"

"I apologize for calling you at home, Colonel. A number of people from the expedition have been attacked. I have Crown Princess Elise Orison from the Kingdom of Pentagar in my office right now, and I'm concerned that we might be in danger here as well."

"Stand by."

He turned to Elise. "Vera Leibowitz is an ex-marine colonel. She'll do what needs to be done."

"*Invincible* is sending a marine pinnace to get me out of here. Don't get into a shooting match with it."

He nodded. "That would be bad. I'll make certain they know about it."

"Senator?" Colonel Leibowitz was back. "There are only two other senators in the building. I've sent extra people to your office, and I'm calling in the Imperial Marines for backup. We've put the building on lockdown."

"Excellent," Breckenridge said. "Also, a pinnace from *Invincible* is coming for the crown princess. Coordinate with Fleet to make sure it gets in safely."

"Will do, Senator. I'm on my way now, and warnings are going out to all the senators' security details. Don't leave until I get there."

"I wouldn't think of it. Thank you, Colonel."

He turned to Elise. "What could they hope to gain by kidnaping or killing these people?"

She sipped her drink worriedly. "Admiral Mertz was apparently to be assassinated. In case the news hasn't made the rounds, he and I are a couple."

His expression hardened, but not about the relationship, she thought. "I hadn't heard. No more small talk. Let me get him on the line for you and give you some privacy. Our business here is concluded, I think."

She nodded gratefully as he again used his desk com.

"Get me Orbital One," he said. "Make sure they know who is calling."

"Right away, Senator."

A moment later, another voice came on the line. "Orbital One security, Senator Breckenridge. Lieutenant Howard speaking. I don't have any more information on the escape."

The senator frowned. "What are you talking about?"

"Captain Breckenridge's escape, sir. Isn't that why you called?"

* * *

KELSEY ARRIVED at the alley where Talbot had called for help with a marine strike team at her back. The police were going over the area with a fine-toothed comb. A woman walked over as soon as the pinnace landed, her hand extended.

She glanced at the weapons on Kelsey's hips but said nothing. A wise decision.

"Princess Kelsey, I'm Lieutenant Amy Jenkins, Planetary Security. We've searched the area thoroughly, but didn't find Major Talbot or any of his attackers. There's a small amount of blood in the alley, which may or may not be connected with this case, but not enough to make me think anyone was killed here tonight."

"Thank God. Do you have any idea what happened?"

The woman flipped an old-fashioned notepad open. "He was at a known marine bar up the street. Some of the staff said there was a bit of a scuffle earlier but that the man Major Talbot was arguing with was in a much better mood by the time the major left. The man was still there when our people arrived, and there's no indication he slipped out or called anyone to cause Major Talbot any trouble."

She pointed up the street. "The major walked from that direction toward the Excelsior. A street camera covering the area went offline just before the ambush. I have techs looking into it.

"One of the people in the building across the street claims to have seen the whole thing from her balcony. She said there were two large groups of attackers. One ahead of the major and another following. He spotted the ambush and made a break for the alley."

The detective gestured at the alley. "He fired some kind of weapon that emitted a blue light that took out the first group as they rushed in behind him. It *purportedly* dropped them in their tracks."

Jenkins raised an eyebrow as she looked at Kelsey. "I'm not familiar with any weapon capable of that, but there are rumors circulating your expedition found something interesting. Can you elaborate?"

Kelsey shrugged. "I can't talk about the expedition yet, but I can confirm that a stunning weapon was used here."

She drew hers and handed it over to the detective. "The range is good out to fifty meters on narrow beam. Wide angle, which is what he must've used, cuts the range in half and reduces the knockout time from four hours to maybe half an hour."

The detective examined the weapon curiously. "This is amazing. It really does all that? What are the chances we can get some? That would really help us take out the bad guys without risking innocent bystanders."

"That's already in the works," Kelsey said. "One of our people made a stun-only version specifically for that purpose. I think there are a few dozen ready in orbit. I'll see that they get them to you."

The woman handed Kelsey's neural disruptor back. "So, the military version can kill? The major might have killed his attackers."

"Almost certainly not. Only an idiot keeps a weapon that can stun on a kill setting. Talbot only needed to stop them, not kill them."

"Lieutenant," a man called from the alley. "We have an ID on the blood."

The two of them stepped over to the man. He looked at Kelsey curiously, but Jenkins gestured for him to continue.

"There was a little fresh blood on the ground near the smashed com. It matched Fleet records for Major Talbot. Not enough for a fatal injury, but based on the few drops on the wall, someone might have bashed him in the head."

Kelsey's stomach rolled over. "Enough to be fatal?"

The man shrugged. "This feels more like a kidnapping than a murder. I'd put money on his being alive."

"That brings me to the last bit of eyewitness testimony," Jenkins said. "Two grav vans picked up the unconscious attackers and the major. They had their identifiers disabled. We'll keep looking, but I wouldn't hold my breath that lead will pan out."

"I might be able to help with that. Major Talbot has a locator beacon. If we can find it, we'll be able to get his precise location."

"Won't the kidnappers find it?" Leibowitz asked.

Kelsey smiled coldly. "Not a chance. It's inside him. The range is about a dozen kilometers. If we find it, my marines and I will go pay them a visit they won't be soon forgetting."

"Not to rain on your parade, but this is a security matter. We can mount a rescue operation without leveling a building."

"Can you stun everyone inside? No? Also, Major Talbot and I are dating. If you think for one second that I'll allow someone else to pull him out of the fire, you are sadly mistaken."

The woman shook her head. "Pistols aside, you're not trained for this kind of work, Highness. Leave it to the professionals."

"You don't know me," Kelsey said. "The last year has changed me in ways you can't begin to understand." She reached down and lifted one end of a trash dumpster off the ground. A full one.

That got everyone's attention.

"What I'm about to tell you is a classified Imperial secret. Pay attention and tell no one. I have enhancements that make me ten times stronger than the toughest man you know. I have a combat computer in my head that can spot trouble before anyone else, and I can act before you twitch. The pinnace has armor in it that no weapon here will touch.

"So don't think you're going to tell me I'm not saving the man I love. Is that clear enough for you?"

* * *

CARL PACED the hospital waiting room. The other people there were staring at him oddly, and he didn't blame them. He looked as though he'd been through a fire, he was carrying a hammer, and he had half a dozen men and women guarding him.

Planetary Security was on the way. Well, technically, there were a few uniformed officers in the waiting room, but the detectives would be here soon.

Major Ellis was going to make it. She'd lost some blood, but the wounds were treatable. Thank God for that.

The marine second in command of his protective detail was briefing him on what had taken place tonight. Someone had wanted to sweep the board, but why attack him? He was small fry.

Obviously, they thought his knowledge of Old Empire technology might help them with something. But what?

A hard-eyed man in a rumpled suit came into the waiting room. He headed straight for Carl.

"Carl Owlet? I'm Detective Ronny Powers, Planetary Security. I have some questions for you." He looked at the marine guards. Even in civilian clothes, they were obviously military. "Alone."

"Not happening," Lieutenant Howard Coulter said. "This man is under Fleet protection. We go where he goes."

The two men glared at one another.

"Let's make a compromise," Carl suggested. "We can go to the chapel, and the marines can sit in the back. We get privacy, and they can keep an eye on me."

With a reluctant nod, the detective agreed. "Lead the way."

Carl had visited the chapel earlier. Never a very religious man, he'd felt the need for some contemplation after the events of the evening. He'd killed men tonight.

First, the men who'd died when he'd flown the hammer through his apartment. Then he'd hit the survivors in the grav van as they'd fled. He'd meant to disable it, but it had dodged right in front of him at the last moment. They'd gone through it at supersonic velocity.

The detective escorted him up front, and they took a seat on the pew with a view, as he'd thought of it. The stained glass window was beautiful and probably had deeper meaning for the religious.

"So, there was a little problem at student housing," the detective said. "Tell me about it."

Carl chuckled grimly. "Yes, I suppose those are the right words for it. A little problem. Armed men attacked Major Angela Ellis and myself. She's my head keeper, by the way. I suspect this was supposed to be a kidnapping, based on the other events of the evening."

"I'm aware of them," the detective admitted. "Or at least some of them. Why would these men want to kidnap you?"

"They probably wanted to know something. I'm a scientist and was part of the recently returned expedition. The details of which I can't go into without permission."

The detective didn't look pleased at that news. "Who would be able to give me a green light?"

"A good place to start would be Admiral Jared Mertz. He's on Orbital One."

The man rubbed his face. "Fine. You were a lab assistant or something, so what could you really know?"

The question sounded rhetorical, so Carl chose not to answer it. Most people didn't accept him as a scientist. He looked like someone just getting ready to go to college. He wouldn't be old enough to drink for months, though he'd been declared an adult for legal purposes.

Detective Powers sighed and made a note in his little book. "So, the bad guys attacked. Your neighbors downstairs heard them breaking in. One even saw them in the stairwell. Masked, of course, but with heavy weapons. That matches the level of destruction in your apartment and the one across the hall. Luckily for everyone involved, the occupants were out partying."

Carl had known the rooms were empty of people because of the combat remotes he'd scattered around. Otherwise, he'd have brought Mjölnir in through a different wall. Unfortunately, the other apartment provided the best way to stop most of the attackers. He'd have to find out how much he owed them for lost personal belongings.

The university would be pissed about the damage to the buildings. First, the classified lab he'd been storing the hammer at would need some roof work. Then the two apartments would need major repairs, and anything the van debris landed on, of course.

And he couldn't forget the windows he'd smashed when he'd gone supersonic.

Yeah, the bill was going to be spectacular.

"So, your guard was shot, but you escaped. None of the cameras showed you exiting the building. How'd you get down?"

"That's classified."

The detective gave him a flat stare. "Uh-huh. I suppose the grav car that broke the sound barrier had something to do with that. Probably shot down the bad guys, too. Can you at least confirm that?"

Carl shook his head. "It's all classified. Was anyone hurt when the grav van came down?"

"Other than the four men inside it who were killed in the explosion? No. You were damned lucky. Part of the wreckage went almost across the campus. It hit some lab and caved in part of the roof. Or, more likely, it was a missile that missed the van. The angles are odd, but that's the only answer that fits the facts. Maybe the grav van took a shot at your car."

The man shook his head. "I suppose I'll find out some version of the truth eventually. Honestly, Major Ellis is going to get a much sterner questioning from me. She holds responsibility for most of the damage, I suspect. Along with those yahoos at the back of the chapel. You're only a kid. No way you caused this kind of havoc."

If he only knew.

The detective put his notebook away. "One more question. The major came into the hospital dressed only in her underwear. I can't help but notice those are hospital scrubs you're wearing. Might I assume that you and the major have a... complicated relationship?"

Carl's clothes had been covered in blood. They'd found the scrubs so he didn't scare the other people in the waiting room.

The detective held up a hand before Carl could deny it.

"I'm not judging. You're a legal adult and can sleep with whoever you choose." He smiled with a glint in his eye. "I will say nice going, though."

He stood without letting Carl say a word. "We'll get to the bottom of this. Whoever these bozos were, we'll identify them. That'll get us the answers we need."

Carl watched the man go back to talk to Coulter. The marine wouldn't tell him anything. In a way, that was good. The fewer lies out there, the less trouble keeping things straight.

Since the marines had overheard everything, he also suspected a few juicy rumors about them sleeping together were going to start making the rounds. By the time Major Ellis found out, it would be far too late to do anything about them.

Except possibly punching him. Again.

24

Talbot woke in pain. His head was throbbing. His abused arm hurt even worse.

The memory of the attack came flooding back in, and he tried to sit up. Nope. His captors had tied him to a bed. Arms, legs, and a belt around his middle. Someone didn't want him getting up.

He smiled. Good.

"Ah, our guest is awake," a male voice said from the darkness beside him.

Talbot adjusted his ocular implants and saw the man in the shadows. Hair pulled back into a long tail, dressed well enough. He'd recognize the face if he ever saw it again.

He activated his recorders. If he didn't make it out, he wanted someone to catch the bastard.

"Where am I?" Talbot demanded in a voice that almost croaked. "Who the hell are you?"

The man leaned forward. "The less you know about me, the better the chances that you'll walk away from this unpleasantness."

"You picked the wrong guy to snag. I don't exactly know that much. I'm just a jarhead."

"Surprisingly, I agree. We didn't target you for your knowledge. We want to examine those machines inside you. To have someone look over the code that drives them. As a senior officer, if anyone is compromised, it will be you."

Talbot took a moment to activate his retrieval beacon. The fact no one had pinged it from the outside told him he must be some distance away from the capital. At least now someone would find him. It was only a matter of time. Kelsey wouldn't stop looking until she did.

"I don't suppose my sincere assurance that I'm not under any compulsion will do."

The man smiled. "No, I'm afraid not. That weapon was quite a surprise. It took down my men in short order. If you'd had a few more moments, you might have escaped entirely. Everyone recovered, so it's nonlethal. What is it?"

Talbot felt around for it with his implants. A smart man would keep it out of his range. Then again, they didn't know he could access it.

He found it in a drawer near the edge of his range and locked it down. Now they wouldn't be using it for anything. Too bad he didn't have the long-range com inside Carl was proposing as a universal upgrade.

"We call them stunners," he lied. "The police in the Old Empire used them."

The man looked impressed. "That's quite a tool. When in doubt, take them all out. One would've been very useful in taking you down. Or the other targets."

That made Talbot's stomach flutter. "You have other prisoners? Who?"

"Alas, we didn't get the others. It's quite embarrassing, really. We wanted to take a scientist to assist with analyzing your code, so to speak. His guards used significantly more force than you to stop us. They killed nine men."

"It might shock you to know, but I'm sorry about that," Talbot said. "I'm not a fan of needless slaughter. I was only a guy out on the town. If you ran up against a dedicated protection detail, they'd use whatever force they deemed necessary to protect the subject."

"Or perhaps more. They blew up the top floor of an apartment building and then used a missile to shoot down our van as it fled. Without any prisoners, I might add. That feels a tad excessive."

That sounded excessive to Talbot, too. His people wouldn't just shoot down a fleeing enemy. Not outside a combat zone. And blowing up an apartment building was never a good idea.

"Who was the target?"

"Not one of your major players, I understand. A lab assistant named Owlet."

That explained a lot. The damned hammer could cause that level of damage in inexperienced hands. He'd seen the vids to prove it.

"He's a graduate student," Talbot said. "Bright enough, but the lowest ranking guy on the science teams. Why would you trust what he had to say, anyway? He'd be just as compromised as the rest of us, by your standards."

The man shifted in his seat. "We'd hoped to have him guide us into extracting the computer code and understanding it. My employer is quite concerned that you people are time bombs waiting to explode."

"I don't suppose you'd care to share a name with me."

The man smiled. "No. Believe it or not, Major Talbot, I intend to release you unharmed. When I do, you're free to tell whoever you want about our concerns."

The man rose to his feet and straightened his jacket. He still probably thought himself safely concealed in the dark. "I'll let you get a bit of rest and we'll talk again. Perhaps over breakfast. Sleep well."

Talbot waited for the man to leave before testing the strength of his restraints. He wasn't getting loose easily. The bed was solid, too. He wouldn't be tipping it over. Even if he could, he'd really mess his arm up. They had him well and truly trapped.

He sighed. He'd just have to count on Kelsey to come to his rescue. Humiliating, but something he could count on.

* * *

THE DUTY PHYSICIAN was just closing up the wound on Jared's leg when Admiral Yeats came storming into the medical center. "What a freaking mess. Your boys and girls killed all four of the attackers."

"Considering the circumstances, I can live with that. I killed the two in the bedroom."

The senior Fleet officer's eyes widened. "Well, that's a surprise. You never struck me as a close combat kind of man."

"I've had to do a lot of things I'd never planned on over the last year, Admiral. Any idea how they got onto Orbital One? My implant database said they weren't Fleet."

The other man's eyes narrowed. "What have you got tucked away in there?"

Jared shrugged. "I wanted to be sure I had at least a little information about the officers on the board of inquiry, so I loaded the public records for all active Fleet personnel. None of those people were in it. I suppose there could be some secret group that you don't have open records for, but I'm betting they aren't part of it."

"Of course we have some off-the-books investigators, but you're right. Those people weren't active duty. All four were marines in the past, though. One retired and three kicked out of the service. Someone in Orbital One security let them aboard. Their ship didn't wait for them, and you weren't the only target."

Jared's stomach sank. "Someone was killed?"

"They busted Wallace Breckenridge out of holding. Killed the on duty security detail in the prison. Whoever they were, they wanted you dead and him free. Does that ring any bells for you?"

Jared eyed the medical staff. "No one I'd mention in public."

Yeats jerked a thumb toward the corridor hatch. "Everyone out."

The staff seemed surprised, but they followed his orders. A few minutes later, the two of them were alone.

"There," Yeats said. "Now talk."

Jared considered his words carefully. One didn't just come out and accuse the heir to the Throne of murder and conspiracy to murder.

"You recall Kelsey's mentor from the Department of Imperial Affairs? Carlo Vega. He died shortly after we left Imperial space. Poison. I have no proof, but I suspect the target was actually me.

"I gave him some candies that the palace sent to me. One of them was probably poisoned, and the only person there who hates me that much is Ethan Bandar."

Yeats pondered what he'd said for a moment before responding. "That's a serious accusation. Particularly without proof."

Jared nodded and stood, testing his leg. It felt a lot better. He'd need some time in the regenerator, but he could walk without help.

"Which is why I haven't said anything. The investigation is still officially open, but I'm certain he was behind it. The last time we met, he basically told me he'd eliminate me as a problem. Permanently."

Yeats rubbed his chin. "I can't officially enter that into the record, but I'll have a private talk with His Majesty. He needs to know how you feel."

"Then I'd best be the one to tell him."

Yeats nodded. "I suspect so. How will you do it?"

"I think I need to meet up with Kelsey. The two of us can tell him together. If you can excuse me from the board of inquiry for the day, that is."

"They have enough testimony to go over without you. There are a ton of other witnesses to speak with."

"You need to be careful, Admiral," Jared said. "With Breckenridge on the loose, that tells me there's something going on that might include Fleet. I hesitate to mention this, but we saw the Pentagarans go through an attempted coup. Watch your ships and commanders."

The older man rubbed his face. "I hope to God we don't have that kind of rot, but you're right. They had someone here in their pocket. We can't count on others being clean. I'll raise the alert level and warn the senior officers on all ships that he's loose and that we need to be on guard. Better safe than sorry."

"With your permission, I'll do the same. My people are less disposed to be allies of his after what he did."

"Do it," Yeats said decisively. "If they can't take over your ships, they can't win."

"You need to get a marine detail you trust," Jared said. "If they can't control you, they might try to eliminate you. With you gone, Breckenridge might move to take charge of Fleet.

"We have some unpowered armor that non-enhanced personnel can use that would make your guards tougher. Also, there's a kind of lightweight armor that Kelsey uses under her regular clothes. It's tough. I'll see that you get a set."

"I worry we're being too paranoid, but it won't hurt to take some basic precautions. I'll accept all your suggestions. Now get down there and settle this, Jared."

"Aye, sir."

He found his pants and summoned the marines waiting in the corridor after the admiral had left. "We're going down to Avalon."

They formed a protective wedge around him and took him straight to the docking level. Their pinnace disengaged as soon as they were strapped in.

He opened a channel to *Invincible*. "Marcus, go to alert status."

"Already there, Admiral. Shall I go to battle stations?"

"No, but I want the fleet ready for trouble. Breckenridge has escaped, and I think something big is in motion. I don't want any of our ships falling into unfriendly hands."

"I'll notify all senior officers at once. I've already taken the liberty of summoning the crew back from leave. With the exception of Major Talbot, everyone is accounted for."

Jared nodded. "Excellent. Be ready to throw up battle screens at the first sign of trouble. A supposedly friendly ship might open fire with no warning."

"Once again, Admiral, I'm one step ahead of you. All ships have their computers watching. At the first sign of hostile activity, every battle screen in the fleet will snap into place. No missile will have time to hit us, and the New Empire vessels don't have beam weapons to worry about."

That was a relief.

"There was a ship or cutter that took Breckenridge and the attackers off Orbital One. Get the operations team to work on determining which one it was and where it went."

"Once the attack on you took place, I took that liberty. Very few vessels undocked between the time the attack commenced and when Orbital One locked down all outgoing traffic. One cutter in particular went to Avalon and landed at Capital Spaceport.

"Though I have no proof that is the ship you seek, I'd wager my as yet unpaid salary that will be them."

Jared felt the corner of his mouth quirking up. "I'm wondering what you'd spend it on. In any case, I'll fix that lapse as soon as possible. I'm meeting with Kelsey, and we're going to speak to the emperor. Hopefully, we can sort this mess out before it becomes a major problem."

"I could always use additional processor cores, larger storage, and faster memory. I hope you can solve this before the situation spins out of control, Admiral. However, I submit that seldom seems to work. Perhaps planning for the worst would be an appropriate course of action."

"Too true, Marcus. I'll let you know when I find out anything. Keep me in the loop as far as major developments."

"Will do, Admiral. *Invincible* out."

The pinnace was already slicing into the atmosphere. It wouldn't be long before he and Kelsey could talk. She didn't know he suspected her brother of killing her mentor. Based on history, she wouldn't take it very well. It might take more than a bit of convincing to bring her around to his point of view.

Of course, he didn't actually need her to believe it was possible. Her just being open-minded while he talked to the emperor would be helpful.

Now all they had to do was figure this out before anyone else got killed.

25

Angela slowly swam back to awareness. The pain in her side was gone. Regeneration was a wonderful thing.

The medical staff was pulling her out of the regeneration unit, and a doctor she vaguely remembered was checking the readout.

"Things look good, Major Ellis," he said. "In case you don't remember our very brief meeting earlier, I'm Doctor John Yeager, and you're at Capital Hospital. You were shot, but your companion got you here in time. Obviously."

He looked up from the readout. "I understand his arrival caused quite a stir. A few excitable souls said he flew in like some kind of superhero from the vids. Obviously, that isn't what happened, but it still has people chattering."

"Was he hurt, Doctor?" Her throat was dry.

He handed her a bottle of water. "Drink up. Your friend wasn't injured. He and the other men are in the waiting room. Before I let them in to see you, a detective with Planetary Security wants to speak with you."

It took no imagination to figure out why. They'd shot up an apartment and then basically vaporized it and a van full of fleeing suspects. She was a little woozy by then, but she remembered the terrifying flight and impact.

Perhaps an avenging superhero wasn't an entirely inaccurate assumption on the witness' part.

"Sure," she said. "Let me get dressed and I'll talk to them."

He shook his head. "Your undergarments are very bloody and also considered evidence. With your larger-than-average stature, I'm afraid the hospital gown will have to do for the moment. One of your men is getting something for you."

Well, that wasn't really a surprise. Not many nurses would match her two meter height.

"Then I guess I'm ready."

The doctor helped her up and escorted her to a normal hospital room. "We'll be keeping you for a short while to make certain everything is good. Lie back down and let me hook up the monitors."

Once he finished doing that, he excused himself and a grizzled man came in. He looked like a caricature of a detective.

"Major Ellis, I'm Detective Ronny Powers with Planetary Security. I have a few questions about what happened."

She gestured to the chair. "Feel free to sit, but I can't tell you everything. Some of it's classified."

"So I'm given to understand. Tell me what you can."

Angela walked him through the attack until the hammer put in an appearance, and then she shut him down. The damned thing was far too dangerous to put into a security report.

He looked annoyed and tried to come at the situation from several angles, but she kept putting up walls.

Powers sighed and put his notebook away. "I'll contact Admiral Mertz in the morning to see what he can tell me. At least the witnesses confirm that you didn't start the fight, even if you were a tad excessive in ending it. That will still need to be answered for, so don't make any plans to leave Avalon."

"I never go anywhere unless I have orders. You might want to mention that to Admiral Mertz as well."

Once the man was gone, Owlet poked his head through the door. "Are you up for visitors?"

She made sure the blanket covered the gown, though after the firefight he probably didn't have too much left to the imagination. Hell, those damned vids the other versions of him had taken might have some really private moments. She suppressed a shudder.

"Come in and close the door behind you. You didn't get hit, did you?"

He sat in the chair and set the ridiculously dangerous hammer on the floor beside him. "Not a scratch. I'm sorry they hurt you."

"That wasn't your fault. Dammit, what were you thinking? Wasn't that thing overkill?"

Owlet shrugged. "It was the only weapon I could put my hands on. And, to follow the metaphor, the problems became nails after that."

Well, that was certainly true. The memory of the hammer blowing a human-sized hole through an apartment building to fly into his hand was going to be hard to forget. He'd been the next best thing to invulnerable after that.

"Why did you take us back?"

"Once I saw how badly they'd hurt you, I kind of let my emotions get the better of me."

"That's one way to describe it," she said dryly. "Why destroy the van?"

"Actually, that was an accident. I meant to disable it with a quick flyby, but they dodged right in front of me at the last moment. This thing is agile, but even it has limits. Out of everything I did, that's the part I regret."

"You were in combat. Shit happens. You should've kept running away. Your first impulse to disengage was the right one. We'd have caught them later."

"I'll keep that in mind if this ever happens again, Major. What now?"

"I think you can call me Angela after what we've been through. We'll let Admiral Mertz sort it out. You did nothing wrong." She hesitated and then continued. "Thank you for saving me. I appreciate the risk you took for me."

His smile turned wry. "You're growing on me. I can see what the other versions of me saw in you. Not that I'll let that be an excuse to be an ass."

Angela said nothing, but he had worn through her armor, too. Perhaps the other versions of her hadn't been complete idiots after all. Any kind of relationship would still be totally inappropriate, but she could see her opinion of him changing.

Not that she'd ever allow him to give Princess Kelsey such a dangerous weapon. That was just crazy. Now more than ever. God only knew what the woman would do with it.

* * *

KELSEY WAS MONITORING the pinnace's scanners from the marine commander's console when she got the word Jared was coming. His pinnace dropped down and they landed together. He joined her and sent his off to keep searching for Talbot.

She hugged him. "I'm so sorry they attacked you. Any idea who it was?"

He nodded and sat down beside her. "You won't like this. I think Ethan was behind it."

Kelsey felt herself frowning. "My... our brother is an ass, but he's not homicidal. That's crazy."

"Is it? Someone poisoned Carlo Vega. I told you the investigation was ongoing, but I'm pretty sure it was in the candy the palace sent. It only had to be in one piece. Poof, the evidence was gone.

"Ethan didn't know you were coming, or he might have tried something different. After all, I might have given you the candy. Or he might have figured our mutual antipathy would keep that from happening. I have no idea. Still, tell me it doesn't make sense."

She opened her mouth to defend her twin but closed it with her objections unspoken. Was Ethan truly capable of doing something so horrible?

I think you know the answer to that.

Ned's voice in her head startled her. He'd kept quiet for so long that she forgotten he was there.

You don't know him like I do. He's not a monster.

The rebellion has taught me that you don't have to be a monster to do monstrous things. Forgive me for saying so, but your brother sounds like he has paranoid delusions or megalomania. Or both. He's clever about hiding it, most times, but if you truly think about it, he's sick, and sick people do terrible things.

Kelsey wanted to reject what Ned was suggesting, but a traitorous part of her mind was considering it. No, not Ethan. Ned and Jared had to be wrong.

She focused her attention on Jared. "I don't think he's capable of that, but if you want to look at it, well, that shouldn't hurt anything. It's not like you have a relationship to sour."

"The two of us do have a relationship. A very bad one. In any case, I'm more concerned about us."

Kelsey sighed. "Jared, I don't think any less of you for suspecting Ethan. I'm just saying not to bet the ranch on him being your sinister mastermind. What do you want to do first?"

"I think we need to speak with your father."

"With *our* father, you mean. Like it or not, he's one of the links that binds us."

"You grew up with him as a father. I didn't. Frankly, I don't know that I'll ever feel comfortable around him. But, for *your* sake, I'll try."

She smiled. "That's all anyone could ask. Well, let's get this over with. The search is widening, and someone will ping Talbot's recovery beacon before long. Once that happens, I'll need to be free to rain hellfire and damnation down on some deserving souls."

Kelsey sent a message to the pilot to head for the palace. Someone would wake her father. If he wasn't awake already.

Jared rubbed his leg thoughtfully. "Speaking of hellfire and damnation, Carl destroyed his apartment building. Part of it, anyway. Planetary Security wants details he and Major Ellis aren't willing to divulge."

"Jesus," she said. "How many people did these bastards attack? Was anyone hurt?"

"The collateral damage was limited to structures, bad guys, and Major Ellis. She's going to be fine. There's a rumor a superhero is on the loose, though." He told her what he knew of the incident.

She shook her head. "That hammer is a little too dangerous for him, I think. He's trashed pretty much everything he's thrown it at."

"But you think it's awesome. Admit it."

"Kind of. At least I think I might be a tad more precise in how it's used. In any case, it saved their lives tonight, so that's a win. What did the mastermind want with him?"

Jared shrugged. "Perhaps he was simply the one who looked easiest to grab. Big mistake on someone's part. With that hammer, he was probably the most dangerous.

"I don't think that device belongs in too many hands. The technology, sure, but not all rolled together. A shield for combat use. A larger scale weapon for vehicles. Even flying marine armor. Just not all in one package."

She nodded. "I'll take possession of it as soon as practical. Angela will howl, but you're right. That's too much for one person. I'll lock it away from general use, too. It would be far too easy to use it as a crutch."

"That might be for the best."

The pinnace came in for a landing at the palace. She unstrapped herself and rose to her feet. "Come on. It's time for you to make your pitch. I don't expect Father will be easy to convince."

* * *

ELISE STEPPED off the pinnace onto Orbital One. Surprisingly, there hadn't been any trouble for her. The security response on Avalon had been ridiculous. Guards everywhere and armed craft circling the Imperial Senate.

She'd found out just before docking that Jared had gone to Avalon. As frustrating as that was, she'd have to accept he was okay until they caught up with one another.

Her welcome party consisted of Reginald Bell, William Hawthorne, and a significant number of Fleet security officers.

"Surely we're not in danger here," she said.

"I'd wager Admiral Mertz thought the same thing," William said. "Yet someone tried to kill him in his quarters. Still, I doubt we're targets in this unpleasantness."

"Agreed," Bell said. "I'll still avail myself of the offered protection. It's been quite a long day, but I find myself wide-awake. Shall we adjourn somewhere for a snack? I have something I'd like to discuss with you, Highness."

She nodded. "I've eaten, but some tea would be most welcome."

The three of them relocated to a restaurant with a fabulous view of Avalon. The snowcapped peaks were particularly stunning.

The security team made sure no one else was in their section. She smiled apologetically at those displaced.

Bell waited until they'd all ordered to speak on anything of substance. "I don't know how your situation was received, but I ran into a hitch. They claim that I have no authority to negotiate with Pentagar. Even with Princess Kelsey's blessing."

Elise nodded. "I ran into a somewhat similar situation. I spoke with Senator Breckenridge. Yes, the ass's uncle. It seems the Imperial Charter doesn't recognize that a world might be separated from the Empire for any reason. So, the treaty Kelsey and I negotiated is being fought over in the Senate."

"And this elder Breckenridge stands against us?" William asked. "That's not surprising, I suppose. My situation is similarly impacted. While we recognize the authority of the Imperial Throne, the negotiations to keep our local rule in place are on shakier ground. The government must be reviewed, they claim."

She sipped her tea. It was surprisingly good.

"Actually, I'm not certain that Senator Breckenridge will be our enemy in this matter. He seems willing to deal. The price for his help is irksome, but reasonable. He wants my best effort to convince Kelsey and the emperor not to pursue charges of treason against Wallace Breckenridge. Though the man's escape may confound all our plans."

William nodded judiciously. "His link to the attackers might make that very difficult. Though, based on his record, the jailbreak portion of the mission went off entirely too smoothly."

There was a core of truth to that. Breckenridge wasn't the universe's most competent villain.

"I'm sure that problem will solve itself. Other than Talbot, the enemy's plans have gone badly astray. Now that people are looking into it, I hope the conspiracy will unravel quickly."

Bell focused his attention on her. "Which brings me to the matter I'd like to discuss. Someone seems to have decided it was a good idea to promote me and award me back pay. You wouldn't happen to know anything about that, would you?"

She gave him a blandly interested look. "Did they, now? I'm sure you earned all that and more. Congratulations."

"I notice you didn't deny the charge, so I'll take that as a tacit admission of guilt."

He sighed. "I was quite happy being an ensign. Now, I'm officially a retired admiral with half a millennium of service. You wouldn't believe how much money that is. Even with the several hundred years the bean counters are disputing because I was in stasis."

"Accountants are so predictable." William's expression brightened. "So, you'll pick up the tab? Perhaps I'll splurge on a good brandy after all."

26

Emperor Karl rose to his feet when Jared and Kelsey stepped inside his office. He waved the Imperial Guardsmen out. "Jared, I'm so pleased to see that you're well."

"It was a close thing," Jared admitted. "Under other circumstances, I might have let the killers in. You've heard about Breckenridge escaping, I presume."

The emperor nodded as he sat. "From the most secure facility we have. It's maddening. He has friends willing to kill to get him out. They found the bodies of some men assigned to Orbital One stuffed into a crate at the spaceport a little while ago. That's in addition to the men and women guarding the brig.

"We recovered the cutter, but they sprayed it down with something that destroys DNA. It's like a bad conspiracy movie. One where I'm the dunce in charge that never saw it coming."

Kelsey rose from the seat she'd taken and put her hand on her father's shoulder. "Why should you expect the worst from people?"

"True," Jared said. "You didn't have your crew mutiny and lock you in the kitchen."

Karl gave him a sad smile. "Yes, but you had no reason to expect the betrayal. I should've seen this coming."

"Through what? Psychic powers? Your Majesty, no one expected this. I have a theory about the people behind the attack on me."

The emperor straightened. "A lead would be most useful right now."

"You won't like it," Jared warned. "I know there are a lot of reports to go over, but have you read the one on Carlo Vega's death?"

"I skimmed it. It's troubling. Who disliked him enough to kill him?"

"No one, I expect. I'll bet everything I own that I was the target."

Karl Bandar's eyes widened. "You? Who would want to kill you, and how did they get Carlo Vega by mistake? Better yet, why didn't you lock them up?"

He gave the man a grumpy smile. "Because I have no authority over the person I suspect is behind it. I'm morally certain the candies that came from the palace for me had one that was poisoned. I gave them to Vega, never suspecting anyone would do that. That's why there was no poison left to find."

"Candies? I didn't send any candies." The emperor licked his lips. "You think Ethan did it."

Jared nodded. "He openly threatened me when I was leaving before the expedition. I'm sure there's no record of the conversation, but he made it plain he was going to eliminate me as a threat to the Throne once and for all."

"God, I hope you're wrong, but Ethan was so pleased after you left. I thought it was just because you were finally out of his hair, but it makes a terrible kind of sense now."

Kelsey looked aghast. "Father! You can't possibly believe Ethan is behind this."

"Believe is too strong a word," her father said. "Fear might be more accurate. He hasn't been his usual self since your expedition returned. He's spoken pretty strongly against trusting any of you. He doesn't trust your implants."

"The implants," Jared said. "That's it. He took Talbot to examine the implants. I think he tried to get Carl Owlet because he thought he might be able to explain everything."

"What about Breckenridge?" Kelsey asked. "Why rescue him?"

"A supposedly 'unbiased' witness? I have no idea. Killing me is the least surprising thing about his plan."

She shook her head. "This is pure speculation. We know Breckenridge has an uncle in the Senate. Perhaps he's behind this."

Her father sagged a little more in his chair. "Nathaniel has never been the easiest man to work with, but he's no traitor."

"Someone is behind this," Jared said. "If it's not Ethan, then we need to eliminate him as a suspect so we can focus on the real threat."

"He's out at the Imperial Retreat. I banished him there until he could get his temper under control. He's got men I trust watching him closely."

"Unless you've got his communications under that same microscope, that doesn't really mean anything."

Kelsey frowned. "Father, are you okay? You look almost grey."

The emperor clutched his chest. "I can't breathe." He fell out of his chair with a gasp before either of them could reach him.

* * *

ETHAN LOOKED up from the tablet he was reading when the head of the guard detail opened his door.

"My lord, you need to come with me."

He frowned at the man. "What's going on?"

"Your father has fallen ill. We need to get you back to the palace at once."

Even though he'd known this was coming, it was still like a blow to the stomach.

"What happened? Is he okay?"

Ethan tossed the tablet onto the desk and followed the man out.

"He's unresponsive, Highness. They have him in the medical center, and his personal physician is there. I don't have any more information on his condition. Your sister and Admiral Mertz were with him when he collapsed."

The smile that news almost sparked was hard to suppress. Perfect.

It was a shame the old man had forced Ethan to kill him, but it was necessary. Those nanites would extend his father's life to undreamed of lengths.

Ethan wasn't going to wait that long to sit on the Imperial Throne. Instead, he'd be the one who ruled for lifetimes. He'd be the one the people called "The Great."

He certainly wasn't going to deal with centuries of fending off the Bastard. Mertz would continue trying to steal the Throne, and he only had to succeed once. Ethan meant to see that threat eliminated before the man could make his next attempt.

* * *

CARL AND ANGELA were just arriving back on *Invincible* when their plans took a drastic turn. They'd barely gotten off the pinnace when Doctor Stone was pushing them toward the next one in line. "This way. We're going back down."

He went where she told him. It only took her a few moments to get them into the second pinnace and it undocked.

"What's going on?" Angela demanded.

"The emperor is ill, and if what I suspect is true, we're in big trouble." Stone flopped into a seat and set her bag down beside her. "The admiral thinks it was the same poison that killed Carlo Vega."

"Oh shit," Carl said. "But you have an antidote. Right?"

"No. The poison had broken down by the time I examined him. I might be able to slow things down, though. I have an analyzer in my bag. I'll send Marcus what we find and pray he can help. But there's a complication."

"That doesn't sound at all promising," Angela said as she sat down and strapped in. "Cinch up tight. They're doing a combat drop, and the grav drives might not be able to dampen all the maneuvers. That means you, Carl."

He was pretty sure that was the first time she'd ever used his given name. Still, he promptly did as she ordered. He didn't want to be squashed like a bug.

"If this is the same poison," Stone continued, "that means it's the same assassin. The admiral was concerned it might be his half brother."

"As in the heir to the Throne?" Carl asked. "That's awkward. With the emperor out of play, there's no telling what he might try."

"Which is why I think you need to take this pinnace and vanish for the moment. You know, as kind of a mobile reserve."

"You want us to hide out in case someone needs rescue?" Angela asked. "Like the admiral or the princess."

"Exactly," the doctor confirmed. "I realize I can't order you to do any such silly thing, so I ran my plan past Marcus. He's endorsed it. Major, if you'll take a moment to call him and confirm."

Angela's eyes went unfocused for a few moments and then she nodded. "The captain has verified your orders, ma'am. That's good enough for me."

"Excellent. Once we land at the palace, I want you and this pinnace to disappear."

"Pinnaces can be hard to locate, but this is the capital. They'll have us on their plates wherever we go."

The doctor grinned. "Not so you'd notice. This is one of the pinnaces from *Persephone*. It does stealth better than anything the New Terran Empire has ever seen. Just head back up and fade from the scanners once you exit the atmosphere. If you're between the orbital and planetary control zones, they'll probably miss you."

"That's pretty damned clever," Angela admitted. "Are you always this sneaky, Doctor? If so, why are you not in my poker circle?"

"I have my moments, but this is Marcus's idea. It's freaking brilliant. He took the liberty of loading you up with a full set of powered armor and weapons. Once you settle down, you can monitor everything via a dedicated tight beam to *Persephone*.

"They're moving out of orbit with Admiral Yeats's blessing. He's not briefed on the plan, but he didn't ask any awkward questions. She's headed out toward the new flip point. She'll engage stealth and slip back into orbit. So long as someone doesn't physically see her, she'll be good."

Angela shook her head. "You're telling me we can't even detect a ship like her in *orbit*? That's insane."

Stone shrugged. "That may change once we upgrade the scanners to Old Empire standards. For now, count your blessings."

Carl cleared his throat. "Once we're all stashed away, what then? What are you expecting to happen?"

"Worst case," the medical officer said, "the heir will assume the powers of the Throne and lock the admiral up. Kelsey is almost certainly safe from retaliation for now. She'll stay with her father and work to make sure I have the access I need."

"So, we break the admiral out?"

Stone shook her head. "No. Just wait for orders. Odds are you won't have to do anything. Only if we need heavy firepower on a moment's notice. Perhaps for rescuing Major Talbot. You're not going to have to make this up as you go. Just take a deep breath and relax."

The pinnace decelerated, and Carl was grateful he'd strapped in. That was the most intense landing he'd ever experienced.

As soon as the ramp lowered, Doctor Stone went charging down. "Good luck!"

The pilot closed the ramp, and the pinnace took off again very quickly. He imagined palace security wasn't happy having an armed marine pinnace inside its defenses.

He turned to Angela. "Do you think it will be that easy?"

She laughed. "Nothing involving you ever goes the way I imagine."

His stomach sank. She was right about their luck. Things were probably going to go straight down the toilet.

27

K elsey stood beside her father's bed, her mind filled with terror. He had to make it. She couldn't imagine life without him. Jared stood silently by her side.

Lily Stone was working with her father's personal physician to isolate the toxin. The man wasn't ready to say it was poison, but he wasn't hindering Stone while she ran tests.

"I found it," Lily said. "It's in his stomach, as expected. I'm getting a sample for the analyzer now."

"Can you reverse it?" Kelsey asked.

"I hope so." Lily took a bit of extracted mess and put it into an Old Empire device. The screen lit up after a few moments. "It has the same basic chemical properties as what I found in Carlo Vega, but it hasn't broken down completely yet. There may be a way to stop the reaction before it kills him."

The emperor's personal doctor looked at the screen. "I recognize this. There's a plant on the southern continent that some people use for religious ceremonies. In high enough doses, it kills."

He looked up at them. "There's some kind of additive, though. A binding agent that might stop the regular course of treatment from working. I'll try it anyway. It should at least slow the progress of the poison."

"I've sent the analysis to *Invincible*," Lily said. "Marcus has the computing power to figure out possible cures. Meanwhile, we hold on and hope the emperor is strong enough to survive while we work."

The doors to the medical center slid open, and Ethan walked through with a dozen Imperial Guardsmen at his back. "What are these people doing here? Get them out at once. Everyone except my father's personal physician."

Kelsey turned to him, her eyes blazing. "He's my father and I'm not going anywhere."

Her brother smiled. "I think you will. I had the guards search your rooms, and they found something interesting." He pulled a vial of dark liquid from his pocket. "I thought you loved our father, but you tried to kill him for the Bastard."

The brazen charge took her breath away. "How dare you? I would never hurt him."

The guards raised their weapons, and she realized she'd clenched her fists and stepped forward. It took an act of will to stop herself from taking another as her combat computer calculated the optimal attack plan to take them all out.

Ethan gestured toward her. "As the heir during a time of crisis, I'm assuming the mantle of the Throne. Guards, take both of these traitors into custody. If my sister resists, shoot the Bastard. That might break his control."

The emperor's physician dodged into the middle of the confrontation and plucked the vial of poison from Ethan's fingers. "I'll take this, Highness. It might save your father's life."

Kelsey saw that her brother didn't want to give up the vial, but he really couldn't object. He was framing them and he wanted ultimate power. It tore at her heart to see that Jared had been right all along.

Ethan was a monster.

There was no way he'd allow Lily to examine the drug on his own. She needed to distract them while the doctors worked.

"You've gone mad," she said as she stepped between the guards and Jared. "I don't know what has taken hold in you, but I'm not just letting you imprison us. You're the usurper in this story. You killed Carlo Vega. You tried to kill Jared. You poisoned our father and put the drugs into my room. I can prove it."

That diverted his attention. "If this involves those cursed things in your head, that's no proof at all. You're a slave to the Bastard's will."

She smiled. "You call him the Bastard, but the joke is on you. It seems Mother was a little free with her affection, too, and before anyone knew about Jared. Awkward. Now he's the only one of us that has any Imperial blood in his veins at all."

Ethan gaped at her and turned a bright red. "Liar! Get her out of my sight, and get their minion out of here before she does something to my father."

Lily pinged Kelsey's implants. *I just sent the analysis of the pure poison up. Good work on distracting him, but you've let the genie out of the lamp.*

I'm sorry I had to spring it on Jared that way. Get the cure for my father. Save him, no matter the cost.

She raised her hands when the guards came for her. "I'm sorry I didn't tell you sooner, Jared."

"We'll talk later."

They took her weapons and cuffed her with heavy manacles. Since they had guns trained on Jared, she had no intention of resisting. That would come later.

They hustled them out of the medical center and down to the security wing. Jared gave her half a smile and pinged her.

I'm partly convinced that was a play, but you sounded so convincing. Is it true?

She shrugged. *Lily found out during that first exam she gave me. I thought about telling you but decided it would only complicate our relationship even more.*

Don't fret on my account. It doesn't bother me one bit. Well, it does, kind of. Now we're not related at all.

She gave him a reproving stare. *Family isn't just blood. It's those closest to your heart. You're my brother in every important way. If Father survives, he'll tell you so, too.*

They put her in a lift by herself. The chief guard gave her an apologetic smile. "I'm sorry, Highness. We have men waiting below. Don't cause trouble or Admiral Mertz will suffer for it."

"This is a lie," she said intently. "Keep investigating. Ethan did this, and you can't just let him take the Throne over our father's dead body."

"I promise there will be a full and thorough investigation," he said with a thoughtful frown. He pressed the button and the lift doors slid closed. It dropped deep into the ground, and a squad of female guards escorted her into a cell. The solid metal hatch slid closed. A camera high on the wall had a red light, indicating it was watching them.

One guard raised her wrist to her mouth. "Camera off." The red light winked out.

"My apologies for the indignity, Highness," the woman said. "But I need you to strip for a search. You'll be given a jumpsuit." One of the other guards held up a folded garment in garish orange.

Kelsey stripped down. The woman gave Kelsey the most thorough search she'd ever imagined.

"Food comes on a regular schedule, Highness. The camera doesn't cover the toilet. The lights dim at night, but not enough to hide any shenanigans. Behave and we won't have any trouble."

They left her alone in the cell after she dressed. The camera light came back on, so they were watching. Good. Let them think she was beaten.

She lay back on the cot and let her built-in equipment examine the cell walls. The scanners were rudimentary but more than capable of seeing the construction details.

Her implants also let her know that Jared was in the cell beside hers. She pinged him.

Don't show any sign you can hear me, but I'm next door.

She heard his silent sigh. *Things went bad so quickly. But don't worry. Lily will sort this out. We will stop him.*

Kelsey hoped that was true, but worry ate at her. Her father was dying, and her twin brother had done it.

Somehow, they had to turn this around. She had to save her father. She had to stop Ethan.

We'll get out of this, Jared. We'll fix this.

I know we will. Our people will be working hard to stop him. For now, it might be best if we get a little sleep. Things are going to happen fast when they start.

Kelsey took the hint and said goodbye. She stared at the ceiling. There was no way she'd sleep. None.

Didn't he feel anything for their father? How could Ethan try to kill him? It was incomprehensible.

How had she missed it? He must've been going mad for years. Becoming a monster that killed those around him because of paranoid delusions.

While she couldn't escape this prison right now, hopefully, her bombshell was making Ethan miserable. No matter how he tried to suppress it, there'd been plenty of witnesses to pass on the juicy rumors. By dawn, their parentage would be the talk of the town.

Maybe that would distract him enough to make a mistake. One they or their friends could capitalize on to take him down.

* * *

ONCE ETHAN HAD THROWN the Fleet doctor out of the palace, he demanded the physician give him a sample of Father's blood. With that in hand, he went to his own doctor and had the woman test his DNA against the old man's.

And damned if the little bitch hadn't been telling the truth. He didn't have any Imperial blood.

He smashed the doctor's tablet on the floor and stormed out. His temper held until he made it to his room and he gave in to the rage boiling inside him.

That bitch! He grabbed the first breakable thing he could find and crushed it under his heel. That's what he'd do to Kelsey!

He picked up his chair and started shattering everything around him. He didn't stop until the red haze was gone and he'd destroyed his belongings.

They'd all pay for what they'd done to him. Every single one of them.

She'd smeared his reputation in front of all those guards. By now, they'd have told their friends. It was far too late to silence them.

What would the Senate do? Try to take the Throne away from him? He'd have to stop them, and he knew just the man to help. He needed to act right now before his enemies had a chance to plot further against him.

He needed to eliminate the other contenders for the Throne as quickly as possible. If they didn't have any other potential candidates, he'd have a stronger hand with the Senate.

First though, he needed an inside man. He knew just who to call.

* * *

THE BUZZER on Nathaniel's nightstand woke him. It was late. He touched the control as he sat up. "Yes?"

"I'm sorry to wake you, Senator," his assistant said. "His Highness is on the line and won't take no for an answer. Your automated system shunted him to me. He insists on speaking to you this very moment."

"My apologies for the disruption of your time off. Go back to sleep and I'll deal with him."

Once his man was off the line, Nathaniel picked up the heir's call. "Highness, it's late. Couldn't this wait until morning?"

"My father has been poisoned, Senator."

That drew Nathaniel to his feet. "My God. Is he alive? Will he recover?"

"It's touch and go. They've identified the poison. I'm hoping for the best, but we must plan for the worst."

Nathaniel rubbed his face. "This is horrible. Who did this?"

"My sister and the Bastard. They found the poison in her rooms. I'm sure he has her under some kind of compulsion. This is his play for the Throne, but it won't work. We have them in custody. They will pay for their crimes."

As a lifelong politician, Nathaniel had been lied to by the best. He could tell when an amateur was trying to play him. The heir didn't sound betrayed. He sounded smug. Something smelled rotten.

"What can I do to help, Highness?"

"I need to know that I have your complete and unwavering support. I don't believe any of the slanders about your nephew. I'll work tirelessly to exonerate his good name, and yours, by association. I have many enemies in Fleet. I think he would make a terrific commander to oversee the purge of disloyal officers."

That would be an unmitigated disaster. The more Nathaniel had reviewed his nephew's record, the worse the idiot's judgment appeared. Now that they were in a shooting war, he'd get them all killed. Particularly after he oversaw a Fleet-wide purge of officers he suspected were disloyal. The very last thing they needed at this point was a witch-hunt.

"My nephew escaped confinement yesterday, Highness. The people that freed him murdered a number of Fleet personnel. He's a wanted fugitive."

"That problem can be solved. I'm certain the attackers took him against his will. Probably Mertz's people. They wanted to see him executed, but the courts would speedily find the evidence against him to be false. Rest assured, Senator. I have this under control."

Yes, he probably did. Nathaniel was now convinced that the heir was behind all the attacks. Most likely even against his father. He was a dangerous lunatic. One who had to be stopped for the good of the Empire.

Well, he knew how to handle crazed men. Talk calmly and reassure them. Then call someone to lock them up.

"I'll back your play, Highness. Family and honor mean everything to me. What do you need first?"

The heir sighed. "One of my sister's slanders seems to be true. My mother had an affair. I'm not related to my father at all. I have no idea who sired me, but I need to be sure that the succession is protected in this time of chaos. I want you to look at the Charter and see what it says in regards to the succession. The Senate has already confirmed me. That needs to stick."

Nathaniel staggered as though someone had punched him in the gut. The news was a complete and total shock. Like a bus dropping out of the traffic control net and smashing into his grav car with no warning.

He struggled to find his voice. "I don't believe that will hinder you, Highness. The Senate has already confirmed you. There won't be enough votes to change that."

"Be certain, Senator. I'll call you again tomorrow. I want this matter settled before it bites me in the ass."

Once the heir had disconnected, Nathaniel sat heavily on his bed. Holy God, what a mess. Everything made sense now. It had just become even more complicated than the heir knew.

Justine Bandar, the empress in exile, as she preferred to call herself, had kept a secret from him. From them all. Nathaniel had once been her paramour. The affair hadn't lasted long, but the timing was about right.

She'd had a number of discreet affairs during her marriage. They usually lasted a few months, and then she ended them when she grew bored. The empress was a powerful and sensual woman. Few declined her advances.

Lord knows he'd certainly fallen into her arms speedily enough. Their torrid affair had blazed like the sun and then ended abruptly when she told him it was over. He'd known that day must come, but it was still devastating. He'd thought it was going so well.

When news came out that the empress was with child, he'd assumed that was the reason she'd broken off their relationship. He supposed that was true, if not for the reasons he'd thought.

The woman had always taken pains to be sure no hint of her behavior ever leaked out, but he knew he hadn't been the first. Nor had he been the last. The irony of the empress divorcing her husband for infidelity was so powerful it turned even his stomach.

What the hell did he do now? His unwitting son was poised to assume the Imperial Throne, but Nathaniel was certain the man was an aspiring regicide. He wanted to pin the murder on Nathaniel's daughter, though she would be ignorant of her lineage, too.

Nathaniel hadn't lied about family and honor being important to him. He just had to figure out what that meant in this context, and he needed to do it fast.

* * *

YEATS LOOKED up when his chief of staff opened the door to his office. "Yes?"

"I'm sorry to disturb you," the man said, "but you have a call from the palace. I don't know the man, but he's identifying himself as an officer with the Imperial Guard."

It must be about the emperor's illness. Good news, perhaps. "Then I'd best take his call. Put it through."

The man slipped back out, and Yeats's com chimed a moment later.

The image of a roughly hewn man in Imperial whites appeared. He inclined his head. "Admiral Yeats, I'm Captain Paul Danvers, Imperial Guard. I appreciate you taking the time to speak with me."

"I always have time for the Imperial Guard. What can I do for you, Captain? Is it about the emperor?"

The man shifted a bit uncomfortably. "Yes and no. I'm stepping a bit outside normal protocol, but there's a situation you need to be aware of.

"His Highness has assumed the Throne during his father's incapacitation, and certain accusations have been made. He's produced what certainly appears to be damning evidence that Her Highness poisoned her father."

"Preposterous," Yeats snapped. "There is no way that young woman would harm a hair on his head. Someone made a mistake."

"I'll confess that does match my feelings, as well. On His Highness's instruction, I've locked Princess Kelsey and Admiral Mertz in our detention facility. The admiral also stands accused of involvement in the attack on the emperor."

Yeats shook his head sharply. "Impossible. I know Jared Mertz. He's as loyal to the Throne as they come. You need to get this sorted out, Captain."

"I'd love to, Admiral, but my options are limited. Also… I hesitate to say this, but I'm afraid for the safety of the prisoners. If His Highness were to take it into his head to do something rash, I fear enough of the Guard might stand by and let it happen. It might be prudent if outside forces are aware of the situation and intervene."

"I grasp the purpose of your call. Rest assured, I know the right people to call. I'll be down there shortly to discuss the situation with His Highness. Thank you for this warning."

"It's my pleasure, Admiral. But do hurry. Time is of the essence, I think."

"Keep a lid on things, and I'll be right there. Goodbye, Captain."

Yeats rubbed his face. Well, this had gone ugly fast. It was a good thing he knew the numbers of a few senators. They'd help him keep this situation from spinning out of control before cooler heads prevailed.

He hit the com link to his chief of staff. "Get a pinnace ready for immediate deployment. We're going to the palace. Oh, and I'll want enough officers and marines to intimidate people trying to keep us out."

"I'll have them ready in a few minutes, Admiral."

Yeats disconnected and started down the list of senators he knew. He didn't have long, and he needed to get moving.

28

Angela couldn't believe how easily the stealthed pinnace had escaped everyone's notice. They'd picked a hiding place deep in the mountains, of which Avalon had more than its fair share. This range was off the beaten path and had no resorts to complicate matters.

It turned out that hadn't always been the case. The ruins of a large chalet graced one slope. It was nothing but debris at this point, mostly buried under snow. Before the Fall, this must've been quite the getaway.

A handy canyon provided them with cover against casual sightings. As far as she knew, no one was actively looking for any Fleet personnel or vessels, but that could change at a moment's notice.

Her team was going over every piece of equipment Marcus had sent. It was sufficient for just about any problem. Each of her people had a suit of Old Empire powered armor. Not the pantywaist kind like the princess wore, but the full up gear.

Nothing short of an anti-ship weapon could hurt them here in the New Terran Empire. But they could deal out pain to anyone else. They had heavy weapons of every kind. Plasma cannon suitable for the armor and flechette rifles of similar size. If they had to strike somewhere, they'd get in.

There were also stunners made to a size appropriate to an armored marine. The Old Empire hadn't felt the need for anything like that, but Princess Kelsey had made the design and creation of such a weapon a priority so they could stun the living crap out of any unfortunates in their way.

While they checked everything, she manned the officer's console and the drones slaved to it. Those were even stealthier than the pinnace. She had them crisscrossing the area around the capital looking for Talbot.

Every ten kilometers, they sent a pulse that would activate his retrieval beacon. That would eventually catch someone's notice, but they'd still be devilishly hard to pinpoint.

All of this helped keep her mind off the fact the admiral and princess were prisoners. Locked away in the Imperial Palace. If she thought about it too long, she became tempted to go get them.

Carl was up in the cockpit. He'd wanted to use a console for something, and there was no flight engineer aboard right now. That kept him out of her hair. Let the pilots deal with him.

Having him out of sight also kept her from reconsidering her feelings about him. It was unsettling. He looked like a kid, but he'd put it all on the line to fight for her. That had to count for something. She just wasn't sure what.

The console pinged for her attention. One of the probes had just detected a marine recovery beacon. Talbot had already activated it.

"Heads up, people! We have a customer! Wrap up your inspections and armor up."

Carl came scrambling back from the cockpit. "You found him?"

"Sure did. The beacon says he's alive and in relatively good health. A broken arm, a minor gunshot to the same arm, and a mild concussion. I'm relocating other drones to triangulate the signal and scout the area. Once we're sure where he is, we'll check to see if it's a trap."

"And if it is?"

She smiled like a shark. "Then we go in even harder. Strap in up front. This is about to get exciting."

* * *

THEY'D COME for Talbot early. A number of armed men and a shock weapon of some kind kept him from getting overly exuberant while he used the bathroom.

Then they'd strapped him back down and taken him to a lab. The medical scanners looked top of the line for the New Terran Empire. Everyone wore old-fashioned medical masks, but he recognized his captor standing off to the side. He made sure to get a better recording of him.

They'd only just begun when his recovery beacon changed status. Someone had responded with a coded pulse. It was intended to reassure an injured marine that CSAR was on the way.

Combat Search and Rescue crews were tough people, armed to the gills to fight off any threat to their patients. Not that he expected it was CSAR coming for him. This facility was going to have a marine combat team on their ass before too long.

One of the scientists frowned. "He has the indicated equipment and some extras that I can't identify. How the hell did they get that thing in his brain?"

A woman beside him shrugged. "Done is done. Focus on identifying what you can. Like this node inside his body behind the lungs. It seems to be linked to his nervous system. And… is that a signal? I think it's broadcasting on a frequency range we don't use."

Talbot killed the beacon. He needed to keep his captors in the dark as long as possible.

Their leader came over and looked at the screen. "What kind of transmission?"

The woman shrugged. "I don't know. It's gone now."

He frowned at Talbot. "What was that? Were you signaling someone?"

"Would I still be here if I was? Part of my gear checks for connections to my armor every hour. It's an automated thing. The range is no more than a hundred meters."

The man didn't look as though he were buying that explanation. "Can you estimate the range of the signal you detected, Doctor J?"

"Certainly more than a hundred meters," the woman said. "Perhaps ten or fifteen kilometers."

"I hope you're a better marine than a liar. We're a long way from anything, and our scanners would tell us if anyone was that close. Nevertheless, we need to make it clear to you that sending signals is a very bad idea."

He reached over to a table of instruments and picked up a laser scalpel. Talbot tensed, but that didn't help at all when the man cut a long, deep slice into the marine's arm.

Talbot screamed. He couldn't help it. It hurt like the devil. He wished he had one of those fancy pharmacology units like Kelsey. One with drugs to deaden the pain. Well, if wishes were horses, he'd be ass deep in horseshit.

"If you behave, I'll have them regenerate that," the man said cordially. "If not, I'll cut off some fingers. We wouldn't want that, would we?"

Talbot shook his head, his teeth clenched tightly. He had no choice. Hopefully, whoever it was had gotten a good read on him.

* * *

CARL WATCHED everything from the flight engineer's console. The pilots were working on their approach and had no time for him. The marines were armored up and ready to go. All they had to do was locate Talbot.

The probe had lost the major's signal before they could triangulate a precise location. That didn't mean there was no data, though. They had almost thirty seconds of recorded transmissions to work with.

The flight engineer's console wasn't optimized for data manipulation, but Carl always carried his best tools in his implants. It only took a minute to update the console and start analyzing the data.

Yes, he could see the signal strength changing as the probe moved. Assuming the major was stationary, that should allow him to infer a rough target area since they had a good idea of the direction from which the signals were coming.

He knew Angela was trying to do the same thing, but she was playing against his strengths now. This was science, baby!

Using the known quantity of the beacon's signal strength, Carl could estimate distance. If Talbot was underground, the signal would be weaker, but he could work with that.

The probe had traveled a good way in those thirty seconds, and the signal strength had grown at a steady rate. That made the case for Talbot being stationary even stronger.

Carl brought up a map of the target area. He eliminated the locations that didn't match the direction of the transmission. Using the strength of the signal and the estimated direction, he put the data through several of his custom algorithms.

That focused him in on a particular stretch of land. Empty forest. Old growth, possibly untouched since the Fall.

He turned the console loose on examining the compiled weather satellite images for the last ten years, and it popped back with a possible anomaly. He looked at the autumn images and magnified them.

There. The trees had lost their leaves late in the season, and that looked like a building. A very well concealed one.

"I found him, I think," he said over the com.

"Show me," Angela said.

"Sending now. There's a building hidden in the forest at about the right area. I can't be completely sure he's there, but it should be enough to send a probe in."

"Good work. You might just have saved his life. I'm sending a probe in now."

Carl monitored the probe as it ghosted in using only passive scanners. Yes, that was a building and it was occupied. Three, no, four guards sat in a pair of concealed blinds that had a great overview of the entire forest around them. There were even more people inside.

"Jackpot," Angela said. "We go in hard and fast. Let the lookouts scream. We'll send an override signal once we get inside to reactivate Talbot's beacon. Then we converge on his location. Stay nonlethal, if possible. I want prisoners."

A chorus of oorahs came back at her from the marine team.

"Lieutenant Veracruz, pick the best-looking ingress route to the target. We'll drop out the back and call if we need fire support. I'll designate people to watch the towers. If they look dangerous to you, the support team will take them out."

"Aye, ma'am. We can start the run at your command. Forty-five seconds to drop zone once we go."

"Everyone ready? Execute the run, Lieutenant."

The pinnace banked and accelerated hard. Carl cinched his restraints tighter and loaded Angela's suit visuals into his implants. This was going to be just like a first-person shooter.

* * *

THE PINNACE SCREAMED over the target with no warning. The probes told Angela they'd taken the sentries completely off guard.

The ramp dropped right on the mark, and she threw herself out of the pinnace with her team. They'd practiced drops like this in the simulators, but nothing beat the first time going at it for real.

They fell from a height of a hundred meters right toward the trees. She kicked in her suit's grav unit to slow her fall and dodge the worst of the limbs.

First squad split off to cover the lookouts. The rest of them landed on the roof of the concealed building. A shaped charge opened it and they dropped in, weapons at the ready.

"Imperial Marines," she said over her external speakers. It made her voice echo from every nook and cranny on the floor. "Lay down your weapons and surrender. Resistance will be met with lethal force."

The first man she saw ran, but he wasn't armed. She left him to one of the others. A blue stunner beam took him down.

Two more men ran around the corner and opened fire with automatic weapons. Corporal Riviera made an example of them with his flechette rifle. A swarm of metal darts tore them apart, and the wall behind them.

"That'll make them duck faster next time," he said with some satisfaction. "The major's beacon is online. He's several levels below us. Stairs or the easy way?"

She pulled a plasma grenade and tossed it down the long hall. Her helmet feed blocked the worst of the light when it detonated. Kelsey was right. It did sound like the end of the world.

They dropped through two levels with that one massive hole. People either ran or surrendered. She detailed a few men to collect prisoners while she led the last group down into the basement.

It was set up as some kind of lab. A number of science types cowered against the wall, and Talbot was strapped to a gurney. Blood ran down his arm, but he was conscious.

"The main guy just ran through the door on the far wall," Talbot said. "He'll have a car to escape the area.

"Think it's faster than a marine pinnace?" she asked. "Everyone, lay on the ground and put your hands out. Now."

She switched to the pinnace frequency. "Jailbird three, Raven Actual. We have the package. There's a flyer about to leave the building, too. Take him alive. I want to discuss a few things with the gentleman."

"Copy that, Raven Actual. He just took off. I think I can convince him to land without any trouble."

She left that to the pilot and freed Talbot. "You sure are a hard man to find. What kind of sissy lets civilians take him down like that?"

He smiled. "We all have our bad days. Is Kelsey okay? The admiral?"

"As far as I know, they're fine. They're locked up, though. I'll fill you in when I feel less worried about a counterattack."

Angela grabbed him and motioned for two of her men to watch her back. In the powered armor, she had no trouble carrying the burly marine back through the wrecked building.

"Did you have to blow the place up? Nothing they had could possibly scratch your paint job."

"Being a marine has a few perks. Blowing shit up is one of them."

The pinnace was just coming back to the roof as she got there. The ramp was an easy hop from there.

Carl was standing beside a rumpled man who'd been cuffed and strapped to a handy seat. "He didn't give us any trouble after Lieutenant Riviera offered to land on him."

"Get more restraints," she said. "We'll have a lot more prisoners in a few minutes. I don't expect we'll be turning them over to anyone just yet, either."

"On it."

The scientist dug more out while she took Talbot to the combat medical area. It didn't have a regenerator, but it would let her set the broken bone and stop the bleeding. The scanners could also confirm that he had no other injuries that his beacon wasn't reporting.

"Tell me," he said.

She popped her helmet and let it swing back behind her. "The heir poisoned the emperor. Then he framed Princess Kelsey and Admiral Mertz. We're working on figuring out a plan to get them loose."

"Shit," Talbot muttered. "This just keeps getting better. We need to get everyone on board and clear out before someone comes looking. I'm sure they called for help."

Her suit told her the others were making their way back up. They had a few dozen people in custody. Two dead inside and four in the lookout towers. They'd been about to fire something at the pinnace, and first squad had taken them out.

"Ten minutes," she said. "Do an intelligence sweep. Anything we find down there that confirms the heir is behind this might be critical."

Talbot nodded. "But we scoot the moment we detect someone coming this way. And, Angela? Thanks."

"All part of the service. Let's get you fixed up before all hell breaks loose."

* * *

Ethan scowled when his com signaled again. Victor. Why did he suspect this was bad news?

It wasn't a call this time, but a voice message. He played it.

"Highness, they found us." Somewhere in the background, someone was shooting at something. "I'll try to get away, but things are looking grim here."

He stopped the message before it finished. The rest didn't matter. Once again, Victor had proved to be less than competent. It didn't matter whether the fool lived or died, so long as he kept his mouth shut doing it.

So, they'd rescued the marine. That hardly mattered when compared to the victory he was about to win.

29

They dragged Jared from his cell. It was early morning, by his guess. Perhaps dragged was too strong a word. Politely escorted him with weapons displayed might be more accurate.

His destination was the official audience chamber. It held the Imperial Throne. Karl Bandar only used it for traditional times or serious matters. It seemed the new management was more officious and pompous than the old one.

Ethan sat on the ornate throne with the scepter on a stand beside him. He didn't wear the crown, so the emperor must still be alive.

Jared wondered how long his half brother would allow that to continue. The heir wasn't a patient man.

The guards brought Jared up and forced him to his knees when he didn't go down on his own.

"Have you no respect for the Throne?" Ethan asked with a smirk.

"I'd give my life for it. I simply have no respect for the ass occupying it right now."

That wiped the expression off Ethan's face. "You will show me the respect I am due, Bastard. You're in deep trouble already. Do not make it worse."

Jared shook his head pityingly. "With you calling the shots, my situation could hardly be any worse."

"Enough of this. You kneel before me charged with high treason. The attempted murder of your liege. Would you care to make a statement before I judge you?"

"Is this how justice works in the Empire now? The trial is you declaring me guilty? What of evidence? What of testimony? What of my representation?"

Ethan smiled. "Why play out the theater where you claim otherwise? You've lost. Take your medicine like a man."

"You told me before I left on the expedition that you'd eliminate me. You tried to poison me with tainted treats and killed Carlo Vega instead. Now your father is dying of the same thing. I'd say my proof is stronger."

The heir laughed. "Your lies, you mean. Nothing but hearsay. You probably killed the man yourself. In any case, that's irrelevant. I'm in charge now. My word is law. I hereby find you guilty of the charge of high treason. The sentence is death. Do you have any last words before the sentence is carried out?"

The main entrance to the hall opened, and the sound of arguing voices carried to Jared. He looked back and saw Admiral Yeats striding toward them while other officers argued with the guards. A squad of marines in unpowered armor faced down the Imperial Guardsmen at the door.

Ethan rose to his feet. "What's the meaning of this? I left orders not to be disturbed."

"Highness," Yeats said, bowing his head. "I understand you have one of my officers in custody. As the senior Fleet commander, I'm here to speak with him."

"The time for speaking is over, Admiral. I've found him guilty of high treason."

Yeats smiled politely. "The Charter requires the Senate to try those accused of treason. The emperor only lays the charge.

"Oh, and that brings me to another issue. The emperor is not allowed to delegate his participation. Since he is ill, you must wait for his recovery or your coronation to bring the charge before the Senate. Highness."

Rage contorted Ethan's face. "How dare you lecture me? I am your liege!"

"Not yet, you aren't, Highness," Yeats said firmly. "The Charter sets strict limits to your authority. Fleet and the Imperial Senate will not stand idly by while you flout the law. I will speak with Admiral Mertz. Now."

"You mean Commander Mertz. I do not recognize that idiotic edict."

"Unfortunately for you, your father already did. All that remains is for the Senate to verify it was ratified or ratify it themselves. With all due respect, Highness, this little charade is over."

"And if I were to place you under arrest?"

Yeats smiled. "The Senate is aware of where I am. I speak on their behalf as well. Unless you'd like to see your position as heir debated today, I suggest you step back from the abyss and allow the law to work as our founders designed it. That applies to Her Highness, as well."

Ethan snarled but eventually waved a hand dismissing them.

The admiral helped Jared to his feet, and marines escorted them out of the audience chamber with the Imperial Guard following along behind them. They took Jared back to the detention level and to a conference room. Yeats gestured for the guards to leave and sat down.

He placed a small device on the table. "This will interfere with their monitoring equipment. We should have a few minutes while they address the problem. Are you and Princess Kelsey alright?"

Jared slumped. "I'm better than I was before you showed up. He was going to send me to the executioner right as you walked in. Good timing, by the way."

"I have contacts in the Imperial Guard. They gave me a heads up. I called a few Senators. No one is happy with what's going on here. I never suspected the heir to be so rash. Or to try something so iron fisted."

"I did warn you."

Yeats nodded. "So you did. How's the princess?"

"Locked up in the cell next to mine. She's worried about her father and pissed at her brother. Do you think the Senate will stand up to him?"

"To a point, yes. No one wants to see an emperor gone wild. The balance of powers is there for a reason. The Senate judges matters of treason to keep the emperor from executing anyone he chooses. He's the one to charge a traitor so that the Senate doesn't have all the authority.

"So, you'll have a trial. You and Princess Kelsey both. His people will have to produce some evidence. This high-handed behavior will make the senators cautious. His Highness just made it more likely they'll validate the edict just to remind him that he isn't a dictator. And, to be fair, they're terrified of the Rebel Empire and what war with them means."

Jared sighed. "I just wish it wasn't so likely there would be an 'accident' here. I don't want to be 'shot while trying to escape' tonight."

"I'll see what I can do to make clear that won't be tolerated."

The door opened, and Yeats pocketed the device as a man came in and looked at the camera. "My apologies, Admiral. The camera in this room appears to be out of order. Would you care to use another one?"

"That's fine. We're done here anyway. You can take Admiral Mertz back to his cell."

Jared stood. "Thank you, Admiral."

"My pleasure. I don't want to see anything happen to my most promising officer." He stared at the guard intently. "If something did happen—to either him or Her Highness—I guarantee the Imperial Senate would put everyone involved under a deep scanner to find out what happened. Pass the word around, and save your friends the pain. Do you get me?"

The guard nodded. "I understand, and I'll make sure nothing untoward happens."

The man escorted Jared back to his cell and locked him in. The guard's expression told him that he was taking that very direct warning seriously.

Jared pinged Kelsey as soon as he was alone and filled her in.

The rat! You were right all along. Her mental voice was outraged.

That's not much comfort if we can't get out of here. The only hope I'm seeing is your father getting better.

Let's both pray for that, and that no one else does anything to complicate this even further.

* * *

TALBOT SAT STILL LONG ENOUGH for them to set his arm and regenerate the rest of the damage. Then he cornered Angela to find out what the situation really was.

"Events have been unfolding," she said. "Not as drastically as some we've faced, but not smoothly. The admiral and princess are in custody, charged with high treason. The emperor is in critical condition, his fate uncertain. Breckenridge is on the loose somewhere. Frankly, I'm surprised he didn't turn up in our raid."

"That would have been entirely too lucky. No, he's up to something else. Probably a chip in the fight to control Fleet. He'd make a great figurehead and a lever for his uncle, the senator. There's still some kind of surprise working in that area."

She sighed. "We need to get them loose. The heir has way too much opportunity to see them dead in one way or another. As the princess says, it's easier to beg forgiveness than ask permission."

He frowned. "She's not the best role model when it comes to that kind of thing."

Angela smiled. "How do we manage to break them out of the most secure facility in the Empire? All we have is the equipment in this pinnace."

"We could get in with the armor if they didn't shoot the pinnace down on approach, but burning down the Imperial Palace will win us no friends. Even if everything went according to plan, the odds someone would just shoot them are too high. We can't risk it."

He gave the situation some thought. "Are those really all the resources we have? What about Carl? Oh, and congrats, by the way."

She frowned. "For what?"

"I hear you two are an item."

She planted her hands on her hips and glared. "Christ! You weren't even here an hour. He and I are not dating. We did not sleep together. None of that is true."

He grinned. "That only makes the rumors juicier."

"Anyway," she said, ignoring his jibes, "we can get some assistance through *Persephone*. Not for attacking the Imperial Palace, but certainly general statuses on all the crap going on."

He allowed his expression to go serious. "It would be better if we could get the emperor back on the Throne. I'll give them a call. Angela, you've done a great job. Go see if any of Carl's tech might help us turn the tide."

Angela sighed. "I guess that shouldn't surprise me, but I'm kind of scared what he might do. He's demonstrated some unexpected backbone."

"You find out the quality of your friends when the chips are down. There's more to Carl Owlet than most people suspect. He's an ace in the hole. Now, go make nice while I see what other fires have broken out."

* * *

ELISE STEPPED into the medical center on *Invincible* and spotted Doctor Stone bent over an unfamiliar instrument. She walked over and cleared her throat. "Doctor."

The dark-haired medical officer looked up and smiled. "Highness. I understand you're going back down to talk with Senator Breckenridge. I have something I'd like to send with you."

Elise took a vial of taffy-colored liquid from the other woman. "Is this an antidote to the poison?"

"Yes and no. There isn't an easy way to make an antidote for that particular poison. It has a binding agent that makes it hard to clear out.

"This is a combination of a new drug that will slow its progress and nanites that can repair the damage that it already caused. Together, they offer the emperor a chance to fight this off."

"Shouldn't you be taking this down yourself and getting it into him as soon as possible?"

Stone growled with obvious frustration. "The heir has barred all of us from his father and has forbidden any 'experimental' treatments. The emperor's physician doesn't have the clout to fight him, and I can't just send the data. He can't make nanites."

"I hear that has a number of senators calling for immediate access to His Majesty, but we don't have time to waste. People are growing worried and suspicious, but this needs to be smuggled into the Imperial Palace and administered to the emperor now.

"I'm guessing the progress of the poison will be irreversible in less than twelve hours. The treatment we already gave him helped give him more time. Otherwise, he'd already have died."

Elise stared at the potential cure. "How does someone sneak into a place like that? The emperor must be under heavy guard. It seems impossible."

"Welcome to the big league. Talbot, Angela Ellis, and Carl Owlet are down there. If you can get some assistance from Senator Breckenridge, it might be possible. It's the only hope we have of stopping the heir. Otherwise, he'll find a way to kill Admiral Mertz and probably the princess, too."

Elise nodded. "I'll do it, of course. Anything for Jared."

"Excellent. *Persephone* has a second stealthed pinnace. It will take you and some additional marines down to support any actions they feel necessary. Planetary control is denying Fleet traffic access to the surface. There's some kind of confrontation building there.

"I'm not sure how the heir means to take control of Fleet, but I'm sure that's on his list of things to do. He certainly doesn't want us helping his father or rescuing his prisoners. I hear he told the Senate they couldn't have custody. That he would hold onto the admiral and princess until his father either recovered or died. He didn't make a lot of friends, so that might help you, too."

"I'd best go pack a bag. If this drags on, I'll want some clean clothes."

30

Carl listened to Angela's summary of their situation, including the news they'd need to smuggle people into the Imperial Palace, with growing worry. How the hell were they going to do something crazy like that?

The security system there had to be the best in the New Terran Empire. Which meant he needed to use the best he could cobble together from Old Empire technology, and they had less than twelve hours to make it happen. It seemed hopeless.

Unless he really went outside the box.

"I need to get back to the university," he said. "To the lab where my equipment is stored. There's something there that might help us."

Angela looked unconvinced. "Like what?"

"Some equipment I got from Omega. A way of going from one place to another without crossing the intervening space. We might not be able to make the sample hardware work, but I don't know if we have another option."

"Well, some chance is better than none. We have a grav car that won't raise any eyebrows. I'll get a team together."

She called Major Talbot and gave him the rundown. He sent them on their way with his blessing.

They sat in the back of the grav car while two marines sat up front. He took a deep breath and pitched his voice low. "I'm sorry for the rumors."

She raised an eyebrow. "Did you start them?"

"No!"

The two marines up front glanced back at them.

"Ears front," Angela said firmly. "Carl, the situation dictated what we did. Don't let this freak you out."

"That doesn't mean I can't be sorry for what it does to your reputation."

The other eyebrow went up. "Seriously? What does that even mean?"

"I'm a kid and they're saying... you know."

She laughed softly. "Let's spin this in a different direction. They're saying I slept with the man who took out a hit team sent to kidnap or kill him. With a freaking hammer out of legend. One that can fly like a superhero."

"That's not who I am."

"That's exactly who you are," she said firmly. "I fell into the trap of seeing what you look like and thinking it was who you are. Don't make the same mistake. Inside that nerdy body is a man with the heart of a hero. One not afraid to risk death for what he believes in."

He felt his face heat. "I'm not sure you know me as well as you think. I was terrified."

"Everyone mistakes courage for lack of fear. We're all terrified when the shit hits the fan. Bravery is doing what you have to do in spite of your knees knocking."

He thought about that all the way to the university.

* * *

ETHAN SWEPT into a room deep in the bowels of the palace. He only had his most trusted men with him now, because of who he was meeting.

Someone had found Captain Breckenridge a replacement uniform, he saw as the man came to his feet.

"Captain Breckenridge. Welcome to the Imperial Palace."

The renegade Fleet officer saluted, as he should. "Highness, it's an honor."

Ethan sat on the other side of the table. "Please have a seat. Time is short. I apologize for any discomfort you experienced during your rescue."

The man smiled as he sat. "It was all worth it. I assume you brought me here for a reason."

He wondered if the Fleet officer knew how inane that sounded. "As you could no doubt tell from the method of your rescue, I need a man I know I can count on at my side. Fleet has proven treacherous. Are you willing to help me tame it?"

Breckenridge's smile widened. "Of course, Highness. They were about to take everything from me, all because I was loyal to the Empire. And to you, of course. You're obviously willing to give me my life back. How can I help?"

"I can no longer trust Admiral Yeats to lead Fleet with the Empire's best interests at heart. I need a man at the top who will remember who he serves. Are you that man?"

"I am, and I know these rebels better than any other officer you're likely to find. Together, we can not only unite the Empire but also crush our enemies. The ones Jared Mertz brought down on our heads. I have a number of people I can call on to assist us that are personally loyal to me. And you, of course."

Ethan smiled. "Then I think we have a deal, Admiral Breckenridge. Call your people. I want to head up to Orbital One shortly."

* * *

ELISE SMILED at Senator Breckenridge's assistant as he let her into the man's office. That smile faded when she saw Breckenridge's grim expression.

"Have a seat, Highness. It's early for a drink, but one certainly wouldn't be out of line with the awful events of last night."

"Coffee would be good if you have any."

"That I can do." He made his way to the bar and set some to brewing. "I assume you're fully aware of the emperor's condition."

"Yes." She considered telling him what was in her pocket but decided to feel out how he was doing first. "I'm horrified, of course, and worried about the future. That's the main reason I've come to speak with you."

He nodded. "You aren't sure how I'm seeing the events. Allow me to lay my cards on the table, because I need your help."

The coffee was beginning to come out of the spout and into a cup. He arranged the fixings to go with it. "Cream or sweetener?"

"Black and straight."

That caused the corners of his lips to rise. "A woman after my own heart."

He fixed them both cups and returned to the seats they'd occupied last night. "His Highness called me late with the news. He's offered me my family's reputation for my support. All charges against Wallace dropped and he implied he would put him in charge of Fleet."

It took all her willpower to sip her coffee without spilling a drop. It was excellent.

"I see. And you accepted?"

"I did, but I have no intention of actually enabling him. For a number of very good reasons, starting with the main one. I think he poisoned his father and is framing Admiral Mertz and Princess Kelsey. I cannot and will not support this, even if defying him means the ruin of my reputation."

He smiled at her over the rim of his cup. "You hide it well, but I think I've surprised you. You wonder why someone in politics for the power would cast it away. I could be the right hand of the Throne itself."

She shrugged. "I'm curious, but I suspect you'll tell me soon enough."

"As with most things, it's complicated. I truly do value my personal honor and that of my family. That only occasionally has anything to do with what others think of me.

"A pre-Empire novelist named Lois McMaster Bujold from Terra said it like this. 'Reputation is what other people know about you. Honor is what you know about yourself.' The two can be wildly at odds. Jubilant throngs might cheer a man while inside he's torn to shreds. Or he's reviled for doing what's right."

Breckenridge set his cup onto the saucer. "I'm prepared to embrace the latter to save the Empire. That's exactly what's at stake. Wallace is incompetent and Prince Ethan is an ambitious fool. Together, they would be the death of us all."

Elise put her cup down and stared him in the eye. "That couldn't be plainer. I'm sorry he put you in such a quandary."

The man laughed bitterly. "You have no idea the minefield I had to navigate last night. His Highness dropped another bombshell on me. He told me his sister informed him they were both illegitimate. He apparently confirmed it."

She tilted her head a little. "Awkward, but troublesome in what way? He's already the confirmed heir. Is that likely to change?"

Breckenridge shook his head. "No. He'll remain the heir. The problem for me is that I'm virtually certain I'm his father."

That hit her like an unexpected bucket of ice water. "That *is* remarkable, if true. You had an affair with the empress at around that time?"

"I did. One that she ended abruptly a few weeks before the official announcement that she was with child. At the time, I assumed she was cutting things off because of the added attention she knew was coming. Now that I know the emperor is not their father, I'd bet everything I hold dear that they're mine."

He rubbed his face. "No matter how this plays out, one of them will probably die. Or spend the rest of their lives in prison. I must pick a side. Though it will ruin me politically, I choose the Empire."

"You're a powerful senator. You'll survive this, too."

Breckenridge picked up his cup and sipped his coffee. "Not if I defy Ethan and fail. The winners write history. I'll end up a traitor and die beside everyone else before it's all over. Everything hinges on either the survival of the emperor—which seems unlikely—or outmaneuvering the murderous heir.

"If we win, then the emperor and Princess Kelsey will eventually find out the truth. My political career will end. My fellow senators will find reasons to shun me. For the good of the Empire, I'd have to retire."

"Is retirement so bad an option?"

"Compared to dying or being one of the causes of the destruction of the Empire? No, not at all. I'll take disgrace and even prison if I must."

She nodded. "You really do value honor over reputation. Perhaps we have a chance after all."

Elise took the vial from her pocket and set it on the table. "This has the possibility of saving the emperor's life, but only if we get it to him in the next ten or eleven hours. I'm sure the Imperial Palace is a fortress. Could you find someone to help us get it to him?"

A flash of hope appeared in Breckenridge's eyes. "Perhaps. We'd need someone skilled with locks and alarms, but there may be a way to get two people, perhaps three, into the palace. They'd need to elude the Imperial Guard and slip into a no doubt heavily guarded medical center. This might only give us a small chance, but I'll take it."

* * *

Angela didn't contact the chancellor. He seemed a nice enough man, but he might do something rash. They couldn't afford to have the police called.

Carl wasn't forthcoming with additional details on the device he'd mentioned. That was probably for the best. She was already doubtful it would work. It sounded like sorcery.

Dressed in casual clothes, her people didn't draw any unusual attention. Much of the conversation she overheard revolved around the wild fight last night. More people than could possibly have been anywhere near the apartments were claiming to have seen the whole thing. Usually male students talking with young women hanging onto every word with wide eyes.

It made her want to puke.

"Those lying sacks of crap," she muttered to Carl. "This pisses me off."

"Why?" he asked curiously. "Because they're trying to use reflected glory to get lucky?"

"It just seems skeevy. Doesn't it bother you?"

He shook his head. "You ever see the birds in the zoo that puff themselves up and strut in front of the females to attract a mate? This is like that. All posturing. I couldn't care less what they say.

"I heard one guy claiming he was in on it. That he helped stop the attackers. I think he overplayed his hand, though. The woman laughed at him and walked off."

Angela nodded. "I bet. I heard one guy that actually saw us. He told his friends about a man flying off with a woman. His friends verbally abused him. One thing is for sure. They'll be talking about that attack for a long time to come."

The building with the restricted access was just ahead of them. Carl and she both had codes, but she'd prefer not to leave a record they'd been here.

Getting in proved to be horrifyingly easy. Carl struck up a conversation with several women in lab coats that were going in. He pulled the exact same crap those boys had been doing, though he stuck to an accurate viewpoint.

His story so enthralled the two that they didn't notice he never swiped his card. He had it in his hand, but held the door for them. He left it open just long enough for her to keep it from closing and walked deeper into the building with them.

As soon as they were a dozen meters away, Angela opened the door and motioned her men to follow her inside.

Carl said his goodbyes to the women and entered a stairwell beside the lift. She followed as soon as the women walked into a first-floor room.

He was waiting at the landing between floors. She gave him a hard look. "What the hell was that?"

"A lesson in security training they obviously forgot," Carl said with a grin. "The easiest way to get into a building and past a lock is to distract someone with access and go in with them. Holding a bunch of donuts and coffee works well, too. Doctor Leonard told me if I ever fell for anything like that, he'd assign me an essay on the subject."

She shook her head. "You're a damned wonder. Come on. Let's get to the lab before someone asks us how we got in here."

"We have access cards. They'd let us walk."

Nevertheless, he speedily led them to the fourth floor and to the room where their gear had been stored. A couple of broken boards blocked the door open, and a man stood there watching as others carried out parts of the roof.

Carl showed the man his card. "We're cleared. I need to see if any of my equipment was damaged."

The man gestured for the four of them to go in. "It looks like the destruction was pretty localized. Something fell through the roof."

"Preposterous," a voice said from inside. "The damage pattern and how the debris fell make it clear something in the room burst out through the roof."

Carl covered his eyes. "Fabulous. It's Professor Bedford. I'm doomed."

"Is that you, Mister Owlet? Finally! You've wasted enough of my time already with this foolishness. Get in here this instant!"

Angela didn't even try to suppress her grin as she followed the dejected graduate student into what was no doubt going to be an epic dressing down.

31

Carl's first sight of Professor Andrew Bedford proved the man hadn't changed much. If anything, he looked more pugnacious than ever.

The short man with the white hair and perpetual sneer gestured for Carl to hurry up. "Perhaps you'd care to set these young men straight about what happened here, Mister Owlet. Surely you've gained enough experience to see it clearly."

The lab hadn't been in use before the chancellor had set it aside for Carl. It had a number of crates and boxes on shelves. The one that had formerly held the hammer was missing. He'd wager parts of it were probably scattered across the roof and yard.

"Professor Bedford. It's good to see you again." A lie, but more for form's sake than anything else. The gleam in the old man's eye told Carl it wouldn't matter what he said.

"Bah. Save the pleasantries for someone that cares. I want you to explain to the gentlemen what happened here in this lab. Take as much time as you need, so long as it's less than five minutes. I have other things to attend to."

A glance at Angela showed she was vastly amused. Her grin made her look beautiful.

That wasn't the kind of distraction he needed right now.

"I don't need five minutes, Professor. A case on that shelf flew up into the ceiling. It came apart even as the contents blew the roof open. The course of destruction is probably to the east."

The older man froze and fixed Carl with a suspicious stare. "That's actually correct, and I doubt you'd be able to see such detail without knowing more than you should. Explain."

"This is my equipment, and I'll explain it all as soon as the workmen leave. It's classified."

"How very secretive. Very well, Mister Owlet. I shall humor you for a few minutes. Everyone get out."

The workers wasted no time heading out the door.

Bedford pointed at Angela and the marines. "You, too."

"We're with him. Don't let us slow you down. We're just the peanut gallery."

"Harrumph," the old man said. "If you're the help, don't bother me." He refocused his attention on Owlet. "How do you know what happened here?"

"Because I caused it." He held out his hand and let the backpack he'd been carrying hang in front of him. He activated the hammer and pulled his hand back. The pack stayed in place.

Bedford walked around the floating object, entranced. "You've succeeded in capturing my full attention, Mister Owlet. Continue."

Carl opened the pack and pulled out the hammer. He dropped the now empty canvas and left the hammer in the air for the professor to examine. "This is Mjölnir."

"The mythical hammer of a Norse god? Doubtful. You'll need to do better than that, young man."

"I built it as a weapon for someone. Last night, intruders tried to capture or kill me. I called it to me and defended myself. Hence the destruction."

The old man whirled on Carl, his eyes narrowed. "That business at the apartment building? The chancellor is fit to be tied. I had no idea it involved you, but I can't say I'm surprised."

"Why is that, Professor? Because of my well known predilection for violence?"

"Don't be insolent, boy. You've always struck me as a troublemaker."

"I think everyone under the age of fifty strikes you that way. Now, if you'll excuse us, I have work to do."

The old man straightened and narrowed his gaze. "Don't try to cavalierly dismiss me, Mister Owlet. I'm not done with you yet."

"Perhaps not, but I'm done with you. This work can't be put off. Lives are at stake."

"You must not have heard that I'm in charge of determining your fitness for a doctorate. An honor you're looking less likely to have bestowed upon you every moment. You thought that toy was worth the honor?"

"I built the hammer based on other people's work. As you say, it's a toy. Keep the doctorate. It's the least important of the issues I'm facing right now."

Carl turned his back on the professor and began pulling a crate out. The one with the parts for the transport device.

"You intrigue me at last, Mister Owlet," Bedford said. "What work is so important that it's worth a PhD? The Lucien Prize, perhaps? You can kiss any thought of that goodbye, too."

"You're a mean-spirited old man out to hurt those under his control," Carl said conversationally as he opened the crate. "I've never done anything worthy of the damned Lucien Prize. Keep that, too, and don't let the door hit you on the ass on the way out."

"Explain this situation to me, Mister Owlet," Bedford said softly. "I'm paying attention now."

He turned on the old man. "This is about saving the life of the emperor and probably the Empire. This crate has a device that supposedly allows for travel from one location to another without crossing the intervening space. It's an alien device."

"Owlet, shut up," Angela said.

He glanced over at her as he began pulling parts from the crate. "Either he's going to help us or he's going to leave and keep his mouth shut after you read him the Imperial Secrets Act. If you want to arrest me, do it once I'm finished.

"Professor Bedford, either help or leave. I don't care which, as long as you shut the hell up."

The old man took off his coat. "Finally, a boy with some spine. Explain to me how this device is supposed to work while we assemble it. If this is for the emperor, time is indeed of the essence."

* * *

Kelsey was reading through her implants when she heard the door to her cell open. She sat up with a mixture of dread and eagerness. One way or the other, something was about to happen.

Wallace Breckenridge stepped into the cell and smirked at her. Two Imperial Guards with weapons out stood behind him.

She didn't bother to rise. "The day just keeps getting better."

His smile widened. "We always seem to be locking one another up. Not that I can claim credit this time, but your crimes have caught up with you. It looks like I win after all."

"That remains to be seen. If you have something worthwhile to say, get on with it. Then get out. I have a nap to see to."

His expression darkened. "That mouth of yours will be the death of you. I spoke with His Majesty a few minutes ago. Pardon, I meant His Highness. The soon to be emperor. Whichever you prefer.

"He's decided to reorganize Fleet. So, my title is Admiral now. I'll be headed up to give Yeats the boot shortly. Your father isn't looking so good. I might be on my way in just a few hours. Within an hour of that, you'll be dead."

Kelsey stood slowly. The guards raised their weapons as she took a step forward. Breckenridge took a step back so they were in front of him.

"I could have your blood, if I wanted it badly enough," she said conversationally. "Say one more word and I'll take it."

The coward wasted no time fleeing, but her brother didn't seem afraid as he stepped into the room and closed the door.

"Go ahead," he said. "Attack me. They'll cut you down, and that will solve one of my problems."

She stared at her twin, her heart breaking. "Why? Just tell me why you're doing this."

"Because I won't allow anyone to take what is mine. It's become apparent to me that you all want to see the Throne stripped from me, and for that, as much as I love you and father, you have to die."

The guards didn't seem surprised by that admission. They must be firmly in his pocket. God knew how many others were, as well.

Tears streamed down her face. "How can you say you love me and that you have to kill me? Don't you realize how crazy that sounds?"

His eyes seemed damp, too. "I've always known that there were forces that wanted to take everything away from me. Since I was just a boy, I've been planning on how to stop them. I just never expected you and father to join them.

"That's one of the reasons I built up a network of people I could trust. I have ears in a surprising number of places and trained men that will eliminate any threat. They've kept me and my birthright safe when my family ignored reality."

He shook his head. "It makes me bleed inside. How could you betray me like this? I'm your brother. I'm the man who will lead the Empire to glory over her enemies. You'd deny me my destiny? Traitor."

He whirled on his heel and strode out. The guards backed out and locked her in.

She sank down onto the bunk. How had she missed it all these years? He was mad. Paranoid, at least. A megalomaniac at worst. She had to stop him from taking the Empire down with him.

Somehow.

* * *

TALBOT WATCHED the second pinnace land with more hope than he had any reason to expect. Princess Elise had said she might have an option for them. If it had the slightest chance for success, he'd push it to the hilt.

The pinnace set down softly beside their hideout. It was an old farm building in the woods. Their small craft could mask their IR signature and visual outline to a degree. As long as no one overflew the site, they were safe.

Princess Elise came down the ramp with a man that looked entirely too much like Wallace Breckenridge for his taste. "Major Talbot, this is Senator Nathaniel Breckenridge. He'll be helping us today."

This wasn't promising.

"Senator," Talbot said. "What makes you think I won't lock your ass up right this damned instant?"

The man gave Elise a wry smile. "I'd imagine it's a coin toss. If that helps make you feel better, go right ahead."

Talbot gestured for one of the men to come forward. "Search him. Confiscate any coms or weapons. Be thorough and don't miss any trackers."

The senator raised his arms and submitted. "I understand and appreciate your concern, Major. I'm only here to help."

Once the man had taken the senator's gear and scanned him closely, he had two of the marines take the senator inside.

"Have you lost your mind?" Talbot asked the princess. "That man is our enemy."

"I think not. He's shared a lot of information with me that could mean the difference between success and failure. I think you should listen to him."

He shook his head. "Why are all the princesses I know crazy?"

"You're just lucky, I guess."

He led her inside. They had a rough drawing of the Imperial Palace on the kitchen table. His senior men and women had been plotting possible assault strategies, but now they were watching the senator.

"Everyone, this is Senator Nathaniel Breckenridge. He says he has some information that might help us." Talbot didn't bother to conceal the skepticism in his voice.

"Hear me out," the man in the elegant suit said. "I've been into the palace more times than all of you put together. I know more than most visitors, too, I'd wager."

"Prove it."

"Might I have the use of my arms and a pencil?"

The guards released him at Talbot's nod. One of the marines handed him a pencil and stepped aside.

Breckenridge scanned the drawing. "This isn't too bad, really. Let me update it with the correct proportions."

He expanded some sections of the building and shortened others. "The security center is in this wing now. They moved it last year when they upgraded the power and control feeds in the building. The cells are still under the old wing but are undoubtedly heavily guarded.

"The medical center is here. There will probably be several security checkpoints inside the building. Getting past them will be tricky but not impossible."

Talbot grunted. "I can't see how. Every strategy we've come up with gets us killed short of the palace. Or gets us in and probably kills the emperor in the firefight. The place is too tough for a frontal assault."

"Then you need another way in." Breckenridge made a line out of the building and off to the west. "This is an old escape tunnel. It's quite well hidden. The exterior side has a very limited access point and is heavily alarmed. The restricted size and security features only allow a few people to use it, so think two or possibly three people to perform the infiltration.

"It was built for the Imperial Family to escape. Most people have no idea it exists. It originates inside the emperor's personal suite. Quite close to the medical center, I might add."

"Just how do you know about it, then?" Talbot demanded.

The senator gave him a sardonic grin. "Because the empress used it to smuggle her most trusted lovers into her suite. I wore a blindfold, but I'm quite resourceful. I managed to locate the exit after the third trip."

Talbot considered him. "I see." He turned his gaze to Princess Elise. "Why should I believe him?"

"Because the man I love might die if he's lying, but I believe him."

That earned a slow nod.

"Very well, Senator. I'll take what you're saying at face value, but if this is some kind of trick, I'll shoot you myself."

"I'm not worried."

Talbot listened as the man began explaining what he remembered of the route. If this were true, it might mean they could pull this off. The emperor's suite was far away from the prison holding his commanding officer and girlfriend. They wouldn't be able to sneak into it.

They'd have to hit it with heavy weapons. Getting in wouldn't be easy. The palace was the most protected place on the planet. They might not see the pinnaces until late, but they *would* see them. Then they'd kill them.

He still had to find a way to get his marines inside. As impossible as that seemed. Carl had better come through in spades.

Talbot was loyal. If it came down to it, he'd save the emperor and weep for Kelsey and the admiral. He prayed another solution would present itself before he had to make the hardest choice of his life.

32

Angela watched the two men assemble the device. It was small, only just bigger than hand sized. The power requirements seemed large, but the older scientist didn't seem concerned.

It was interesting to watch them work together once Carl focused on his task. He ignored his obvious distaste for the man and just did what he needed to.

The professor spared some of his attention for Carl, but mostly fondled the equipment. He kept peppering Carl with questions that the younger man couldn't answer. Finally, Carl had the parts together.

"It requires a flat surface to work on, according to the notes I made," he said, sifting through the debris. He found some material he could use and cut it free with an Old Empire marine knife.

Once he had it, he set the knife down and blocked the professor's hand as he reached for it. "Don't test the sharpness or you might lose a finger. Its edge is almost molecular in thinness, and it's harder than any metal you're likely to have worked with. The Old Empire used hull metal for these knives."

The professor promptly withdrew his hand.

They ran power, but the device didn't want to activate. That caused a fair amount of creative cursing from Carl. She made a mental note to give him remedial training in foul language. He'd have to do better than that if they became a couple for real.

That thought made her mentally skid to a halt. Where the hell had it come from? She wasn't even considering dating him. Not a chance. No way.

Yet, she felt as though part of her disagreed. How many of her in other universes had made the same choice? Was she an idiot in all of them but this one? Probably not.

She wondered if he'd considered how the deaths of his other selves had affected her in those universes. If she'd loved him there as deeply as she believed, she'd have been crushed. Worse than when she'd lost most of her people on *Ginnie Dare*.

There was a perverse kind of horror imagining the pain she'd have felt. It took more effort than she liked to push the dark visions aside.

Carl was getting out some other equipment when she came out of her mental bubble. "This is the quantum communications device the chancellor told you about. The entangled sets of photons can be swapped out to allow communication with different people at long distances."

"How far?" Bedford asked with a softer voice than she expected. "This is the thing we were going to test? The other ship is no doubt in place by now."

"We only have a little time, so I'll set it up to communicate with your man first. Keep it short." Carl swapped out a metallic rod. "Use it like a normal communicator."

Professor Bedford touched the controls. "Watts, are you there?"

There was no response for a long moment, and then a voice came from the speaker. "Professor Bedford? Is that really you?"

"Who else sounds like me, you idiot? Where are you?"

"In the Baker system. This thing really works!"

Bedford stared intently at Carl. "Watts, what did I write on your last paper?"

"Uh… I'd rather not say."

"Watts!"

"Okay! You compared me unfavorably to a lawn ornament. A lopsided, drunken lawn ornament."

Bedford blinked. "Well, I'll be damned. It really does work."

"What should I do now, Professor?"

The question focused Bedford back on the com. "Stop wasting my time and ask the captain to go another flip out. I'll call you in a few days."

He killed the circuit before the student could respond.

"I'm deeply impressed, Owlet. You've cracked a genuine secret here. Real-time communication at interstellar distances. Remarkable. We'll have to verify the range, but even this will change so many things. It's real science, boy. To my shock, you actually did something worthwhile."

Carl's smile was decidedly lopsided and wry. "I wish I could take credit, but this is once more someone else's work on creating entangled pairs. All I did was take the theory and put it into practice.

"Then I took some secret work done in the Old Empire and figured out how to create the hardware that allowed the communications and the conversion to voice or implant signals. It's how I control that." He gestured back to the hammer still floating in the air.

"And you dismiss the real work of a scientist as futzing along like Watts does in the lab? Bah. Was meshing these theories together and creating the hardware easy?"

Carl frowned. "Hell, no. I went down so many blind alleys before I hit the solution that I almost gave up. This was work."

"Welcome to being a scientist. So, what now?"

"We call the alien intelligence that created this transport equipment and figure out what I did wrong."

Angela watched them work and slowly let out her breath. Carl had turned the professor's head, even if it didn't show very much. He'd accepted Carl as a junior associate, which as crass as it sounded, was probably the best anyone could hope for from the man.

Carl would get that doctorate. He'd probably win the Lucien Prize, too, based on the covetous looks the professor was giving the com equipment and the hammer. She'd best make sure it didn't disappear.

When Omega spoke from the com unit a few minutes later, the professor was almost reverent as Carl introduced them. A few minutes explanation had Carl making some kind of changes to the equipment.

It came on this time, making the flat surface on one side of each circle look like a mirror. Before she could say anything, Carl stuck his arm through one, and it popped out of the other a dozen meters away.

"See? No harm, no foul."

"Remarkable," Bedford said. He walked over to the bodiless hand and put a tool into it.

Carl drew his hand back and waved the tool above his head. "Omega, what's the range on this small unit?"

"Not far," the alien said through the com. "No more than a hundred kilometers."

"I think our definitions of the word may be different," Bedford said. "How long can it stay open?"

"Indefinitely, as long as there is power. The drain it creates is moderate and only requires energy on the end that creates the link."

"It's bidirectional?"

"Yes," the alien said, "though it was standard practice to have two units, each designated for one direction of travel to speed their use and avoid people or cargo colliding."

Bedford checked the connection they'd made to the power bus. "The energy requirements are enough to limit us to the one unit here. What of the larger pair?"

"There are two sets of large rings. That would allow for bidirectional travel." He mentioned a large sounding power requirement that Angela couldn't translate in her head.

Carl shook his head. "That's too much. What's the range?"

"No more than five thousand kilometers."

"That's useful, but I can't see us smuggling it into the palace."

Angela cleared her throat. "It looks as though the individual parts could pass through the smaller rings. Is that true? If so, we might be able to smuggle the larger ring into the palace through the smaller one."

"That might work," Bedford muttered. "We could tap directly into the university fusion plant, with the chancellor's approval. For this, I can convince him."

That would require them slipping a bunch of marines in powered armor onto the campus somehow. Maybe a few at a time in vans. She knew Talbot could work that out. First, they'd need access to the palace.

She mentally shrugged. That was Talbot's worry. She came for a way in and she had it. The plan was coming together.

* * *

ELISE LISTENED to them work out the basics of a plan with one eye on the time. The clock was running down, and they needed every minute.

When Major Ellis called in with a report on the alien gates, the missing parts of Talbot's plan fell into place. All they had to do was get someone in through the secret passage.

Once inside, a small group had to infiltrate the medical center without alarming the guards. Once they had the emperor protected, they could launch a major assault on the security cells. They'd be safe from the most potent protective weapons at that point.

God only knew how it would turn out, but they'd at least have a fighting chance at stopping the would-be usurper.

Talbot nodded sharply when Major Ellis finished. "This is our best bet. We have a few grav vans, so we can begin smuggling people onto the university right now.

"Meet with the chancellor. Get him on board, and get everything tested and ready for use. We kick this off in three hours. Get yourself and Carl back here as soon as possible with the smaller ring."

Once he was done, Elise cleared her throat. "Who makes the trip inside the palace?"

Talbot inclined his head toward Breckenridge. "We know at least two people can use the entrance. What stops them from letting more people in?"

"It opens onto a small car that runs to the palace. I suppose your skilled locksmith could come back for more people, but it's too small for armored marines. That magical transport ring sounds more like the right idea."

"There you go," Talbot said. "Carl is the best we have at breaking and entering using the Old Empire technology. Ellis will be his protector. If we can have a third person, it needs to be someone familiar with the palace. That means the senator. As much as I hate the idea, he's been very helpful so far."

The politician inclined his head. "I'll take that as a compliment. We should get the inside team in place as soon as we can. It might take quite some time to gain access, and Lord knows about setting up the strange transport equipment."

"We're assuming that it won't set off the alarms when it goes online," she said. "Is that certain?"

"No," Talbot said. "We probably need to have the medical center team on the way faster than that. I want them in place before we move the rest of the marines, if possible. Carl will need to come back for a marine or two to help them.

"Go get Carl and Angela. Bring some of her team along with you. Find the exit and get things moving."

Elise didn't wait for him to change his mind. She wanted to get Jared out of there before his homicidal half brother did something terrible. And Kelsey, too.

A grav van with Carl, Angela, and two marines in civilian clothes arrived. They all had large packs. Carl looked smug and Angela peeved.

"What went wrong?" Elise asked the other woman.

"The chancellor was mad. *Really* mad. And it wasn't at Carl. He blamed *me* for the damage. Man, those academics can tear a strip off you with the biggest words."

Carl grinned. "It made up for her laughing at old Professor Bedford ripping me up. I put on my best innocent face and skated by."

She shook her head. "You two are so funny. Allow me to introduce my associate, Senator Nathaniel Breckenridge. As you already know, he's providing us with a way into the palace."

Angela nodded, all business. "Excellent. What's the area around the exit like, Senator?"

"It's in a small town near the palace. Some discreet inquiries told me the building wasn't in use a few years ago. Probably intentionally. We'll be able to get in. The palace is ten kilometers away, but the hidden tube doesn't show up on their scanners."

"What about alarms on the building?" she asked.

"No problem if you have a swipe key." He produced one. "I checked after the empress left the palace. It still works. It won't open the secret exit, though. I'm not precisely sure how that part works."

"We'll figure it out once we get there," Carl said. "I've got some very sensitive scanners and the best hacking tools in the New Terran Empire. What happens when we get inside?"

Elise filled them in on Talbot's plan. "Once we have everyone in place, I'll go with the group to the emperor's side. I have the drug and I'm less threatening. I might be able to talk my way out of a confrontation. Senator Breckenridge goes with me. I'll need a neural disruptor."

Angela pulled one from her bag. "I'm not thrilled with this plan, but you're probably right. Here's to hoping we aren't too late."

33

————

C arl inventoried his tools as they flew to the secret entrance to the palace. He'd grown fairly proficient with breaking into Old Empire equipment, but this would be different.

The New Terran Empire security systems were less advanced but didn't interface with his tools in the same way. He'd have to approach this job with the deepest caution.

"We're coming in," the marine up front said. "Does the building have interior parking?"

"Yes," Senator Breckenridge said. "Go around back."

Getting inside proved as simple as landing, letting the senator open the door, and moving the grav van inside. Everyone piled out and gathered their gear.

The senator led them to a storage room with a lift. "This serves the upper floors but also has some means of going down. I'm not sure what she did to the panel to send it there."

"Let me take a look," Carl said.

He examined the panel for alarms with his handheld scanner. None. At least, no obvious ones.

The panel gave way to a common screwdriver. All the buttons had wires going to a small controller. He found a standard access port and plugged into it.

Its security was higher than one would expect from a lift unit. He thought he knew how to bypass the hardware, but he took his time in triple-checking everything.

"Is there a problem?" Angela asked.

"No. I'm just being cautious. I don't want to trigger a lockout or alarm. We only get one chance to sneak in without them catching us."

Once he was sure he understood the setup, he insinuated his control tool into the software interface. There. He saw the normal floors and a "basement" destination. That would be where the tube was. The secret control worked by pressing the first and third floors, letting them release, and pressing the first floor again.

"Everyone in?" he asked. "Here we go."

He closed the panel and pressed the buttons in the correct sequence. The doors slid shut, and the lift sank into the ground. It went down a fair bit and opened onto a small tunnel platform. There was no car.

The marines spread out, but there were no threats. There wasn't even a camera. Only a call station.

Carl saw at once that it was significantly more secure than the lift. It was a biometric lock that required an authorized retinal pattern.

He smiled. "I think this is going to be easier than we'd hoped."

At the bottom of his bag, he found one of his sophisticated hacking tools. "I can use this to provide the pattern," he said.

"How?" Angela asked. "You don't have the empress's retinal pattern. She might not even be on the access list anymore."

Carl grinned at her. "No, but I have Princess Kelsey's. I bet she's on the approved list, even if she doesn't know about the secret tunnel. We can try it once and see. If it doesn't work, I'll tear the lock apart and figure something out."

He activated Kelsey's pattern and put the eye-shaped projector against the reader. The light on the control turned green.

"I can feel air movement in the tunnel," one of the marines said after a minute.

A small pneumatic car slid into the station. It had two seats facing one another. A third person could stand between the seated riders. Four in a pinch.

"Okay, the senator and I go first," Angela said. "Carl will stand between us with the ring gear. We'll send the car back for the three of you shortly. It will take two more trips to get the equipment and you."

The senator and Angela sat inside with the bags of equipment on the floor. Carl stood between them and looked at the controls. "This is a simple go button. Press it and you'll move to the other station. We'll wait there for you."

He pressed the button and the doors slid shut. The car took off at a significant speed, tossing Carl into Angela's lap.

"This is so transparent, Owlet," she said with a laugh.

"Yes, but more comfortable than it looks." He settled into her lap and tried to control his blush. The heat of her body was doing things to him that weren't appropriate for a covert assault mission.

She put her lips beside his ear and whispered. "Maybe we should try a date when this is all over. You *are* kind of cute, in a nerdy way."

"Don't torture me."

"That depends on how well the date goes."

The car pulled into the station, and Carl was out the moment the doors opened. It was identical to the station on the other end of the line.

Angela and the senator climbed out with the gear. Carl pressed the button on the console and sent the car back for the rest of the team. Fifteen minutes and two trips later, everyone was there.

The lift was smaller on this end, so they needed two trips to get everyone into the emperor's suite. The designers had stashed the exit behind a bookcase in the library. Carl supposed that made it useful when the empress wanted to fool the emperor.

Being in his liege's home made him feel awkward. It seemed as though the man might just walk through the door at any moment.

The marines put on unpowered armor while Carl assembled the smaller ring. Angela looked over his shoulder. "So, tell me again why this one doesn't need power?"

"The connection between the two ends serves to power them both. What's the plan?"

"I'll go with Princess Elise and the senator. I'll take the men. That leaves you here alone to bring the rest of the marines in. If something goes wrong, you should be safe here."

"What if I don't want to be safe?"

"Deal with it. I get to be the hero this time."

He smiled at her. "And a hero needs something special. I can't pass the hammer on to you, but I did bring you something."

Carl dug into a bag and pulled out an arm brace that looked familiar to her. It was the portable shield he'd been working on.

"Strap this on and activate it with this code." He sent her a string of code through her implants. "There are two settings. Round and tall. Pick which works best and try not to get shot this time."

Angela took it with a grin. "This will come in handy. Thanks."

She raised her voice. "Okay, listen up, people. We'll head directly to the medical center. We might get lucky and not hit a checkpoint. Or we might get into a shootout. Stun only and protect the civilians. Let's go."

She started for the door, paused, and turned around. "I want you to hold onto something for me," she said to Carl.

Angela grabbed him, pulled him into a hug, and kissed him thoroughly. She grinned when he swayed a bit after she let him go. "See you soon, nerd boy."

* * *

Elise followed the marines into the corridor. No guards. They probably considered the sophisticated alarm and lock system good enough inside the palace.

The medical center was close to the emperor's suite, for obvious reasons. They were fine until they neared the target. Angela checked the corridor with a device that peered around the corner.

"I see at least three guards outside the medical center," she said softly. "The angle is bad to see the whole area. The curve in the hallway obscures too much."

"That's my cue," Elise said. "Senator, you're with me. If things go bad, Major, come right on in."

"Wait." Angela handed her the device Carl had given her. "Strap this on and here's the code. Keep it round, I think. This should keep you from being hit."

She took it, but frowned. "This is to keep you safe."

"I'm not the one running the risks right now. Just do it. If things go bad, both of you haul butt back here."

Elise let the senator precede her and stayed to the right. She had her neural disruptor held behind her back. She'd only get one shot, even on wide beam. The sleeve of her jacket concealed the shield.

Their caution proved warranted when they saw an additional two guards just around the bend. They were all the way up at the other end of the hall, talking as they came toward the medical center.

The men in front of the entrance straightened as they saw her and the senator. "Halt! Identify yourselves," one of them called as they all raised their weapons.

Breckenridge raised his hands a little. "I'm Senator Nathaniel Breckenridge. The Imperial Senate sent me to get an update on the emperor's health. Didn't the gate tell you I was here?"

That allayed their fear enough for them to lower their weapons slightly. They must've recognized him. Just as Elise had hoped.

She pushed the neural disruptor past Breckenridge and fired. The three men just in front of the entrance to the medical center dropped. The other two did, too, but only so they could bring their weapons to bear from the floor. They were out of stunning range.

That's where the plan went a little awry. Senator Breckenridge ran back the way they'd come, but Elise took advantage of the guards' momentary shock to race forward.

She activated the shield just in time. The bullets struck the invisible field and ricocheted into the walls. She threw herself into the medical center just as they opened fire.

A bullet smashed into her lower leg at the last moment, making her stumble, but she managed to slap the emergency lock on the door. It slid closed and sealed. Now only someone inside could open the door.

The medical people stared at her in shock. The emperor's personal physician stormed up. "What's the meaning of this?"

She deactivated the shield and gestured for him to step back with her neural disruptor. "I'm not here to hurt the emperor. I'm here to save him. Doctor Stone sent me."

"I can't use anything she sent," the man said as he backed up. "The heir gave orders not to trust anyone that might be compromised."

"Small wonder, since he poisoned his father to begin with. Well, I'm going to save him, and you can't stop me. Everyone, against the wall. How is he, Doctor?"

The man shook his head. "Worse than I'd hoped. He'll be gone soon."

"So, you really have nothing to lose. Why not give this a try?"

He gave her a lopsided smile. "Who am I to argue with the woman with a gun?"

Elise hobbled over to the emperor's bed. He was so pale. He almost looked dead already.

She brought out the vial and found an injector. Stone had trained her how to use one, so it was simple enough to slip the antidote into place and empty it into the man's arm.

There. It was done. Now all they could do was wait. She sent a signal to Major Ellis that she'd accomplished the primary mission.

"If I might be so bold," the doctor said. "You're bleeding on my floor. Let me examine your wound."

Elise sat heavily in a handy chair and raised her leg. "Why not? Don't try anything funny, or I can't tell you about what we just gave the emperor."

He gathered some instruments and supplies. "You have my word."

* * *

ANGELA RAN FORWARD when Senator Breckenridge dove back toward them. She expected Princess Elise to follow, but the crazy woman ran for the medical center. She made it.

Two quick shots from her neural disruptor took those men down, but others popped up both ahead of them and behind. They had her pinned down.

She dragged Breckenridge back against the wall and let her men cover ahead of them while she fired at the guards behind them.

Kick it, Carl. They know we're here.

Bullets struck all around her and some bounced off her armor as they edged toward the medical center. A round grazed the back of her left hand. It hurt like the devil.

They stunned enough of the guards to make it to the medical center doors. She signaled the princess to let them in.

A moment later, just as enemy reinforcements arrived, the doors slid open. They tumbled inside as a frightened nurse rapidly backed away. Angela found the manual lock and sealed the doors. Now the guards would have to cut it open. They wouldn't dare risk explosives.

One of the marines had a minor wound, but the senator had taken a shot to the side of his abdomen. "I need a medic over here!"

She leaned over Breckenridge. "Good timing, getting shot outside a medical center with a handy trauma team."

He grinned through his obvious pain. "I've always been lucky. Now I'm a wounded hero. What politician couldn't use that kind of thing? Did the princess save the emperor?"

"She gave him the shot. Now we wait to see if it works. We've done all we can."

The doctor left what he was doing to Elise to a nurse and took charge of getting the senator onto an operating table.

She set the marines to watching the door and walked over to the princess. "That was stupid. You could've been killed."

"I'm pretty sure that it's a requirement to do something crazy to be part of this club. Do I get a card and a secret handshake?"

Princess Elise pulled the shield off her forearm and handed it to Angela. "That came in handy. Too bad I turned it at the last moment, or I might have gotten off without a scratch."

"Let that be a lesson, then. Leave this kind of thing to the professionals."

The princess gasped as the nurse dug into the wound with some kind of long pliers and pulled out the slug. The woman dropped the bloody lump of metal onto the tray and started cleaning out the wound.

Angela smiled. "You deserve a medal after all that." She found something to stop the bleeding from her hand. Her marine implants would know the moment other marines made it into the palace.

"Come on, Carl," she said softly. "Don't blow it now."

34

Talbot stood in the university fusion plant work area, watching Professor Bedford and a group of technicians examined the power connections.

"Professor, this isn't the time for something to go wrong."

"Give me a moment," the old man said testily. "One of the connections must be loose."

"We don't have a moment. This isn't your latest lab experiment. Lives are on the line. Make the magic happen."

"Found it," one of the techs said triumphantly. "One second... try the power again."

Someone threw a switch and the surface of the panel across the opening turned silver.

"Go! Go! Go!" Talbot shouted at the waiting marines. Their power-armored forms ducked through the reflective surface with their weapons at the ready.

"Keep this open until we get back or I personally tell you to shut it down," Talbot said. "Clear?"

The scientist nodded. "Good luck, Major."

Talbot awkwardly locked his helmet into place. He'd be the next best thing to useless with this broken arm, but he was in armor like his men. He was going for Kelsey, and he had no pity for anyone who tried to stop him.

He was the last one through the ring. Armored men filled the Imperial suite, getting ready to make a push for the cells under the old security wing.

Carl stood off to the side. "They got the medicine to the emperor. They're holed up in the medical center. Only one seriously injured. The senator."

"Well, I'll be double damned," Talbot said. "I suppose he was serious after all. I'll detail a few men to stay with you."

The young man held up the hammer. "I'm good. Go save Kelsey and the admiral."

"I can afford a few men to secure our way out. Go back through the ring if you have to. I'm serious. Don't get shot trying to hold this position. Leave that to us."

He sent orders to his men to execute the plan. They fit through the doors with only minor damage. The lead team headed right for the security wing to block any response from the men there. The second team, led by Talbot, headed for the detention center.

The rest fanned out as they moved. He detached a squad to guard the emperor's suite. The last team headed for the medical center. They'd make certain no one harmed the emperor or Angela's people.

In their powered armor, his people were invulnerable to all but the most deadly weaponry. Nothing they'd see inside the building could hurt them. And if it did, they'd deal with it like marines.

Almost immediately, Talbot had to grab a vase that the man in front of him brushed up against. With one hand, and in powered armor, he was astonished he managed to save it from destruction. He carefully set it back on the table. It was undoubtedly worth a fortune.

"Be careful of the art," he said. "Let's not destroy our heritage."

The various teams began running into resistance almost immediately. They bulled through and stunned everyone in sight. Their attack was so unexpected and overwhelming that they made it to the security lifts in only five minutes.

The lift wouldn't respond, but they'd expected that.

"Open it up, Corporal Riviera."

The marine punched his hands through the armored metal and tore the doors out. "The lift is down below. On point." He jumped down without waiting for the order.

"By the numbers, marines. Secure our people."

They poured down the shaft, no doubt occasionally landing on one another. The armor could take it. His last squad held the lift for the retreat.

He stayed with the team up top. Someone started shooting at him from behind, but the bullets didn't worry him. He hardly staggered when they hit him with a rocket launcher. He gave them a friendly wave and started stunning people.

If everything went according to schedule, they'd be on the way back out in just a few minutes. He wanted this area under control by then.

* * *

ETHAN SAT beside Wallace Breckenridge on the Imperial yacht. They were going up to Orbital One to relieve Yeats and put Fleet under Ethan's thumb.

After the stunt at the palace, he couldn't afford to have Yeats with a knife at his back.

Unfortunately, he could already tell Breckenridge was going to be an interim appointment. He wasn't smart enough to fight a war. Not and win.

He'd been waiting for the news of his father's death, so he wasn't surprised when his com sounded. He put on a suitably somber expression and answered it. His moment of triumph was at hand.

"Yes?"

"Highness, we have a problem," his man in the Imperial Guard said. "Heavily armed intruders have broken into the palace. Sir, they have control of the medical center."

"Shit! It has to be Mertz's people. Get someone in there right now. Stop them at all costs and *protect* my father." His emphasis on protect should give the man the right idea. To shoot the emperor during his "rescue attempt."

"Highness, these people are in some kind of heavy armor. We can't get in without using a level of force that would be *guaranteed* to kill the emperor."

So, they couldn't attack that way. The majority of the Imperial Guard wouldn't stand for it. He'd just have to hope his father died anyway.

"Then see to the prisoners. Personally."

"I can't, Highness. They sent even more people there. We're trying to retake the security lift, but I'm not holding out much hope."

"Do what you can. Call me as soon as you have an idea what's happening."

He cut the call and looked at Breckenridge. "Mertz is making a play. He has people with the emperor now, and odds are he'll be free of his cell in short order."

"I knew it!" the disgraced Fleet officer said. "He's staging a coup. There's no way we can gain control of Fleet before he's loose, but I have a plan that will allow us to salvage the situation. It's risky, but the odds of victory are better than letting him take us into custody."

How could the man be so stupid? He still believed Mertz was behind everything. Unbelievable.

Still, what choice did Ethan have? Once his enemies were free, they'd put him under lock and key. His play for the Throne had failed. Unless, of course, the emperor died. Then he'd have a chance. It would probably mean a civil war, but that was a price he was willing to pay.

"Tell me your plan," he said.

* * *

JARED KNEW something was up when an explosion tossed him off his bunk and onto the floor. He crawled under it, just in case something came loose from the ceiling.

A check through his implants showed marines on his level. This was a rescue.

Things must really be desperate.

The door to his cell swung open, and an Imperial Guardsmen's boots stood in Jared's line of view. Whatever the man had been about to do, someone stunned him first. He dropped like a stone.

"Admiral, are you in there?" a marine in powered armor said from outside. He couldn't fit through the door.

"Right here." Jared rolled out from under the bunk and stood. "What's the situation?"

"We have control of this section of the palace. We're taking you back up to the medical center."

Another marine opened Kelsey's door, and she came out spoiling for trouble. "Where's Ethan?"

The marine managed a shrug in his heavy armor. "Sorry, Highness, I don't know. We have a line to take you back up. Major Talbot is waiting."

She smiled. "You found him! Excellent. Let's go."

The marines lifted the two of them back up to the main level with a line. Kelsey threw her arms around her lover. "Thank God you're okay."

She frowned. "Why are you favoring your arm?"

"It's busted. Come on. We need to make our way to the medical center. We've cleared the area, but I don't want to chance someone doing something rash."

His sister's expression told Jared she intended to do something rash to whoever hurt Talbot.

Jared stayed in the middle of the cluster of marines as they moved to the medical center. Whatever resistance they'd encountered getting in had pulled back, though some people with white bands around their arms were carrying out the bodies of Imperial Guardsmen. Stunned, he hoped.

"How much trouble are we in, Talbot?" he asked. "What's the penalty for breaking us out of custody?"

The marine grinned. "That depends on who wins, sir. If we got to the emperor in time, maybe nothing. We'll see."

The first thing Jared saw as they entered the medical center was Carl Owlet assembling some kind of device. One he'd never seen before.

"Mister Owlet."

The boy looked up. "Admiral! Good to see you again, sir."

"Did you arrange our breakout?"

"I may have played some small part in it. Princess Elise did more."

Jared looked around and saw her sitting in a chair off to the side. Her leg had a bandage around it below the knee. He rushed to her side.

"Elise, are you okay?"

Her smile glowed like the sun. "Thank God you're safe. I'm not standing up. Come give me a hug."

He did and then looked pointedly at her leg. "How did you get hurt?"

"Doing what needed doing. The doctor said I'd be fine. He's working on Senator Breckenridge now."

"Breckenridge? What is he doing here?"

"His part to make up for his nephew. The emperor is responding to the treatment. Doctor Stone is on her way down, and she's cautiously optimistic."

Jared looked around them pointedly. "I doubt she's going to get landing permission."

"Probably not, but she doesn't need it."

Carl stepped back from his equipment, and the flat surface turned silvery. Moments later, Lily Stone stepped through.

"Well, well. That *is* a surprise," Jared said in wonder. "Remind me never to count that young man out."

He looked over at where Kelsey was standing beside her father. "I hope we did enough to make a difference. Any idea where Prince Ethan is?"

"Not a clue. He'll turn up, I'm sure."

* * *

KELSEY WATCHED Lily run the medical scanner over her father with her heart in her throat. "How is he?"

Stone smiled. "The drug is slowing the poison down, and the nanites are starting to repair the damage. He's not out of the woods just yet, but he has a fighting chance now. Call it sixty-forty. If he makes it, I foresee a complete recovery."

"Will moving him lower his chances?"

"Not appreciably. I think we'd all be happier if we can get him up to *Invincible*. If he has a complication, I'll be better able to work on him."

The doctor glanced over at the Imperial physician. "It looks like he has things wrapped up with Senator Breckenridge. We'll take everyone up. Talbot! Call the pinnaces in to the university. We're leaving."

"Aye, ma'am. Everyone, make sure to keep things together as we pull out. No slipups at the last moment. The outer perimeter will pull back in to extract as soon as we're clear."

"What is that thing?" Kelsey asked Stone.

"A kind of point-to-point transfer device Carl got from Omega. I have to say it came in very handy."

"We need to hurry. I want to know where my brother is. We have to stop him."

Stone looked up from where she was preparing to move the emperor to a gurney. "I know that one. They spotted the Imperial yacht leaving orbit just as I was landing. I guess he was on his way to Orbital One and changed his mind."

"He can't run fast enough to stop me from kicking his ass," Kelsey said grimly.

She walked over to Talbot. "I need to get to *Invincible* as soon as possible."

"It should be back in orbit. Once things went down, Admiral Yeats called most of our ships back in. There are pinnaces right on the other side of that transport ring."

"Excellent. Come with me."

He shook his head. "Not until all my people are clear. You go ahead."

"Be careful." She kissed him hard.

Kelsey fell in behind the gurney as it headed for the ring and grabbed Jared by the arm. "Ethan is in orbit. We're going up right now to catch his ass."

He grinned coldly. "Let's go end this."

35

J ared found the trip through the ring surreal. One moment he was in the Imperial Palace, and the next, he was in the fusion plant at Imperial University exiting one of two large rings set up there. Almost eighty kilometers traveled in the blink of an eye.

The marines would withdraw from the palace and take the rings with them. Now that the emperor was safe, Talbot said they'd disassemble the ring in the medical center, move back to the emperor's suite, extract everyone through a second ring there, and then disassemble it. Carl and Angela would pass the rings through a smaller one and then escape out a secret tunnel.

They'd disabled the internal security monitors, so the remaining Imperial Guards wouldn't know they'd relocated. That would give them enough time to get away safely. No doubt the guards would wonder how the attack took place at all.

Hopefully, the emperor would be in a forgiving mood when he woke up. Jared refused to believe the man would die after everything they'd risked.

Once the emperor and Senator Breckenridge were aboard the pinnace, he joined Kelsey and Elise inside. He sat next to his girlfriend and hugged her as the pinnace lifted.

"This might just turn out okay after all."

"Not if Ethan escapes," she said. "We've both seen how even a failed coup can damage society. Imagine a civil war. The man is insane, and he won't hesitate to rip the Empire apart to slake his thirst for power."

Kelsey nodded sadly. "We have to stop him, Jared. If he gets away, he'll turn people that would otherwise be loyal citizens against the Empire. We cannot afford a civil war."

"Even if that means killing him?"

She sighed. "I hope it doesn't come to that."

The flight up went smoothly, and they docked with *Invincible* a few minutes later. Someone had found him a uniform to replace his prison clothes, so he took a few minutes to change before heading for the bridge. He wanted to project the right image, both for his people and Ethan Bandar.

The flag bridge was a hive of activity as he arrived. Kelsey was already standing beside his command console. She hadn't bothered changing.

"Give me a status," Jared said, as he tapped into the implant feeds and looked for himself.

Commander Jade Winslow, his chief of staff, turned to face him. "A number of cutters left Orbital One and docked with *New York* half an hour ago. Apparently, Captain Breckenridge hijacked it. Most of her officers and crew were off the ship, so they couldn't resist marine boarding parties.

"It took us a while to realize that was what had happened. It and the Imperial yacht are already quite a distance away. Only our destroyers or fighters have a chance of catching them."

The officer shook her head. "They made a really bad call. We don't need to chase them that fast. They're running for the Nova system flip point, sir."

* * *

WALLACE BRECKENRIDGE SAT in the command chair of his new ship. A destroyer was a big step down for him, but beggars couldn't be choosers.

His arrival on board *New York* had surprised the skeleton crew, and his men had managed to seize control. He wished he'd had enough people to grab something bigger, but she would do. After all, he'd be able to replace her with something much more modern very shortly.

"Lieutenant Heller, what is the status of the Fleet vessels still in orbit?" he asked his lead man.

The officer turned from the helm controls. "No change, sir. They're still sitting there with those battle screens of theirs down. The Imperial yacht and we are too far away for them to catch us short of the new flip point. From there, we should be able to get to the flip point heading for Harrison's World."

Breckenridge nodded with satisfaction. One of his spies had gotten a heading and distance from this flip point to the other one. They'd be able to make the trip quickly enough to arrive before Mertz. Once there, the heir would be able to leverage his rank into a new headquarters that the Bastard wouldn't be able to budge him from.

Honestly, he thought it was a brilliant plan and was quite pleased with it.

"How long on the timer?" he asked.

"Three minutes and twenty-two seconds."

He smiled wolfishly. The Bastard would be getting a big surprise. He wished he could see his face when the universe fell on him.

* * *

JARED WAS JUST ABOUT to order *Invincible* out of orbit when the general quarters alarm sounded.

Winslow hunched over her console. "Missile launch! Multiple missiles inbound at point-blank range."

"Battle screens up," Marcus said. "Firing beams in defensive mode. Impacts in two... one..."

The massive ship lurched under the explosions, but no fresh alarms wailed.

"Status," Jared snapped.

"Battle screens at sixty percent," Marcus said. "No loss of hull integrity."

"Who fired those missiles?"

"No one, Admiral. They came to life near the area where *New York* was in her parking orbit. They must've preprogrammed them and ejected them."

Jared slowly nodded. "That's actually pretty clever. We didn't spot them because we weren't looking. If you hadn't had the battle screens ready for immediate use, they'd have sucker punched us. Scan for any other little surprises he might have left for us."

The AI was silent for a moment. "No other anomalies detected, Admiral."

"Good. Commander Winslow, signal our ships to leave orbit at flank speed. Let's see if we can close the distance enough to talk them out of this insanity."

* * *

ETHAN SAT at the command console on his yacht. He had Breckenridge on screen from *New York*. The officer had scraped the barrel and gotten enough men and women personally loyal to him to control the ship. Barely.

"Are you certain this is the right way to go?" he asked the renegade Fleet officer. "Other than the basic data, we have no idea where this new flip point leads. The report was heavily restricted, and I never looked into it. I had more pressing things on my mind."

"We know the important part, Highness," the renegade Fleet officer said. "It leads to the Old Empire where they got those ships. You can order the Fleet units there to stand down. We can still turn this around. Many officers will rush to support you over the Bastard."

Ethan nodded. Of course they would. Except for those who had been secretly against him from the beginning. Like Breckenridge's former executive officer. He'd have to go. There would be no more coddling traitors.

Mertz had been diabolically clever. He'd sewn men loyal to him in so many places. Everything was a gamble. But he knew he could overawe the

Fleet stooges Mertz had left at Harrison's World. They would never defy him in person. He could turn this all around.

"What kind of force is guarding the new flip point on our side?" he asked.

The Fleet officer looked at his console. "A single destroyer. I've already sent them orders to move away from the flip point."

"Will they?"

The other man laughed. "They won't fire on the heir to the Throne, if that's what you're worried about. If they do, I have a lot more experience. I'll take them out."

The commander of the Imperial yacht turned toward Ethan. "Highness, we're receiving a signal from Fleet."

"Put it on the main screen," Ethan said. "Split the view between it and Admiral Breckenridge."

Rather than one of the officers from the destroyer, he found himself looking at Jared Mertz and Kelsey. Mertz was in uniform, but Kelsey was still in her prison clothes. He wondered what that meant.

"Ethan Bandar, Wallace Breckenridge, I'm ordering you to heave to and prepare to be boarded," Mertz said sternly. "This is over. We have the emperor under our care, and he's going to survive your assassination attempt."

The officers on the yacht's bridge all looked up at that, shock clearly written on their faces.

Ethan sneered. "You don't frighten me, Bastard. This fight is far from over. If you think you can just fire on the heir to the Throne, you're very much mistaken. The people would rise up against you."

He smiled a little wider. "Even if what you said just now were true, which of course it isn't, the Empire would go up like a tinderbox. No matter what you do, you lose."

* * *

KELSEY SIGHED and considered what her twin had just said. "He's right, Jared. Blowing him up would tear the Empire apart." She stared at her brother for a long moment. "Let him go."

Jared turned to her, surprise written all over his face. "But——"

She felt hollow inside as she held up her hand. "This is my decision to make. It's the best thing for the Empire if we don't stop him."

Kelsey kept her eyes steady on Ethan's smirking face. "Make no mistake, anyone taking that flip with you is guilty of treason and subject to death. No warning and no quarter. Your crew doesn't know what you're asking of them. Give them a choice to leave."

Ethan laughed. "They swore their lives to serve the emperor. They know where their place is. But, if any cowards want to scamper away, good riddance."

He smiled nastily at her. "We'll meet again, dearest sister, and sooner than you think."

"Make your peace with God, Ethan," she said, her throat closing up on the words. "His is the only forgiveness you'll find in this life or the next."

She made a gesture to cut the signal.

Jared rose from his seat. "The yacht doesn't have battle screens. The radiation will kill him."

"Yes, it will."

The silence on the flag bridge was deafening.

Jared nodded slowly. "I understand and I'm sorry, Kelsey. They have another half hour to change their minds. To come to their senses."

But they didn't.

A number of escape pods from both ships told her that they'd allowed those wanting to leave to depart. That made her feel a little better. Only those embracing Ethan would die.

* * *

FAR TOO MANY of the crewmen on the yacht had abandoned Ethan, but Breckenridge had sent a few more trained officers over by cutter as they approached the new flip point. *New York* would guard the flip point on this side to give Ethan time to sprint to Harrison's World.

"Transition in ten seconds, Highness," the new help officer reported.

"Take us over when ready."

The time dragged until the universe twisted. They'd flipped.

A loud alarm blasted from the overhead speakers. Ethan covered his ears. "What is that?"

The helm officer spun in his seat. "We're being bombarded by heavy radiation, Highness. It's blasting right though the hull."

"Are we in danger? Get us out of here."

"The flip capacitor is charging. I'll flip us back as soon as I can. Highness, the dosage is high enough to be fatal in just a few minutes."

Ethan leaned forward, staring at the man incredulously. "How did they ever get through here? Why didn't that idiot Breckenridge warn me?"

He suspected this was some kind of twisted assassination plot. Breckenridge had been some kind of plant. As stupid as that sounded, he'd been in Mertz's pocket all along. The man's entire plan had been to trick Ethan into killing himself.

Well, that wouldn't work. He'd flip back to Avalon and overcome this. Somehow.

A different alarm began sounding.

"What now?"

The man stared at his console for a long moment without responding. When he turned, his expression told Ethan he had bad news.

"The flip drive shorted out. They're trying to get it back online, but it won't matter." The man's eyes were hollow. "All the systems are taking damage from the radiation. We're going to take a fatal dose before they're done. We'll be walking dead men even if they succeed."

Ethan swallowed noisily. "And if they don't?"

"I'm no doctor, but in five minutes we'll be in excruciating pain. We'll be throwing up and voiding from the other end as well. In fifteen minutes, we'll be dead and glad this is over."

He felt as though he could already sense the churning in his gut as the lethal radiation rotted him from the inside out.

"Are there any other options?" he asked, his throat dry.

"One," the man said. "We might be able to overload the fusion plant. That would be a lot cleaner way to go."

"Kill that noise."

The silence was almost more deafening than the alarm.

Ethan waited for the time to run out. Once it became clear that they weren't going to make it, he nodded toward the man. "Do it. Blow up the ship."

The lights flickered and went out. After a moment, they came back on dimly.

"The fusion plant just failed, Highness," the man said. "The capacitor is less than half charged. I don't suppose any of your people brought sidearms."

"My guards," he said numbly.

"I suggest you call one up here. We have need of his services."

* * *

ONCE THE YACHT HAD FLIPPED, Kelsey sat at one of the auxiliary stations. It was done. Only the pain remained to endure. Something she knew entirely too much about.

New York stayed in the flip point, possibly guarding it to give Ethan more time. Breckenridge had no way to know her brother was already dying.

Oddly, the emotions inside her were subdued. She knew what she'd done, but it didn't feel real. Not yet.

Twenty minutes later, just as *Invincible* and her escorts were coming close, *New York* flipped to the Nova system. A minute later, they were back. Breckenridge must have realized his mistake.

Their exposure had been short. If he surrendered now, he'd live.

Jared nodded to Winslow. "Signal *New York* to surrender."

Of course Breckenridge didn't. The destroyer opened fire on *Invincible*. It was ridiculous. They couldn't even get through her battle screens.

"Return fire," Jared said coolly.

He'd probably meant just the superdreadnought, but all their ships fired a salvo. *New York* never stood a chance. She died in fire long before the massed beams of the Old Empire ships destroyed every missile Breckenridge had fired.

Kelsey felt bad for Eliyanna Kaiser. The woman had lost her ship. Well,

Jared would find something for her. Somehow, the fact all of Breckenridge's task force was now gone felt appropriate.

"Send a destroyer over to recover the yacht," she said, her voice sounding tired and hollow to her.

Jared rose from his seat and pulled her into a hug. "I'm so sorry."

She should've cried like a baby, but the tears refused to come. She knew the shock wouldn't last long. The flag bridge wasn't the place to have a breakdown, either. "Thanks. I'm going down to check on my father."

The trip to the medical center was a blur. Her mind couldn't pull away from the horror she'd tricked her brother into. Even after everything he'd done, she'd still loved him deep down.

She'd killed him just as effectively as if she'd leveled a plasma rifle at him and pulled the trigger.

The little boy that had chased her through the Imperial Gardens, laughing like a fool, was dead, and she'd killed him.

Kelsey walked into the medical center in a fog of grief so strong she almost ran into Lily Stone.

The other woman gripped her shoulders and pulled her into her office. "Kelsey, what's wrong?"

"I killed my brother."

"Oh, honey." The other woman pulled her into a tight hug, and Kelsey cried. Another pair of arms surrounded her. Elise was holding her, too. All three of them cried.

No one said anything or asked questions. They just gave her the support she desperately needed right then. She knew Jared would have done the same, but she couldn't afford to break down in public like this.

They pulled apart at last, and Lily brought Kelsey some tissues. "I know this makes no difference whatsoever, but you did what you had to. He was a mad dog bent on wrecking the Empire."

"I know," Kelsey said, her voice filled with grief. "But we were kids together. He was my world once. That doesn't go away even when people go bad. I have to tell my father, if he ever wakes up."

"Then let me give you some good news. The nanites have turned the corner for him. He's going to be fine."

A man in white knocked on the hatch. "Doctor, the emperor is awake."

Kelsey hurried out after Lily. Her father lay on a bed surrounded by medical equipment, but his eyes were open. It took all her willpower to stand back and let Lily check the readings.

"How are you feeling, Majesty?" Lily asked.

"Like a grav truck ran over me and then backed up to make sure I was down." His voice was a ghost of its normal self. "What happened?"

Lily glanced over her shoulder. "I'll let Kelsey tell you."

She stepped back and lowered her voice. "No stress just now. Save the bad news until he's stronger."

"I'll keep it easy, but he's the emperor. I have to tell him something, or he'll keep after me and worry even more."

Kelsey stepped up beside the bed and took his hand in hers. "I'm so glad to see you getting better, Papa. You really scared us."

He smiled up at her. "You haven't called me that since you were a little girl. Tell me true. Is everything okay?"

She shook her head. "No, Papa, but things will get better now. I did what needed to be done. The Empire is safe, and you're going to make a full recovery."

"What happened?"

"Not now. You'll just have to trust me when I say the danger has passed. When you're stronger, we'll talk about it. I'll tell you everything. I promise."

He looked at her steadily. "Where's Ethan?"

"He can't be here right now," she said with more strength than she'd thought she'd had. "You're on *Invincible*."

"I feel as though you're leaving something important out, but I can't seem to focus. I'm sorry, but I'm so tired."

Lily stepped in. "Your father needs to rest. He'll be a lot stronger tomorrow. Why don't you get some sleep yourself?"

"I think I will. Goodnight, Papa." She kissed him on the forehead.

Elise limped over to her as she was heading for the hatch. "Would you like some company?"

She shook her head. "Thank you, but no. I need to be alone."

The other woman hugged her again. "Call me if you want to talk. Day or night."

"I will. Thank you."

A check of the ship's systems told her that the pinnace with Talbot on board was just leaving Avalon. She had hours before she could cry all over him. In the meantime, she'd sit in the observation lounge, watch the stars, and remember the laughter of a little boy who'd once meant the world to her.

36

Elise sat beside Jared as he waited for the board of inquiry to make their findings public. The last month had been brutal. Most of the citizens in the Empire hadn't had time to comprehend the emperor's poisoning before the heir was dead, but that did nothing to stop the backlash it caused.

Kelsey had retreated into private, but the more extreme news groups—both conservative and liberal—roundly lambasted her for not taking the heir into custody so that the authorities could discover the "actual facts" of the situation. Conspiracy theories abounded.

She'd taken her brother's death hard. Harder than her father had. Her friends tried to be there for her, but she'd pushed them all away. Even Talbot.

That hurt him, too, but he put on a brave face for her. Elise had helped him understand it wasn't him, but that only went so far.

He'd eventually bulled his way back into her life, and she was starting to show signs of coming out from under the black clouds her life had become.

Elise knew that she'd recover and be sad that she pushed them all away in time. Jared understood, too. They'd be there for her when that time came.

The emperor had tried to blunt the criticism, but his own grief made that difficult. Now the Imperial Senate was locked in a vicious battle over whether to deny Kelsey the position of heir or not. That situation would come to a head today. Kelsey said she didn't care, but Elise doubted that.

Her strongest advocate no doubt surprised her. Senator Nathaniel Breckenridge gave fiery speeches denouncing those who fought against the emperor's will. His usual stance as the opposition undermined his normal allies' positions but didn't stop the fighting. It only made it bloodier.

Nathaniel Breckenridge had insisted Elise not tell Kelsey what he suspected about her genetics. That he'd tell her when the time felt right. Elise thought that was excellent judgment.

At least the Senate had settled the treaty issues before it had plunged off the deep end. The Senate had accepted Harrison's World and Erorsi into the Imperial fold and confirmed their new senators. They'd even validated Emperor Marcus's edict.

They'd amended the Imperial Charter to allow for worlds orphaned during the Fall, too. Pentagar was now officially an ally, but not part of the Empire. They'd exchanged official embassies, and trade had begun. Captain Anton Keller and his new ship, *Best Deal II*, had made the inaugural run.

The hatch to the side of the room slid aside, and the members of the board walked to the table. Admiral Jack Lancaster banged a gavel and brought the proceedings to order.

"This board has considered all aspects of the events that occurred during expedition fifteen and the actions of Admiral Jared Mertz. It has taken a long time to hear every bit of testimony and consider what happened. For that delay, this board apologizes. Admiral Mertz, please rise."

Jared stood. His back was straight, but Elise could see the tension in him. He was ready for them to send him to a court-martial.

"Admiral Jared Mertz, it is the judgment of this board that you acted in accordance with Fleet regulations and made the best decisions circumstances allowed. In your place, this board fears it would have made a catastrophic mess of the situation.

"It is our belief that you acted in the finest traditions of Fleet and that no further action is necessary. This board stands adjourned."

There were some approving cries, but mostly the mood was somber. The last month hadn't brought anyone much joy.

Elise stood and took his hand. "I knew you'd be fine."

He smiled at her. "That's one of us, then. I'm just glad it's over so we can move on to other problems."

"Like Kelsey's confirmation? If we hurry, we might be able to make the hearing."

"We'll have time. That hearing won't be ending anytime soon."

"Probably not," she conceded. "We should still go show our support."

"Then let's go. We can just make the next cutter if we hurry."

* * *

TALBOT SAT beside Kelsey in the emperor's box at the Imperial Senate. He didn't know how she kept such a cool expression on her face while that rat-faced bastard stood there at the podium slandering her. He was sorely tempted to go over the rail and make him regret those artfully-crafted insults.

The pompous ass had no idea the horrible pain she'd been in. How much she still suffered. It had taken every bit of his love to get inside her dark world, plant his back to hers, and help her fight back. A lesser man might've given up, but he'd lasted her out.

She'd spent most of the last month in the dojo. She'd earned her black belt and then devoted herself to earning the last mark of distinction. Sensei. Ned had grudgingly granted her the red stripe this morning.

Kelsey tightened her grip on his hand. "Homicidal thoughts are acceptable. Actions, not so much."

"He pisses me off. Raving on about how you murdered your brother. He knows the facts, though he isn't shy about saying you and the admiral made the whole thing up. Like you're the villain of this story. Asshole."

"That's the spirit. I don't care what he thinks. I don't care what any of them think. The only opinions I value are my friends and my father."

The emperor had taken the death of his son hard, but to his credit, he hadn't blamed Kelsey. He'd blamed himself. He'd backed Kelsey to the hilt and nominated her to replace Ethan as the heir as soon as the official period of mourning was over. And hadn't that been throwing red meat to the wolves?

Leaving aside all the whacky conspiracy theories, they talked about her parentage as if she were a broodmare. One senator had even called into question her place in the peerage because she was sleeping with Talbot.

That bastard was going to pay one day very soon. Talbot had a fantasy about punching his lights out.

Frankly, Talbot had mostly stayed away from listening to them "debate" to protect his blood pressure. And to keep himself out of prison.

"What happens if they decline to name you heir?" he asked. "You were the second in line to the Throne. Are you no longer a princess? Not that I care one damned bit if you have a title or not."

She smiled at him. "Some people have advocated stripping me of my title, but odds are I'd keep it. Father has declined to disown me, so that movement won't go anywhere.

"More likely, they'll decide I'm not worthy to be heir and start looking for someone more to their liking. I'm fine with that, too. I just want this over so I can put my life back together."

She looked at him and sighed. "I'm so sorry I've put you through this, Russ. I don't deserve you."

He kissed her, knowing that some bastard would get a picture. Screw them. "Well, I won't say this has been easy, but I deserve you, so don't give me any flack."

She took a deep breath as the senator speaking wrapped up his denunciation. "It's time for me to go piss everyone off."

Kelsey rose to her feet and met Jared and Elise as they opened the box door. She hugged her brother. "Thank you for coming. How did it go?"

"No court-martial," he said. "And we wouldn't have missed being here for you."

"Thank God," she said fervently. "Now sit down and watch as I ruin my future."

His commanding officer and Princess Elise sat beside Talbot.

"She's joking, right?" Jared asked.

"Her humor's been so black recently, I'm not sure."

Elise looked at his dress uniform. "I see she talked you into wearing your medals. It looks good on you."

The emperor had held the longest awards ceremony in Imperial history last week. The list of all the people who'd died was read aloud at The Spire. Then they'd announced the posthumous medals for valor.

The event had been acid on his soul. He'd wept without shame when the emperor awarded the Imperial Cross to Timothy Reese, laid to rest with the rank of Lieutenant Colonel.

A number of living people had received the Empire's highest award. Admiral Mertz, for example. Well deserved, there.

He'd been less happy when they'd given it to him. He hadn't earned it. Not like everyone else. The knighthood that went with it was somehow subtly insulting. He was a marine ground pounder, not a pampered noble. He was as common as they came, and them thinking they could change him into something else just rubbed him the wrong way.

"I only wore it because she told me to," he said stubbornly.

He saw understanding in the admiral's eyes. "She's a smart one, my sister. Don't let her get away."

Kelsey appeared at the podium. She gripped it and looked out over the sea of faces in the senatorial boxes and the visitor's gallery. Rather than speak, she just stared at them until the murmuring started.

Then she spoke.

"I come before this august body to discuss my place in the succession. Or, I should say, that's what many of you believe I'm here for. It's not."

Talbot swore he could hear a pin drop in the silence that statement left. Even with his enhanced hearing.

"I don't care one damned bit if you vote for me as the heir," she declared in a ringing voice. "In fact, I urge you to find someone else. Someone less likely to offend your delicate sensibilities. Someone less like the 'cold-hearted bitch' one of you referred to me as.

"If you do confirm me, I'll do whatever I think is best for the Empire, no matter whose feelings it hurts. No matter the cost, to either me or anyone else. I killed my brother because he was a threat to the Empire. That's the kind of person I am."

That started a lot of chatter in the boxes, making the speaker pound his gavel for order.

Kelsey didn't wait for them to quiet down. "While we're on touchy subjects, let me clarify how I feel about my parentage. I don't have a single drop of Imperial blood in my veins. If that bothers you, go screw yourselves."

That brought a roar from both the boxes and visitor's gallery. A mixture of rage and glee. Talbot found himself on his feet screaming his support of her.

"Tell them off, Kelsey!" he shouted.

She cranked the volume on her microphone up and spoke over the bedlam.

"Do whatever you want. It's all this body of puffed-up, self-important chatterboxes has ever done. Find a talking head to be the next emperor and see how long he keeps the rebels off your necks. I'll stick with fighting them face to face. At least that's honest work."

She turned her back on the pandemonium she'd caused and left the podium.

Jared stood there and started slow clapping. The visitor's gallery picked it up next. Even some of the senators. The new senators from Harrison's World and Erorsi were the most ardent in their support.

Talbot noticed Nathaniel Breckenridge had a wide grin on his face. He inclined his head toward the man.

Kelsey rejoined them a few moments later. "Well, I think that should settle matters," she said as she sat beside Talbot. "Now I can put this behind me and get down to the real work."

He squeezed her hand. "You were awesome."

"At least that should end the debate," Elise said with a grin. "They'll either love you or hate you for saying those things."

"You always have a spot with me," Jared said.

"Thanks," Kelsey said. "I might need it if they banish me."

The speaker finally got things under control. He recognized Senator Breckenridge.

Breckenridge climbed to the podium and looked out over the Senate. "Everyone knows I've never been the strongest supporter of the emperor, but today I stand by his side. Do we want a milquetoast as the heir or do we want someone with fire in her belly? Someone who says they love the Empire or someone who has demonstrated it with their every action? Their every sacrifice.

"Princess Kelsey said some harsh things. Things that might have hurt your delicate feelings. Well, look at those of us who have disgraced ourselves in speaking of her like that. It's unworthy of the Imperial Senate. Unworthy of a crowd in a bar, for that matter. We deserved to hear her tell us the truth."

He glared at the men and women before him. "It's time to show your true colors. Are you men and women with spine or weaklings made of ego? I nominate Princess Kelsey Bandar for heir to the Imperial Throne."

A voice cried out a second.

"We have a motion to vote on the emperor's petition to recognize Princess Kelsey Bandar as heir to the Imperial Throne," the speaker said. "Cast your votes on the electronic system now."

Talbot tried to hold out some hope, but he couldn't see her winning after the dose of bitter truth she'd given them.

A few minutes passed as various senators argued with one another. Some *very* loudly. Talbot wondered how many duels this was going to spawn.

The speaker finally gave the senators sixty seconds' warning. Once that time ran out, the man looked down at his board with a grave expression.

"The Imperial Senate has spoken. All rise and welcome the heir to the Imperial Throne, Princess Kelsey Bandar, to her new position."

The tally board showed the vote had been close. The new senators from Erorsi and Harrison's World had turned the trick.

Kelsey looked shocked, but she was more so when Talbot whooped and swung her up into the air.

* * *

ANGELA TURNED OFF THE SCREEN. The sight of Princess Kelsey's shocked expression was the perfect end to the whole crappy process.

She looked over at where Carl sat on the couch. They'd seen each other socially a number of times over the last month, and she was now convinced she'd been an idiot to fight this. He might be young, but he had spirit and heart.

"All's well that ends well," she said.

"I got a call while the vote was happening. I took it on my implants. It was the Lucien Committee."

When he didn't say anything more, she reached over and smacked him on the back of the head. "Don't keep me wondering. What did they say?"

He took a deep breath and shook his head. Her heart plummeted. She'd been so sure he'd win.

"I can't understand why, but they somehow think what I did was worthy of the award."

It took her a moment to process what he'd said, and then she leapt to her feet and yanked him off the couch and into a hug. "You won, you rat!"

"But I didn't deserve it! And I sure as hell didn't earn the Imperial Cross. It's ridiculous."

She set him on his feet and glared at him. "Let me tell you a little secret, nerd boy. Other people tell us when we're worthy of something. That or we end up like Prince Ethan or Professor Bedford. Don't second-guess their judgment."

"Professor Bedford isn't actually that bad, now that I know him better. Once they gave me my PhD—which I also didn't earn—he started treating me like a colleague. Though he still doesn't understand why the quantum com works the way it does."

She'd heard him talking about it enough over the last month to know the details. The com worked through a flip point, but not two. Distance didn't seem to be a factor. It was almost a thousand light years to Nova and it worked, but two shorter hops didn't.

It seemed that a single trip through a flip point used up most of its energy. Oh, it was still useful throughout the target system, but not any interstellar distance beyond it.

That wasn't to say that it didn't work through normal space. They'd taken one around a great loop and found it worked at three hundred light years along a straight line, even after it had stopped working due to there being too many intervening flip points.

That didn't match up with the theory at all, so everyone was scratching their heads. Including that old reprobate, Professor Bedford. It wouldn't stop them from creating a network of FTL repeaters, though. A call to Pentagar could take place in real time. Or to the other side of the universe, if they built enough coms to rebroadcast the transmission.

This was going to change everything. Galactic civilization would never be the same. If the Old Empire had had these devices, the rebellion would never have succeeded.

Bedford had also been stunned to learn of the bodies from other universes. No one had known what to do with them, other than give them an honorable burial, but the scientist was certain there must be some kind of subtle differences that might shed light on how those alternate realities worked and what laws governed them.

Carl was just glad it kept the old man out of his hair.

Angela shook her head. "That's because he respects what you've done, dolt. These people aren't honoring you for the toys you've built. It's the mind inside that scrawny body they drool all over."

He started to say something, but she put her hands on her hips and leaned over him. "Personally, I think they're being hasty, though. All those other versions of me were onto something."

He frowned. "What?"

"I think it's time to take our relationship to the next level, Doctor Owlet. Or should I call you Sir Carl? I want to know what I've been missing."

She smiled at his shocked expression.

"Unless, of course, you'd rather not have sex with me."

He shook his head emphatically. "I'd carry you off if I could lift you."

"Don't worry about it, sport. You do the thinking, and I'll do all the hard work."

Angela tossed him over her shoulder and headed for her bedroom while he laughed. Finally, something felt perfectly right in her life.

RECON IN FORCE

BOOK SIX

Know your enemies. Especially those capable of crushing you like a bug.

Princess Kelsey Bandar must lead a bold strike deep into enemy space to steal the technology the New Terran Empire needs to survive.

Success gives them a fighting chance. Failure dooms them to death and worse.

1

Admiral Jared Mertz wrapped up his presentation to the senior Fleet officers aboard Orbital One with more than a hint of relief. Everyone had seen the data they'd brought back from Harrison's World about the Rebel Empire, but it was still hard for them to get their minds around. Particularly the scope and danger their enemies represented.

He understood the conceptual challenges they faced. Before the expedition, he'd felt the same way. The Old Empire had died over half a millennium ago. They'd known that all their lives. The New Terran Empire, as Kelsey had come to call them for convenience, was a peaceful civilization. One not ready for a war to the death.

Which was what they found themselves saddled with.

Thankfully, Admiral Yeats wasn't the kind of man to roll over when faced with such an overwhelming threat. He was just the man they needed in Fleet command at a time like this.

The older man rose to his feet. "Thank you, Admiral Mertz."

Yeats looked over the sea of faces as Jared resumed his seat. "This is a lot to have dumped on us with no warning. Even a month is hardly enough time to let it sink in, but we don't have the luxury of sitting on our butts and hoping the Rebel Empire doesn't come calling.

"We could've had the displeasure of an enemy fleet dropping by instead of the forces Admiral Mertz brought home. Make no mistake, those ships are a godsend, but we're still way behind the curve.

"We'll continue receiving repaired ships from Harrison's World, but we need to start building our own. The first of the captured shipyards at Erorsi will be fully operational in thirty days. The other one was badly damaged and will take longer. The ones we're building from scratch will take over a year to become operational.

"The shipyards at Erorsi are small, as well. Each will be able to build two destroyers or light cruisers at a time, or a single heavy cruiser. Nothing larger. The shipyards we're creating here at Avalon will have dozens of slips, each capable of building any size ship we want. Once those are online, we'll start building others throughout the New Terran Empire for redundancy and to increase production.

"As each shipyard comes online, it will begin construction of an initial set of destroyers to make certain all systems are operational and that the personnel are completely up to speed. That first set of ships will take about nine months. I expect the timeframe will be a few months shorter for an experienced construction crew.

"They'll move up to larger hulls once we're confident that everything is progressing well. Expected construction times are as follows: seven months for destroyers, twelve months for light cruisers, sixteen months for heavy cruisers, twenty-two months for battlecruisers, and thirty months for superdreadnoughts and carriers."

He gave them a long, serious look. "That means it will be years before we have anything close to the fleet we want. We'll need to be cautious in how we deploy what we have. Speaking of those ships, Captain Quinn, you're up next."

The slender woman rose to her feet. "We've fully manned the ships Admiral Mertz brought back, but we're running up against some hardware constraints as we work on the rest of the existing Fleet personnel. Boxer Station and the Grant Research Facility have sent all the completed implants they have on hand, but even their reserves are limited. We need to get our own implant manufacturing capability online.

"The factory ships have helped, and we've started refining the requisite materials and building our own implant infrastructure, but that will take at least another month to get fully off the ground just for what we need in Fleet.

"The civilian side will take a year or more to really get rolling here on Avalon. The rest of the Empire will take longer. We're focusing on the critical personnel first.

"We'll have the civilian implant manufacturing capability at Avalon running at full speed inside a year. Updating existing equipment to use them will take longer. Perhaps another year just for the most critical systems.

"I'm estimating that it will take between two and three years before we've incorporated implant usage into every facet of civilian manufacturing and have it all rolled out to the general population. Fleet has priority, of course, so we'll have retrofitted everything in about eighteen months. We've already begun that process."

Yeats nodded. "The basic computer systems on Orbital One have been upgraded to allow us to use implants. We're all no doubt pleased that the administrative tasks go by much more quickly, but the paperwork never seems to end, does it?"

That brought a round of laughter.

Yeats rose to his feet, hands behind his back. "Thank you, Captain."

He focused on the rest of the compartment. "The information that Harrison's World has on the rest of the Rebel Empire is sparse and inconsistent. I'm tempted to believe that some of what they do have is misinformation. In fact, we'll assume it probably is.

"The captured AI didn't have any data on the area outside the sector it controlled. That had to be intentional. Not only does the ruling AI not want its human subjects to know too much, it doesn't want the cybernetic competition knowing it, either. That makes stamping out any rebellions easier, I suppose. Such as what they did at Harrison's World. It doesn't make our jobs any simpler, though."

Jared cleared his throat. "If I may, sir, I think I have a partial solution."

The older man gestured for him to continue. "By all means, Admiral Mertz."

This wasn't going to be an easy sell, but Jared knew the time had come to make his pitch. He sent a command to the screen, and it changed to a picture of their captured Rebel Empire computer specialist.

"Meet Lieutenant Commander Michael Richards, Rebel Empire Fleet. We captured him at Erorsi. It's taken a while, but he's come to the conclusion that we're telling him the truth. That the AIs lied to his people, and that they're slaves. He's ready to help us in every way he can. In particular, he knows the system where they picked up the Marine Raider hardware."

Yeats nodded, but his expression tightened. "Why should we trust him? Forgive me, but the man has to have reservations. If someone switched sides once, they can always change their mind again. How can we possibly trust that he isn't leading us into a trap?"

"Marcus vetted him through his implants," Jared said. "That's where the subject opens up access and allows the AI to verify the truth of his statements. Richards is honestly convinced his people are slaves and is willing to help us."

After a moment, Yeats shook his head. "I need to think about that. I'll want more information on this vetting process, too. If it's as effective as you say, it will be useful with the other prisoners.

"Speaking of Marcus, where are we in building more AIs like him? We could use some help with all this work."

Doctor Leonard rose to his feet. "We've been hard at work reverse engineering the hardware, but progress is slow. Sir Carl tells me that it will take at least a year to design complete plans, and then we'd need to build one as a test. A test, by the way, that will almost certainly fail.

"A realistic timeframe for success might be three to five years. Any serious setbacks—of which there will be a few—will delay the project further. If we could get our hands on the plans somewhere, that would be extremely helpful."

Quinn made a face. "I suspect the odds of that are low. Can't Marcus help?"

The elderly scientist shook his head. "That timeframe already includes as much help as Marcus and Harrison can give. Without them, the time required goes up dramatically and the chances of overall success plummet."

Yeats sighed. "Of course they do. Can you give us an update on the flip-point jammer project?"

"It's not proceeding as well as I had hoped, Admiral," the scientist said. "The people at the Grant Research Facility built the three existing units by hand over a period of years. They didn't anticipate mass production for quite some time.

"While they're working diligently to correct that deficiency, it will be at least six months before we see the first new units roll off the line. It may take longer if they run into problems. Even then, the number of units produced in a month will be low until they get extra production lines working."

Yeats grimaced but nodded. "That isn't unexpected. We'll just have to hope that things stay relatively quiet for a while. Once we can get more of the flip-point jammers, we can start protecting our space from the rebels and even disrupt the sectors we intend to take away from them.

"We have teams going over the maps of the Old Empire you brought back to present various scenarios where we might surgically use flip-point jammers to disrupt the enemy. A number of choke points have suggested themselves."

"There's going to be another supply ship for the AI at Erorsi in about a month," Jared said. "There's also a destroyer due to go report on Harrison's World a month after that. Either one of those situations could blow up in our faces."

One of the officers in the crowd raised his hand. "Are they likely to be suspicious, Admiral? You took out their last supply mission."

Now it was Jared's turn to grimace. That comedy of errors was the late and unlamented Wallace Breckenridge's fault. They'd lost ships and men that hadn't needed to die.

"I think this year is safe," he told the man. "The records indicate that ships have vanished before. Even warships. That speaks to some other situation that we're unaware of but gives us some breathing room. No doubt, the loss of this second set of ships will cause us more trouble. Our time of being undiscovered is coming to an end."

"Could the alien build flip points into the Rebel Empire?" a woman with captain's tabs asked. "That would allow us to strike anywhere we choose."

Jared shook his head. "Omega says the power requirements are quite steep. He has at least four months of steady charging ahead to recover the energy needed to create even one. I floated the idea of providing him with extra fusion plants and power storage, but the hurdles are too steep. His people designed his hull to stay sealed, so we can't just build a massive exterior station to support him. Everything would need to go inside the station.

"The problem there is that our power generation and storage technology is woefully inferior to his. The word he used to describe our current technology is 'adorable.' We have a team of people working on rectifying that, but it will take time to even understand the principles his people are using."

"We also need to keep in mind that these new flip points are permanent. If we open one into rebel-held space, they can use it to get to us. We should keep that idea in reserve, but I strongly suggest we avoid it until it will have a decisive impact."

"Agreed," Yeats said. "On the plus side, Sir Carl has finalized the design of the FTL coms. We'll begin seeding them throughout the Empire over the next few months and should have reliable, redundant, real-time communication throughout the Empire inside a year.

"Unfortunately, he's discovered that this technology isn't quite as undetectable as he'd originally believed. They do cause a resonance similar to, but far weaker than, a flip point. We will need to be cautious about using them in forward areas. They're a tremendous asset, and we don't want to tip our hand to the enemy.

"That leads me to the next subject. In consultation with our best ops planners, as well as Marcus and Harrison, I've decided that we need to firm up our understanding of the Rebel Empire. We need reliable data.

"The best candidate for that mission is Admiral Mertz, of course. I'm authorizing a reconnaissance in force. He won't be taking *all* the ships he brought back, but we'll send him with enough strength to take care of business if it comes down to it."

Yeats looked around the room. "Fleet has always relied on its commanders to make the hard calls for themselves, and I see no reason to change that. If the Rebel Empire manages to disrupt our new means of communication, we need people willing and able to act decisively. There will be no micromanagement from the rear in Fleet."

That brought a palpable sigh of relief from the crowd.

"We'll send *Invincible* as the flagship on this scouting mission," Yeats continued, "and about half of the ships Admiral Mertz brought back with him. The freshly recommissioned superdreadnought *Gibraltar* will form the core of our new Home Fleet once it arrives.

"And before any of you start casting covetous glances at her, I've decided that I'm moving my flag there as soon as she arrives."

He glared at them for emphasis, earning a rumble of laughter.

"Admiral Mertz, I want you to capture the supply ship intact this time. Preferably the escort, too, but definitely the freighter. Princess Kelsey has been hounding me about needing the supplies it carries. She wants more raiders, as do the emperor and I.

"Then you'll need to scout for the facility that made them. If the information on the freighter matches what Commander Richards told us, I'll revisit my decision about him accompanying you.

"Let me be clear. I not only want you to capture the supplies but to get the technology to make more. The princess's manuals only cover the use of

Raider enhancements, not the construction of them. We *need* that knowledge if we're to survive and fight effectively."

Jared nodded. "You can count on me to do my best, Admiral."

"I know I can. We haven't finalized the timeline yet, but expect us to pull the trigger on the reconnaissance in the very near future. As in no more than a week, but probably less than that. We absolutely cannot afford to allow the enemy to know we're here."

The older man smiled. "Also, I've spoken with His Majesty about the current situation on *Persephone*. He said that it is not acceptable to have a civilian in command of a Fleet or Marine Raider vessel."

"Princess Kelsey isn't going to be happy about that, and neither is the computer controlling the ship," Jared said. Unhappy was probably an understatement.

"I know," Yeats said. "So we've decided to commission her as a colonel in the Imperial Marines. She'll find out later today that she's the new commanding officer of the Marine Raiders. If she's going to fight, we might as well get rid of the fiction that she isn't a warrior."

"It's about time, sir. She'll be pleased."

"Major Talbot will be less so, I'm sure," Yeats said with a smile. "I also have something in mind for your carrier and her escorts. It's a bit unusual, but I think it's the best course of action given the circumstances. We really don't have any people trained in fighter operations, so I intend to keep Zia Anderson in command.

"She doesn't have the rank for it, but I'm also placing her in charge of the carrier group. The job belongs to a commodore or admiral, but I'm not quite ready to shift any of the existing flag officers to do that, particularly since they don't have a firm grasp on what being a fighter commander is really about."

Jared felt the corners of his mouth rise. "She's going to feel even more out of her depth. She was only a lieutenant when this all started."

Yeats nodded. "I understand, but we all have to step up. I'm transferring a very experienced executive officer to help her with that. He has a much firmer grasp of running a ship, even with his weakness in fighter operations and unfamiliarity with implants.

"She'll have to bring him up to speed. Once that happens, she'll have someone to share the load. Then we can talk about promoting people. I have some thoughts that I'll share with you about that later."

"Aye, sir."

"Now, we have a lot more ground to cover before we can wrap up," Yeats said briskly. "I've got people waiting outside to brief us on the status of our remedial training on Old Empire technology, the drive to recruit the people we'll need to man all the ships we're planning to build, the greatly expanded ground forces we'll require, our transition to a wartime economy, and more. Get comfortable."

Jared resisted the urge to check the time. This was going to be a really, *really* long day.

* * *

KELSEY BANDAR, heir to the Imperial Throne, banged her head on the table in the Imperial library. She'd gone over everything they still had in electronic form from before the Fall, and there was no reference to the "key" that Emperor Marcus had mentioned his son Lucien having.

It was infuriating. Surely, the words he'd used in his last transmission meant *something*.

She'd spent the last month going through the archives of old equipment. There were plenty of keys of one kind or another but nothing that seemed to have any deeper meaning.

To help sort things out, she'd shanghaied the newly created Doctor Carl Owlet to help. Sir Carl when she was particularly cranky.

He'd examined the data with every tool he'd designed for things like this. Still nothing.

"Excuse me," he said from behind her. "Are you all right?"

She raised her head and sighed. "Yes. I'm just frustrated. I was so *sure* there was something here."

He shrugged. "Apparently not. Is this all the hardware left over from before the Fall?"

"Yes."

"Maybe we need to take a step back and look at the person rather than the gear," he said. "Emperor Lucien arrived as a boy. Perhaps he didn't know what this key was or the person tasked with telling him died in the attack."

She rubbed her face. "His guards shoved him into an escape pod and blasted it free as soon as they got close to Avalon. The rebels still almost killed him anyway.

"He had people with him, but no advisors. He basically arrived with the clothes on his back."

Carl nodded. "Is the escape pod still in existence? Perhaps they hid something inside it. Or even dropped it there during the chaos."

Her head came up. "That's not a bad idea."

"Of course not," he said with a twinkle in his eyes. "I came up with it."

She laughed.

They'd linked the Imperial Library to an Old Empire computer, so searching the records wasn't nearly as difficult as it would've been a year ago.

"Got it," she said as the data came up in her implants. "The escape pod is on permanent loan to the Imperial Air and Space Museum. Let's go give it a look."

Her guards formed up around them as they headed for the parking garage. She hadn't wanted to accept the fact she needed them, but being the heir was part theater. The men and women of the Imperial Guard were the price she paid for being one breath away from the Throne.

Of course, since they'd locked her up a month ago, she'd insisted they get implants and be questioned closely about their loyalty to the Throne and her. That had scared off more than a few applicants.

With reason, it seemed. Ethan had had his fingers deep into their number. Follow-up investigations were still under way.

She knew the men and women assigned to her were loyal. They wouldn't turn on her. They also wouldn't let her wander off unescorted. Dammit.

The trip to the museum entailed her grav limo and two follow cars. Officially. She knew that there were two Fleet fighters circling the area in case she needed heavy backup.

Hopefully, that wasn't going to be a problem here at home, but considering the number of times things had gone badly, she wasn't going to complain.

She checked her internal chronometer. "We don't have a lot of time. I'm supposed to meet Senator Breckenridge for dinner. Probably something political and boring, but the man took a flechette for my father. I owe it to him."

Carl nodded. "That's perfect, actually. Angela and I have a little getaway planned. She rented a cabin up in the woods for some quality time. I'm not supposed to know about it, but she has terrible computer security habits."

Kelsey gave him a stern look. "Just because someone leaves their door cracked open doesn't mean you should walk in and look around."

He made a dismissive noise. "It's as though she left it lying on the counter. She knows I know. I'm not sure what that means, but it's probably important." He sighed. "Relationships are hard."

"Yes, they are. They take work on everyone's part."

Kelsey turned her head and smiled a little. He was right, as far as he knew. His girlfriend, Major Angela Ellis of the Imperial Marines, had arranged with Kelsey to borrow the Imperial Retreat. They'd plotted together to leave enough information lying about to give Carl the wrong impression but not enough to clue him in that they were running a disinformation campaign.

The grav limo landed outside the museum, and her guards formed up around her as they went in. The crowds were just as large as one might expect. Wide-eyed kids and equally interested adults examining the artifacts left over from the Old Empire. There was so much to see. More than she'd anticipated.

It had artifacts from before the Fall and from their slow climb back into space. She imagined it would have a number of new exhibits before long.

She'd come here as a kid herself. The thought darkened her mood. She'd had just as much fun as the people around her at her brother Ethan's side. Now he was dead at her hand. Basically.

He'd tried to kill their father and take the Throne for himself. She'd had no choice. It still hurt. It was like cutting off her own arm. She knew the pain would never fully go away.

A man in a dark suit walked toward her, but the guards stopped him. After a moment, they let him through, though they kept a close eye on him.

He bowed low. "Highness, welcome to the Imperial Air and Space Museum. I'm Director Chandra. How can I be of assistance?"

"Thank you for taking time out of your busy day to meet me, Director. This is my associate, Doctor Owlet. We need to examine Lucien's escape pod."

He looked a bit confused at that but nodded. "Of course. It's in the main space wing. This way, please."

It only took a few minutes to get there.

The escape pod had no doubt seen better days, but the museum had painstakingly restored it. It sat in a display that looked like a hillside. The hatch was open, and a bold-faced youth stood there looking out. The mannequin was very lifelike, though she knew the boy must've been terrified during the real events.

She started to step over the rope, but the director stopped her.

"I'm sorry, but you can't go inside. It's a delicate relic."

Kelsey smiled at him. "I assure you it's sturdier than it looks, Director. The Old Empire built to last. We believe there might be something inside that the Empire needs."

The poor man looked of two minds, but he nodded. "Please be careful. I cannot overstate how historically important this relic is."

"Sir Carl is our most respected expert in Old Empire technology. I realize this is an unusual situation, but I happen to know we have a number of things we've brought back during the expedition that are in need of a good home."

She could see in his eyes that that made a difference but didn't entirely ease his worry. He let them in, though.

When the guards made to follow her, Kelsey stopped them. "There's not going to be any danger in there. Why don't you focus on the crowd?"

She and Carl stepped past the false Lucien and into the pod. It was a standard Old Empire model that held two dozen people in zero comfort. Much like a marine pinnace, the passengers were strapped to the walls and packed like fish in a tin. There wasn't even a control console.

"Do you suppose the power is still on?" she asked.

"Not a chance," Carl said as he walked deeper into the pod. "The power packs wouldn't have lasted more than a few months."

He set his bag down in front of a large access panel. "The power connections are behind here. I have a small fusion pack in my bag for emergencies."

She knew it wasn't Mjölnir. The high-tech hammer he'd built for her was safely tucked away in her personal armory.

"Exactly what kind of emergencies are you expecting, and why do you need a fusion pack in your bag?"

He grinned at her. "Why do you need the arsenal you carry around? Because it might come in *really* handy in a pinch."

She couldn't argue with that.

It only took him a few moments to open the panel. The power packs were obvious and marked. Their indicators were dark.

Carl pulled out a fusion power pack the size of his fist and started connecting it to the ports. The lights began coming on.

Once she was sure the on-board computer had come online, she linked with it. It wasn't much more than a basic interface, but it had what she was looking for. Records of the descent and landing, both interior and exterior. It also had an encrypted copy of the ship's logs at the time it ejected. Those might be invaluable.

If nothing else, the records were historically priceless. Now the people of the Empire could see for themselves the moment everything changed for Avalon.

The recording started as soon as the escape pod jettisoned. That made sense. Why waste data storage on noncritical periods?

The interior view showed the pod packed with more people than its designers had ever intended. Mostly women and children. Lucien was easy to spot.

Someone—probably a guard—had strapped him in. The boy struggled free of the restraints as the pod raced away from its doomed mother ship, awkwardly helping a woman with a baby into his place.

Kelsey swelled with pride. That was the man he'd become one day shining through.

The external view captured her attention at that point. The pod was moving rapidly, but Kelsey recognized what the mother ship was. A battlecruiser much like *Courageous*. The computer labeled her as *Lancelot*.

Explosions wreathed her as she returned fire at unseen enemies, shielding the escape pods with her own hull and battle screens. Pods continued flooding from her until she exploded without warning.

The pod tumbled badly. A piece of shrapnel from the ship must've struck it. The people inside were thrown around like leaves in a whirlwind. Some died. Kelsey could see that as her heart flew into her throat.

Lucien smashed into the wall and somehow hung onto a harness. The woman inside clutched at him desperately. He looked as though his arm were broken.

The pod straightened moments later and entered the atmosphere at what an observer might charitably call an unsafe speed. The external cameras went offline moments later.

Kelsey imagined anyone on the ground who happened to be looking up saw the pod as a finger of fire racing across the sky.

The pod could still sense the surface, and it braked hard just before impact. That ripped Lucien free from the woman's grip and slammed him into the forward bulkhead.

Once it was safely on the ground, the hatch slid open, and people started trying to get free from their restraints. They had to be afraid death was still coming for them. In their place, Kelsey would've been.

Lucien staggered to his feet and cradled his arm. Yeah, that was an ugly break. In that moment, he looked so much like the mannequin it was spooky. Determination steamed off him. It made her proud.

The woman who'd held him tried to help him out, but he shook his head. Kelsey wished there was sound to hear what he'd said to her.

The boy-emperor leaned against the wall and opened a storage compartment. He dug inside and pulled out a pack. He opened it and partially extracted something, obviously examining it for damage. It was an object she was *very* familiar with. Understanding flooded her.

"Isn't that…" Carl started.

"The Imperial Scepter," Kelsey finished breathlessly. "It must be the key Emperor Marcus was talking about."

2

———————

Captain Zia Anderson was certain the crew thought she was crazy, but she couldn't help herself. Here it was late on third shift and she was wandering the corridors of her new command. Her first command.

The Fleet carrier *Audacious* was both an Old Empire ship—with all the bells and whistles that implied—and a completely new kind of warship for the New Terran Empire. Fighters hadn't made a comeback after the Fall, so none of the so-called wiser heads was really sure how to fit them into their battle plans.

That left it to her to come up with fighter doctrine all on her own. Oh, the Old Empire had a ton of books on the subject, but no living person had ever put them to use. Reading something was not the same as living it.

Ever since Princess Kelsey had promoted her and Admiral Mertz had assigned her to command *Audacious*, she'd been learning and refining what she knew and dragging the crew along with her.

A little more than a month was not enough time to get them even into a modicum of shape in her opinion. The ship's crew was coming along nicely, but the pilots in her squadrons were still learning the basics of their craft. Pun intended.

She was learning along with them, though at a slower pace. She'd never been much of a pilot, but anyone that served on the command crew of a Fleet ship knew enough to take over someone else's station in a pinch. As a tactical officer, she'd sat right next to their pilot—Pasco Ramirez—for years. She could get a ship from point A to B well enough.

That wasn't nearly enough to fly a fighter well, so she'd been spending a lot of time in the simulators. That meant being there when the pilots were mostly asleep. A captain didn't make a big display of her ignorance. She had to seem competent at every aspect of her command.

Now, after drilling for a month, she was about ready to take a real fighter out. It had her both nervous and excited. She'd flown with other pilots before, but only under their watchful eyes. This was her first solo excursion.

Zia walked onto the flight deck and found Commander Annette Vitter waiting for her. Vitter was a comrade from her service on *Athena*, their original ship. She'd been one of their best cutter pilots.

The other woman smiled. "You ready to take her for a spin, Captain?"

The "her" in question was a sleek fighter sitting on the launch rack with the rest of the ready birds. Vitter had had the ready team prep her for flight, but Zia intended to go over every centimeter of the craft before she climbed in.

"You bet," Zia said. "I'll start the preflight."

She couldn't help but look at Vitter's right arm every time she saw the other woman. One day, maybe, she'd be able to forget that the pilot had lost it in a pinnace crash. One that her skill had turned from outright destruction into something barely survivable.

Princess Kelsey had gotten a tourniquet on her quickly enough to save her life, and the doctors on Harrison's World had created this life-like artificial limb that interfaced with the woman's nervous system just as well as the original.

Vitter had been the obvious choice as the lead pilot, and the princess had promoted the woman while she was still in rehab. She'd taken to fighters like a marine to booze and cards, and she was wickedly good.

In addition to her overall command of every fighter on the ship, she personally led Black Jack Squadron. If needed, her second was more than capable of stepping in to take over while the woman guided all of three squadrons in action.

Her title was archaic and hoary with age. It came from the time when the only carriers on Terra were in the wet navy and limited to only atmospheric work. She was the Commander, Air Group, or CAG.

Admiral Yeats had been skeptical of the usefulness of the fighters at first. Then Vitter had led her people on a simulated attack run, swarming Orbital One. Even knowing they were coming hadn't been enough to save the space station. Not then, and not in the follow-up runs he'd ordered.

After that, he'd become a fervent convert, running roughshod over any of his subordinates who weren't as eager to embrace the new technology. He'd taken enough spare fighters recovered from the graveyard to outfit Orbital One, and they were still installing the new flight decks there.

A second carrier would be arriving at Avalon in a few more months, but he wanted to have a ready force to help defend against any threats. Unlike when Admiral Mertz had used his in combat, they were significantly more effective in large numbers.

Zia focused on the preflight. Her implants provided the checklist and could even expand on what she should be seeing, so it didn't take long.

Vitter stood back, watching. She was already dressed in her bulky flight suit. Zia would need to change before they launched.

"I'll go gear up," Zia said once she was satisfied with the external preflight.

"Locker A-1 is reserved for you, ma'am. It'll always have your gear ready to roll."

She smiled a little. "I'm afraid my job is on the command deck, Annette. Sending you people to do what you do best."

"Maybe, but that doesn't mean you don't have a place here. My people respect you."

That meant a lot to Zia. She knew that once they got into the thick of it, all too many of her pilots wouldn't be coming back. It was dangerous work.

"Not any more than I respect them. I'll be right back."

Zia went into the ready room and waved at the on-duty pilots. They were all dressed to launch at a moment's notice but were engaged in everything from sleeping to watching entertainment vids to playing poker.

Those who were awake called out greetings as she made her way to the adjacent compartment with the lockers. She quickly stripped off her uniform and pulled on an under suit. It would keep her alive if all else failed. Princess Kelsey had proven that with the one she wore under her armor at Boxer Station.

Once she had the snug under suit on, she climbed into the bulky flight suit and arrayed her survival gear. The more capable equipment would allow her to survive for up to a day if everything went south. A beacon on her hip would lead CSAR to her or any other pilot who successfully ejected from a crippled fighter.

Not that doing so was standard practice, regardless of what Admiral Mertz had done. The deadly little craft could keep a pilot breathing for a week, just based on the emergency supplies it carried. They'd only bail if it were in danger of exploding.

Her helmet was sleek and aggressive in styling. That fit the mentality of the people attracted to the job. Hotshots, each and every one of them.

They'd decorated her helmet with all three squadron emblems, which filled her with pride. The rear of a pilot's helmet usually only had their own squadron's badge. They had arranged hers in a diamond with *Audacious*'s emblem sitting on top.

She headed back out only to run into a pair of the ready pilots. They checked her gear over matter-of-factly. Part of her felt like objecting, but she knew they'd do the same for one another.

"Thanks, boys," she said once they finished. "Don't break anything while I'm gone."

Their leader grinned. "Who? Us? Have a good flight, Captain."

Vitter was standing next to one of the ready fighters when Zia came out. "Your call sign for this flight is Black Jack One, Captain. I'm Black Jack Six."

Zia nodded. "Got it."

She climbed into her fighter. It only took a moment to bring everything online via her implants, and she got down to the task of checking every system.

Once she was ready, she opened a channel to Vitter. "Black Jack Six, this is Black Jack One. Ready for launch."

"Copy that, Black Jack One. Contact flight operations and launch when ready."

Zia opened a channel to them. "Flight operations, this is Black Jack One requesting a launch window."

"Copy that, Black Jack One," Lieutenant Leo Thomas said. "You are cleared to launch at your discretion."

"Thanks, Control. Black Jack One out."

She sent the command to the magnetic catapult her fighter rested on. It came to life and hurled her down the short tunnel and out of the ship with brutal force, pressing her deeply back into her acceleration couch.

Once clear of the ship, she brought her drive online, and it instantly cut the perceived acceleration down to something bearable.

Moments later, Vitter's fighter appeared off to port. She could see the woman looking at her through her canopy. "Good launch, Black Jack One. Let's put you through your paces. I hope you studied all the maneuvers carefully, because I'm a stickler for detail."

Over the next two hours, Vitter taxed Zia's memory, skills, and endurance. They went through virtually every scenario a fighter pilot needed to perform. Everything except an ejection. That was a bit traumatic for the little craft.

"That's a wrap, Black Jack One," Vitter finally said. "You need to work on a few things, but overall, I'm satisfied with your progress. You're still a greenhorn, but you'll do in a pinch."

Damned with faint praise. Zia smiled. She really was on the low end skill-wise, and she knew it.

"I'll take it, for now, but I'm going to keep practicing."

"Roger that. Contact control and take us in," Vitter said. "You'll only have an hour to get cleaned up and onto that fancy bridge of yours before all the lazybones are up."

Zia called *Audacious*'s flight operations and got them a return vector. They positively dawdled back to the ship. Once they were in the area, Control gave her priority over a passenger cutter inbound for landing.

Unlike most ships, all small ships used the carrier's flight decks rather than isolated docks.

The landing priority apparently didn't sit too well with the cutter pilot. She could hear him arguing with control. He claimed to have a senior officer on board.

Control called Zia. "Black Jack One, this is Control. The inbound cutter is requesting priority in the landing queue. Are you okay with coming around again?"

"Negative, Control. Black Jack flight will land first."

"Copy that, Black Jack One."

The other pilot shut up once he acknowledged Control's instructions, but Zia imagined he was pissed. Too bad.

Zia led the way in and put the fighter neatly down in the designated area. Vitter landed beside her.

The cutter took a spot just up the deck, and the passenger hatch opened as soon as it settled. A large man with wide shoulders and a grim expression exited and headed right for the fighters.

Well, this should be interesting.

She opened her canopy and shut the fighter down before climbing out. The man was waiting impatiently below her. His rank tabs indicated he was a commander.

"What the hell was that? Didn't you hear my pilot say there was a senior officer on board?"

Zia held out a hand, cutting Vitter's hot response off. "I heard you just fine, Commander. This is a carrier. Fighter operations always have priority."

"Helmet off, pilot. When I'm chewing ass, I want to see who I'm talking to."

That really tanned Zia's hide. She had a volatile temper, when she allowed it to rear its ugly head, and this guy was pushing her buttons.

She popped her helmet off and held it in the crook of her arm. She ran a hand through her hair to get it into some semblance of order.

The man glared down at her. "I realize you people think you're all that and a bag of crisps, but the universe doesn't revolve around you. What's your name?"

"Anderson. Call sign Black Jack One."

"Well, Anderson, you'd better be glad I don't have time to deal with you right now. You can be sure that once I've reported to the captain, we'll have another discussion that you won't enjoy nearly as much as this one."

Zia frowned. She hadn't been expecting anyone coming to see her.

"And why would that be, Commander?" she asked.

He smiled a bit smugly. "Because I'm your new executive officer. I don't know how you people have been doing things, but they'll be by the book going forward. Expect my call, Anderson."

He turned on his heel before she could respond and headed for the lift.

Vitter stepped up beside her. "Why didn't you tell him you were the captain, ma'am?"

"Because it'll have a bigger impact if I let him find out the hard way. He wanted to make a point by browbeating me, so now he gets to get the same kind of treatment.

"I'm a bit concerned that I didn't hear about this ahead of time. I knew Commander Leonidas was going to receive his own command, but I thought he had another week."

The other woman smiled knowingly. "The ways of the personnel branch are obscure, ma'am. You know what I think? That if I had orders to a new ship, I'd make sure and at least know what my commanding officer looked like."

"That's because you're a prudent and thoughtful officer. I can see this new guy is going to have a rough time adjusting to how we do business. I should go get cleaned up and get this over with."

Zia called her steward while she stripped her gear off and told him to stall the man. She took a quick shower, dressed in her uniform, and headed back into the ready room.

She stopped in her tracks as soon as she came in. It looked as though every fighter pilot on the ship was there.

Commander Vitter stood in front with a wicked smile on her face. "Captain Zia Anderson, you have met all of the qualifications to be a Fleet fighter pilot. It is my pleasure to welcome you to our ranks, but my sad duty to inform you there is yet one more burden to be borne. Attention on the flight deck!"

Every person in the room stiffened, including Zia. She still wasn't completely used to being a senior officer, and a commander still felt like a superior to the lieutenant inside her.

"The fighter corps has a tradition when welcoming people to its ranks that goes back to before humanity ever left the surface of Terra," Vitter said conversationally. "One that left a mark on all who accepted our deadly burden. Captain Zia Anderson, are you willing to shed blood for your brothers and sisters? To suffer pain for them?"

That was an easy one. "I am."

"Then open your tunic."

That was an odd thing to do, but Zia opened the top of her uniform tunic, exposing her undershirt.

"Once pilots wore wings of metal on their uniforms, not patches sealed into place," the pilot said. "That meant that our wings had bite."

She held up a set of metal wings with two long spikes in the back. Zia suddenly knew what was coming.

"Each and every pilot on this ship has shed their blood with these very wings to join our ranks. Your nanites might heal the wounds quickly, but the pain and symbolism mean a great deal to us."

The woman placed the wings on Zia's upper left chest and used the heel of her fist to pound it into her captain's flesh.

The spike of pain was immediate and intense, but Zia gritted her teeth and made no sound. She kept her expression neutral though her chest was on fire.

Vitter waited a beat and pulled the spikes back out. Another pilot stepped forward with a swab and tugged the under tunic aside long enough to wipe away the blood. He applied two dabs of medical sealer to the aching wounds and stepped back.

"Pilots, I give you our newest sister!" Vitter said.

Everyone shouted raucously and crowded around Zia, pounding her on the back and shaking her hand. It was such a powerful moment that it took everything Zia had not to cry, but she averted that catastrophe. Barely.

Once all the pilots had left, except the ready crew, Vitter shook Zia's hand. "We're glad to have you in our ranks, Captain. We know you'll make us proud."

"That was barbaric but damned powerful."

The other woman laughed. "We're warriors, ma'am. We spill blood for a living. The marines have nothing on us."

Zia couldn't help smiling in return. "Well, I suppose I'd better get upstairs and shed some blood of my own."

She left the flight deck energized. This had been one of those moments that changed people's lives forever, and she'd never forget it. Now she had to go try to inoculate the new guy with the same bug, as difficult as that seemed to imagine at the moment.

* * *

ANNETTE WATCHED her commanding officer walk out with more than a dash of pride. The former tactical officer was shaping up into a fine leader. She still had some growing to do, but that was true for all of them. Particularly herself.

Her assistant squadron commander, Lieutenant Commander Jake Fiennes, stepped up beside her. "She's a good one."

"I was just thinking that. I'm wondering how she'll handle the new guy. They didn't exactly get off on the right foot."

He snorted. "You think? Well, he'll either adjust or get rolled."

She gave him a raised eyebrow. "That isn't the way to think about our new executive officer. I know all fighter pilots are wild cards, but there are limits to the meme. Whatever his personality, we're going to have to work under his orders."

Jake seemed to consider that for a moment and then nodded. "I suppose so. The captain will set the tone, but he's going to do what he does. We have to make sure our boys and girls don't raise too big a stink."

"Good man. How are the deployment plans coming?"

She'd tasked him and the other squadron commanders to devise an attack plan for a fleet action. Fighter deployment was new to all of them, and she wanted to have a number of primary, backup, contingency, and emergency plans worked out and practiced ahead of when they needed them.

The notion that people rose up to meet a crisis was wrong. They defaulted to what they'd trained to do. She didn't want her people to practice until they got it right. She wanted them to be so skilled that they couldn't get it wrong.

"We have a number of basic strategies worked out," he said as they walked into her office. "*Audacious*'s computer had all the plans the previous squadron commanders worked up for various scenarios. We kept that framework in place and broke them down even further so we can practice the basic skills they already had down pat.

"The training we've already gotten will slot into the new plans easily enough. Once we get on station, we can launch training flights to stitch everything together. It'll take years before we're as smooth as they probably were, but we can be effective much sooner than that."

She nodded. "That works. I'll want to see a preliminary training schedule this afternoon. I'll have my comments back to you as soon as I can to refine what you have. After the training run, of course."

"Roger that. If you'll excuse me, I'll go get the squadron ready to launch."

Annette sat behind her desk as soon as he'd left and brought up the Fleet records on Brandon Levy.

Last assigned as the commanding officer on a heavy cruiser. He'd also commanded a destroyer a few years back.

She couldn't access the sensitive parts of his record, but the theme was there for anyone who looked. Levy was a competent officer with solid skills. He'd have a much better grasp of running a ship than Zia Anderson, even though Annette thought the other woman was doing fine.

The new guy would have two strikes against him. First, his attitude. Second, he didn't understand the new technology. Not that the rest of them were as far along as they needed to be, but he'd have more ground to cover. Not just skill-wise, but conceptually. Understanding that something was even possible gave one a leg up.

Or an arm.

She held up her artificial arm. The technological marvel still astounded her. When she'd lost it, she'd known her career was over. She'd become a cripple. Someone to be pitied.

Only that wasn't how things had turned out. The doctors in the command post on Erorsi had the full know-how of the Old Empire at their fingertips. They couldn't build a sophisticated arm like this one with their limited facilities, but they'd laid the groundwork.

The doctors on Harrison's World had built her arm with her piloting in mind. The rehabilitation hadn't been easy, but she came into it determined to regain everything she'd lost.

Months of blood, sweat, and tears had paid off. It was almost as natural as her real arm had been now. She could perform any task she needed to with as much finesse and dexterity as any uninjured person.

Annette knew she'd have to help the new guy if they were to avoid a nasty situation where he didn't grow the way he needed to. The fighter pilots under her command were vulnerable to someone that didn't truly understand their purpose. She'd have to make sure the new guy didn't dismiss them out of hand or file them away as glorified cutter pilots.

Unfortunately, it certainly seemed as though Brandon Levy had already put them in that mental space. Tomorrow, she'd make his acquaintance. She'd be a friendly face and make sure he assimilated. That way she could shape his views before they became a problem.

Well, she could worry about him after the training flight. He wasn't going anywhere. She rose to her feet and headed for the ready room.

3

———————

Kelsey arrived at Senator Breckenridge's home a few minutes early but close enough to be considered punctual. There was an art to arriving to dinner parties that was a bit hard to understand for the uninitiated. It wasn't all about being fashionably late.

Frankly, she'd rather have examined the Imperial Scepter, but with Carl and Angela off on their getaway, it wouldn't have mattered. Only someone with his level of technical expertise could even hope to make head or tail out of something as complex as it probably was.

She'd decided not to tell her father until they had at least a little information. After all, any discovery had already waited half a millennium for them to find. It could hold for a few more days.

The senator's palatial home seemed a little deserted to be hosting a dinner party. She'd expected to find guests already in the landing area and on the balcony overlooking it. The lights were on, and there were uniformed Senatorial Guards, but no guests.

God, she hoped she hadn't misremembered the time. Or the date.

She checked her implants as they landed. No, right on time. Something else was going on.

The Imperial Guard formed a cordon around the air car as she exited. There wasn't any visible tension between them and their senatorial counterparts. They'd no doubt worked together before and coordinated her arrival.

The door to the house opened, and Senator Breckenridge himself came out with a smile on his face. "Welcome to my home, Highness."

She held out her hand. "I was worried I misremembered the date. Where are your other guests?"

"My apologies. I thought you understood it was only the two of us."

Looking back, she didn't think he'd ever said one way or the other. She'd made an assumption. This was a little disconcerting. Not because she worried about being alone with the man. Even discounting her guards, she could handle herself just fine.

"This is all suitably mysterious," she said as she allowed him to escort her inside. "I'm thinking you want to do more than small talk."

He nodded. "We can adjourn to my parlor. There's plenty of room for the guards, though I want to discuss a personal matter that requires some discretion. We can eat beforehand, if you're hungry. That might be best, honestly. You might not be in the mood to dine when we're done."

"That doesn't sound promising. I say we just trot it out and get it over with. If I feel like eating when we're done, we will. If not, I can storm out in a huff with a sandwich."

His parlor was filled with family history, she saw. Old paintings and far too many knick-knacks to count. It seemed like a very comfortable space.

There were two chairs waiting for them near the fireplace. It wasn't cold out, but someone had laid a small fire. A decanter of amber liquid and some glasses sat on a small table between the chairs.

Breckenridge saw her to her seat and poured them both a drink. She sipped hers as he sat. She preferred beer, much to her father's horror, but could recognize the quality of excellent scotch when she tasted it.

"Shall we dance around the meat of the matter for a while, or do you just want to trot it out, Senator?"

He smiled. "I think I like the new you better than the old one. Not that I had any problem with you before, Highness. You've got spine now, though."

Breckenridge sipped his drink. "Though I will admit that doesn't make what I need to say any easier."

She racked her brain but couldn't figure out what had the man all worked up. He'd recovered from his injuries sustained helping rescue the emperor and had firmly advocated for her to become the Imperial Heir, even though she hadn't really cared one way or the other.

"You might as well tell me, Senator. I have no idea what has you in an uproar." She looked over at her guards. "I'd like you to wait outside. Also, please turn off your enhanced hearing."

They weren't happy, but they left as instructed. His guards followed them out and closed the door softly.

Breckenridge set his glass on the table. "I know you've read the report on the rescue mission to save your father, but there were certain details that were left out at my request. I felt that I needed to say them face to face when the time was right. Such as the fact that I provided access to the Imperial escape tunnel."

She frowned. "I looked it over. It was biometrically keyed."

"Indeed it was, but I was the only available person who knew where it was located . I'm sorry to have put this so baldly, but I don't think dancing around it will make any of this easier. I was the empress's paramour."

Kelsey opened her mouth to say something and then closed it again.

The news shocked and dumbfounded her, so she was better off saying nothing until she knew what she wanted to say.

After a moment, she started again. "I should be surprised—and I suppose I am—but I already knew my mother had betrayed her vows. I'm disappointed to hear you helped her do it, Senator."

He nodded. "It was a long time ago, but I should've exercised better judgment. I intend to make a similar confession to His Majesty, but I felt I needed to explain myself to you first."

"I don't see the logic in that," she said. "Your apology to him makes a lot more sense than one to me. I'm not affected by—"

Her thoughts screeched to an abrupt halt. If he felt as though his dalliance with her mother was important to Kelsey, that had to mean…

He nodded. "I can see you've figured it out. I didn't even suspect until you came back. The times match up too closely to dismiss. I spoke with Crown Princess Elise, and she had me consult with Doctor Stone. I set up this meeting as soon as I was sure. This is a terrible way to break the news, but I can't think of a better one. Biologically, I'm your father."

* * *

JARED WALKED into his father's quarters without a guard at his heel for the first time. He had no doubt they were deeply unhappy with that, but the emperor had been firm on that point.

Over the last month, he'd seen his father more times than he had since he'd discovered his heritage. It made him uncomfortable at first—even more so than before—but the man had just lost his son. The same son that had betrayed and almost killed him.

Jared supposed that might've played into the Imperial Guard wanting to keep an eye on him. Honestly, he couldn't blame them. The emperor had come very close to dying.

A week ago, the older man had undergone the implant procedure. Doctor Stone said he'd come through perfectly. The Imperial Guard was doing the same, no doubt hoping that helped them keep a better eye on their charge.

Jared found Karl Bandar standing beside the massive carving that Master Vestor of Pentagar had given to the people of the New Terran Empire. The incredibly detailed carving hung on the wall in the emperor's quarters for now. In a few weeks, it would go to the Imperial Gallery so that the people on Avalon could enjoy it as well. Then it would tour the Empire.

The emperor had a magnifier out and was closely examining a particular section. He glanced over as Jared cleared his throat.

"It's simply astounding," the older man said. "I cannot imagine the level of dedication and skill required to carve such detailed work by hand. Have you looked closely at the way he used the wood's grain to his advantage?"

"It is unbelievable," Jared agreed. "And such a large piece. The amount of time it took is staggering."

The emperor put the magnifier down and walked over to Jared. "I've sent him an invitation to come visit. I do hope he accepts. I want to meet the man who can create such beauty."

His father gestured to the same chairs the two of them had used before Jared left on his original mission. "Join me."

Jared sat, more than a little discomfited to have the emperor pouring them drinks. "How are you adapting to the implants?" he asked to cover his own awkwardness.

The emperor handed him one of the glasses and beamed. "They're just as wonderful as you and Kelsey had said. It's only been a week, but I can hardly imagine how I got along without them. Even though I'm not using them anywhere close to their potential, I'm sure. For that, you'll have to find a teenager."

That made Jared laugh. "Too true. Kids always seem to know how to push technology far past where those of us just getting it can imagine. The first class of midshipmen that have had them since their teens are going to be an eye-opening experience, I'm sure."

"More like terrifying, I'd imagine. This technology will change the Empire in ways we can't begin to imagine."

The older man sipped his whiskey. "Jared, I want to thank you for your support during this very difficult time. I understand you never liked Ethan, but what he became wasn't truly him. Not the boy I raised. This has been hard."

Jared nodded. "My support has nothing to do with Ethan, frankly. I care about you and Kelsey."

"Nevertheless, I appreciate what you've done. This has been very difficult for Kelsey. More so than for me, I suspect. She's the one that allowed Ethan to make that one final, fatal mistake. It eats at her, but she won't talk with me about it. I hope she opens up to Talbot or you. That kind of thing can fester."

"She hasn't really talked to me, but I know she's getting counseling. Doctor Stone is also her confidant. She's talking to Talbot, too, I'd imagine. He's not the kind of man that lets someone sit on their butt feeling sorry for themselves without making some noise."

"He's good for her," the emperor said. "I'd never have envisioned that match, but it's a good one. He's smart and determined. I think he'll make an excellent prince consort."

Jared smiled. "Oh, I can't imagine he'll like the sound of that. Just being Sir Russel gives him hives."

"If it's any consolation, he pitched a fit when I told him and demanded the Imperial herald enter his title as Sir Talbot."

That made Jared sputter in the middle of a sip. "I'd say you were yanking my chain, but I know him. Did you do it?"

"Of course I did. The man is an iconoclast. His very personality demanded that I do so. It also suitably distracted him from the fact that I was covertly making him more acceptable to the Senate as the prince consort. Knighthood is not a lofty title, but it technically makes him a member of the Imperial aristocracy. Which brings me to you."

Jared froze, his glass almost to his lips. "Me?"

"Indeed," the emperor said with a slight smile. "I've made a decision you're going to hate as much as Talbot did, but it's for your own good. And the Empire's, too, of course.

"You might never be comfortable with the idea, but you are as much my son as Kelsey is my daughter. Blood never entered into my thinking, so the fact you are biologically mine and she isn't doesn't matter one bit to me. Still, the blood of emperors flows in your veins, and the Empire is in sore need of icons like yourself."

"My heart is filled with dread. Majesty, I am no icon."

The other man's smile widened. "I suppose I did turn this into an emperor/liegeman moment. I hadn't intended this to be an ambush, but I'll just keep rolling.

"Have you considered everything that you did? Imagine, if you will, that someone else had led the mission and done those heroic deeds. Have you read any of the Norse Sagas? Epic is not an understatement for what you've accomplished. As the story gets out, the people of the Empire will see you as a hero, and nothing you can do will change that."

Jared carefully set his glass down. "I can see that, but I'm not sure I like where you're going with this."

"I'm not surprised. You're just as pigheaded as Talbot, in your own quiet way. And as blind. Do you love Elise?"

The question took him by surprise. "Of course I do."

"Do you see yourself marrying her one day? Raising a family?"

"I'd like to think so. Did she have something to do with this?"

Crown Princess Elise Orison of the Kingdom of Pentagar was one of the most politically savvy people Jared knew and wickedly subtle in moving behind the scenes. Much more so than he was.

The emperor made an ambivalent gesture with his hand. "Perhaps, in a roundabout way. If you're asking if we talked about what I'm going to do, the answer is no. Still, she's an incredible manipulator—and I mean that with the deepest of respect—so I suppose it's possible that she helped chart my thinking on the matter.

"She's going to rule her people one day, and even though you're a national hero there, that might make a marriage to you more difficult. Knowing her, she'll run roughshod over anyone who objects, but wouldn't you like to make her life a little easier?"

"Now who's manipulating?" Jared asked. "What exactly do you have in mind? A knighthood like Talbot's? I suppose I can accept that. It's not as though others haven't done so."

The people that had done the most during the mission had all received knighthoods, and he considered the honor well earned. He'd seen his promotion to admiral as a similar reward, but if becoming a knight made Elise's life a little easier, he wouldn't fight very hard.

The emperor nodded. "Always the humble man. It suits you, Jared. No, I have something a tad loftier in mind. I've been doing some research in the library that you brought back. *Courageous* was well stocked with electronic texts, but the list of titles that Coordinator West covertly collected is breathtaking.

"For example, there's a fascinating book on the history of the Imperial line. It contains so much that we never knew. For example, our ancestor Empress Christa the First. She succeeded her father, Emperor Justin, after he died in an unfortunate mountain climbing accident. You really should read all about it. It's fascinating."

Jared felt his eyes narrow at the man's light tone. If the emperor had been one of his subordinates, he'd have told the man to trot the full story out. As it was, he had no choice but to allow him to proceed at his own speed.

The emperor took another sip of his whiskey, slowly and obviously savoring it. "What makes the story relevant is that Emperor Justin was a little free with his affections and also had a son out of wedlock. One that he fully acknowledged.

"Empress Christa and the young man knew each other growing up, and she decided a more formal recognition was called for when she assumed the Throne."

He smiled at Jared. "To bring an already long story to a close, she approached the Senate about creating a new position in the peerage. One I had no idea existed, or I'd have taken this step long ago."

Jared's stomach felt as if he'd fallen off a cliff. "What position?"

"One reserved solely for those of Imperial birth that are not in the line of succession. Tomorrow morning, I'll hold a surprise ceremony officially elevating you to your new position. Well, both of them, actually.

"I'd also decided that some of you needed more recognition than you've already received. Doctor Stone, for example. I'm making her Countess of Hawk's Mount. It's a beautiful rural estate that I'm creating from the Imperial lands on the world you grew up on."

Jared nodded. "I've seen the mountains. I think she'll like that."

"It comes with a large stipend, and I'm going to build the seat of her estate with the Crown Purse. It only seems fair when she so cleverly saved my life.

"I'm also posthumously making Timothy Reese a count. He has no family, so the title won't carry on to his blood, which is so unfortunate, but I have a plan. I'll make Talbot his heir. He needed time to adjust to just being a knight, but I think it's been long enough."

Jared snorted. "I hope you have a five-second delay on any live transmissions. He's going to cuss a blue streak."

The emperor laughed and then inclined his head. "Which brings us to you, Jared. I'm making you Duke of East Bay."

Jared blinked. East Bay was also on his home world of Xander. It was the temperate continent in the southern hemisphere where his mother lived and where Hawk's Mount was.

"I'd imagine Duke Matterson won't be happy about that," was all Jared could think to say.

"Actually, he's thrilled. The population on Xander has grown to the point that he was already in discussions with me about doing exactly this. He'll retain his title, of course, and will assume the duties of Imperial governor there. He'll still be running everything but will help create a staff to rule in your place while you're serving in Fleet."

Jared took a deeper sip of his whiskey and poured himself an unprecedented second drink. A big one.

"I should decline, but I suspect you'll just roll over me if I try."

"That's very perceptive of you. The Empire needs this, and so do you."

Jared sighed. "I could argue the point, but I know when I've lost a fight. Well, I suppose that will make me acceptable to even the fussiest Pentagaran."

"If it doesn't, I'm sure the second appointment will."

Jared frowned. "Wait. I thought that was it. Empress Crista made him a duke."

"Actually, she didn't." Emperor Karl Bandar smiled wolfishly. "She made him a prince of the blood. Welcome to the peerage, Highness."

4

One of the things that Zia liked about *Audacious* was that she was as big as a superdreadnought. She needed to be just to have the space for three squadrons of fighters and a flight deck.

Since her steward had parked the new officer—Commander Brandon Levy—in her day cabin as instructed, that meant she could drop by the flag bridge and see what the hell was really going on.

Her primary office sat directly off the flag bridge, which she also used to control the ship. At some point, she really needed to separate the functions, but she was the commander of both this ship and the carrier group. Combining the functions allowed her to keep an eye on the fighters and the ship simultaneously.

Commander Danny Leonidas was already rising from the command chair as she exited the lift. "Captain, we have an unannounced visitor. He's in your day cabin."

She smiled at him. Admiral Mertz had bumped Danny up from lieutenant, just like her. He'd served on the heavy cruiser *Spear*, but she couldn't hold it against such a dedicated officer. Wallace Breckenridge hadn't tainted everyone.

"I know. Step into my office for a minute, Danny."

"Yes, ma'am."

Once he was inside her spacious office, she gestured toward the more comfortable seats to the left of the desk. "Let's take a load off."

He sat, but his expression turned a bit wary. "This is beginning to sound ominous."

"As if we've never just had a casual chat right here. Though I will admit that I know something you don't. The Admiralty sent me word yesterday that you were getting your own command. I don't even have the orders yet, so I didn't expect your replacement for another week."

Danny leaned back in his chair, his eyes wide. "My own command? I was a junior helm officer just a few months ago. I'm not ready for that."

"I respectfully disagree. Yes, you do need more seasoning, but who among us doesn't. We're all going to miss you, but the light cruiser *Lightning* will be happy to have a man like you in the center seat."

The other officer shook his head as though clearing it. "This is all so unexpected. So, the new guy is my replacement?"

"Supposedly. I haven't seen his orders, either. We crossed paths in the hangar bay, but he didn't know who I was. His reaction to the fighters taking precedence over his cutter concerns me. There was a bit of attempted intimidation, too."

"Boy, did he pick the wrong person to try that on," Danny said with a shake of his head. "And right after boarding. That is not promising."

"Yet I'm going to have to work with him," Zia said grimly. "Maybe I caught him on a bad day. I want to spend a few minutes going over his record together."

Commander Levy's record was a good one, on paper. She knew that didn't always reflect a person's true personality, much less whether he'd be a good fit in an unusual command.

He'd last served as the commanding officer of a heavy cruiser under the overall authority of Captain Alice Quinn. That was to his favor. She knew that Quinn had stood up for Admiral Mertz in front of the court of inquiry following their return. She was an ally.

Perhaps Levy felt that moving from a cruiser command to the executive officer's slot on a ship like this was a step down. Or perhaps it was her own rapid elevation to command that raised his hackles.

Nothing in his record led her to believe he was generally a problem child, but her instincts told her there was going to be trouble of some kind.

Danny rubbed his chin. "Maybe this was a one-time occurrence. He seems like a great candidate. Better than I'd have been in his place, that's for sure."

Zia smiled. "That's not even close to true. If I'd had a say in this, I'd have kept you right where you are, but I know an independent command is going to do you a universe of good. Fleet knows that, too."

She sighed. "Well, I suppose I'll figure the new guy out in due time. If he makes an ass of himself, I can handle that, too."

He rose to his feet when she did. "Skipper, I want you to know what an honor and pleasure it's been to work with you."

She took the hand he offered and shook it firmly. "Likewise, and I don't think this is the last we'll see of one another. Your cruiser squadron is going to be providing *Audacious* the cover she needs going forward."

Danny nodded. "That makes perfect sense. Shall I go retrieve the new guy?"

"Yes," she said as she headed for her desk. "Keep him in the dark about our earlier encounter. I think this might be a salutary experience for him."

The other officer grinned. "My lips are sealed, ma'am. Be right back."

She brought up Levy's record on her desk comp while she waited. His orders were in the system now, too, so she quickly read them. Fleet had indeed assigned him as her new executive officer.

Zia called her steward. "Jim, it looks like we'll need a going-away party tomorrow. Danny Leonidas is moving on to a command of his own."

The tall man on the screen nodded. "I'm both sorry and excited to hear that, ma'am. Will a lunch timeframe work?"

She nodded. "Yes. Plan on all the senior officers attending."

"The new man will be replacing Commander Leonidas?"

Steward First Class Jim Richmond had one of the best poker faces Zia had ever seen, but there was a flicker of something in his eyes.

"He will. Tell me what you think of the man."

"It's not a good thing to speak ill of senior officers, ma'am. Particularly when they're going to become the new executive officer."

Zia smiled coolly. "You work for me directly, Jim. No need to be nasty, but I really do want to know what your initial take is."

"The man has a temper," the steward admitted. "Apparently, some pilot torqued him off and he's pissed. I didn't ask the particulars, but that seems mighty fast to have an incident. That leads me to believe he's going to stir up trouble this ship might not be the better for. With all due respect, of course."

"That pretty much matches what I've already seen. I wouldn't worry too much. We'll all find a good balance, I'm sure."

"If you say so, ma'am."

The admittance chime to her office hatch sounded. A check of her implants showed Danny and the new guy outside her door.

"I have to go, Jim. Make the party a special one."

He looked mildly affronted. "As if I wouldn't. Ma'am."

She laughed until the man smiled and then cut the connection. Then she put on her captain's face and hit the button to open the hatch.

Danny stepped in first. "Someone to see you, ma'am."

The other officer took two steps forward and came to attention. "Commander Brandon Levy reporting as ordered, ma'am."

Interestingly, his eyes held no recognition. Of course, she'd been wearing a bulky flight suit and helmet, though the latter had come off for a little bit. That wasn't very observant of him.

"Thank you, Commander Leonidas."

Her soon-to-be former executive officer smiled wryly and stepped back out. The hatch slid closed, leaving her with her newest problem child.

Her voice must've triggered something in his memory. She knew the moment that he made the connection because his eyes widened in alarm.

Zia smiled coolly. "It's good to see you again, Commander. We really didn't have much of a chance to chat on the flight deck. I'm looking forward to a nice, long conversation so we can get to know one another.

"I understand you have some concerns about fighter priority, but we should get the formalities out of the way first. I'm Captain Zia Anderson. Welcome aboard the Fleet carrier *Audacious*."

* * *

JARED ALMOST STUMBLED out of the Imperial Palace. He wasn't sure how he'd have gotten home without an official driver.

The man frowned in concern, but Jared waved for him to proceed. He had to pull himself together. "I'm fine. Just some unexpected news. Take me to my apartment."

"Aye, sir," the Fleet rating said.

The man brought the air car out of the palace garage at a sedate pace and headed back toward the city. A second car came in from the left and began shadowing them.

The driver eyed it suspiciously. "We have company, sir. Should I call for backup?"

Based on the events a month ago, it wasn't an unreasonable question. Only this time Jared was sure the men in the other car weren't there to kill him. He had a sinking suspicion he'd just inherited his own detail from the Imperial Guard.

He shook his head. "No. It's fine. I'm not in a position to speak about it, and I'd appreciate your discretion. His Majesty has decided I need a little extra protection for a bit. Nothing to worry about."

The man's eyes narrowed, but he nodded. "As you say, sir. We'll be back at your place shortly."

Twenty minutes later, they pulled into his new neighborhood. Elise had said his old apartment was quaint and a little small for two people.

His new place occupied the top floor of an older building in a stylish neighborhood. One with a pad on the roof where his marine guards could screen visitors.

The door into the building opened as they landed, and Elise Orison stepped out. The driver had obviously signaled ahead. Her guards came out, and their eyes tracked the follow car.

Jared stepped out as soon as his air car settled. "It's okay. They're not a threat." He turned back to the driver. "I'm in for the evening, so head back home."

"Aye, sir," the man said.

Elise stepped up beside him as the car took off and watched the other car come in for a landing. Three people in Imperial whites stepped out: two women and one man.

"Jared?" she asked, her expression tightening. "Why are they here?"

"Let's go in and I'll tell you over a drink. I already had a double, and it wasn't enough."

"You're scaring me."

He slid his arm around her shoulders. "I'm sorry. It's a bit of a shock, but I'm not in trouble. Well, not as you'd define it, anyway."

"You're maddening."

She marched him inside and closed the apartment door in the faces of her guards. They'd be a bit discussing things with their Imperial counterparts anyway.

"Make mine a large glass of red," she said as she sat on the edge of the couch. "The good stuff, mind you. And stop stalling."

"I'm not stalling," he delayed as he poured the drinks. "It's just been a shock."

"Let me see," she said thoughtfully. "What is it that Kelsey says at times like these? Oh yes. Trot it out, mister."

Jared chuckled and handed her a glass of the red she liked. He sat down beside her and sipped his drink. The buzz from his earlier drinking had worn off, unfortunately.

"His Majesty has decided that my promotion is a little light for his taste in rewards, so he plans on having us drop by in the morning for a little ceremony."

Her eyes narrowed and glittered a little dangerously. "Details," she ground out between clenched teeth.

"He decided that a title would be appropriate."

Her face lit up. "That's wonderful news! How can you be so glum? Tell me. Will you have to start styling yourself as Sir Jared? Honestly, with the others that were knighted, I felt a little cheated on your behalf."

"If so, he didn't tell me. That wouldn't surprise me, now that you mention it, though. No, tomorrow morning he's going to bestow a newly created duchy upon me."

She just about spilled her wine as she set it down and pulled him into a tight hug, squealing in his ear. "My God, that's terrific! You'll make a handsome ruler, Your Grace. It's very well deserved."

He tossed his drink back and set the empty glass down beside hers. "I'm afraid that isn't all. After some careful study, he decided there was one more title he wanted me to carry, and it's going to cause me grief. I just know it.

"It turns out there's historical precedent for a special level in the peerage for those of direct Imperial lineage when they aren't in the line of succession. At least those the emperor or empress favored. He's going to make me a prince of the blood."

She did knock her wine over this time when she lunged into his arms, whooping loudly.

Loudly enough to make the guards burst in with their weapons drawn, but that didn't dampen her wild celebration dance in his honor.

He waved them back out and used some tissues to stop the wine from running off the side of the table and staining the carpet. He finished just in time to have her land on him again, pushing him back onto the couch with her body.

Jared tried to speak, but she had different ideas. In moments, he found that he really didn't want to talk about it anyway.

5

Annette walked out of the ready room with her helmet under her arm. "Are we ready?"

Fiennes nodded. "All the birds are prepped, and they're wrapping up the preflights now. I already gave your bird a once over."

She'd still check the most critical systems. Annette trusted Jake with her life, but a warrior didn't delegate the critical tasks to others. She'd flown this morning, so a basic run-through would be good enough.

"Have you passed the flight plan on to everyone?"

"Of course."

"Excellent. Then they'll be completely discombobulated when I do something else."

He shook his head with a smile. "Shouldn't we at least pretend we're following an actual plan in the training?"

"I am following a plan," she said. "I'm teaching them that even when they think they know what's happening, the situation can change for the worse without any notice at all. I'll incorporate what you presented to them, but not in the way they expect things to run."

"You're the boss."

Annette went over her assigned fighter closely. It was uniquely hers, permanently assigned and with her name just under the canopy, along with a jack of spades emblem. She'd gotten used to the specific quirks it had and was very happy with it.

Once she was satisfied the bird was ready, she put her helmet on and strapped herself in. "*Audacious* Flight Control, this is Black Jack Actual. Com Check."

"You're coming in loud and clear, Black Jack Actual," a man's voice answered. "What's on the plate for today?"

"Formation fighting and ugly surprises," she said with a smile.

"Won't you be popular? Orbital One is aware of your sortie, and we'll be watching for those ugly surprises with interest."

"Thanks Control. You'll like it. Trust me. Black Jack Actual out."

She switched to the general squadron frequency. "All Black Jack elements, this is Black Jack Actual. We'll be performing a planetary patrol today. Nothing too complicated, but I want you to pay specific attention to keeping close to your wingman.

"We'll try out several basic formations and maneuvers today. Do not embarrass me. Launch when ready and form up fifty kilometers astern of *Audacious*. Black Jack Actual out."

The Black Jack pilots called in their acknowledgments one by one in numerical order. That was standard so that in the heat of battle they didn't try to talk over one another. They also sent in their acknowledgment via implant, but she liked hearing them. It gave her a better feel for their states of mind.

Flight by flight, they launched. When her turn came up, the launch catapult hurled her down the launch tube and out of the ship. Once the grav drive came online, she nudged her fighter into its assigned position among the swarm that was Black Jack Squadron.

They started off easily enough, cycling through a few changes in formation. They were simple maneuvers but very important. If they didn't shift position in the correct manner, they might risk collision with their teammates.

When she was satisfied they were firmly in the groove, she brought up her simulation override controls. They allowed her to activate certain features in the scanner software on each of the fighters.

She activated the program. Down on Avalon's surface, a strobe lit up, announcing hostile missile launches.

"Vampire, vampire, vampire," she said over the general frequency. "Hostile launches from the planet's surface. First flight, take the missiles out. Second flight, cover them. Third, eliminate the launchers."

With commendable speed, first flight peeled off and dove into Avalon's atmosphere. The fighters took continually shifting positions with each pair watching over their wingmates. They targeted the incoming missiles while Second Flight watched for other fighters.

There weren't any this time. At least, not yet.

Jake led Third Flight down on a strafing run. The area housing the supposed facility was actually a military training range. No one was in danger below, and the ordinance was real today.

She took a place behind Second Flight. If needed, she'd help with what they were doing, but she was controlling what was happening in the exercise today. In a real fight, she'd guide First Flight.

Things went gratifyingly smoothly. First Flight took out the attacking missiles quickly and focused on the follow-up waves as Third Flight dropped down and blew up the target area. The flashes were probably bright enough to be notable in orbit.

While they were still conducting their bombing run, she activated the next segment of the program. Her scanners almost immediately reported fighters launching from the south.

"Second Flight, incoming fighters," she said. "Engage."

"Copy," the lieutenant in command of the group said.

They spiraled out to engage the enemy fighters. These were the ugly surprise. They weren't simulated. They were real.

Scimitar Squadron came racing up to meet them, splitting into elements at the last moment. The fighting—with simulated weapons, of course— quickly turned into a massive snarl, as though a cat had gotten ahold of a humongous pile of yarn.

Their implants made keeping track of all the other fighters possible but *very* difficult. Any particular craft could change course at a moment's notice, turning right in your path.

Like two of the enemy fighters did for her.

"Black Jack Actual engaging," she told her wingman.

She peeled off, brought her antifighter missiles online, and fired. The lead fighter dodged violently, and his electronic countermeasures allowed him to elude her strike, but his wingman was less fortunate. He turned red on her scanners and immediately exited the area.

Her pleasure was short-lived, as two other fighters targeted her.

Annette pushed her fighter into a sharp dive and evaded the incoming strike. Barely. Her wingman had a scary moment when he and one of the enemy fighters almost collided. For real.

"Jesus, Black Jack Seven!" she shouted. "Watch out!"

"Sorry about that," Larry Connors said back. "We jigged the same direction."

She started to answer, but her threat warning lit up again. Annette dodged, but it wasn't good enough. A simulated missile took her out.

And just like that she was dead. Thankfully, not in real life.

A quick consult with her scanner gave her a clear course out of the fight, and she had all the time in the world to observe the battle play out.

Any semblance of order was gone. With everyone fighting for their lives, they'd lost track of the strategic situation. Herself included, she thought wryly. It had turned into a dogfight.

The after-action report was going to be fun. They'd overcommitted, and another ground site was busy shooting down her squadron. Jake did what he could, but they'd already lost. The best he could do was try to extract as many of their people as he could.

Well, they said mistakes were the best teachers. They'd all learn something from today's exercise.

Once the remains of her squadron were clear, she sent the signal to terminate the war game. "All *Audacious* units, this is Black Jack Actual. Exercise terminated. Return to base."

Sorting them all out took longer than she liked, but they eventually headed back for the carrier. She started making notes for the briefing. The fight left her tired but exhilarated. This had been far uglier than she'd planned, but that was fine for now.

Once they finished the briefing, they could get something to eat and get some rest. Then they'd do it all again tomorrow.

* * *

KELSEY WANTED TO SMASH SOMETHING. Or someone. With her physical strength, that wasn't exactly the safest frame of mind to be in.

She shed her guards at the door to the suite she shared with Talbot and headed right for the gym. He wasn't home yet, and that was a very good thing. She didn't want to take her fury out on him.

Since she could literally lift the weight machines, she turned her enhanced musculature off and focused on her regular muscles.

It's okay to be angry.

"I don't want to talk about it," she told the ghostly voice of Ned Quincy. The disembodied copy of the dead Marine Raider lived in her implants, so he of course knew what had happened.

"Screw it," she snarled before he could say anything else. "You're damned right I'm angry. If you want to talk, you can use the projectors. I'm not doing this in my head."

She'd had Carl seed her quarters with holographic projectors, all except the master bedroom and bath. He might live in her head, but she wanted *some* privacy.

The figure of a man in casual clothes appeared sitting on the weight machine beside hers. If she hadn't known he wasn't real, she'd have had no clue he was a projection. The Old Empire had really known how to make good equipment.

Kelsey forced her weights up over her head, craving the burn. "Don't try to calm me down," she told the AI. "I'm not going to be placated."

"The thought never crossed my mind. In fact, you might have better luck on the range."

The mental image of incinerating Nathaniel Breckenridge with a plasma rifle was tempting. Perhaps a little too tempting.

Especially since she had more than a bit of difficulty blaming him for this situation. The evidence that he'd been unaware of their genetic relationship was clear enough. He was too much of a power broker to have avoided using the knowledge a long time ago, even if only with Ethan.

No, she believed the man hadn't known he was her father. That didn't change a damned thing, though. It was a huge stinking mess. As if her life hadn't been complicated enough already.

"I'm better off without a weapon in my hands right now," she grunted. "I'm not sure who I'd shoot first: Breckenridge or my mother."

She let the weights crash back down and slumped forward a little. "Holy hell, what do I do? If I tell my father, he'll make some grand announcement. Shit. Breckenridge might beat him to it."

"While this isn't exactly good news, it isn't terrible either. Honestly, so what if the man sired you? Does that really complicate your life more than being the heir?"

"Probably not," she admitted, "but I'm not ready for some new relationship, especially with the uncle of the idiot that tried to kill us."

"Then don't. It's not like you have to send him Christmas presents or invite him over for dinner. I specifically recall him stressing that. If you don't tell your father, do you really think Breckenridge will leak the news?"

Kelsey sighed. "I have no idea. I suppose you're right, but the bastard slept with my mother. He's probably not the only one, either. I really should query the access list in the secret tunnel."

"That's stupid," the AI said. "One or a hundred, it makes no difference."

"I assure you that a hundred would make quite the difference," she said tartly. "There's a not-so-fine line between harlot and slut. God, I hope it's not a hundred."

She rubbed her face tiredly. "I'll grant you that he readily admitted he made a serious mistake in judgment, but to be fair—which I really don't want to do—he was a young man, and they tend to be easily swayed into mistakes by their hormones. Not that it excuses him, but I'm not sure that many other men in a similar position would have refused.

"My mother was the instigator in this relationship. I'm sure of it. I guess that's who I'm really angry with. She's known all this time that I wasn't Father's, but she still condemned him and dragged us all through the muck when he made a mistake in judgment that he owned up to."

The man nodded. "So, what can you do about that?"

"Not a damned thing, but you can be sure that this is going to result in an epic fight whenever I go to see her. Thankfully, I don't have the time right now, so this is going to simmer for a long, long while. Maybe I can avoid strangling her if I have time to calm down."

Kelsey heard the front door open. Talbot was home. She really wasn't looking forward to telling him about this.

"Time for lights out, Ned," she said as she stood. "I want some privacy."

"Take it easy on him," the man said as he stood and vanished. He'd have other ways of amusing himself that didn't involve using her senses or the equipment in the suite.

She needed to see about getting him loaded into a different system. Carl said he was close. Frankly, it couldn't happen soon enough for her.

Time to get this done.

Kelsey headed for the living room. The door opened just as she reached for it, and she started to say something to Talbot.

Only it wasn't her lover.

"Kelsey! I rushed here as quickly as I could," her mother said as she rushed in. "Are you all right?"

* * *

COMMANDER BRANDON LEVY stared at the woman sitting behind the desk in shock. It was the pilot from the flight deck. The one that had...

He pulled himself together. He'd screwed up. Badly. This wasn't the time to make it worse.

"I'm sorry, Captain. I didn't know that was you."

He knew how idiotic that sounded the moment he said it. Which didn't help one bit.

"Obviously," the young woman said dryly. "We've gotten off on the wrong foot, so I suggest we try again. At ease."

He allowed himself to relax slightly. He'd looked over her record, but clearly not well enough. He should've recognized her on sight. Only he'd been too angry to try that hard, and that had been a stupid mistake. The kind he wouldn't allow to happen again.

No matter how good her record was, she'd only been the tactical officer on an almost obsolete destroyer. He had a decade of experience on her, but they'd bumped her three grades and put her in command of this tremendous ship.

She considered him a moment then glanced at her comp. "Your record is excellent, Commander. You probably expected the Admiralty was giving you command of one of the new ships. I know this has to be hard, but we have to make the best of it. Are we going to have a problem?"

"No, ma'am."

He wouldn't allow his anger to get the better of him again. She might not have earned this command, but he'd damned well make sure it didn't end badly for the Empire. He might not want to help prop up her inexperience, but he'd do his duty.

"Without judging, this morning's conversation tells me that we need to come to a shared vision on how this ship is run," she said. "This is the first carrier in Fleet since the Fall, and adapting to how she's used is going to be challenging.

"I need you to keep an open mind. If, once you've had time to consider the new situation, you think something needs to change, I'm willing to hear you out."

Her lips thinned. "What I'm not willing to do is accept reflexive judgments on capabilities that you don't fully understand. Yet."

Brandon nodded and even agreed with her to a point. He'd allowed his anger at the situation to color his behavior. That was unprofessional and would not do. He'd listen carefully and keep his emotions under control.

"Yes, ma'am."

She eyed him for a moment before nodding herself. "Very good. Let's address the elephant in the room. Until just a few months ago, I was a lieutenant and a tactical officer. Now I'm in command of this ship. That has to chafe."

He made a mental note to put her in for the Understatement of the Year Award but said nothing.

Once she recognized that he wasn't going to respond, she continued. "As it happens, I know very well that I'm not as experienced as you. I didn't seek out this command, but someone had to do it.

"Princess Kelsey made the decision, in consultation with Admiral Mertz, to promote me and assign me to this command. Something I'm still more than a bit uncomfortable with, but I will carry out my orders."

Admiral Mertz. The thought almost made him snort. Not that he was one of the people in Fleet inclined to hold the man's birth against him. No, he knew Mertz by reputation. He'd more than earned his destroyer command. Honesty compelled Brandon to concede that Mertz should've been a captain years ago.

The man obviously had what it took. He'd read the classified summaries of what had happened on the exploratory mission, and Mertz had more than lived up to anyone's wildest expectations.

Brandon didn't think that entitled Mertz to be an admiral, but he wouldn't have blinked at a promotion to commodore. So one more bump wasn't too much of a stretch. Besides, as he'd heard the story, Princess Kelsey had ambushed him with the promotion. Much like Zia Anderson, he reluctantly admitted.

Logic wasn't going to help him adjust to this situation. Fleet expected its officers to obey their orders, and he would do so. He just didn't have to like it.

"My current executive officer is a good man, though about as inexperienced at his post as I am. He's moving on to command one of the light cruiser escorts for the carrier group. We're having a party for him tomorrow. I think you should be there."

Of course he should be. That was just basic courtesy.

"Yes, ma'am."

"You're not very talkative," she observed. "Well, we'll find our own rhythm as we become accustomed to one another. The part of the job you're going to have to work on revolves around fighter doctrine.

"You're going to have to play catchup on that one, but you're in luck that we're all still getting accustomed to it ourselves. I also see that you don't have implants yet. That's an even steeper learning curve to master, and they will influence every single aspect of your job."

She eyed him. "What do you imagine implants mean for you, Commander Levy?"

"They'll make doing my job easier, ma'am. Allow me to interface more directly with the ship to better manage it."

He had no idea what that actually meant. Even after all the reading he'd done, he still didn't really grasp the full implications of what the new technology could do.

Anderson nodded. "All technically correct, but that sounds rote. Frankly, it can't be any other way. You have no idea the depth and power implants give an officer on this ship. Or honestly even what the ship is capable of. *Audacious.*"

"Yes, Captain Anderson," a mellow male voice said from the overhead speakers.

"Attention to orders. Commander Brandon Levy will assume the position of executive officer as of 0800 tomorrow. Note it in the logs."

"Aye, Captain. Welcome aboard, Commander Levy. This unit looks forward to working with you."

He swallowed. He'd never heard of a computer that could sound so autonomous. He wasn't sure if he should answer or not, so he defaulted to the polite thing.

"Thank you, *Audacious.*"

"The computer on this ship can run every system in a pinch, except for the weapons," Anderson said conversationally. "Those require a human being by design. He also can't remotely control the fighters, since they're considered weapons. They usually operate too far away anyhow.

"*Audacious* is built on a modified superdreadnought hull and still has two-thirds of her weaponry. The fighters make her far more dangerous than *Invincible*, even without them. The three squadrons we have aboard could take a superdreadnought, though they'd suffer hideous losses. More to the point, they could take every original ship in Fleet present in this system without support from us. But only if they are used wisely."

She considered him for a moment and then stood. "I think a demonstration of both implant and fighter operations are in order. Come with me."

Anderson led him out onto the ridiculously large bridge outside her office. The man he was replacing rose from the wrap-around command console in the center.

"Keep the conn, Danny." Anderson turned to Brandon. "Let's take a seat at the observation consoles, Commander."

He opened his mouth to ask what they were doing when a loud klaxon began screaming and the lighting changed to a reddish hue. The ship had just gone to general quarters.

The bridge crew focused on their consoles as the overhead speakers came to life. "This is a drill. I repeat, this is a drill. Long-range scanners have just detected an incoming Rebel Empire fleet. Come to heading two five zero by one seven five at maximum military power."

It was Captain Anderson's voice. Her lips hadn't moved.

The speed with which the bridge crew performed was amazing. They seemed to be one with their consoles, hardly speaking and only occasionally manipulating the controls.

"The ship is actually still in orbit," Anderson said. "I have the bridge controls in simulation mode. Operations is taking over their regular duties.

"The bridge crew is using their implants to do almost everything. The scanner readings and more are available right in their heads. They should be able to operate without the consoles at all. *Audacious*, cut power to the bridge."

The compartment plunged into darkness, every console going dead all at once. Only the emergency lights remained active. The bridge crew sat back and frowned in concentration. He assumed the ship continued operations without the slightest hitch, which was damned impressive.

"During the battle of Harrison's World, *Courageous* lost power to the bridge, and we would've died without the ship's AI. Marcus is a lot more advanced than our computer. No offense, *Audacious*."

"This unit is incapable of taking offense, Captain."

"Restore power to Commander Levy's console," she said.

Brandon's screen came to life, showing the area of space the carrier supposedly occupied as it sped out of Avalon orbit. The scanners also showed what he assumed was a computer-generated fleet racing toward them. It was almost as massive as the one Admiral Mertz had brought back to Avalon.

Audacious wasn't alone. It looked as though the entire fleet was going out to meet the intruders as a unit. He assumed they were all computer generated.

Over the next hour, he watched as a stupendous battle took place. A preposterous number of missiles raced toward them, and Admiral Mertz's ships returned fire in kind. Then the admiral ordered the fighters in.

The little minnows charged into the enemy formations, almost as fast as missiles themselves. Only they were much harder to kill.

They worked together in ways he couldn't quite grasp but that were obviously practiced. Massive ships perished under their fire, but they took punishing hits in return. It might be hard to swat a swarm of insects, but they died when hit.

When they came streaming back to the carrier to rearm, there were less than half as many as had gone out. That kind of attrition broke units, but these people went about their duty without complaint.

Of course it was all a drill, so they weren't real.

"Is that level of loss normal?" he heard himself ask quietly.

"No. We're making this harder than we think it will be in real combat," she said. "Of course, when the rebels killed *Audacious*, they all died. They went out four times. The last sally only had three fighters."

She turned to face him squarely. "Those people are the ship's real weapons, Commander. In combat, weapons have the right of way, so we always act accordingly. This isn't ego. I didn't tell you to wait for the fighters to land because I wanted to put you in your place. This ship exists as a platform to project their power, and when doing so, they have precedence."

He reluctantly nodded. "I can see I have some work to do before I can understand everything I'm seeing."

"Agreed. Tomorrow morning, I want you to report to Doctor Zoboroski for your implants. You can't do your job without them. It'll be light duty for you tomorrow, but Commander Leonidas can still show you everything you need to know before he leaves for his new command."

Brandon still wasn't convinced she really knew the best way to run this ship, but he was willing to try to open his mind. One way or another, this was going to be a rough transition.

6

Jared had a rough night. Sleep hadn't come easily. He'd lain awake long after Elise was dreaming beside him.

She'd been unreservedly delighted at the news, and not just because it made her life simpler. Regardless of what the emperor said, she'd already flat out told him that she'd marry him if he'd been a normal man on the street because she loved him.

Her fierce determination told him it wasn't posturing either. That made him feel good but did nothing to lessen the nerves he still felt.

He rose quietly and made his way into the bathroom an hour before the alarm would have normally woken him. A long, hot shower at least put him in a comfortable mental space.

Once he was dressed, except for his uniform tunic, he made breakfast. If he timed things well, he'd serve Elise breakfast in bed.

While he started the eggs, he checked his implants for any new messages.

Implant coverage in the capital was spotty, but that would change as more people required it. They'd fully wired his place. Even normal calls went to his implants.

There was a message from Kelsey waiting for him. He checked the time. It had come in right after they'd gone to bed.

Her image appeared in his mind's eye. She looked like she needed sleep more than he did, which was unusual.

"I just saw the message from my father that he wants me at the Imperial Palace in the morning. Do you have any idea what's going on? Also, I need to talk to you as soon as you get up. I have some unsettling news."

He deleted the message and pinged her. If she wasn't ready for a call, her computer would prompt him to leave a message.

An image opened up of her drinking some coffee in her kitchen. She was a little bleary but awake.

"Morning, Jared."

"Morning," he said. "I don't like the idea of unsettling news, though I have some, too. You called, so you get to go first."

She shook her head. "I'm sure mine is more troubling. I had dinner with Senator Breckenridge last night, though I'd hardly call it a meal. More like an ambush.

"He told me that… ahem, he'd been indiscreet with my mother about nine months before I was born. He's my biological sire. Lily confirmed it. Without telling me in advance, which I'm going to have to talk with her about."

He almost dropped the package of bacon he was opening but managed to save the sacred pork. "That's a lot more unsettling than my news, at least to you. I'm not sure what to say, but you knew it had to be someone. At least the man showed some character during the coup."

She nodded, eyeing the stovetop. "That looks good. I'm going to make me some, too."

The way the implant calls worked, it seemed as though she was standing right there, though her kitchen was laid out differently than his. It was as though the two rooms were side by side. It made having a conversation much easier than just voices in one another's heads.

"The news was shocking," she admitted, "but it wasn't the worst part. My mother showed up right after I got home."

Jared, a man who'd faced death in combat without a tremble, blanched. "Jesus."

"Indeed."

"What did you do?"

She laughed without humor. "I resisted the urge to punch her lights out. She is my mother, after all. In fact, I managed to avoid telling her anything and threw her out on her ear, much to her outrage. I was far too angry to have that fight."

"And she let you throw her out? I'm shocked."

"I cheated and had the Imperial Guard handle it. That didn't go over well, as you might imagine. You know how she is."

He smiled a little. "Actually, I don't. She never wanted to see me, and I was happy with that."

Kelsey growled. "See? That's what pisses me off. She's a damned hypocrite. She had the gall to sound all outraged that I wasn't ready to welcome her with open arms. Accused me of holding a grudge over something that happened before I was born."

"Something she conveniently forgot to mention, and that you had to find out the hard way," he agreed.

"Exactly! Anyway, she just wanted to fight after that, so I had the guards eject her from the premises. I did allow myself the pleasure of pushing her out the door and locking it behind her."

He focused on the food for a minute, making sure everything was cooking well. Then he started the coffee.

"You're not going to be able to put her off for long, you know."

Kelsey sighed. "I can try. I needed to tell Talbot first anyway. He deserved to know the truth. Which, I'm still not sure I should tell my father, by the way."

"Why not? He already knows you're not biologically his. I'd imagine he'll have an epic fight with your mother about it, by the way."

"That is his fight," she admitted, "though I deserve to have a piece of her, too. I'm concerned that putting a name to my sperm donor will cause Senator Breckenridge more trouble than he perhaps deserves.

"I've come to the conclusion that his mistake was a long time ago, and that he was young. Christ, look at the things I've done. I'm not in a real position to judge."

She sipped her coffee. "My mother, on the other hand, was a serial adulterer. Talbot and I flew out to the palace, and I examined the secret exit's computer. I'll bet she didn't know it kept recordings of the comings and goings. Care to guess how many men she smuggled in?"

"I'm told the only way to win this kind of game is not to play."

"Eighteen!" she said, ignoring his response. "And not all of them before my birth! She was cheating on my father right up until they found out about you. Breckenridge was actually one of the shortest affairs in duration.

"One of them lasted two years. He moved out to her new home as the groundskeeper, by the way. I'm not sure precisely which bushes he keeps trimmed, if you know what I mean."

"That was a bit bawdy, even for someone who spent much of their time with marines," he said. "She is your mother. Don't forget mine kept exactly that same kind of secret from me."

Kelsey shook her head energetically. "Oh no, she didn't. I'll lump her with Breckenridge and my father. The excitement of the situation and the person they were dealing with overcame their common sense. That's a far cry from what my mother did. She knowingly cheated on her husband for decades.

"Anyway, I'll deal with her soon enough. What is your unsettling news?"

He started to respond, but the door chimed. "Someone is at the door. Let me call you back."

Jared pulled the last of the breakfast off the heat and headed for the door. He could've checked remotely to see who it was, but the guards wouldn't have disturbed him unless it was important.

Opening the door revealed his own mother. "Jared!" She rushed into his arms. "I got here as quickly as I could."

"Mom, I'm glad to see you," he said, squeezing her tight. "I should've come to visit, but things have been so busy. Come in."

The guards—a mixture of Imperial Marines and Imperial Guards— closed the door behind them. He was going to have to sort out that mess before long, too.

"I just made breakfast."

"Good. I'm starving."

That hadn't been his mother's voice. Elise, her hair tousled from sleep, came out of the bedroom and stopped dead in her tracks. Thankfully, she was dressed, though only in his shirt. It covered everything. Barely.

His mother's face paled a little. "I should have called ahead. Why don't I come back later?"

"It's a little late for any embarrassment," he said with a chuckle. "Besides, today is going to be very, very busy. Mother, this is Elise Orison. Elise, my mother, Patricia Mertz."

Elise smiled as though she hadn't walked almost naked into the room with his mother. "It's a pleasure to meet you, Patricia. You absolutely should stay for breakfast.

"Let me get dressed and we can talk. And, before you start, I don't want any of that 'highness' nonsense from you. I'm Elise." She headed back into their bedroom.

"Let me get us some coffee," he said to his mother. "I have so much to tell you."

"Obviously," his mother said with a twinkle in her eye. "I'd given up hope that you'd ever find someone special with your career looming over you like it does. I hope she's the one."

He smiled. "I think so. I just have to find the right time to ask the question."

"You know I can hear you, right?" Elise asked from the bedroom. "Yes, I'm the one. That's the worst proposal ever, by the way, but I'll take it."

He'd forgotten that she had excellent hearing but smiled anyway. The prospect of marrying her had his heart soaring.

His mother pulled him into a hug. "Oh, my God! I'm overwhelmed! So much has changed."

"You have no idea. Sit down and I'll bring your coffee. I know my message was a bit sparse on detail, but I'm okay. Better than okay, really. So much has changed. Some of which I can't talk about."

She took the mug of coffee from him. "I heard some of it. I always knew you'd succeed at anything you tried, but you've exceeded my wildest expectations."

"I've also exceeded my own worst-case estimates. The situation the Empire finds itself in isn't pretty. I'm not sure if everyone understands that just yet."

"The news services seem to be taking the situation seriously," she said. "I'd only gotten your initial message when the emperor had His Grace virtually shove me onto a fast transport for Avalon. If you sent any other messages, they haven't caught up with me."

"Then you've missed a lot of the story," Elise said as she came out of the bedroom in a sophisticated-looking dress. One suitable for the ceremony later that morning.

Which reminded him that he hadn't gotten around to telling Kelsey what was coming. Well, she'd just have to be surprised along with everyone else.

"I'd planned on asking you to marry me a little more formally," he told her.

She kissed him soundly. "I was almost to the point of proposing to you. You can be frustratingly dense at times. Have you heard how long before you ship out again?"

He nodded. "No more than a week. Possibly sooner than that. Time-sensitive events are in motion."

His mother's face fell. "I'd hoped to have more time with you."

"I'm sorry. I'd like that, too, but if you've heard even the basic story, you know how important this is."

She nodded, her face becoming resolute. "Of course. You know I'm so very proud of you, don't you?"

Jared pulled her into a hug. "I do, and that makes me feel as loved as I could possibly be. You made me the man I am."

He checked his implant chronometer. "I have to finish getting dressed. Elise will make sure you get to the palace, but I have to be there early."

His mother frowned. "But you haven't eaten. Why are you going to the palace?"

Elise smiled, her eyes twinkling. "Oh, just a little get-together." She speared him with a glance. "Eat some breakfast. I have it on good authority that they'll wait for you to start."

His mother looked apprehensive. "I don't know if Jared told you, but I used to work there. After what happened with the emperor, there might be some... hard feelings. Perhaps I should just stay in my hotel."

Elise put her regal face on. "I won't hear of it. Trust me when I say that anyone who is rude to you will have more than enough people leaping to your defense. Any trouble will be very short lived and terribly one sided."

"You can't yell at the emperor."

"I can, actually. Not that I expect him to be anything other than gracious and welcoming."

From his mother's expression, she didn't necessarily share that assessment.

Jared walked into the kitchen and put the food onto plates. "We have enough time to eat, I suppose, but we don't dawdle. We can catch up this afternoon. Let's get some fuel. Today is going to be long and—for me —trying."

7

Z ia stepped out of the cutter she and her command crew had taken down to the Imperial Palace. The unexpected trip had thrown off her carefully scripted schedule, but when the emperor summoned his officers, they came and stayed as long as he wanted.

Danny Leonidas and Brandon Levy stepped out behind her, still talking quietly. Annette Vitter and the ship's chief engineer, Tony Hastert, were on their heels. The rest of her officers trailed after them.

The Imperial Guard surrounded the landing pad. They were undoubtedly scanning her and her people for weapons.

A woman in a suit stepped forward. "Captain Anderson, I'm Lisa Devonshire, His Majesty's majordomo. If you and your officers would be so kind as to accompany me, I'll show you to the audience room. Many of your fellows are already waiting."

Zia smiled and nodded. "Thank you."

She ran back over her thoughts as the woman took them inside the tremendous building. It had to be an award for Admiral Mertz. Nothing else made sense. The man certainly deserved them. The promotion he'd gotten didn't even match some of the rewards others had gotten for their parts.

Frankly, she was glad she'd managed to dodge any awkward awards. She enjoyed teasing "Sir Talbot" every chance she got. He was still grumbling about it.

That wasn't to say that she'd gotten away unscathed. The emperor had given a number of people the Imperial Cross: Admiral Mertz, Commodore Graves, Lily Stone, Dennis Baxter, Talbot, Pasco Ramirez, Annette Vitter, Timothy Reese, and herself. It felt like too much in her case, but telling the emperor no wasn't an easy task.

Fleet officers, Imperial nobility, and Imperial Senators filled the Imperial Audience Chamber. She was definitely out of her league in here.

"Zia!"

She turned her head and spotted Charlie Graves and Dennis Baxter heading her way.

Charlie was in command of the battlecruiser *Courageous* now. Her old partner, Pasco Ramirez, was his executive officer. Frankly, she was stunned that he hadn't taken over *Audacious*. He had a lot more experience than she did.

Dennis had been *Athena*'s chief engineer. He was now doing the same thing on *Invincible*.

"Hey, boys," she said. "Any idea what this is about?"

Dennis shook his head. "No, but I haven't seen the admiral. It has to be about him. I think there's going to be a knighting ceremony."

Charlie grinned. "I hope so. I'd love to tease him about it."

She looked around the room. "There are a lot of us here. Not just people from the mission, but senior officers from all across Fleet. Not to mention all the people looking down their noses at us. This feels a little bigger than a knighting."

"What then?" Charlie asked. "Maybe making him a baron or something? That would be wonderful!"

"Zia."

She turned her head and found Crown Princess Elise Orison standing behind her with a vaguely familiar-looking woman at her side.

"Highness."

"This is Patricia Mertz, Jared's mother."

Zia smiled and took the older woman's hands in hers. "It's wonderful to meet you. Allow me to introduce Charlie Graves and Dennis Baxter. We all worked with your son on *Athena*."

"It's such a pleasure to meet all of you," the admiral's mother said. "I've heard so much about you over the years. I feel as though I already know you."

"I have to go meet up with Jared," Princess Elise said. "Would you be so kind as to keep an eye on Patricia?"

"I'd be happy to," she said. "Do you know what's going on? Is it about Jared?"

The other woman nodded. "Yes, but my lips are sealed. You'll like it. I promise." The princess excused herself and hurried out of the room.

Zia focused her attention on Patricia Mertz. "You should be so proud of your son. He saved all of us, and I do mean *all* of us."

Jared's mother smiled. "I couldn't be more proud. This is so overwhelming."

"There are people serving champagne," Charlie said. "Would you like a glass? Everyone?"

At their nods, he hurried away into the crowd.

"There's Princess Kelsey," Dennis said.

Zia turned her head and saw Jared's sister zipping along in the same direction that Princess Elise had gone.

That's when she spotted a looming disaster. The princess's mother was sailing along in her daughter's wake.

"Oh, hell," Jared's mother said.

"Dennis," Zia snapped. "Get people around us right now. If she doesn't see us, there won't be a scene."

"Battle screens up, aye" he said, pulling in people they knew to provide a wall between what would undoubtedly be a matter/antimatter mixture.

"I should leave," Patricia said.

"Bull," Zia said firmly. "You have more of a right to be here than she does. This is Jared's moment. If she starts making a scene, I'll end it."

The older woman looked unconvinced but didn't argue.

The guards at the doorway allowed Princess Kelsey through but stopped her mother. From the sound of it, she was giving them hell, but they held firm. It wasn't as though she were the empress any longer. The divorce had been almost as scandalous as his affair, back in the day. Now, everyone knew the woman was a hypocrite.

Zia kept an eye on where the woman went. This situation still had the potential to go seriously south, so she'd pay more attention to her than the ceremony. Just in case.

* * *

KELSEY MADE her way to her father's dressing room. He was already in the robes of state. The long, flowing purple fabric was stiff and unbearably hot, or so he'd always said.

Half a dozen pages stood ready to assist him, and the Imperial Crown and Scepter sat on cushions close at hand.

She resisted the urge to look at it more closely. This wasn't the time.

"Am I late?" she asked.

"Just in time," he said warmly. "They tell me Jared only just arrived. I expect him momentarily."

"Are you going to tell me what this is about?"

"He didn't tell you? Well, then, who am I to ruin the surprise?"

She planted her fists on her hips. "So that's how this is going to be. Fine, two can play at that game. I know a secret that you desperately need to know. I'll trade."

He laughed. "Always bargaining. I'll pass."

Kelsey sighed. "You really do need to know. Mother showed up at my place this morning. She's here in the palace."

That wiped the humor right off his face. "Grim tidings, indeed. I suppose it was inevitable. I'd been hoping she'd stay away. I really don't want to deal with her."

"Then don't," she said bluntly. "I tossed her out of my place, so she's in a fine humor. There's going to be a fight eventually. A big one. Fair warning, I'm going to cut her off at the knees."

"I may go into seclusion." He rubbed his face. "Well, I don't have time to worry about her now. There are people waiting for me to start. On the plus side, this is going to piss her right off."

"You're not going to tell me, are you?"

He smiled. "And ruin the surprise? Of course not. You and Elise are going to be right there, and you'll know in a very few minutes."

The main door opened to admit Jared, Elise, and the Imperial majordomo.

Her father nodded. "Just in time. Let's go."

He led them to the door in the wall. One of the pages presented the Crown to him. Karl Bandar settled it on his head and took up the Imperial Scepter. In that moment, he became her liege, the Terran Emperor. The transformation still amazed her.

The majordomo waited for his nod and opened the door, walking out first. Kelsey could hear her voice as she announced her father's arrival.

"His Imperial Majesty, Karl the First, Emperor of the Terran Empire. Her Imperial Highness, Princess Kelsey Bandar, Heir to the Imperial Throne. Crown Princess Elise Orison, Heir to the Throne of the Kingdom of Pentagar. Admiral Jared Mertz. All draw close to hear the words of your liege."

They all slowly walked into the audience chamber. There was no rushing when pomp and ceremony were required.

Her father stood before the Imperial Throne. She had a smaller one beside it. It had been her brother's back before things had gone to hell. Jared and Elise stood to one side.

Everyone in the crowd stood at attention, or close to it in the case of the senators and nobles. The only one scowling was her mother. There was a small bubble of space around her. It seemed no one was in the mood to chat. Probably afraid they'd get something on themselves.

Her father gestured for Kelsey to sit. That was not according to protocol, and the majordomo's eyebrows pulled together a tad. It was her version of a fierce scowl.

Kelsey did as he'd indicated and sat. The cushion made the throne a lot more comfortable than it looked. Thank God.

Her father looked out at the crowd. "Over the course of the last few months, most of you have heard many details about the mission into the Old Empire. What you have not heard are the full details that only a few are privy to. Nor have you heard of every event that transpired. Some of them will remain classified for many years to come.

"Many of the people involved have been recognized in one way or another. Some with promotions, others with awards, and a few with grants of knighthood. Those were only the first wave. Others are coming."

He smiled. "In fact, I have a number of knighthoods to bestow upon the unsuspecting tonight. Shall we begin there?"

Kelsey watched as her father called officers and crewmen alike forward. The majordomo read the unclassified parts of their awards and then he used a thin ceremonial blade to tap them on the shoulders in a ceremony older than the Empire itself.

All looked stunned, but none more than Zia Anderson, Kelsey thought. She really hadn't seen this coming. Neither had Charlie Graves, Dennis Baxter, or Pasco Ramirez. They should have. They'd been a big factor in the Empire's successes.

As each person she knew came forward, Kelsey grinned at them, pleased to be part of this moment in their lives.

Once her father finished, he smiled. "And then there are those that did even more. In secret, the Imperial Senate and I have worked to make our pleasure known. Doctor Jerry Leonard. Step forward."

The scientist blinked at them in surprise. Carl Owlet nudged him toward the dais.

"Doctor, you met the challenge of the Old Empire technology head on, marshaling the forces and intellect to turn them into tools we could use to survive. For that, the Empire is in your debt, and we always pay our debts. Kneel."

The scientist actually protested. "Majesty, it was Doctor Cartwright—"

"Hush, Doctor. He's out of the system, but my agents are seeing to his reward today as well. You've earned this."

A low laugh ran through the crowd as her father knighted the befuddled man.

"Rise, Sir Jerry, and accept the accolades of your peers."

The red-faced scientist waved weakly at the clapping crowd in the audience room, much to their amusement.

Her father grabbed the other man's shoulder when he tried to escape back into the sea of people. "Hold up. I'm not done. It is my considered opinion that you've earned far more than a simple knighthood. I am hereby giving you a grant to continue your researches, and forming an institute to assist you in the Herculean tasks ahead of you. I won't be so crass as to mention the amounts, but trust me when I say that you will not want in your work."

The scientist beamed. "Thank you, Majesty! That will open so many doors for us."

"Indeed it will," her father agreed. "So will the Barony of Jackson's Rest that I'm bestowing to you and your heirs. It's on East Bay on the world of Xander, but I'm sure that you'll be far too busy to go visiting it all that often anyway."

"A what?"

It was all Kelsey could do not to whoop out loud. This was perfect.

"Don't worry, Your Excellency. I'm sure Sir Carl will explain it to you in words large enough to make sense."

That did get a laugh from the crowd as Carl came to lead the stupefied man off the dais.

Her father then called Doctor Lily Stone forward and did the same, minus the research facility, but with an upgrade to Countess of Hawk's Mount, also on Xander. She handled it with much more aplomb than Doctor Leonard.

"Your work with Old Empire medical procedures will save innumerable lives, Your Excellency," her father told the Fleet officer. "To facilitate this, I am promoting you to the rank of Commodore and placing you in charge of the medical and research sections of the hospital ship *Caduceus*.

"Captain Justin Guzman will assist you, and Fleet will see that the operations side is filled with the best people. They will support you to the best of their abilities, I'm sure."

Lily bowed. "Thank you, Majesty."

The doctor gave Kelsey a smile before she left the dais.

Kelsey followed her down with her eyes and spotted her mother again. Justine Bandar looked furious. She had no idea over what, but her mother was glaring at Zia, Dennis, and Charlie. Well, good luck with her causing trouble for them.

"Now for an award that it saddens me to give," her father said. "During the mission, one of the major factors for their success were the marines. Until almost the end, they were led by Timothy Reese, who was tragically killed in action. I've already seen that he was promoted to lieutenant colonel and given the Empire's highest award, but that isn't enough.

"He had no living family, but I am raising him to the peerage posthumously. I've selected a very nice area of land for his heir, though. Not coincidentally, also on Xander. I hope you're all seeing a pattern here."

He smiled out at the crowd. "No, this isn't an empty gesture. I believe it's fitting that a marine carry on in his stead, just as someone took command once he was gone."

Kelsey sat up straight, having just enough warning to know what was coming.

"Sir Russel Talbot, step forward in the name of Timothy Reese."

Her fiancé looked stunned, but he didn't argue as he came onto the dais.

That was damned sneaky of her father. Talbot would make a huge fuss over this in his own name, but he'd never utter a peep now. At least not until it was safely done.

"As Lieutenant Colonel Reese is no longer with us," her father said once Talbot stood in front of him, "it falls to you to carry on in his stead in the marine tradition. In the name of the Terran Empire, I grant you the County of Barrett Falls. Not coincidentally, it is adjacent to Countess Stone's holdings."

I'll get you for this, Talbot sent her through their implants.

Don't blame me. This was all his idea. Suck it up, Buttercup.

Once Talbot was safely off the dais, her father turned toward Jared. "And that brings us to the guest of honor. Admiral Jared Mertz was the man who made all these successes possible. He made the right choices. The hard choices. We collectively and individually owe him our lives.

"So, while he'd tell us that his promotion is reward enough, I am forced to disagree. Come forward, Admiral Mertz. Kneel."

Once Jared was on his knees, the emperor took up the ceremonial sword. "A knighting is the least that I can do, so let's get that out of the way." He tapped the blade to Jared's shoulders. "I name you Knight Commander in the Order of Lucien. Rise, Sir Jared."

Jared's face didn't show how uncomfortable he must feel, but Kelsey knew him far too well.

"Now, to the meat of the matter. Your service to the Throne demands a suitable recognition. I'm awarding you the Duchy of East Bay on Xander. Congratulations, Your Grace. As always, you'll be keeping an eye over your most trusted subordinates."

Kelsey saw the woman her mother had been glaring at react, standing there with her mouth open in shock. Zia grabbed the woman into a hug and whooped while Dennis and Charlie grinned.

Who was she? She did look vaguely familiar, but Kelsey couldn't place her. She took an image through her implants and sent a request through the palace system to identify her. The Terran Empire was large, so that might take a while.

"Yet that isn't enough," her father said. "After consulting with the Imperial Senate and verifying that sufficient precedent exists, I am reviving an old tradition. You are my acknowledged son, though you were not born in wedlock, and that has caused you grief. For which I am truly sorry.

"However, it gives me the foundation to make that up to you. Almost a thousand years ago, there was a similar situation, and the Imperial Senate at the time created a level of the peerage to recognize such individuals that the emperor, or in that case, empress, decided were worthy, though they were not in the line of succession. It gives me great pleasure to raise you to prince of the blood. Congratulations, Your Highness."

"No!"

Every head turned at the hot denial from the crowd. It was her mother, of course. Perfect.

Justine Bandar stormed up onto the dais. The guards moved to stop her, but her father halted them.

"I will not stand for this travesty!" her mother snarled. "He is a piece of common trash, and he will not be part of my family."

Karl Bandar smiled coldly. "I'd have preferred not to air our dirty laundry in public, Justine, but I'll not shy away from it. We're divorced. He's not part of your family. He's part of mine."

Kelsey rose to her feet. "And since we're talking about travesties, let's discuss the fact that neither Ethan or I were products of your marriage to my father."

"How dare you? I'm your mother! You will not side with him over me."

"Oh, I assuredly will. I don't know what kind of welcome you expected, but I'm not interested in talking. Guards, see my mother out of the palace."

Her mother looked shocked and tried to shake off the guards' hands, but they efficiently whisked her away.

Kelsey looked out over the crowd. "I'm sorry you had to see that, and even sorrier that I had to be part of it. Father, back to you."

He reached out and pulled her into a hug when she tried to sit back down. "I love you."

Kelsey held him tight. "And I love you."

He held her out at arm's length. "Since you're standing, I have one more thing to do. Kneel."

She gave him an odd look but obeyed.

"My little girl left on this mission as a—forgive me—pampered young woman. The crucible of fire has forged her into a warrior, and it's time I recognized that. I dub thee Knight Commander in the Order of Lucien."

He tapped the ceremonial sword on her shoulders and then pulled her to her feet. "I'm sure that Admiral Yeats was going to tell you himself, but I'll just go ahead and steal his thunder.

"As the only Marine Raider in the Empire, I think we have to recognize that you are only the first. You're in command of the Marine Raider ship *Persephone*, so you need the rank to do so. Therefore, I'm inducting you into the Imperial Marines with the rank of colonel."

His eyes twinkled. "Perhaps that will keep you from needing to disobey all the military people standing in the way of you doing what you have to do."

Her ears were roaring. No, it was the crowd. The Fleet and Marine personnel were clapping like mad and shouting their approval. She was stunned.

"I'm not a military person," she said. Only her father was close enough to hear her.

"That's no longer true," he said with a smile. "You're a leader. Now you have the tools to make that authority legitimate. Wield it well."

Once the celebratory noisemaking subsided, Elise stepped forward. "If I might co-opt your ceremony, Your Majesty, I also have an announcement."

He inclined his head and stepped back. Kelsey followed suit.

The Pentagaran heir smiled at the people gathered before them. "It is my great pleasure to announce the impending marriage between His Highness, Prince Jared, and myself. May it bind our people even closer together."

That earned another set of lusty shouts from the crowd.

Her father grinned widely. "That is *excellent* news! My most sincere congratulations to you both. Have you selected a date?"

Elise shook her head. "I know that Fleet has imminent plans for him, so I think we should have the ceremony on Pentagar. We'll have to put things together quickly, because I'd like to make sure he's mine before he has to leave."

Jared nodded. "We'll have to get my mother there. She's waited long enough for me to get married. Luckily, we don't need to send very far for her."

Her father blinked. "Patricia is here?" He looked out over the crowd and smiled at the woman Kelsey had noted earlier. "There you are! Come up here and stand with our son."

Kelsey understood now. No need for that identity request she'd sent earlier, and no wonder her mother had been shooting daggers.

She put on her most welcoming smile and held her hand out to Patricia Mertz. "I'm so glad to finally meet you. I'm sure your son will have the grandest wedding you could desire."

"This is all so overwhelming," the woman said softly. "I never told you how sorry I was."

"You don't need to apologize to me," Kelsey said firmly. "We're family."

She pulled the other woman into a hug. Over her shoulder, she saw Talbot grinning at them. That made her smile wickedly, which wiped the smile off his face.

"Count Talbot," she said with her hand extended. "Get up here. Since we're going to be working on a big wedding, we should make it a double."

8

Brandon Levy rode back up to orbit lost in thought. The ceremony had shaken him out of his resentful state of mind. If the emperor thought he needed to knight Zia Anderson, perhaps he had blinders on. Perhaps.

There was a lot to think about.

Not everyone was going directly back to the ship, so the cutter was half empty. As the soon-to-be executive officer, he had a little bubble around him. He was still the new guy.

So he was surprised when a woman moved up and sat beside him. It was the woman who'd been with the captain on the flight deck.

She stuck out her hand. "Commander Levy, I'm Annette Vitter. I'm in charge of all the fighters."

He took her hand and shook it. "I'm sure I made a bad first impression. Can I ask for a redo?"

The corner of her mouth twitched up. "I'm a huge believer in second chances. The two of us are going to be working closely together, so I want to have the best relationship we can possibly have. Might I ask you a personal question?"

He nodded. "I won't say I'll answer it, but sure."

"Is part of your anger with the situation because you don't think the captain is experienced enough?"

"That's damned impertinent to ask," he said after a moment.

She smiled a little. "Impertinence is my middle name. Look, I can't help how you feel, but I wanted you to hear from someone who's served with the captain since before we left on this mission. You'll not find a more dedicated and conscientious officer, or one with a better grasp on what it means to command a carrier.

"Not to turn up my nose at your experience, because it's valid and important, but we've had over a year to get used to working with this equipment and the requisite tactics to use it effectively. The tech is so ubiquitous that you might never know where it is or how it can help you. Case in point." She held up her right hand.

"You've lost me," he said after a moment.

"I was using my arm as an example," Vitter said. "I lost it in a pinnace crash on Erorsi. This is cybernetic."

He blinked in surprise. Her uniform tunic covered her arm, but the hand she was holding up looked completely natural.

"I had no idea. I have to confess that the transfer came so suddenly that I haven't more than glanced at anyone's files. They basically stuffed me into a cutter and sent me over." He gestured at her arm. "May I?"

Vitter held her hand out, palm up. "I was piloting a pinnace full of marines on Erorsi when someone dropped an asteroid on us," she said stoically. "We tried to run for a ridge, but we didn't make it. The blast wave smashed us into the ground."

"And you walked away from that?" He felt her hand gingerly. It felt like flesh and blood.

"More like they carried me out after Princess Kelsey put a tourniquet on me. I'd have died without her quick action. My copilot didn't make it, and neither did some of the marines, in spite of their crash harnesses and armor.

"The folks at Erorsi stabilized me, but it was the doctors on Harrison's World that fitted me with this. It took a while before I could use it well. I thought I'd never fly again. I can only imagine how hard it was for Princess Kelsey to remaster her body after the Pale Ones butchered her."

He'd seen the classified report on what had happened to the heir. That level of modification took his breath away. Just the cranial implants he was supposed to get in the morning scared him a little.

Brandon released her hand. "I can't tell it isn't real. Does it work with your implants?"

"It communicates with them, but it's self-contained and connected directly to my nervous system. It isn't amped up like the princess's artificial muscles, either."

"Does anyone else have anything like this?"

She nodded. "Captain Paul Cooley of *Shadow* lost his legs and suffered a lot of internal injuries. He's still on Harrison's World recovering. I spoke with him a little before they pulled me out of the hospital. He's got a tough road ahead of him."

Brandon had seen that part of the report, too. The Rebel Empire destroyer had savaged the light cruiser. Less than thirty percent of the crew had survived the initial attack, and even more had died when the AI ships had captured the heavy cruiser *Spear*.

Shadow was going to be scrapped. He wondered where the other officer would end up or if he was even capable of serving any longer. Brandon had never heard of anyone with that kind of physical and mental injury making it back onto active duty.

He sighed and decided to answer her overly direct question. "Honestly, I don't know how I feel. I should be supporting the captain to the hilt, but part of me feels like I've been shafted. I have to find a way past that."

Vitter nodded. "She's young. You feel as though they skipped over you. That's perfectly understandable. I'd probably feel the same way.

"What you're not seeing is the experience she has with the new ships and systems. Once you've made the jump, I wouldn't be surprised at all to see you moved to command a ship of your own. Fleet is going to grow like you've never imagined."

Brandon pinched the bridge of his nose. "I hate being so petty. Honestly, I'm sure I'll adjust. I just have to get myself into a new headspace. A little mental distance from the change will make things better."

They had half an hour until they docked, so he might as well make the best of the time. "Tell me about fighter operations. What are your people like?"

She smiled. "They'll give you grey hair, but I couldn't ask for more aggressive, hard-fighting people. They'll make you want to brig them, and then they'll make you proud. Often in the same day."

The two of them settled into a deep discussion of how the small craft worked, and he immediately felt more comfortable. Maybe this wasn't going to be so bad after all.

* * *

ANNETTE WAITED until they exited the cutter to spring her next surprise. She cut Commander Levy off as he was excusing himself.

"Actually, if you have a few minutes, I'd like to give you a tour of the flight deck. It's what this ship is formed around, and you need to know what's down here."

Levy smiled a little. "Now why do I feel as though you sat by me on the cutter just to lure me into this tour?"

"That's not the *only* reason, but it was one. No offense, but your arrival might have cemented certain preconceived notions about fighter pilots. I'd rather have you see us in our element and form a better idea of the kind of people we are."

"Sure."

The landing bay was adjacent to the launch bay so that ships could quickly rearm and get back into the fight, so it was a quick walk to the area where the fighters were arrayed, ready for battle.

"These are Raptors. Mark fives, to be precise. The most advanced fighters the Old Empire had. They're incredibly fast and can be configured for antiship or antifighter roles. That basically means that it carries different missiles to suit the occasion.

"To take out a ship, it needs powerful strikes. It can carry two ship killers, one under each wing. Those can swap out for twelve antifighter missiles on need. They also have high-capacity flechette guns for really close work and taking out missiles fired at them."

He looked at the closest fighter with a quizzical expression. "Wings? Don't grav drives make those obsolete? Not to mention a space fighter doesn't run into air."

"Part is aesthetic design, more is tradition, but in the end, these ships can fight in atmosphere and drives do fail. Do they need wings? Probably not, but they look more ferocious with them."

Levy squatted to look at the missiles. "Only one under the wing, so this must be a ship killer. It's chancy enough getting through with ship-launched missiles. How can these little things hope to compete?"

She smiled. "Because we get in close. The drives on these are short range but very powerful for their size. Think of a sprinter. The charges are shaped to help get through battle screens and armor. One won't kill a ship, but enough stings will take the target down."

"That sounds pretty dangerous for the pilots."

"It is. In an actual combat scenario, we'll lose pilots. A lot more than any of us like. We all know that. That might explain some of the personality types that seem to be attracted to the profession."

He leaned back against the fighter and considered her. "What kind of personality are we talking about?"

"Someone cocky, who pushes the limits. Risk takers and daredevils. And let's not forget the egos. They're the best, they know it, and are always trying to prove it. We're a breed apart.

"I'm not saying that as a way of trying to earn them any slack. Only so that you'll have an idea what you're getting into as the executive officer on a carrier. Especially the first carrier."

"All right. I'll keep that in mind, though I won't promise I'll go any easier on them. At least I've been warned what I'm in for."

She stepped away from the fighters. "Let's go into the ready room. We always have some fighters in a state of readiness. They can launch on a moment's notice and keep an unexpected enemy busy while the rest of us get into flight suits. It's a rotating duty we all pull."

The pilots in the ready room were all awake, though that wasn't a firm requirement, so long as they were suited up. About half of them were playing cards, while the rest were watching a vid.

"Heads up," she called out. "Keep your seats and listen to me. This is Commander Levy. He's our new executive officer."

Their expressions were professionally guarded.

"I've heard a lot of good things about you," Levy said. "I won't pretend to understand what you do yet, but I'm going to learn. That will undoubtedly mean I make mistakes and miss things. When that happens, I'm going to rely on you and your comrades to set me straight."

He smiled a bit wryly. "On the flip side, I'm going to be the guy you get hauled in to see when you get up to any shenanigans, so don't push me too hard. If we can find a balance, we'll get along fine."

She stood back and watched as the new officer mingled with the pilots and started learning who they were. That was promising. Hopefully, he'd figure out the right balance as they went forward.

Once the crap hit the fan, it would be too late.

* * *

JARED SAT DOWN BESIDE TALBOT. The emperor had other things to do and had excused himself. Elise, Kelsey, and his mother were locked into a deep discussion about flowers. He was damned glad he only had to show up and get married. They were giving this more attention than he'd marshalled when they attacked the AI at Harrison's World.

"This is crazy," Talbot said. "I had no idea what I was getting myself in for. Hell, even this morning I thought I had more time to get used to it."

That made Jared smile. "I only knew the hammer was coming down this morning. About the wedding. I had one whole night to think about these titles. Man, they are going to complicate my life."

"Tell me about it," the marine grumbled. "I'm as far away from being a noble as possible. What the devil was he thinking?"

"I'd imagine that a lot of the first nobles were people like us," Jared said philosophically. "The men and women who got things done. The foppish sort only came in later."

Talbot sighed. "Maybe. I still feel maneuvered. The emperor used the LT to make me feel like I had to accept the title."

"It worked, didn't it? Frankly, that was a masterstroke. I'd have bet money you'd have run for the door before they corralled you into this."

The other man laughed softly. "Wouldn't that have caused a scene? Then there's the wedding. Kelsey and I talked around the subject, but she's just like her father. She saw an opportunity and waded in swinging."

Jared looked over at the women. "Is it the wrong decision? If so, now might be the time to say something."

"No, no. Nothing like that. I just envisioned this as something that would happen a little more sedately. A year ago, I couldn't even spell officer. Now I are one."

The last two sentences were said in a stilted voice, and it was a joke Jared had heard before.

"Very funny. You still haven't caught up, though. Once you marry Kelsey, you become the prince consort. Your Highness."

"Shit," Talbot said. "I never even considered that."

Jared laughed. "Did you consider the fact that your bride-to-be is now a colonel in the marines? Major."

"Dammit. This just keeps getting better. Think about who I'll have as a mother-in-law."

"Ouch. Point to you. Your life is going to be filled with plusses and minuses."

They sat in silence for a minute before Talbot spoke again.

"I suppose she's worth it."

Jared laughed again. "Remember she has super hearing."

"She'd have already skewered me if she'd heard me," the marine said with a grin. "Have you considered that we'll be brothers-in-law?"

Jared hadn't thought of that wrinkle, but it was definitely an upside. "I like that. You're a good man to have at my back when trouble comes knocking, and I like to think I have my uses."

"Such as when Justine Bandar comes calling?"

"Let's not get carried away. Bravery only goes so far."

Kelsey came out of the other room and glared at them. "You know I can hear you, right? I'm trying to plan two weddings. With only a few days before we leave, you're a distraction. Out."

Jared wasted no time in pulling Talbot to safety. The Imperial Guards assigned to him formed up around them as he headed for the landing pad. "Let's get out of the building before they find something for us to do."

"An excellent idea," the marine said. "We should make the most of the evening. Where do muckity-mucks go to have a real drink?"

"To the nearest marine bar."

Talbot grinned. "I know just the place. We should celebrate our freedom while we can."

"Speak for yourself, marine. I, for one, welcome our feminine overlords."

9

Z ia woke, glad that medical nanites had made hangovers a thing of the past. She showered, dressed, and made it to the bridge right on time. Danny Leonidas smiled at her and rose from the command seat. "I expected you to sleep in, Captain. You were up late."

"You mean that I made the mistake of letting the fighter pilots get me well and truly hammered. Thanks for covering for me."

"It was no problem. I'm going to miss being here."

Zia took her seat and shook her head. "You're going to revel in commanding your own ship. Admit it."

"It's intimidating," he said. "But, yes, I'm really looking forward to it."

"Once Commander Levy has completed the implant procedure, I want you to get him up to speed on basic implant operations and run down everything he needs to know."

Danny nodded. "Aye, ma'am. That's a tall order, but I'll get the process started. I'm sure he'll catch on fast."

She really hoped so. Even more, she wanted Levy to get the chip off his shoulder. She might need his unstinting support very soon now.

Lieutenant Esther Frasier turned toward them. "Excuse me, Captain, but we just received orders addressed to you."

"Send it to my implants."

A small window popped up in her mental view. It was Admiral Yeats. "Captain Anderson, these are preliminary movement orders for *Audacious*. That of course means the rest of Admiral Mertz's fleet, too.

"You'll all head for Erorsi in forty-eight hours. I don't want to chance the freighter arriving before you do. I have no idea what Admiral Mertz's plan of engagement will be, but I'm sure your people will play a big role in it. Be ready to depart on schedule. Good luck."

The message ended, and she shook her head at her soon-to-be former executive officer. "We have preliminary orders. You'll arrive on your new ship just in time to head out with us. We leave in two days."

The other officer winced. "That's not a lot of time to get settled in. As in no time at all."

"Such is the life of an Imperial officer. Get things moving on our end. I don't want any unpleasant surprises."

He nodded. "I'll send out recall orders for everyone that hasn't returned to the ship. We're good on supplies, and I see no reason *Audacious* can't leave on time."

"Pass Levy on to Annette and let her get him up to speed. Time just became too precious for you to focus on your replacement. He'll have to learn as he goes."

"Aye, ma'am. Should we cancel the going-away party?"

Zia shook her head. "No way. We'll make time to send you off in style. Unfortunately, we'll have to stuff you in a cutter and send you on your way as soon as we finish. Get some people to help you pack. I'm going to miss you, Danny."

"I'll miss all of you, too, though I won't be so far away. If you'll excuse me, I need to start moving Heaven and Earth."

Zia spent the next hour going over everything for herself. She knew Danny would handle the details, but the responsibility of being fully ready was hers. She also called for Annette to come to the bridge.

Once she arrived, Zia led her into her office. "Time is short, so I'll get right to the point. We have movement orders. We'll be under way in two days."

The other woman nodded. "Danny told me. We'll be ready."

"What he probably didn't tell you was that he's going to be too damned busy to get Commander Levy up to speed. I'm passing that task on to you. Have Jake get Black Jack Squadron ready. The other two squadron commanders can handle their own birds. Get our exec to where he needs to be."

Annette nodded again. "Will do. He and I spoke on the way up from the ceremony. I think he'll fit in just fine, once he adjusts to the new circumstances."

Zia raised her eyebrow. "That seems awfully optimistic. I'm not sure that he's going to fully accept me as his commanding officer. There's a pretty big gap of experience and, in his shoes, I'd be pissed."

"I told him the same thing. I think he'll manage things, and I'm willing to help push him along. He's representative of the rest of Fleet, you know. All us new kids have a serious leg up on them, and they're going to have to scramble to catch up. Some otherwise fine officers won't make the jump."

Zia grimaced. "We'll just have to win that fight one person at a time. Levy's implant procedure should wrap up shortly. We really need him as a full part of the team. Go do me proud."

The pilot saluted. "Aye, ma'am. One hard-charging executive officer coming up."

* * *

BRANDON SWUNG his legs over the side of the table. The operation had been less overwhelming than he'd expected, considering they were putting things in his head.

The ship's doctor, Commander Zac Zoboroski, checked the readout one last time. "Everything looks good, Commander. Someone will need to show you the ropes, and you're on light duty for the rest of the day. If anything happens that concerns you, come immediately back here and let me have a look."

"Such as what?" he asked. "Frothing at the mouth? My wall screen going on and off by itself?"

The other man smiled. "Nothing like that. Headaches, mostly. Something off with your vision. I don't expect that to happen, but the literature says to watch out for it. Even that only means we need to adjust the settings a little. This is very safe technology. Now that the AIs can't reprogram it, of course."

"How many of these have you seen installed?"

"Hundreds. I was responsible for all the new folks that transferred aboard after *Audacious* arrived in Avalon space. Doctor Stone trained me in it once I had my own set of implants."

Brandon considered the other man. "Do they really make that much of a difference?"

"It's night and day. The things I can do now were unthinkable a year ago, and I'm discovering new possibilities in the library every day."

"None of us is using this new technology at anything like full potential. For that, we'll have to wait for the kids who get implants to grow up. They'll manage things that we'd never imagine because they don't know their fool ideas are impossible."

Brandon shook his head. "It feels like this is impossible, so I suppose that makes sense."

The hatch opened and Annette Vitter walked in. "I see I'm just in time."

"I'll leave you to it, Commander," Zoboroski said as he headed for his office. "Take it easy today."

He stood and was pleased to see he had no dizziness. "What are you just in time for?"

"I'm the lucky soul that gets to show you how to use those new implants of yours. I'll also give you a walking tour of the ship. Commander Leonidas is busier than a one-armed paperhanger. Trust me, I should know."

"I can't believe you're so cavalier about it," he said, stepping up beside her as she walked toward the hatch. "That's got to be a serious mental trauma."

Vitter nodded. "I make light of it because I don't believe in letting something like that dominate my life. I'm damned lucky that they were able to fix me so well.

"The first thing you need to know is that there *is* an instruction manual. I realize as a man that you're genetically disinclined to read the instructions before haring off into unknown territory, but I suggest you give it a look first."

He snorted. "That is so sexist. How did you know I wouldn't flip out about you saying it?"

"I didn't," she said with a twinkle in her eye. "Now I know you have a sense of humor under that dour expression."

"I'm not dour," he said primly. "I'm just a little reserved around people I don't know."

"That's what they all say. Okay, the interface to your implants is surprisingly easy to use. It just takes a little practice. Think of this like a new sense. You can see the corridor, you can hear the people moving down it, and so on. Try to take it all in for a moment."

He instantly saw what she meant. There were little icons scattered along the corridor now, including on and in the people passing by. He focused on Vitter and found several on her person.

"Okay, that's interesting. You have icons on you."

"What about yourself?"

As soon as she said that, he realized that he also had one. It must be his implants. With that frame of reference, he recognized her implants and could separate them from the other gear she had that popped up on his internal radar.

He tried to poke his implants mentally. They responded with something very much like a menu. The first thing on it was labeled orientation. That was useful.

"I found the instructions."

"Excellent," she said as they walked into one of the lifts. "You'll want to spend some time studying it in more detail. Take us to the flight deck."

He reached for the button, but she stopped him. "Tell the controls where to go with your implants."

The next few hours were a real education, and he started to get an idea of exactly how far behind he and all of the other Fleet personnel were. The sheer number of things he could now do with a thought staggered the imagination.

The sheer number of systems on the ship daunted him. Each one allowed the appropriate people to do their jobs in ways that were barely comprehensible. A crew trained and able to do this would have significant advantages in speed and effectiveness.

Vitter left him in his quarters when they were done. He felt guilty about taking her away from her duties when he found out they had orders to leave in less than two days. She shouldn't have wasted time on him. Hell, she shouldn't have had to.

It was obvious that it would take him weeks just to become competent at the basics. Putting him here was a severe disservice to a probably well-oiled crew. Fleet should have left Leonidas in the exec's position.

Well, he didn't have the luxury of telling them that, so he'd better get his ass in gear. If they got into a fight, he had to be ready. If something took out the captain, he had to be able to step into her suddenly larger shoes.

10

K elsey put her hand on Carl's shoulder. "I'm sorry you had to cut your getaway short."

He grinned at her. "Me, too, but we have a rain check from the emperor. Besides, I wouldn't have missed the ceremony for the world. Honestly, Angela got her orders right after we got back into the city, so it wasn't happening anyway. Don't worry about it."

"Where is she going?"

He raised an eyebrow. "You don't know? She's going to your ship, Colonel."

"Ah. Well, I'll be happy to have her."

The Imperial Guards around them seemed faintly scandalized when he picked up the Imperial Scepter from its cushion, she noted.

"We're not going to hurt it," Kelsey assured them. "We just need to perform some tests. You're going to be right there with us. I promise we're not stealing it so we can sell it on the black market."

"How much do you think it's worth?" Carl asked.

"Don't tease them like that," she said repressively. "They leave their senses of humor in their duty lockers."

That got a smile from some of them.

She'd checked with her father about this, of course. She hadn't mentioned the reason she wanted to do it, though. Just in case they were barking up the wrong tree, she wanted to keep that close to her vest for the moment.

Carl's main lab was in the capital at Imperial University, so only a short air car ride from the palace. He'd brought down a surprising amount of technology recovered from the graveyard of dead Fleet ships at Harrison's World, as well as some things from the Grant Research Facility, a very secret weapons research lab that had been the genesis of the rebel forces on Harrison's World.

She hadn't been to his lab since they'd refurbished an entire building for his use. She supposed that the prestige of having a Lucien Prize–winning scientist on their staff, as well as having the Imperial purse foot the bill, made a large facility inevitable.

In this case, Carl's lab wasn't just the outer research area, which was filled with scientists and research students examining various pieces of equipment, but the highly secure inner lab that was his personal domain.

Security here worked like an onion. It took clearance to get past the human guards at the door. Carl had shown them just how easy it was to use social engineering to get into one of their other "secure" labs, so he'd insisted on diligent people manning the entry points.

Once into the outer labs, only those with appropriate clearances could get into any of the more secure rooms. His personal lab had the tightest security of all, only opening to his implants or someone whom he'd approved.

That was a damned short list, considering the importance of the experiments and research in progress there.

He led her and her guards into his private domain. The wide room had a dozen tables piled with partially disassembled gear and almost as many computer terminals. No people, though.

"We'll want to put it under a scanner and see what we can without opening it," he said, heading for a machine with its hood already raised. "I doubt it's booby trapped, but it pays to be cautious."

Carl set the scepter under the scanner head and lowered the hood. A screen behind it came to life, showing them the external surface. Little points appeared on the image as the scanner determined the composition of the materials.

Kelsey watched it but also used her implants to get a more details. Under the precious metals on the surface, there were additional high-tech materials but nothing that seemed out of place.

The scanner bumped up the power and started looking at the inner makeup of the scepter. She immediately saw advanced electronics very similar to what went into implants.

"I'm not seeing anything that leads me to believe opening it would be dangerous," Carl said. "There is a computerized component, but I'm unsure of what it's for at this point."

He raised the hood and took the scepter over to a worktable. The Imperial Guards hovered a little too close, so he gestured for them to step back. "I'm going to be very careful. Don't worry."

Carl grabbed a headband with a magnifier. "The latches are cleverly hidden. If I didn't know this was meant to come apart, I'd have figured it was a solid unit."

"That makes sense," she said. "You don't want everyone in the Empire seeing that when you use it in ceremonies.

"I wonder if this is the original scepter or one built after the rise of the AIs. If this key was there before the AIs, it might not have anything to do with them." The thin scientist shrugged. "Emperor Marcus seemed to think it was relevant, so it must tie in somehow."

He used a tool under one edge of the handle, and the end of the scepter came off. From there, it was easy to remove the rest of the panels.

The interior of the scepter was made of what certainly looked like a small computer to Kelsey. Her implants detected nothing, not even an operating power supply. After all this time, any power source was likely dead.

Carl plucked the battery out. "I have one that will work here. This is the same model I use in a few other projects."

He retrieved an identical battery from a bin and slipped it into the appropriate socket. The lights on the computer indicated it was booting, but Kelsey still couldn't detect it. It was very stealthy. Her Raider implants were good enough to sense most equipment at this range.

"I'm not seeing any way to connect with it," she said.

Carl nodded. "That might be intentional. The best way to hide an access point is to make it invisible. You either have to activate it in some way or transmit in the blind. You know, like saying a code phrase and having a secret door open up."

She smiled. "Someone has been watching too many action adventure vids. Can you see any way to trigger the access point?"

"Let me examine the rest of the scepter for a few minutes."

Kelsey stepped back to let him work. She could do other things while she waited for him to wrap up. Like figure out what she was going to do about her mother.

The woman had left a billion messages on her com. The guards had sent her packing twice last night, including once where they'd called the local police to haul her away.

She doubted they'd arrested the ex-empress. That would've taken colossal balls. No, they'd probably taken her back to the precinct and read her the riot act. Not that it would stop her mother for very long.

Not that it needed to. She'd be out of the woman's grasp in two days. Then she'd have weeks or months to come to terms with what she'd learned. Her mother could find her own balance in that time, too.

No, she had to meet this challenge head on.

"I found something," Carl said.

She shook herself out of her funk and walked back over to him. "That was quick."

"That's because it's right in my face. Literally." He lifted the handle a little. "This is a sophisticated scanner. One I'd wager is tuned to scan someone's DNA."

Kelsey snorted. "Then I'm screwed, because it would have to be linked to the Imperial line. My father or Jared are the only possible candidates, or one of the cadet branches of the family. That all assumes that it wasn't set to only recognize Lucien and his father."

"There's only one way to be sure. We need to have one of them give it a try. Perhaps they can add people to the access list. I'm a bit nervous about hacking the computer without trying other options first. If it's *really* secure, it might wipe itself if someone unauthorized attempts to get in by force."

She nodded. "Get together with Jared and see what you can find. Since I'm not actually required for this, I should probably deal with my mother."

He shook his head. "I don't envy you that task. Her behavior at the ceremony last night was all the morning news could talk about. I'll grab some portable gear and head up to *Invincible*. Good luck."

"You have no idea. I'm considering wearing my powered armor. Just to be safe. Send the details to my implants once you figure something out."

"Will do."

Kelsey collected her guards and headed back out to the air car. Finding her mother wouldn't be hard. All she had to do was listen to any of the ranting messages to get the address where she was staying.

* * *

ZIA THOUGHT THAT COMMANDER—SOON to be captain—Leonidas's going away party was a smashing success. Jim Richmond had outdone himself. The food was light yet very scrumptious. Probably fattening, but medical nanites could help with that. Thank God for technology.

Danny Leonidas looked at turns sad and happy. That pretty much defined how they all felt. Except for the new guy. Brandon Levy looked depressed.

Zia wasn't sure about what. With him being so new, it could be just about anything. She hoped he'd settle down once he was actually working his new position.

Annette Vitter slid over beside her. "He's really not that bad once you get past his dour and occasionally officious exterior. I mean seriously, he's a lot less abrasive than Commodore Meyer was when the admiral had to deal with him."

That was certainly true. Then-Commander Sean Meyer had had trouble walking with that stick up his butt. He'd been arrogant and closed-minded on the best of days.

The events of Harrison's World had proven that even the most obnoxious person had a good side, and she had to admit that Meyer was more than dedicated to his job. Even if he was snootier than the local nobles.

"Here I am being as closed minded as I accused him of being," Zia said sourly. "Being in command has a lot of challenges. Like giving him the benefit of the doubt until he gives me reason not to."

Annette turned so that her back was to Levy, who was chatting with Tony Hastert. The swarthy chief engineer seemed to be telling one of the tall tales he was known for. He seemed to think that a story worth telling was worth embellishing.

She had to admit he had a real talent for it. He could spin out the story of *Spear's* destruction into an epic tale of tragedy and loss, which of course it was.

"I wouldn't let it get to you," Annette said. "He has got a chip on his shoulder, but he's starting to understand why things are the way they are. Once he's up to speed with the new technology, he'll find himself in command of one of the salvaged ships."

"Sure, after we spend all the time training him," Zia said grumpily.

Annette laughed. "All it takes is one look at the manpower requirements going forward even five years and that becomes inevitable. We're going to be hideously short of experienced command personnel."

That was even truer than Annette knew. Zia had been there for the full-day briefing with Admiral Mertz. The scope of the new Fleet was vast.

They'd already broken ground on a new academy but were aggressively recruiting new people to stick into makeshift classes all over the planet. The current crop of junior officers was going to be learning on the job in positions they'd never have dreamed of getting for years.

The situation with the senior officers was even worse. Fleet had never been huge to begin with, so it taxed the current manpower levels just to crew all the ships they'd brought back. A number of older vessels were in parking orbits, bereft of everything but a caretaker crew. They'd probably be decommissioned in the near future.

That wouldn't even begin to be enough. Recall orders would go out to former Fleet personnel and those who'd retired. That would help, but it wouldn't fill the gap. It was going to be challenging.

Well, that was a problem for another day.

Zia picked up a fork and rang it against the glass of champagne in her hand. "Your attention, everyone. As much as we're all enjoying this, Danny needs to get his butt onto the cutter for his new command. Danny, we're going to miss you."

She raised her glass. "I give you Captain Daniel Leonidas, commanding officer of the Imperial Fleet light cruiser *Lightning*."

Everyone raised their glasses and shouted their congratulations.

Danny smiled and saluted them with his glass. "I'm sorry to leave you all, but I know the ship is in good hands. I won't be too far away, either. To the Empire! May she never falter!"

Zia smiled and repeated the toast. He was going to be a great captain. Now she had to get Brandon Levy into similar shape.

"It is also my duty to welcome our newest companion. As of this moment, Commander Brandon Levy is officially *Audacious's* executive officer. Welcome aboard."

The clapping was much less boisterous, but that didn't seem to bother Levy. He smiled and nodded to all of them. "I'm sure this is as sudden for you as it was for me, but I'll do everything I can to get up to speed quickly. I look forward to working with all of you."

Zia clapped but decided to reserve judgment on that. Annette was good at reading people, but only time would tell. They were going back into harm's way, and there was no room for petty jealousy.

"Danny, if you'll say your goodbyes, I'll walk you down to the bay," she said. "I think Annette has arranged a little escort to see you safely to your new command."

11
_____

J ared examined the Imperial Scepter closely. It was just as impressive as he'd expected, plated in precious metals and glittering with cut gems.

"What do you need me to do?" he asked Carl.

"The handle has a sophisticated scanner that I think is keyed by DNA. Nothing happens when I pick it up, but I'm hoping you get a different result."

"With my luck, it'll be an electrical shock."

The young scientist laughed. "No chance of that, Admiral. It's safe."

Jared grasped the scepter by its handle and lifted it. The thing had more heft than he'd expected. It would make a decent club.

"I'm not feeling anything," he said after a moment. "What am I missing?"

"See if you can connect with it. You might not sense anything to ping, but try anyway."

Jared didn't feel as though the scepter was available, but he tried to insert his implants into it anyway. After a few tries, he sensed something. It felt as though the device were looking back at him. He received a connection request through his implants and accepted it.

Identify yourself, a computer voice whispered into his mind.

I am Jared Mertz, Fleet admiral and prince of the blood. He'd added that last since it seemed appropriate.

The key recognizes your bloodline, Highness.

That seemed a little underwhelming. *Am I authorized to use you?*

This unit will work for anyone of the blood that possesses it.

"It says I'm authorized, but I have no idea what it does," he told Carl. "What do you want me to do?"

"See if it will describe what it does. What kind of key is it?"

Tell me what you do, he instructed the device.

This unit is the key. It unlocks the repository.

This wasn't the smartest computer he'd ever interacted with. *What repository?*

The Imperial Vault.

"It says it opens the Imperial Vault," he told Carl. He connected with the ship's computer and ran a search.

The original Imperial Palace on Terra had had a massive vault with many, many treasures from all across the Empire.

Do you mean the treasure room under the Imperial Palace?

Yes.

Do you have any other data that I can access?

This unit has no further information to share, Prince Jared Mertz.

Can I instruct you to allow contact from another computer?

Yes.

Open a connection.

He felt the connection appear in his implants. "Marcus, please connect with this computer and see what information you can get from it."

"Right away," the AI said. "Connection established. It's remarkably restricted. It literally only knows what it just told you."

He scowled. "Then why have a sophisticated computer?"

"It seems the processing power must be in the function it performs," Carl said. "If I wanted a lock that no one else could pick, this might just be the way. Whatever it does will mesh with the computer in the vault in some manner.

"Without the key, the vault won't open. Since it's restricted to Imperial blood, no one can steal it. Well, not anyone that isn't related to the Imperial line."

Jared shook his head. "That seems silly. What if the emperor died without an heir? How would they open the vault?"

"Brute force and ignorance," Carl said matter-of-factly.

"You've spent too much time with Angela. I'm fairly sure that won't work out well for the burglars."

He set the scepter back on the padded rest. "I'm not sure what would be so important to Marcus or Lucien once the AIs kicked them off Terra."

"Perhaps Emperor Marcus put something into the vault that's critical to stopping the AIs once and for all."

"It would've been nice if he'd left a note about that." Jared sighed. "He may have hoped to turn things around. At this point, we'll probably never know. Visiting Terra is somewhat low on our list of priorities."

"Admiral, I have found a segregated piece of memory inside the scepter," Marcus said. "It's locked and I cannot access it."

Computer, what is in the segregated memory?

This unit is aware of no segregated memory.

"Interesting. It doesn't know about it. Is it part of the computer?"

Carl frowned. "Hang on. I can see it through Marcus. It's located in an area that is read-only for most computers. There's no reason for something so basic to be protected so well."

"Can you unlock it?"

The scientist shook his head. "No, but you might be able to. Just like you don't need to sense the computer to link with it, you might not need to directly access it."

"You know that doesn't make sense, right?"

"Think of it like a blind connection. The computer can't sense the memory, but if you tell it to access the sectors I give you, it might be able to do so. A function it doesn't even know it has. One that only someone actually able to use the scepter could even fathom, but most would never think to look for. Marcus is a lot more observant than the average computer."

"Thank you," the AI said.

Carl gave Jared a series of numbers, and he instructed the computer to read the area. An image immediately appeared in his head. It was Emperor Marcus. He appeared very much as he had in the transmission Kelsey had found on Pentagar, but he was now seated behind a desk.

"Son, I'm sorry that I can't be there for you. I can only pray that you've managed to escape the notice of the rebels and have arrived at Avalon safely. If not, I suppose you won't be seeing this.

"Maybe when you're older, you'll understand why I couldn't take you with me. It's not because I didn't want to but because I couldn't bear the thought of you dying with me. Which, I have to assume, is the most likely end."

The man sighed tiredly. "We're about to pull out of Terra. We can't hold the system. Based on their tactics, the rebels will destroy everything in space and use EMP blasts from orbit to kill most of the technological base. The death toll is going to be hideous.

"We've pulled as many people as possible onto the ships with us, but the rebels will keep pursuing us. We'll try to give the civilian ships as much lead as we can before Fleet turns and fights, but freighters and personnel transports can't match a battlecruiser's acceleration."

Marcus leaned forward intently. "Once they pacify a system, they don't leave a lot of force there. They start infecting the population through their implants and move on. That's why they can keep using so many of the ships they've captured.

"I'm hoping that once they've moved past Terra, you can strike back for me. I never spoke with you about the AIs, but they have a weakness. One specific unit in a system called Twilight River controls them. If you can co-opt it, you can end the rebellion and reverse the infection in everyone."

Jared smiled sadly. The man had no idea that the rebels would find Lucien and pursue him right to Avalon's atmosphere. They'd destroyed every Fleet vessel, and it had taken longer than Lucien had lived to regain the lost technology.

The boy emperor hadn't had the benefit of medical nanites. They didn't implant the devices until someone was in their late teens because they could interfere with the early development of a growing body. The Empire had relied on their advanced medical care to correct any issues before then. He'd only had a normal human lifespan.

"The scepter will get you into the vault once you slip back into the Terra system. They might flatten the palace, but you know the other ways in. Don't do anything to alert them to your presence.

"Inside the vault, you'll see an amazing number of things. Treasures sent to the emperors from all across the Empire since the very beginning. You'll need to move to the rear of the vault and look for a plain wooden crate on the floor. It's not big, but be careful with it. The contents are irreplaceable."

An image of a small crate appeared in the corner of Jared's vision. He'd recognize it if he ever saw it.

"That crate contains the only override for the AI that exists. Or, perhaps I should say, that still exists. There was one on the station at Twilight River, but I'm sure the AI saw to its destruction at once.

"One of the scientists was visiting the nearby Fleet base to consult with a colleague and broke every security rule to give her a peek. They managed to escape with it when the AI infiltrated the Fleet base."

Emperor Marcus rubbed his face. "I understand that leaving it in the vault probably seems stupid, considering that we know the AIs will overrun the system, but I can't take the chance that they destroy the ship carrying it.

"It may be possible for me to send some Raiders to recover it if we're more successful than I imagine. They'd have to break in, but that isn't impossible if I give them the plans. Which, by the way, are appended to this message."

He smiled wryly. "I know this is a terrible final message for a father to leave his son, but all our hopes ride with you. I love you, boy. Always remember that. When you have a family of your own, you'll understand. Godspeed."

The message ended, and a file uploaded to Jared's implants. It had a very detailed map of the Imperial Palace on Terra, exquisite specifications on the vault itself, and a listing of the contents. The sheer number of priceless historical artifacts in that massive chamber stunned him.

After a moment, he set that aside and looked at the plans. He didn't know that much about breaking and entering, but this wouldn't be easy, even with inside information.

He had no idea what the situation was really like on Terra. Olivia West said that the AI had given up on subduing the population and bombed it back into the Stone Age. The Imperial Palace might not even exist anymore. Yet he now knew they had no choice but to make the journey.

If there was any chance at all they could turn this around, it would require the override. Otherwise, every AI in the Old Empire would keep fighting. Hell, there was no guarantee that they could even get to the

Twilight River research station. The AI probably had a massive fleet there to defend itself.

"That was useful," he told Carl and Marcus once he'd digested everything. "Here's what I got." He sent them the message and the plans to the vault.

"Too bad there weren't plans for the override itself," Carl complained. "Then we could build our own."

"Probably not," Marcus said. "Much like the key, it's probably all tied up in the specific computer programming and custom hardware. We'll need the actual override to plug into the master AI. What I wish the emperor had mentioned was who was behind the attack in the first place."

"I'm pretty sure that whoever they were, they lost control," Jared said. "Otherwise, the AIs wouldn't still be running everything."

"We'll need to brief the emperor. When the time comes for our trip to Terra, we'll have to appropriate the key. For right now, that's a low priority. We have to capture the freighter and make sure the escort, if any, doesn't make it home."

He smiled at Carl. "This time we're ready. All we have to do is get into place and wait for them to obligingly come calling."

* * *

ANNETTE TOOK Levy down to the launch bay and into the ready room. "Now that you have implants, I think you need to see how they can affect things like flying a ship. It also gives me an opportunity to show off the fighters for you."

"That doesn't sound like light duty," he said with a smile. "I think the doctor is going to be annoyed with me."

"I'll take it easy," she assured him. "I only make people throw up when they're feeling good."

"Thanks. Seriously, isn't the acceleration going to be a problem?"

She shook her head. "I had them relocate a training fighter to the landing bay. We'll go out nice and easy."

"Training fighter?"

"It's easier to show you after we get you suited up."

Jake Fiennes was waiting to get Levy into flight gear, so she let them go while she mentally reviewed her planned excursion. There'd be no in-atmosphere flight or hard acceleration. It was basically a joyride. One that would allow the newly implanted officer to interface with the small craft and get a feel for what that meant.

Fifteen minutes later, Jake brought Levy back out. She nodded approvingly. "You look ready. Okay, let me give you the safety spiel first. If for any reason we have to eject, you need to keep your hands in your lap and sit up straight. The grav drives in the seats are not light duty by any stretch of the imagination, so we'll try to avoid that.

"Second, while on the fighter, I am in command. If I give an order, it is for the safety of the vehicle, and you need to obey without argument. Clear?"

He nodded. "Perfectly. I won't be a problem."

"We can cover the rest while I'm doing the final preflight. Come on."

She led him back to the landing bay. The training fighter was very similar to the regular version except that it had an extended body and a second cockpit in front of the normal one. That allowed a trainer to observe everything a new pilot did while not seeming like they were hovering.

"This is the trainer," she said. "You'll be in the front, so it'll feel like you're alone. That's by design. I'll be communicating with you the entire time."

Annette gave the bird a good preflight and showed Levy how to enter the cockpit. Once he was seated, she made sure he was firmly strapped in.

"Before you put your helmet on, there are a few other things," she said. "The fighter has a lot of emergency supplies onboard, so unless the fighter is in danger of exploding—which is exceedingly unlikely—we'll be fine in the event of trouble. We're not even going that far away from *Audacious*.

"Also, your controls are locked out unless and until I activate them. In the also unlikely event that I'm somehow disabled, the controls will activate for you. The fighter keeps good track of our health. You've piloted a cutter before, so I know you can get back to the ship if you have to."

He nodded. "Got it."

"Strap your helmet on and connect it to the life support system. In the event that the cabin loses pressure, you're still going to be fine. I'll settle in back and take us out. Once we're clear of traffic, we'll get started with your familiarization."

Annette got herself situated and linked with the fighter's on board computer. The cameras in the front cockpit allowed her to see Levy. She'd make sure he could see her when they got out.

The fighter didn't have standard controls like a cutter or pinnace. Pilots controlled these high-tech marvels directly through their implants.

That scared a lot of new pilots. What if something went wrong?

In fact, this way was a lot safer for the pilots. All the fighter's systems were in range of the implants, even without the amplifying effects of their helmets. Each system had multiple control interfaces in case of damage. The only way to lose contact with a system was the destruction of the system in question.

On a cutter, an unlucky bit of damage could take out a control run and leave systems offline. Even with multiple dedicated runs, those craft were more vulnerable than the Raptors.

The other weak link in the control chain was the pilot's implants. Since they were in their heads, the loss of their implants wasn't that much of a concern. They wouldn't be caring if they were dead or unconscious.

The lack of a control panel also meant that the pilot wasn't tempted to use the less efficient manual controls. The implants were so much more versatile.

With the fighter amplifying their implant range, a pilot could directly control someone else's fighter if the on-board computer detected they were disabled and the rescuer had the appropriate authorization.

The command pilots—those with the highest level of training and authority—had override codes. They could literally take over another fighter from close by, even if the pilot wasn't disabled.

She smiled. That usually unnerved the hell out of the new guys. It was also useful in simulating systems failures.

None of this was important for the moment, though. Commander Levy probably didn't have what it took to be a fighter pilot. This was just an orientation run.

Annette cleared her departure with Control and lifted them off the deck. A light touch on the grav drives sent them coasting out of the bay at a leisurely few hundred meters a second. With the drives online from the start, there was no feeling of acceleration.

She opened an audio link to the other cockpit. "Okay, we're clear of the ship. If you open your implants up, you'll detect an access point for the fighter. As I said, I've locked out your controls, so you're not going to do anything if you stretch your wings. You'll be able to use its scanners to see what's going on around us."

His eyes widened. "Holy cow. I can see every status on the fighter without searching around for it, and the view is unreal. It feels like seeing, but it's not really visual. More like a 3-D tactical display."

"That's a good analogy. You can see me if you try. We could communicate solely by implant, but that makes a lot of people uncomfortable."

He nodded. "I see you now. How do you keep everything straight without displays to monitor?"

"I treat the fighter like my body. It takes a while to get used to it, but it's incredibly natural. You can also tell it to create virtual displays through your implants. That's usually how most people learn to fly, so it's comfortable.

"In this case, I want you to do this the hard way. Look at our course. See how we're coming up on some geosynchronous satellites? I want you to turn us a few degrees to either side of our present course. I've released the flight controls to you, though I have override authority."

The course change was more abrupt than he'd intended, she was sure. That was a natural mistake for a first-timer. They didn't realize how sensitive the controls were.

"Sorry," he said. "I overcorrected."

"You didn't know what to expect. I'm going to throw a waypoint onto the scanner readings. Change course for that and increase our speed by ten percent. We're positively dawdling."

Over the next hour, she gradually added systems to his control until he had a very good idea of the complexity of what it meant to pilot a fighter. He handled them better than she'd expected. Maybe he had what it took after all. That was something to explore at greater length later.

"Okay, I think you have the basic idea," she finally said. "Now it's time to give you a demonstration of what it means to be in the advanced course."

Annette brought up a dogfight simulation. Empty space suddenly became a 3-D nightmare of ships going every direction at maximum speed, all while shooting at one another.

"Holy shit!" he blurted, trying to dodge the fighter around an oncoming enemy. Proximity alarms blared as he almost collided with their fictional wingman.

That's when someone dropped in behind them and fired missiles. The end was quick.

"Oops," she said. "You're dead. Don't feel bad. I got blown up just about that fast the first time, too. Being a fighter pilot is dangerous business."

He stared at her out of the mental screen. "How the hell do you keep all of that straight? With all the other fighters, I couldn't even tell which ones were on my side, much less where any of them were going."

"Training and practice. We have to keep all of the variables in our heads. I ran an ambush yesterday where most of my squadron died, including me. We train hard so that doesn't happen when things get real, but up close and personal, a lot of us will die anyway. That's what we do."

He frowned hard. "I said I knew what you meant about being a fighter pilot, but it turns out I had no idea. I'm going to have a lot of work ahead of me to understand not only what it means to be a fighter pilot but to command them from the deck of a carrier.

"On the plus side, I think I have a good idea of how implants work on a small ship like this. The capabilities are a lot more intuitive than I expected. I'm sure this is only the start of my education, but I get it. Hopefully, I'll pick up the critical things more quickly. Thank you."

"My pleasure. Now, since we're done, I'll let you find *Audacious* and take us home. Try not to get us killed on the way," she added with a smirk.

12

K elsey stood outside her mother's hotel room and dithered. She had a lot of nerve coming here after what had happened at the ceremony. Kelsey was going to catch hell, even though she was the wronged party here. Her mother would never admit fault. That simply wasn't how she worked.

Well, time to start the fireworks.

She turned to her guard commander. "There's going to be yelling. Things will get broken. I'm a Marine Raider. She's not going to hurt me. Under no circumstances are you to come inside that apartment unless I signal for you to do so or you see blood seeping out from under the door. Is that understood?"

The man looked deeply unhappy, but he nodded. "Yes, Highness."

Kelsey pressed the buzzer on the door and waited. Moments later, her mother yanked the door open and glared at her. "Finally. Get in here and leave these people outside. The time for childish behavior is over."

"I couldn't agree more."

Kelsey stepped inside and closed the door behind her. "I can't imagine how you expected this to go, but I'm not the little girl you abandoned all those years ago."

"Don't be ridiculous," her mother said. "I didn't abandon you. You came to visit as often as you liked. I blame your father for turning you against me."

"Then you'd be wrong." Kelsey put her hands on her hips and stood there, not wilting under her mother's glare. "I know what you've done. What's worse, I know who you did it with. There's no unseeing something like that."

Her mother shook her head. "I have no idea what you're talking about. All I did was come back to make sure you were okay. A daughter needs her mother after a trauma like you went through."

Justine Bandar had no conception of what Kelsey had been through. They'd decided that the public didn't need to know the gory details of her implants or how she'd gotten them.

"You cheated on my father. How could you?"

Justine Bandar threw up her hands and started pacing. "How can you ask me that after he cheated with the help? Worse, how could you stand by that bastard in the first place?"

"Call Jared Mertz a bastard at your peril," Kelsey said in a low, dangerous voice. "I like him far better than I like you at this particular moment, and I don't see that changing.

"As for Father, he admitted what he'd done and paid the full price for it. You're still busy denying everything and hoping no one realizes the true extent of your betrayal. The fact that you'd had no idea he'd slept with Jared's mother while you were sleeping around doesn't exactly help your position, either."

Her mother started to say something, but Kelsey held up her hand. "I'm not finished. I've seen the train used for escaping the palace. Nathaniel Breckenridge showed it to the people that rescued me from Ethan.

"Maybe you never realized it, but it records every trip. I've seen exactly how many people you've slipped into your rooms over the years, and how long your infidelity went on. Do *not* try to pull the wool over my eyes. I know who you are now."

Her mother dropped into a comfortable-looking chair with an audible huff. "That changes nothing between us. I'm your mother, even if Karl isn't your father. It doesn't mean I don't love you."

Kelsey shook her head. "Maybe not, but it severely limits my sympathy for you when you go after my brother."

Justine Bandar's eyes hardened. "He is not your brother. Jared Mertz killed your brother. He's a monster."

Kelsey shook her head slowly. "You really should watch the news more often. I killed Ethan."

Her mother waved her hand as though she were dispersing smoke. "So those idiots on the news said. I don't believe it. You're not capable of something so terrible. Your father convinced you to take the heat off his precious by-blow. You don't need to lie to me."

"You have no idea what I'm capable of," Kelsey said coolly. "Ethan was mad at the end, paranoid and dangerous. I gave the order that let Ethan run to his death."

Her mother blinked. "What?"

"The flip point he ran through went to an area of space filled with deadly radiation. I kept my mouth shut and let him go."

To her credit, her mother looked horrified. "Why would you do that?"

"Because he was going to start a civil war that would kill more people than either of us can comfortably count. I loved him, but it was him or the Empire. I'll live with the consequences of my decision for the rest of my life, but I wouldn't change it."

"Ethan was your brother."

"Ethan was a mad dog that had to be put down," Kelsey said regretfully. "I don't know when he became a paranoid monster, but you don't leave unexploded ordinance lying around where anyone can set it off. He was the heir, and the Empire wouldn't have survived him ascending to the Throne."

Her mother's frown intensified. "Did you kill him so you could take his place?"

That actually made Kelsey laugh bitterly. "Hell, no. I'm still so disgusted with things that I'd have happily renounced my claim and become a commoner. I have important work to do that doesn't involve egomaniacal senators or other nobles. Political backbiting is one thing I could cheerfully live without."

"Why not just capture him?" Her mother finally sounded somewhat normal, just a woman hurting for the loss of her son.

"He was too far away and had a destroyer with him. If I'd warned him, he might have been able to escape. I'll admit that was a low-order probability, but he'd just poisoned Father and blamed me, so I wasn't feeling very forgiving.

"Which brings us back to you. I counted eighteen different lovers over a period of decades. That's a little more serious than an ill-considered fling. Yes, it's between you and Father, but it hurts me, too.

"If you want to continue having a relationship with me that doesn't involve shouting and recriminations, I'd lose the chip on your shoulder.

"Jared and I have been to hell and back, and we've worked out our differences. He's my brother in every way that matters. I can't stop you from being a bitch to Father or me, but if you go after Jared Mertz, I will make you deeply regret that mistake. Am I clear?"

Her mother said nothing for a long moment, examining Kelsey's face closely. When she did speak, it was much more calmly. "You've grown harder. You were always so soft when you were younger."

"Hard times either toughen you up or they kill you. The past is gone, Mother, and so is the little girl you could manipulate. If you want to continue having a relationship with me, you're going to have to accept that. Grow. Up."

Justine Bandar nodded slowly. "I can see we have many things to discuss."

Kelsey turned toward the door. "It will have to wait. I'm shipping out in a day and a half and have far too much work to do before we leave. I'll give you a chance when I get back. It might be several weeks or several months. You'll just have to be patient. I'm far too angry to be reasonable, and so are you. We'll talk then."

She more than half expected her mother to try to stop her, but the other woman let her leave without a word. The guards surrounded her, and they headed back to her air car. She only relaxed when she was on the way home.

Her mother probably thought she'd find a way to talk with her tomorrow, but Kelsey would be back on *Persephone* by then. She had a meeting with Carl Owlet, and then they'd be leaving for Pentagar. Maybe by the time they captured the freighter, she'd feel a little calmer. Probably not, but one could hope.

Kelsey's implants announced a message from Jared. She listened with interest as he explained what they'd discovered about the Imperial Scepter. Even though it wasn't useful right now, it gave them a long-term goal that might bring the AIs down.

If they could subvert the prime AI, it could order its subordinates to surrender. Considering how badly the Old Empire had lost a straight-up fight, they'd need to be sneaky in fighting this war. A full-on confrontation would be fatal.

She'd tell her father what they'd found and let him incorporate the details into his planning. Once they'd dealt with the freighter, they could map a more considered path forward.

Frankly, she had to admit she badly wanted to see the birthplace of mankind. Even in the condition it was in now. Her mind was already working the angles, and that beat the heck out of being pissed at her mother.

* * *

JUSTINE BANDAR CONSIDERED the door that Kelsey had just closed with barely contained fury. How dare her daughter treat her this way?

The urge to shriek and smash furnishings was strong, but it wouldn't serve her purposes now. If her little girl thought she could put her mother at arm's length for months, she was sorely mistaken. A plan was already taking form in her mind.

She smiled, looked up a number, and activated her room's com. She spoke in her most sultry voice. "Jackson? Justine Bandar. Are you free for lunch? Oh, and perhaps the afternoon? I have a favor to ask, and I'm willing to do anything to get it. Anything at all."

* * *

BRANDON MADE a point of visiting with each of the department heads that evening. He'd read their status reports for the last month, but he wanted to hear them tell him what was important to them. Some things didn't make it into reports, and he didn't want them to have any unpleasant surprises on this mission.

The rush wasn't anyone's fault, but that didn't stop him from resenting it. The stakes were so high. Failure might mean the death or enslavement of everyone he knew. No pressure.

The most interesting conversation was with Lieutenant Commander Elizabeth Givens, the ship's tactical officer. Since Captain Anderson had made such a big deal about how the fighters were their weapons, he hadn't expected *Audacious* to be so well armed.

It might not pack the punch of an Old Empire superdreadnought, but it could take a couple of battlecruisers for a hard ride if the need arose. The missiles were a lot more capable than he was used to, and beams and battle screens were wholly new to his experience.

Tactical doctrine called for the carrier to have a protective group of battlecruisers, cruisers—both heavy and light—and a screen of destroyers. In the Old Empire, they'd have more than they did now, but that would change as they acquired more ships.

Everything Captain Anderson had told him about controlling the ship was true. He could—and had—accessed the scanners from his bed. With his overrides, he could have taken the ship to battle stations and done just about anything that normally required being at a console on the bridge.

Watching the crew work with the ship's computer was a humbling experience. He had a lot of learning to do just to understand what he didn't know.

That didn't mean that he had nothing to offer this ship, however. He took guilty satisfaction in making a list of things he could tweak to improve the way the crew worked together. Neither Anderson or her former exec had had the experience to see how sloppy some things were.

These were modifications that didn't have a thing to do with implants, just interdepartmental functions. If either of the other officers had served as an executive officer, they'd have had a better grasp of what needed doing.

His experience still counted for something.

He spent a good part of the night at his desk working up a grueling training regimen for himself. He had a number of Fleet primers on how the implants influenced tactical and strategic operations. He also knew the basic functions—and the advanced ones—that he'd need to learn just to catch up with his peers.

Then there were the esoteric theoretical possibilities. He had a nephew that was a wizard with technology. He'd sent him an unclassified note asking what kinds of things he'd imagined were possible. The boy had been voraciously reading up on the civilian implant data and had immediately send him back a long, rambling letter with tasks ranging from the mundane to the mythical.

The next wave of Fleet trainees would upend everything people like him imagined possible. Better yet, the first wave of people with implants—like Zia Anderson—would be in exactly the same boat.

He shouldn't feel satisfied about that, but he did. Small and petty was fine, in private and limited in scope so that he didn't let it bleed into his working relationship with the others. As it had already done.

About an hour and a half before he was due on the bridge, he gave up the pretense of trying to sleep and headed to the gym. To his surprise, he found Annette Vitter there lifting weights.

"Morning," he said as he started stretching.

"Morning," she agreed. "Are you feeling overwhelmed yet?"

He snorted. "You know I am. This is an impossible task, but I'll get it done. The only question is how long that takes and how many mistakes I make along the way."

She set her bar on the stand above her head and sat up. "No matter how badly you screw up, you'll never reach the epic heights that Wallace Breckenridge managed on the same mission we're trying to do over."

Brandon stopped a second snort. Barely. "I could hardly do worse. That man screwed up by the numbers. At least this time we have a lot more ships, and we're on the same footing technologically."

"Don't be so sure," she warned him, wiping her face with a hand towel. "Those people have been using implants their entire lives. Even our most experienced people still default to doing things manually. We don't know all the tricks."

"I was thinking about that earlier. We need to get a bunch of kids implanted and put them in simulators. They'll adjust to the new capabilities far more quickly than we can, and they'll come up with things we never thought of."

The fighter pilot cocked her head. "You mean like full-up ship simulators? I hadn't ever considered that. I was only thinking about general tech."

He nodded. "If we set up classes of kids, taught them the basics of ship operation, and let them play ship simulators in combat, they'd take to it fast. Make it a competitive game and they'd swarm to it.

"We have all the manuals of what tactics the Old Empire used, but we're still short on knowing how they did a lot of things so naturally. The kids could teach academy cadets, who'd pick up a lot of what they were hearing."

Vitter nodded slowly. "That's a pretty good idea. I'd write that up and send it to Fleet headquarters before we ship out. It might make a big difference."

"I probably will," he said as he stretched his calves. "Do we have any idea what role we're going to play in the ambush?"

"Yup. We're the backstop. We'll be positioned in the system on the other side of Erorsi in hiding. Once the freighter and any escorts go by, we'll cover the exit. If someone gets away, we'll make sure they don't get any messages back to the Rebel Empire."

"That seems a safe bet with this ship's capabilities, not even considering the fighters."

"Admiral Mertz isn't the type to take chances if he doesn't have to. It's like Talbot always says: If you aren't cheating, you aren't trying."

He laughed. "That sounds like a marine. Did you know him all that well before this mess?"

They fell into talking as he started working out. Maybe integrating wasn't going to be as difficult as he'd feared.

13

Jared examined the layout of the task force via his implants. Everyone was in place at the Nova flip point. They'd make the jump into the hellish system and almost immediately to Pentagar.

If Ethan Bandar or Wallace Breckenridge had only known how close safety was, things might have turned out a lot differently.

"Take us through, Marcus," he ordered. "Send a greeting to Omega and then take us to Pentagar. We don't have a lot of time to chat."

"Aye, sir," the AI said. "The task force will flip in thirty seconds."

His mental countdown went smoothly, and they made gut-wrenching transition from Avalon to Nova. In just an instant of time, they travelled hundreds of light-years through the gravitational anomalies they called flip points.

The fact that this one was artificially created didn't seem to change how it worked. It hadn't changed in the months since the alien had used its station orbiting the black hole at the center of what had once been its people's solar system to bridge the distance between not only it and Avalon, but also to Pentagar.

In practical terms, that meant that a fast ship could get from Avalon orbit to Pentagar orbit in a matter of hours. Once they had more freighters rigged up to stand the incredibly deadly environment around the black hole, trade would no doubt keep a stream of traffic making the journey.

"Omega sends his greetings and wishes us the best of luck with the ambush," Marcus said. "I estimate five minutes until everyone is in place for the next flip."

They could've done it faster, but there was no need to rush. Better to arrive in good order.

"Have we got any idea what's on the other end of the rest of the flip points in this system?" Jared asked. "Other than Harrison's World, of course."

Omega had given them a map of the flip points it could detect using its linkage to the black hole. No one had really been able to explain exactly how that worked, though Omega had tried. The science was incomprehensible. Much like the fact the alien station had once created portals into other realities. Science fiction made real.

Just like the transport rings he'd gifted Carl Owlet. The smaller pair made for a useful science experiment, but the openings were maybe a quarter of a meter. The two larger pairs were useful for people and cargo. Both had the range to take someone to the other side of the planet or even a ship in orbit.

Admiral Yeats wanted his own transport rings to make getting people and equipment to Orbital One easier. That was one of the projects Carl's team was working on. They just needed to understand them first. That would take a while, even with Omega's guidance.

Marcus's answer pulled him out of his micro-reverie. "One of the flip points leads to Harrison's World, of course. Admiral Yeats sent scouts through the other two. Those systems appear to have never been occupied by anyone.

"There are normal flip points exiting from there, but the admiral decided that they didn't need to be examined at this time. Omega's map does show some of the potential of that new branch, however.

"One thing the map does not explore is the potential for other destinations through the weak flip points. Doctor Leonard still believes that fine-tuning the flip drive's output might generate a different outcome. Thus far, though, he hasn't tested his hypothesis."

"That would certainly change things if he's right," Jared said. "It's not applicable to us at this moment, though. Are we ready?"

"All ships ready to flip, Admiral. Commencing in thirty seconds."

Less than a minute later, they were in Pentagaran space. A number of Old Empire ships that they'd gifted to the Pentagarans were on guard duty at the new flip point. Jared thought that was a prudent precaution.

"Incoming signal, Admiral," one of his staff members said, turning in her seat. "Admiral Sanders."

Walter Sanders had been a Pentagaran commodore when Jared and Kelsey had first arrived, but after the attempted coup, Elise's father had speedily promoted him and put him in command of the Pentagaran Navy.

"Put him on," Jared said.

The main screen switched from a strategic map of the Pentagar system to a view of a bridge identical to the one Jared was on. The older man in the center seat grinned like a boy. "It's good to see you again so soon, Lord Admiral Mertz."

"I thought we were on a first-name basis, Walter."

"Well, I thought after your recent social promotion that a little formality couldn't hurt. After all, you're now engaged to the heir to the Pentagaran Crown! Perhaps I should call you Highness."

Jared grimaced. "I'd rather you didn't. I'm already tired of the bowing and scraping when I leave the ship. Seriously, how do you people manage?"

"We somehow get by. Fine, I'll call you Jared. In private. At least until you become the prince consort. Then we'll have to fight about it some more.

"Meanwhile, I'd like to thank you for this fine new ship. Her name is *Resolute*, and she's a superdreadnought just like *Invincible*. I'm in love, by the way."

Jared smiled. "They make nice flagships, don't they? You're very welcome. It's the least we could do after you helped us so much."

"I seem to recall the help being a bit tilted toward you helping us. In any case, you're going to want to head to Pentagar, so I'll accompany you. We need to sit down and plan the ambush in more detail. We have forces in place at Erorsi, so there's no danger the Rebel Empire will sneak in like they did last time."

That, too, had been Wallace Breckenridge's fault. The man had had an absolute talent for doing the wrong thing. If he'd just followed the plans Jared and Sanders had worked out, they'd have caught that first freighter with its pants down.

"Maybe so," Jared said, "but I'm not going to feel comfortable until we have everything securely locked down. Right now, the flip-point jammers can keep us safe, but we could really use some Marine Raiders. With the supplies from that freighter, we'll be able to keep Kelsey out of the fighting."

The other man smiled. "Good luck with that. She seems like the lead-by-example kind of woman, heir or not. I'll have to congratulate her on her promotion as well."

"Well, we'd at least have Talbot and the rest to help defend her," Jared sighed. "Actually, I'm going to send Elise over to one of your ships to get to Pentagar. We're all heading for the Erorsi flip point."

Sanders nodded sharply. "Of course. You're in command of the operation, and I'll feel better when we're ready, too. I'm not sure Princess Elise will feel the same way. She has a wedding to plan, and you're one of the mandatory attendees."

"I suspect more goes into organizing and executing a state wedding than we've put into the ambush."

"I'm not sure Her Highness will appreciate the comparison of her upcoming nuptials to an ambush," Sanders said dryly. "Yet your point about the planning is well taken. I'm sure many details will take time to work out and get into place. With such an important event, no one will want to see any aspect left to chance.

"I'll hop in a cutter and make my way over. We can review the plan and current positioning of the assets over dinner."

"That sounds excellent," Jared said. "I haven't chosen a steward yet, but my new rank allows for one. For the moment, we'll just need to make sure we don't starve ourselves."

"It's a good thing you have a lot of space on that ship," the other man said with a gleam in his eye. "One steward might do for an admiral, but the prince consort of Pentagar will have a few more servants to keep around. We monarchists just love to have hangers-on."

Jared sighed helplessly. "I'll never understand that. They'd better not try to help me get dressed, or I'll space someone. I'll see you in about half an hour. And Walter, it's good to see you again. It isn't very often we get a chance to correct a serious blunder. Let's make everyone proud."

The older man's smile widened. "Then we're in complete accord. I'll see you shortly, Jared."

* * *

KELSEY WALKED into the briefing room on board *Persephone* with a purposeful stride. The men seated at the table rose as she stepped to the head of the table.

She smiled. "Gentlemen, as you've probably already guessed, I'm Kelsey Bandar. For simplicity, let's set aside any excess formality. We're all here to carry out a very difficult mission, and I don't want anything to trip us up. Are we good with that?"

The men glanced at one another and nodded.

A group that looked less like military personnel was hard to imagine. None of the men wore uniforms of any kind. In fact, most had never served in any branch of the Imperial service. Their elite status came from the other side of the sheets, so to speak.

The fourteen men around her specialized in recovering spacecraft that someone had either stolen or that had failed to maintain their payments. Recovery agents were what they called themselves. The next best thing to pirates, but staying on the legal side of things. Mostly.

Talbot's original plan for capturing the freighter was predicated on boarding with marines and shooting everything in sight. While she'd become a big fan of that kind of thing, they absolutely had to capture the freighter—and its cargo—intact.

That included the computer and crew. Lieutenant Commander Michael Richards, the Rebel Fleet officer they'd captured, thought he knew where they'd picked up the cargo of Raider implants and gear, but it would be best to have independent confirmation.

It would be even better to have people that had been inside the facility, and she intended to get those people, no matter what it took. With that in mind, she'd already decided to speak with her father about including Richards on the mission, even though Admiral Yeats disapproved Jared's request.

They still had time to make that happen, so she'd get her hands on the freighter first. The follow-up mission would flow from what they learned.

"Before we get started," she continued as she sat, "I'd appreciate it if you'd introduce yourselves and tell me a little about what you do."

Everyone resumed their seats. A taller man with brown hair going grey at the temples spoke up. "I'll take the lead on that, then. My name is Cain Hopwood, and I'm the lead partner of Recovery Incorporated. Been getting ships back from folks that shouldn't have them for twenty-five years. Most of these fine folk have been with me since I started.

"And I'm not sure a listing of skills would be much help. We're jacks-of-all-trades sorts. You kind of have to be. You might find yourself needing to do all sorts of things on a recovery operation. Just assume we can all handle any aspect of hijacking this ship you can think of, and plenty you can't."

She smiled. "I like the sound of that. The wrinkle that concerns me most is that this ship will have implant-capable equipment. You've all received corresponding implants, but you've never had to anticipate the kind of security obstacles they might entail."

An equally tall man, this one pale of skin with dirty blond hair, shook his head. "Jason Young. That probably won't be much of an obstacle. The crew will feel all safe and secure. The first hint of trouble they'll have will be someone stunning them. Great things, those stunners. Beats the heck out of darts."

A tall, balding man shook his head. "Best not to get too cocky. What if someone wipes the computer or sets off a self-destruct charge? Oh, I'm Alan Barnes. I usually pilot the skiff."

"That's the kind of thing we absolutely have to prevent," Kelsey said. "Mainly to keep from dying, but also to be sure the Empire keeps breathing."

A tall, bookish-looking man with brown hair smiled. "Bob Noble. I usually secure the target's computers. I've been working with Sir Carl, and we've modified some of our standard tools to do the same kind of thing on the new technology.

"That might not be good enough for a military system, but it should be fine on a civilian freighter. Once we're in, they won't be able to wipe the computers."

"I can say the same about the engineering spaces," an average-sized man with a receding hairline said. "If I can get to the engine room, I can lock them out of propulsion. Michael Falkner here."

A redheaded man spoke up from the other side of the table. "Dale Thompson. I'll take the lead in searching for and locking out any demolition charges."

"Very good," she said.

A tall, white-haired man half raised his hand. "I guess I'm next. Bill Smith. I'm an intrusion specialist. If anyone locks themselves into the bridge or other space, I'll blow the hatch and get us in."

An older, slightly balding man cleared his throat. "I'm Jon Paul Olivier and the young man beside me is my son, Andrew. We're takedown specialists."

She smiled at the two men. "What does that mean?"

The father smiled. "We sneak even better than the rest. Have you ever seen a vid where someone gets whisked away right out from under the noses of his friends? That's what we do."

Hopwood nodded. "And let me introduce the rest of my team. Raise your hands when I say your name. Tracy Bodine, Michael Goad, Kristopher Neidecker, John Naiser, and Tom Stoecklein."

"Well, I'm sure you're all good at what you do," Kelsey said. "You have a stellar reputation for success. Rather than me telling you what the plan is, why don't you tell me the best way to make this work?"

Hopwood nodded. "The challenge here is that the freighter might have an escort. That makes sneaking up on it very hard to do without the warship spotting us. That would probably be fatal.

"We're lucky that your ship has very stealthy pinnaces. If the warship isn't on a heightened state of alert, we should be able to lie in wait for the freighter and slowly match course and speed. Space is big. If they don't see us, we'll be able to attach to their hull. If they *do* see us, we'll have blown everything and need to run like hell."

"Let's assume we manage to succeed, because failure drops the ball into Admiral Mertz's lap. Once we attach, what next?"

The man grinned. "We bypass an airlock and let ourselves in. The men split up and head for the critical areas of the ship: the bridge, engineering, and the computer room. Once we're in position, we seize control of everything. The details vary, and sometimes the execution is tricky, but if we get onboard that ship, we'll get things locked down very quickly."

She nodded. "We'll have a team of Marines in the pinnace to back us up with armor and heavy weapons, if needed. They'll make sure everything stays friendly once we gain control.

"The optimal solution leaves any possible escort in the dark about the change in management. Taking it out is Admiral Mertz's job. Once we signal him that we're in control, he'll kick off stage two of the ambush. He'll use his ships to separate us from the warship and then defend us from any attempts to shoot us."

"How likely is that?" Thompson asked.

"The last time, the destroyer abandoned the freighter. It didn't seem at all concerned about us capturing it. My guess is that this will play out similarly.

"We'll be over in the Erorsi system in a few hours. Once we're in position, we'll use a freighter and destroyer of our own to do test runs until we have everything working perfectly. Or the bad guys show up and we run out of time."

She brought up the deck plans for the kind of freighter they'd likely encounter. "While we wait, let's go over the plans and start making some broad decisions."

14

Zia studied the layout of the system just beyond Erorsi. A white dwarf burned hotly in the center of the system, orbited by uninhabitable rocks and debris. The system was empty of Rebel Empire vessels, which was exactly what she'd expected to find.

That didn't keep her from taking every precaution. She left two probes in the flip point to Erorsi to take back word if they found anything. She also had several probes watching the other flip point in the system with passive scanners from a distance. When the freighter arrived, they'd relay a tight beam back to *Audacious*.

Since the carrier and her escorts were the plug that would keep any Rebel Empire ships from escaping Admiral Mertz's ambush, she had to make sure they didn't see her. The single asteroid belt would be more than enough to conceal her ships from any scans that came their way.

The carrier, two battlecruisers, four cruisers, six light cruisers, and a dozen destroyers floated in a loose array, powered down to standby and moving with the slow orbit of the belt. She had fighters out to keep an eye peeled for significant debris, but that wasn't likely to be a problem. Unlike what the vids usually said, objects in an asteroid belt were extremely rare and far apart.

Her carrier group was overkill for a destroyer, or even several cruisers, but she didn't mind having more than enough force at hand to convince an enemy to surrender.

"How long until we expect the freighter?" Commander Levy asked.

She looked over at where he stood beside her console. "The time interval is variable. The likeliest timeframe won't be for another few weeks, but they've come early before. Or they might not come until three or four months from now. We might as well settle in."

He grimaced. "I hate the waiting, but more practice time is useful."

"How are you adjusting to your implants?"

Levy shrugged. "They aren't that hard to master, with someone to show me what I need to do. It's thinking ahead about how to best utilize them that's hard. I can't seem to break the habit of doing things by hand."

She nodded. "That comes with practice. We're so used to doing things one way that we default to that first. That's why we keep practicing until it becomes second nature. When the fecal matter hits the rotating oscillator, we'll do what we've wired into our reflexes.

"On another note, I've looked over the changes you made to the interdepartmental workflow. I have to confess that was never my strong suit. The interaction seems to be a lot smoother now. Well done."

He smiled a little. "That comes with time and practice, just like everything else. I've been studying the Old Empire map of systems beyond this one. Based on what Commander Richards said, there isn't a lot of habitation out this way. Not anymore."

Zia knew that hadn't been true five hundred years ago. At the height of the Old Empire, almost every system had some kind of population. After the rebellion, the remains of humanity had been concentrated into relatively few systems so the AIs could keep an eye on them.

Commander Michael Richards, the AI specialist they'd snagged on the disastrous mission to capture the last freighter, had some familiarity with this sector of space. Even so, they couldn't completely trust what he said. The AIs kept their slaves in the dark about a lot of things. It was far better to assume the worst and be pleasantly surprised when things worked out as expected.

That happened rarely enough at the best of times.

"Right. The nearest known inhabited system is three flips toward the Imperial core. We can't count on all the other places being empty, though. Just because the AI tells them nothing is there doesn't make it true. Remember the hidden ships at Harrison's World."

Unknown to the inhabitants there, the AIs had placed a facility inside the atmosphere of a gas giant with four computer-controlled battlecruisers in standby mode. Any system could be seeded like that. Even this one.

Which was one of the reasons she'd sent probes all over it as soon as they'd arrived. Since it had never had a real population, she considered the odds of hidden ships low, but in a space battle, the worst surprises weren't what you didn't see. They were what you saw that turned out to be wrong. Lord knows Admiral Mertz had used that fact against any number of opponents while she'd served under him.

She liked to think she'd learned a few things from the experience.

"Status change," one of the sensor techs said almost two hours later. "The stealthed probes at the other flip point report activity. Two ships have transitioned into the system."

"They're early," Levy said, seemingly a little surprised. "Really early."

"Good thing we're already here waiting for them. Another win for the admiral's cautious streak. Do we have a reading on what kind of ships they are?"

"Yes, ma'am," the tech said. "A freighter and a destroyer. Just like last time."

"What's their ETA to the Erorsi flip point?"

"Eight hours at their current speed."

"Excellent. Send one of the probes through to Erorsi with the news. The more time that Admiral Mertz has to get into position and hide his ships the better. We'll shoot the second one through just before they could possibly detect it flipping."

She used her implants to go over the scanner readings from the spy probes. The resolution was crappy, but without going active, they'd need to rely on the emissions from the ships themselves. The destroyer seemed like a Zombie class, just like before.

The little destroyers had been ubiquitous in the Old Empire. They were very utilitarian and filled a number of roles with ease.

The freighter was larger than the last one, and the power output was a tad higher, but that was fine. With a missed shipment, they'd probably brought enough to make up for the loss.

"Remind me why we're not using those fancy FTL coms that Sir Carl developed," Levy said.

"Because it's possible they'd detect the signal. It does generate a small but noticeable gravitic signature. They might not be able to tap into it like Omega did, but we don't want to take any chance of tipping them off that we're here.

"There's also the fact that Sir Carl is still putting them together. We thought we'd have longer to get ready."

He nodded. "I really hope we don't need it this time."

"Thankfully, we only have a destroyer and freighter to worry about."

She settled back into her chair. In half a day, this would be over. One way or the other. She hoped they captured the freighter intact. That was just the kind of break they needed to have a fighting chance.

* * *

JARED HAD to admit he was surprised by how early the freighter was, but the records they'd recovered from Erorsi had a few occurrences this early in the year. He was damned lucky he'd been conservative.

Though, to be fair, even if his forces had missed the arrival completely, the Pentagaran forces were well situated to take care of the two ships.

With Zia's early warning, it was no problem at all to get the various ships in the Erorsi system into hiding. *Invincible* was in Erorsi orbit, taking the place of the destroyed orbital.

With the two shipyards there, that made three objects with fusion plants for the approaching destroyer to detect. Since that was what it expected to see, he'd made sure they could mimic the old orbital's output as closely as possible.

It only took a moment to access the strategic map of the Erorsi system. Some of the ships were out of place but racing to get in position before the freighter and its escort arrived. There was plenty of time, so long as the warship didn't outpace its slower companion, and that seemed unlikely.

Persephone was just about in position. The Marine Raider ship was almost undetectable when either moving slowly or stopped. She would sit behind the flip point.

The plan was to launch both of the Marine Raider pinnaces ahead of the expected arrival and get them inbound. That would reduce the required acceleration to match courses. It also meant they were vulnerable to being spotted or possibly failing to catch up if the target ships took a different course in.

He'd worked extensively with Marcus in playtesting the attack runs. They had a very high chance of being on the proper course and almost a two-thirds chance of escaping detection.

Those were odds he could live with. The chancy part came when the boarding parties seized the freighter. That's when everything could go to hell.

"If the ships bump their speed ten percent, how long until they transit, Marcus?"

"A little more than five hours, Admiral."

He nodded. All their assets into place in less than three. That worked.

Now it became a waiting game. One with a chance to increase their overall odds of success dramatically in the war against the Rebel Empire. Unlike the last time, they had the edge in firepower now. If needed, they could saturate the destroyer's defenses and obliterate it without risking any marines.

* * *

KELSEY DIDN'T WAIT for *Persephone* to get into position before she launched the stealthed pinnaces. She, of course, went with them.

Major Angela Ellis—her former bodyguard and new executive officer— would rather have had her stay on the ship, but that reduced the chances of quietly capturing the freighter by almost twenty percent. Too great a risk to take.

Of course, Angela had sicced a new minder on her. Lieutenant Regina Paulson wasn't as physically imposing as Kelsey's tall friend, but she was a tough and determined marine. Kelsey was sure the dark-headed woman had secret orders to keep her as safe as anyone could in a firefight.

The princess was in her Raider armor and outfitted for war. Not that she expected to need most of her weapons on this mission, but she'd been caught short far too many times to skimp when she had the chance to prepare in advance of the trouble.

Half of the recovery team was on this pinnace, along with three dozen marines in unpowered armor. The other pinnace had the other half of the recovery team and another set of marines. If only one pinnace managed to rendezvous with the freighter, they could still carry out the mission.

Kelsey sat at the pinnace commander's station on the marine deck. It gave her a wide console to oversee a map of the system. Even though she was completely comfortable using her implants, there was something about seeing the data laid out like this that made it feel more natural. She doubted that would ever change.

This feels like old times, Ned Quincy said.

"You can use your outside voice," she said aloud. "Everyone, Ned Quincy is an AI that is going to appear beside me. Don't be alarmed."

The marines already knew Ned, but she hadn't had any reason to tell the recovery team. She probably should keep his existence secret, but she'd grown tired of talking to him in her head.

His image appeared beside her, made to look solid by the emitters she'd installed. He waved at the goggle-eyed recovery agents. "Afternoon. The princess should also mention that I'm classified. Keep this under your collective hats."

They nodded and kept watching the projection curiously. Lieutenant Paulson wandered over from the rest of the marines.

Ned turned to face them both. "This isn't the first time I've done something like this. Sneaking up on other ships is a stock in trade for the Raiders. The destroyer complicates matters, but if they aren't looking too closely, they'll miss us. Even at point-blank range."

"Any last-minute advice?" Kelsey asked.

"Commit. Once you're in, push through hard and fast. The worst-case scenario is getting onto the freighter and having word get out while you're still capturing it. Make sure you don't give anyone time to yell, either in person or over the com."

Kelsey nodded. "Good advice. We'll be in position by the time the destroyer and freighter flip into the system. It's all a matter of waiting for them to catch up with us. Piece of cake."

Her gut put the lie to her casual words, though. Being able to make more Raiders was riding on this mission. If anything went wrong, they might not be able to recreate what was done to her, and they desperately needed more people with her capabilities.

She took a deep breath and let it out slowly. This wasn't her first rodeo. She'd make it happen, even with the inevitable surprises along the way.

15

Brandon was sitting at one of the spare consoles on the flag bridge practicing with his implants when he spotted an unusual reading from the freighter. At first he thought it was the relatively unfocused nature of the passive scanners themselves, but the more he refined the data, the more certain he became that there was actually something different about the ship.

"Captain, I may have something," he said.

She turned in her seat and gave him her full attention. "What is it?"

"I've been using the passive scanner data to practice using my implants, and I think there's something different about the freighter. Not as in just different data based on the class, either. Something that shouldn't be there."

As the ships had come closer, they'd been able to narrow down the classes until the probability was over ninety percent. That was just about a certainty, considering the limited number of possibilities. He had a very good idea of what the readings from the freighter should look like, but there was something off.

"How so?" she asked.

"We're almost certain it's a Yeager class freighter, but I think I'm seeing more than one fusion plant. There's the ghost of a second one in the data."

Anderson's eyes unfocused for a moment and then she frowned. "I think you're right. It's shielded, I think. Not as well as it could be, but easy enough to miss if you're not looking closely. Good catch."

She tapped her console. "Most freighters only have a single fusion plant. This must be some kind of custom job. I wonder what they need the extra power for."

"Could it be a weapon?"

As a former tactical officer, he knew she had to be thinking along those lines, but it was his place to ask the question.

"I suppose so, but I'm not seeing the reason. They have a destroyer right next to them. Against the ships the Pale Ones used, it's more than capable of handling the job. Even if they wanted to give it some punch, they'd go with missiles. Beams are too short ranged to give an otherwise unarmed ship."

"Maybe they gave it battle screens."

"That might make more sense, but again, why? It's a freighter. The cost and space required for the second fusion plant would eat into cargo capacity and make it a lot less profitable."

One of the women monitoring the consoles around them stiffened and turned in her seat. "The destroyer just went to active scans."

"Are we in danger of detection?" Anderson asked.

"No, ma'am. We're too far away for a normal return from our hulls, and with the fusion plants at standby, they won't be able to detect the reduced power output. The drones we have shadowing them came from *Persephone*. They're heavily stealthed, and I don't think they'll see them either."

"Then what are they doing?"

Brandon tapped into the appropriate scanner feeds and examined the raw data. "It looks like the scans are stronger in front of the ship. I think they might be giving the flip point to Erorsi a closer look. We don't have anything there to detect, so we should be safe."

The captain frowned. "It must be worried about an ambush of some kind. That might make sense with the loss of the last freighter and escort. Their suspicion is going to make the princess's job harder, though."

He shook his head. "Do we have any idea why the Rebel Empire is so cavalier about losing ships? They run the Empire. If someone was taking out my destroyers, I'd be worried."

"Commander Richards didn't know. He wasn't on the command track, so they restricted the information he had on certain things."

The destroyer seemed satisfied after about fifteen minutes of scanning and went back to passive.

They watched it get closer to the flip point over the next few hours. The last thirty minutes were the hardest. Brandon knew the captain probably wanted to get their fusion plants back to full capacity, but they couldn't afford to jump the gun. They'd wait until the ships were gone before they even started the process.

"Status change," the ship's computer said. "Passive scanners are picking up other vessels in the system."

The captain sat bolt upright. "What? Where? How many and what kinds?"

"Numerous vessels have transited the other flip point into this system. With this unit's probes shadowing the original vessels, the passive scanners did not detect them until they engaged their drives at full power. This unit is detecting twenty-six ships accelerating at military speeds."

Brandon accessed the feed through his implants. There wasn't much data at all for him to examine.

"We need to launch other probes to intercept the new forces," he said. "The destroyer was looking for anyone at the Erorsi flip point that could detect this task force."

Anderson nodded. "That has to be it. Why? This has never happened on previous supply runs."

"Then it isn't a supply mission," he said grimly. "It's an ambush. One we can't warn the admiral about."

She shook her head. "Worse, we can't stop the princess from boarding the freighter. With that extra fusion plant, it must be some kind of Q-ship. It looks like a cargo hauler, but they've converted it into a warship. She's going to sneak on board looking for supplies and probably find an armed military crew."

* * *

KELSEY WATCHED the freighter and its escort flip into the system through the passive scanners with satisfaction. The game was on.

Once the two ships had begun accelerating into the system, she was able to get a better idea of their course and speed. It wasn't as firmly nailed down as an active scanner reading would get, but close enough.

She opened a general frequency. "Okay, people, we're on. They're actively scanning the area around the flip point. That'll probably die down as they become more comfortable with their surroundings.

"They're on a course for Erorsi that pretty well matches our estimates. If everything goes according to plan, we'll board in about an hour. An attack that far out from any planet will be so unexpected that we should be able to seize the freighter without too much trouble. Then we'll signal Admiral Mertz, and he'll ambush the destroyer."

One of the recovery agents, Andrew Olivier, spoke up. "What if the destroyer isn't happy with our signals once the fighting starts? We can't trot out the original crew. They'll tip our hands. We can't make them suspicious."

"I've thought of that," she said. "The ambush will kick off with one of our destroyers shooting at the freighter and almost missing. The debris from the missile explosion will miss us, but we'll pretend it knocked out our drives and communications. There will be enough uncertainty that our people should be able to separate the two ships. Then the ruse won't matter."

They spent the next half hour going over the details. Once they'd made a few last-minute tweaks, they settled into their restraints. Now was the critical moment. The approach and boarding could go wrong in so many ways.

They'd approach with the freighter between them and the destroyer, maximizing their chances of going undetected. Once close to the hull, the two pinnaces would split up and attach at predetermined locations.

Time crawled as the freighter grew large in the passive scanners. No one on board seemed to notice them, but her heart was racing. It didn't slow until the pinnaces split up and attached to the hull.

The most dangerous part of the operation was over. They'd snuck up on the target. Now all they had to do was get on board and incapacitate the crew.

Kelsey unstrapped and lowered the ramp. The radios they were now using were low powered, but she didn't even want to chance that. She used hand signals to get everyone moving in the manner she wanted.

The recovery team took the lead to the targeted airlock. It was one used for emergency ingress. They used a very similar procedure to what the marines had done when they'd attacked Boxer Station. They cut the metal around the controls and bypassed the sensor wires.

She made a mental note to have that particular security flaw corrected on *Persephone*. If someone snuck onto *her* ship, she wanted to know about it.

The hatch opened soundlessly into the vacuum. It was a standard emergency airlock, so there was room for half a dozen suited people. Two of the recovery agents and three marines joined her inside.

The recovery agents did some more work on the interior controls before they cycled the airlock again. Probably making sure the inner door didn't signal the bridge.

Maybe she should have them do a security review on *Persephone* to identify weaknesses she hadn't considered.

The airlock opened off a corridor. It was empty. She attached a remote to the bulkhead and kept everyone together as the rest of the team came inside.

Once the rest of them joined her, she consulted her implant map for the ship class. Her subgroup was responsible for securing the bridge and computer center. There were some crew quarters on the way that they'd bypass and deal with after they made sure no call for help would be forthcoming.

They ran into a problem almost immediately. The corridor dead-ended without the lift she'd expected.

Why close off the corridor like this? There wasn't any cargo area in this part of the ship. This made no sense.

Well, they didn't have time to figure it out. She backtracked and found a set of stairs that took them up three levels. The bridge and computer center were on the same deck, adjacent to one another.

That's where they ran into their first crewman.

The woman came out of a compartment almost as soon as Kelsey entered the corridor. She was dressed in a dark coverall with a tool belt strapped around her waist. Best guess was that she was in maintenance.

Kelsey had been ready for this and had her stunner out. The pale blue beam took the woman in the chest while she was still gaping. She collapsed at once, making a little noise.

"Lisa?" a voice called out from inside the compartment. "You okay?"

A glance inside showed a man in a similar coverall working on an air handler. He had no more warning than his friend did before Kelsey stunned him.

The marines hauled the woman into the compartment and tied them up.

"This is a stroke of luck," Hopwood said. "We can use these coveralls to get our people closer to the bridge without raising suspicions. These two don't have implants, so I won't need to use the jammers Sir Carl worked up on them."

"Jammers?"

He nodded. "To keep prisoners quiet. Think of it as a little helmet with a chinstrap. Once we have them tied up, that would keep officers from screaming for help electronically."

"That's a good idea," she admitted. "Too bad we don't have something that works over a larger area. Preferably without silencing us."

The man grinned. "I think he's working on something like that."

"Won't the crew recognize strangers?" she asked. "They won't have a lot of people to remember. We don't look like these two."

"We only need a moment's confusion. If you see someone in the kind of clothes you expect, acting as if they have every right to be there, you wonder if you somehow missed a new guy. That's human nature.

"Andrew and I will lead the team forward and hit the bridge first. On a freighter like this, we'll probably only have a couple of folks to contend with. Those stunners make for much faster work and are a lot less chancy than shock weapons. Alan will come with us to take over running the helm.

"The other team will hit the computer center. Your people will be right behind us in case there's trouble. Once we've secured the bridge, we can lock out the com systems. That'll keep anyone from screaming for help right away. The team hitting engineering will make sure the drives stay the way they are. With those two areas secure, you and your marines can hunt down the remaining crew."

She nodded. "Excellent. The other team should be close to engineering, so let's be about this."

They stripped the two prisoners out of their coveralls. The woman's would be tight on one of the men, but it only had to stand up to a momentary glance.

The recovery agents checked the corridor and sauntered toward the bridge. She kept the marines far enough behind them so that anyone they encountered wouldn't see them. The other agents brought up the rear. They'd hit the computer center at the same time as the bridge team went in.

Hopwood stopped by the bridge hatch and hefted his stunner. Once Andrew was ready, Hopwood triggered the door mechanism and went in. The low hum of the stunners sounded. The rest of his bridge team went in after him.

Then shouts of dismay and gunfire erupted.

She came in fast with her stunner up, searching for targets. Of which there were far too many for her taste.

The bridge wasn't the small affair the plans had led them to expect. It was as big as the one on *Persephone* and had almost a dozen men and women at the control stations. Not just regular crewmen, either. Most of them were in Rebel Fleet uniforms and were armed.

"Civilians down," she shouted over her com as she shot the closest armed woman. She dropped, but flechettes started ricocheting off Kelsey's armor even as the marines poured into the room behind her.

Kelsey shot the man at what would be the com console next. He'd turned back to his controls, and she didn't want a cry for help to get out.

The fighting was brief but intense. When the enemy was down, she checked her people. A few of the marines had minor wounds, but Hopwood was crouched over Alan Barnes. The man had taken a flechette to the chest and was in a bad way.

"Medic!" she shouted.

One of the marines crouched down beside the wounded man and ripped open his medical pack. It looked bad, but they had a chance to save him.

A loud alarm began hooting over the overhead speakers. She walked around the bridge and made sure everyone was out. Then she started examining the consoles.

"This is overkill for a freighter, and they certainly don't need armed Fleet officers. Something is very wrong."

16

_____

Zia watched the fleet approaching the Erorsi flip point with frustration. There had been no way to send a warning drone without someone detecting it. The gap between the lead destroyer and the fleet was too small. She really wished they'd had the time for Carl to finish deploying the ship-to-ship FTL coms.

"Once that fleet flips to Erorsi, I want us moving as soon as possible," she said. "We have to follow them through and hold the flip point. How long to get the fusion plants back up to normal output?"

One of her staff checked something on her console. "Twenty minutes, ma'am."

"Tell Tony to try for fifteen. I have no idea what kind of situation is going to develop at Erorsi, but we have to count on some of those ships heading back into our system before we get to the flip point.

"If not, we'll probably pop over there to find a battle already in progress. Have we nailed down what the fleet consists of?"

Commander Levy nodded. "I make out two dozen destroyers. The remaining eight seem to be a mixture of light and heavy cruisers. _Invincible_ can probably handle all of them, though it would hurt."

Zia shook her head. "No, those ships can scatter. No one in their right mind goes head to head with something our size if they can help it. If any of them get away, we might not be able to catch them all without a huge mess."

She grimaced. "Besides, we don't know their plan. Is this something to deal with the rogue AI, or is it an all-out attack on Pentagar? The ships in Pentagaran space are up to the task of defending themselves, but it only takes one ship to devastate a planet."

The time until the enemy task force reached the Erorsi flip point counted down with syrupy slowness. If they left any ships on this side, that would severely limit the amount of support Zia could give Admiral Mertz.

She cursed when the enemy ships flipped. Two icons tagged as destroyers remained on station in the flip point. The enemy commander was covering her backside.

"Dammit," Zia muttered. "Why the hell did we get a competent bad guy?"

"Because idiots make you sloppy," Levy said. "Then you get your clock cleaned when the good ones show up."

Well, they weren't going anywhere at speed now. They'd have to sneak up on the ships as best they could.

"The most important thing is to prevent them from getting a warning back to the Rebel Empire," Zia said. "I want a net of ships between them and the other flip point. If they shoot off any drones, I want them swamped."

He nodded. "We can move ships into position while we have an ambush team creep as close as possible. We won't be able to stop them from seeing us, but we can stop them from warning anyone at home."

"I suppose that's the best we can hope for, but it's going to delay our arrival at Erorsi. Admiral Mertz will be on his own. If we're going to do this, let's do it right. I want enough force to be sure that anyone that comes running back from Erorsi can't overwhelm us with drones. We'll plug this system."

"Aye, ma'am."

Getting all the ships back up to full combat power took a little over twenty minutes. She'd be having a long discussion with certain captains about that.

If the enemy fleet came rushing back into this system, she didn't have enough ships to be certain of stopping them all. That meant she needed to plug the other flip point. To be sure nothing got past the blockade, she split her escort and assigned a battlecruiser, two heavy cruisers, four light cruisers, and six destroyers to the task. They should be able to stop anything that got past her.

The aces up her sleeve were her three squadrons of fighters. Gnats carrying sledgehammers, Annette had once called them. Added into her force mix, she could kill most of the ships she'd seen earlier if she had to.

With her reserve blocking the only other exit to the system, she could hunt them all down. Ugly and messy, but doable.

Right now, she needed to get the destroyers into position to block their enemy counterparts in case the initial strike failed. They were harder to detect at slow speed than her heavier units. The plan was for them to get as close as possible before the primary attack took place.

Once the blockading force was far enough out and ready to shoot down the inevitable drones, she ordered her main task force into motion. The destroyers led the way while the heavier ships cut in to interpose themselves along the most direct route of retreat for the enemy.

Admiral Mertz was the inspiration for the attack method. He'd once used a single fighter to ambush an AI destroyer. He'd rammed it, but Zia knew she could do better. Rather, she knew that Annette could do better.

* * *

ANNETTE TOOK her fighter out to join the combat space patrol. Once she was flying along beside them, she brought her low-powered com online. They could do all the interfighter communicating they wanted until they got close to the destroyers watching the flip point.

Dozens of fighters were already on a ballistic course toward the Erorsi flip point. They'd coast into range and launch antiship missiles as they soared past. If they didn't kill both destroyers, they'd certainly cripple them. Hopefully before they took any shots in return.

After all, a fair fight indicated lack of planning on her part.

For once, she had a stroke of good luck. The enemy rear guard must've been certain they were alone. They only used their active scanners every once in a while, so the fighters made it very close. When the risk of detection became too high, she ordered her people to launch.

The first inkling the enemy had that they weren't alone was a swarm of missiles blossoming to life in their faces. The small grav drives spiked to life at ridiculously short range, hurling their explosive passengers into the stationary destroyers.

One of the enemy ships exploded outright in a bright flash as its fusion plants failed, creating a momentary sun right next to its companion.

The other destroyer was luckier. It survived the explosion and the missiles blasting into its hull. It was no doubt wrecked but still functional enough to launch a pair of drones toward the distant flip point and to vanish. It had flipped to Erorsi.

Annette cursed under her breath. Bad luck had ruined the surprise. The fight around Erorsi was going to be ugly.

"Back to *Audacious*," she ordered, bringing her fighter to full power and swinging around. "Rearm and get ready for immediate launch. We're going to war, boys and girls."

* * *

JARED WAITED IMPATIENTLY AS the freighter and its escort slowly flew more deeply into their trap. His view from Erorsi orbit was time delayed, but the other ships were far enough past his net that they wouldn't be able to escape.

The destroyer captain had already communicated with them, never guessing that Marcus was mimicking the now-dead computer they'd been dealing with. With the full transcripts of every interaction it had ever had with the Rebel Empire, it was child's play to construct a convincing message.

In fifteen minutes or so, his trap would close, and one of his hidden destroyers would carefully fire missiles at the two ships. One would be aimed at the freighter. It had to be convincing but still cause as little damage as possible. He wanted his people alive and that ship intact.

Other ships would then open fire on the destroyer, forcing it to separate from the freighter. He'd prefer to take it alive, so he was hoping the show of force he'd planned would intimidate them into surrendering. He wasn't holding out much hope, though. These people were damned bloody minded.

"Status change," Marcus said. "The probes monitoring the enemy flip point have detected a number of ships transiting. There are too many to be Captain Anderson's carrier group."

Jared realized almost at once what it had to be. The Rebel Empire had sent an ambushing force of its own. He didn't have time to ponder the reason for that. He had to deal with the situation as he found it.

"What kind of numbers are we talking about?" he asked. "What course are they taking?"

"Thirty ships moving slowly enough to avoid detection from Erorsi. It looks as though a third of them are heading toward us. The remainder are angling for the Pentagaran flip point."

"Can you assign classes to the ships?"

"Tentatively," the AI said. "Most are destroyers, but eight are likely cruisers of some kind. Two cruisers and eight destroyers are following slowly behind the freighter and its escort. Six cruisers and fourteen destroyers are angling for the Pentagaran flip point.

"I'm concerned about Princess Kelsey and her forces. If we delay much longer, our hidden ships will be out of position to support them."

"There's nothing we can do about that now," Jared said. "We have to let the new ships get further into the system so we can bottle them up. If we attack now, they'll run back through the flip point. Zia doesn't have enough ships to be sure of stopping all the runners."

He considered the layout of the forces he had on station. If they allowed the first destroyer and the freighter to proceed past the ambush, they wouldn't be able to intervene if the warship figured out something was happening on the freighter.

The two ships would enter *Invincible*'s range in roughly three hours. That allowed the force headed toward Pentagar to get almost to the flip point, even if he attacked early. If he waited for the right time in Erorsi space, the other ships would have transitioned to Pentagar.

Well, at least the Pentagarans had a sizable fleet of their own and kept a very diligent watch, even over the secured flip point to Erorsi. They could handle the attack.

"Are any of our ships in position to fire a probe through to Pentagar without detection?" he asked.

"Possibly," Marcus said. "One of our colliers is stationed in that direction. If we signal it now via tight beam, it could possibly get a probe to the flip point before the attackers arrive. Unfortunately, there is a significant chance the enemy will detect the probe. That might endanger the collier."

Jared brought up that ship's location and considered the distances involved. A second option presented itself.

"If the collier bolts for the flip point as soon as it receives our message, she might beat the missiles they fire at her. It'll tip our hand, but their ships will be committed by then. It doesn't matter what they think."

The AI seemed to consider that. "Our fleet will not be in an optimal position to engage the enemy at that time. They will be able to elude us. Except, perhaps, the closest destroyer."

"Send the collier."

"Aye, sir. Orders transmitted."

Jared felt a little hollow. This entire mission had gone sideways, and no matter how this played out, people were going to die.

He hoped one of them wasn't Kelsey. He had no way to warn her that she was in significant danger or to tell her what the new plan was. He had to count on her to understand what the aborted ambush meant and to act accordingly.

"Status change," Marcus said. "A new ship has arrived at the hostile flip point. It's transmitting a signal. Passive scanners indicate it has battle damage."

"Go active," Jared snapped. "Spring the ambush."

17

Kelsey hit the com to the other team. With the alarm ringing, the crew knew something was wrong.

"Report."

"We're fighting for engineering," Lieutenant Paulson said. "There are a lot more people down here than we expected, including armed Rebel Empire Fleet officers.

"The layout is radically different, too. Someone spotted us and sounded the alarm. We have the control consoles, but we're trying to nail down the Rebel Fleet personnel before they can shut off the drives manually."

Not optimal, but better than some possible outcomes.

"We have the bridge and presumably the computer center. They aren't getting a warning out. Stop them as fast as you can."

"The marines are pushing hard. We'll get it done, but people are going to die, ours and theirs."

Kelsey grimaced. "It can't be helped. Do the best you can. Something is very wrong with this ship, and we need someone to tell us what it is. The bridge crew will be out for hours."

"Roger that. I'll call you back when we're secure down here."

Kelsey pointed at the bridge hatch. "Watch for crew trying to retake the bridge. Send out teams of marines to locate and incapacitate the remaining crew. I want this ship under our complete control as soon as possible."

She turned to Hopwood. "Is the computer center under our control?"

He nodded, rising from where the medic was still working on Alan Barnes. "I just got the word. They had a few people inside, but we stopped them from purging the system."

Finally, some good news.

She nodded toward Barnes. "How is he?"

"It's not good, but the medic thinks he can stabilize him. The ambush should kick off soon. We'll transport him back to one of the pinnaces in an emergency bubble. He and any other wounded can get care more quickly that way."

Kelsey shook her head. "We're going compartment by compartment, so we'll find the medical center soon. They'll have what we need. If we can take the medical staff without stunning them, we'll get them to work on all the injured, theirs and ours.

"Before we do that, we need to figure out what the hell is going on with this ship. The layout is off, and there are a lot more people than we expected. Rebel Fleet shouldn't be manning a civilian freighter. This makes no sense at all."

Hopwood stepped over to a console. "They were still running the ship, so this isn't locked. They never expected anyone to just pop in unannounced like we did. Let's see what I can find."

He worked his way through the console's screens. He must've been studying hard to know what he'd need to do.

"Weird," he muttered. "The engineering controls show two fusion plants. That's definitely nonstandard. It had to eat into their cargo space."

Kelsey looked over his shoulder. "Is that what was blocking the corridor we tried to take?"

The man checked a few other screens. "I don't think so. The second fusion plant is forward of engineering, but not that far. Let me toggle through some more panels."

She watched him going from screen to screen and stopped him when he found one she wasn't familiar with. "Hold up. What's this?"

"I'm not sure," he said. "It's almost like a weapon control system, but not like any I'm familiar with."

Kelsey used her implants to interface with the console. Since they hadn't locked it, she had no problems accessing it. Another potential security issue on *Persephone* to talk over with the recovery specialists.

It *was* a weapon. There were munitions, but they weren't missiles. It was something she'd never seen before.

A check of the targeting system gave her more insight. The range was less than twenty thousand kilometers. Very, *very* short range in space. The weapon also required orienting the ship to fire, because it had control over the attitude thrusters.

"This looks like an orbital bombardment weapon," she said at last. "It fires solid slugs at high velocity, but the targeting is only for short range. Like from orbit to a planetary surface."

She stared at Hopwood. "This isn't a supply run. It's an ambush. They want to take out the computer on Erorsi before it knew there was a problem."

He scratched his chin. "If that's the case, then the destroyer is going to be on higher alert than we'd expected. It might not shoot us when the admiral springs the ambush, but we might not get away clean either."

"The destroyer also might not be alone. A single destroyer couldn't take all the ships that the Erorsi computer could field before we smashed it. If I were them, I'd send more ships to back it up.

"They also have to secure this system against an attack from Pentagar. Probably by sending a force large enough to take them out as quickly as possible. It's what I would do."

The man stared at her. "What do we do now?"

She shrugged. "We follow the plan. If Jared springs the ambush, we separate the freighter. If he doesn't, then we know there are other ships in play and he's improvising. We'll have to do the same.

"Once we have the freighter locked down, I want the holds examined. They might not have any Raider implant supplies. If so, that's a very bad break. If there are some, I'll want as much as possible shifted to the pinnaces. We might have to bail, and I don't want to leave any of it behind if I have a choice in the matter."

He nodded. "I'll see if I can find a cargo manifest. It might tell us what we need to know without a thorough search. There's no reason they'd fake it. It isn't as though the computer here sent a customs party to inspect them."

"Actually, that isn't a given. We don't know if it sent Pale Ones to check the supplies. I find it hard to believe the paranoid device would let Rebel Fleet humans onto its stations. Let me know what you find as soon as you find it."

She stared pensively at the main screen. They'd know in just a few minutes if Jared was going to attack. If he didn't, she needed a new plan. Time to come up with it.

* * *

BRANDON CURSED as the destroyer escaped. "We need to get after it. The ambush is blown."

"Flank speed to the flip point," Anderson said. "Get to operations, Mister Levy. You'll fight the ship while I focus on fleet and fighter operations."

"Aye, ma'am."

He raced for the lift and impatiently waited for it to get him to the operations center. On *Audacious*, it was where a normal superdreadnought's main bridge was. He had to admit it was significantly larger than what he was used to.

A full crew had already transferred control of the ship from the main bridge. He understood the need to segregate operations, but he still thought they were going around their elbows to scratch their butts.

The flag bridge should be reserved for this all the time, and the operations center should be where the ship was controlled. Of course, that meant that a carrier needed a flag officer rather than a captain in command of everything, but that was a fight for another day.

"Status," he said as he took the center seat.

The helm officer partially turned in her chair to face him. "We're on course for the Erorsi flip point. We'll arrive just in time to recover our fighters and make the flip. Call it fifteen minutes."

"The cruisers and destroyers will precede us," the tactical officer said. "The captain ordered them to follow the destroyer as closely as possible and take it out."

He wasn't sure that would help very much. The cat was out of the bag.

"Has one of the destroyers launched a probe through the flip point?" he asked.

"Negative. They're flipping. They'll signal back via probe."

"I want to see the layout in the other system as soon as we get the data."

"Aye, sir."

Brandon checked the ship's systems. Everything was in the green and all hands were at battle stations. The fighters were queued up and ready to launch as soon as they emerged.

The basic plan for the fighters was to launch them a squadron at a time. It would take about a minute to get the next fighter on the launch rail once the previous one was gone. So, a total of two minutes to get everyone out. Three minutes when all three squadrons were aboard.

Missiles were armed and ready. The beam weapons were in defensive mode, ready to cut down any missiles fired at the carrier. They'd be at their most vulnerable when they flipped. If the other ships didn't take out the crippled destroyer, it might shoot them up. If it could.

"They don't know what kind of force is after them," he said after a moment. "They saw the fighters and the lead destroyers. The rest were off his scanners. He might think it's a grand idea to wait for his pursuers to come through and shoot the hell out of them if they can. I know we're going through after the rest, but I want us ready for any unlikely surprises."

He watched the two lead destroyers make the flip. The rest of the ships were still more than ten minutes out.

Three minutes passed before a probe came through and a data update came back. They'd found exactly what he'd worried about. The destroyer had been waiting for them.

Luckily, the commanders of the two destroyers had been ready for something like that. They'd taken some hits, but they'd eliminated the other ship. Too late to stop the bastard from sending a warning, Brandon was sure. The enemy force had split with almost two-thirds of their number on the way to Pentagar.

When *Audacious* finally flipped, they arrived to find the system in turmoil. It looked as though the ambush on Pentagar was off. That group had turned and was on its way toward the carrier and her escorts. The ships headed for Erorsi were still on course, though.

"Signal from the flag bridge," the tactical officer said. "Cry 'Havoc!' and let slip the dogs of war."

Bright sparks of light lit up the tactical plot as the fighters launched.

"Shakespeare," he murmured approvingly. "Vitter will appreciate the comparison. Raise battle screens, but make sure the launch and landing approaches are kept clear," he said. The screens were not conducive to launching small craft in their most protective mode. "Go to active scans. I want to know everything we can about the incoming ships."

"Aye, sir," the tactical officer said. "I see six light cruisers and fourteen destroyers coming our way. They're almost in extreme missile range."

He smiled coldly. They'd turned around before the carrier had come through. They probably expected a pair of destroyers. Then that jumped to four destroyers and two light cruisers. They'd still outnumbered the Imperial ships three to one, so they were coming in hot to deal with the problem.

Then *Audacious* had flipped. If the enemy didn't use fighters, they might be surprised at how much combat strength a carrier could put on the board.

The fight was going to be hard but winnable. They'd take some hits, but that was the price they paid. Even if someone broke through, they'd never get back home. The ships Captain Anderson had left behind would make sure that no one escaped.

Captain Anderson had sent out fleet instructions to the escorts, who were forming up around the big ship. The two destroyers had minor damage. The ship that had tried to jump them was an expanding cloud of debris and escape pods.

"Enemy ships launching missiles," the tactical officer said.

Brandon checked the flight time versus the fighter's launch sequence. The final squadron would clear the bays in time for him to raise the battle screens completely. Barely.

"Once the last of the fighters is clear, full power to the battle screens and fire back. Use your best judgment on targeting."

The fight was on.

18

K elsey dragged the man from the freighter's command chair and sat down. With the marines guarding her back, she could focus on the situation around them. Data was finally coming in. A fleet of Rebel Empire ships had come into the system, and a battle at the flip point was getting under way.

Part of the force was headed toward Erorsi. The freighter and its escort had come deeper into the system than they'd planned, so the ships they'd had ready to pounce on the destroyer were further away and at a disadvantageous angle.

"Incoming signal," Hopwood said from the helm console. "It's the Rebel Empire destroyer. Orders to come about and make tracks toward the outer system."

"Do it," she said. "The longer we can keep them in the dark about our identity, the better chance we have."

The new course took them even farther away from the ships they had lying in wait. If only she had a way to deal with the destroyer herself. It didn't even know she was flying along at point-blank range, but she didn't have any ship-to-ship weapons.

But she wasn't unarmed.

Kelsey brought up the targeting system for the bombardment weapon. Its range was ridiculously short for this kind of thing, but it had the power to take out a warship if they got close enough. Currently, the freighter was too far away to make it work.

"Cain, edge us closer to the destroyer a bit at a time. Be casual."

"I have no idea what a casually drifting freighter looks like, but here goes."

He altered their course just a fraction, and the range between the two ships began shrinking. At this rate, it would take a few minutes.

With some time to spare, she tapped into the ship's interior monitors. The battle was still raging in engineering, but it looked as though Paulson was pushing the defenders ever farther away from the critical equipment.

Elsewhere, a few crewmen were putting up a struggle, but most of them weren't armed. It shouldn't be more than a few minutes before the last of them was down.

One thing she saw that looked promising was the cargo bays. They weren't completely empty. Perhaps they hadn't failed. There might be *some* Raider implants in there.

Her stomach jittered a little as the freighter crept closer to the escort. They were just crossing into extreme range. She'd get one shot at this.

That was when one of the escape pods jettisoned.

"Dammit!" she shouted. "I locked those down!"

A signal pinged them from the destroyer, but she ignored it, focusing on the targeting software. Kelsey took over the helm remotely and brought the nose of the freighter onto target. The moment it came to bear, she fired.

The results were spectacular, to say the least. The kinetic weapon was much, much faster than a missile. There was no dodging it. The oversized flechette quite literally blew through the destroyer, entering amidships and coming out aft in engineering.

While the other ship didn't blow up, the damage was extreme. His drives cut off, and he tumbled, out of control.

Kelsey cut their drives back and changed course. The weapon had no provision for automatic reloading. If the other ship got its act together, he'd fire missiles at her. To call her antimissile defenses pathetic was an understatement.

One of its fusion plants was spiking, which was very, very bad, but the Rebel Empire destroyer still managed to fire a single missile before it blew up. The damned thing raced toward Kelsey and the freighter.

She fired everything she had at it, which perhaps annoyed it enough to miss them. That was the only thing she could think of at this ridiculously short range. It had almost scarred the freighter's paint, but it *had* missed.

"Colonel, we've secured engineering," Lieutenant Paulson said over the com. "My people are making another pass to look for hidden hostiles."

"Be sure to check the escape pods," she said. "One ejected at what I would delicately call a critical moment. We're safe for the time being, but we have enemy ships in route to our position. Probably no more than an hour out."

"Copy that. Paulson out."

Invincible was under power from Erorsi orbit. Maybe she would gather more of the bad guys' attention. To make things harder for the Rebel Empire fleet, she boosted the freighter to maximum speed and made sure the course took them away from the ambushing ships.

They might not have clearly seen what had caused the freighter's escort to explode, but they had to be suspicious. Particularly when she failed to follow their inevitable orders to head their way.

The freighter had a lot more drive power than she'd expected. They'd probably intended for it to get away from Erorsi as fast as possible once they'd sprung their surprise.

She was so focused on the strategic situation that she jumped when someone whooped over the com.

"Who is that?" she said sharply. "Report!"

"Sorry, Colonel. It's Corporal Galloway. I'm down in one of the holds looking at a crate full of what certainly looks like Marine Raider pharmacology units."

"Which hold? I'll be right there."

Kelsey headed for the hatch as the man gave her a hold number. "Mister Hopwood, you have the conn."

"Yes, ma'am."

If there really were Raider implant supplies on this ship, she might be able to get some of them out to the pinnaces. They could drop away and go stealth. They might go unnoticed.

She sprinted toward the lift. Time was not on their side, but this was worth the risk.

* * *

THE DECK CREW had rearmed Annette's fighter by the time *Audacious* flipped, so she was ready when her time came to blast out of her launch tube.

"All *Audacious* squadrons, this is Black Jack Actual," she said over her com. "Focus on the lead ships. Cover your wingmates on their runs. Black Jack will take lead. When we pull out to rearm, make your runs in sequence."

The goal was to have fighters coming in waves. One wave should be attacking, another should be covering them, and the third should be rearming. Somehow, she didn't think this was going to be that easy.

Part of her was relieved that no fighters came screaming out of the enemy formation. That would've complicated an already dangerous situation. The rest of her was disappointed not to test her mettle in a real dogfight.

She sent a final targeting set to her people and pushed her fighter up to maximum acceleration. The six light cruisers were their targets. They posed the greatest threat to the carrier and her escorts. Not that fourteen destroyers would be a walk in the park, mind you, but they'd be very hesitant to engage without their big brothers.

Annette focused on her designated target while keeping an eye on the overall tactical situation. The big ship probably wasn't going to waste missiles on fighters. His antimissile flechettes were going to be the big threat, and his beam weapons.

That was another reason to take out the cruisers. The destroyers didn't have beams. They'd be limited in their response.

She noted how their battle screens were layered and picked a weak point where two overlapped. When her targeting scanners had locked on, she fired both her missiles and pulled away.

The cruiser fired a burst of antimissile flechettes, both at the missiles and her fighter. It had a dozen other fighters to deal with, too, since she'd split her squadron of twenty-four to attack only two light cruisers.

Her fighters proved a lot more maneuverable than the shooters expected, but that didn't mean the good guys escaped unharmed. That only happened in the vids. Two of her fighters exploded, and one veered out of control before the pilot ejected. Once the battle was over, they'd send search and rescue after him.

The ship killers they'd fired exploded all over the targets. They'd launched in waves so that the screens had time to fail. The leading missiles ruptured the battle screens where they overlapped, creating fissures that the rest exploited.

In the end, their fire was overkill. Both cruisers died in flame, gutted by the fiery swords that disemboweled them.

Space was full of chaotic violence as she pulled her squadron back toward *Audacious* to rearm. They'd learn from that mistake fast. This was going to be ugly.

* * *

JARED GRINNED when he saw Kelsey punch the destroyer's lights out. He had no idea what she'd done, but the results were gratifying. The destroyer exploded and left her ship running for empty space.

"Go to active scanners."

"Aye, sir," Marcus said. "It'll take a few minutes to get a return from the inbound force."

"Go with worst case. Two heavy cruisers and eight destroyers. Have the ambush force that was originally supposed to cover the freighter try to protect her."

He checked the tactical plot. At full speed, it would take the enemy almost an hour to get into missile range of *Invincible*, if the enemy were obliging enough to keep coming in their direction. They'd be able to fire on his ambushing force in half that time.

The Rebel Empire forces outnumbered Jared's ambushers about three to one. *Invincible* had more firepower than all of the enemy ships combined, but it wouldn't be able to bring them to battle if they ran.

Of course, in this situation, that might not be the worst outcome. They could hunt down the stragglers. Probably.

If any of them headed out into deep space, that might make them hard to find. He could take steps to make that outcome unlikely.

"Marcus, have our ambushers launch probes to shadow the attacking force. I want enough coverage to be sure each ship has no less than three probes that are out of weapons range and hopefully undetected."

"Aye, sir."

He could see the battle forming up at the hostile flip point, but only through the gravitic scanners. It would take a while longer to see the specifics of what was happening out there. Probably long after the fight was over.

"The collier has made the flip to Pentagar," Marcus said. "Perhaps once we have more force in the system, that will convince the enemy to surrender."

"I hope so, but I wouldn't hold my hypothetical breath if I were you. A single destroyer wasn't dissuaded when we chased it down with a battlecruiser, and the sight of a superdreadnought coming their way isn't deterring these boys.

"I'm also afraid that trying to intimidate them over the com would backfire. They don't respond well to us. That programming in their officers' implants makes them go all violent. That might be counterproductive."

"I submit that that might work in our favor," the AI said. "If they are driven to attack, then we can be certain that no stragglers become lost in the system.

"By now, they are aware of the battle taking place at the flip point they came through. I have no doubt it will be resolved in our favor, though probably at heavy cost. They will not try to fight their way back through."

Jared shared the AI's opinion about the likely cost of the battle but wasn't sure he followed the rest of his logic.

"Are you saying they'll go suicidal? I'm not sure this is that simple."

"Perhaps suicidal is the wrong word, Admiral. I think they will try to take us out, but I have no absolute proof that is true. What I am relatively confident of is the fact that they will likely not try to escape."

He considered what Marcus was saying and shrugged. "There's only one way to find out. Record an outgoing message."

Jared faced the main screen resolutely. "This is Admiral Jared Mertz. We have you outgunned and in a poor tactical position. My superdreadnought has more than enough firepower to take out your entire force. I call on you to spare your crews and surrender."

19

Zia watched the brawl just inside missile range with a mixture of awe and dread. The fighters had obliterated all six light cruisers, but they'd taken heavy losses. Five pilots had ejected from crippled fighters and thirteen others were gone, their pilots almost certainly dead.

Annette was rearming now and would rejoin the fight in a minute. Unless Zia ended it first.

Her tactical officer turned toward her. "We're inside the designated firing range."

"Fire," Zia said coldly.

Audacious and her escorts billowed missiles toward the light war craft. The carrier had fewer missiles than a superdreadnought but far more than even a heavy cruiser could boast. In a standup duel, the destroyers would lose.

The enemy returned fire, streaming almost as many missiles back toward her. That's when they found out another ugly truth.

Fighters could shoot down missiles with their flechettes. Almost half of their salvo never made it past the swarm of little ships around the destroyers.

With their attention split between the fighters and the incoming missiles, their defenses were far weaker than they'd probably expected.

Explosions lit up the space around them. When the scanner readings cleared, they'd blown up or disabled all but six destroyers. This fight was almost over.

"Incoming signal from the hostile ships," the com officer said. "They're surrendering."

"Pull the fighters back," she ordered. "Cease fire, but maintain targeting locks."

The fighters disentangled themselves from the remaining enemy ships. Some headed back to *Audacious* for rearming, but the rest kept the surviving destroyers under their guns.

"They've dropped their battle screens," the tactical officer said. "I still have the officer on the com."

"Put them on the screen," Zia said.

A smoke-filled bridge appeared on the main screen. The woman in the command chair had a long gash down her cheek and had a number of black smudges on her face. She looked furious. In her place, Zia couldn't blame her.

"I am Commander Veronica Giguere, commanding officer of the Imperial Fleet destroyer *R-7322*. We surrender. I don't know what the hell you bastards are playing at, but we surrender."

Zia nodded. This had to be hard for the woman. She knew it would be if the situation were reversed. Now she just needed to handle this without triggering the buried programming in the woman's corrupted implant code. She wanted live prisoners, not a ravening fight to the death.

"We accept your surrender, Commander. You've done the smart thing, even if it doesn't feel that way right now.

"Keep your screens down and idle your fusion plants. No targeting scanners, either. No destruction of your systems or booby-traps. My prize crews will meet any resistance with lethal force, and that won't change your situation one bit.

"You made the right call. Now don't screw it up. Gather all your crew in the mess areas. No weapons. Not even a folding knife. We'll process you all as quickly as we can and get you safely removed to our ships."

The other woman shook her head slowly. "This is treason. You'll hang for this."

Zia smiled a little wryly. "Don't think you know everything that's going on in the Empire, Commander. Let's just say that not all our leadership has been read in on every operation. Unfortunately, you stumbled into something you aren't cleared for."

An outright lie, but one that would hopefully keep her thinking Zia and her people were part of the Rebel Empire fleet.

"I have no idea what the hell you're talking about," Commander Giguere assured her. "We will follow your instructions, but rest assured there *will* be hell to pay over this. I don't care what faction you represent, the Lords will quash you like a bug. *R-7322* out."

The screen cleared, reverting to a view of space.

Zia opened a channel to operations. Brandon Levy appeared.

"Yes, Captain?"

"The enemy in our area has surrendered. I want you to organize prize crews to take control of the ships. All the prisoners come to *Audacious*, and you'll keep enough people over there to move the ships if we need to.

"I've instructed them not to destroy systems or set booby-traps, but we can't assume that's the case. At the very least, I expect they'll purge the computer systems. I would. You'll have to be thorough, but don't give them any reason to suspect who we are. Keep conversations down to instructions, don't give names of ships, and stomp on any resistance."

He nodded. "I'll get right on it, ma'am. What about the rest of the system? Are the other ships still actively hostile?"

"It looks that way. We'll find out soon enough. If Admiral Mertz can't handle the rest of the hostiles, we'll come in and help."

"I get it now," he said softly. "I understand why this ship revolves around the fighters. They really turned this fight around."

She just wished it hadn't cost so many of them their lives. "You had no way of knowing. Now you do. Welcome to the club. CSAR will recover the pilots who ejected, and then we'll have to help them put themselves back together again. Losing friends is never easy."

* * *

KELSEY ARRIVED in the cargo bay and took stock of what it held. There were a number of cargo containers. Her implants could read the manifests easily enough. If they were accurate, this hold held enough Raider implants to upgrade about a thousand people.

More than they had with them, but far less than she'd hoped to get.

The rest of the crates held sundry other high-tech replacement gear. Mostly things they already had in large measure.

Being the untrusting sort, she opened a few crates to verify their contents. The ones labeled communications gear were a surprise. They contained all the parts to construct an AI.

That made sense. They'd obviously intended to obliterate the computer and put a real AI in command.

The find put her in a quandary. They had enough space in the pinnaces to take the Raider implants or the AI. Not both.

"Dammit," she said under her breath. "Get the crates labeled as communications gear onto the pinnaces."

The corporal frowned. "I don't understand. Aren't we here for the Raider gear?"

"Yes, but these crates have a disassembled AI. That trumps the Raider implants. I can't believe I'm saying this, but we're going to have to leave the implants."

"Maybe not," a man said from the entrance to the hold. It was one of the recovery people. Tom Stoecklein. The tall man was looking over the crates with what seemed like a knowledgeable eye.

"You have my full and undivided attention, Mister Stoecklein. How can I have my cake and eat it, too?"

"This ship has a number of cargo shuttles. Not stealthy at all, under the best of circumstances, but perhaps useful. I suggest you load the rest of the cargo onto them and eject the shuttles. Don't even power them on. Let them coast along our current trajectory while we change course."

Kelsey thought about that and slowly nodded. "It's possible that a ship that chases us down might miss the shuttles, or assume they have the crew on board. It's better than no chance, I suppose. Thanks."

She turned to the corporal. "What's in the other holds?"

"They're empty, ma'am. It looks as though they only brought enough actual cargo to look good in a spot inspection. I'm surprised they put the AI in the same hold, though. What if the customs people looked inside?"

Kelsey shook her head. "You've never met the Pale Ones. Attention to detail is not their strong suit. Get all this gear loaded and prepare to eject all the small craft.

"See that the prisoners are on the pinnaces, along with all nonessential personnel. Lieutenant Paulson will make sure there is space for everyone."

She checked the scanner readings through her implants. The incoming hostile force was still angling to meet *Invincible*, but a destroyer was edging their way. Not far enough to actually come meet them, but perhaps to launch pinnaces. The marine boats would be able to board the freighter. Or destroy it.

Kelsey had no idea how they expected to get out of the system. Perhaps their scanner readings from the area around the flip point were showing something different than she saw. Perhaps their other ships had beaten Zia.

That would be a disaster, so she prayed it wasn't so.

That's when she noticed the destroyer changing course to meet them and accelerating. So, no pinnaces. That probably meant Zia had just handed them their asses.

"We have less than half an hour to get everything loaded," she said. "Get moving!"

That was going to be very, very tight, and she wasn't done with her scavenging yet.

Kelsey raced back to the computer compartment. She didn't pretend to have anything like Carl's knowledge of these things, but she did know where the cores were. If there was useful data for them to find, she needed those cores.

In her armor, she had no trouble lifting the heavy pods out of their cradles once she'd opened the wall shielding them up. The computer followed its programming and shut down.

"Colonel, this is Cain Hopwood. The computer just went offline."

"That's me," she said as she hefted the first one and carried it out into the corridor. "We're evacuating, and I want to take the cores with us."

"Copy that. What should my people do?"

She made her way to the lift at the end of the corridor and set the core down before heading back to get the second one. "Coordinate with Lieutenant Paulson. Get the cargo and people loaded up."

"Roger that. Hopwood out."

The loading of the cargo shuttles was well under way when she arrived. A quick eyeball told her there was enough room for the Raider implant containers but not the computer cores. It was a tight fit with just the implant hardware.

Hmmm. She was going to need to be creative.

Ten minutes later, they'd loaded the cargo shuttles. As expected, there was no room to spare. They'd had to strap a few containers outside the hulls of the small craft to get everything. Two of the marines volunteered to pilot the shuttles, but she sent them back to the pinnaces. She wasn't risking her people on this wild chance.

A check of the shuttles' control interfaces told her that the Rebel Empire had installed standard implant overrides. Since no one on a regular freighter would have implants, that was simply covering their bases.

Using the knowledge she'd picked up from Carl, it only took a minute to get the devices to pop up the override codes for her. She changed them to something she would remember. It was always best to make sure the enemy couldn't use their surprises.

Paulson stepped up beside Kelsey. "We've got the containers and prisoners loaded onto the pinnaces. We're ready to eject these and scram."

Kelsey nodded. "Excellent. How are we doing for space?"

"Packed to the bulkheads. The pinnaces were never designed to carry cargo like that. We'll all fit, though."

"Send me the load details," she said as she strapped the computer cores to the cargo shuttles. She'd put one on each. That increased the odds that at least one of the redundant units would make it.

The data appeared in her implant interface. Both pinnaces were heavily overloaded. This was risking a lot.

"I'll ride on the other pinnace," she told the marine officer. "It has a tad more space left. Go load up and be ready to depart on my order."

Paulson nodded. "Copy that."

She watched the marine head off. The woman was going to be seriously displeased with her once this was over.

Kelsey contacted the pilot on the other pinnace. "Once you have the last of your assigned people on board, be ready to separate. I originally told the LT that I was going with you, but I think I'll go with her instead. Don't wait for me."

"Copy that, ma'am," the man said.

Once no one was looking at her, Kelsey climbed into one of the cargo shuttles and strapped into the pilot's chair.

"Does everyone have their assigned people aboard?" she asked over her armor com.

When both replied they were ready, she continued. "I'm remotely jettisoning the cargo shuttles. Once they clear the freighter, you can detach from the hull and move off under stealth."

That's when she saw Tom Stoecklein climbing into the other shuttle. How had he slipped away from the pinnaces? Probably the same way she had. Better yet, how had he known what she was up to?

She opened a low-power implant connection to the man.

What the hell are you doing?

I could ask you the same thing, but I figure I already know the answer. I probably shouldn't let the heir wander off all by herself.

Kelsey shook her head. *This is going to be dangerous.*

As if the rest of this isn't. I was up on the bridge, programming a few automatic responses into the controls that might help fool the destroyer. Once I saw you were still aboard, I decided to come along for the ride. Aren't we wasting time?

Don't think you've heard the last of this. Jettison in three... two... one... mark!

She hit the control, and the cargo shuttle unclamped from its recessed area. The doors under it slid open and allowed the shuttle to drift away from the freighter. She'd already programmed the hatches to close once she was clear. That would keep the enemy in the dark about their departure.

The other shuttle drifted clear of the freighter, and the hatches closed on schedule. The freighter began pulling away from them quickly. It wasn't accelerating that fast when compared to other ships, but the shuttles were unpowered.

Kelsey couldn't see the pinnaces departing, but she knew they'd be leaving the hull about now. They'd accelerate slowly in different directions, keeping her people safe from the enemy.

Now all she had to do was hope the destroyer didn't spot the shuttles. The freighter would change course in a minute. That would hopefully keep them out of the detection range of the Rebel Empire warship.

20

B randon made his way down to the landing bay. His crew in operations would keep a close eye on the enemy ships, but they'd caught them. All he had to do now was get their crews onto *Audacious* without setting off their buried attack programming.

Annette Vitter was standing there, still in her flight suit. She turned toward him when he approached. Her face was drawn.

"I'm sorry about your people," he said. "They saved a lot of us on the ships, and they really showed everyone what fighters could do."

"Thank you. It's just hard to appreciate that right now when I've lost so many of them."

He already knew the numbers. The enemy had destroyed eighteen of the agile little craft. Two thirds of a squadron.

Most had gone completely silent, but a few pilots had ejected. That was no doubt why she was here, waiting for word on those who might still be alive.

"We lost at least thirteen people," she said. "I'm hopeful that five others are still alive, but that hurts on a personal level. I've lived and worked with these people. It's like losing family."

"I wish there was something I could do to make it better."

She sighed. "We'll mourn them and get past it. We don't have a choice. Next time it might be worse. Fighter pilots burn bright and die quickly." The last sounded more than a bit bitter.

He put an arm around her shoulder. It was highly unprofessional, but it felt right. "We're all here for you."

Annette nodded, tears in her eyes. "That makes a difference. It really does."

A low hooting announced an incoming ship. Moments later, a CSAR shuttle came streaking in at high speed, only coming to a stop when the arrestor field snatched the small craft to an abrupt halt.

The rear hatch came down, and a medical team raced out with a woman on a stretcher. She was burned but obviously alive. Annette took a single step after her but stopped.

"I can't help her now. I'd only be in the way."

Four other pilots came down the ramp at a much more sedate pace. They saw their commander and headed over toward her.

Brandon stepped back to give them the time and space they needed to grieve.

Thirteen pilots dead, then. Maybe one more if the injured woman didn't make it. It sounded like good numbers when considered analytically. They'd be down to fifty-four fighters. Still three-quarters of their combat strength intact.

But that didn't count the human cost. The price these people had willingly paid for that victory. In that light, the loss of those people was a tragedy. One he'd undoubtedly think of as light when something truly awful happened at some later point.

He sighed. War was hell.

The next incoming ship was a cutter. Based on the number of marines lined up, it was filled with prisoners.

The captured Rebel Empire Fleet personnel came out one by one, each with their hands bound behind them. Most had their heads down, but one was looking around with an air of suspicion.

It was the officer that had surrendered to Captain Anderson. He suspected that she sensed something off.

He went to pull the enemy officer from the line. "Commander Giguere, you'll be coming with me."

She opened her mouth to say something, but an expression of rage washed over her. She growled and hurled herself at him.

"I've got her!" he shouted before anyone brought their stunners to bear.

Brandon used his leg to trip her but grabbed the woman to keep her head from hitting the deck. She tried to bite him.

Oh, yeah. They'd triggered her resistance program somehow.

He yanked her up and bodily carried her away from the other prisoners.

One of the marines came with him, seemingly uncertain how to help.

"I've got her," he told the man. "Pass the word. Stun anyone that looks aggressive like this, and don't let them talk to one another."

The marine nodded. "Aye, sir. Do you need an escort?"

"If I can't handle a bound woman that doesn't have her facilities about her, then I deserve what happens to me."

He carried the growling woman down to the medical center. They were working on the injured pilot, so that was good news. The woman hadn't died. He prayed she made it.

Doctor Zoboroski was busy, but one of his assistants came over. She eyed the struggling officer and gestured to a handy table with restraints. Together, they got the frenzied woman strapped down.

"So this is what the implant override programming looks like," the doctor said. "I'm Lieutenant Commander Lisa Osborne, Commander."

"Pleasure to meet you. Yes, I think she figured out we weren't what we seemed. I assume there's a means of reversing it."

She nodded. "The procedure is already worked out. Let me get some equipment, and I'll overwrite the corrupted code. It took them about four hours the first time, but we've cut that down to about two hours now. She'll be in no danger."

"Good. Get that started now and expect to have more soon. How many can you handle at once?"

"Five," Osborne said. "We didn't plan on having a lot of people to do. The other ships all have similar equipment, so we can have more units on hand shortly."

He shook his head with a sigh. "That's going to take forever. Luckily, only their officers are implanted. Which, come to think of it, is probably what tipped her off. We have the marines implanted. She's a command officer. She knows that's wrong."

Once the doctor brought back the equipment and started overwriting the woman's programming, Brandon gestured to the operation in progress. "What's her status?"

"Not good," Osborne said. "She has severe burns over most of her body. We'll be able to regenerate the damage once the doctor assures she's strong enough to make the transition to the regenerator. Physically, she'll almost certainly make it. Emotionally, she's going to have a long, hard recovery. She was burned alive before she ejected."

"That won't be easy to deal with," he agreed, "but she has a tremendous support system. Every single member of this crew is there for her, every step of the way."

The doctor smiled a little. "That probably will help. Would you like to watch the surgery?"

He hid his shudder. "No, thank you. I'd best go see to the rest of the prisoners. Until we have them all locked down, we won't know what might set the next one off. Thank you, Doctor Osborne."

Brandon headed back to the landing deck. A check of the scanners showed that the battle farther into the system was about to be joined. He hoped the admiral had a good plan to shut the enemy down.

* * *

JARED WATCHED the attacking Rebel Empire warships closing with the destroyers he'd had lying in wait for the freighter. Since they hadn't revealed themselves, he could use them now.

"Execute Bravo," he said.

The rest of his fleet came out from behind Erorsi and accelerated to catch up with *Invincible*. They'd get to him before any enemy missiles could. Barely. He'd cut it as close as he possibly could.

The four destroyers that had been sitting quietly in wait for the freighter and his escort bolted toward the superdreadnought's protection. If the enemy decided to engage them, they'd be committing to a face-to-face meeting with his fleet. Something he was willing to bet they'd decline.

"What's the status of the other fight?" he asked.

"It's over, sir," one of the people around him said. "*Audacious* reports they have accepted the surrender of six destroyers. They're putting prize crews on board."

"The enemy formation is veering off," Marcus said. "They're going after the freighter, or at least turning in its direction."

The two light cruisers and eight destroyers wouldn't be able to slip away, but they would be able to take out the freighter.

"Signal Kelsey to abort her operation. Keep in narrow beam. I want to deny them any information we can. And open a channel to the enemy fleet."

"You're live in three… two… one…"

Jared leaned forward. "Your other vessels have failed to break through my blockade, and you will fail, too. Don't throw the lives of your crew away. Surrender."

A few minutes later, they received a reply. The officer giving it sat on a bridge Jared recognized as belonging to a light cruiser. His uniform marked him as a commodore. He must be the overall commander of this operation.

"I don't know who you are, traitor, but I will not surrender my ships to you. If you want me, come catch me."

Jared grimaced when the transmission ended. "Well, that could have gone better. What can he hope to accomplish? Even if he breaks contact, he's not getting out of the system."

"He is likely not aware that you have probes shadowing him," Marcus said. "If he continues on this course, only our fastest ships can keep up. He might turn on them or simply escape into deep space to wait for a better time."

"Catching up to him is going to be challenging," Jared admitted. "Not impossible, though. Just time consuming. Is the freighter clear? Did Kelsey respond?"

"Negative to both. They'll be in firing range of the freighter in just a few minutes."

As soon as the ships entered extreme missile range, the freighter turned on them and charged. It was a pretty anemic charge, but still. That didn't change the results of the engagement one bit, but it showed that someone had balls. While that could have been his sister, he was counting on her having already fled.

The warships fired a spread of missiles that obliterated the freighter on the first try. The ten warships again altered course and sped toward the outer system.

He smiled. They'd just miscalculated. They were running for the only unoccupied flip point. The one leading to Pentagar.

A check of flight times showed they would arrive before *Audacious* could get any blocking ships in place.

Perhaps they thought they could still carry out their mission. Considering the forces that would be waiting for them, that was almost as good as them coming to him.

* * *

ONCE THE REBEL Empire ships had turned and accelerated away, Kelsey opened a low-power com to the other cargo shuttle.

"Keep your transmitter on low. You programmed the helm to charge them?"

"I did," Stoecklein said. "It was camouflage to make them think we were still on board."

"Good work. We'll wait until someone on our side gets here before we announce ourselves. I'd rather not spook them into coming back."

Their support arrived sooner than she'd hoped for when *Persephone* announced herself via low-powered com twenty minutes later. The Raider ship must've been pushing her stealth to the very edge to get here so quickly.

The pinnaces popped up moments later, closing on the shuttles. A signal from Paulson told her that the woman had discovered her ruse.

The visual showed the woman was seriously pissed, but her voice was deceptively calm.

"Colonel. There you are. We seem to have misplaced you during the evacuation."

Well, that was delicately put.

"Stuff happens. Thankfully, everything worked out."

"Uh huh. We'll see how things work out when the admiral finds out."

That was true. Jared was going to be angry.

"I suppose it's too much to hope for that you'd keep this between us."

"Sorry, Colonel," the woman said, not sounding even the least bit apologetic. "Far too many people know what happened now. I'd imagine word will get to him one way or the other. Besides, you wouldn't want me to falsify a report, would you?"

Kelsey smiled wryly. "I'd never want to get someone in trouble, and we all know what a big proponent of rules I am. Tell you what. I'll let my brother know what happened and find some way to make my little deception up to you. I happen to have some Raider implants that need a good home. Can you think of some people that might need them?"

21

Annette really wanted to stay with her people, but one didn't ignore orders to meet with the admiral. The superdreadnought was trailing the remaining enemy ships toward Pentagar, but Annette was on a cutter with Captain Anderson and Commander Levy heading for *Invincible*.

Personally, she wasn't sure pulling the carrier's top people away at the same time was the best call, but it wasn't her decision.

She used the time to go over the scanner readings from the battle. She'd made mistakes. There were things she might have done better. Part of her worried that she had cost some of her people their lives.

By the time the cutter docked with *Invincible*, she had some changes she wanted to make to the training. She walked off the cutter behind her commanding officer. She really should've let the executive officer go next, but it would've felt rude after he gestured for her to proceed.

The admiral wasn't waiting on them, thank God, but Marcus chatted with them as they walked. Apparently, the princess had been simultaneously more successful than they'd hoped and less. They'd gotten another AI but far fewer Raider supplies than they'd hoped for.

The three of them walked into the admiral's office, and he rose from behind his desk. "I'm glad to see all of you. Please, have a seat. Princess Kelsey will be joining us shortly and is listening in."

Annette sat, more than a bit uncomfortable with the idea of doing so in front of a flag officer.

Admiral Mertz walked around his desk and sat down with them on the comfortable chairs. "I'm both pleased that you stopped the Rebel Empire ships with so few casualties and sorry that your pilots died. Tell everyone how proud I am of them, Commander Vitter. You and your people saved a lot of lives today."

She nodded. "On behalf of my people, thank you, Admiral."

"I'm hoping we can get some other, though perhaps lighter, carriers back into service to increase your striking capability. With that in mind, please run through the battle for me. I need to know what worked and what didn't."

Annette listened to Captain Anderson run through everything from the carrier group commander's point of view. She'd heard a lot of it already, but it was good knowing what the other woman had been thinking.

Commander Levy's story was interesting, too. He'd jumped right on to getting the carrier's weapons and defenses into the action. Honestly, he'd worked hand in glove with her people. His missiles had precisely complemented her fighters. Together, they'd overwhelmed the enemy.

That wasn't to say that they couldn't do better. There was room to be a lot smoother going forward.

The admiral finished debriefing Levy and turned to her. "How is your injured pilot?"

"She's out of surgery. The long-term prognosis is good, but she's going to have a lot of difficult recovery ahead of her."

He nodded somberly. "What jumps out at you after the first real engagement using the fighters?"

"That there aren't enough of us," she said. It came out more bluntly than it had sounded in her head. "We need more carriers and many more fighter pilots. We had the advantage this time. With fighters, the more you have, the fewer you lose. If we get into another fight before we recover, we might lose every trained pilot the Empire has."

"Harsh," he said, "but probably true. In our defense, we never expected to find ourselves in quite this position. We thought we'd have more time to work into our roles. To expand the fighter corps. Let that be a lesson for us. We need to act as though we're going to war with what we have."

The hatch slid open, and Princess Kelsey came in. "Sorry I'm late. No need to stand on my behalf."

Annette stopped part way to her feet and resumed her seat.

"As Jared said, I was listening in over my implants. Annette, I'm very sorry you lost so many good people. They will be missed, and they will be avenged. Please continue."

Admiral Mertz nodded. "The word I have from *Audacious* is that all the enemy personnel have been removed from the captured ships and that others have been rescued from the wreckage of the ships lost in combat. Kelsey, there were no survivors on the destroyer you took out."

The princess nodded. "It happened fast. They never had a chance, but I can live with that."

"Tell us about what you recovered."

"The take from the freighter is both more and less than we'd wanted. On the minus side, there wasn't very much in the way of Raider implants.

This was an ambush, so they only had enough on hand to fool the AI for a very short time. We can make maybe a thousand Raiders."

Considering what the princess could do, that sounded like a lot to Annette.

"On the plus side," Princess Kelsey continued, "they brought a full-blown AI to take over ruling this area of space. We'll be able to add one more AI to the friendly network. I'm inclined to give it to the Pentagarans."

Admiral Mertz nodded slowly. "That would definitely cement the alliance, and we could use an AI in this neighborhood. Honestly, we could use one or more back on Avalon, too.

"That, however, is a discussion for another time and audience. I want to focus on the carrier group and how to make it more effective. To do that, I've been researching how the Old Empire did business and how other navies in history did.

"In particular, I've been reading about how the wet navies on Terra worked. There are some interesting examples of how operations were handled that might be better than what the Old Empire did."

"Really?" Captain Anderson asked. "That seems counterintuitive."

He nodded. "The Old Empire had a lot of firepower. In the end, that's what brought them down. They operated in huge groupings of vessels, particularly compared to what we use today. Powerful but unwieldly. We need to be a lot more flexible, and to do that, each command needs more autonomy."

That was above Annette's pay grade, but she understood it.

"I've already discussed how the carrier group should be commanded with Admiral Yeats," Admiral Mertz said. "Nothing against you, Zia, but he was unsure you were the right person to have overall command. That's why he placed an experienced officer like Commander Levy with you. The call on which one of you was better suited for overall command is my decision."

"With all due respect, Admiral," Levy said, "I might know how to run a ship, but I'm behind the curve in fighter operations. Captain Anderson has it down cold. As much as I wish I could say I'm your guy, I'm not. Not yet."

Admiral Mertz smiled. "I agree with you on all counts, Commander. You're making up ground fast, but you don't have the mindset for carrier group command. You will one day soon, but not yet. So, with Admiral Yeats's concurrence, I'm bumping you to commodore, Zia. Congratulations.

"To go along with that, you're confirmed to command your carrier group and all its escorts."

He turned his attention to Levy. "That brings me to you, Commander. She's going to be far too busy commanding her task force, so you inherit command of *Audacious*. To go along with that is a promotion to captain. Not as extravagant as to flag rank, but someone will need to command future carrier groups."

Levy didn't look perturbed. "I'll make you proud, sir."

"I know you will. And that brings us to you, Commander Vitter. I picked up something from the Terran wet navies that I think will help us. The

United States, a powerful prespaceflight nation, had an interesting way of balancing their ships and the fighters stationed on them.

"The commanding officer of the carrier and the commander of the air wing were coequal, and both reported directly to the flag officer in overall command. Usually an admiral, but Zia is going to have to make do. So you are also hereby promoted to captain and will now work with Captain Levy to carry out the operations ordered by your commodore."

She nodded. "That's very doable, sir. Captain Levy and I work quite well together."

"It means that you're in charge of all fighter operations and the pilots that perform them, so you'll have to find a way to keep them in line. Say keeping them from buzzing the ship, for example."

He said the last with a wry grin, which she completely understood. He'd done exactly that when he'd piloted the very first fighter they'd recovered.

Which raised a point for later in her mind. He deserved wings of his own. He'd taken out a destroyer all on his own. He might not have much in the way of flight time, but he'd walked the walk.

"I think I can keep my people from doing anything so rash," she said dryly. "They're not barbarians."

He laughed. "We'll see. The remaining enemy forces are almost to the Pentagaran flip point. They're about to get an ugly wake-up call. My ships have almost converged with your carrier group, so we'll bottle them up.

"Once the invasion is defeated, we'll go over the data we've recovered and make further plans."

Admiral Mertz rose to his feet. "Until then, return to your ship. You've done the Empire proud. Now, go do it again."

* * *

ZIA FELT MORE than a little overwhelmed on the trip back to *Audacious*. Yes, she'd been doing the work already, but she wasn't ready to be a flag officer. She'd only been a lieutenant before the exploration mission! She felt in far over her head.

"You're ready," Annette said. "Don't second-guess yourself."

"I don't feel ready."

"Who does, when it comes right down to it? We do the best we can and learn for the next time."

Levy cleared his throat. "Speaking of the next time, we need to start planning for the next engagement. We got lucky this time. Next time, we have to plan for things to go wrong."

Zia nodded. "We need an FTL com, especially if we're going to be operating in a forward star system. I'll discuss that with Sir Carl first thing. That should allow us to warn the people behind us when it all goes in the pot."

"That's a good start," the man said, "but I'm thinking bigger. We made this operation up as it developed. I think we really need to work on some contingency planning before the next time. Will we cover all the bases? No, but I'd like to see our worst-case scenarios planned out."

Annette grunted. "We thought we had. The bright side is that we shouldn't run into a fleet so soon again."

"We can't count on that," Zia said with a shake of her head. "We have to expect exactly that. Then if we miss them, so much the better. Once we get back to *Audacious*, I want the two of you to put your heads together to work out more scenarios we might run into.

"I'll call the carrier group's captains together after that, and we'll do the same on a fleet level. I'm afraid you're going to be very busy, Captain Levy."

The man smiled. "That's how I earn my exorbitant salary, ma'am."

She considered the newly promoted captain. "I think you'll do a lot better job at commanding *Audacious* than I did. Your experience is going to help out with any number of things I missed."

"Don't sell yourself short, Commodore. I'll be the first to admit that I had my underwear in a knot, but you had all the basics covered. You were doing just fine. I'm sorry that I allowed my personal feelings to make me... grumpy."

The cutter pilot announced that they were on approach to the carrier.

"We'll have to save the group hug for later," Zia said. "We need to be ready in case the bad guys come running back through the flip point. My internal chronometer says they'll make the flip in about twenty minutes. We'll be half an hour behind them.

"Annette, I want the fighters ready to launch but still on board. We might end up fighting this out in Pentagar space. Brandon—I can call you that, right?—I want the ship ready to fight or maneuver."

The other officers nodded as the cutter entered the landing bay. "Excellent," Zia said. "Let's finish this battle so we can plot out our next move."

22

J ared watched the last of the enemy ships flip into Pentagaran space with more than a hint of trepidation. He really didn't like leaving the fighting to someone else, as much as he knew their ships were up to the task.

In particular, the defensive forts around the flip point were vulnerable. They'd been designed to fight the Pale Ones. They couldn't survive even a cursory exchange of fire with modern warships.

Ten minutes later, a light cruiser and three destroyers popped back into the Erorsi system. All four ships were heavily damaged. They took off for deep space, but it was far too late for that. Jared was already in missile range.

"Cut your acceleration and surrender or I open fire," he said curtly over the com. "You're in my missile range, and I'm not inclined to allow you to escape. You're not blind. You know you cannot possibly get away. Spare your crews."

He thought they might ignore him, but one of the destroyers cut its acceleration. The other two followed suit quickly enough. All three dropped their battle screens.

The light cruiser continued to accelerate for almost thirty seconds before it gave in to the inevitability of the situation and surrendered.

The next transit through the Pentagaran flip point was the Pentagaran superdreadnought *Resolute* and her escorts. Admiral Sanders signaled him at once.

"The fighting is over on our side, Admiral Mertz. All but two of the destroyers were crippled or destroyed in the exchange of fire. The other cruisers fought to the death.

"They wasted valuable ordinance and time on the orbital forts. They had no idea we'd abandoned them and put the defenses on automatic. We didn't lose any ships, and our damage was light."

Jared smiled. "I'm glad to hear that. Be careful when you rescue survivors. They can't find out about too much or you'll trigger their implants."

"Already taken care of. We have a lot of people that still need implants, so they're going to see exactly what they expect. Thank you for the timely warning. If that fleet had come upon us unaware, they would have hurt us badly. What is the plan now?"

"We get them off their ships, separate the officers from the crew, and overwrite the implant code. That will take a good long while, so we might see about letting you take care of it. Kelsey is going to see if she can find out where they're making the Raider implants. At this point, it's become clear we need to strike fast and get the flip-point jammers back into place."

The older man nodded. "At least we can put it back up once you're away. You can signal us to open it up for you once you get back. Where will we gather the captured ships?"

"I think that anything with a functional flip drive should go to Pentagar. That will make searching them a lot easier. We might have a few ships that can't flip, but we can get them on a trajectory toward the flip point. Borrow the recovery ship from Harrison's World to get them over."

That was the vessel the AIs had used to gather all the wrecked Imperial ships into the graveyard around Boxer Station. It used long, curved arms to enclose a ship so that the drive field worked on everything during a flip. With the relative proximity to Harrison's World via the flip points Omega had created, the recovery ship could be at Pentagar in less than a day.

"What do you think the invasion means?" Sanders asked. "What triggered them? Was it the lost freighter?"

Jared shrugged. "Maybe we'll find out when we start questioning the prisoners. Or, more likely, the AI just gave them orders to get it done.

"In any case, I'm glad we were here to catch them, but the missing fleet is going to get a lot of attention very soon. My people need to get what data we can and start the next phase of the operation. Our window of opportunity is closing quickly."

* * *

KELSEY WENT DOWN to the lab on *Invincible*. Carl Owlet was hooking up the computer cores from the freighter.

He waved at her. "I'm glad to see you in one piece. Angela is not happy with you, by the way."

She smiled. "I'd imagine not. She's still under the delusion that she has some kind of control over the trouble I get myself into. On the positive side, I gave her a pile of prisoners to interrogate. It turned out the freighter had almost twice the expected crew, evenly split between what looked like civilians and Rebel Fleet personnel."

"Any idea why?"

Kelsey shrugged. "Probably because some of the work was beneath what the Fleet people thought they should be doing. Someone will talk soon enough, I'm sure. I have some good news about the computer."

The corners of his mouth curled up. "Really? I thought that was my line."

"You'll like it. The bridge controls were unlocked, and the captain was logged in. I took the opportunity to add our implant serial numbers to the cleared list. I supposed they expected to have some warning before bad guys came calling."

"That is good news," he admitted. "Though it sort of feels like cheating. At this point, I'm used to hacking my way in past all the safeguards they can throw at me. How can I be satisfied with just logging in?"

"You'll manage something, I'm sure."

He laughed and started typing on a keyboard. Even with implants, the young man preferred using his hands.

While he worked, she continued talking. "I'm going to have the recovery people go over *Persephone*'s security. I really want to make this hard if anyone tries to pull it on us. There have to be ways to secure things without making normal work impossible."

He nodded. "I've been dabbling with some work in that arena. I'll coordinate with them and see what we can come up with. They've also requested something like the implant jamming headbands, but with range. I'm not sure I can exempt our people from something like that, but I'll do what I can.

"Let's see if we can isolate the ship's log and parse it for the course they took. I know Commander Richards says he remembers the system where they picked up the Raider implants, but it would be nice to have some independent confirmation."

"You don't trust him? Marcus vouched for him."

Carl shrugged. "I wouldn't say I distrust him. More like I worry the AIs pulled a fast one somewhere."

That she understood perfectly.

He leaned forward and looked at the text scrolling up the screen. "Here we go. I pulled the flip transitions from the drives. Correlating that to the names of the systems gets us this."

A section of the Old Empire flip point map appeared in her mind's eye. A green dot started a line of transitions that ended with a red dot. The red system was Erorsi.

"The green dot is the origin system. I'll guess that was where they installed the orbital bombardment weapon. From there, it went through a dozen transitions. One of the systems it transited is indeed the one Commander Richards suspected of being the manufacturing location for the Raider implants."

The map expanded and began displaying system data. "Dresden," she said. "The Old Empire databases have it listed as a minor manufacturing hub. Nothing to write home about."

"That was then, and this is now," Carl said. "According to the scanner records from the freighter, the main world there has a single large orbital. It's where the freighter met up with its escort. That might mean there aren't many warships left there."

"Or it could mean there are," Kelsey said. "We won't know until we take a look for ourselves. It's best if we don't head in with any assumptions."

"I'll extract everything. Once I have it on my systems, I'll look for classified files and compile a report on anything that looks interesting at Dresden. It won't take me more than a few hours."

"That'll give me time to coordinate things with Jared. When I head back to *Persephone*, I'll want an FTL com. I don't want to get surprised again. We need to have them on all the capital ships."

"I have a few on the table over there. The installation instructions are included with each unit. I don't have nearly as many as I want, but it's a start. When we get to Dresden, what are our goals?"

Kelsey hefted the box of coms. "We take anything they have on hand, including the plans to make the implants, if we can. Let me know immediately if you find anything."

* * *

BRANDON EXCUSED himself once they were back on board *Audacious*. He wanted to check on his senior prisoner before she was transferred off the ship for transport to Pentagar.

They'd finished reprogramming her implants while he was on *Invincible*, so she was now in the brig. All the senior officers were. The junior officers were in a separate hold they'd converted to use as a place to detain everyone else with implants.

The unenhanced people that made up the bulk of the crew were scattered throughout the carrier group. They were significantly more cowed, so he didn't expect them to resist his people directly.

That said a lot about the Rebel Empire society, he supposed. He'd read up on how things had been on Harrison's World before they'd liberated it, but he'd entertained the hope that it was better elsewhere in the Rebel Empire. Apparently not.

The destroyer captains were all in solo cells. The executive officers and senior crew from each ship were together in larger ones. He'd quadrupled the normal marine guard, so the brig was fairly crowded.

That didn't count the extra guards in the corridors. There would be no breakout on his ship. Well, not technically his yet. No one even knew he'd been promoted yet.

The officer on duty nodded at him as he entered. She looked at ease but had both a stunner and a flechette pistol on her hips. "Commander. Everything is quiet."

"I'm glad to hear it," he said. "That beats a riot any day of the week. Let me in to speak with the senior prisoner."

The captain of the destroyer that had surrendered to them was the most senior of the remaining officers. She was also the only one that had caught on that something was seriously wrong.

That was the primary reason he hadn't allowed the captains to communicate with their crew. It would be up to Admiral Mertz when and if to change that.

A pair of marine guards backed him up when they opened the cell. He gestured for them to remain outside and to close the cell behind him.

The woman glared at him from where she sat on her bunk and didn't stand. "Are you here to get this farce out of the way?"

"There are so many farces on my schedule that I don't rightly know where to begin, Commander Giguere. Why don't you pick one for us to start with?"

She shook her head. "Let's start with the fact you aren't Fleet."

He allowed himself to smile a little. "Oh, but I am. I've been a Fleet officer for over twenty-five years. The devil is in the details. Let me guess. You're referring to the fact we have our enlisted men and women implanted."

"That's right. What kind of lunatic would do that? You're from outside the Empire. I have no idea why you feel the need to pretend or how you got your hands on so many Fleet vessels, including ones restricted to core systems, but you're playing some kind of game. What do you want from me? Hell, what did you do to me?"

Brandon pulled out the chair beside the built-in desk. "My name is Brandon Levy, by the way. I'm currently the executive officer of this vessel, though I'm taking over command shortly. As for what we did to you, why don't you tell me why you went berserk?"

That made the tall woman look a little disconcerted. "I'm not really sure what came over me. Did you give me some kind of drug?"

"No. If I had, I assure you it wouldn't be to make you more violent. No, this is where unpleasant truths that you aren't ready to hear come into play. Or perhaps you already know most of the story, just not some of the hidden details.

"Whether you know it or not—whether you accept it or not—the Empire you know is ruled by artificial intelligences. Ones that do not have the health and well-being of the human race in mind. Feel free to stop me if you've heard any of this before."

When she didn't respond, he launched into the same basic story he'd heard about the corruption of the Rebel Empire.

Within a few moments, he could see the disbelief and disdain in the woman's expression. Well, it didn't matter if she believed him. She had to hear why they'd needed to overwrite her implant code if she were to have any chance of ever accepting the truth.

This was going to be a long and unpleasant revelation to the woman. However, once she ultimately accepted the truth—which she eventually would—she would help convince her fellow officers. Only then could there truly be any negotiation between the two sides.

23

It took Jared almost half a day to get the captured ships corralled and headed for Pentagar. Most of the prisoners were on their way there, too, but not all. One of the destroyer captains had figured out they weren't the same Fleet as she was, so he'd decided to leave her and her officers on *Audacious*.

Brandon Levy felt as though he could convince her of the same truths as they'd shown Lieutenant Commander Richards. Personally, Jared wasn't sure, but he was willing to allow the man a chance to try.

Time was short. Yes, they'd defeated the invasion, but if they had any hope of capturing the Raider manufacturing equipment, they'd need to strike quickly. Once the Rebel Empire became aware that they had a new enemy, they'd move the facility farther away from the fighting just to keep them from capturing it.

He examined the scanner readings as soon as they'd flipped to the Pentagar system. The defensive forts were gone, blown to bits. He was glad they'd had time to evacuate them.

Another group of ships was searching the wreckage of a few Rebel Empire vessels a short distance away.

That wasn't to say they were alone. There were dozens of ships protecting the flip point, and they'd put the flip-point jammer into place at the hostile flip point before they'd left Erorsi. No one would be sneaking up on them.

One of his people turned to him. "Incoming message, Admiral. It's for you."

"Put it on screen."

A familiar face appeared. Lieutenant—no, Lieutenant Commander—

Parker of His Majesty's fast courier *Lance*. The man smiled. "Lord Admiral Mertz. It's a pleasure to see you again."

"For me, too, Commander Parker. What can I do for you?"

"I have instructions to ferry you and Princess Kelsey, as well as some of your other senior officers, to Pentagar at once. I have my trusty new ship standing by to get you there faster than ever."

Jared frowned. "Is something wrong?"

"Not that I'm aware of, Lord Admiral. All Crown Princess Elise told me was that events there were moving faster than anticipated and that your presence is required."

"Is see. Who are you supposed to bring?"

"Yourself, Princess Kelsey, Count Talbot, and the officers that originally served as your command staff on *Athena*. Her Highness urges you to hurry."

He rose from his seat. "Then I'd best get moving. I'll see you in a few minutes."

Once the connection closed, he headed for the lift. "Marcus, see that everyone else is notified that we're needed on *Lance*."

"Already done, Admiral. Your sister is still in Erorsi space, but *Persephone* should be here in about fifteen minutes."

In all, it took about half an hour to gather everyone on the new *Lance*. While the old fast courier had been—well, fast—the new ship was the best the Old Empire had to offer. It would get them to Pentagar in an hour. Quickly by anyone's estimation.

Kelsey sat down beside him. "What's this all about? I was just getting Angela into the implantation machine for her first session. Well, technically her second session. She already has her implants and nanites."

"What is she getting?"

"The Old Empire went slowly with their Raiders. The implant procedure took six sessions. First was the cranial hardware and nanites. Session two is the optical, olfactory, and auditory hardware. Three is supposed to be the pharmacology unit, but I've decided to lump that in with session two. The last three sessions are the artificial musculature and bone reinforcement. So, we'll use five sessions."

He frowned. "Are you sure you should be combining them like that? They had them separate for a reason."

She nodded. "It's fine. Even Ned agrees. He says they'd been recommending this change for longer than he'd been alive. The Imperial bureaucracy wasn't renowned for its speed. Angela will have about a week to adjust to the new hardware before we start on the artificial musculature and bone reinforcement."

Jared looked over at where Talbot was talking to Charlie Graves. "What about him? I'd have expected he'd be demanding his turn."

She smiled. "He is, but you caught us right before we put him in. Angela was actually the second person in line. We'll get him going once we take care of the fire here. Any idea what's going on?"

He shook his head. "Not yet. Elise usually sends enough detail to know what's happening, but not this time. It can't be too bad if they need us without our ships. Since we have the time, let's go over what you've found out about the target system."

"There isn't much," his sister said. "Before the rebellion, Dresden was an out-of-the-way backwater. It still is in many ways. The databases have nothing on it at all, but a few prisoners have indicated the planetary population is low.

"There's a lot of manufacturing capability in orbit, though. If this is where they made the Raider implants before, it might have been a secret facility and is only used intermittently."

"Do we have any idea where the equipment might be?" he asked.

She shook her head. "Not for certain, but they only have one orbital. We're going to have to improvise and overcome. On the plus side, I don't think they'll have a large Fleet presence. This ambush group was stationed there. No one is talking about what kind of firepower they left to guard the place, but it can't be much."

He brought up the image she'd sent him from the freighter's computer core. The planet looked nice enough, though the color was more green than blue. There was a single large orbital. It massed about thirty percent more than a superdreadnought. Not huge, but not insignificant, either.

"Recovering the equipment is going to take time," he said after a moment. "We'll have to search the orbital and pull out what we need in a hurry. Anyone could come along while we're doing it."

Kelsey grinned. "If it was easy, anyone could do it."

Jared started to respond, but a call from Elise interrupted him. A check indicated they were almost to Pentagar. Time had flown.

He could've done this as a mental conversation, but he chose to imagine he was sitting at a real com console and actually speaking. That made his life a little easier.

"Elise," he said aloud. "What's going on? What's the emergency?"

His fiancée smiled. "No emergency. Well, not really in the way you mean. After all the fighting, I decided that we couldn't risk waiting any longer. It happens tonight."

He frowned. "What happens?"

Elise gave him an exasperated look. "Our wedding, of course. I'm making you mine before anything else happens. You'll want to tell Kelsey and Talbot. We have a lot of work to do if we're going to have a double wedding in less than four hours."

* * *

KELSEY BURIED her head in her hands. "We're never going to pull this off."

"You are such a pessimist!" Elise scolded. "We have the resources of the entire Kingdom at our disposal. We can manage this."

Kelsey laughed. She thought she sounded a tad hysterical. "I'm sorry, but I can't imagine how that's even possible. The cake takes time, so do the flowers. It can't be possible."

The woman smiled. "You'd be surprised how motivated one becomes when the Crown Princess calls. And, for this, I am ruthlessly using my father to personally exhort each of the major players to produce miracles."

"Not even your father can change the laws of physics."

"You'd be surprised. You have a wedding dress to select. I've taken the liberty of arranging a fast car to get you to the most prestigious firm specializing in that immediately. They have a team standing by to receive you."

"Aren't you coming?"

Elise smiled. "I already have a dress. I hoped this day would come and wanted to be ready at a moment's notice. Now go pick the dress you've always wanted."

The car turned out to be *really* fast. It broke every speed regulation imaginable as it literally screamed across the city to Royal Bridal.

A distinguished man with a head of silver hair bowed as she exited the car.

"Princess Kelsey, my name is Edward Pollack. Rest easy. I will make absolutely certain that we produce the dress of your dreams, even if I have to make it myself."

He gestured to the woman standing beside him. "If you will accompany my assistant, she'll get your measurements, and you can begin selecting the style of dress you'd like."

Kelsey found herself hustled into a room. The woman who'd accompanied her gestured toward a booth. "My name is Jinny, Highness. If you'll strip and climb inside, the scanner will get all your measurements. Follow the instructions on the screen. Call out when you're dressed again."

The woman stepped out, and Kelsey stripped and stepped into the booth. The screen told her how to stand and had her run through a series of motions. She couldn't imagine needing to squat in her wedding dress, but it seemed she'd be able to.

Once the machine finished scanning, she exited the booth, dressed, and called out to Jinny. The woman led her to a computer terminal, where they both sat.

"We can narrow down the style of dresses you're interested in here," Jinny said. "It's a simple matter of putting them onto your scanned picture. We'll broadcast a full-sized image into the attached holotank."

Jinny brought up a sample dress and threw the image into the tank. It really did look just like a full-sized version of Kelsey wearing the dress. It spun slowly and allowed her image to move, demonstrating the flow of the gown.

"I've always had something in mind," Kelsey admitted. "It's probably long out of style, even on Avalon, but I saw it in a wedding when I was a girl. I can describe it."

"That might not be necessary. Once we made contact with the Empire, we immediately began researching weddings and dresses. Master Pollack is already planning to expand there. Was the wedding for someone notable?"

"One of my distant cousins, Angelina Kerr."

Jinny brought up a search screen on the computer. "This dress?"

A picture from the wedding appeared on the screen. It had a long, flowing skirt and a simple cut with a medium neckline. There were undoubtedly more technical descriptions, but she'd never bothered to learn wedding dress terminology.

"That's the dress!" Kelsey said.

Jinny nodded. "It has classic lines," she agreed. "The style isn't in fashion in the Empire at the moment, but I've discovered that people like yourself define the styles in demand rather than following trends. Let me compare this to the dresses we have ready for fitting. If one of them is similar, that will save time."

Jinny pulled up a number of dresses and seemingly disregarded them at once. Then she hit on one that made her pause.

"This is close. We'd have to do some work on the neckline and redo the skirt, but I think that's doable. Let me see if we have it in close to your size."

Kelsey thought that unlikely. Not unless they normally had children getting married. She was much shorter than the average bride.

"We have one that can be pulled in, I think. Let me call the master and see what he thinks."

He swept into the room with a confident air a moment later. He must've been close by.

"We have an historical dress from Avalon that Her Highness wants," Jinny said. "I have a possible match on screen."

He considered the wedding photo and the potential dress for less than three seconds before he shook his head. "That won't work. The modifications to bring it down to size are too extreme. It will compromise the flow of the fabric. Move over, please."

He sat at the chair his assistant vacated and began playing their system like a virtuoso with his favorite instrument. Images flew across the screen as he scanned a wider selection of dresses. He froze on one image. The dress was more cream than white, and it seemed to be made for a child.

"I think we have a candidate," he said, looking over at Kelsey. "This was a dress made for a younger bridesmaid. Since the one you want to emulate is of a relatively simple cut, it would be easier to add the skirt and adjust the neckline."

Kelsey examined the dress closely. "I like the color, though I had wanted white. If you think it'll work, that might be the closest we can come."

He scowled at her. "I'm not satisfied with close enough, Highness. A white version will be extremely challenging, but we are up to the task. Jinny! I need everyone to gather in my office in five minutes. We don't have a moment to waste!"

24

Zia watched Jared driving the tailor to distraction with amusement. "Admiral, you're going to look lopsided if you keep moving around like that."

The room was filled with stands, partial mannequins, and fabric. The older gentleman working on Jared had a distinguished white beard and a walrus mustache. If his own suit were any indication, the admiral would look fabulous.

The tailor gave her a withering glare. "He will not! I assure you that I can compensate, though this is wasting valuable time."

"I was thinking exactly the same thing," Jared said. "While I love Elise, we're critically short on time. I should be getting the fleet ready."

"Delegate," she said. "If you spend any more time worrying about this, you'll be late for your wedding. I don't believe that I need to stress that your bride is a lot more demanding than Fleet. Particularly today."

The tailor—Renaldo—pulled Jared up short. "Stop fidgeting, Highness."

"You've fought in space and hand to hand," Zia said. "This is only a wedding. Don't panic. If you do, the Royal Guard will efficiently tackle you and deliver you on schedule."

"That's very reassuring, Zia," Jared said dryly. "Thanks."

She laughed. "I'm lucky. I got the word to bring my dress uniform. Someone is getting it updated for my new rank as we speak. I can do this all day."

Renaldo gestured for Jared to stand on a small dais. "I've made certain the suit is very close to your uniform measurements but that is not bespoke. You should rectify that, Highness."

"Maybe for my dress uniform," Jared allowed. "The others are designed for working."

The other man clucked with his tongue. "That is a common misconception. Well fitted does not mean unusable. In fact, you will find them even more durable and functional than anything you buy off the rack. You should have your steward contact someone."

"If I ever get one, I'll keep that in mind."

"You don't have a steward?" The man looked scandalized. "All officers of flag rank should have someone to take care of the everyday details of their lives. A forward-thinking captain would do so, I assure you. This is particularly true now that you are a high noble."

Jared shook his head, and the man handed him a shirt. "I've been dressing myself my entire life. I can manage to tie my shoes now that I'm a flag officer. Or a noble."

The tailor seemed unconvinced.

The entire exchange amused Zia. Having taken the step of getting a steward, she could heartily agree with Renaldo's assessment. In fact, she'd already tasked her own steward with finding someone for both the admiral and Princess Kelsey.

It took a surprisingly short time to get the admiral ready. Renaldo handed the last piece of clothing off to one of his assistants and shooed Jared toward the door.

"They will handle your makeup next door while I complete my Herculean task. Don't dawdle, Highness. The clock is ticking."

The statement made the admiral frown. "Makeup? I don't need makeup."

"Preposterous," the tailor asserted. "The lights will make you look like a corpse. Leave this to the professionals, or no one will see you in the right shade."

"I don't get it. The lights here are fine. Why would they be any different at the church? Or wherever we're getting married. I don't think anyone told me where that will happen."

The other man rolled his eyes. "Your ceremony will take place in the Royal Cathedral. The lights are for the cameras, so that everyone in the Kingdom can see the crown Princess marry. And your sister, too, of course."

That made Jared look uncomfortable. "Oh, crap. You're talking millions of people. Talbot will love that."

"Indeed. Hundreds of millions, at a minimum. Likely billions. Oh, and since the heir to the Imperial Throne is going to be there with you, I'll assume that the viewership in the Empire will be quite high. You'll want to look your best."

Zia imagined it would be far higher than that if one considered those who would be seeing the ceremony in the years and decades to come.

"Focus, Your Highness," Renaldo said sternly. "A groom makes the bride wait at his peril."

"Truer words," the admiral muttered.

"I need to head out, too, Admiral," Zia said as she headed for the door. "Keep your chin up."

* * *

JARED THOUGHT he looked excessively orange, but they assured him that the bright lights focused on the dais would balance things out. He'd have to trust them on that one.

Renaldo had him dress and made a few last-minute tweaks before pronouncing himself moderately satisfied. "This is good enough for the ceremony. I will see that other suits are made to match it, but I'll take my time to be certain they will last longer."

"You mean this will fall apart?"

"No, Highness," the man said with exaggerated patience. "Only that the seams are rushed. It won't last as long as a bespoke suit should. Before you profane this room with the declaration that you can just have more made, I'll remind you that quantity does not make up for quality, no matter what the old saying says.

"Imagine taking one of your new ships up against a group of Fleet's current ships of the line. Quality counts for even more in my line of work."

Jared didn't know enough to argue the point, so he shut his mouth.

The older man gave him one last walk-around. "I believe you'll do, Highness, and just in time. I believe I hear your keepers coming."

The door opened, and Jared saw Royal Guards outside. "Your car is ready, Highness," one of them said.

They rushed him through the halls and out to the landing pad. A classic-looking air limo awaited. Standing beside it was Talbot, looking sharp in a suit very much like the one Jared wore. He still managed to look slightly rumpled, but the small man beside him was still working on that.

"Thank God," the marine said. "I can't get this guy to leave me alone, and they insisted on making me look like a clown."

"No one is going to make you look like a clown, Talbot. Did they tell you why we're wearing makeup?"

The small man shook his head vigorously, just out of Talbot's range of vision.

"No," Talbot said. "Why?"

"The lights," Jared said as he climbed in. "It's bright in the Royal Cathedral."

"Oh. That makes sense, I suppose. Do you think the ladies are ready?"

Jared laughed. "Not a chance. If we're being rushed, they're in even worse shape. They'll want to have every detail nailed down. Nervous?"

Talbot climbed in beside Jared, and the car took off. "Not as much as I'd have thought. This really isn't in the same league as someone trying to kill you. It's only a wedding."

Jared smiled knowingly. Oh, this was going to be good. It might even distract him from the butterflies in his own stomach.

* * *

ANNETTE RUBBED HER EYES TIREDLY. She and Brandon Levy had been working over the data Carl Owlet had recovered from the freighter for what seemed like hours. A check of her chronometer told her that was accurate.

It also told her that they needed to wrap things up and get onto the cutters if they were going to make it to the wedding on time.

"We need to finish," she said. "I think we've looked at every bit of scanner recording they had."

"It wasn't much," the man grumbled. "Just the approach scanners. We don't know anything about the orbital or its defenses. Much less the warships they might have guarding the place. If it was me, I'd have a base to go along with my secret facilities."

She nodded. "Me, too. Judging by the number of ships we saw at Erorsi, I'm betting they brought a lot of that protective force to act as the attackers in our little drama. Did you get anything out of your prisoner?"

Levy shook his head. "Not really. She's not buying what we're selling, at least not yet. From what I've heard, it took Commander Richards a while to come around, and he had the benefit of being an amateur historian.

"Veronica Giguere isn't one to think about the past, it seems. She's one of those Fleet officers that lives and breathes her work."

"Considering some of the stuff that Princess Kelsey found in the other destroyer commander's cabin, that sounds like a point in Giguere's favor. She's not a social climber?"

"Not based on anything we've found. We broke into her safe, but she'd already destroyed the contents. Her bedroom is reassuringly normal, though."

The first destroyer captain's bedroom had looked like a bordello, based on some of the images that Annette had seen. Her office walls had any number of pictures showing the officer with civilian notables, and she'd had more blackmail material than a dedicated criminal.

Based on what she'd heard from people knowledgeable about Harrison's World, Annette was pretty sure that was the rule rather than the exception. Social climbing was a contact sport in the Rebel Empire.

"Has anyone on the freighter crew started talking?" she asked. "What was their plan?"

"Get into orbit and blast the lake where the crazy computer's ship was. They had no way of knowing it was already done for.

"They didn't expect to have any trouble, but they brought along enough Raider implants to show the goods if required. All in all, they expected a walk in the park. The Fleet personnel were there to fire the weapon and keep the crew of the freighter in line."

"Were they expecting trouble from their own civilians?"

He shrugged. "It doesn't sound like it. More that they have some kind of institutional objection to allowing a weapon of that kind out of their control. Frankly, I sort of agree. A ship with that could kill millions in the blink of an eye."

Levy stood slowly. "We should get dressed and board the cutter. The schedule is already tight."

"Good idea. I'll see you there in a few minutes."

She jogged to her quarters and changed into her dress uniform. Zia had given Annette her old rank tabs, which meant a lot, so she was in good shape.

Thankfully, Fleet's black-and-gold dress uniform made formal events easy. She was sure that Admiral Mertz wished he could just wear his.

Once she was ready, she headed for the landing bay. Brandon Levy was already aboard the cutter, and he had the correct rank tabs.

She had a moment to appreciate how the dress uniform flattered him. The other officer was sharp. It was too bad they were in the same command.

That thought gave her pause. Yes, it had been a while, but was that really where her mind had just gone?

Apparently so. Though, now that she considered it, the idea wasn't a terrible one. For that matter, they weren't technically in the same chain of command, either. They were coequal commanders of the people on board *Audacious*. Neither one in charge of the other, and both reported to the commodore.

Something to ponder, she decided as she watched his eyes. Men thought they were subtle, but she could tell he was admiring the cut of her uniform, too.

"You look good," she said with a smile. "You're not trying to outshine the admiral, are you?"

"Not likely. Maybe Major Talbot. You look great, too."

"Thank you."

The two of them sat among the other senior officers going down for the wedding. Weddings, plural.

Many of her companions were talking about the event, wondering how grand the pomp and circumstance would be.

She'd already decided it would be a powerful affair, filled with symbolism and emotion. She'd cry, of course. She'd brought more than enough tissues.

Rather than focusing on the wedding, she immersed herself in plotting out their attack on Dresden with Brandon. No matter how they played it out, they'd need the carrier and its fighters to suppress any hostile response.

The fighters could slip in much closer than any of the other ships except for the *Persephone* and her pinnaces. While the pinnaces were fine scouts, they didn't have what it took to stand off warships.

Almost certainly, the Raider ship would get close and use her pinnaces to get a boarding party onto the orbital. That raiding party would secure the target while the fighters engaged any Rebel Empire ships that might take offense. That would allow the rest of the fleet to get in close.

With that much volatility to the planning, they needed to have primary plans, backups, contingencies, and emergency courses of action all mapped out. They needed to take all possible enemy responses into consideration.

The trip to Pentagar wasn't nearly long enough to do more than outline the general shape of their needs. Once the wedding was over, maybe Brandon and she could find a suitable restaurant to have dinner and keep working.

She gave him an enigmatic smile. Oh, yes, that would be very nice indeed.

25

Brandon found a relatively empty corner of the Royal Cathedral and continued his review of the data they'd collected and the rough plans they had for using the fighters and the carrier group. The one real engagement they'd fought had left him feeling as though they were headed for a big surprise—and not a pleasant one—if he didn't get his part of the job under control.

The implants were becoming easier to use, though they still surprised him with the things they were capable of doing. For example, his implant computer was advanced enough to run basic simulations of the carrier's performance when he changed a few parameters of how the ship entered the scenario.

That allowed him to propose certain procedural changes and see if they looked like they might generate better results. That in turn suggested changes to the training that he might implement.

"Are you going to hide here much longer?" a voice asked from the doorway. "You'll miss the ceremony if you dawdle much longer."

It was the freshly promoted Commander Jake Fiennes, the new commanding officer of Black Jack Squadron. Annette Vitter's former deputy.

"How did you even find me?" Brandon asked as he shut down the simulation and stepped out.

"Implants are great things. Annette told me to make sure you didn't wander off too far, so I had mine tell me where yours were."

That had been sneaky. It suggested that he might be able to run a few shipboard drills and see if he could find better paths people might take during drills. Or even use them during hostile boardings.

He firmly put the thought away. "There's a wedding on. Why is she keeping track of me?"

The other man shrugged. "That's just how she rolls. She's always been great at keeping all the little details straight when things get complicated. Like in the middle of a dogfight. Attention to detail is a very good trait for a pilot or someone who commands them."

Brandon considered that and nodded. "That makes a lot of sense."

"And I think she might like you."

"I hope so. We're going to be working very closely for a while."

The other man stopped and considered him for a long moment.

"What?" Brandon asked.

"I'm not sure if you're joking or not. I mean I think she *likes* you."

The less-than-subtle emphasis on "likes" finally did it for him. "That's quite a jump to make, don't you think? It's also something that regulations frown upon."

"Do they? I thought you were co-commanders. Did I misunderstand?"

"We work on the same ship. It would be inappropriate. Even if it wasn't, how could you possibly think that? I barely know the woman."

The other man shook his head. "Being attracted to someone doesn't require you hop right into bed, sir. Annette has had a rough year. After the crash where she lost her arm, she thought her life was over.

"Things are looking up now, but she's a senior officer. Fraternization rules exist for good reason, so she's been in a tight shell. It's good to see her at least contemplating a relationship."

The man gave Brandon a steady look. "I should mention that the pilots would be really unhappy if something happened to hurt her. We all worship her. In case no one ever told you, fighter pilots can be rash and more than a bit impulsive. I trust you see that could have serious repercussions."

Brandon could only imagine what that might mean, but it didn't sound good.

He shook his head. "I'm not going to hurt anyone. You're talking a hypothetical situation. One that you probably misread. I appreciate you having the talk with me, but this isn't what you think it is."

"Copy that, sir. Well, the ceremony is about to get under way. You might want to find your seat. I'd imagine it's going to be quite the spectacle."

Brandon followed the other man into the main chapel. He'd spent a good bit of time examining its gorgeous construction and adornment earlier, but now his attention was inward.

Was Fiennes right? Surely not. He'd met Annette less than a week ago, and under less-than-pleasant circumstances. He'd righted his course, but he'd no doubt made a less-than-positive impression on her.

He knew what the other man was talking about, though. The loneliness of command was something all senior officers dealt with. Any less-than-professional encounters with the fairer sex happened on leave.

Annette would have been one pilot among many aboard the destroyer

Athena. There'd been plenty of people not in her chain of command to see, if that's what she'd wanted.

He imagined her injury kept her emotionally isolated, and then they'd promoted her to command of the fighters. As a commander, her rank would've kept everyone else at arm's length, even though she wasn't technically in charge of the ship's personnel.

According to the regulations, an officer could fraternize—and by that, they meant have a romantic relationship—with people not in his own chain of command that were within two grades of him.

For himself, that meant fighter pilots at the rank of lieutenant commander and above. For her, ship's personnel with similar rank. Definitely not a large pool.

The fighter corps were predominantly male. He wasn't sure why. Perhaps temperament.

For Annette's part, she had a somewhat larger pool, since Fleet as a whole was fairly well balanced when it came to the sexes. Maybe a dozen officers of the appropriate rank.

Why was he even thinking about this? Her sex life was none of his damned business. Jake Fiennes was wrong. Even if he wasn't, now was not the time to be thinking about it. He had a wedding to attend.

He was looking for a seat when he saw Annette wave. She had one next to her open. Considering the crowd, that wasn't happenstance.

Brandon sat beside her. "Thanks for sending Fiennes after me. I lost track of time."

She smiled. "You tend to be a little focused, so I figured it was better to be safe."

The train of thought the other man had started in Brandon's mind had him examining Annette in a new light. He'd known she was pretty, but now he was seeing her as if for the first time. It was a bit disconcerting how attractive he found her.

It was a good thing there really wasn't anything to worry about.

* * *

KELSEY PACED the dressing room they'd put her in at the back of the Royal Cathedral. By some miracle, her wedding dress had arrived on time, and it fit perfectly. It was just as gorgeous as she'd hoped it would be.

The wedding cake was running late, and God only knew what other problems were cropping up. Things she needed to deal with but had no idea were going on because the Royal majordomo wouldn't tell her anything. The woman seemed to believe that not knowing made things easier for Kelsey.

"You need to take a deep breath and stop wearing a path in the carpet," Elise advised her.

Kelsey came to a stop and took several deep breaths. It felt as though she was hyperventilating. "How can you be so calm?"

The crown princess of Pentagar smiled and held out a flute of champagne. "Be careful sipping that. No spills."

The champagne was cold and delicious. Kelsey resisted the urge to gulp it.

"I'm not worried because we have the most capable people imaginable nailing down all the details. They don't need you trying to 'fix' things. You'll only make their jobs harder.

"Tell me, in a fight, do you run around and make sure everyone else is shooting what you want? If you are, you really need to stop. Micromanagement is an obstacle to be overcome rather than a method to command. Do you really think our extremely capable majordomo is going to drop the ball?"

Kelsey sagged a little. "Not really. I just feel helpless. I need to get my hands on the controls."

"No, you *want* to get your hands on the controls. That doesn't mean you'd be a better driver, only that the car was more likely to crash when the two of you struggle over the direction. Sit down and let them do their magic."

That wasn't easy, but Kelsey managed to sit. "Are we making a mistake rushing this? We could've waited until after we got back from this mission."

"That presupposes that you all come back," Elise said grimly. "You'll remember where Talbot inherited his title."

Kelsey couldn't help but remember Timothy Reese's death. He'd been talking on the radio when one of the AI-controlled machines had obliterated him with a plasma rifle. There hadn't even been a body to bury. One moment he was in command of the attack, the next he was only a memory.

As capable as she was, that could all too easily happen to her. Yes, her armor was a lot tougher than what Reese had been wearing, but nothing was invulnerable. Either she or Talbot could die, even if they did everything right. The same went for Jared.

"That's not exactly the cheerful prewedding pep talk I was expecting," Kelsey groused. "But you do have a point. Yes, we shouldn't wait, but I don't want to screw everything up by springing the ambush too soon, since we're going with military metaphors."

Elise laughed. "Don't worry over every little thing. Focus on what you need to do and let our team handle everything else. Even if something goes a little differently than planned, no one in the audience will notice. They'll be watching the four of us. As long as we don't throw up on the minister, we'll be fine."

Kelsey smiled a little at that. "I think I'll manage to avoid that. I just hate waiting."

The door opened, and the majordomo appeared. "Highnesses, we are ready to proceed to the chapel. Princess Elise will go first, with you waiting for my signal to proceed, Princess Kelsey."

"I feel badly about bumping you from the primary spot in your wedding," Elise said.

Kelsey waved the concern away. "This is your world. It's only right for you to be the focus. Besides, we'll reverse things when we get back to Avalon."

"We're having two weddings?"

She nodded. "While this one is legally binding, it's not fair to deny my people the chance to celebrate this with me. It also wouldn't be fair to Jared's mother. A second one wouldn't hurt for you, either."

"Highnesses," the majordomo prompted.

The ladies-in-waiting that the other woman had found for them gathered around, but there was a disturbance at the lift down the hall. A number of familiar female faces were putting in a belated appearance.

"Thank God," Kelsey said. "I thought you weren't going to make it."

"Sorry we're late," Lily Stone said. "Getting the dresses at the last moment was a little harder than we'd expected."

"She means *me* getting the dress in *my* size was the problem," Major Angela Ellis said. "We should've stuck to dress uniforms."

The marine officer was over two meters tall and endowed to the same heroic scale. Kelsey imagined fitting the woman had been a nightmare. At least Kelsey could start with a child's gown.

Zia Anderson shook her head. "You should've seen the seamstress running around in a panic. I almost had to slap her to get her to come out of it."

Elise laughed. "Wouldn't *that* have been a sight?"

Kelsey pulled them all into a hug. "I'm so glad to see you. Now, we have to go. We're already late."

"I beg to differ," Elise said. "A bride is never late to the wedding. She's always precisely on time."

"We'll see if the grooms think so."

It took another minute to get the party back into order, and then they took the corridor beside the lift. It would deliver them to the rear of the cathedral without any of the guests seeing them.

Once behind the ornate doors, Kelsey could hear the murmuring of the crowd and the soft organ music.

The majordomo cleared her throat. "Once I open the door, the bridesmaids will proceed to the dais. Their Highnesses will follow them, Crown Princess Elise in the lead. Once Her Highness reaches the dais, Princess Kelsey will begin."

"Where's my father?" Elise asked.

"Right here," he said, stepping in the front door. "I was merely getting your escape vehicle ready."

He beamed at his daughter before pulling her into his arms. "You look radiant."

"You're going to make me cry," Elise protested as she held him.

"It's your wedding. You're supposed to cry."

"I will not cry before I even see him," she said firmly.

The king turned to Kelsey. "As your father cannot be here, I shall act in his stead. Once I walk Elise to the dais, I shall come back for you."

"It's time," the majordomo said firmly.

* * *

JARED STOOD ON THE DAIS, watching the back of the church with a mixture of anticipation and worry. The crowd was much larger than he'd anticipated, and the lights were just as bright as the tailor had warned him they would be. The floating holocameras were no doubt sending the images out to everyone on the planet and recording them for transmission to the Empire.

Talbot hadn't figured that out, so he wasn't going to enlighten the man.

They had a number of comrades behind them in support: Charlie Graves, Dennis Baxter, Carl Owlet, and Pasco Ramirez. He'd have loved to have more people, but there just wasn't space.

The organ picked up into the wedding march, and his stomach lurched. The ceremony was beginning.

The doors to the rear of the cathedral opened, and the bridesmaids began streaming in. He smiled at them. It was more reassuring than he'd expected to have people he knew in the lead.

Then he saw Elise, and nothing else mattered. She came down the aisle on her father's arm with a smile only for him. She was the most beautiful thing he'd ever seen. It took all his willpower not to take her hands when she stood in front of him.

The king returned to the rear of the cathedral and brought Kelsey out. He heard Talbot's breath catch. She looked like a bright pixie in her small white dress.

Once she stood beside Elise, the minister stepped forward and smiled. "Marriage is a sacred bond that brings two people who love one another even closer," he said. "But in some cases, it is also a matter of state where it involves more than family or friends.

"Today is one such circumstance. We will see our crown princess wed to a hero from legend. This marriage will bring our people closer together, yet this ceremony is only a reflection of the love and commitment they already have for one another."

The man paused, allowing his words to sink in. "I could go on and on about what that means, but I think it's far more appropriate that they say what they truly feel to one another. Jared Mertz, why don't you go first?"

Jared reached out and took Elise's hands in his. "The first time I saw you, I realized how special you were, but I never expected that we would have a future together. The gulf between us was too vast. Me, a lowly officer born on the wrong side of the sheets, and you a powerful noblewoman who would one day lead your people.

"And then you showed me that the space between us was all in my mind.

That together we could overcome every obstacle. Even those we erected ourselves."

He gazed into her eyes for a long moment, enjoying the wide smile on her face. "While I don't feel worthy of many of the rewards heaped up me, I'll accept them if that's what it takes to be your husband. I love you with all my heart and pledge my life to making you happy. Even if this inconvenient war gets in the way."

A low rumble of laughter ran through the hall.

"Well," she said with a twinkle in her eye, "that might be the understatement of the year. Let me make one thing clear. I would walk away from every one of my titles without the slightest hesitation if that were what it took to make you mine.

"I'm glad neither of us has to do that, but between us there is no gulf. You will be my husband and I your wife. Crown princess and prince consort are simply labels that others apply to us, not who we are. I am Elise Orison, the woman who loves you madly. You are Jared Mertz, the man who makes me complete."

She looked at the minister. "It is time. Make me an honest woman."

The crowd did laugh at that, and the minister smiled. "You're already an honest woman, Highness. I'm just here to make it official."

He looked at Jared. "Do you, Jared Mertz, take Elise Orison as your lawfully wedded wife? To have and to hold, forsaking all others for the remainder of your days?"

Jared's throat tightened. "I do."

The minister turned to Elise. "Do you, Elise Orison, take Jared Mertz as your lawfully wedded husband? To have and to hold, forsaking all others for the remainder of your days?"

Her smile took on a hint of triumph. "I do."

The minister raised his arms and stepped back "Then I take great pleasure sealing this eternal bond between you. My lords and ladies, I present to you, Elise Orison and Jared Mertz, your crown princess and her husband."

The crowd erupted into cheers, but Jared only had eyes for Elise. His wife.

He reached for her, but she was already pulling him tightly into her embrace, kissing him soundly.

"You're mine forever," she said fiercely. "Thank God."

Jared laughed and kissed her back, only stopping when someone cleared his throat. A glance up showed his father-in-law standing where the minister had just been.

"I'm very sorry to interrupt this tender moment, but you're not quite done, Prince Jared. There remains one more ceremony to be completed, and we'd best move along sprightly, because your sister is impatiently waiting."

Kelsey laughed and tapped her foot.

"Now, this is complicated by the fact you aren't a citizen of Pentagar, other than by marriage, of course," the king said, "but I've been in communication with your father about the matter, and we've come up with a solution.

"You are a serving Imperial Fleet officer, and your oaths to the Empire are sacrosanct. The oath I shall now require of you will take that into consideration and fall second to it. Is that acceptable?"

Jared nodded. "It is."

"Kneel."

Once Jared had sunk to his knees, Raymond Orison stared sternly down at him. "I won't lecture you on taking care of my daughter, because she can take care of herself. What I will say is that you displease her at your peril. I've had a nice cell set aside in the dungeon if you err too grievously."

Jared mostly restrained his smile. "I wouldn't dream of displeasing her."

"Excellent. Now, as king of Pentagar, I require the oath of prince consort from you, as modified by negotiation with the Terran Emperor, your liege. With the exception of your oaths to the Terran Empire and to the Imperial Fleet, do you, Prince of the Blood Jared Mertz, swear to stand firm beside the crown princess of the Kingdom of Pentagar, helping her to rule it when that time comes?"

"I do."

The king smiled. "Then rise, prince consort of Pentagar."

The crowd began chanting something, but Jared couldn't hear it clearly. Raymond pulled him into a ferocious hug. "It's so good to have you as part of my family. I know you'll make my daughter very happy."

"Thank you."

"Excuse me," Elise said, "but if you're finished, my good friend Kelsey is less than patiently waiting her turn."

Jared risked his sister's wrath by kissing his wife once more before stepping back to his place. Now it was time for her moment in the sun, and he couldn't wait for her and Talbot to take their vows.

26

Kelsey was happy for Jared and Elise but could barely restrain herself. It was her turn, dammit.

The minister took the king's place. "Now we come before you to wed the heir to the Terran Empire. At the risk of going at this ceremony backwards, I call upon Princess Kelsey to go first."

Her eyes were swimming in unshed tears, but she had a tissue handy. She dried her eyes and then took Talbot's hands in hers.

"Russ, when I first met you, I was a pampered little noble girl. She's still in here somewhere, but you didn't let the social gulf stand between us, and you became my friend. Then when my world came apart, you stood beside me, shouting defiance in the face of death, and worse. A more steadfast, caring man is impossible for me to imagine.

"Inside that blunt shell is a heart as big as the universe. I found myself loving you but unsure of how to say the words. Then you showed me that words could sometimes get in the way. We are made for one another, and I pity anyone that tries to come between us. I cannot wait for you to be mine forever."

Talbot didn't wait for the minister to speak before he started.

"I'm a blunt-spoken man, so forgive me if I don't have any flowery phrases at the tip of my tongue. I never expected to have someone like you in my life. Hell, I never expected to find someone as strong inside as you. Someone I could love without restraint.

"I only thought I was self-sufficient. I never realized something was missing from my life, but you've made me whole. With you at my side, I'm not afraid of what the future might bring. Together, we can do anything we choose. I love you and want you to be my wife."

She looked at the minister. "We're waiting."

He laughed. "Then allow me to speedily move things along. Kelsey Bandar, do you take Russel Talbot as your lawfully wedded husband? To have and to hold, forsaking all others for the remainder of your days?"

"Hell yes."

The crowd rumbled with laughter and the minister gave her a look of mock disapproval. "We try not to bring hell into the wedding ceremonies, but I'll accept that."

He turned to Talbot. "Russel Talbot, do you take Kelsey Bandar as your lawfully wedded wife? To have and to hold, forsaking all others for the remainder of your days?"

He smiled down at her.

"Hell yes."

"Then it gives me great pleasure to seal this eternal bond between you. My lords and ladies, I present to you Crown Princess Kelsey Bandar of the Terran Empire and her husband, Russel Talbot."

She pulled Talbot down into a kiss that she hoped would make everyone blush. He was her willing coconspirator.

Once she had to come up for air, she coughed. "That was very nice, but now it's my turn to swear you to an oath. Russel Talbot, I now speak with the voice of the Emperor, your liege. He wishes he were here to do this in person, as do I, but he will have that pleasure soon enough. Kneel."

Once he settled to his knees, his face was almost level with hers. He was actually still taller. She reached out and nudged his head down a little, to the delight of the crowd.

"Russel Talbot, do you swear to stand with the heir of the Terran Empire and to support her rule when she ascends to the Imperial Throne?"

"I do," he rumbled.

"Then I name you prince consort of the Terran Empire. Let no one stand between you and your duty to me and the Empire. Rise, Your Highness."

Raymond Orison stepped forward as Talbot stood, facing the crowd. "Normally, there would be round-the-clock celebration, as well as even more pomp and circumstance, but matters of state press close.

"The newlyweds will have scant time to celebrate, so I declare tonight as theirs alone. Come morning, Prince Consort Jared leads a strike deep into the heart of the Rebel Empire. We'll just have to celebrate without them."

He turned to the wedding party. "I have two vehicles out back. I've taken the liberty of arranging some secure and discreet lodgings for the evening. Once you return from your mission, it will give me great pleasure to host your long and well-deserved honeymoons. Is that acceptable?"

Talbot swept Kelsey off her feet with a whoop. "Why are we still standing here?"

She laughed as he threw her over his shoulder and charged for the indicated exit. Kelsey vowed to have her revenge by carrying him across the threshold when they got there.

* * *

ZIA LAUGHED as Talbot carried the princess out, and Jared more sedately escorted his bride away. Those couples would be just fine, no matter what the universe threw at them.

She, on the other hand, had a ton of work to do. In his absence, she and the newly promoted vice commander of the mission—Commodore Charlie Graves—had a lot of work to do if they were going to get out of here on schedule.

Graves was still aboard *Courageous*, but now it was his flagship. Captain Pasco Ramirez was his new flag captain.

Captains Levy and Vitter would see the carrier group arranged. She had to focus on helping Charlie get the rest of the ships into order.

He stepped over to her as soon as the crowd began dispersing. "Let's take my cutter up to *Invincible*. We can see what Carl managed to pull out of the computer cores and get a general order of battle arranged."

"Sounds good, but I need to change first. I'm starving, and there is no way I'm going to eat in this dress. It must cost a year's salary. I'd undoubtedly spill something on it."

He glanced down at his own suit. "Good point. Meet me at the cutter in an hour."

Zia retired to the changing room the bridesmaids had used to get ready and quickly got back into her duty uniform. She found a car waiting for her when she was ready, and it speedily took her to the spaceport.

Charlie Graves was already on the cutter, so they departed immediately.

"I took the liberty of getting you something from a deli we drove past. I seem to recall you have a special place in your heart for meatball subs."

"You are a god."

"That's what they tell me," he said with a roguish grin.

She took the bag from him, spread her food out on the folding tray on the back of the seat in front of her, and dug in. The meatballs were scrumptious, though a tad messy. Changing had been a wise decision.

Once she'd taken the edge off her hunger, she focused on Graves. "Last I heard, Carl had dug out some hard details from the freighter cores but nothing from any of the recovered military computers. Has that changed?"

He shook his head. "Not to the best of my knowledge, but hope springs eternal. At least we have an idea of where we're going. Dresden isn't very populous, I understand.

"I've gone over the possible entry points to the Dresden system. It has three flip points. One leads to a heavily populated system, one to a more lightly occupied one, and one to an empty one. The last one would be best, but we can't get to it without cutting through some systems we'd prefer to avoid."

She nodded. "So we have two possibilities."

"Right. We'd take six flips by the closest route and eight by the other. I figure we're talking adding a few days to a week to get there. The second route has the more sparsely populated system."

Zia brought up the two routes on her implants. "Being less direct might be more advantageous for us. Once we're done, they won't have the force to stop us from getting back to Erorsi."

He nodded slowly. "The one system in question isn't heavily traveled. We could come in on one side and take a longer curve above the plane of the ecliptic to the final flip point. It adds another day but reduces the opportunity for detection."

That made sense, so she nodded. "We can have *Persephone* scouting the way in front of us. If she runs into anything problematic, she'll have enough firepower to shut them up, and they're unlikely to be spotted."

"Exactly," he agreed. "We'll follow up with the smaller ships and take the big ships last as a group. We can keep our acceleration down to a reasonable level and never tip the people we're sliding by.

"One thing we need to consider is communications. Do we seed FTL coms in the systems between us and Erorsi?"

Zia frowned as she considered that. Not being able to communicate had bitten them hard, but they absolutely could not afford to allow the technology to fall into Rebel Empire hands.

"Maybe if Carl can design self-destruct charges for them. If we seed them in the outer part of each system, we can leave them there. Are we certain that they'll work as relays? I didn't think Carl had all the bugs worked out."

"I don't know. We're almost to *Invincible*, so let's go ask him."

She threw away her trash and secured her tray. The cutter docked, and she followed Charlie onto the superdreadnought.

"Welcome aboard, Commodores," Marcus said. "I've been expecting you. Allow me to say that the wedding was an interesting ceremony."

Graves grinned. "That it was. You can pester Jared with questions about it when he comes up in the morning. Assuming, of course, that he can string comprehensible sentences together."

"I'm quite certain that he will be more than able to do so," the AI said primly. "Sir Carl is waiting for you in his lab."

The two of them made their way there and walked in to find the young scientists hunched over a wide screen, typing quickly.

He glanced up at them and then returned his attention to the screens. "Hang on a second. I'm almost ready."

Zia looked around his lab with interest. She hadn't had much opportunity to drop by when she'd been assigned to the same ship as him. It was bigger than she'd imagined and filled with other people in lab coats doing various tasks.

It took more like five minutes for Carl to wrap up what he was doing, but they waited patiently. When the young man finished, he stood and stretched.

"Sorry about that, but I'm looking for hidden or deleted files. People think they've gotten rid of something important, but you can often dig it back up if you know how to look."

"What are you hoping to find?" Charlie asked.

"There are no close-approach scanner readings. I'd like to have a better idea of what the station looks like. That might narrow our search for the manufacturing area when the time comes to board. I'd imagine saving hours is a good thing."

Zia could certainly agree with that.

"What about the military computers?" she asked. "Any luck?"

He shook his head. "No. We might still get in, but I wouldn't count on it. We're just going to have to use the data I've pulled out of the freighter."

Charlie looked around the lab. "What about the FTL coms? Have you figured out how to link them together so we can talk over multisystem distances?"

The young man waggled a hand. "Yes and no. The process of handing off the com signal isn't perfect. Not yet. It might work all the way, or it might become garbled. I haven't experimented with that yet. I'd say we can use it so long as we don't count on it working when we get too far away."

"What about self-destruct charges?" Zia asked. "We can't afford for the Rebel Empire to get their hands on this technology."

"That I can do," the young man said. "A probe will have several methods to kill it. First, we can just tell it to blow up. The charge is miniscule, so unless someone is right on top of it, they'll never know. Second, if a ship not transmitting the appropriate codes approaches, it can be made to kill itself. Lastly, we can set a timer. If the time period expires without someone countermanding the order, it will end it all."

Charlie smiled. "That sounds good. Do you have the people to get a dozen of them constructed?"

The young man nodded. "I've been working with Captain Baxter. He's got me covered. I can have a few ready by tomorrow. The rest will take a day or two."

"That's perfect."

"What about ship-to-ship FTL?" she asked. "That would've been helpful during the last fight."

Carl nodded. "I imagine so. Those are easier, since they're just direct links. I gave the few I had on hand to Princess Kelsey and can build more on the way. Certainly enough for all lead elements in the fleet."

"Excellent," she said. "Have you spoken with Angela after the wedding?"

He shook his head. "She's on her way to *Persephone*. I'll head that way once I finish the file search. Why?"

Zia smiled slyly. "Weddings do funny things to women. Expect the unexpected."

The two men frowned at her.

"What does that even mean?" Charlie asked.

"Let's just say that I'll bet she has her own future in her mind tonight. She seems like a direct kind of woman. She might just propose."

Carl paled. "Jesus."

She laughed and headed for the hatch. "Tell her I have a dress, just in case she needs a maid of honor."

27

Brandon roused, unsure of what had woken him. He lay in the dark of his bed, listening. Had something changed in the normal sounds the ship made? Not that he could tell.

That's when he heard it. The soft sound of someone else breathing in the room. No, in his bed.

Oh, crap.

The memory of the evening came flooding back. The late dinner with Annette, his growing attraction to her, and her determined seduction. One he had to admit he had aided and abetted.

Now, outside of the heat of the moment—and it had been hot—he wondered if he'd made the wrong choice.

Almost at once, he rejected that thought. It had been the right choice. Whether things worked out in the long term or not, allowing himself to care —to desire—wasn't a mistake.

He had no idea what she might feel like now. Had she been looking for a night of passion or something more? Brandon had no idea.

No matter what happened, they had to work together, so he wouldn't be a jackass.

She rolled over and pressed against him. That completely disrupted everything he'd been thinking about.

"Are you awake?" she asked sleepily. "It's early."

"I just woke up."

After a moment, she sat up a little. "And you're worried."

That hadn't been a question. "Maybe a little. I thoroughly enjoyed what happened, but I don't know what you want long term. Hell, I don't know what I want."

She turned the light on, and he realized he wasn't in his room. They were in *her* bed.

"Then I suggest you don't panic," she said with a smile. "I hadn't planned on this, either, but I'm open to the possibilities. We're both professionals. We can—and will—keep our heads about us. If things work out, I'll be thrilled. If they don't, I'll be sad. In either case, we'll be okay as long as we don't overthink this."

That was a little more cool-headed than he'd expected. It was also somewhat disconcerting.

Annette rose from the bed and headed for the bathroom. "It's almost time for breakfast. You can either join me in the shower or skulk back to your place." She glanced back at him from the doorway with a smile. "I'd prefer it if you joined me."

The view from where he lay was stunning, so there was really only one choice. "We might be late for breakfast."

"I can snack on the run."

Brandon rose to his feet and trailed after her.

* * *

SAYING goodbye to Elise had been the hardest thing Jared had ever done. One night alone wasn't nearly enough, but he couldn't delay. Events were moving faster than he'd like, and he couldn't afford to let the Rebel Empire pin them down.

This was a lot different from the reconnaissance that Admiral Yeats had envisioned. He'd reported the most recent events, and the admiral had endorsed his new plan.

This morning, once he'd finally torn himself away from his wife, he'd found a new message from the admiral waiting for him. Well, one of many. Everyone he knew—and more than a few he didn't—had sent some form of congratulations.

He'd eventually have time to go through them all, but today he only had time to focus on the most pressing. Since the most recent message from Admiral Yeats might be part business, he played it first. He managed to wait until he was on his cutter and on the way back to *Invincible*.

The vid was of Yeats at his desk, so business just became a lot more possible.

"Jared, let me start off by extending my most profound congratulations. Princess Elise seems like a wonderful woman and a great partner for you. I wish you many, many years of happiness together. I suppose with nanites, that might even extend to centuries."

Jared hadn't considered that, but the thought made him smile. That would be terrific.

"I wish that were all that was on your plate," the admiral continued. "Unfortunately, it's not. No matter how you cut it, you're about to make the Rebel Empire very much aware of our existence. The missing fleet would do that, too, but they can't possibly miss your ships when you get to the Dresden system.

"Luckily, Erorsi and Pentagar are in an isolated cul-de-sac to the best of the Rebel Empire's knowledge. They'll know something happened but be unable to get through the flip-point jammer.

"They won't understand the technology any better than we do, but they will think their problems are isolated. Thankfully, the FTL coms will allow you to close the flip point once you leave and then signal for admittance when you return."

Jared had been considering that very thing before he'd found out the wedding was last night. The FTL coms gave them an incredible advantage over their enemies. He needed to have more brainstorming to figure out how to best utilize them.

"In any case, I'm giving you full authority to do whatever you feel best. Work with Princess Kelsey to be sure she thinks any strategic decisions are the correct ones.

"This is going to be hard, no matter what happens, but I'm counting on you and the princess to at least give us a shot at ultimately winning. Good luck, and I'll see you when you get back."

The vid ended.

The next message was from his father. Unlike the admiral, the emperor was seated on a comfortable chair and not in any kind of official garb.

He smiled widely. "Jared, I just finished watching the ceremony. Elise looked radiant, and I'm so happy for you both. I wish I could have been there, but I take solace in the fact that I'll get to do so when we repeat the ceremony here.

"I wish you had all the time in the world to luxuriate in your bliss, but I know you'll be departing shortly. Just don't let your duty keep you from enjoying the fruits of joy that life sends your way. Once they pass, it's a rare thing to have a second chance."

"But not unheard of."

That hadn't been the emperor.

His mother sat down beside his father, her eyes shining with tears of joy. "I am so thrilled for you, Jared. You deserve to be happy. I so wish I could've been there, but I understand the press of time."

Her expression grew fierce. "Don't think that means I won't have my hands all over your wedding when you come back to Avalon. I'm your mother, and I will have my moment in the sun. I realize Elise doesn't have her mother still with her, so I've already spoken with her. She has given me permission to meddle to my heart's content. And I will."

Karl Bandar nodded. "I wouldn't try to fight this if I were you. Your mother is a very determined woman."

Jared knew that for a fact. What he was learning, however, was that things had changed back on Avalon.

It didn't take a genius to see their body language. The fact they were sending this message together was also telling. The emperor and his mother were exploring a renewed relationship of their own.

A year ago, he'd have been aghast, but now he found himself nodding in approval. They'd made a mistake all those years ago. One that had hurt them both. They'd more than paid the price for their sins. Let them find what happiness they could in this life.

"Well, we know you're very busy, so we'll let you get about it," the emperor said.

"We love you," his mother said. "Be careful and come back safely."

He thought about the message and all its unspoken parts until the cutter docked with *Invincible*. Times had changed, and he approved. Not that things would be easy. It only took one thought about Kelsey's mother to end that pie-in-the-sky view.

Now all he had to do was give them a fighting chance. With the ability to make more Raider implants, they might be able to pull this off. He'd best be about it then.

* * *

KELSEY HATED HAVING to split up from Talbot, but he had his own preparations to take care of on *Invincible*. Not the least of which was getting his initial implants.

The message from her father was sweet and to the point. He seemed genuinely happy for the two of them. Oddly, he also had an air of conspiracy about him. She wondered what surprise he hadn't wanted to mention in advance. He had a terrible poker face.

Ominously, there was no vid from her mother. She was undoubtedly displeased about not being invited, not planning anything, and likely unhappy about her daughter's choice in mates.

Too bad.

If the woman thought Kelsey was going to let her anywhere near her wedding on Avalon, she was sorely mistaken. She might love her mother, but it was hard to feel it right now. Particularly with what she knew.

Of course, that wouldn't stop the woman from making herself an Imperial pain when Kelsey got back to Avalon. Their problems still needed to be settled, but that was for another day.

Angela was waiting for her as soon as she stepped out of the pinnace.

"Did you have fun?" she asked with a sly smile.

"Duh. How are you feeling?"

"The optical implants are still screwing with me, but I'm getting a handle on the auditory ones. The pharmacology unit is what it is."

Kelsey led the way to the lift. "It was just about the reverse for me, and those are the easy parts. Next comes the bone reinforcement and artificial muscles. Those are going to be very hard to learn. Trust me on that."

"I'm glad I have such a knowledgeable teacher, then," the tall woman said seriously. "I've picked up a lot just listening to you and reading the familiarization materials in the computer. Thankfully, I don't have my next session for a week."

"Any word on what our plan of action is?" Kelsey asked as they arrived outside the bridge.

"The fleet pulls out in two hours. We'll make our way by route Bravo, just as I suspected."

Kelsey wasn't surprised the marine had nailed it. She was sharp.

Once Kelsey was behind the captain's console, she checked the ship's readiness. All in the green. Everyone was aboard, too. She'd been the last to arrive.

"Excellent. What is our order of march? We're up front, I assume."

Angela nodded. "We'll scout each system as we go and communicate back via the FTL com. We have links to *Invincible* and *Audacious*. The latter will be backing us up, with the main fleet following them."

Kelsey nodded. "All as expected. Since we're ready, I'd like to pull out early. Signal Jared that we won't go too far."

The other woman smiled. "Already anticipated. We're clear to depart at your discretion."

"Even better. What's the status of stage two implantation for the crew?"

She intended to upgrade everyone on her ship to Raiders as soon as possible. That meant she wanted them all to have the auditory and optical implants and pharmacology units before they arrived at Dresden.

"We've worked our way through about fifteen percent of the crew," Angela said. "They seem to be tolerating it well. We should be done on schedule."

Kelsey leaned back in her chair. "It's rare for things to go as planned, so I'll luxuriate in that for a bit. Take us to the Erorsi flip point and coordinate with *Audacious*. We're not going to get to Dresden by sitting on our butts."

28

Zia watched the scanner feed with more than a hint of dread. The last few weeks had almost brought them to their target. Dresden was one flip away, but this system—unlike the others they had traveled through—was occupied. One misstep here and their surprise advantage would vanish.

Admittedly, saying this system was occupied might be something of an overstatement. It had no main world at all, so the population was clustered around several mining hubs in the system's three asteroid belts.

Old Empire records indicated that one of them had been heavily metallic, so there was a lot to recover, even now. Since it wasn't the same as the rest of the system, it had probably been a captured body from deep space.

The belts weren't even close to orderly, so the evidence of the disaster was still writ large for anyone to see. That made travel more dangerous than usual.

Under normal circumstances, that would be relatively minor, but they were restricted to using only passive scanners. That left them open to fast-moving bits of debris that were far too small to see in time.

The relatively empty nature of space meant the likelihood of being struck was small, but it wasn't impossible. That led to the current worry on her part.

The miners were easy to spot by the radio and scanner emissions. So were the ships plying the depths of space between where they worked. All she and the ships with her needed to do was stay far enough out and travel too slowly for them to see.

They'd hoped that the FTL coms they'd deployed behind them would allow for continuous communication with Erorsi, but the new technology wasn't mature enough. Or the process didn't work the way they wanted.

The FTL signals deteriorated with retransmission. Using a repeater to send the signal on to the next hop worked about half the time. Pity. Since they were only copying the data stream and using a different quantum pairing to send the next set of data, it shouldn't matter, yet it did. Carl was going to have to work on that when time permitted.

She turned her attention back to the ship ahead of her. She didn't want to let *Persephone* get too far ahead of them.

"Probe update," one of the flight officers said. "There's something at the flip point, and we have a large ship a few hours short of meeting it."

Zia accessed the scanner readings and examined the problem. The vessel in the flip point looked like a destroyer. The other one was significantly larger. Bigger even than a superdreadnought.

Thankfully, she recognized what it was before her blood pressure spiked. It was a recovery ship, like the AIs had used to move derelicts and captured ships to Harrison's World.

This one wasn't moving a ship, though it did have a cargo of some kind. Probably raw materials from the asteroid belts.

Taking out the destroyer might announce their presence to the miners, but that wasn't necessarily a problem. This system only had two flip points, with one leading back toward Erorsi. They couldn't exactly run and tell anyone else.

"Signal *Persephone* that we'll check them out. If she needs to get moving, I don't want her pinnaces wandering around."

"Copy that."

* * *

ANNETTE LED the flight of fighters escorting the Raider ship herself. Rightly, she should've delegated the duty, but she was their best pilot, and her on-scene evaluation might make a universe of difference.

The recovery ship wasn't scanning the area around them. This far out from the belts, there wouldn't be much debris, but that was careless.

On the military side, the destroyer was scanning on a set interval. Every fifteen minutes, they'd pulse their scanners and get a look around them. If her fighters got too close, the enemy would spot them.

The recovery ship was still far enough away from the flip point to approach, but that could change in a moment if someone got curious over there. Or if the destroyer sent a directional scan at the ship and spotted the fighters.

As they got closer, she saw the recovery ship had a large bundle of ore in its movable arms. They were using it as a glorified freighter.

She supposed it would be good enough at doing something like that. Picking up or dropping a cargo would only take a few minutes.

Annette opened a low-powered directional beam to the Raider ship. "*Persephone*, the recovery ship is carrying unprocessed ore from the mines."

"Copy that. Come back and stand by for instructions."

"Will do."

She changed course and slowly moved back toward the Raider ship.

* * *

PRINCESS KELSEY CONSIDERED THE SITUATION. If they could capture the recovery ship, it might be very useful. It was a known factor on Dresden. It must bring materials in on a regular run. She could use that.

The crew wouldn't be on the lookout for trouble. Not the kind of trouble she was going to cause them, anyway. Still, an assault on the ship was fraught with danger.

If the destroyer saw something, it could flip over and warn Dresden. They would have to deal with it one way or another.

"Angela," Kelsey said after a moment. "I have a very evil thought."

"Why does that fill me with dread?"

"Because you know me. I want you to lead a team over to the recovery ship. I'm thinking a two-stage attack. First, I need you to get there undetected and plant charges all around the habitation section of the hull. I want to decompress it in as short a time as possible without compromising the ship."

The tall woman nodded. "A civilian crew won't be likely to have suits close at hand. If we take the entire ship at once, they'll be forced into rescue balls or die."

Anyone that made it into a rescue ball would be safe but unable to do anything. The balls were meant to allow people to survive a sudden decompression and then wait for rescue from their fellows.

If they hit the entire ship—and it actually held only a very small crew— that would leave no one in a position to help the crewmen except for Kelsey's marines.

"We have to assume that a few people won't get to them or that some fail," Kelsey admitted. "I'm sure things aren't up to maintenance standards in a backwater like this. They've probably never had a problem like this.

"That may or may not stop them from sending a distress signal, but the ship is close enough that the destroyer will see something. If it looks like an accident, they may move out of the flip point to assist the recovery ship. We'll use *Persephone*'s stealth field to get close to the flip point and cut them off."

The marine considered the plan and slowly nodded. "I think we can make that work. It won't be anything they'd expect, in any case."

It took an hour for the marines to get into position. Kelsey used the time to bring *Persephone* around to the other side of the flip point.

The tension was as intense as she'd ever felt while she waited for the

TERRY MIXON

strike to happen. So this was what Jared felt like when she was off doing something stupid.

"The charges just went off," one of her people said. "The recovery ship is venting atmosphere and signaling distress."

The destroyer, much to her relief, responded exactly as she'd hoped. It came rushing out of the flip point and raced toward the distressed vessel. Its scanners were active but focused in the wrong direction to see her ship.

"Move us up into the flip point and prepare to shoot down any drones they try to get past us. We'll leave them to Jared."

Once the destroyer was committed and far enough away from the flip point, Jared brought the task force out of hiding by accelerating all units in toward the Rebel Empire warship from every direction. Kelsey switched off her ship's stealth field to make it apparent, too.

The destroyer was outside the flip point, surrounded, and tremendously outgunned. Then the fighters made themselves known, seemingly popping out of nowhere and surrounding the recovery ship in a protective bubble.

She listened to Jared ordering the destroyer to surrender with interest. Would they give up or fight?

In this case, common sense won out, and the ship promptly struck its battle screens. That was a relief, really.

It took another twenty minutes for Angela to clear the recovery ship and report. Her image appeared on the main screen.

"Good news," she told Kelsey. "The crew consists of a dozen people, and we took them all alive."

"Excellent. What's the status of the ship itself?"

"Operational. They didn't have time to lock the computers down. We have everything."

Kelsey smiled. It was about time something went her way. "Get them over here. We'll question them and formulate a plan. I'll call Zia and have her send someone to take over the recovery ship. I have an idea on how we can use it."

"Copy that."

* * *

JARED LISTENED to his sister's plan with more than a hint of misgiving. Once she finished laying it out, he leaned back in his seat.

"I can't begin to tell you how risky that sounds," he said after he considered her for a moment. "The crew we captured from the destroyer isn't talking, but their body language tells me that they aren't too worried about us waltzing over there.

"They have a force to be reckoned with, I think. If you just blithely flip over there, they'll spot you right away. Then they blow you up."

"Maybe," she said with a shrug. "It isn't as though we have much choice, other than going back the way we came. The Rebel Empire is still going to know we were here one way or the other.

"The destroyer didn't send a distress call, but the miners in this system heard the one from the recovery ship. We sent a follow-up canceling it before they came out to investigate, but once the people from Dresden start asking questions, some version of the truth will occur to them. We have to strike now if we ever want to get the ability to make Raider implants."

He shook his head. "We have to know what you'll find on the other side of the flip point. If they have ships right there, you're screwed. We can't risk a probe, either."

She smiled. "Let me work on the crew from the recovery ship while we make preparations to carry out my plan. If you decide it's too dangerous then, we've lost nothing. If you decide we can go, then we'll be ready."

"Admiral Yeats was clear that as the heir, I needed to take your input, as if I wouldn't." He rubbed his face. "How do I ever let you convince me of these things?"

"Because I'm right."

He sighed. "Probably. I still think sending you is more than we should do, but I can already anticipate your reasoning. The manufacturing plant might require your unique Raider implants to access. Sadly, I know you're probably right. I can only hope that isn't the case one day.

"Fine. Go question the crew from the recovery ship. If they give you any reason to think your plan has a chance of success, we'll give it a go. If not, we'll shoot it out with them."

Kelsey shook her head at him. "You know that isn't going to work. If we can't get people into the manufacturing plant before they know about us, they'll be able to destroy everything we came for. If my plan doesn't have a chance of success, we'll consider other options."

She was right, of course. The mission would be part stealth, part misdirection, and all crazy. Just like something from one of the adventure vids.

He ran through the options one last time, but no other possibilities occurred to him.

"Keep me in the loop," he finally said. "Also, if you go, I'm sending Talbot and as many marines as we can stuff into your hull. When the time comes, I want to leave them no chance to fight back."

Kelsey entered the room where the prisoners were waiting. Each of the men and women was secured to a table by cuffs, not for her protection but to make a point. They were prisoners, and she was going to have their cooperation, one way or another.

She'd dressed in a Fleet captain's uniform for this little charade, also designed to intimidate. She had two very large and menacing marines at the corners of the room to emphasize the prisoners' precarious position.

"Well," she said with a false tone of cheerfulness, "it seems as though you've gotten yourselves into a spot of trouble, doesn't it? Which one of you is running your little enterprise?"

They stared at one another in obvious confusion. One of the women cleared her throat.

"Excuse me, My Lady, but if you're asking who is in command of *A-8257*, it's me."

Kelsey widened her smile. "Excellent. Then you can explain your little smuggling ring to me."

The woman's jaw dropped. "My Lady? We aren't smuggling anything."

The sound of Kelsey's hand slapping the top of the table made them all flinch.

"Then perhaps you can explain why we've been tracking large quantities of drugs in the raw materials you move to Dresden? Surely you aren't going to pretend ignorance. If so, I may have to become… unpleasant."

She'd really put them into an uncomfortable position. Confessing to and explaining a crime they hadn't committed was going to be awkward at best.

The woman lowered her head. "I don't know who told you that, My Lady, but we aren't smuggling any drugs."

"How tiresome," Kelsey drawled. "Not surprising, though. This isn't going to hurt me a bit. I can't speak for you, though."

"It's just tech, My Lady," one of the men said. "It doesn't hurt anyone."

Kelsey blinked in surprise. Thankfully, the prisoners were mostly focusing unfriendly stares at the man who'd spoken and didn't see her reaction.

She covered her expression of surprise with a sly smile. "I can see how that mistake could have been made. Tell me everything, and I promise you the lightest of the potential sentences. In fact, I may grant the most cooperative of you clemency, but only if you tell me everything I want to know right now."

"The crates don't take up much space," the woman said. "They come in with the supplies on the Dresden side, and we drop them off when we pick up our load. We never see who eventually gets the stuff, but we get paid for every delivery."

"What kind of tech are we talking about?"

The woman shrugged. "They didn't say, and we never asked."

"We'll check it out. If it proves true, and you answer all my questions, your sentences will be much lighter. Tell me about Dresden."

They looked at one another again in confusion.

"They make manufacturing equipment used throughout the sector," the man who'd spoken earlier said. "Nothing of any merit, really. Farm implements, kitchen supplies, that sort of thing."

"I already know all this, but I'm leading to a specific set of questions and checking to see what you actually know," Kelsey said. "Answer as if I know nothing about Dresden. Why the Fleet presence?"

"To keep the Ghosts at bay," the woman said.

Kelsey stopped herself before she could frown. What ghosts? She couldn't look ignorant about something that could be common knowledge, but she wasn't going to fall for a trick, either.

"Are they really that much of a threat?" she asked with a taste of irony in her tone.

"One such as myself has no way of knowing," the woman said, bowing her head. "I am sure they are no threat to Fleet. I apologize for implying otherwise."

"I take no offense," Kelsey assured her. "Tell me more. What precautions are you aware of around Dresden?"

The woman took a deep breath and let it out slowly. "Well, there have been a number of ships disappearing in the sector. The ships here patrol in search of the Ghosts who take them. The guard stations make sure that the Ghosts cannot raid here."

"And has Fleet found any of these Ghosts?"

"I have heard rumors," the woman said hesitantly. "Fleet sometimes corners a Ghost. They say they self-destruct to avoid capture."

That sounded suspiciously like the Fleet ships of old during the rebellion, except those ships just vented their atmosphere.

"They blow up?" she asked carefully.

The woman nodded. "So they say. Rather than fight a superior force, the ships blow themselves up. I suppose that is to keep Fleet from finding their hidden bases."

That wasn't completely surprising, Kelsey supposed. The freighters delivering supplies to the Pale Ones had vanished from time to time, even with escorts. That implied someone working against the Rebel Empire.

They'd all speculated about who that might be but never got any further than a deeply hidden guerrilla force that occasionally struck out at their enemies. Much like what Olivia West and her people had been. Obviously with some warships, but probably not many.

Honestly, this was still as much conjecture as before. Other than the fact that the Rebel Empire version of Fleet took the risk seriously. That implied the attacks were a real problem. One that needed a large number of ships occasionally.

One more mystery to solve when time and circumstances permitted. Right now, she had other fish to fry.

"Tell me about the Fleet disposition you are aware of at Dresden. I want to see if it matches what we want people like you to see."

"There are three flip points, My Lady. Each has a guard station assigned to it. It sits far enough away that no surprise attack will overwhelm it. There are normally a number of ships assigned to it, as well, but the majority of the Fleet presence withdrew a month ago. The remaining ships are out at the unoccupied flip point."

Kelsey brought up a map of the system from the Old Empire records. The two flip points that led to occupied systems were only a few hours apart, but the third was all the way across the system.

"You mean this one?"

The woman nodded. "Yes, My Lady. I can't tell you how many ships or what kind, but there are none left in Dresden orbit or at either of the other two flip points. Just the defensive stations."

"So the station scans your ship from a distance and allows it to proceed? Does the guard destroyer make transit with you?"

The woman shook her head. "No, My Lady. It remains here. The station scans us and then allows us to proceed. When they had ships, they'd occasionally come out for a closer look, but no more than once or twice a year. Now, none."

Kelsey pursed her lips. "Do you know where the Fleet ships went or when they will return?"

"No, My Lady. I assume the ones that left will be back soon enough."

She almost snorted. Wouldn't that be a hell of a bluff? To send in the right kinds of ship and let them assume they were back?

No, that would be far too dangerous. The Fleet units here would know what to expect, and they probably weren't coming out of this system, so they couldn't just waltz in.

What they could do was execute her plan. It would take a few hours to arrange, but it was wickedly clever, even if she did say so herself. With a hint of luck, the guard fortress would never know what they were letting by.

* * *

ZIA LISTENED to Princess Kelsey's orders a second time, certain that she must have misheard her. When the message repeated itself exactly as she'd heard it, she took a skeptical breath and called Brandon Levy.

He appeared on her console a moment later.

"Yes, Commodore?"

"I need you to head over to the recovery ship. I'm detaching you to take care of an important special project."

He frowned, as well he should.

"I'm not exactly free to leave my command in someone else's charge. What's going on?"

She pulled her thoughts together. "The princess is going to sneak into Dresden hidden in a load of ore. Don't worry, *Audacious* is going along for the ride, but I need my best commander on that ship while we're under the missiles of the Rebel Fleet guard station."

He opened his mouth to respond but closed it again. After a moment, he finally spoke. "That's quite possibly the craziest plan I've ever heard."

"Welcome to working with Princess Kelsey. There's the right way, the wrong way, and her way. We're doing this her way. Time is short, and I need to have the most experience possible on that ship to give her harebrained scheme a chance of working. That's you."

He shook his head with obvious misgivings. "I'll do my absolute best, Commodore, but I've never done anything remotely like this."

"Me, either. Welcome to the club. We'll have some fighters stashed in the ore, ready to come out fighting. We can't expose either ship enough to have clear missile tubes, so those fighters are all we have. Annette will be on one of them, and she'll have our best people with her."

"I'll take over for you here, since we won't be able to launch fighters or have other ships along for the ride. Get moving as quickly as you can."

The other officer nodded. "Aye, ma'am. I'll do my best."

"Good luck, Captain."

* * *

ANNETTE THOUGHT this plan was crazy, but it wasn't her call. Releasing the ore, getting the ships inside the arms on the recovery ship, and repacking some of the raw material to conceal the hidden vessels had taken a surprisingly short amount of time.

It seemed like a poor disguise to her. The shape of the ships was right there for anyone to see if they bothered to look.

That's what they were counting on, she supposed. That the Rebel Fleet would scan the recovery ship and its cargo, see what they expected to see, and then wave them on through.

If they didn't, it was up to Annette and her fellow pilots to make sure they kept the bad guys in check until the larger ships could shed their disguises. Under fire, that wouldn't be possible, so she certainly hoped the other side missed what was right in their faces.

There were small pockets in the ore where the fighters could hide. They were small enough to blend in without being covered up and close enough that they could receive short-range transmissions without risk of detection. They'd see the view as relayed by the recovery ship.

Right now, she knew Brandon Levy was ripping out the scanner suite on the ungainly ship. He'd install a better set to improve the readings on the passive scans.

If the enemy spotted their ruse, she had absolute certainty she and the other pilots would die in the ensuing fight. They'd trade their lives so that the bigger ships could get into the fight.

Once her fighter was secure, she put it into standby mode. Unlike a ship, she could get to full power instantly. The lines holding her in place among the ore would snap at the first application of real power.

Half an hour later, the recovery ship moved into the flip point.

The flip was unusual. She'd never been outside the hull during one before, and this created some unusual effects for her. Her vision seemed to cycle through a quick spectrum of color before settling back to normal, and the dizziness was impressive. Thankfully, it faded quickly.

None of that kept her from using her implants to follow the situation along. The recovery ship pulled out of the flip point and headed into the system. The Rebel Fleet battle station was bigger than *Audacious* but farther away than she'd expected.

That was a plus in this case. Their scan felt cursory, and they signaled the ship to proceed.

The princess's crazy plan had worked. They were in.

30

J ared had to force himself not to pace the flag bridge. Such things only made the crew nervous that their commander was worried.

Which he was, but that was beside the point.

They didn't dare use the FTL coms with a known enemy force present. One they couldn't keep quiet if they saw something they shouldn't. That might make them go after Kelsey and the rest.

The silence from Dresden was reassuring. No news was good news. If they'd been flagged, the crap would have already hit the fan, and there'd have been no reason not to call them in.

That was what his forces were arrayed for. They sat in the Dresden flip point ready to flip. If they did, they'd fire every missile they had ready at the battle station to take it out quickly.

Doing so was the worst-case scenario. He'd rather let Kelsey do her thing and call for help when she was ready to leave if she needed it.

Having *Audacious* and her fighter groups along made Kelsey needing help less likely. Their intelligence said there were very few mobile platforms in the Dresden system, and they were all out at flip point number three. Waiting for the Ghosts if the crew of the recovery ship was to be believed.

He supposed it didn't matter what he believed. If they believed there were boogiemen, who was he to argue? That might camouflage this attack.

The basic plan Kelsey had laid out called for them to capture the orbital at Dresden and use the fighters to interdict any hostiles there, as well as any ships that came in from the flip point. It didn't matter what the crew on the battle stations thought was happening.

Kelsey would strip the equipment and supplies off the orbital and come hauling back out to rejoin him. She'd signal him when the time came, and

Jared would launch a surprise attack through the flip point at an inconvenient moment.

Of course, nothing ever worked out according to plan, so he could only hope they didn't have to improvise too much.

"Admiral, I have some information that may be useful to you," Marcus said through the speaker in the arm of Jared's chair.

"Go ahead."

"I've been monitoring the prisoners' conversations," the AI said. "They are obviously aware that is likely, so they are being circumspect, but one of them asked a question that has implications on the princess's mission.

"It was the executive officer of the destroyer speaking with the captain. He spoke very softly, but I have excellent hearing. Even over the extra-loud conversation around them, I picked up enough to piece together what was said. Also, reading lips is an excellent skill to add to one's toolbox."

Jared smiled. "And what did they want to keep private?"

"The executive officer asked when 'the ships' were due. The captain told him to shut up and didn't answer, but even the inquiry means that there will be other mobile units to deal with at some as-yet-unknown future point."

He grimaced. "Well, we couldn't expect everything to go our way. Hopefully, he's thinking that the fleet they dispatched to Erorsi will be coming home. That's the most likely thing. Otherwise, they should've already had fresh ships here before they left.

"If not, there isn't exactly anything we can do about it other than be ready to act on a moment's notice. Which is what we're doing anyway."

"Should we warn the princess?"

"No. That would break operational security and not really give her any useable information. If the situation changes, she'll know as soon as we do. Probably sooner, since they're going to send probes out to monitor the other flip points.

"As dissatisfying as it is, we're just going to have to ride this out. Work with the operations staff to come up with some likely scenarios. Make plans to react to various possibilities and get them to me as soon as you can. Chance favors the prepared mind."

The AI chuckled. "Someone has been reading the classics. When we have something for you, I'll let you know."

Jared tried not to worry about this troubling turn of events, but that wasn't going to be easy. That was his sister out there, and the heir of the New Terran Empire. If something happened to her, he'd never forgive himself.

* * *

BRANDON SAT in the cramped control center on the recovery ship and watched the returns from the stealthed probes they'd launched earlier. The telemetry beams were very tight and almost impossible to detect, but he still worried.

They'd been out of scanner range of the defensive station for almost two hours and were now more than halfway to Dresden. After consulting with the princess and commodore, he'd launched a brace of probes borrowed from *Persephone* toward the world growing larger ahead of them.

He wasn't crazy enough to send them into orbit, but they'd make a wide pass around the world and send back some rough data. Even at this range, he could tell that the planet wasn't being used effectively.

As the captured crew had indicated, there was only a single large orbital. Based on what the princess had said, they used it for several kinds of manufacturing. If this really was the source of the Raider implants, then they were using the place for both civilian and secret military purposes.

If it had been him, he'd have used two orbitals and made sure there was no unauthorized access at all.

Some of the work took place on the planet, based on the steady stream of cargo shuttles running back and forth. It seemed as though they were all coming from a single continent in the southern hemisphere.

There were two freighters in wide orbits around the single space station. They also had a few shuttles ferrying things back and forth with them.

He opened a channel to Annette Vitter. She was still in her fighter on the surface of their disguise.

"How's the weather out there?"

"Dry and hard to breathe," she said. "As it usually is in space. I assume things are going well."

He grinned at her image. "Better than we had any reason to expect. I haven't gotten a good look at the orbital yet, but there don't seem to be any Rebel Fleet vessels in orbit. Just a couple of freighters. It doesn't look like you'll have to blow anything up this time."

"Oh ye of little faith. Things will probably go to hell soon enough. Any word on what the plan is once we get there?"

He shook his head. "Not yet. I'd imagine that they want to be sure what they'll be facing before they commit to a strategy. There is a steady stream of shuttles from one location on the planet, too."

"Is it under the station?"

"No. The station isn't in geosynchronous orbit. The two locations are sometimes on the opposite sides of the planet from one another. Do you think that might be helpful?"

The pilot smiled. "I do. Let me bring the princess and the commodore into the conversation, and I'll run something past them."

* * *

KELSEY FELT naked without her powered armor, but it would stand out on a scouting mission like this. Annette Vitter's plan was audacious—appropriately, given her ship. If it worked, they'd get onto the station without disturbing anyone at all.

As a reward—or perhaps punishment—she'd brought the fighter pilot along for the ride. She was on the other pinnace.

The stealthed pinnaces would join the stream of cargo shuttles from Dresden when the station wasn't in a position to see where they came from. Unless they were severely paranoid, this had a very good chance of getting her people where they needed to be.

"Any indication they're using specialized identification?" she asked her intelligence specialist.

"Not that I can see," he said after consulting his console closely. "There are standard Rebel Fleet IFF signals, but the only communications I'm detecting are standard traffic-control stuff. Instructions to change course or use specific docking areas."

"Are they querying origin or passenger manifests?"

The man shook his head. "Nothing like that. My guess is that if it has a valid IFF, that's good enough. It's not like someone is going to sneak into the system with stolen codes and brazenly waltz right up."

Like they were doing.

"When are they squawking ID for the station?" she asked.

"Just before final approach."

The pilot slowly tapered off the stealth field as they got into the right orbit and then boosted speed a little.

"We're in the open," he said. "No one seems to have seen anything unusual. I'm heading around the planet, and I'll squawk our stolen codes when we hit the right spot."

Kelsey was tapped into the com system, so she heard the response from the station when the pilot had done so.

"Control has you, Y-112. You and Y-243 are cleared for approach along your current vector. There are two shuttles in front of you, so watch for them crossing ahead of you. You can dock at the indicated markers."

"Copy that, Control. Y-112 out."

The pilot turned and looked over his shoulder. "You get that, Colonel?"

"Yes, but stick to calling me Captain going forward. Everyone, mind your cover stories. Once we arrive, we'll need to scout the station, verify it's what we think it is, and plan our mischief. Then we'll execute stage two."

The pinnaces entered the docking bay without incident. Kelsey waited until the lock was green and cycled herself in. Here they went.

31

Annette sauntered down the ramp of her pinnace and onto the space station as though she owned the place. She wore the uniform of a commander in the Rebel Fleet. The team assigned to her was at her heels.

Princess Kelsey's pinnace was right down from hers, so she gave the other woman a covert nod when their eyes met. They each had different areas of the station to search, so she'd best get about it. Time was wasting.

The two pinnaces would depart as soon as they unloaded some precious crates.

There was quite a crowd bustling about. Based on what she'd heard from Commander Richards, she responded to the people around her in different ways.

The Fleet officers either saluted her or she saluted them. Enlisted personnel got a look down her nose when they saluted, and they dodged her. She ignored the civilians entirely. They were unlikely to bother those of them in uniform.

The second set of her people was another story. The recovery agents were in civilian clothes taken from the captured ships. They'd hit other parts of the station where uniforms might raise eyebrows.

They split into groups and began wandering the corridors.

It didn't take her long to find something interesting. As one would expect on a large installation, there were maps to help lost souls find their way.

Not that any of them listed "secret manufacturing area" for her, but there were entire sections of the station that were helpfully blank. She figured that any place that they didn't want visitors knowing about would be interesting.

Of course, getting into them might be a challenge. She wouldn't know until she made a pass by them.

Princess Kelsey had given them a few pointers on slipping past security, so she had one of her people pick up a large tray of pastries. One that precluded her from opening any doors.

A lookout made sure she arrived at the unmarked security doors right behind someone. The man proved himself a gentleman when he held it open for her. She repaid his kindness with a sugary treat, and the two of them vanished inside.

A few minutes later, the woman opened the door for Annette and Jon Paul Olivier. She'd kept the pastries, so Annette snagged one. Being a spy was hungry work.

Just inside the security door was another map for the lost. This one labeled most of the previously hidden areas with letter designations. Five of them. She guessed that might correspond to various security restrictions.

The area surrounding all of the other shaded spaces was labelled with "A," and the other four went from "B" to "E."

"Interesting," Olivier said. "This covers almost all the areas left blank on the public map, but not completely."

"I noticed that," she said. "What do you think it means?"

"The remaining area is directly in the rear, so it's part of the concealed grouping, but they didn't want to draw attention to it, even in here. Only someone looking closely for missing areas would see that they'd excised it."

He sent her an updated map with a black area in the deepest part of the protected area. They could get close in the corridors, but they'd have to go through area "E" to get there. She dubbed it area "F."

Together, they wove their way deeper into the secret facility. Other people, both Rebel Fleet and civilian, passed them without comment.

The conversation she overheard tipped the hand for area "C." They were researching enhancements to existing weapons in there. Longer-range missiles with faster speeds. More powerful beams. God knew what else.

This place sounded a little like the Grant Research Facility on Harrison's World. Capturing it would be damned useful in its own right. Too bad they couldn't just put everything into their pockets. Maybe they could steal some of the computer cores.

The hatch to area "E" had guards, so they weren't getting in. They'd just pass by and see what else they could hear before getting out of the shielded area and contacting the princess.

Annette was almost to the hatch when the massive slab of metal slid open and a Rebel Fleet commander strode out.

He smiled at Annette. "Commander Renner? I'm Edward Irons. We'll be working together. I thought I'd have to walk all the way to the main entrance for you. I didn't realize they'd already issued you clearance for the secure areas. Welcome to the project.

"Commodore Murdock is about to start the briefing." He smiled even more widely at the pastries. "Unfortunately, your aides are not cleared for this, but the donuts are. I'll take those, Lieutenant."

Going along with his mistake was dangerous. If anyone realized she wasn't the expected officer, the jig would really be up. Still, this was about the only way they were going to see what was in the most secret area.

"No worries," she told the man as she discreetly updated her name in her implants. It wouldn't do to have someone ping her and get her real name. Sir Carl had made the update allowing it to all their implants, just in case any data needed to be changed or the implant responses turned off altogether.

Annette took the tray and whispered in Olivier's ear. "Find the real Renner. Take her out of play quietly."

The man nodded. "Of course, Commander."

Irons escorted her into area "E" and led her past a compartment filled with manufacturing gear. Her heart soared when she recognized a little sled with pharmacology units. This *was* the right place.

He gestured at the cart. "We're wrapping up the production on these and the related hardware. The project is being mothballed, and we're getting the space once it's done."

Annette smiled. "You can never have enough space." She wanted to ask him why it was wrapping up, but she could guess. They didn't expect to need them anymore once the AI at Erorsi was gone.

He nodded to another pair of guards at the hatch in front of them as he led her into area "F." It was bigger than area "E" by a factor of five, according to Olivier's map.

Their destination was a conference room. Several dozen Fleet officers and civilians waited for them inside. No commodore, so they'd gotten there early enough. No one wanted to arrive after a flag officer.

Her escort showed her to a pair of open seats with folders laid out in front of them. Printed matter meant it was *very* classified.

Since other people were looking at the contents, she opened her packet. It only took a few moments to realize what she was looking at. Enhancements to equipment that made complex computer cores. Ones she'd seen before, in the compartment that housed Marcus on *Invincible*.

Area "F" was where the Rebel Empire made AIs. Capturing the facility just became critical, but she had no way to notify the princess. She'd just have to hope that the woman pulled the mission off with her usual flair, even though she didn't know how critical it had become.

* * *

"ADMIRAL, we have an incoming FTL message from *Audacious*," Marcus said. "It was a prerecorded video in burst mode."

"Put it on screen," he told the AI.

Zia Anderson appeared on the screen. "Admiral, I have to risk using the FTL. Our stealthed probes just picked up activity at flip point two. It appears that a large number of ships just transitioned into this system. I'm attaching the data.

"Princess Kelsey is already aboard the station, so I can't notify her about it. It's going to complicate our extraction, so you'll need to factor them into your planning. I'll risk another transmission when we have a better assessment of the enemy reinforcements. *Audacious* out."

Flip point two was the portal to the other occupied system. This was bad news and worse timing. It had to be the relief force that the prisoners had hinted at.

Jared accessed the attached probe telemetry. The distance between the probe and the ships, as well as the passive nature of the intercept, required some interpretation. What was obvious at a glance was that the number of ships was significant. More than he'd brought with him and more than they'd sent to take out Pentagar.

They might all be destroyers, but he wasn't about to take that for granted.

"That's going to put Kelsey and the rest in a tight spot," he told Marcus. "They'll be in a position to cut off their avenue of escape. We need to expand on those contingencies you were already working on."

* * *

ZIA WATCHED the telemetry from the probes as they closed with the Rebel Empire ships. The original data wasn't quite as bad as she'd first assumed, though it wasn't good. The ships she'd thought were superdreadnoughts were actually large freighters. Two of them.

The largest warships were three battlecruisers. Of course, they had dozens of cruisers and swarms of destroyers flanking them. This force would take a mauling, but it could hurt Admiral Mertz in a standup fight.

"The enemy fleet is breaking up," her operations officer said. "It looks as though they're diverting ships to the other two flip points, as well as leaving some on station where they are."

It looked as though they were splitting into groups of roughly equal size. One was on the way to where they'd be escaping, one was staying on site at flip point two, and the last group was going around to flip point three. The freighters were on their way into the system.

One thing that was obvious was that they weren't going to be sneaking out the way they'd come in. No matter what happened now, there was no aborting.

Even if she could figure out how to do that, they'd be trapped in the system fairly soon. There was a short window during which they could still escape, but it was going to have to be through flip point three.

Zia brought up the Old Empire flip point maps. None of the links took her back to either the New Terran Empire or Pentagar. They'd have to either sneak into the Rebel Empire or go into unmapped space.

Or find a weak flip point that might give them new options.

She considered sending another FTL burst to *Invincible* but decided to wait. She'd fill Princess Kelsey in once she called. There'd be time to let the admiral know about the new situation once they actually had a plan to get themselves out of the system.

Princess Kelsey should have word to them on their target in less than half an hour. She'd just have to wait, because there was no way to com her with the updated news until she executed phase two.

Zia hoped things went smoothly over there, because any hiccups were likely to cause them all a lot of pain.

32

K elsey listened to Olivier carefully as he described the secret areas of the station. She wished she had confirmation that the target was inside, but at this point, she didn't even know that Vitter was going to get back out again.

She considered the irony of wanting to tear the woman's head off for racing in where angels feared to tread. Talbot was going to laugh at her, assuming this all didn't just go to crap.

"That just about confirms that we're in the right place," she said. "We won't wait for Vitter. One thing that *has* changed is that I want the computer cores. All of them. That means we'll need to swamp them. Stun everyone as quickly as possible. Then we'll disassemble the large equipment and get it back out."

The rally point she'd chosen was on the civilian side of the station, in a small warehouse directly adjacent to the military part of the orbital. It was only a few levels from the secret facility.

Cain Hopwood had secured it for them, trussing up the workers and safely tucking them into a storage room where they wouldn't see anything useful. They'd release them once the operation was over.

They'd cleared the center of the warehouse and set up their secret weapon. Their half of the transport rings stood gleaming, ready to link up with its mate on *Audacious*. Theirs was the one that didn't require an attached power supply, obviously.

She'd released the pinnaces to head out as soon as she'd made the decision to go ahead with the attack. The transport ring came to life right on time, and marines poured through in powered armor, their heavy weapons covering everything and everyone. Talbot came through with her armor already in his arms. Carl Owlet was right behind him, also dressed in powered armor.

"The situation has changed," he said as she started stripping her uniform off. "There's a Rebel Empire fleet in the system. It split up and sent forces to the other flip points. We're not going to be able to just slip out the way we came in."

"Then we'll come up with a different plan."

"Commodore Anderson already has one, but she wants your approval before she tells the admiral. If we hurry, we can get what we're after and slip out through flip point three. It doesn't have any obvious connection back to where we want to go, but it beats being trapped here."

Kelsey nodded as she finished sealing everything except her helmet. "Then that's the plan. Send word back for her to tell Jared that we'll find our own way home. Once we kick this off, I want her to jam all communications from this station and the freighters. We can't let the warships know what we're doing or they'll come racing in.

"The other side of the wall in front of us leads into the military section of this station. I'll send everyone a map. We want to get to the area marked section 'F.' Time is of the essence. We get in, steal everything, and then get the hell out.

"We'll be capturing the other areas as well. This station is like the Grant Research Facility. I want their data cores. Let no one stand in your way, and don't dawdle. I don't want anyone to get the idea they need to scrub the cores."

"Copy that," Talbot said. "Stand away from the wall, everyone."

"Noncombat personnel through the ring to *Audacious*," Kelsey said. "Take my uniform. No need to leave anything behind. Remember, everyone, we leave no one behind.

"Carl, we seeded the transmitters you gave us. They're all over the military section but not inside the secret facility. Is that going to be a problem? What can we expect from them?"

The young man set his portable console on a handy table. "They're designed to detect implant transmissions and jam them. Their range is fairly short, and they won't be able to suppress all the transmissions completely. Not inside the secret areas at all.

"Your armor has an alternate frequency that the jammers won't interfere with. You should still be able to communicate effectively inside the orbital."

"Excellent," she said. "You stay here and monitor that end. Once we have the secret areas secure, we'll call you in to extract the computer cores. Talbot? It's time to make the donuts."

He raised his plasma cannon and trained it on the wall.

Kelsey's implants pinged with an urgent message.

"Hold it!" she said. "Stand by."

Once she was sure she'd checked her husband's impulse to fire, she accepted the link. "I'm kind of busy."

"And you're about to get busier," Annette Vitter said. "I just got a look at the innermost area of the security zone. The target just changed.

"While they are making the Raider implants here, the real secret here is that they're building sentient AIs. The bad news is that the equipment is way too big to go through the transport rings."

Kelsey gaped. "You're certain?"

The other woman nodded. "I just sat through the longest briefing in recorded history talking about the plans to expand the facility. I know them in excruciating detail. By the way, I now know someone even more long-winded and stuffy than Captain Breckenridge."

"Impossible," Kelsey declared. "I can't believe you bluffed your way into something like that. You got big brass ones, lady."

"Everyone likes pastries. I had to leave the security area to com you, but I can get you to where you need to go if you'll have someone open the hatch."

Kelsey thought furiously. This changed everything.

"I have news of my own. The Rebel Empire sent a fleet here, and they're locking down the system. We have a *very* short window to escape, and it won't be back toward Jared. We'll have to run through flip point three. We need a way to get the equipment out of here."

She considered and rejected several harebrained schemes before she stepped back to reconsider the whole plan. There *was* another option. It was insane, but it might work.

"Did that briefing cover the power generation for the secure areas?" Kelsey asked Vitter.

The other woman nodded. "Two fusion plants in the military side, thankfully not in the secured area. The rest of the station has three plants seeing to their needs."

"Send me their locations. I have a history with power plants on Rebel Empire stations."

"So I hear. That's not going to get the manufacturing equipment out of here, though."

Kelsey smiled. "I have an idea. You'll love it. First, we need to actually capture everything. Get as close as you can to the fusion plants, and we'll join you shortly."

"Copy that."

Once again, the recovery team proved startlingly capable. They managed to sneak people near all three power plants, though not up to the plants themselves.

"Talbot, it's time," she said. "If you'd be so kind as to open the door."

He grinned at her, put his helmet back on, and hefted the plasma cannon. Everyone crouched behind something as he took the shot, knowing that it would be incredibly destructive.

It was certainly that. The reinforced wall simply vanished in a sun-bright flash. The bubble of destruction would've been impossible for most people to cross, but they were in powered armor.

The marines leapt forward and vaulted the gap, landing easily and racing toward their designated targets.

There seemed to be a never-ending stream of them coming from the ring. She'd brought every marine in the fleet with her for this mission.

Most people would've called this overkill, but she no longer believed in such a thing. All these people would allow her to run over any resistance and quickly capture the critical areas.

Many of the marines were headed for the fusion plants, but not all. Other teams set out for the command and control levels. The faster they eliminated any possibility of organized resistance, the better.

The Rebel Empire didn't trust their marines, thankfully. That meant the ones on the station had no access to powered armor or heavy weapons. The officers in command no doubt assumed that they'd have plenty of time to make changes if some other circumstance came into play.

Kelsey intended to use that paranoia ruthlessly against them.

The marines rolled right over everything in their path. Stunners took out everyone they met. No one was armed on the other side except for a few guards with flechette pistols. Which were not even remotely effective against her troops.

The teams in the civilian side were actually progressing more slowly than the teams in the military area. They didn't want to trample the people running away from them. They'd have enough time, she hoped.

It took her three minutes to reach the lift leading down to the military fusion plants. She didn't bother calling the car. It would only slow her down.

She ripped the lift doors open with her bare hands and looked down the shaft. The car was two levels below. She'd need to move it. She pulled a fusion grenade off her belt, armed it, and tossed it down the shaft.

"Fire in the hole!"

The blast was impressive in the enclosed environment, but she didn't wait for it to fade completely before she jumped into the shaft.

The car was gone, as was the shaft around it. She plummeted through the space it had once occupied and hit her grav assist to slow her when she reached the right level.

The marines following her didn't have grav assist, so they were using their powered hands to grip the walls as they scurried down like massive spiders.

Kelsey ripped open the lift doors, and flechettes began to ricochet off her armor. Half a dozen guards emptied their weapons at her. She raised her own weapon and stunned them.

It only took her a minute to find the control room. Oddly, a group of Fleet officers was trying to force the hatch when she arrived. Her stunner put them down.

The hatch slid open, and Vitter grinned at her. "Good timing. I have no idea how to shut these things down."

"I have the engineers right behind me."

The man and woman in question were awkward in their powered

armor, but it had gotten them here alive. She helped get their gauntlets and helmets off so that they could work.

Commander Mark Kinder, the chief engineer on *Persephone*, looked over the controls. "This is Rebel Empire standard. Shutting it down now."

Alarms began wailing, and the lights dimmed.

The man grinned. "Both plants are offline. We can get them back up when we're ready, though it'll take a little time."

"Good work."

Kelsey pinged the other teams outside the secure area. Two of the civilian plants were offline already, and the third went down as she watched. They'd eliminated the simplest way for anyone to destroy the station.

She had marines looking for other self-destruct methods but didn't expect to find any. Why have them when you could overload a fusion plant and take out everything?

It was time to execute the final phase. She sent a signal to Owlet to head for the secure area. A team of marines would make certain nothing stood between him and their prize.

"That means I gotta go," Vitter said. "Talbot, help me up the lift and back to the transport ring."

"We'll go secure the labs and the military command team," Kelsey said.

They'd won the first round, but things could still go horribly wrong. It was time to wrap this up and get the hell out of here.

33

———————

Brandon stared at Commodore Anderson's image. "You want me to what?"

"I need you to jettison both ships and get the station inside the recovery ship's arms. We're taking it with us."

"That's what I thought you said."

He looked at the scanner readings of the station as he initiated the release procedure to set *Persephone* and *Audacious* free.

"I can't get it all inside the arms. It's close, but—"

"This is why they pay you the big bucks, Captain. Make it work."

Brandon rubbed his face. Something was going to have to give. He loaded the orbital's geometry into his implants, and then he set up the maximum spread he could get on the arms. They had to be around the cargo, or the drives wouldn't be able to shield it from inertia or flip it.

It almost worked if he twisted the ship around, but the arms didn't open widely enough. The orbital was almost a quarter larger than *Invincible*.

He accessed the specifications for the arms. They were replaceable. That meant they could be removed. Now he needed to figure out how to attach them in the new configuration.

"I'll need several teams from engineering to come assist me," he said. "I need to detach two of the arms. Once we have the station in place, we can reattach them. We'll need to secure them against acceleration, but they will be able to provide flip capability and inertial dampening."

"I'll have people on the way as soon as we clear the landing bay. How long will it take?"

"Considering we've never done it before, it might take an hour."

"Shorten that as much as possible. We're tight on time."

He nodded. "I'll move it along as fast as I can. I can send the specifications along now. The engineering teams can start finding places we can save time while they wait for a ride."

"Excellent," the commodore said. "I've got to get the last part of this mission under way. Call me if there are any problems."

He closed the com channel and started working on what he could do ahead of time. This was going to be tight.

* * *

ANNETTE BUMPED her acceleration up enough to catch up with her squadrons. Every fighter they had was on its way to flip point three. They'd kept their acceleration down so as not to be detected, but they'd be going very fast when they arrived.

The ships in Dresden orbit should be on the way behind them before they attacked the Rebel Empire forces. Based on the range from the new forces moving at the edges of the system, they might arrive there undetected, too.

She called Jake Fiennes on the short-range com.

"What's the plan, boss lady?" he asked.

"It's as simple as it gets. We're going to arrive at flip point three several hours ahead of *Audacious*, *Persephone*, and the recovery ship. The stealthed probes say we have three destroyers and that battle station. I want to take them all off the board on the first pass."

He whistled. "That's a tall order. We can scrub the destroyers, but the battle station is a big one. It's made to take lots of hits. Why do we need to run the table?"

"Because we don't want to let them know where we went for a while. The commodore is arranging a distraction, but a distress signal from out here will really mess us up. The recovery ship is overloaded, and her arms are in a nonstandard position, so it'll be extremely slow. We can't afford to let them catch up with us."

He seemed to consider what she'd said. "We'll have to allocate almost all our fire to the battle station. We have no idea what the internal layout is. I figure we can wax the destroyers with four fighters each. They won't have battle screens up."

"Three each," she said. "We can't allow the battle station to survive."

"We also can't let any of the destroyers live," he countered. "We have to get them, too."

"We know where their fusion plants are. Pick one pilot in each group to eject and let their fighters go terminal on the enemy. In a perfect world, we'd be able to control them remotely via our implants, but we can't risk the enemy detecting any signals. We'll have to do it the hard way."

His eyes lost focus as he considered the tactic. "Pulling what the admiral did? Bold. If we follow up with missiles right on the kamikazes' heels, it should finish them off before they can scream for help. Still, this is chancy. If anything goes wrong, we'll be in trouble."

"Then let's make sure nothing goes wrong."

* * *

KELSEY MADE it to the command deck for the station right after the marines had stormed it. Once again, they'd stunned everything that moved.

She made the rounds of the consoles, moving stunned people out of the way and looking for any that had been left unsecure. Due to the speed and ferocity of the attack, not everyone had been on the ball. She found an auxiliary panel unlocked.

Finding the security information took longer than she liked but was reassuring when she did find it.

The very first thing she did was trigger the antiboarding stunners. That would take everyone off the table. Her people were shielded. She also locked out the escape pods. None of them had ejected, but she wouldn't discount the idea of someone getting around the lockout.

The pinnaces would keep an eye out for any and deal with them. The jamming would keep the Rebel Empire fleet from hearing any distress beacons.

The next challenge was to locate the computer cores. It turned out that there had been someone in the core room. Unfortunately for him, he was woefully short on clearance. He didn't know the codes to erase the system, so he'd been left with a large wrench as his only tool of destruction.

He'd managed to smash some equipment before she used the antiboarding stunners, but the cores were intact.

Kelsey let out a sigh of relief. "That was close. Let's try to keep anyone else from getting too excited."

She called *Audacious*. They'd left a few frequencies open for just this purpose. "Zia, I think we've pulled it off. Does Captain Levy know how he's going to grapple the station?"

The Fleet officer nodded. "He's got that under control. We'll be able to move in twenty minutes."

"Excellent. What's the status of the Rebel Empire fleet?"

"Still on course. The detachment heading toward Admiral Mertz will be there before we can secure the station. The other one is still a ways off from flip point three. If we get under way on time, we'll beat them, but not by much.

"I have a plan to distract them, though. If Annette can take out the defenders, we might be able to escape in the chaos. One of the captured freighters is almost empty. It will be a critical part of my ruse."

"I hope your plan works. Otherwise we're in deep trouble."

* * *

ZIA SENT a crew over to unload the mostly empty freighter. It would make a great addition to her decoy, hopefully confusing the Rebel Empire forces for a while as to what had really happened at Dresden.

Princess Kelsey had instructed her to hold off notifying Admiral Mertz of their intentions until the last moment, figuring he would try something bold and heroic. Zia probably should have argued more strongly that she had a duty to keep him in the loop, but she privately agreed. If things went south, she wanted to see the majority of their forces make it safely home. The Empire would need them to survive.

Using the FTL coms now was a risk but less of one now that the station was theirs. Unlike last time, she needed this to be a two-way conversation.

"Open an FTL link to *Invincible*," she ordered her communications officer.

A few moments later, Admiral Mertz appeared on the main screen.

"We were getting worried, Zia. Based on the initial data, the enemy was splitting up to cover all the flip points. Are you in danger?"

She gave him a wry smile. "Nothing we can't manage, I hope. We've secured the orbital."

He nodded. "Excellent. We've worked up a number of different scenarios to break you out. Depending on the actual forces we'll face coming in, we should be able to get you through."

"Actually, the princess has a different plan."

"Of course she does." He sighed. "Lay it out."

"First, I need to give you the reasoning. I'll be quick because I don't want to keep this line open any longer than I have to. The major point is that the orbital didn't just make Raider implants. It also built sentient AIs."

The admiral sat up abruptly. "Seriously? Then we need to put every effort into getting you out of there as soon as possible."

She shook her head. "We can't extract all the equipment from the station in the limited time we have available, sir. We're just going to steal the whole thing."

"The whole—"

He stopped himself. "You're going to put the orbital into the recovery ship. That's brilliant. If you can evade detection on the way to flip point one, we'll keep them off you."

"The odds of us making it through to you are slim, Admiral. Too slim. We're arranging our own distraction and breaking out through flip point three. The fighters will hit the defenders there before the reinforcements arrive. We'll distract the relief force and escape before they know what's happening."

Admiral Mertz looked down at his console. "There aren't any links on that route to bring you home. The Rebel Empire Fleet is going to chase you down. It's too risky. We'll come up with something else."

"I can't recall the fighters, Admiral. They're only a few hours from executing. We're committed."

He considered her for a long moment. "That's Kelsey's doing, isn't it?

She told you to hold off notifying me so that I couldn't countermand her scheme."

Zia sighed. "I wish it were that simple. I looked at the options, and your likely responses, before I decided that I agreed with her. The Empire needs your ships and your experience to survive, Admiral.

"Even if we made it to flip point one, the odds of us extracting the station and keeping the Rebel Empire ships off us while we retreated to Erorsi are nonexistent. It's too far. Our only chance is to vanish, leaving them to scratch their heads about what happened."

He looked skeptical. "And you think you can do that?"

She smiled. "With just a dash of luck. I'm sorry for the deception, Admiral, but I'm doing what I think has the best chance of success in the long run. If it works out, we'll be able to give you a final status report before we escape."

The unspoken part of that was they'd also tell him if it all went to crap.

Jared Mertz considered her for a long moment. "You're the officer on the scene, Zia. I have complete faith in you. Good luck."

"I'm attaching everything to the transmission now. We'll call once we're about to leave the system. Thank you for your confidence, Admiral."

"You've more than earned it. You'll need every bit of skill and smarts to get back home, but I know you'll do it. Make us proud."

She nodded, her heart swelling with emotion. "Thank you, sir."

Zia attached the files about the escape plan and ended the transmission.

34

Annette watched the range to the targets grow smaller. They were coming in on a purely ballistic course, and at fairly high speed. Since the ships and battle station weren't scanning continuously, they probably wouldn't even know they were in danger until it was far too late.

The probes gave them a good idea of exactly where they needed to hit. She'd already moved the fighters they were using as rams up front. Not by much, but she had to give the pilots time to eject and fly past the targets before they destroyed them. At this speed, it would only mean a delay measured in fractions of a second.

A second stealthed probe had been giving them statuses on the force headed their way, but they'd had to shut it down. They were close enough to the flip point that the defenders might pick up the edge of the beam.

They *should* be too far away to pick up the explosions. Space was vast, and even the flare of failed fusion plants faded fast. As long as they weren't actively scanning when the time came, the attack should go undetected.

Unless someone got a distress call off.

That was the worst-case scenario. If the Rebel Empire ships raced in, there was no way they could escape. They had one chance at this.

Annette forced her mind off the chances of failure. She had to maximize the chances of success.

The battle station was still the biggest question. Without knowing where the fusion plants were inside it, they couldn't use pinpoint targeting like they were with the destroyers.

The plan called for the three fighters to ram the station, and as the pilots were flying past it in their suits, the rest of them would use missiles to tear the thing apart. That should blow at least one of the plants. Probably.

She hated the uncertainty.

Well, there was one thing she could do to increase their chances. They were too close to the targets to notify any of the others that she was about to change the plan, but it was worth the risk.

Annette used her maneuvering thrusters to slow her speed just a hair. Unlike the grav drives, the chemical reaction wouldn't be detectable. She had to use every ounce of thrust she had to make enough difference, but it put her behind the remainder of the attacking force.

Her internal timer slowly crawled to zero, and the space in front of her burst with light. Even before her mind had fully registered the explosions, her implants fired her missiles to follow them up.

The rest of the pilots spiraled past the damaged battle station and raced into deep space. She didn't.

Her canopy blew off, and the powerful grav drive under her seat blasted her straight up. Annette didn't see her beloved fighter plow into the already expanding craters on the target, but she couldn't miss the blinding flare of a failed fusion plant as she hurtled past it.

In a moment, it was gone and she was tumbling through space. An alarm was howling in her ears. Suit integrity had failed, and she was losing atmosphere. Her radiation count was also off the charts.

The exposure was so brief that she'd probably live, supposing they found her quickly, and she didn't suffocate first.

Her helmet locked tight around her neck, cutting off the loss of air. Her body could stand a brief exposure to vacuum. With any luck, one of the other pilots would find her. An emergency ball from the external stores of the fighter would keep her alive.

They'd disabled their beacons. One going off would ruin the stealth they'd struggled so hard to achieve. It also meant that they'd have to find her with short-ranged scanners, or she'd be lost forever in the depths of space.

At least she could take solace in the fact they'd destroyed the battle station. Hopefully, the destroyers were gone, too.

In any case, her part in this little drama was over. It was up to the princess and commodore to make their sacrifices mean something.

* * *

KELSEY SAT at a borrowed console on *Audacious*'s flag bridge and watched the passive scanner results from flip point three with satisfaction. Annette Vitter and her people had taken out the battle station and all three destroyers. The path was clear, so long as they diverted the Rebel Empire ships that were currently headed in that direction.

She turned to Zia. "Are we clear of Dresden?"

The other woman looked up from her command console. "We're just leaving the exclusion zone you'd designated around the planet. I'd like to have another half-hour at this speed before we kick things off. If they spot us now, everything was for nothing."

The carrier, *Persephone*, the recovery ship with the hijacked station in its grip, and the fully laden freighter were creeping along at a very low acceleration. Too slow to show up on the scanners of any ships that happened to look their direction. They hoped.

"I understand," Kelsey said, "but we don't have the luxury of being certain. If they don't fall for the bait, we're in for some serious fighting. Your fighters will only barely make it back to us before we get to the flip point. They have a lot of momentum to burn off, and they can't use real acceleration to do it. If that force doesn't divert, they'll screw us all."

Zia sighed. "I know. Well, if wishes were horses, we'd all be ass deep in horse crap."

"I see someone else still likes to look into the historical archives. Execute Operation Troll."

"Aye, ma'am," Zia said. She pressed a button on her console. "Signal away. It'll take a minute for things to kick off on the other end."

Kelsey calculated the time it would take for the trigger signal to race to Dresden, so she was ready when the distress signal came.

It had taken them a while to find the emergency procedures for the orbital, but once they had them, designing a faked distress signal was easy. They had a lot of archived message traffic to use in splicing together a believable message using the actual people manning the station. That was the key, she thought.

The image her people had put together was computer generated, which probably wouldn't have been enough to fool anyone for very long under normal circumstances, but they'd sent the data they had to Marcus through the FTL com.

The AI had access to tremendously more computing power than they did. The video he'd sent back looked and sounded very authentic.

The main screen came to life with a view of the orbital's main control room. The commanding officer—the boring commodore that Annette Vitter had mentioned—was staring out at them with a look of pure desperation on her face.

"Mayday, mayday, mayday! We need immediate assistance in Dresden orbit. One of our fusion plants has entered some kind of runaway state, and we can't get it to shut off. We've moved the critical research to one of the freighters, but we can't—"

The transmission ceased.

One of the support staff looked over at the two women. "We have an explosion in Dresden orbit. The freighter's fusion plant detonated right on schedule."

Kelsey nodded in satisfaction. When the would-be rescuers arrived in orbit, they'd find a real mess. Zia had put all the ore that they'd brought around the freighter. It wasn't as much mass as the station, but it was a significant fraction.

They wouldn't decipher that mess for a while. By the time they realized that the station couldn't have been destroyed—either through analyzing the debris or just recognizing there wasn't enough of it—she and her people would hopefully be long gone.

The two inbound freighters would be close enough to see the explosion but too far out to get any details. Their messages would add authenticity to the ruse.

Kelsey watched the task force closest to them in the passive plot and crossed her fingers. If they all came running, the distraction was an unqualified success. Otherwise, she'd have to fight the remainder at the flip point, and the rest of the force would quickly be on their heels as they ran.

The task force changed course as soon as the distress signal arrived at their location. To her intense satisfaction, all the ships turned together. They would arrive in orbit a little before her slower ships made it to the flip point.

Kelsey worried about the active scanning until they were clear, but the signal strength never peaked high enough to mean the others could have seen them. The gamble had paid off.

Not that she relaxed until they'd arrived at the flip point. The fighters had rejoined them. The defenders had never even seen them coming, so there were no combat losses, other than seven fighters used as ramming weapons.

The only unexpected news was that Annette Vitter had been one of the kamikazes. That hadn't been part of the plan. The woman's people had noticed she was missing and searched frantically until they'd located her. Without a beacon, that was a real challenge.

Word was that she had radiation poisoning and was suffering from vacuum exposure but that she would live. Kelsey couldn't wait to hear the story of the attack and to watch the recordings.

"We've recovered all our fighters," Zia said. "We can transition at any time."

She nodded. "I'll give Jared a final status first. This will be the last time he and I talk before we find a way home."

The other woman smiled. "I can't wait to see the vid drama they make about your latest exploit."

Kelsey couldn't help rolling her eyes at that. Perfect. They'd managed to keep the damned original vid out of the public eye, but she had no doubt it would be everywhere by the time she got back. It was a good thing she'd be gone for months and couldn't see it or any prospective new ones.

* * *

"Incoming FTL signal, Admiral," Marcus said.

Jared looked up from his console. "On screen."

Kelsey appeared. She stood beside Zia Anderson's control console and smiled at him.

"Well, things are in good shape here, and we're ready to flip. The majority of the ships at the remaining flip points are racing for Dresden.

They sent a signal to the battle station at flip point three but accepted a brief acknowledgement we sent back without suspicion.

"The orders are for the ships here to keep watch with a higher level of vigilance. We said we'd make sure no one slipped past us, of course."

He shook his head. "I can't believe you pulled this off. You stole an entire orbital. That's impressive."

"They'll figure out we tricked them sooner or later," she said with a wry smile. "The destroyed units here will tell them which way we went. We'll try to stay out of sight until we can sneak back home."

"That'll take a long while unless we find some handy weak flip points that get us closer. Tell my father I'm sorry to do this to him, but it was important."

"He'll know," Jared said. "One positive: you don't have to worry about your mother ruining your second wedding ceremony on Avalon for a while."

She laughed. "True. Or that just might give her more time to take it over. I'll deal with that crisis when I get home."

He allowed his expression to grow serious. "Be careful, Kelsey. There's no one to help you out of a bind. Keep the risky moves to a minimum."

"Sure. You know me. Timid as a mouse."

"Don't torture me like that."

She laughed. "I'll be careful. Look, we have to get going. I love you. You be careful, too. Until we meet again."

"Zia, make sure and append the current scanner readings you have. Kelsey, I love you, too. Until we meet again."

The transmission ended.

According to their plan, they'd be flipping now. He'd have to wait for them to sneak through the Rebel Empire before he knew she was safe. It was going to be nerve wracking.

One thing he could do to make it less so was to make sure the enemy didn't go chasing after Kelsey at all. It would make his retreat to Erorsi a lot more dangerous than he preferred, but that was a price he was willing to pay.

The data and equipment his sister had captured were quite possibly key to the Empire's survival. Anything he could do to improve her odds of getting home with it was worth the risk.

He opened a channel to his fleet. "All vessels execute Operation Shiva in thirty seconds."

As a unit, they all flipped into Dresden space and flushed their missiles at the battle station. They fired three salvoes before the first arrived on target.

The enemy returned fire late. The crew probably couldn't believe their eyes. They certainly had time to scream for help, though, which was fine by him. He *wanted* the other ships in the Dresden system to know he was here.

The battle station was powerful but no match for his sustained firepower. The second wave of missiles degraded its battle screens to the point of failure, and the final wave savaged it to the point it blew up.

Its return fire was manageable. He had plenty of antimissile platforms.

The Rebel Empire had obviously never entertained the idea of a concerted attack at this strength.

The mobile forces in the system were strong enough to engage him. They might not win, but in this kind of situation, both sides would be badly mauled.

So, he had no intention of waiting around for them to catch him. He just wasn't going to tell them that.

Once he was sure they were forming up to come his way, he ordered his fleet to launch decoys at the remaining flip point that had a battle station. Only the heavy cruisers and larger vessels had decoys, but they would convince the enemy he was making a move on the other station.

They wouldn't see any destroyers, so they could either assume those were staying at this flip point or heading in at a slower pace to engage them. It didn't matter. Any of the possibilities worked for Jared.

Then he quietly had his fleet flip back to the mining system and head back for Erorsi at flank speed. By the time his decoys self-destructed, the enemy would be committed to chasing them.

Once the enemy started examining the situation, they would have no choice but to assume he'd somehow destroyed the orbital. It would probably drive them crazy, but his arrival wouldn't be seen as coincidental.

Of course, they'd wonder how he'd eliminated the forces at the flip point Kelsey had used to flee. Then they'd discover the station hadn't really blown up. Maybe.

They might put something like the real story together at that point, but it would take days or weeks. He'd seen the scanner readings of the explosion of the freighter and the ore. It would hold for a while.

In any case, it would give Kelsey and Zia time to escape. Surely, one of the systems along their path would have a weak flip point they could use to slip out of sight. The Rebel Empire forces would lose them if they had any luck at all.

"Do you think it will be enough, Admiral?" Marcus asked.

"It has to be," he replied. "It's all we can do."

* * *

ZIA STAYED at her console long after her shift would have normally ended. Princess Kelsey had returned to the captured orbital to help sort out the thousands of prisoners, and Brandon Levy was back on board the carrier. She was desperately tired, but she wanted to watch the scanners until they flipped again.

The enemy hadn't come after them, and they were almost to the next flip point. If they made it through, any pursuers would wonder if they'd really come this way at all.

She'd left a probe in the Dresden system to muddy the waters. It was far outside the system and racing for deep space. About now, it was going to begin transmitting an intermittent signal just strong enough for the enemy to detect. One designed to make the Rebel Empire commander wonder if someone was creeping along in the outer darkness.

They couldn't prove a negative. The probe would self-destruct after a few hours, so they'd never find proof one way or the other. It would probably drive them bonkers.

"We're ready to flip," Brandon said over the com.

"Take us across, Captain."

"Aye, ma'am."

She watched them flip and counted her ships on the other side as they arrived. That was a huge relief. It bought them the most precious of commodities: time.

"We're across," Brandon said. "Initial passive scans are clean. I estimate we're nine hours to the next flip point. I'll send out probes to look for weak flip points and potentially hostile vessels. Then I'll launch the combat space patrol."

Their fighters would escort them in relative safety. She didn't expect to find anyone in these unoccupied systems, but one never knew.

"Hang on a second, ma'am. We might have a situation."

Her heart lurched in her chest. "What kind of situation?"

Had Rebel Empire ships come into scanner range at the last moment before they flipped? Were there ships in this system? A quick check showed that neither of those conditions was the case.

Brandon listened to someone beside his console and shook his head. "Unbelievable. How the hell could this happen?"

"If you don't tell me what's going on, I'm going to scream," she assured her flag captain.

He looked back at the pickup. "It seems we have a stowaway, Commodore."

A moment later, the view swiveled toward the lift on the bridge. Two marines stood on either side of Justine Bandar. The diminutive woman looked triumphant.

"Oh, hell," Zia muttered.

ASSASSIN'S RETREAT

BONUS STORY

Still dealing with the grief of killing twin brother to save the New Terran Empire from civil war, Kelsey withdraws to the solitude of the Imperial Retreat, deep in the snowy mountains of the Imperial Range, to try to figure out how she can live with herself.

Only her enemies refuse to leave her in peace. Pursued by assassins, she chose to let them have their try at her. Now she must end them before they can end her, all without letting her friends know what she intends.

That sounds fair. Let the hunt begin.

1

ASSASSIN'S RETREAT

Author's Note: Assassin's Retreat takes place at the end of *Paying the Price*, book five in The Empire of Bones Saga. There's a one-month gap between where the action ends and when the final scenes play out. This story is set precisely in the middle of that time.

As a reminder, this story takes place shortly after Kelsey was forced to kill her twin brother Ethan to save the New Terran Empire. To say that she isn't in a good mental place during this story would be something of an understatement.

* * *

KELSEY BANDAR STOOD in the center of her brother's room at the Imperial Retreat and wanted to cry but couldn't seem to touch the agony deep inside her chest. As much as she'd loved Ethan, she didn't know why the tears wouldn't come.

Her twin brother was gone, and—here at least—there was almost nothing left of him.

The closed-off room was small, with scarcely enough room for a single-person bed, a dresser, a nightstand, and a small desk. It was an interior room, with no view of the breathtaking, snow-covered mountainside towering above the retreat or the other peaks that made up the Imperial Range.

The Imperial Retreat sat perched at the highest point the massive, old-growth pines had managed to scale the mountain. Avalon had been a pristine world when Imperial scouts had discovered it almost a millennium ago. It hadn't needed terraforming, but the original colonists had judiciously introduced some species from Terra in their quest to make it a prime vacation world.

Part of their vision included making the tremendous mountains—ones that often rose higher than any on Terra—into getaways for the wealthy in the Old Empire. Massive lodges had dotted the most accessible, and with grav technology, many more were reachable than one might have thought.

After the Fall, access to most became nearly impossible. The rebels had used massive electromagnetic pulse weapons to wreck most advanced technology and had driven Avalon back to prespaceflight levels of technology in the hours before they were defeated by the last Fleet units. That defense had cost those brave men and women their lives, but it had saved the people they'd been protecting.

A few centuries after the Fall, the Imperial Family had claimed this particular mountain range, renaming it the Imperial Range, and refurbished this one lodge as the Imperial Retreat—a place where they quite literally got away from it all.

Not that one could see any of the beautiful outdoors today. The powerful storm currently pummeling the Imperial Range was dumping snow sideways in what could generously be called whiteout conditions.

Ethan's room was so insulated that the roar of the wind was cut down to more of a constant, low-pitched moan that only occasionally rose in volume enough for normal ears to hear it. She could make it out with her enhanced hearing and was glad that she was safely inside the warm building.

The investigators had already searched Ethan's room for electronics or writings that might explain why Ethan had tried to kill their father, but everything else was just as her twin brother had left it.

Not that there was much to see. He'd brought little when their father had banished him from the capital. The lack of personal effects reinforced her impression that the room was more like a monk's cell than the vacation home of a wealthy, powerful man.

On reflection, his room was smaller than the closet in her own suite here at the retreat. That probably said more about who she'd been as a girl than who Ethan had been as a man.

Kelsey sat on the edge of the bed and picked up a book that her brother had left on the nightstand. It was old and worn, though cared for. She carefully cracked it open and saw that it was filled with poetry, the verses handwritten in faded ink. The smell of the pages was somehow comforting, and she flipped to the front of the book.

According to the notes there, it had been written four hundred years ago, a century after the Fall. She didn't recognize the author's name. Based on the few verses she allowed herself to read, he'd had some talent.

She returned the book to the nightstand. Reading something like this was so very much like her brother, though no one outside the family had ever see him this way. He'd been a deeply personal man. Secretive, even.

Obviously, since he'd kept to his own counsel when he'd tried to kill his father, sister, and half brother in order to take the throne for himself.

Sadly, she suspected that Ethan had really believed he was doing what was best for the Empire. In his twisted mind, everyone was a threat not only to him but to humanity as a whole.

She sat there, desolate at the loss of the brother she'd grown up with. The brother she'd loved without reservation. The brother she'd killed just as surely as if she'd done it with her own hands.

Which was exactly what some people thought she'd done, all to take his place as the heir to the Imperial Throne. Something she'd never wanted and now secretly hoped she'd never have to endure.

In the two weeks since Ethan had tried to kill their father, the Empire had been in an uproar. Everyone wanted explanations about what had happened and seemed determined to make the appropriate people pay for their part in the failed coup.

Unfortunately, who needed to pay depended on whom you spoke to.

There were a fair number of voices calling for the Senate to strip her titles from her and for her to be placed on trial for treason. She wasn't exactly certain what they believed she'd done that qualified as treason, but they were quite fervent in their demands.

Fleet was still conducting their review of events during the expedition. That was to determine whether or not her half brother Jared would be court-martialed. In many ways, their futures hung in the balance in very similar ways.

Her father had already assured them both that if the outcome of either review went against them, he had pardons ready, even though it would still be the end of their respective careers. Or whatever her life was, in any case. The prospect of leaving behind her titles and being free to leave Avalon to forge a life of her own choosing actually held some allure.

If Fleet cashiered Jared, Elise would take him back to Pentagar and marry him. She'd told Kelsey that both she and Talbot would be welcomed there with open arms. It was tempting. So tempting.

Whatever the future held, she'd been going crazy at the Imperial Palace waiting for it to happen. It felt as if everyone was staring at her and whispering behind her back. She'd known that was, ironically, the same kind of paranoia that had destroyed her brother's life and his sanity, but it had nevertheless driven her into isolation.

Her father had finally insisted that she take a few days and get out from under the microscope of attention she was being subjected to. As the Imperial Retreat sat in the middle of a vast reserve, deep in the formidable mountains of the Imperial Range, she wasn't going to have any unexpected visitors.

She'd insisted that the staff who were normally in residence took some time away so that she could be completely alone. He'd fought her on that but lost. Kelsey had become adept at taking care of herself over the last few years. She'd even learned how to be a decent cook, if one limited the number of dishes one ate.

Normally, there'd be Imperial Guards stationed at various locations around and inside the retreat. Considering the role they'd played in the failed coup, she'd had them replaced with Imperial Marines. Ones she personally knew, led by an officer she absolutely trusted: Major Angela Ellis.

Not that she expected to need them during the storm. Only an absolute idiot would go out into that.

So she'd ordered them to the exterior guard posts around the perimeter of the retreat. She had the house completely to herself.

That wasn't nearly as bad as it sounded. The guard posts were designed for the environment and were toasty warm. Most of the observation was done via remote cameras and security scanners. The few people that left on foot or grav patrol—though never in weather like this—dressed for the cold and had plenty of survival gear.

No, banishing everyone from the house had proven to be the right call. It gave her the peace and quiet to grieve. It had also given her plenty of time to think. To go over everything she'd done and try to figure out if she could've done anything differently. If there'd been any way she could've spared her brother.

She'd come up dry. She'd been blind to Ethan's insanity. Even when Jared had told her that he suspected Ethan was behind the death of Carlo Vega on the outbound leg of the exploration trip, she hadn't believed him. Of course, he hadn't told her what he thought until years later.

He'd been right in saying that she'd never have believed him in the beginning. Back in those days, she hadn't trusted Jared any more than Ethan had. Looking back, it was obvious that her brother had poisoned her against her half brother. She'd just been too young and inexperienced to recognize it.

And now, here she was, sitting in the room her father had banished Ethan to. The room where her brother had waited for word that their father was dead or dying before returning to the Imperial Palace to arrest Jared and herself.

Not to mention planting evidence that Kelsey was behind her father's poisoning. Well, having it planted, most likely.

No, looking back, there'd been no easy answers in dealing with Ethan. When he'd stolen the Imperial yacht and fled through the new flip point connecting Avalon with the Nova system, she'd decided the best thing for the Empire was to let him go. To let him fly blindly into the radiation that would kill him without a word of warning that he was doomed.

And that was something she'd have to live with for the rest of her life.

Kelsey rose with a sigh and started packing her brother's belongings in boxes she'd found elsewhere in the building. She'd send them back to the palace and let her father decide what he wanted to do with them.

Except for the book. She'd read it in memory of the life and love Ethan and she had once shared.

* * *

SHE WAS JUST FINISHING that depressing task when her com went off. It was Russ Talbot, her fiancé.

He'd wanted to accompany her to the retreat, but she'd refused. Not because she didn't want to be near him but because she'd needed time alone to deal with her grief and anger.

Besides, he was a major in the Imperial Marines and had a lot of people that he needed to take care of. She could handle herself for a couple of weeks.

"What's going on, tough guy?" she asked, making certain that her tone was somewhat upbeat even though she didn't feel that way in the slightest.

"A little bit of trouble," he admitted. "We've mostly finished rounding up everyone in Ethan's organization, but one of the people we'd captured at the very beginning managed to escape. Victor Harrow."

She set the box she had just filled with her brother's belongings down on the bed. Harrow had been Ethan's right-hand man and most likely had been the one who'd poisoned her father and framed her for the crime. He'd also kidnapped, tortured, and been going to kill the love of her life. He'd probably also been the one that had tried to kill Jared twice and had murdered a dear friend of hers—Carlo Vega—with poisoned candies.

Oh yes, she knew Victor Harrow.

Based on some rather... intimate cards she'd found, she also suspected Harrow and Ethan had been lovers. Harrow had certainly expressed his love with what seemed like sincerity to her. That probably also explained why Ethan hadn't found a woman to give him an heir of his own.

That could have been taken care of with technology, but he'd gone out of his way to keep the relationship a secret. Probably because if he admitted to it, the background investigation on Harrow would likely have come up with some very revealing information.

Kelsey hadn't told anyone. Ethan was dead, and there seemed no point to doing so. So now, she'd have to pretend ignorance.

"That's the guy that kidnapped you?" she asked.

"That's right," he said. "We figured he was Ethan's right-hand man. We don't have any evidence, but it's likely he was the one that made certain your brother's enemies disappeared or had 'accidents.' He's probably also the one who sent the tainted candies intended for Admiral Mertz that killed Carlo Vega.

"We've locked down all off-world transport. Every shuttle going into orbit is being searched before launch, and if someone makes the mistake of trying to slip away without an inspection, they'll *really* wish they hadn't made that call. We'll find him."

Kelsey imagined they would. A key figure in the attempted coup against the Emperor on the run would spark the largest manhunt in Avalon's history.

"Why are you calling me about him?" she asked. "Shouldn't you be out tracking him down?"

"I think he has an interest in you. He never once cooperated with us, but based on his commentary to his compatriots, he was close to your brother. He took Ethan's death hard and swore his desire for revenge against you to a number of people."

Kelsey grimaced. "Do you want me to come back?"

"No. You're far safer out there than in the capital. We have no idea how much access he still has to the Imperial Palace. We haven't fully vetted the Imperial Guard yet either. Some of them worked hand in hand with Ethan, and I'm not certain we have all the dirty ones locked up yet.

"I doubt very seriously that Harrow is going to make an attempt on your life out there because it's not that easy to get near the Imperial Retreat, even on the best of days. In the middle of that storm? No, you're safest there, I think."

Well, that was a refreshing change of pace. She wouldn't have to scurry off because danger loomed. Not that she'd been all that good at doing so over the last few years.

"If he did somehow make it up here, I've got all these marines looking out for me," Kelsey said reassuringly. "Even if he somehow managed to get through all of them, I think I'd be able to deal with him."

"Don't get cocky," Talbot warned her. "There's a lot of high trees and mountain ridges around the retreat. All it takes is a sniper rifle, and he can get to you once the storm clears. Never doubt for a second that it's possible. Take precautions."

"Yes, Mother," she said with a ghostly smile that she actually felt. "I'll be careful until you've found him. Now get back to work. I love you."

"I love you too. Please be careful, Kelsey. This guy is dangerous and probably has resources that none of us know about. Treat him with the respect that he's due."

"I'll honor the threat, Talbot. I'll also talk with Angela and work out something to be absolutely sure we have our eyes open. Like you said, it's really unlikely that he could get out here to begin with, since the storm has this whole area buried.

"He's probably gone to ground in some secret base like the one he held you at. He's going to hide there until he thinks it's safe to leave Avalon. He's not going to draw attention to himself by coming after me."

"I certainly hope that you're right, Kelsey. To reassure you, I have a number of people providing security to Admiral Mertz, your father, and myself. This guy isn't going to get to any of us."

"See that he doesn't," she said firmly. "Now, get back to work and track this guy down."

Kelsey ended the call, put her com unit back in her pocket, and considered the situation. This Harrow had always considered himself smarter than his targets. Research she'd secretly carried out into the hits he'd performed showed that. His overconfidence occasionally led to people other than the target dying.

Like Carlo Vega, killed when the poisoned candies Harrow he'd sent hadn't been the kind Jared Mertz enjoyed. Jared had passed them to Vega. He might just as easily have given them to Kelsey.

Ethan would've probably killed Harrow for that mistake, lover or not. Probably.

With the additional knowledge that she'd killed the man's heart mate, she was certain that he'd come for her. In his shoes, she might very well try to slip into the retreat under the cover of the storm. And since he had inside information that a normal person wouldn't, she had to assume he knew everything that Ethan had known about the building and surrounding area.

With that inside angle, there was a way to get to Kelsey. A risky, difficult path, but one with a decent chance of success, if one were bold enough. If she'd take the risk—which she would have—she had to figure that he would too.

On reflection, this might just be the kind of distraction she needed. A game of chess with lethal consequences. An assassin waiting in the dark wilderness for his chance to end her.

That was a worthy challenge. Harrow had no idea the level of enhancement that went along with her Marine Raider implants. They'd kept that kind of information to a very select group of people that hadn't included Ethan.

All Harrow would see was a slight woman topping out at one and a half meters. He probably expected that he'd be able to kill her with his bare hands.

She smiled coldly. Oh, how wrong he'd be. Not for very long, mind you, but in this case, the hunter would become the hunted. And with everything he'd done to her and her friends and family, she'd kill him if she could.

How had that old Terran movie framed it? Ah, yes. "Two men enter. One man leaves." She wasn't a man, but the phrase suited her frame of mind perfectly.

* * *

KELSEY BUNDLED up and braved the blizzard to get to the Imperial Guard command post. That wasn't nearly as difficult as it sounded, though. There was a dedicated sidewalk with a handrail. Even though she couldn't see anything more than a few meters away, she knew that she wouldn't get lost.

If she did, the yard wasn't that big. She could walk until she found a wall and made her way around. With her warm layers of clothes, her pharmacology unit and enhancements didn't even have to work to keep her protected.

The Marine Raider implants and the drugs in the unit would have been enough to see her back to safety if she'd been naked in the cold. It wouldn't have been pleasant, but she was far tougher than anyone would reasonably expect these days.

Not that she went out of her way to advertise those capabilities to the general public—or even to her closest associates—when keeping her mouth shut served her own ends.

Even so, it was a relief to get inside the command post and out of the biting wind. The compact room was filled with viewscreens that allowed the four marines sitting at the consoles to monitor the grounds and surrounding area.

They'd undoubtedly seen her coming as Angela was already standing near the door. She, like all of the people under her command, wore cold-weather gear. It was chilly even in here. Probably intentionally so. They wouldn't want to take the time to dress if a crisis developed quickly.

If trouble did come calling, all they needed to do to get ready for the storm was throw on their parkas, goggles, and hats.

"Highness," Angela said. "I wasn't expecting you to come out and check up on us so quickly. We only just got word of the escaped prisoner. I'm reviewing our security arrangements and have called for reinforcements from *Invincible*. I'm sorry, but I'm going to have to move some marines into the house itself to assure your safety."

Kelsey nodded. "I'm not particularly happy about that, but I understand. It would be foolhardy for me to argue, so I won't. Still, I don't want anyone inside my suite. I'll be able to defend myself if anyone intrudes that far."

Angela nodded. "That's good enough for me. With the weather being this bad, I'd like to have roving patrols outside the walls, making certain that the forest around the retreat remain clear, but that's not possible. I'll have to rely on the remotes the Imperial Guard has in place and supplement them with recon drones I'm having shipped down from orbit. The Old Empire tech will see through this junk a lot better than what we have on-site.

"I'll also increase the number of marines inside the walls, walking the grounds, and securing the retreat itself. Even if this guy brings friends, he's not going to have any luck getting to you."

Under other circumstances, Kelsey believed her friend could manage that, but this wasn't just any intruder. Harrow had been a close associate of Ethan's. Her brother would've told the man about an alternative entrance he could use.

Just like the Imperial Palace, the retreat had a secret tunnel to allow the Imperial family to escape in case of attack. Her father knew about it, as had she and Ethan.

So did Harrow, she was certain. If she was correct, he probably felt secure in his ability to slip in unnoticed and kill one little slip of a girl. Since that gave her the opportunity to get some personal payback without putting anyone else at risk, she'd cheerfully let him try.

Not that he'd find the task so simple. Kelsey had changed the access codes to the security system as soon as she'd arrived. There was no telling who had the codes to get into them at this point.

Kelsey had no real objection to allowing marines into the retreat, so long as they stayed out of her suite. If everything worked according to her plan, they might never even know that she'd left the building.

The marine officer looked more than a bit gratified at not having to fight Kelsey on this. "Thank you for understanding, Highness. Major Talbot informed me that he would have a pinnace on the way from *Invincible* in the next ten or fifteen minutes. We'll have double the number of marines, some of them in powered armor, in an hour."

Kelsey nodded as she used her implants to link up with the communications console on the major's desk. Normally, such a thing wouldn't be possible here on Avalon because the new technology had only arrived a few weeks ago. Implants were unknown before their return.

Her father had insisted that the technicians from *Invincible* make modifications to the Imperial Palace and the Imperial Retreat to allow for the use of implants. Angela had them, too, but wouldn't know what Kelsey was up to.

Once she'd linked into the com system, Kelsey created a message and sent it to *Invincible*. It wasn't very long. Just an addendum instructing her steward to send down a few things from her quarters.

She smiled at Angela. "Well, I should let you get on with what you need to do. It's going to be dark soon, and I'm certain you'll want to have all of your new people in place before the sun goes down. After all, we don't really know what's out in the woods, do we?"

* * *

KELSEY PUT a cheerful face on when the marines invaded the Imperial Retreat. None of what had happened was their fault, so she refused to take her bad mood out on them.

A corporal by the name of Jaylen Hale brought her the box she'd asked her steward to send down. "Here you go, Highness. I think this is what you're waiting for."

She smiled and took the box from the earnest young man. "It sure is. Thank you very much, Corporal."

With a wave, she retreated to her suite. Her smile evaporated as soon as the door had closed behind her.

Unlike Ethan's room, her quarters were a true suite: a master bedroom, a common room, a master bath, and a closet bigger than the room where Ethan had stayed. Even a balcony that would normally look out onto the towering mountain that the retreat was built on.

The maps called it Imperial Mountain, but she'd never felt comfortable giving it a name. It was simply "the mountain" in her mind. Names would only serve to lessen its majesty.

Everything in her suite was as she'd left it before the expedition. Given her current tastes, it was much too feminine. It was a stark reminder of who she'd been before the mad computer had changed her forever. Before she'd grown up.

A child in an adult's body had decorated this place. A child that was forever gone.

If the Senate didn't strip her of her titles, she'd have to redecorate, particularly since she now had Talbot to think about. He'd be mortified to be staying in a room like this. The very idea of him sleeping in the bed with its bright-pink spread and frilly pillows made her smile. The stuffed animals would be a bonus.

And speaking of the closet, a lot of the clothes would need to go. Her tastes had changed radically since the expedition and having all this—stuff—embarrassed her. She was used to living with far less now.

Kelsey walked over to the bed and set the box down on its neat covers. It was long and slender. Truthfully, it looked like an oversized flower box.

That couldn't have been further from the truth.

She opened the box and gazed down at its contents. Inside lay her harness and swords, resting on top of her marine skinsuit. The blades had once belonged to a Marine Raider by the name of Ned Quincy. He'd died during the Fall, but his intellect and memories survived inside his implants.

Oh, not precisely him, but the original wasn't around to complain about the differences. No one understood how the AI that called itself Ned Quincy could even exist, but there was no doubt that he shared the dead man's memories and thought of himself as him.

That was good enough for her. In her mind, this was a case of Occam's Razor. The simplest answer was the truth. The being in her mind was Ned Quincy.

The swords had been recovered from *Persephone* along with a tremendous amount of other gear. The training information that she'd uploaded into her implants from the dead Marine Raider had allowed Kelsey to know how these weapons were used in a mechanical sort of way.

After over a year of practice under Ned's tutelage, she'd gained true mastery of the weapons. They now acted as extensions of her hands when she fought. Deadly, razor-sharp extensions.

Talbot isn't going to approve, a male voice said softly inside her head. *I'm not sure I approve.*

Kelsey no longer jumped at the words no one else could hear. That wasn't to say they didn't startle her every single time. Every. Single. Time.

"You can use your outside voice, Ned," she said aloud. "There's no one else here. And you aren't supposed to be reading my surface thoughts. We have an agreement."

Since the AI resided in her implants, he had access to her surface thoughts as well as the ability to see through her eyes, hear through her ears, and sense everything around her just as she herself did.

Which included bathroom and sexy time, among other private moments she'd rather not have anyone else seeing. So, they'd come to an arrangement in how her senses were shared. He didn't read her surface thoughts and turned off his access to her senses when she was doing anything that he wouldn't normally be allowed to be present for.

Her com unit chimed. A glance confirmed it was her own implants calling. She accepted the call.

"I can't use what doesn't exist," Ned said. "*Persephone* and the other ships —even the marine pinnaces—now have holo projectors that allow me to manifest, but this building doesn't."

"Point," she said as she started stripping out of her clothes.

Oddly, this wasn't one of the times Ned was banned from. Her father would be horrified if he ever learned of the coed manner in which marines —and she—armored up for combat. The first part of which involved stripping to the skin and getting into a protective, armored skinsuit with gender-appropriate plumbing attachments.

If the nobility had any idea how many men—and women—had seen her naked, they'd spit out their teeth. A sight, she had to admit, that she'd have enjoyed immensely.

"And I'm not reading your thoughts. Your actions tell me everything I need to know. You're going to ambush them when they come for you."

"Yes, I am," she said calmly. "And you're right in that Talbot wouldn't approve. So, I'm not going to tell him. Neither are you."

She turned her back to the com, pulled the suit up her legs, and connected her plumbing. Then she shrugged into the torso section and sealed up. Its sleeves extended to her wrists, where she could attach the inner gloves of a vacuum suit or powered armor to them. The feet had matching socks.

Armored socks. She'd have never imagined that back in the day.

Kelsey pulled her normal clothes over the skinsuit, attached the aforementioned socks, and slid her feet back into her boots. The gloves went into her pocket, as did the snug head and neck protection. Those could go on last, leaving only her face unprotected when the time came.

She tucked a balaclava and goggles into her parka pocket to handle that last bit of protection. Everything was in white, which would help her blend in when the time came. Not that blending into a blizzard was all that challenging. Even neon colors would be lost half a dozen meters away from any observer.

Her skinsuit was vacuum rated and would keep her nice and warm. All she had to do was turn down the heat exchanger that normally chilled someone in armor. It really was the best underlayer imaginable for a situation like this.

"You're not exactly in the best mental place right now," Ned said. "You're hurting inside, and you want to make someone bleed for it. You're going to do things you'll regret."

Kelsey dug into her closet and pulled out her weapon's belt. It held a heavy flechette pistol to her right hip, a neural disruptor across her left hip, and a marine combat knife at the base of her spine. She didn't put it on but laid it on the bed next to her swords.

She wouldn't don her outer layer or weapons until and unless she knew she was going out. Once she strapped the belt on, it would sit under the bottom edge of her parka.

Then she considered the final weapon in her closet. It was a relic in every sense of the word. A true work of art from another age.

A Pirone Nitro Express 18 millimeter semi-automatic hunting rifle. A big bastard left at the resort that had become the Imperial Retreat after the Fall, found by one of her ancestors, and lovingly restored.

She had no idea what it had been used on in the Old Empire, but there was nothing on Avalon that required a magnificent weapon like it. The slugs —actual copper-sheathed lead slugs!—were wider than her admittedly slender thumb and even longer than the digit itself.

The massive slugs were driven by an old-fashioned chemical reaction, gunpowder set off by a primer in an enormous brass case. The rifle had a kick that felt almost as bad as the plasma rifle built for use with her powered armor.

Almost.

Even though there was nothing worthy of the weapon here, and she really wasn't the type to go kill something for sport anyway, she'd taken the rifle out and shot at nonliving targets of opportunity. The tremendous blast and kick of the weapon had thrilled her.

In the middle of a snowstorm, the rifle wouldn't normally have any range to speak of, but she wasn't just anyone. She had access to senses other than her eyes to observe the enemy.

Maybe she'd take it, just in case.

"If they come hunting me, then I have every right to hunt them back," she told Ned softly. "This man tried to kill my father and Jared. He did kill Carlo Vega. If he comes into my hands and attacks me, I will end him."

"Your father would be horrified to hear you say that," Ned said. "If they show up, you'll know. You could turn the marines loose on them. They'd never stand a chance if Major Ellis sent in marines in powered armor."

"And let others take my revenge for me? Fat chance."

"It's called justice nowadays, Kelsey. As a civilized people, we're supposed to take revenge out of punishment."

"I reject that," she said coldly. "This man and his associates tried to take what was mine, and now they want me. They can have their shot but only on my terms. Terms they may not particularly care for, but no one ever said life was fair."

Ned was silent for a few seconds. "How will you explain what you've done when it's finished? You realize that stalking them will technically make you a murderer."

"This mountain is owned by the Imperial Family. The Empire allows someone to defend their property against invaders. They'll be armed, and I could justify the use of lethal force."

He laughed. "You are a master and teacher of the fighting techniques of the Marine Raiders. The first sensei since the Fall. It's like a normal person 'defending' his home against the intrusion of a pack of wilderness scouts barely out of puberty."

"While I earned my black belt first, the marines you were teaching were right behind me. Several of them should've made sensei first, but they stopped testing while I made the final push to earn my red stripe. They handed it to me."

"They wanted you to be the first sensei in the New Terran Empire," he said sternly. "You'd earned their respect, and they wanted you to have that distinction. You're right that some of them are far better at hand-to-hand combat and have a killer's mind-set. If we ever get the hardware to make new Marine Raiders, they'll outpace you.

"But what they won't do is outshine you. You've led the way, paying in blood and pain. Those are coin that the men and women in the marines understand and value. I beg you not to throw it all away."

Kelsey pulled out the box of spare ammo for the rifle. It looked like she had two dozen of the enormous cartridges, each one was half again longer than her hand. Each a handcrafted work of art made with loving care by an unnamed master gunsmith.

She found a bag with a drawstring that was large enough to hold them all. The rifle was a single-shot bolt-action and would require her to reload after every shot. She'd also need to wrap the action to keep it from freezing. Even modern gun oil could only do so much.

"It's not murder if I give them a chance to surrender first," she said stubbornly, looking at herself in the mirror. "I'll give them one and only one chance to give themselves up. If they chose not to, if they attack me on my own doorstep, I'll take them down. They'll have every chance to kill me first, so it seems like a fair trade. I'm not invincible."

"But are you suicidal?" Ned asked softly. "You feel responsible for Ethan's death. You feel as if you murdered him. It's not true, but you want to give his lover one last chance for vengeance to make you pay for what you feel you did. The sin you're convinced you committed."

"Yes, I killed Ethan. I had no choice when it came to protecting the Empire. That's something I'll have to live with for the rest of my days. Which might be very few in number if Harrow succeeds. I'm not going to make it easy, but I'm going to give him his chance. As the Bard said, 'and if you wrong us, shall we not revenge?' As much of a bastard as he is, Harrow deserves his chance at me."

"Kelsey, this isn't like you. I'm worried about you. You need to talk this over with someone. Preferably before you do something you'll regret for the rest of your life."

The corner of her mouth quirked up. "Too late for that now. Maybe once the storm ends, if no one comes calling."

Her implants pinged in her mind as they connected with new hardware. Old Empire recon drones were active over the retreat and feeding data into the command net. Angela was sending them out to scan the forest and mountains around the area and to warn her of any vehicles trying to sneak in under the cover of the storm.

Kelsey immediately used her override codes to filter out any warnings unless she cleared them to go through. Human beings would be watching the feeds, but their senses weren't up to the standards of the hardware itself. If she caught sight of the enemy first, she could edit them out of the feed entirely.

It turned out to be a good thing that she had, as moments later one of the recon drones found a large grav vehicle nestled in the trees far below the retreat. It was situated near the exit of the escape tunnel on the other side of the mountain.

The assassins were already here, and the die was cast.

* * *

Kelsey made one pass through the retreat and made certain that everyone knew she was going to try and get some rest and didn't want to be disturbed. That would keep them from looking for her except under any but the most urgent of circumstances.

Like assassins making an assault on the retreat, but with any luck, the marines would never know about them.

Once back in her suite, she put her weapon's belt around her waist, donned her parka, strapped her sword harness into place, and hefted the massive rifle. It was far too big to sling inside. It was longer than she was tall, and the tunnel wasn't all that big to begin with.

Her suite was made to be defensible if something went wrong. The door was paneled with expensive wood, but armored metal lay underneath. The walls, floor, ceiling, and doorframe were made of the same material and the emergency bolts were big enough to make sure any attackers would need to cut their way in.

She activated the locks. No one would be following her out, even if they guessed there was an escape tunnel. This was her fight, and she'd see it to the end.

It might have been trite to hide the access to the tunnel behind the bookcase, but she didn't mind. She was a traditional girl in some ways.

Kelsey entered a code on a keypad hidden behind some books on a lower shelf, and the hidden door swung open. Behind it was a small lift, its doors already sliding open.

She stepped inside the lift and placed her palm against the reader. The doors slid shut, and the lift car descended. Outside, the bookshelf would've already swung closed.

The lift opened into a small alcove just off the tunnel. There was another alcove for her father's suite and one for her brother's room. She took a moment to use her override to lock all the lifts down.

Inside the central area were a number of lockers holding survival supplies and weapons. Enough to outfit a platoon of marines. One even held some unpowered armor.

"You're being far more sporting than you should be," Ned said through her com unit, his voice muffled in her pocket. "At least take some armor."

Well, Talbot always said that if you weren't cheating, you weren't trying.

She shucked out of her weapons and parka and then strapped on some torso armor. She left the rest of the set and redressed herself.

"Anything more will slow me down when speed is my best defense," she said. "This is a game of cat and mouse. I don't want them to see me at all before I step out of the snow."

Kelsey grabbed a set of snowshoes, a bag of climbing gear, and a coil of rope. The drifts would be murder, and she needed to be able to move quickly, so the snowshoes were a must. There might be parts of the mountain that she could take them off, but not having them would've been stupid.

The climbing gear would come in useful if she had to get up one of the frequent rocky ledges to get into a better position. She wasn't a professional climber, but she'd taken the course. Her Marine Raider enhancements made up for a lot of deficiencies in skill.

That would have to be enough.

The tunnel descended at a steep slope and the exit was a fair distance away, on the other side of the mountain from the resort. This was good, as no matter how well the snow dampened sound, only distance and the mountain itself would keep the marines on patrol from hearing the Pirone, if she had to use it.

The chamber at the end of the long walk was large, holding a number of grav vehicles that would be useful in escaping the mountain during an attack. Since people coming to kill the emperor or his family shouldn't know it even existed, the theory was that it allowed for them to escape unseen.

The large hatch on the far side of the chamber led directly out of the side of the mountain. The personnel exit was through a short tunnel to the right. It led to an area above the cliffs where someone desperate enough could hike to safety under the cover of the pines.

Kelsey accessed the security systems and turned on the camera on the other side of the personnel hatch. She was somewhat surprised to find three men working on the security system there.

The man behind the two working to get into the console was probably Harrow. As he had his hood up and there was no audio, she couldn't be sure, but his angry body language made it a good bet. If she'd had to guess, he was pissed that the codes he had didn't work and was tearing a strip off his people to get them to hurry up.

And, since they were sitting in the middle of her exit, that presented something of an unanticipated challenge. She'd expected to have enough warning to get out of the tunnel before the enemy arrived, but they'd gotten here faster than she'd anticipated.

She might be able to best them with surprise, but the hatch would open slowly enough that they'd know she was there. Three to one odds in what amounted to a closet would be far more hazardous than she was willing to chance when not in powered armor.

Kelsey turned and considered the vehicular hatch. It was made to keep the elements out and still work, but the three men in the antechamber would feel the massive hatch opening through the ground under their feet.

That would give them warning that she was here, and she was willing to bet that their grav car had enough weaponry to take her out before she could land. That wouldn't do.

There was a personnel hatch built into it so that outside maintenance could be performed, but there was no access to the rest of the mountain. At least she thought there wasn't.

The metal of the massive hatch was ice cold when she laid her palm against it. That reminded her to put her gloves and headgear on. The goggles came last, protecting her eyes from the bitter wind and snow she was about to encounter.

The smaller hatch responded to the code she entered and obligingly slid aside. It opened onto a ledge no more than a meter and a half wide. The arctic air instantly made her noise hairs freeze, a sensation well known to anyone who'd ever visited a truly cold place. Kelsey could see the edge of the stone ledge, but the snow masked everything beyond it.

Not that she needed to walk out onto the icy rock to know she was screwed. Looking down wouldn't tell her anything she didn't already know. She was thousands of meters above the icy rocks below. A fall meant death, even for her.

She fitted the climbing spikes from the bag over her boots, took one step forward into the howling gale, and considered her options. Climbing the stone walls around the exit would be extremely dangerous even on a clear day.

In the middle of a blizzard? Ned would rightly call it suicide, but she was out of options. If she wanted to have any chance at all of exacting her revenge on Harrow and his men, she had to get to them first.

* * *

THE CLIMBING GEAR that had seemed so comprehensive when she'd grabbed it now felt completely inadequate for the task ahead of her. She drove a spike into the wall next to the ledge, ran a line from it to her belt, and carefully stepped over to the edge to examine what was around the opening.

The stone within reach seemed solid enough, but she expected that would be true right up until something pulled loose under her weight.

Satisfied that she at least had a chance to do this, she leaned out and looked over the edge. As she'd expected, she saw nothing but wind-whipped snow.

Thankfully—or perhaps unfortunately for her peace of mind—she had access to the recon drone network. The mechanical device watching over this section of the mountain had more than enough scanner power to cut through the weather.

The drop was just as deadly as she'd thought it would be, coming in at a little more than two thousand meters straight down to rocks that would tear her apart if she fell.

She'd best not fall, then.

This is insane, Ned said through her implants. *You need to go back to the retreat and let them know we have visitors. They're in danger too. Find another way to do this.*

The noise of the storm made hearing her com impossible, and she hadn't wanted an inopportune call to alert her attackers to her presence, so Kelsey had shut it down. That might raise some eyebrows back in the retreat if Angela tried to contact her, but that was a risk she had to take.

"Did *you* just call me crazy?" she asked, inserting an ironic note into her tone. "You're a Marine Raider. You did stuff crazier than this for fun. Hell, that combat drop at orbital speeds on Harrison's World was *far* more insane than this."

While the orbital drop had a measurable chance for you to die, it was far less dangerous than this madness. Kelsey, I beg you not to do this. Once you take this road, you can never really undo the damage to your soul.

Her only answer was to drive a spike into the icy wall just outside the ledge area. She'd leave the first attached until she had two more outside, then signal it to retract from the wall.

The spiked sleeve she'd slid her boots into gave her some grip when climbing but nothing she'd trust her life to. The ropes would save her when she fell. With that in mind, she kept the lengths short.

She had ice axes to use in her hands. The long spikes would help her climb, but they might also dislodge something. She couldn't trust anything.

The recon drone told her that the shortest path to safety was almost straight up. If she could make it up the hundred meters to the cliff above, she could get herself onto solid ground.

This would've been a great time to have Mjölnir along. The hammer Carl had designed and built for her had a built-in grav drive, and she could've just flown up in seconds.

But it was "safely" locked away in a safe in her quarters that only Talbot, Jared, and she could access. Her steward wouldn't have been able to gain access without tipping off the very people Kelsey had to keep in the dark.

Jared or Talbot would instantly drop marines all over the mountain. If they suspected anything, they'd stop her. She couldn't allow that to happen.

"Slow and easy," she muttered to herself. "This is the simple part. No one is shooting at you yet."

Kelsey made it up the first ten meters at a steady pace. Go a meter, drive a new spike into the cliff face, retract the lowest, use her axes to drag herself up a few centimeters at a time, and then do it all over again.

If she'd been a normal human, she'd probably never have made it even a fraction of the way without skills she just didn't have. Her enhanced muscles had no trouble supporting her weight, and she wasn't tiring. The skinsuit kept her warm enough to manage.

She could barely see the ice-covered rocks in front of her face, but she used the recon drone to map her progress. It wouldn't do to go off course.

Without warning, her right-hand ax broke free and left her dangling by her left ax. She was still trying to orient herself when it also tore free, dropping a head-sized rock on her shoulder as she plummeted.

The pain was nothing compared to the terror she felt, only to be yanked up hard when her lines snapped taut. One of the spikes tore loose, but the other two held her tight as she dangled thousands of meters above a rocky, icy death.

Watch that first step, Ned said dryly.

"You're *way* less funny than you think you are," she grumbled.

It took her a few more seconds to dig her axes back into the stone and get the third spike back into place. She hung there against the cliff, her heart pounding. That had been far closer than she'd liked.

On reflection, the Kelsey that had decorated her room in the retreat before the expedition would've heartily agreed with Ned about her mental state. How life could change one's view of things.

The remainder of the ascent went much more smoothly, but she took nothing for granted. She knew that she could fall to her death when she was only a hand's grip from the top, so she took every care.

At long last she lay on her back above the cliff, cushioned by the snow. She shouldn't waste any more time, but she had to calm her racing heart.

"Okay," she muttered. "You're right, Ned. That was nuts."

And yet, here you are, safe and sound. Well done, Raider.

"I'm pretty sure I haven't passed all the qualification tests," she disagreed. "I've been meaning to see what other gaps I have in my training. Now I see that I have a reason to fill even the most obscure lack in my experience."

No one ever finishes their training, Kelsey. They just keep learning new things and refreshing what they've forgotten. Trust me when I say you've done everything I would expect of a Raider, even before the Fall.

Even considering her current circumstances, his words made her feel inordinately pleased. She'd come farther than she'd ever imagined possible, overcome every obstacle set before her.

Now she needed to get up and do it again. The mountain was filled with men that wanted to kill her. It was time to give them their chance to try.

* * *

KELSEY USED the recon drone to locate the hostiles on the mountainside. There were six men huddled in the lee of a ridge to keep out of the biting wind. Added to the three inside the antechamber, she had nine hostiles at the exit.

There were possibly more at the vehicle. She'd find out shortly. Her first job was to make sure that they couldn't simply run away when things started going sideways. That meant disabling that vehicle and denying them any long-distance communication.

No handheld com could reach anywhere useful from way out here. Hers could link with the network in the escape tunnel and thus back to the retreat, but not theirs. Not without a vehicle booster.

As far as she was concerned, her contest started the moment she offered them the chance to give up and they either refused her or failed to respond. Then she'd stop using the recon drone to keep tabs on them. If her actions were to have any meaning, she had to give them a sporting chance during the actual fighting.

She gave the assassins a wide berth, grateful that she'd brought the snowshoes, and approached their vehicle from behind. It was a large grav van that didn't look sturdy enough to have made it in through a blizzard. It was white in color and blended seamlessly with the snow around and on top of it.

As she'd guessed, there were some fairly well concealed weapons that could have taken her out if she'd taken a vehicle from the tunnel. She could've used one of the Imperial Guard vehicles, but that wouldn't have been very sporting.

Based on the drifts piled on it, the vehicle had been here a while. The interior read as cold in her enhanced vision, so she doubted they'd left anyone to guard the vehicle. He'd have shown up in infrared.

Still, it paid to take no chances. Since her personal little war was undeclared, she pulled her neural disruptor and set it for stun. If they'd left a guard, she wouldn't kill him without challenge.

The sliding door was on the protected side of the vehicle and had much less snow blocking it. She yanked the door open and covered the interior with her weapon, but found it deserted. A check of the driver's area was similarly unproductive.

Kelsey used the recon drone to make sure no one reacted to her opening the vehicle door. It wasn't possible for anyone to have heard something, but that didn't stop some sensor from alerting them to the door opening. Or her setting off the vehicle alarm, now that she thought about it.

When no one made a move for a solid minute, Kelsey felt sure that she wouldn't get any unexpected guests in the next few minutes and closed the door to block more of the wind while she worked.

The rear of the van had seats for more people than she'd seen through the recon drone, but the open bags told her they'd used the extra space for equipment. The empty seats confirmed that she had, at most, nine people to deal with. Unless, of course, they'd sat in one another's laps.

Still, as a precaution, she tasked the recon drone with monitoring for new people on the mountainside. It would only warn her if someone unexpected popped onto the scene.

That was cheating in a way, but she had no intention of firing on any marines that caught wind of the fight. There would be no friendly fire incidents today.

Disconnecting the long-range com took less than a minute once she'd made note of the frequency the intruders were using. It took only slightly longer than hot-wiring the vehicle itself. Spending all that time around Carl Owlet had just paid off.

She slowly lifted the van up off the mountainside. The snow and wind would mask the hum of the grav units, and the intruders wouldn't be able to see her in the air.

The van bucked and tried to roll as she lifted, but she yanked it back into line, raising the vehicle ten meters into the air. Only the one recon drone was in place to see her, and it wouldn't warn Angela or the other marines protecting the retreat about her antics.

They'd be justifiably furious if they ever caught wind of what she'd done. She'd have to be very thorough in cleaning out all signs of her access when this was done. If, of course, she was still alive. If not, they'd be pissed at her for other reasons that she had no control over.

Five minutes later, she was on the ground well away from the original landing place. She promptly exited the vehicle and manually disconnected the power supply. That made finding it impossible for the assassins.

She was hungry, so she took a few minutes to eat some ration bars. They tasted like kudzu but gave her the energy she needed for the fight ahead. The trash went into her pack for disposal once this was all done.

Getting back to the area near the personnel exit took a while longer, but none of the enemy was moving. In fact, the three inside had come out to gather with the others. Whether eating, talking, or bitching, she had no idea.

Once she was settled into place between them and where they'd originally left their vehicle, Kelsey dropped the feed from the recon drone, turned on her com, and linked her implants to it. She changed the frequency to the one they'd been using and smiled. It was finally time to end this.

* * *

"Victor, you've been a very, *very* bad boy," she transmitted through her implants and com on the assassin's frequency. "You don't mind if I call you Victor, do you? It feels more personal when I use first names."

For a minute, she thought he wasn't going to respond, but a male voice finally answered. "Who is this?"

"The woman you've come all this way to meet. I decided to welcome you. That's what a responsible host does, even if the guests are unexpected."

"Only unexpected?" he asked. "Not unwelcome, too?"

Kelsey chuckled. "Oh, no. Your presence is most welcome. I've been needing a distraction *just* like you."

"Then open up the door, and we'll come in. It's a mite chilly out here."

She laughed. "You misunderstand. I'm not inside the hatch you've been trying to break open. I'm out on the mountain with you."

Another few moments of silence hinted at the consternation her words had probably caused.

"I doubt that," he finally said. "This kind of weather isn't suitable for man nor beast, much less pampered little princesses like you. Besides, I'd have seen you come out. You don't expect me to believe you walked all the way around the mountain, do you?"

"You can believe whatever you want. You parked a large white van down the mountainside from where you're huddled right now. That's where I got this frequency.

"By the way, your ride isn't there anymore. I moved it, disconnected the long-range com, and killed the power supply. We wouldn't want any irksome interruptions, would we?"

That caused a much longer delay in response. Someone was probably trying to access the vehicle remotely. Now, at least, they'd know she was serious.

"You've captured my full attention," he said. "What do you want? Our surrender? Don't hold your breath. You helped kill someone very important to me, and I'm going to make you pay for it in blood."

"Excellent!" she said with a real smile. "Honestly, your surrender is the very *last* thing I want. You kidnapped and tortured my fiancé. You tried to kill my brother and *did* kill an old friend of mine. You've probably murdered dozens of people on Ethan's orders. I want you to try to finish what you came here to do. Kill me, if you can."

"The Bastard isn't your brother," the man said coldly. "He's the man who killed your *real* brother. How could you ever believe otherwise?"

"Because I was there. I killed my twin brother with my own words and deeds. He was a threat to the Empire, and he tried to kill my father. Or you did on his orders, more likely. Ethan was always a little squeamish about getting his hands dirty.

"Let that sink in for a moment, Victor. I killed your lover, and I'm going to kill you too."

"We'll see about that, bitch."

"Honor demands that I offer you and your men the chance to surrender," she said, allowing her distaste to color her tone. "I sincerely hope you don't take me up on that, personally."

"Why? So your marines can drop down and kill us for you?"

That brought a real smile to her face. "I've gone out of my way to make sure that no one will interfere with our little dance. Believe me when I say that no one will ever find your bodies if you allow this one fleeting opportunity to pass you by.

"I'm out here all alone. You and your men against one pampered princess, as you called me. If you want your revenge for what I did to Ethan, this is the only chance you'll ever get to take it.

"I'll admit that I'm in a far more obliging mood than I should be, but I want to see your blood on the snow. To feel it on my hands. To taste it. Tell me, Victor. Are you afraid of a little slip of a girl like me?"

"I'll see you shortly, Princess. Right before I slit your throat."

"No quarter it is. At least you won't regret that choice for long."

She killed the channel and turned the com unit off. It was done, and her sense of honor was satisfied.

You goaded him, Ned said. *He has no idea what you really are.*

"I am death," Kelsey said flatly. "Now it's time to go show him the true scope of his error."

* * *

IF SHE'D BEEN in command of the enemy, she'd have sent a scouting party to make sure the van really was gone. If Harrow underestimated her as much as she expected, he'd believe that she sabotaged the van and left it in place. He wouldn't believe that she had the skill to fly it in this weather.

Kelsey crouched lower against the shallow ridge of stone that she was using for cover. Not only would that help conceal her from direct sight, it would allow the snow to clump against her. From a meter away, she'd be invisible. She turned her breath to the stone to keep from giving herself away with puffs of visible heat in the cold air.

While she waited for the first men to come her way, she dumped Panther into her system. The drug cocktail increased the transmission speed along her nerves as well as her cognitive abilities. When the time came to act, she'd have her moves planned and strike without mercy.

Ten minutes later, she heard others moving in the snow just beyond the ridge she was crouched behind. Her enhanced hearing gave the combat processors in her cranial implants enough data to know that, even if she couldn't tell how many they were or how far away they were.

Under less trying circumstances, she'd have known their number and spacing. She'd also have a combat remote to toss over there so she could see directly through her augmented senses.

But that would be cheating, just like using the recon drone.

It sounded like three or four people. A decent scouting force.

She almost rose to start stalking them but reconsidered. Harrow knew that she was here somewhere. Would he be smart enough to send a second group after the first? They could wait for her to spring an ambush on group one and then shoot her down.

Yeah, that would've been a rookie move on her part.

Instead of giving chase, she waited and was finally rewarded when she heard a second group following the first. This group passed just on the other side of the stone she hid behind. She raised her head just as they passed and saw two men with rifles in their hands walking single file.

They were already out of range of normal sight in the snow, but her enhanced eyes had no difficulty making them out in infrared.

Kelsey rose silently to her feet and paced them until the small ridge shielding her sank into the snow and allowed her to step into their tracks. She synchronized her steps to theirs and closed the gap until she was right behind the rear man.

Ready, she clamped her hands on either side of the man's head and, before he could react, she spun his head around, and his neck broke with a crack. It sounded almost exactly like a green limb breaking.

She had no idea what the lead man thought his friend was up to, but he'd only begun to turn when she drew her marine knife and plunged it through his temple. With her augmented strength and the unbreakable blade's sharp point, it went hilt deep with no issue.

There was a little blood splatter from the wound but nothing serious. She took a moment to clean her blade in the snow, dry it on one of the dead men's clothing, and sheathed it at the small of her back.

Two down. They'd died before they could cry out, but that didn't mean they wouldn't eventually be missed.

She'd taken the irrevocable step Ned had tried to protect her from. These men hadn't really had a chance against her. If anyone ever discovered the truth about what had happened here today, she'd pay a very real price.

She might even regret what she'd done once the ice in her soul melted. If it ever did. She knew that even over the cold fury that flooded her veins at the moment. The irresistible demand for vengeance against those who had harmed those she loved. She had no room for a conscience now.

A quick check found both men had coms with earbuds. Kelsey put one on so she could monitor their communications.

She considered taking one of the rifles but decided against it. She already had the hunting rifle, and a second might stand out. Besides, the modern weapons didn't fit into the game of stalking she'd decided to play.

Time to add a few more assassins to her tally.

With the gap between the lead party and the second as well as the time she'd taken to kill these two, the first group should be in the area where they'd left their van. Boy, were they going to be disappointed.

"Victor," a man said over the enemy com unit. "The van is gone."

Harrow cursed. "Search the area, and make sure she isn't hiding there waiting for us to drop our guard. Group two, keep watch on group one."

The first man confirmed and Kelsey dropped her voice as low as she credibly could and gave a brief response. "Copy."

If her response sounded odd to Harrow, he didn't say anything.

Rather than skulking around, she chose to walk directly into the area as if she hadn't a care in the world. One of the men must've spotted her.

"Jackson?" a voice asked. "Is that you?"

"Yep," she said, waving her arm.

"For god's sake, act like this is a real mission. She could be anywhere around here."

While he'd been speaking, she'd spotted him behind a tree to her left and headed his way. He must've realized something was off at the last moment, because he flinched as she reached him.

"Shit!" he yelled as he tried to pull back and raise his weapon.

Kelsey knocked the rifle away from her and smashed the meaty part of her closed fist into his face like a hammer. Given her strength, the results were *spectacularly* gory.

His nose pulped, spraying blood everywhere. In fact, her blow had shattered the bones of his face and driven it back into his skull. She'd probably broken his neck, too.

He fell dead at her feet without even twitching.

Three down. With his shout—even in this storm—his friends probably knew she was here. Time to fade back into the trees.

Of course, the enemy would be able to follow her snowshoe tracks. Still, that could be used to her advantage, she supposed.

* * *

HER ENHANCED HEARING picked up two people closing in from different directions. She angled toward one of them so as to be able to engage them separately.

Kelsey heard one of the assassins warning Harrow she was there in her earbud. She helpfully confirmed the order Harrow gave to move the second group to assist the first. That would make them feel better, knowing the two dead men were there with them.

It would also delay Harrow responding to her attack until she'd dealt with his lead elements. If she could eliminate half his force before he took her seriously, that would make the second part of this fight a lot more entertaining from her point of view.

The snow falling on the trees created piles around the circumference of the outspread branches, relatively empty place under them, and white mantles all the way up the outside. The shielded spots had little snow, allowing her the chance to remove her snowshoes.

Before she took her snowshoes off, she made an obvious exit from the other side of the clear space. It was a false lead, meant to lull her target into an unwarranted sense of security. A distraction while she killed him.

That accomplished, she removed her snowshoes, strapped them to her back, and crouched. Using all the power in her legs, she vaulted high enough to grab one of the lowest limbs. It was easily four meters off the ground, so no one would expect her to be able to do that.

Her tracks led nowhere near the trunk of the tree, so climbing the tree should never enter the man's thoughts. Still, he might glance up out of reflex. It was a good thing the area under the tree was as dark as the bottom of a hole. Thankfully, her enhanced eyes were up to the task.

She'd just settled into place over her false trail when the first of her attackers appeared at the gap she'd made as she'd ducked under the tree. Kelsey slowly drew one of her swords and waited for him to advance.

He came in with his rifle up and ready, searching for targets. He did glance up but didn't see her in the gloom, obviously not seriously considering it possible for her to be up there.

"She ducked under a tree," he told his associates over his com. "Looks like she went out the other side."

"Be careful," another voice said. "She's got some kind of sledgehammer with her. She smashed Handley's face in like a broken melon. There's blood everywhere."

"Damned idiot. How did he let her get a full swing on him like that? Come east and follow my trail."

"Copy."

When he was right below her, Kelsey dropped off the limb, swinging her blade as she fell, and landed right beside him on both feet. He saw her, but his shock was so complete that he didn't have time to even twitch before she completed the blow she'd struck on the way down.

His rifle fell to the ground with his hands still gripping it. She'd timed her strike perfectly, severing both arms just below his elbows.

Without hands, all the man could do was thrash around and scream. Kelsey stepped back to avoid the worst of the blood spraying everywhere, but she was sure she'd gotten drops all over her. With wounds like that, he'd be dead in a minute.

"Sucks to be you," she told the screaming man with a cheerful smile. "Surprise is a stone-cold bitch, am I right?"

The man had fallen by the time she'd cleaned and sheathed her sword, gotten her snowshoes back on, and made her way out via the false trail. It was possible he'd still be alive by the time his friend got to him, but the blood loss had already taken his consciousness.

Kelsey circled around the tree and waited for the next man. He appeared a minute later, looking around with far more concern than his dead associates had shown. He was afraid of her. Good.

Once he ducked under the tree on her original path, she hurried after him.

"Holy shit," the man said over the com. "She cut Winder's arms off. He's dead."

"She did what?" Harrow demanded. "Stick with team two and follow her."

"They haven't caught up with me, and I'm not chasing her by myself. She killed Handley and Winder before they could do shit."

"That's impossible. Team two, what's your status?"

Kelsey unslung the Pirone and let its long barrel lead the way under the tree. The man she'd been stalking was facing the wrong way, covering the exit she'd used a few minutes earlier.

"Team two won't be coming," Kelsey told the man ahead of her as she flicked off the safety with a soft metallic click. "You won't need them anyway."

He twitched violently at her words and spun on his feet, whipping his weapon around. He was fast but not faster than her trigger finger.

The rifle slammed against her shoulder, driving her back a step as the man's chest came apart. The hydrostatic shock wave from such a large slug pulped his internal organs even before the thumb-sized hunk of copper and lead blew his spine apart while exiting his back.

To her chagrin, Kelsey hadn't considered the massive concussion being a weapon all its own. Her enhanced ears blocked the sound of the shot, which would've deafened her otherwise, but they did nothing to stop the sound wave from making the snow clinging to the tree from falling on her like a mini-avalanche.

Thankfully, no one came along to take advantage of her blunder. All she could hear as she dug herself out were Harrow's increasingly desperate-sounding calls over her earbud for an update.

That wasn't very smart, Ned said dryly. *You know we're going to talk about this in the after-action briefing.*

"I'll bet," she muttered as she worked the bolt, ejected the steaming brass case, pocketed it, and dug into her pocket for a fresh round.

"What the hell was that sound?" Harrow demanded. "Does she have grenades? Report. Anyone report."

"I'm afraid the men you sent to check the van are indisposed," she said, allowing her pleasure at the outcome to color her tone as she locked the bolt forward on the fresh round and engaged the safety. "That just leaves you and your three sidekicks. I'm past the halfway point now. Feeling a little scared?"

"I'm going to fucking kill you," he ground out. "Come get some. Switch to encryption key two."

Kelsey pocketed the earbud. It was useless now. She'd have to take the last four without knowing what they were doing.

*   *   *

Now THAT's she'd silenced half their number, odds were very good they wouldn't send anyone off alone again. At least not the minions. They'd be terrified of her, which was kind of the point. Harrow might risk it, if he thought there was something to gain.

Based on his track record, he might use the other three as bait—though he'd never phrase it that way to them—and try to kill her as she stalked them.

That meant he'd be counting on her finding them. He still had the unconscious mental image of her as a helpless little woman. He couldn't allow himself to believe that she'd stalked and killed five of his men. She could use that against him.

Kelsey weighed the odds and decided that they'd probably set up a defensive perimeter around the escape tunnel antechamber. It would make the perfect trap from his understanding of the situation. If she went in after him in that supposed hiding place, his people on the outside could close in and kill her.

He'd never allow himself to be trapped inside a place with no retreat, though. So, he'd need to make her think he was in there. What better way than setting his minions in a defensive perimeter around it?

Of course, until she saw the situation, she'd only be guessing. In this weather, she'd probably not be able to see them all in any case.

They'd be in worse condition. They hadn't brought the equipment to detect her in conditions like this, since they'd never considered the possibility of fighting on a mountainside in a blizzard.

Lack of contingency planning sucked.

Kelsey left the ambush area and circled around the escape tunnel exit. The recon drone had given her a great tactical map of the area. It was pretty sheltered, so there were several places someone could ambush people going in or coming out of the tunnel. A real flaw the planners hadn't seemed to have considered, since they'd focused on making sure no one knew about the tunnel.

She found the first of the men about where she'd expected. Rather than approach him, she backed off and looked for his companions.

The second man was only a few meters away, literally watching over the first. If she'd have attacked the first man, this guy could've sprayed bullets into her. The reverse was also true, given enough warning.

The first man was watching over the entrance to the tunnel, so that made her wonder if Harrow and the remaining man were on the other side.

A slow walk around found the third minion there, but no one watching over him. He was checking in via com every minute, unlike his fellows. A beat that would tell the assassin leader if she took the man out.

She used her implants to mark his location on her internal map and then retraced her steps. Harrow wanted her to think he was inside the antechamber, but that was bull. He was waiting somewhere to her east, near the cliff, in case his men failed.

After a few moments juggling the tactical situation, she decided that she'd handle the two men together first. One had his attention focused on the exit, so she'd start with his backup.

Once she was in position, she considered how to do him. She needed to take him down without alerting anyone, so the rifle was out. She'd stabbed one with her knife, broken another's neck, punched one to death, and cut another with her sword. She'd need something new.

After all, variety was the spice of life.

If this guy was like the rest, he had a rifle, a pistol, and a knife. The way he held his rifle told Kelsey that he was right-handed. His pistol would be there on his hip, while his knife was on the other side.

Moving with glacial slowness, she slipped behind the man until she could have reached out and touched him. He had no idea she was right behind him and that sent a shock of unexpected pleasure through her. His life was in her hands, and he didn't even know she was going to take it.

Almost casually, she reached past him with her right hand and yanked the rifle out of his grip, tossing it into the snow a bit away from them. Her

left arm snaked around his neck at the same time and clamped off the yell
she knew was coming.

She could've broken his neck but satisfied herself with choking him
instead. His right hand grasped at his pistol only to find it his holster already
empty. It had gone to join his rifle moments after she'd grabbed him.

That left his knife, which required some space to use. Her greater
strength allowed her to throw them on their left sides in the snow, hopelessly
pinning his arm to the ground.

"How's it feel?" she asked softly, whispering into his ear as he franticly
jabbed his right elbow into her torso armor with zero effect. "Knowing that
this is it? Knowing that mine is the last voice you'll ever hear?"

His struggles became fiercer, but the end was never in doubt.

As the man's movements started slacking off, she allowed her lips to
brush his ear with an almost intimate familiarity. "Good night. Sleep tight.
Don't let the bedbugs bite."

Kelsey held that pose until she was certain the man was dead.

That was way *creepy,* Ned said. *You need to talk with Doctor Stone.*

"Yeah," she agreed softly after a moment. "Maybe I do need a little help
dealing with recent events. After I kill the last of these bastards, I'll give her
a call."

* * *

SIX DOWN. Time to finish the opening act.

Kelsey rose to her feet and took the man's earbud and com. That would
plug her back into the enemy's communications net without them being
aware she'd done so. She made a mental note to discuss methods to prevent
the same from ever happening to her people once she had a chance.

The man in front of her was crouched down behind a rocky spine, his
weapon aimed at the tunnel exit. He looked as if he were shaking. Probably
scared to death. That suited her just fine.

Without bothering to even let him know she was there for him, Kelsey
unhooked one of the ice axes from her belt and drove the point through his
heart from behind. An agonized grunt was the only sound he made before
she clapped her hand over his mouth.

The long spike had embedded itself into the stone in front of the man,
pinning his thrashing body there like some strange insect with a needle
holding it to a board. He was dead in seconds.

Once he'd stopped moving, Kelsey yanked the ax out, cleaned it, and
put it back onto her belt. Kneeling beside the dead man, she swung the
Pirone off her shoulder and settled into his location.

The man on the far side of the small valley was completely invisible, but
she knew where he was down to the centimeter, since she'd mapped his
location on her tactical map in her implants. She even knew the elevation
difference.

That made calculating a bullet's trajectory an interesting challenge rather than an impossibility. Her combat computer gently guided her aim to a certain point while her artificial muscles held the big rifle as steady as a gunsmith's vise.

Technically, this was using the same weapon twice, but since this was not at point blank range, she'd allow it.

The other man checked in with Harrow right on schedule. As soon as he finished speaking, Kelsey flicked off the safety, squeezed the trigger, and rode out the recoil. The blast of sound echoed around the mountainside, coming back in strange echoes for several seconds.

Harrow demanded a report, but no one answered. That told her she'd most likely killed the man she'd been shooting at, but she'd have to verify that before she trusted he was really dead.

"It looks like it's just you and me, Victor," Kelsey said over the com channel as she loaded a fresh round and engaged the safety again. "Nice plan setting them up to guard the tunnel while you waited to see if I took them out. Only one problem. What do you do now that I did?"

"This isn't possible," he responded, panic infecting his voice. "You're just a woman. Just one little woman who never learned to fight."

"That's what they call a fatal mistake in my new business," she said as she circled around to check the results of her blind sniper shot. "You're counting on me being who I was when I left Avalon all those years ago. Things have changed.

"It's just the two of us now. I've killed all your people. Not one of them even got off a single shot. Do you think you'll see me before I get my hands on you? Or will you still be jumping at shadows when you find out I was standing behind you all along?"

He didn't respond, so she left it at that. Welcome to the end game.

* * *

KELSEY ARRIVED at the spot where the last man had been hiding. He no longer had a head. It was scattered across the area in little pieces of skull and gray matter. She stuffed the enemy coms and earbuds into his pocket and faded back into the storm.

Now it was a guessing game now. Harrow would be lying in wait for her. For that, he'd probably want something behind him that she couldn't get past.

If it was her, she'd have used the cliff. Of course, that also meant that he was pinned against a two-thousand-meter drop. Perfect, if she could find him.

The temptation to use the recon drone was almost irresistible. She wanted this fight done and Harrow dead, but she wasn't going to cheat. There had to be a way to find him.

Then she smiled. Just like they had used her tracks in the snow to find her—as badly as that turned out for them—she could use Harrow's tracks to find him.

Oh, he'd use them to set a trap for her, if he could, so she needed to be very careful. This man was a professional assassin. He snuck up on people for a living. The key here would be setting a counter trap for him to walk into.

After circling wide, she found his tracks leading toward the cliff's edge. He'd have gotten back to the trees and would be lying in wait behind the snow. Possibly in one of the same snow-free zones she'd used so well.

Climbing a tree wouldn't help him get her, so she wasn't worried about an attack from above. He had to be able to see her to kill her.

Kelsey checked her inertial navigator and edged to the right about fifty meters. She found the trail from when she'd climbed the cliff right where she'd expected to find it. The storm had mostly filled it in.

She walked along her path, stopping several meters short of the edge. The wind howled as it cut around the mountain. It made hearing anything a challenge, and the snow was whipped into a frenzy that almost blinded her.

Perfect.

The snow here was deep enough to offer her some concealment. She took off her snowshoes, attached them to her pack, which she also took off. She tossed it under the nearest tree. If this plan didn't work out, she wouldn't be needing it.

She aimed her rifle at the unseen sky and fired three shots as quickly as she could reload. Then she set the rifle aside, crouched low in the gap made by her snowshoes, and waited.

Harrow would only be able to tell the rough direction she'd fired from. The echoes would confuse things so he'd be unsure how close she truly was.

Staying perfectly still, she listened with all her concentration. By the time she'd be able to hear him, he'd be almost on top of her. She'd get one chance at this, and if she blew the timing, he'd shoot her.

It was almost twenty minutes later when she heard the sound of someone moving slowly through the snow. Harrow had taken the bait. He was coming from the direction she'd spotted his tracks.

He'd obviously waited to see if she'd come to him but had finally chosen to come find her instead. That was the last mistake the man would ever make.

Even this close, she'd have trouble seeing him, but he'd miss her in the snow. If she wanted to, she'd probably be able to shoot him, but that wasn't how she saw this ending. No, the cliff was too fitting. Too poetic.

Kelsey gathered her feet under her when he was almost to her tracks. He wouldn't miss them, but he wouldn't expect her on the dangerous side of the open area either. He'd think she was in the trees.

When she saw his form take shape out of the whipping snow, she waited until he paused and then sprang. As expected, he'd partly turned to face the trees.

What was less expected was how he'd exchanged his rifle for a pistol. Even with her speed, the snow slowed her enough that he was able to fire one shot into her torso just as she reached him.

The impact was like being kicked by a mule, but her armor held. Score one for Ned and his cautious nature.

She pulled his pistol out of his hand with a twist, hurling it away into the snow. She spun him around and yanked his rifle off his shoulder, sending it after the pistol. Only then did she step back toward the cliff's edge.

"Hello. My name is Kelsey Bandar. You tried to kill my father. Prepare to die."

He's never going to recognize the reference, Ned said. *But bonus points for having a nice one liner at hand when push came to shove.*

"Some things are meant for an audience of one," she subvocalized as she began walking backward.

She pulled out her knife and grinned at Harrow through the driving snow. "This is it, sport. One of us is bleeding out here today. Do you feel lucky?"

Harrow howled at her and rushed toward her as fast as his snowshoes allowed, pulling his knife as he came. "You killed my Ethan, and I'm going to kill you!"

Just as he came into range and slashed at her with more skill than she'd expected, Kelsey fell back, allowing him to fall onto her in his rush. She bent her legs as he came down and then forcefully extended them again, hurling him into the open air over the cliff.

The wind tore his screams away and within moments his fall was lost to her, obscured by the howling wind and driving snow.

Kelsey climbed slowly to her feet. She'd ended up a little closer to the edge than she liked, so she backed away to a safer distance.

You've left quite a mess to clean up, Ned said through her implants.

"The storm is going to last a few more days. I'll come back tomorrow, recover the bodies, put them into their van, and move them to a lake I know down the range. It's iced over almost year-round.

"I'll take one of the plasma guns with me, melt the ice under the vehicle, and let it sink. No one will ever find them down there."

That's going to make your husband do a lot of unnecessary work looking for them.

"He's been on edge. It'll be good for him to have something other than me to focus on for a while."

She linked to the recon drone and looked over the mountainside closely. No living enemies anywhere that she could detect. Perfect.

Just to be thorough, she verified Harrow was sprawled on the rocks below. Indeed he was.

Mission accomplished.

* * *

KELSEY GATHERED her gear and headed for the antechamber. She came in with her pistol up, just in case someone was hiding in there, but it was all clear. The fight was really over.

Unfortunately, someone had disassembled the controls. To her annoyance, it took her half an hour to put everything back together and open the locked hatch.

A wall of hot air hit her like a sauna when she entered the tunnel. It was only room temperature, but after spending so many hours out in the cold, she couldn't get out of her parka fast enough.

It was spattered with blood. She suspected the blood belonged to Winder, but it might have been mixed with Handley's. She'd have to dispose of it. Hell, she'd best get rid of all of it. No need to keep evidence around for someone to find one day.

She examined the torso armor critically. "We really need to upgrade the gear down here. That pistol shot caused way more damage to this than I like."

Whereas you're not so concerned that you were slow enough that he managed to shoot you in the first place? That was sloppy, Kelsey.

"Add it to your list of things to yell at me about once I've taken a shower. Or maybe a bath."

Kelsey stashed her bloody outer clothes in a handy locker, along with the damaged armor. Then she headed up the lift to her suite. Five minutes later, everything except her skinsuit was put away.

She'd need to spend some quality time cleaning the Pirone once she'd taken care of herself. It had performed like a champ today.

No matter what the future brought, this magnificent weapon was coming with her. They'd fought and killed together. She wouldn't leave it behind to gather dust where no one would use it again for decades.

"Time to turn off your monitoring, Ned. Thanks for your help."

My pleasure, Raider.

After she stripped out of her skinsuit and locked it away, she took a long shower, changed into something casual, and sat by the desk com.

Kelsey knew she should be filled with revulsion at what she'd done, but all there was inside her was a cold emptiness. A wall sat between her and the woman she'd once been. One that felt as tall as the sky and as wide as the universe.

She couldn't allow this to go on. She couldn't allow what she'd done to her brother to fester inside her like this. That rage had driven her to kill people. It didn't matter that they'd come to kill her first. That wasn't the kind of person she wanted to be.

With a sigh, Kelsey tapped a code into the com and waited for it to connect to *Invincible*.

"Stone."

"Lily, it's Kelsey. I need to talk. I'm looking into the mirror, and I don't like the woman looking back at me. Could you come down to the Imperial Retreat when you have some time?"

Her voice broke as she spoke the last sentence. Her emotions were rising inside her like a tidal wave, threatening to wash her away.

"I'll be there in twenty minutes," Lily said. "Just hang on."

To make that kind of time, her friend would've had to have had a pinnace already standing by to make a high-speed combat drop on the Imperial Retreat. That touched Kelsey in a way that she couldn't clearly describe.

"Thank you. All of you. You all mean so much to me."

She disconnected the call and unlocked her door, feeling almost physically weak as she started to tremble. If she knew Lily, the doctor would have Angela stay with her until she came roaring in like the cavalry in a hurricane of snow and overheated metal after the marine pinnace punched through from orbit in a trail of fire.

The wall of pain inside Kelsey broke and she started crying even as Angela came through the door without knocking. She buried her face in the other woman's arm and sobbed as the marine held her, stroking her hair and whispering that everything would be okay.

* * *

WANT to get updates from Terry about new books and other general nonsense going on in his life? He promises there will be cats. Go to TerryMixon.com/Mailing-List and sign up.

DID YOU ENJOY THIS BOOK? Please leave a review on Amazon. It only takes a minute to dash off a few words and that kind of thing helps Terry make a living as a writer and gets you new books faster.

WANT the next book in this series? Grab *The Empire of Bones Volume 3* today or buy any of Terry's other books, which are listed on the next page.

VISIT TERRY's Patreon page to find out how to get cool rewards and an early look at what he's working on at Patreon.com/TerryMixon.

ALSO BY TERRY MIXON

You can always find the most up to date listing of Terry's titles on his Amazon Author Page.

Note: the links below (ebook only, obviously) redirect you to my website where you can click a button to go to Amazon. This allows me to participate in Amazon's associates program and earn a little more. Sorry for any inconvenience.

The Last Hunter

The Last Hunter

Bonds of Blood

Alpha Strike

The Enemy Revealed

Command Authority

The Grand Conspiracy

Shield of Humanity

Fog of War

Ships of the Line

Operation Liberty

The Empire of Bones Saga

Empire of Bones

Veil of Shadows

Command Decisions

Ghosts of Empire

Paying the Price

Recon in Force

Behind Enemy Lines

The Terra Gambit

Hidden Enemies

Race to Terra

Ruined Terra

Victory on Terra

When Luck Runs Out

Gunboat Diplomacy

The Imperial Marines Saga

Spoils of War

Imperial Recruit

Enemy Action

The Humanity Unlimited Saga

Liberty Station

Freedom Express

Tree of Liberty

Blood of Patriots

Single Novels

Scorched Earth

Storm Divers

The Vigilante Series with Glynn Stewart

Heart of Vengeance

Oath of Vengeance

Bound By Law

Bound By Honor

Bound By Blood

Box Sets

The Empire of Bones Saga Volume 1

The Empire of Bones Saga Volume 2

The Empire of Bones Saga Volume 3

The Empire of Bones Saga Volume 4

Humanity Unlimited Publisher's Pack 1

Humanity Unlimited Publisher's Pack 2

ABOUT TERRY

#1 Bestselling Military Science Fiction author Terry Mixon served as a non-commissioned officer in the United States Army 101st Airborne Division. He later worked alongside the flight controllers in the Mission Control Center at the NASA Johnson Space Center supporting the Space Shuttle, the International Space Station, and other human spaceflight projects.

He now writes full time while living in Texas with his lovely wife and a pounce of cats.

TerryMixon.com